The
PRAIRIE STATE
Friends
TRILOGY

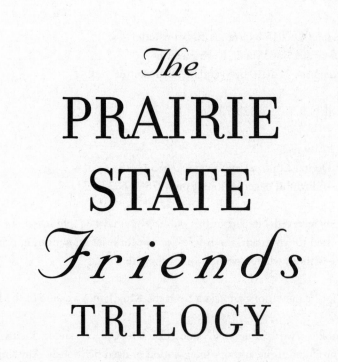

The PRAIRIE STATE Friends TRILOGY

WANDA E. BRUNSTETTER

BARBOUR BOOKS
An Imprint of Barbour Publishing, Inc.

Print ISBN 978-1-68322-736-6

eBook Editions:
Adobe Digital Edition (.epub) 978-1-68322-738-0
Kindle and MobiPocket Edition (.prc) 978-1-68322-737-3

All scripture quotations are taken from the King James Version of the Bible.

This book is a work of fiction. Names, characters, places, and incidents are either products of the author's imagination or used fictitiously. Any similarity to actual people, organizations, and/or events is purely coincidental.

For more information about Wanda E. Brunstetter, please access the author's website at www.wandabrunstetter.com

Cover Design: Faceout Studio, www.faceoutstudio.com

Published by Barbour Books, an imprint of Barbour Publishing, Inc., 1810 Barbour Drive, Uhrichsville, Ohio 44683, www.barbourbooks.com

Our mission is to inspire the world with the life-changing message of the Bible.

Printed in the United States of America.

The DECISION

To caregivers everywhere, who selflessly give to others.

Blessed are the merciful: for they shall obtain mercy.
MATTHEW 5:7

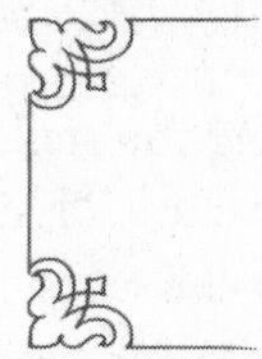

PROLOGUE

Arthur, Illinois

Elaine Schrock shivered and pulled her woolen shawl tightly around her shoulders as she stepped out of the house Saturday evening. The air was cold and windy, like it had been most of the winter, yet it was two weeks into spring. They ought to be having warmer weather by now, but winter didn't seem to want to give in just yet. Last week, the temperatures rose into the upper seventies, and everyone caught spring fever. Neighbors and friends began preparing their gardens, and fields had already been plowed and were ready to be planted. Green shoots from flowers were coming up, and buds on the maples had turned red. Unfortunately, this time of year it wasn't unusual for the weather to tease people into thinking winter was finally gone. The calendar might say it was April, but Mother Nature said otherwise.

Heading toward the barn, where her grandfather had gone to check on the horses, Elaine hurried her footsteps. The wind howled noisily. She glanced toward the darkening sky and shivered. It almost felt like it could snow.

Elaine entered the barn and headed for the horses' stalls. "Grandpa," she called, seeing no sign of him in the first stall where Grandma's horse, Misty, had bedded down for the night.

She stopped to listen, but there was no response.

Moving on to the stall where her own horse, Daisy, was kept, Elaine still saw no sign of Grandpa. When she reached across the gate to stroke the mare's head, she heard a low moan coming from the next stall.

Hurrying over, Elaine gasped. Grandpa lay in the straw a few feet from his horse, Dusty. "Grandpa, what happened? Did you slip and fall?" she asked, opening the gate and quickly entering the stall.

Grandpa's eyelids fluttered, and he clutched his chest. "Lainie," he murmured, using the nickname he'd given her when she was a girl.

"I'm here, Grandpa," she said, dropping to her knees beside him. "Please, tell me what's wrong."

"I—I am *katzodemich*," he mumbled.

"You're short of breath?" Elaine's heart pounded when he gave a feeble nod. Although she tried to remain calm, she couldn't help noticing Grandpa's pale skin and the bluish tint to his fingers and lips.

"Lie still, Grandpa," she murmured. "I'll run out to the phone shanty and call for help."

"No, wait," he said, clasping her hand. "There's something I need to ask you."

"What is it?" Elaine leaned closer to him, barely able to make out his words.

"If I don't make it—will you promise me something?" Grandpa's voice seemed to be growing weaker.

"Of course, Grandpa. What is it?"

"Look after your grandma for me. She—she'll need someone to care for her now. C–can you promise me that?"

Tears welled in Elaine's eyes as she held his cold hand. "I promise that I'll always be there for Grandma, no matter what." She gave his fingers a reassuring squeeze. "Help will be here soon, Grandpa. Don't worry, you're going to be fine."

Elaine rose to her feet and dashed out of the barn. It had begun to rain hard, and the bleakness of her mood matched that of the foreboding sky. Tension mounted in her chest as she raced on shaky legs toward the phone shanty. The cold, wet drops made it hard to hurry as she slipped along, trying not to lose her footing. "Dear Lord," she prayed out loud, "please let my grandpa be okay. Grandma needs him, and so do I."

CHAPTER 1

Tears coursed down Elaine's cheeks and dripped onto the front of her black mourning dress. The mourners had arrived at the cemetery a few minutes ago, ready to put Grandpa Schrock's body to rest in the ground. He'd died of an apparent heart attack just moments after the paramedics arrived Saturday evening. This morning, because Grandma wanted it that way, Grandpa's funeral service had been held in a large tent outside their home, rather than in the Otto Center, where some local Amish funerals took place.

During the service, one of the ministers quoted Matthew 5:7: "Blessed are the merciful: for they shall obtain mercy." Grandpa had always been merciful to others, and so had Grandma. When Elaine was five years old and her parents had been killed in a buggy accident, her father's parents had taken her in. They'd been wonderful substitute parents, teaching, loving, and nurturing Elaine, yet asking so little in return. She only hoped she could live a life that would be pleasing not only to Grandma, but also to God.

If I'd only found Grandpa sooner, could he have been saved? Elaine wondered. *Oh, Grandpa, I already miss you so much.*

Elaine glanced over at her grandmother, standing to her left with hands folded, as though praying. Her eyes brimmed with tears. Grandma Schrock was a strong woman, but the grief she felt over losing her husband of forty-five years was evident on her face. And why wouldn't it be? Elaine's grandparents always had a deep, abiding love for each other, and it showed in everything they said and did as a couple. Elaine hoped to experience that kind of love when she got married someday.

Taking Grandma's hand, Elaine's throat constricted as Grandpa's simply crafted wooden coffin was placed inside a rough pine box that had already been set in the opening of the grave. Death for the earthly body was final, yet she was confident that Grandpa's soul lived on and that he now resided in a much better place. Grandpa had lived the Christian life in every sense of the word, and he'd told Elaine many times that he loved the Lord with all his heart, soul, and mind. Yes, Elaine felt certain that Grandpa was in heaven with Jesus right now and perhaps even looking down on them with a smile. Did Grandma feel it, too? Quite possibly she did, for she gave Elaine's fingers a gentle squeeze as she turned her face toward the blue sky. *Thank You, Lord, for giving us a sunny day to say our good-byes,* Elaine prayed.

A slight chill hung in the air, but at least it wasn't raining, and only a gentle breeze whispered among the many headstones surrounding them. A bird chirped from a tree outside the fenced-in graveyard, as though offering comfort and a hope for the future.

A group of men from their church district began to sing while the grave was filled in by the pallbearers. Elaine winced. Although she had been quite young when her parents died, she still remembered standing in the cemetery during the burial, holding her grandparents' hands. Elaine's maternal grandparents, who had since died, had been living in Oklahoma back then. They had decided not to uproot Elaine from the only home she'd known, and she was grateful that Grandma and Grandpa Schrock had been more than willing to take her in. As the last shovelful of dirt was placed over the coffin, Elaine remembered her final words with Grandpa and her promise to take care of Grandma. *And I will,* Elaine reminded herself. *For as long as Grandma needs me, I will be there for her.*

Bishop Levi Kauffman asked the congregation to pray the Lord's Prayer silently, which concluded the graveside service. It was time to start back to the house for the funeral meal their friends and neighbors had prepared, but Elaine had no appetite. She'd be going through the motions and doing what was expected of her. Grandma would no doubt do the same.

Scanning the faces of close friends and church members, Elaine saw that the heartache she and Grandma felt today was shared by all. Although nothing had been said during the funeral service earlier this morning about Grandpa's attributes, everyone knew that Lloyd Schrock was a kind, caring man. Having farmed in this community from the time he'd married Grandma until his recent retirement, Grandpa had proved his strong work ethic and commitment to the community. How many times had Elaine witnessed him getting up at the crack of dawn to head out to the fields without a word of complaint? Grandma always got up with him and made sure he ate a hearty breakfast before beginning another busy day. She'd done the same for Elaine throughout her school days.

Elaine would miss their shared meals, as well as Grandpa's smile and the stories he often told. On cold winter evenings, they would sit by the fire, enjoying apple cider and some of Grandma's delicious pumpkin or apple pie. All the wonderful times the three of them had together would be cherished memories.

As folks turned from the grave site and began walking back to their buggies, Elaine's friends Priscilla Herschberger and Leah Mast approached Elaine and her grandmother and hugged them warmly. No words were necessary. These two young women had been Elaine's best friends since they were children, and even though at twenty-two Elaine was the youngest of the three, they'd always gotten along well.

"Are you coming over to our house for the meal?" Elaine asked.

Priscilla and Leah both nodded.

"We'll do whatever we can to help out today so you and your grandma can relax and visit with those who attend." Leah, whose hair was golden brown like a chestnut, gave Elaine's arm a tender squeeze.

"You can count on us, not just for today, but in the days ahead as you and your grandma strive to adjust." Priscilla's dark eyes, matching the color of her hair, revealed the depth of her love.

"*Danki*, I appreciate you both so much." Given a choice, Elaine would prefer to keep busy, but she'd be expected to visit with the guests, so she wouldn't think of turning down her friends' offer of help.

"I am grateful for you, too," Grandma said, her voice trembling a bit. "I value all of our friends in this community."

As Elaine and Grandma moved slowly toward their buggy, Elaine caught sight of Jonah Miller heading her way. For nearly a year, she and Jonah had been courting, and Elaine was fairly certain it was just a matter of time before he proposed marriage. A week ago, she would have eagerly agreed to marry Jonah if he'd asked. But with Grandpa dying, she needed to be there for Grandma. Perhaps later, once Grandma had recovered sufficiently, Elaine would be ready for marriage. But she would continue to look after Grandma, making sure that all of her needs were met.

"I'm sorry for your loss," Jonah said, his coffee-colored eyes showing the depth of his concern as he looked first at Grandma and then Elaine. "If there's anything I can do for either of you, please let me know," he added, pulling his fingers through the back of his thick, curly black hair, sticking out from under the brim of his black dress hat.

"We will," Grandma murmured. "Danki."

All Elaine could manage was a brief nod. If she spoke to Jonah, her tears would flow, and she might not be able to stop them. There would be time for her and Jonah to talk—perhaps later this afternoon or evening if he stayed around after the meal that long. Jonah had a business to run, and he might need to get back to work this afternoon.

As though reading her thoughts, Jonah touched Elaine's arm and said, "I'll see you back at your house." Nodding in Grandma's direction, he sprinted for his horse and buggy.

As Jonah stepped into his buggy and picked up the reins, he thought about Elaine and her grandmother and wondered what they would do now that Lloyd was gone. Would they continue to offer sit-down dinners in their home for curious tourists, or would Elaine find some other employment in order to help out financially? Although Lloyd had retired from farming, he'd continued to earn money by selling a good deal of the produce they raised to a local store where many Amish, as well as some English, shopped. He wondered if Elaine would end up taking over that responsibility.

I could ask Elaine to marry me now. That would solve any financial worries she and her grandma might have. Jonah smiled. *It would also make me a happy man.*

Jonah had been unlucky in love—at least when he'd lived in Pennsylvania. He had fallen in love with Meredith, a beautiful young woman whom he'd met several years before while visiting Florida. Meredith had believed that her husband was killed in a tragic bus accident, and after a suitable time of courting, Jonah and Meredith made plans to be married. But on the eve of their wedding, Meredith's husband, Luke, showed up. It turned out that he hadn't been on that bus after all, but had suffered from amnesia because of a beating he'd received at the Philadelphia bus station. For over a year, Meredith had grieved for Luke, until she'd finally given her heart to Jonah. When Luke showed up, claiming his wife and child, Jonah's whole world had turned upside down. Knowing he needed to get away from Lancaster County and begin again, a year and a half ago Jonah had moved to Arthur, Illinois, where his twin sister, Jean, lived with her family. Jean had also suffered a great loss when her first husband, Silas, was killed in a tragic accident. But since then, she had remarried. Jean had two children, Rebecca and Stephen by her first husband, and now she and Nathan had a baby boy named Ezekiel.

Jonah's bishop from childhood used to say, "Everything happens for a reason. God can take the tragedies in our lives and use them for something good." That was true in his sister's life, for she seemed happy and content. Jonah had also found happiness and love again when he'd met Elaine. He looked forward to the future and hoped to make the pretty blond his wife someday. But while she and her grandma were recovering from this great loss, he wouldn't bring up the subject of marriage. Instead, he'd be there for her, offering support in every way. When the time was right, he'd propose.

Thinking about the others who had been at the cemetery, Jonah reflected on how Sara Stutzman had looked as though she might break down at any moment. Sara's husband, Harley, had been killed by a falling tree ten months ago. Attending Lloyd's funeral and going to the graveside service must have been difficult for her, especially given that Harley's grave wasn't more than ten feet from where Lloyd was buried.

It was hard for Jonah, too, because he and Harley had been good friends. Since Jonah was courting Elaine, he had to be careful not to offer Sara too much support. But he, as well as several other men from their community, had gone over to Sara's several times to help out with chores. Jonah still dropped by occasionally to check on Sara and her two-year-old son, Mark. Usually Jonah's sister, Jean, was with him, as she and Sara were good friends. He wondered if Sara would get married again, since it would be better for Mark if he had a father.

But that's really none of my business, Jonah told himself. *If it's meant for Sara to marry again, she'll choose the right man when the time comes.*

Back at the house, Elaine visited a bit and then headed for her bedroom to retrieve a gift she'd purchased the week before for Leah. As she walked down the hall, each step was a struggle. Walking into her room on the main floor, Elaine quietly closed the door. The voices from those who had gathered in the yard, as well as from inside the house, became muffled.

She stood by the bedroom window, her head leaning against the cool glass. Gazing outside at the people who were visiting in the yard, she was overwhelmed by how many friends Grandpa had made over the years. Elaine watched with blurry vision as Priscilla and Leah and a few other women dashed around, making sure food and drinks were readily available for everyone. It was nice to see Grandma receiving so much support on such a difficult day. For Elaine, it was like losing her father all over again, only worse because she'd been with Grandpa a lot longer. Grandma's heart was aching, too. It would take some time to work through all of this, and they would need to rely on God.

Away from well-meaning people, the tears Elaine had held in for most of the morning pushed quickly to the surface. Quietly, she let them fall, covering her mouth to stifle the cries. Grandpa was gone, yet it seemed as though he were still here. His presence would be felt in this house for a long time. Grandpa's voice seemed to whisper in Elaine's ear: *"Make each day count, Lainie, no matter what. Things happen for a reason, and although we may not understand it, in time, you'll find the answers you seek."*

Grandma used to remind Elaine of similar things, often saying, *"The Lord knows what is best for each of His children."*

God, is all of this really what's best for me? Elaine's jaw clenched. *First, You took my parents, and now You've taken Grandpa, whom we need so much. I feel like I'm in a dark tunnel without any light to guide me out.*

She could stand in her bedroom and sob all day, but she had to get ahold of herself. It was time for her to support Grandma, just as she and Grandpa had always been there for her.

Elaine wiped away the tears with her apron and went to her closet to get Leah's gift, a bag of daffodil bulbs from the market. Leah's favorite color was yellow, and Elaine thought her friend would enjoy planting them and seeing them bloom every spring. She had enough bulbs to give half to Priscilla. She hadn't planned it this way, but it would be her way of saying thank you for all they were doing to make things easier on her and Grandma. She would ask them to plant the flowers in memory of Grandpa.

Elaine hesitated, wishing she could stay in her room a little longer. She took a deep breath, squeezing her eyes tightly shut. Grandma must want to be alone in her grief, too, and yet throughout the funeral, graveside service, and now here for the meal, she had put on a brave face in the presence of others.

How can one go on after losing their soul mate and partner for life? Elaine wondered. *How does a wife begin each new day, knowing her husband is gone and won't be coming back?* First Grandma had lost her only son, and now her husband was gone. *Oh, Lord,* Elaine prayed, *help me to be there for her in every way, offering all of the comfort and care she will need in order to get through each day.*

Elaine thought of Jonah and wondered what it would be like if she'd never met him. She cared deeply for Jonah and hoped to have a future with him, but how fair would it be for him to have to help her care for Grandma? The most difficult part of today was behind her, but now the real work would begin. It was time to pick up the pieces of their lives and try to move on.

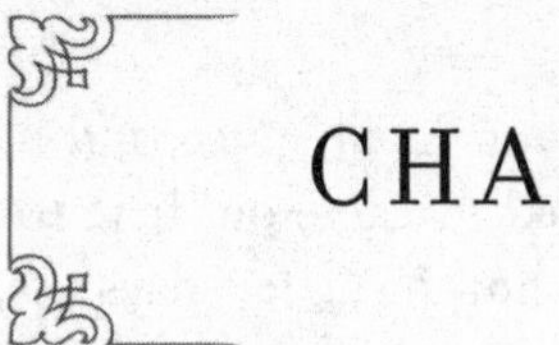
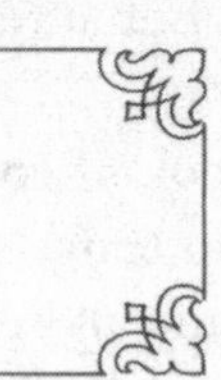

CHAPTER 2

That evening after all the food was cleared away and everyone had gone home, Elaine went out to the barn to feed the horses. The sound of her steady stride had apparently alerted the animals of feeding time and sent the buggy horses into whinnying and kicking at their stalls. Patches and two of their other barn cats seemed excited to see Elaine, as they skittered across the lawn and pawed at the hem of her dress. "Not now, you three. I'm too busy to play right now."

When Elaine stepped inside, she was greeted by familiar smells—grain, hay, dust, and the strong odor of horseflesh and urine from the horses' stalls. They really needed to be cleaned, but that could wait for another day. She was too tired to lift a pitchfork, and it would be all she could manage just to feed the horses this evening.

As Elaine approached the stall where Grandpa's horse was kept, she bit back a huge sob. This was the last place she'd seen her grandfather alive, when he'd asked her to look out for Grandma. Grandpa had obviously known he was dying.

"I will be here to help Grandma through her grief," Elaine murmured. "And she'll be here for me."

A rustling noise behind Elaine caused her to jump. "*Ach*, Jonah! I thought you had gone home," she said as he moved toward her.

"I left to make sure my sister got home safely," Jonah explained. "Her horse was acting up, and since Nathan had to work and couldn't be with her today, I decided to follow Jean and her *kinner* home. Then I came back to check on you and your grandma and see if you needed my help with anything." He walked over to an open bale of hay and removed a few chunks to give Elaine's horse.

"Danki, Jonah." She stepped closer to him, feeling comforted and choked up by his consideration.

A look of concern showed clearly on Jonah's face, and it brought Elaine to tears. "Oh, Jonah," she sobbed, "I came out here to feed the horses, and all I could think about was how just a few days ago, I found Grandpa dying in his horse's stall."

Jonah drew Elaine into his arms and gently patted her back. "Losing a loved one is never easy, but God will give you the strength to endure it, for He understands your grief."

She nodded, pulling slowly back and gazing up at his tender expression. "As much as I hurt right now, I know that Grandma is hurting even more."

"*Jah*," Jonah agreed, "and she will need to deal with the pain of losing Lloyd in her own way, in a time frame we can't control."

"Are you saying there's nothing I can do to help her get through this terrible loss?" Elaine could hardly believe Jonah would hint at such a thing.

"I'm not saying that at all," he said with a shake of his head. "I just meant that Edna will have to deal with Lloyd's passing in her own way."

"I know, but I made a promise to Grandpa that I would be here for Grandma, and I plan to keep that commitment."

Jonah nodded as though he understood and reached for her hand. "Why don't you go back to the house and let me take care of the horses? You've had a long day, and I'm sure you're exhausted."

"You're right about that," she agreed with a weary sigh. "And if you're sure you don't mind, I think I will go inside and make sure that Grandma's okay. I'll fix some chamomile tea, which will hopefully help us both get to sleep."

Jonah bent and kissed Elaine on the cheek. "I'll be back sometime tomorrow to see how you're both doing."

"Danki, that means a lot." As Elaine left the barn, she thanked God for bringing Jonah into her life. He was such a kind, compassionate man. She hoped that he wouldn't ask her to marry him anytime soon, for if he did, her answer would have to be no. For however long it took, Elaine's first obligation was to Grandma, which meant her own needs and wants must be put on hold.

Sara Stutzman stood in front of her bedroom window, staring at the inky blackness of the night sky. Attending Lloyd Schrock's funeral today had been hard on her, as it brought back memories of when she'd had to watch her own husband's body being buried. She and Harley had been married a little over two years when his life was snuffed out by a falling tree, leaving Sara to raise their son, Mark, by herself. Life could be hard, and disasters could occur when least expected. But life continued, and Sara had a reason to live lying right there in his crib across the hall.

Her precious dark-haired little boy would never know his father, but she would make sure to tell him what a wonderful, loving man his dad had been. At moments like this, Sara wished she had a picture of Harley so she could share it with Mark when he got older. But posing for a photo was frowned upon in her church district, so she would do her best to describe to her son what his father looked like.

Biting her lip to keep tears from flowing, Sara wondered if it was right to continue living in Illinois or if it would be better to return to Goshen, Indiana, where her parents and siblings lived.

Sara had met Harley when he'd gone to Goshen to work for his uncle Abner one summer. They'd quickly fallen in love, and when Harley went back to Illinois, they kept in touch through letters and phone calls. He came back to Goshen to visit several times, and a year later, Harley had asked Sara to marry him. They'd lived in Indiana for six months before moving to his hometown, where he'd started a new business making windows. Sara liked Illinois, and she'd made many friends in the area, including Jean Mast, whom she considered to be her closest friend. If Sara went back to Indiana, where she'd been born and raised, it would be hard to say good-bye to those she'd become close to here. Still, was it fair to Mark to live so far from his mother's parents, whom he would never know as well as his father's parents?

So many decisions to make, Sara thought. *But I don't want to make any permanent changes just yet.* Like Harley's mother had said a few weeks after his death, *"It's best not to make any quick decisions about the future until you have had sufficient time to grieve."*

Betty was right. She still grieved the loss of her eldest son, just as Harley's father and younger siblings did. It had not been an easy time for any of them, but Sara was thankful they had each other's support, for without Harley's family, she wouldn't have made it this far. And having Mark close by helped Betty, because her grandson was the only part of Harley she had left.

Even though it was dark, in her mind's eye Sara could see every inch of the property. This home, this land was where she and Harley had planned to live, raise a family, and grow old together. Sara's heart was in this place as much as her husband's had been, and in the time they'd lived here, so many good memories had been made. But then this very land they'd loved so much had taken her husband's life. Would she be able to continue forcing herself to look at the trees lining their property without letting that horrible day override the sweet memories they'd made in such a short period of time?

Sara was thankful she'd been able to lease out part of their land to a neighboring Amish man who farmed for a living. The income from that, as well as money they had saved in the bank, was helping her get by. In addition, both Sara's parents and Harley's had given some money to help out.

My year of mourning is almost up, and I'll need to make my decision soon about whether I should stay here or move back to Indiana, Sara told herself after she'd pulled the covers aside and crawled into bed. *In the meantime, I need to find an additional way to support myself and Mark, because my savings won't last forever, and I can't rely on my in-laws' or parents' help indefinitely. I need to ask God for His guidance and strength each day.*

Grandma and Elaine had retired to their rooms a few hours ago, but Elaine was still standing at her window, looking toward the heavens and asking God for answers about what the future might hold. The stars seemed to be twinkling more brightly, perhaps just for her. *Lord, help me to be strong for Grandma. Help me not to lose hope and to understand why, when things seemed to be going so well, everything suddenly fell apart.* Elaine's body was tired, yet her mind whirled with a multitude of questions.

Finally, Elaine willed herself toward the bed, knowing she needed to get off her aching feet. Pulling back the covers, she slipped into the linens that still smelled like fresh air. Grandma always hung the sheets outside after washing them, and they held their fragrance for several days. Elaine loved to bury her nose into the pillowcase and breathe deeply of its freshness. It was almost like falling asleep outdoors.

She tucked the quilt, lovingly made by her grandmother, under her chin, while wiggling her toes to get the cramps out. What she wouldn't do right now for her friend Leah to give her a good foot massage. Leah practiced reflexology and was quite good at it. Reflexology dealt with a lot more than massaging feet, but right now, Elaine would have settled for just that.

She reflected on how Leah and Priscilla had been happy with the daffodil bulbs she'd given them. Even before Elaine had suggested it, both friends had said the flowers would be planted in memory of Grandpa Schrock, an affectionate name they had called him by all these years.

Elaine closed her eyes, and even with both doors tightly shut, she heard Grandma's muffled crying from the room across the hall. As Elaine drifted fitfully to sleep, her last words of prayer were for Grandma to find the strength to go on.

Elaine sat straight up in bed and glanced at the clock on her dresser. It was nearly midnight, and she'd only been asleep a few hours. A noise seemed to be coming from the kitchen. She tipped her head and listened, trying to make out what it was.

Then Elaine caught a whiff of something cooking. But that was impossible; Grandma had gone to bed hours ago.

Pushing her covers aside, Elaine crawled out of bed and put her robe and slippers on. Opening her bedroom door, she padded down the hall toward the kitchen.

When she stepped into the room, she was surprised to see Grandma standing in front of the stove, flipping pancakes with an oversized spatula.

"Grandma, what are you doing out of bed, and why are you making pancakes at this time of night?" Elaine asked, joining her at the stove.

Grandma turned to look at Elaine. "I'm sorry, dear. Did I wake you?"

"Well, I. . ."

Grandma placed one hand on her stomach and gave it a pat. "I'm *hungerich*, and I had a craving for *pannekuche*. Would you like some, too?"

Elaine shook her head. "I'm not hungry, and after the long day we've had, you should be tired, too."

"I couldn't sleep, and I was thirsty." Grandma's mouth twisted grimly. "My bed seems empty without my dear husband to share it."

Elaine wanted to say that she understood, but having never been married, she couldn't fully comprehend the scope of what Grandma must be feeling right now. "Would it help if you slept in one of the guest rooms upstairs?" she suggested.

Grandma shook her head vigorously. "I am not leaving the bedroom your grandpa and I shared for so many years." She sighed and turned off the propane-operated stove. "It'll take me awhile to get used to sleeping alone, but I'll manage somehow."

Grandma placed the pancakes on a plate, grabbed the syrup bottle from the cupboard, and sat at the table. "Even in my loss, I can give thanks for all that the Lord provides." She bowed her head and closed her eyes. When she opened them again, Elaine took a seat beside her.

"Are you sure you're not hungerich?" Grandma asked, taking a drink of water from the glass she'd placed on the table. "I'd be happy to share some of these pannekuche with you."

"No. I'll just sit here and watch you eat," Elaine replied. She guessed it was good that Grandma was eating now, as she hadn't had much to eat at the meal after Grandpa's graveside service, and neither had Elaine.

"As you like." Grandma poured syrup over the pancakes and took her first bite. "Your grandpa loved pure maple syrup. He liked buttermilk pancakes the best, but I think he would have eaten any kind that was set before him." Grandma chuckled. "As much as that man liked to eat, it was amazing that he didn't have a problem with his weight."

"I guess it was because he always worked so hard," Elaine commented.

"Jah, and before he retired from farming, he labored in the fields, so it was no wonder he had such a hearty appetite."

Grandma went on to talk about how she and Grandpa had met

at a young people's singing many years ago—a story Elaine had heard several times. But she listened patiently, knowing it did Grandma good to reminisce like this, and it would no doubt help the healing process. Truthfully, Elaine never tired of hearing it. She was comforted by hearing about how things had been when Grandpa and Grandma were young.

When the grandfather clock in the living room struck one, Elaine suggested that they both head back to bed.

Grandma yawned. "I guess you're right; I am awfully tired. Danki for sitting here so patiently while I rambled on and on about the past."

Elaine placed her hand over Grandma's. "It's all right. You needed to talk, and I hope you'll share things about Grandpa with me whenever you want, because I enjoy hearing them."

Tears welled in Grandma's eyes. "We who grieve will never forget the ones we've lost, but we can be thankful for the years we had with your *grossdaadi*, for he filled our lives with love and laughter and gave me a sense of joy beyond compare." She squeezed Elaine's fingers. "And if I'm not mistaken, someday soon you'll find that same kind of love, laughter, and joy with Jonah Miller."

"I hope so," Elaine said in a near whisper. Truth was, she wasn't sure Jonah would be willing to wait until she felt ready for marriage. And if he wasn't, she wouldn't blame him for that.

CHAPTER 3

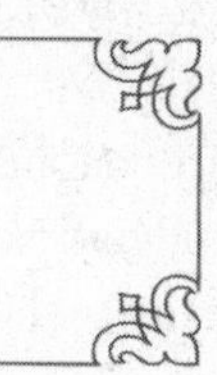

When Elaine entered the kitchen the following morning, she found a stack of Grandma's good dishes sitting on the table, and Grandma was at the sink, washing glasses.

"*Guder mariye*, Grandma."

"Good morning."

"Why do you have the good dishes out?" Elaine questioned.

"Have you forgotten that we have a group of tourists coming here on Friday?"

"Well, no, but. . ."

"Thought I would get a jump on the dishes while I have some time to clean them. That way, they'll be ready for our guests. Then I'll take them out to the dining-room table." Grandma turned and offered Elaine a weak smile. Dark circles rimmed her pale blue eyes, and Elaine was sure she hadn't slept well, if at all, last night.

"Oh, Grandma, I think it's too soon for that. I had planned on calling the tour group director this morning and canceling our Friday-night dinner."

Grandma shook her head determinedly. "We made a commitment, Elaine, and we need to stick to it. Besides, we could sure use the money."

Elaine couldn't argue with that, but she wasn't up to cooking a big meal for fifty people, and she didn't think Grandma was, either. "Maybe we can reschedule it for another time," Elaine suggested, moving closer to the sink.

"No, we can't." Grandma reached for another glass to wash, carefully immersing it in the soapy water. "The people who'll be coming are from out of town, not to mention that they've paid for their meal in advance."

Elaine sighed deeply, picking up the dish towel to dry what Grandma had washed. "We can refund their money, Grandma, and I'm sure once I explain the circumstances to the tour director, she'll understand."

"We need the money," Grandma repeated.

"There will be other tour groups, and we're not going to starve." Elaine's frustration mounted. Didn't Grandma realize that neither of them was up to hosting a big dinner right now? Not only would they have the meal to prepare, but while the tourists were eating, Elaine and Grandma would be expected to say a few words and answer any questions they were asked about the Amish way of life. They'd both be exhausted by the end of the evening.

"I know you're worried that I'm not up to this," Grandma said, "but keeping busy will help me not to think so much about missing your grossdaadi. I think it would be good for you, too. Maybe we'll both get a good night's sleep after entertaining the group."

"Okay, we'll do the dinner," Elaine finally conceded. "Guess I'd better head over to Rockome Garden Foods and pick up a few things that we still need for the dinner."

Soon after Elaine left, Edna carried her good dishes out to the room where she and Elaine hosted their dinners. She wouldn't set the table today, but wanted to have everything here and ready to put in place on Friday morning. As Edna covered the stack of dinnerware with one of the embroidered cloth napkins to keep the dishes free of dust, she thought about what else she could do before Friday's gathering.

As she glanced around the spacious room, a lump formed in her throat. With the help of several men in their district, Lloyd had built this extra-large dining room to accommodate up to one hundred people. In addition to being used for their sit-down dinners, the add-on had served them whenever it was their turn to host one of their biweekly church services. It was also used on days when Edna would invite a group of women into her home for a quilting party or some other function.

She moved over to the large window, looking out at the field Lloyd had rented to one of their neighbors after he'd retired from farming. It had been planted in alfalfa and was already growing nicely. When Lloyd used to work the fields, Edna enjoyed going out to see how he was doing or bringing him water and a snack to eat. He'd always been appreciative and hadn't seemed to mind the interruption. Lloyd used to tell Edna he was glad for the break and that it was a good opportunity for them to visit awhile.

Edna's gaze went to their giant oak tree. A swing Lloyd had put up for Elaine many years ago still hung from a lower branch. It had provided hours of fun for their granddaughter through the years. Even though Elaine was twenty-two years old, she still took time to enjoy that swing and gleefully giggled as she swung back and forth.

Pushing her thoughts aside lest she give in to threatening tears, Edna left the room and headed back to the kitchen. Although difficult to face, she was glad there were so many reminders of Lloyd all around, for each one held a special memory. Memories of him would help keep her going.

Edna was just getting ready to take a stack of napkins and a box of silverware to set by the dishes when she heard a horse and buggy coming up the lane.

Peeking out the kitchen window, she watched as the driver parked his rig near the barn. When the young Amish man got out of the buggy and secured his horse to the hitching rack, Edna realized that it was Jonah Miller. No doubt he had come here to see Elaine. Too bad he'd just missed her.

"If you're looking for my granddaughter, she's not here right now," Edna said after she'd answered Jonah's knock.

"Came by to check on both of you," Jonah replied with a grin.

Such a nice-looking, thoughtful young man, Edna mused. *He reminds me of Lloyd at that age. Not just in looks, but in his kindness for others. I'm so glad Elaine is being courted by him.*

She opened the door wider and asked him to come in. "I'm sorry, Jonah. Where are my manners? Good morning to you, and would you like a cup of coffee? I made it fresh this morning." Edna's face heated, for she felt a bit rattled right now.

"Some coffee sounds good." He removed his straw hat, placing it on the wall peg near the back door. "So where's Elaine off to this morning?" he asked, taking a seat at the kitchen table.

"She went over to Rockome Garden Foods," Edna replied, filling a cup with coffee and handing it to Jonah. "There are a few things we need for the group of tourists who'll be coming here Friday evening."

Jonah quirked an eyebrow. "You're hosting a dinner so soon?"

She gave a brief nod.

"Couldn't you have rescheduled it for a better time? I'm sure you and Elaine are both emotionally drained."

"I'll admit, we're tired physically and mentally, but we'll be fine," she said, pouring herself some coffee. "Like I told my granddaughter, it helps to keep busy, and we don't want to disappoint the people who have paid in advance to have dinner in an Amish home. For some who live out of town, this might be the only chance they'll have to visit our Amish community."

Jonah blew on his coffee and took a sip. "I see what you mean. Keeping busy in stressful situations has worked for me on more than one occasion. When you're good and tired, it helps you fall asleep quickly, too."

"Were you referring to situations in your work as a buggy maker or to more personal matters?" Edna asked.

"Both." Jonah went on to tell Edna how stressful it had been for him when he'd first moved to Arthur and didn't know anyone but his sister. "Then I made friends with Harley Stutzman and, of course, Elaine, and everything changed." He smiled. "Just being with her makes me feel calm and relaxed."

"I understand. My granddaughter has a sweet spirit and a special way about her that is calming." Edna handed Jonah a plate of brownies someone had brought by when offering condolences. "Whenever I was with Lloyd, I felt a sense of peace." She sighed deeply. "I'm grateful for all the wonderful years we had together."

Jonah nodded and took one of the brownies. "I look forward to having a relationship like yours and Lloyd's with my future wife someday. And I hope to be blessed with many good memories, like I'm sure you have, and my parents do, too."

Edna was tempted to ask if Jonah planned to ask Elaine to marry him, but thought better of it. If they were meant to be together, it would happen at the right time without her interference. Of course, she was hoping Jonah would eventually pop the question, and was almost certain that Elaine would say yes. She'd noticed the way they looked at each other whenever they thought no one was watching.

"Is there anything you'd like me to do for you before I go?" Jonah asked after he'd eaten a brownie and finished his coffee.

Edna shook her head. "I can't think of anything at the moment, but danki for asking."

Jonah rose from his chair. "Think I'll stop by Rockome Garden Foods and see if I can catch Elaine there before I head back to the buggy shop."

"You're welcome to wait for her here if you want, but I'm not sure how long she will be."

"That's okay. Think I'll just drop by the store. There are a few things I could pick up there anyway, and then I'll need to head back to my shop and get some work done, or else I'll end up getting behind on my orders."

"All right then. It was nice seeing you, Jonah."

"Same here. And don't forget, Edna, if you ever need anything, just let me know. Even though I'm busy at work, I'll always make time for you and Elaine."

Arcola, Illinois

Elaine had only been browsing the shelves at Rockome Garden Foods a few minutes when she spotted her friend Priscilla talking to one of the clerks. Elaine waited until they were finished, then walked over and asked, "*Wie geht's?*"

Priscilla, looking quite surprised, replied, "I'm fine. How are you?"

Elaine shrugged. "Doing okay, I guess. What brings you here today?"

"I'm delivering some of our homemade strawberry jam," Priscilla replied. "We have more canned goods than we need for our small store, and the owner here said they could use some jam. Why are you here?"

"Grandma and I have a group of tourists coming to our house Friday evening, and I'm picking up a few things we're out of. Maybe I should get some of that jam, too, because I think we're nearly out."

Priscilla's brows furrowed as she put her hand on Elaine's shoulder. "Are you sure you're up to that? I mean, with your grandpa dying, I figured you would put all dinners on hold for a while."

"I wanted to." Elaine sighed heavily. "But Grandma insisted on hosting this meal. I think she wants to keep busy so she won't have time to think about how much she misses Grandpa. She reminded me, too, that we need the money."

"If you're struggling financially, others in the community will help out," Priscilla said.

"I'm sure they would, but Grandma's an independent woman, and she won't accept money from others as long as we can provide for ourselves."

"I understand." Priscilla spoke in an encouraging tone while giving Elaine's arm a tender squeeze. "If you and Edna need help preparing for the dinner, or even cooking and serving the meal, let me know. I'm not doing anything Friday afternoon or evening, so it wouldn't be a problem at all."

"Danki for the kind offer, but I think we can manage." Elaine's throat tightened. Like Grandma, she wanted to be independent, although she still wasn't sure either of them was up to hosting another dinner so soon. All it took was one sympathetic look from her friend and she felt like she could break down in tears. *I wonder what Grandma would say if Priscilla did come to help. She'd probably tell her that we can do the dinner on our own. Maybe it's best if I don't press the issue and just see how the meal goes.*

"Well, guess I'd better get what I came here for and head back home." Elaine moved over to the cooler to select some cheese. "I don't want to leave Grandma alone for too long. She's likely to do more than she should while I'm gone."

The sounds of screeching tires and a shrill horn interrupted their conversation.

Elaine and Priscilla rushed to the window to see what had happened. "Oh no," Elaine gasped. "It looks like a car hit someone's buggy! I hope no one is seriously hurt."

CHAPTER 4

Jonah whistled as he headed toward Rockome Gardens with his horse, Sassy, pulling his buggy. The Amish museum and other facilities, including their restaurant, would open next week, but Rockome Garden Foods, where they sold baked goods, bulk foods, various kinds of cheese, candy, and several other items, was open to the public all year.

Jonah was fascinated by Rockome Gardens and its history. He had visited the museum not long after he'd moved to Illinois and learned that the 208 acres of land had once been used for farming. It had been purchased by Arthur and Elizabeth Martin, who had a dream of creating the largest flower garden in Douglas County. They used seven acres of the farm to plant flowers, create rock formations, and build their summer cottage. Work began in 1937, but it was slowed by the Great Depression and the start of World War II. The Martins continued to expand, planting more flowers and creating additional rock formations. In 1952, they gave Rockome Gardens to the Mennonite Board of Missions and Charities of Elkhart, Indiana, and it was used as a retirement village for missionaries. A few years later, it was sold to Elvan and Irene Yoder, who opened it to the public, adding buggy rides, tours of an Amish home, and a small gift shop. Other attractions, such as a tree house, lookout tower, antique museum, and ice-cream shop were added. Whenever the Yoders traveled, they returned to Rockome with new ideas for rock formations and other attractions. In 2005, the Yoders sold the property to a group of investors. It was sold two more times, and then in 2011, Steve and Bev Maher took over. The couple had visited the gardens many times and realized it was in need of restoration.

Jonah smiled as the gardens came into view. Each of the rock formations was truly unique. This was a place where families could come to relax and find inspiration. He'd hoped to bring Elaine here, maybe sometime this summer, because she liked the gardens, too.

As he neared Rockome Garden Foods, Jonah caught his breath. An Amish buggy was flipped over on its side, and the car that had hit the buggy was parked nearby. His heart pounded. A group of people had gathered around, and one of them was Elaine, who was crouched on the ground next to Priscilla. His nerves calmed, seeing that Elaine and her friend seemed to be okay. But someone was injured, and he wondered who it was they were assisting.

Jonah halted Sassy and leaped from the buggy, but his hands didn't want to cooperate as he secured the horse's reins. He'd seen one too many buggy accidents. Some were minor, while others involved fatalities. Once he'd managed to tie Sassy to the hitching rack, Jonah sprinted to the scene of the accident, where he discovered Sara Stutzman's mother-in-law, Betty, lying on the ground in front of Elaine and Priscilla. She was conscious but gritting her teeth.

"What happened? Is she seriously injured?" Jonah asked, kneeling beside Elaine.

"We're not sure how it happened, but Betty's buggy was hit." Elaine motioned to the car, then back to Betty. "Her leg appears to be broken, and she could have some internal injuries, but we won't know for sure until she's been seen by a doctor."

"Did someone call for help?" Jonah questioned.

"Jah. The paramedics should be here soon," Priscilla interjected.

"I'll check around the scene and make sure all of Betty's things are picked up and taken back to her place." Jonah stood and looked toward the road. "What happened to Betty's horse? I don't see it anywhere."

"We don't know yet if her horse was injured, but a passerby stopped and said he saw the mare running into a field down the road," Elaine replied. "The man offered to go after the horse, and hopefully he'll be able to bring her back without a problem."

"Looks like that might be him coming now." Jonah pointed. "At the pace they're moving, it doesn't look like the horse is seriously injured."

"That's a relief." Priscilla looked toward the stranger leading Betty's horse.

"Betty's family needs to be notified," Elaine said. "We could call and leave a message, but they might not check the answering machine in the phone shanty for several hours."

"You're right," Jonah agreed. "I'll drive over to the Stutzmans' right now and let them know about Betty. I'll tie the mare to the back of my buggy and take her with me."

Arthur

"Wie geht's?" Leah called when she rode her bicycle into the Schrocks' yard and saw Edna hanging laundry on the line.

"I'm keeping busy," Edna replied. "That's the best cure for depression, I'm told."

Leah wondered who had given Edna that advice, but she didn't ask. Instead, after parking her bike, she said, "Would you like some help with those wet clothes?"

Edna shook her head. "I can manage. Besides, I'm almost done. It's nice to have your company, though."

Edna is so independent, Leah thought. *It's no wonder Elaine is like that. She probably learned from her grandma's example.*

"Where's your granddaughter? Is she busy inside?" Leah asked, clasping her hands behind her back so she wouldn't be tempted to grab a few towels and hang them on the line.

"Oh, Nancy went shopping today. We need a few things for the dinner we'll be hosting this Friday."

Leah tipped her head. "Nancy? Did you say Nancy went shopping?"

Edna's face reddened. "I—I meant Elaine. Guess I must have been thinking about my son's wife, Nancy. Even after all these years, I still miss her and Milton. Elaine lost out on so much, growing up without her parents." She sighed deeply and pushed an errant strand of silver-gray hair back under her covering. "There are times when Elaine reminds me of her mother, and during her childhood, I slipped a time or two and called her Nancy. I haven't done it much lately, though." Edna readjusted the loosened clothespin that held up one side of an oversized bath towel.

Leah slipped her arm around Edna's waist. "Elaine was fortunate to have you and Lloyd, and I'm sure she knows it."

Edna nodded. "It's been a blessing to raise our only grandchild. I pray every day that Elaine will find the same happiness with Jonah that I had with my dear husband."

Leah's mouth opened slightly. "Has Jonah asked Elaine to marry him?"

"Well, no, not yet, but I'm sure it's just a matter of time." Edna reached into the basket and clipped another towel to the line. "It's obvious that they're very much in love. I can see it every time they look at each other."

"I've noticed that, too. And they seem to have a lot in common," Leah agreed. "They both enjoy flowers, and Jonah admires the unusual rocks Elaine has found and painted, like that one she made to look like a bear. I think he mentioned to Elaine that he plans to take her to Rockome Gardens sometime. They sure have a lot of rocks to look at."

"Jah." Edna gestured to the now-empty laundry basket. "Since that chore is done and I'm feeling the need for a little break, should we go up to the house and have a cup of coffee?"

"None for me, thanks," Leah said. "It's never been my cup of tea." She snickered. "You may remember how I used to invite Priscilla and Elaine over to my house for tea parties when we were girls."

Edna smiled. "Oh, that's right. Instead of coffee, let's share a pot of tea while we wait for Elaine to come home."

Leah smiled. "That sounds nice."

"We can have some of that moist and delicious banana bread someone gave us the other day, too," Edna said as they headed toward the house. She yawned noisily and covered her mouth. "Sorry about that. I didn't get much sleep last night and got up for some water and decided to make pannekuche."

"You made pancakes for breakfast this morning?" Leah asked.

"Not for breakfast. It was sometime during the night, but I can't remember what time it was. I was hungerich and decided to make myself something to eat." Edna smiled briefly, but her expression sobered. "Lloyd loved pancakes. Elaine didn't eat with me, but she sat and listened while I shared some memories, and then we both went back to bed."

"Oh, I see." Leah couldn't help but notice that even though Edna was trying to put on a brave front, she looked exhausted and seemed kind of forgetful. No doubt the stress and pain of losing her husband was the cause.

When they entered the kitchen, Leah went to the cupboard and got out two cups for their tea. She turned just in time to grab hold of Edna, who all of a sudden had turned pale and seemed unsteady on her feet.

"Dear me," Edna said, holding her head. "I must have stood up too quickly when I put the clothes basket down. Either that or I'm feeling a bit woozy because I've gone too long without something to eat. It's been awhile since Elaine and I had breakfast."

"Let me take care of making the tea and cutting the banana bread," Leah said as she guided Edna to a kitchen chair. "You've been through a lot this past week, and it's okay to rely on others. After all, that's what friends are for."

Rather than pushing herself to keep busy, Edna ought to take time to rest and allow herself to grieve, Leah thought. Once again, she didn't voice her concerns, figuring Edna might not appreciate it. She would, however, keep Edna and Elaine in her prayers and stop by whenever she could to help out.

"We're going to see your Grandma Stutzman today," Sara said, lifting her son up to the buggy seat. Betty had invited them over for lunch, and Sara looked forward to the visit. Spending time with her in-laws made her feel closer to Harley—at least the memory of him. Betty always had humorous stories to tell about things Harley had said or done when he was a boy. Just the familiarity of being at the Stutzmans' place, where Sara and Harley had visited so many times, gave her comfort.

Riding down the lane before getting to the main road, Sara glanced in the direction of the small grove of trees on the far side of their property. Quickly, she turned away. She couldn't avoid seeing that area every time she went to and from her home. Hopefully, instead of the constant reminder that her husband's life had ended there, someday happy memories would override the bad ones and remind her of the joys they'd treasured among their once-cherished woods. Harley and Sara had enjoyed Sunday picnics there, and during the week, it was a resting place where they had many times shared lunch during warmer weather. Sara had delighted in looking up at the leaf-covered branches while relaxing on a blanket beside Harley. The steady currents from the gentle breeze made the leaves move in a beautiful, hypnotic dance as Harley and Sara talked about their future. Sometimes they'd enjoyed simply relaxing in the shade's coolness before getting back to work again. They had even flown kites one spring day, and Sara would never forget the fun they'd had.

They'd enjoyed bringing Mark to their special woodland spot as well. The baby seemed to love the fresh air, and while nestled on a blanket, cushioned by the soft grass underneath, he would kick his little legs and giggle. Like a store-bought mobile, the wafting leaves above kept him content. It never took Mark long to fall into a relaxing sleep.

"Someday, perhaps, I'll be able to smile again when I see those woods of ours," Sara said out loud, as if her husband sat right next to her. But for now, it was a constant reminder of how her life had changed in a split second of time.

Mark's sleepy blue eyes closed soon after Sara pulled onto Route 133, and he slouched in his seat. She smiled. Either her son was very tired, or the rocking motion of the buggy had put him to sleep.

As Sara guided her horse down the road, she thought about stopping to see how Edna and Elaine were doing. But she'd left the house a little later than planned and didn't want to be late for lunch. Besides, Mark was napping, and Sara wanted her precious boy to rest. She could stop by the Schrocks' either on the way home or sometime later in the week.

When Sara pulled onto the graveled driveway leading to her in-laws' house, she saw Harley's eighteen-year-old brother, Andy, coming out of the phone shanty. Sara waved but waited until she'd pulled her horse and buggy up to the hitching rack near the barn before speaking. Andy had followed her up the driveway, and he held the horse while

Sara got out of the buggy.

"Harley's friend Jonah was here a few minutes ago, delivering some bad news." His forehead creased with wrinkles. "My *mamm*'s buggy got hit in front of Rockome Garden Foods, and she's been taken to the hospital. I called my *daed* at work and let him know right away."

Sara's fingers touched her parted lips as she drew in a sharp breath. "I'm sorry to hear about Betty. Was she seriously hurt?"

"I—I'm not sure. Jonah said Elaine Schrock and Priscilla Herschberger were there when the accident happened, and they thought Mom's left leg might be broken. Jonah also mentioned that she was pretty banged up. We won't know till we get to see Mom, and since Dad's on his way home now, I called one of our drivers to take us to the hospital in the next half hour or so." Andy gulped in a quick breath before slowly shaking his head. "I can't believe this happened. We aren't over losing Harley, and now Mom is hurt. What more could go wrong?"

"I know, it's hard," Sara agreed, "but at least your mamm's life was spared."

"Jah, and I'm thankful for that."

"I'll have to go home and get some things, but I'll be back in time to greet the children when they get home from school today," Sara offered.

"Try not to scare 'em with the news about Mom," Andy said. "Don't think they need to know a lot till we have all the facts."

"I understand, and don't worry about anything here. I'll take care of everyone until you and your daed return home." Harley's siblings had taken his death pretty hard, and if they thought they might lose their mother, they'd really be upset.

"By the way," Andy added, "Jonah brought Mom's horse back with him. It broke away when the buggy was hit, but the mare seems to be okay. Said he stopped by your place, but somehow you must have missed each other."

"I wonder how that happened," Sara pondered. "I took the main road here."

"Oh, I remember now." Andy scratched the side of his head. "Jonah did mention that he'd taken the back road. Guess he thought it'd be better, since he had Mom's horse tied to the back of his buggy, and there'd be less traffic and all."

Dear Lord, Sara prayed as she lifted her sleeping son from the buggy, *I hope and pray that Betty's injuries aren't serious. This family has already had to deal with one tragedy, and we sure don't need another.*

CHAPTER 5

When Elaine got home, she found Grandma and Leah sitting on the porch, drinking tea.

"It seemed like you were gone a long time," Grandma said. "Did you make more than one stop?"

"No, I just went to Rockome Garden Foods." Elaine set the paper sack she held on the wicker table and took a seat beside Leah. "I was visiting with Priscilla there when we heard a loud crash and looked out. A buggy had been hit by a car in front of the store."

"*Ach*, no!" Grandma's face paled. "Was it someone we know?"

"I'm afraid so. Betty Stutzman was driving the buggy, and we stayed with her until the ambulance arrived."

"Was she badly hurt?" Leah's thoughtful expression revealed her concern.

Elaine bit her lip. "It appeared that her leg was broken, and I heard one of the paramedics say that he thought she might have some cracked ribs, as well as some possible internal injuries."

"I hope they don't lose her." Grandma stared across the yard as she got the wicker rocking chair moving rhythmically back and forth. Was she thinking about Grandpa? Grandma's face looked pale, and from the droop of her shoulders, Elaine thought she appeared to be tired—even more so than she had earlier this morning.

"I'm sure they'll take good care of her at the hospital," Elaine reassured her.

"Betty and her family have been through. . .losing their son. I hope she'll. . .be okay, because. . ." Grandma teared up as she fumbled for words to express how she felt.

Elaine reached over and gently touched Grandma's arm. "You look *mied*. Why don't you go inside and try to take a nap?"

"That's a good idea," Leah put in. "You do look as if you could use some rest."

Grandma slowly rose to her feet. "All right then, I'll take the items you got at the store and put them away. Then I'm going to my room to lie down awhile. Please let me know when it's time to fix supper so I can help."

As Grandma took the paper sack and shuffled into the house, Elaine glanced curiously at Leah and said, "If she sleeps that long, I'll be surprised. It's not even lunchtime yet."

"Maybe she's *verhuddelt* about what time it is. She does seem a bit confused today."

"In what way?" Elaine asked.

"At times while we were visiting, Edna had a hard time focusing and remembering things."

"That makes sense, don't you think? I mean, it's only been a few days since Grandpa died. Since then, I don't think either of us has had much sleep. And with the funeral being just yesterday, well. . ." Elaine paused, looking out over the yard where she had played as a child.

"I realize that, but there was something else, too. Your grandma became quite wobbly when we came into the kitchen. I grabbed hold of her before she lost her balance."

"What?" Elaine eyed Leah with newfound concern. "I wonder what caused that."

"I'm not sure. Edna said she thought it was because she stood up too quickly after putting the clothes basket down."

"I guess that could have caused her to be light-headed. I've done that myself sometimes, standing up too quickly, and then the blood leaves my head." Elaine twisted her head-covering ties around her finger. "Of course, it could be because she hasn't had enough sleep or even just from being under too much stress. Grandma is emotionally and physically drained, and so am I."

"That's understandable, but she bent to set the empty basket down before we went to the kitchen," Leah explained. "Her wooziness didn't occur until after we'd gone in there to brew some tea. Edna also mentioned not having anything to eat since early this morning, so I'm wondering if her blood sugar was low. If so, that may have been the cause."

Elaine sighed deeply. "I'm so worried about Grandma."

"I am, too, which is why I think it's way too soon for you and Edna to be hosting a sit-down dinner this Friday night." Leah tapped her fingers on the arm of her chair.

"She told you about that?"

Leah nodded. "Said she needed to keep busy."

"We both do." Elaine clenched her hands tightly together in her lap, watching as a bumblebee flew lazily across the porch. She didn't like where this conversation was going and figured she was probably in for a lecture.

"I understand that to a point," Leah said, "but you need to rest and take time to heal emotionally. Pushing yourself to keep going and doing is not the answer, Elaine. And it's fairly obvious, even to you, that your grandma needs to rest."

"I appreciate your concern, but Grandma's insistent on us doing this dinner, and no matter how I feel about it, I won't go against her wishes."

"Where's Mom? I didn't see her buggy parked outside, and it's not in the buggy shed, either. Do you know why she isn't here?" twelve-year-old Paul asked Sara when he and his sisters arrived home from school that afternoon.

Sara removed a tray of ginger cookies from the oven and turned to face the children. "Your mamm is at the hospital."

Paul's mouth dropped open. "What? How come?"

"Her buggy was hit by a car this morning."

Marla, age seven, let out a sharp scream. "Oh no! Is our mamm gonna die?" Tears pooled in the little girl's blue eyes and splashed onto her cheeks.

"No, she'll be fine once her injuries are taken care of." Sara gathered the child into her arms. "She broke her leg and has some other sore places, so she'll have to stay in the hospital overnight, but her injuries aren't life-threatening."

"That's *baremlich*." Carolyn, who was nine, frowned deeply.

"You're right, it is terrible," her brother agreed.

"Guess I'll have to stay home from school tomorrow so I can take care of things while Mom is gone," Carolyn said.

"That won't be necessary," Sara assured the child. "I went home after lunch today and got a few things so Mark and I can stay here overnight. In fact," she added, trying to sound as cheerful as possible, "we'll stay for as long as we're needed."

"I'm glad you're stayin', but where's little Mark?" Carolyn glanced around, as though she expected to see him appear.

"He's taking a nap in the other room." Sara placed several cookies on a plate and set it on the table. "Would anyone like some *kichlin* and milk?"

The children nodded eagerly and hurried to wash their hands before taking seats at the table.

"Are Timothy and Andy out in the barn?" Paul asked.

"Timothy is, but Andy's at the hospital with your daed. He said he'd be home later this evening, but your daed plans to spend the night at the hospital with your mamm."

Sara decided to join the children at the table, knowing they would probably have more questions about their mother. She was glad she'd thought to check the Stutzmans' answering machine earlier and had listened to Andy's message. If there was one thing Sara knew, she wouldn't be moving back to Indiana anytime soon, because Betty and her family needed her now.

"Let's go, boy! Now quit your dallying!" Jonah called to his horse as he headed down the road toward the Schrocks' house. He was anxious to see Elaine this evening, and of course, Sassy chose this time to go into his plodding mode. There were moments like this when Jonah wished he'd bought a different horse when he arrived in Arthur. Since the last horse he'd owned, when he lived in Pennsylvania, had belonged to Meredith's husband, Jonah had felt the need to return it to Luke when he came home, recovered from amnesia.

"What's the matter with you, Sassy?" Jonah snapped the reins.

"You'll get fat and lazy if you don't do a little running once in a while. Guess I shoulda named you Poky instead of Sassy, because you're sure poking along today."

The horse picked up speed, and Jonah smiled. "That's better, ol' boy." Even though he'd seen Elaine at Rockome Garden Foods, he hadn't been able to visit with her due to the accident. He had left right away to let Sara know. Unfortunately, she hadn't been home. He'd wasted no time in getting to Herschel's to notify Betty's family and return her horse, but he'd promised Elaine he would stop by her house this evening to visit awhile and let her know how Betty was doing. Only trouble was, he hadn't heard anything about Betty's condition, so he planned to stop by the Stutzmans' place on his way to Elaine's and see what he could find out.

Redirecting his thoughts, Jonah smiled as he passed a sign along the side of the road. It read: YOU'RE A STRANGER ONLY ONCE. He had seen that sign when he'd first come to Arthur, and it had made him feel as welcomed then as it did now. Of course, the folks in this community had welcomed him, too, and that made his transition much easier. Moving from Pennsylvania and starting over here had been a good thing for Jonah, especially after he'd met and fallen in love with Elaine. If only he felt free to ask her to marry him.

Just try to have patience, Jonah told himself. *I'll know when the time is right to propose to Elaine, and hopefully she'll say yes when I do.*

A short time later, the Stutzmans' place came into view, so Jonah guided his horse onto the path leading to their house. When he secured Sassy to the hitching rack, he noticed another buggy parked nearby and figured it must belong to Herschel or one of his boys.

Taking the steps two at a time, Jonah stepped onto the Stutzmans' porch and knocked on the door. He was surprised when Sara answered his knock.

"Afternoon," Jonah said. "Is Herschel here? I was wondering if there's any news on how Betty is doing."

"Herschel's at the hospital with Betty," Sara replied, her brown eyes downcast. "She has a broken leg, some fractured ribs, and several bruises and contusions, so they're keeping her overnight."

"I'm sorry to hear that," Jonah said, "but at least her injuries aren't life threatening. It could have been so much worse."

Sara nodded and lifted a slender arm as she swatted at a bothersome fly. "I wonder how the English woman who ran into Betty's buggy is fairing."

"From what I saw, she wasn't hurt, just shook up pretty bad."

"That's understandable. Do you know how or why she hit the buggy?" Sara questioned.

"When the police came, I heard the woman say she'd started to pass the buggy and didn't realize it was turning into Rockome Garden Food's parking lot." Jonah frowned. "It seems like there are so many accidents involving our horses and buggies. Makes me wish there were no cars on the road."

"I've thought that many times myself, but I guess it's just wishful thinking. I can't imagine that the Englishers would ever give up their cars in favor of driving a horse-pulled carriage, or that we would decide to give up our horses and start driving cars."

"I think you're right about that, Sara," Jonah agreed. "So are you here to take care of the kinner?"

"Jah. Mark and I will be staying until Betty's well enough to take over running her household again. Oh, and before I forget," Sara added, "I heard you stopped by my place before bringing Betty's horse home. I appreciate you doing that, and I'm sorry I missed you."

"It's okay." Jonah smiled. "I took a back road because Betty's mare was tied to the back of my buggy. Didn't want traffic to spook the horse any more than she was. After being in that accident earlier, the poor animal was scared enough."

"That was good thinking." Sara paused a moment. "Anyway, I'm here for however long Harley's family needs me."

"I'm sure your help will be appreciated."

Although Sara was a small-boned woman, not more than five feet tall, she had a determined spirit as well as a generous heart. Jonah didn't doubt for a minute that she would help in whatever way she could. He studied Sara for a moment, noting that her brown eyes were a shade darker than her hair. She was a good-looking woman, for sure, and Harley had often said he was a lucky man. But Jonah was lucky, too, having fallen in love with Elaine, who was every bit as pretty as Sara.

"Helping each other out is what families are supposed to do," Sara said. "Betty and Herschel have helped me plenty since Harley died, and of course several others in our community have done that as well."

People helping people, Jonah thought. *That's what the Bible teaches.* Right now, though, assisting Elaine and her grandma was uppermost in his mind, because whether they wanted it or not, help from him and others in their community was what they both needed right now.

After Jonah left the Stutzmans' and was on his way to Elaine's, he thought more about Sara. She was only twenty-four and already a widow. On top of that, she had a little boy to care for. Sara was fortunate to have her husband's family close by. Harley had been gone ten months already, but his family was still healing. From what Jonah had heard, they'd been a big help to Sara and her little boy. Now she would be helping them while Betty recuperated. It was good they had each other to lean on. Jonah would continue to be available if she needed anything, too.

He switched his thoughts back to Elaine, hoping that by next year at this time, they might be married and living in the house he'd purchased not long ago. Jonah was anxious to get started on a few minor improvements, but other than repainting some of the rooms, the house didn't need a whole lot done to it. The place was actually in move-in condition. He also wanted to sand the living-room floor and finish it with a new coat of varnish. His goal was to get that and the painting completed before he and Elaine got married, but Jonah was confident that he had plenty of time.

The lane leading up to his home was edged by bushes that turned to a brilliant red in the fall. Those needed a bit of trimming, but he'd decided to wait on that until early in the new year. Knowing there would be little red berries on the bushes over the winter, Jonah didn't want to take a natural food source away from the birds. The property had a small barn that someday he hoped to enlarge, giving him more space for his buggy business. A pond behind the house was stocked with plenty of fish.

Jonah's mind wandered to the future. He pictured children sitting next to him as he taught them to fish and swim during the hot days of summer. On chilly winter evenings, he envisioned sitting around the bonfire at the far end of the pond, roasting hot dogs and marshmallows after ice skating with his wife and children. The house Jonah purchased had four large bedrooms on the second floor and two downstairs. Jonah smiled thinking of the children who would one day fill those upstairs rooms. He couldn't wait to become a father and give his children a loving home, just like his parents had given him. Elaine would be a good mother. Even though she'd lost her parents at a tender age, because of Elaine's grandparents, she understood what it was like to be loved and raised in a secure environment.

Jonah's thoughts did a reverse, and he wondered how his parents were doing back in Pennsylvania. He even reflected on his folks' border collie, Herbie. Jonah missed having a dog around, and soon after he and Elaine got married, he planned for them to get a dog. For now, though, Jonah just needed to be there for Elaine and Edna, helping them in any way he could.

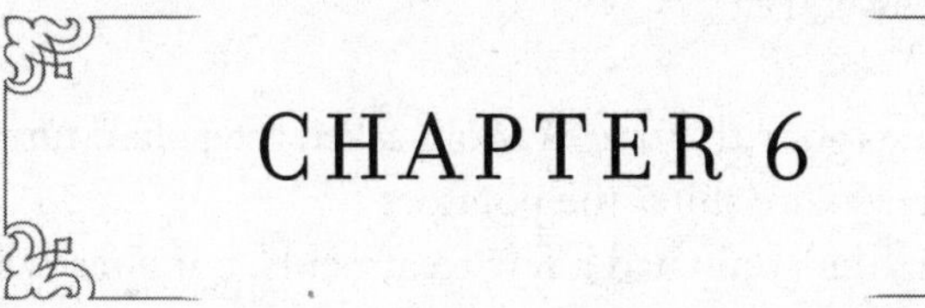

CHAPTER 6

Leah had just come up from the basement of her parents' home, where she gave reflexology treatments, when her mother called from the kitchen, asking for help getting supper on the table.

"Okay, Mom, I'll be there as soon as I wash my hands," Leah responded. Ten minutes ago, she'd seen her last patient for the day, Susan Diener, an elderly woman from their church district. After Susan had left, Leah had put away her massage lotion and repositioned the recliner people sat in while she worked on their feet. As she always did after the final appointment, she checked her schedule to see who would be coming for the next treatment session and made sure the basement area was ready and in order. It was Friday, so there would be no more patients until next week.

Leah had learned reflexology from her maternal grandmother, who'd since passed away, and Leah saw her ability as a gift to help others through this unique method of healing. At least, that's what her grandmother had always called it. Reflexology wasn't a replacement for a doctor's care, but by massaging and pressing certain reflex zones on people's feet, she'd seen recoveries from various ailments.

When Leah finished up in the bathroom, she went straight to the kitchen to see what she could do to help out. "What do you need me to do?" she asked her mother, who was busy stirring a pan of gravy on the stove.

"You can make a tossed green salad and then set the table," Mom answered. Her brown eyes appeared even darker than usual in the dimness of the room.

"No problem." Leah first turned on the gas lamp that hung over the table. Then she took out the salad ingredients from the refrigerator, placing them on the counter next to the sink.

"How'd things go with Susan?" Mom asked after she'd turned down the stove and started mashing the potatoes.

"Fairly well. She's only had a few treatments, but already her sinus issues seem to have improved."

Mom looked over her shoulder and smiled. "That's good to hear, Leah."

After Leah washed the head of lettuce and started tearing its leaves into a bowl, she glanced at the perpetual calendar sitting on the windowsill. Elaine and Edna would be busy getting last-minute things done before their dinner guests arrived. Closing her eyes, she lifted a prayer on their behalf.

Upon entering his sister's cozy, two-story house, Jonah sniffed the air. "Is that baked ham I smell?"

Jean, who'd been setting the dining-room table, blinked her dark eyes rapidly and smiled at him. "Jah, and I chose ham because I know how much you like it, dear brother."

He stepped up beside Jean and gave her a hug. "I'm blessed to have such a thoughtful sister."

"And I feel blessed to have her as my *fraa*," Jean's husband, Nathan, proclaimed when he entered the room with their three children. Rebecca, the oldest, who had recently turned four, ran over to Jonah and clutched his hand. "Horsey ride?" she asked in their traditional Pennsylvania-Dutch language.

"Jah, sure." Jonah got down on his hands and knees and told the cute little dark-haired girl to climb onto his back. The next thing Jonah knew, two-year-old Stephen gave a whoop and climbed on, too.

"Giddyup, horsey, let's go for a ride!" Rebecca hollered, gripping Jonah's shoulders.

Putting one hand in front of the other, Jonah made his way around the dining room, avoiding the table; then he headed down the hallway, made a U-turn, and came back again. The children giggled and shouted commands for their horsey to go as fast as he could. It was fun hearing his niece and nephew giggle, but Jonah hoped his knees wouldn't give out.

By the time they'd made it back to the dining room, Jonah was ready for the game to end, and equally relieved when Jean said it was time to eat supper.

"Come on, children, give your uncle a rest." Jean winked at Jonah and smiled. "I'm sure Uncle Jonah had a tiring day."

Jonah had a great sister, and they'd always looked out for each other. Truth was, he'd do just about anything for his twin.

After Nathan put their six-month-old son, Zeke, into his playpen, the rest of them gathered at the table, with Stephen in his high chair. After silent prayer, Jean passed the ham and baked potatoes, followed by a bowl of fruit salad, some rolls, and a dish of creamed peas.

Jonah took a bite of ham and smacked his lips. "Sure wish I had someone in my house who could cook as well as you do, Jean."

"Danki, Jonah." She smiled and blotted her lips on a napkin. "Our mamm taught me well, and if you'd hung around the kitchen a bit more when we were kinner, you could probably cook as well as I do."

Jonah grunted. "I doubt it, but I get by well enough, and I don't go hungry, so guess I can't really complain."

"Maybe you oughta find a good fraa," Nathan said, reaching over to place more peas on the tray of Stephen's high chair. Jonah was surprised when the boy ate them, and eagerly, too. When he was growing up, he'd always hated peas. Green beans, too, for that matter.

"Did ya hear what I said about finding a good wife?" Nathan asked, bumping Jonah's arm with his elbow.

"Jah, I heard, and I've been thinkin' on it."

"So you haven't asked her yet, huh?" This question came from Jean.

"Asked who?" Jonah grabbed his glass of water and took a drink. He didn't want to talk about this right now, but his sister probably wouldn't give up until he answered.

Jean squinted her brown eyes at him. "I was talking about Elaine. She's the one you've been courting, right?"

Jonah gave a nod.

"Well, when are you going to ask her to marry you?" Jean persisted.

"Whenever I feel the time is right." Jonah grabbed a roll and slathered it with strawberry jam. "With the recent passing of Elaine's grossdaadi, now is not a good time."

❧

"What's for supper? What's for supper? Pretty bird. . .pretty bird. . . What's for supper?"

Elaine grimaced, rolling her eyes. "I hope that silly parakeet isn't going to carry on like that all evening while the tourists are here." She didn't know why she felt so edgy tonight. Maybe it was just her fatigue.

"Millie's excited because she knows we're cooking supper." Grandma glanced across the room at her parakeet's cage. "If she gets too noisy, I'll have to cover her cage."

"That's a good idea," Elaine agreed. "Maybe we should cover it before our guests arrive. Better yet, why don't you take her to your bedroom where she'll be out of sight?"

"She might really get to squawking if she's all by herself; I may just cover the cage." Grandma drank a second glass of water, even though just moments ago she'd emptied her first. "Just remind me, though. I've been kind of forgetful lately. And I don't know what's making me so thirsty. Guess I must have eaten something salty today."

Elaine couldn't deny that Grandma had been forgetful. Even before Grandpa's death, Grandma had seemed a bit absentminded at times. Elaine figured it was part of growing older, although she herself had times when she couldn't remember where she'd put something. Just the other day, she'd gone upstairs to retrieve an item, but by the time she got to the top step, she'd forgotten what she went up there for. The thing that concerned Elaine the most about Grandma were the symptoms Leah had observed the other day. When Elaine had asked Grandma about the dizziness she'd felt, Grandma made light of the situation, saying she'd gotten up too quickly after setting her laundry basket down, but felt better once she'd had something to eat.

"How would it be if I called next week and made you a doctor's appointment?" Elaine asked, reaching for the basket to fill it with the rolls she'd made earlier.

The wrinkles in Grandma's forehead deepened. "Whatever for? Is it because I'm thirsty and said I must have eaten something salty earlier today?"

"No, of course not. I'm worried about that woozy spell you had the other day, and I think it would be a good idea if you saw the doctor, just in case."

Grandma set aside the pickles she'd been slicing. "In case what?"

"In case your light-headedness was caused by something more than just bending down and standing up too quickly."

Grandma frowned and poured herself more water. "I don't want to go to the doctor. They poke and prod too much. Maybe I should see Leah and get my feet worked on."

Elaine lifted her shoulders with hands palms up. "If you see the doctor first and he doesn't find anything beyond the scope of Leah's abilities, then I'm in agreement with you letting her work on your feet."

Grandma folded her arms in a stubborn pose. "I'll think about it." Then she quickly unfolded her arms and gestured to the kitchen window. "Right now, we need to greet our guests, because the tour bus has pulled in."

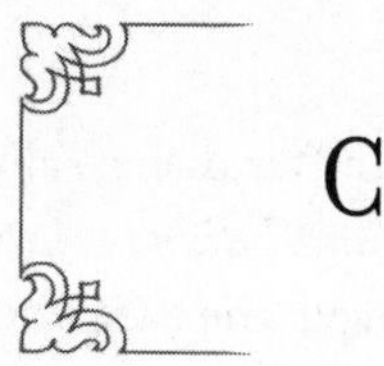

CHAPTER 7

After Sharon Sullivan, the tour guide, had introduced Edna and Elaine to the people who'd come for dinner, Edna smiled and said, "I hope you're all hungerich, because there's enough food here for everyone to have seconds and maybe even thirds."

"What does *hungerich* mean?" a young woman who wore her hair in a ponytail questioned.

"Oops!" Edna felt her cheeks warm, embarrassed by her slip of the tongue. "*Hungerich* is the Pennsylvania-Dutch word for *hungry*, which is what I really meant to say." She glanced at Elaine to see her reaction, but she had just placed bowls of mashed potatoes on both tables and made no comment.

Edna quickly followed with the gravy, and then she set a bowl of creamed corn beside it. When everything had been put on both tables—potatoes, gravy, corn, fried chicken, roast beef, bread, and pickles, she returned to the kitchen to get some butter and jam. Edna didn't know why she felt so rattled this evening, but her hands were damp with perspiration, and her stomach did little flip-flops, like it used to when she'd first started hosting dinners for tour groups and was unsure of herself. She'd been doing this for a good many years now, so there was no reason to feel apprehensive or jittery. Maybe it was too soon to be doing this. It would be a week tomorrow since Lloyd had died. Maybe Edna was wrong in thinking she needed to stay busy in order to deal with her loss. Perhaps she shouldn't have worried about trying to fulfill her obligation to the tour group. Well, it was too late for speculations. The people were here now, and she'd make it through the evening somehow.

"That's strange," Edna muttered when she discovered there was no butter on the counter. She was sure she'd taken two sticks of butter from the refrigerator earlier and put them on butter dishes, along with knives. *Maybe Elaine took it into the other room and I didn't see it there.*

Edna opened the refrigerator and removed the strawberry jam Elaine had bought the other day. After she'd divided the jam into two dishes, she took them to the dining room and placed one on each table. Scanning the length of both tables, she saw no sign of the butter, which meant that Elaine had not brought them in. *That's so odd. I wonder what happened to them.*

Feeling even more flustered, Edna headed back to the kitchen and opened the refrigerator again, thinking she might have just thought she had taken the butter out earlier.

"What are you looking for, Grandma?"

Edna jumped. She hadn't realized Elaine had come into the room. "I'm searching for the *budder*. I was sure I had set the dishes on the kitchen counter, but now they are nowhere to be found."

"I haven't seen the butter," Elaine said. "They are probably still in the refrigerator."

"No, they're not." Edna shook her head vigorously. "Come see for yourself if you don't believe me."

"It isn't that I don't believe you, Grandma." Elaine moved across the room. "I just can't think of anywhere else the butter would be."

Edna moved aside and let Elaine look over the contents of the refrigerator. A few seconds later, Elaine stepped back and said, "You're right, there's no butter in there. Do you remember taking them out of the refrigerator?"

"I—I thought I did." At the moment, Edna wasn't sure about anything. To make matters worse, she was beginning to feel woozy, like she had the other day.

Elaine clasped Edna's arm. "You look pale, Grandma. Are you feeling *grank*?"

"Well, I. . ." Edna grabbed the back of a chair for support, fearful that she might topple over. "I don't think I'm sick, but I do feel a bit light-headed."

"Sit down and put your head between your knees," Elaine instructed, helping Edna into a chair. "Are you feeling the way you did when Leah was here the other day?"

Edna lowered her head. "Jah, but I felt better after I'd had something to eat."

"I'll fix you a plate of food right now and see if that helps. If not, then it might be best if you go to your room and lie down."

"I'm not going to bed and leave you here to wait on all those people by yourself."

"I'm sure I can manage."

"You might make it through, but then you'd be more exhausted then I am right now. I'm sure that once I've had something to eat, I'll be fine," Edna insisted.

"As you wish." Elaine took a plate from the cupboard and dished up some potatoes, corn, and gravy that had been keeping warm on the stove. Then she took a piece of chicken from the oven and added that to the plate. "Here you go, Grandma." She set the food on the table in front of Edna, along with a knife and fork.

Edna offered a brief silent prayer and quickly ate a piece of chicken. "Yum. This tastes as good as it looks. I hope our guests are enjoying their meal."

"I'm sure they are, Grandma, but right now, I am more worried about you."

Edna ate a few bites of potatoes and flapped her hand. "I'm fine. Feeling better already, but I would like a glass of water."

"I'll get it." Elaine opened the cupboard where the glasses were kept, but instead of removing a glass and turning on the water, she lifted out the butter dishes and held them toward Edna. "It looks as though you may have accidentally put these in the cupboard when you took down the glasses to set the table for our guests."

Edna gasped and covered her mouth. "Ach, could I really have done something so *dumm*?"

"It wasn't dumb," Elaine said, shaking her head. "You've been a little absentminded since Grandpa died, but that's perfectly understandable." She started toward the other room with the butter, calling over her shoulder, "I'll take care of things in there while you finish what's on your plate."

Edna didn't argue. Her stomach seemed to appreciate the food, as did the rest of her body. In fact, with each bite she took, she felt her strength returning. *It's a simple matter, really. Just don't go too long without eating.*

Elaine hurried into the other room. After she'd placed the butter dishes on the tables, she checked on the vegetable bowls and meat platters to see if any were empty.

"Yuk! What did I just bite into?" A freckle-faced boy crinkled his nose and spit something out of his mouth. "What was that in my mashed potatoes?"

Elaine hurried over to the table, perspiration dripping down the back of her neck. She knew one thing: her bed would never feel better than when she crawled under those covers tonight. *We shouldn't have hosted this dinner. It would have been better to have a nice quiet Friday evening, just me and Grandma.*

As Elaine looked at what the boy held in his hand, she let out a breath of relief. "I'm sorry about that," she said, "but I think it's just a seasoned chicken cube that must have gotten into the potatoes by mistake. You didn't break a tooth on it, did you?"

He shook his head. "Naw, I'm fine. Just freaked me out when I bit into it."

Elaine said a silent prayer. *Please help us get through the rest of this evening without any more mishaps.*

Seeing that the gravy was the only item that seemed to be getting low, Elaine paused to answer a few questions from an elderly woman, and then she picked up the gravy bowls and went back to the kitchen.

"Are you doing okay, Grandma? Do you need something more to eat?" she asked, noting that Grandma's plate was empty.

"No, I'm fine." Grandma wiped her hands on a napkin. "I feel much better now." She gestured to the chair beside her. "Why don't you have something to eat, and I'll go check on our visitors?"

Elaine shook her head. "That's okay. I'm not hungry right now." Usually she and Grandma waited until their guests had gone home to eat their supper. But at least one of them needed to get back in the other room to make sure the food was being passed around for a second time and then to bring in the pies for dessert. "Why don't you stay here and relax?" she suggested. "I'll take care of everything else that needs to be done." Elaine kept the mashed potato incident to herself, not wanting to upset Grandma further.

Grandma gave a stubborn shake of her head. "We always work together as a team."

"I know, but if you need to rest, I can manage by myself this time." Even though Grandma had said she was feeling better, she still looked pale, and Grandma's droopy eyelids betrayed her exhaustion.

"I won't hear of it." Grandma pushed away from the table and put her dishes in the sink. "Is it time to take the pies in yet?"

"Not quite. I need to make sure everyone has all the meat and vegetables they want, and then I'll clear away the dishes."

"That will go quicker if we both do it." Walking slowly, Grandma left the kitchen. Elaine followed.

While their guests finished eating, Elaine and Grandma answered more questions about the Amish way of life, and then they excused themselves to clear away the dishes and bring in the desserts.

"I'll carry the sour-cream peach pies I made, and you can take the strawberry-rhubarb ones that you baked," Grandma told Elaine.

Just inside the kitchen, Elaine paused. "Actually, Grandma, you made chocolate–peanut butter pies this morning."

"Now that I think of it, I had wanted to make the peach pies, but since there are no ripe peaches on our trees yet, I changed my mind and made chocolate–peanut butter instead. Of course, I could have used some of our frozen peaches." Grandma nudged Elaine's arm. "Well, don't dawdle, now. You'd better get busy."

"Okay," Elaine replied, feeling suddenly like she was a young girl again and Grandma was completely in charge. Grandma had never been bossy, but she'd always let Elaine know that she was the one to make the final decision on things. Out of love and respect, Elaine had never questioned Grandma's authority.

They'd just stepped into the other room with the pies when Elaine heard a shrill screech, followed by, "Pretty bird. . .pretty bird. . . Where's the pie? Where's the pie?"

"Why, there must be a parrot somewhere in the house," the elderly woman who'd asked a question before said.

"Millie's my grandma's parakeet," Elaine explained.

Grandma's once pale face colored to a bright pink. "Oh dear, I must have forgotten to cover Millie's cage before everyone got here." She placed one of the chocolate–peanut butter pies on the first table and was approaching the second table when she tripped on one of their throw rugs and the pie fell on the floor. "Oh no!" she gasped, tears of obvious embarrassment running down her cheeks. "How clumsy of me. I—I'd better get something to clean up this mess." She hurried back to the kitchen, walking faster than she had all evening.

Elaine quickly followed. "It's okay, Grandma. I'll clean up in the other room. Why don't you stay in the kitchen and rest awhile longer?"

"I don't need to rest." Grandma shook her head determinedly. "I feel like such a *dappich naar*, tripping like that."

"You're not a clumsy fool. An accident like that could have happened to anyone." Elaine motioned to a chair at the table. "Please sit and relax. After I've cleaned up the floor, I'll bring in that extra pie we baked earlier today."

Grandma sighed heavily and sank into a chair. "Whatever you say. I do feel like I need to sit awhile."

Elaine grabbed a large spatula and a serving tray to put the remains of the pie on, as well as a bucket and mop to clean the floor. Then she rushed back to the dining room.

"Let me help you with that," Sharon, the tour guide, said when Elaine knelt on the floor.

"My grandmother isn't quite herself tonight, and she feels terrible about this," Elaine explained as the two of them began to clean up the pie. "You see, my grandfather died just a week ago, and—"

Sharon's eyes widened. "Oh dear, I hadn't heard. Why didn't you call and cancel this dinner?"

"I suggested that to Grandma, but she insisted on carrying through.

And since she'd already scheduled it with you, Grandma didn't think it would be right to back out at the last minute."

"I would have made some other arrangements for this group, and I won't schedule any more dinners here for at least a month, or until you let me know that you're ready," Sharon was quick to say. "You and Edna need time to grieve, and I'm so very sorry for your loss."

"Thank you." Elaine blinked against tears threatening to spill over. She wished she had tried harder to talk Grandma out of hosting this meal or at the very least taken Priscilla and Leah up on their offer to help. The way Grandma had been acting this evening was proof that she wasn't ready to entertain yet.

I wonder if Leah's concerns about Grandma are founded, Elaine thought as she headed back to the kitchen with the remains of the chocolate–peanut butter pie. *She does seem quite forgetful, not to mention how pale and woozy she got earlier. I think when I see Leah at church this Sunday, I'll ask her to have a talk with Grandma about going to the doctor.* Grandma put a lot of faith in Leah's foot doctoring, so she might be more willing to listen to her than Elaine. At least Elaine hoped that would be the case, because if Grandma refused to see their doctor, then Elaine might ask if he would be willing to make a house call. One thing was for certain, she wanted to make sure Grandma was okay.

Back in the kitchen, Elaine found Grandma standing in front of the sink, staring out the window. "Are you all right?" Elaine questioned, dropping the pie mess into the garbage can.

"I was just thinking about your grandpa. If he were still here, he'd probably be in the other room right now, entertaining our guests with a few songs he liked to play on his mouth harp."

"You're right about that." The tourists had always enjoyed listening to Grandpa's music. "Well, guess I'd better take that other pie out to our guests now," she said, removing the third chocolate–peanut butter pie from the refrigerator. "If you'd rather stay here, Grandma, I think I can manage on my own for the rest of the evening."

Grandma shook her head. "I won't hear of it. But before I go back in, I'm going to get out a bowl of fresh fruit for anyone who doesn't want pie."

Just then, one of their guests walked into the kitchen with an empty cup. "Would there be any coffee or tea to go with our pie?" She set her cup down on the table.

Elaine gave a nod. "Yes, of course. I'll bring it right in."

Returning to their guests, Elaine placed the coffeepot and pie on the table. "While you finish eating your dessert, perhaps some of you have more questions you'd like to ask."

"I do," said a middle-aged woman who'd introduced herself earlier as a schoolteacher from North Carolina.

"What is it you would like to know?" Elaine asked as she cut the pie.

"I heard that Amish children only attend school until the eighth grade. Is that true?"

Elaine nodded. "After they graduate, the young men learn a trade, and in addition to learning how to run a household, the girls will often find jobs outside the home. Sometimes if a family member has their own business, a young girl or boy might help in the store."

Just then, Grandma walked into the room, and Millie flew in right behind her. "Where's the pie? Where's the pie?" the bird shrieked.

This caused a round of laughter from some of the tourists and a few screams from others, while some of the people ducked their heads.

Oh no, now what? Elaine cringed. "Grandma, I thought you had covered her cage."

"Dear me!" Grandma exclaimed, red-faced and looking quite flustered. "I think I must have opened the cage door by mistake." Grandma stood in the archway with her arm extended, which Millie usually landed on immediately, but not so this evening. The parakeet flew this way and that, while Elaine and a few others ran around the room chasing her. Elaine could not believe what was happening. Not only did she feel like a fool, trying to catch the crazy bird, but most of the people laughed, as though they were enjoying the show. Some were rude, however, and took pictures, even though they'd been told that it wasn't permitted. Elaine couldn't really blame them, though. How often did a person get photos of a desperate Amish lady chasing after a bird? This was entertainment the tourists hadn't expected. Elaine hoped she wouldn't end up on the front page of their local newspaper. She could read the headline now: "Parakeet Invades Amish Dinner."

CHAPTER 8

Jonah tried to concentrate on the song they were singing, but he couldn't help watching Elaine. She sat between her friends Leah and Priscilla on a backless wooden bench in Thomas Diener's barn, where church was being held. Although she sang along with the others, Elaine's heart didn't seem to be in it this morning. Jonah could tell by the slump of her shoulders and her droopy eyes that she was struggling to stay awake. He glanced at the chairs that had been provided for some of the older women, and noticed that Elaine's grandmother also looked tired.

I wonder how things went with the dinner they hosted Friday night, Jonah thought as he shifted on his bench, trying to find a more comfortable position. He'd planned to go over to the Schrocks' on Saturday to check on Elaine and Edna, but he'd gotten busy in the buggy shop and let time slip away. By the time Jonah was done for the day and had taken a shower and eaten supper, it was almost nine o'clock—too late to be making a call on anyone, he'd decided. Hopefully after church let out, he would have a chance to speak with Elaine. He'd been concerned when he'd heard that Elaine and Edna would be hosting a dinner. Jonah didn't understand why they were so determined to do it so soon after Lloyd's death. Elaine and her grandma hadn't had time to grieve properly. Hosting a big meal must have been a drain on the women, and if they weren't careful, one or both of them would end up getting sick.

During the noon meal after church was over, Elaine took a seat beside Leah. "I need to ask a favor of you," she said, leaning close to her friend.

"What is it?" Leah asked.

"Things didn't go well during our dinner for the tourists the other night, and in addition to forgetting several things, Grandma had another dizzy spell."

Leah's forehead wrinkled. "I'm sorry to hear that. What happened?"

Elaine gave her friend a recap of the events, then said, "I was so glad when the evening finally came to an end."

"I think your grandma ought to see the doctor."

"So do I, and I suggested that to her, but she wouldn't agree to it." Elaine touched Leah's arm. "Grandma's been coming to you for foot treatments for some time, and she has confidence in you, so I was hoping you might have a talk with her about this."

"When she got dizzy last week, I did suggest that she see the doctor, but I can try again if you like."

"I would appreciate it. I'm worried about Grandma."

"Why don't you bring Edna over to our place tomorrow morning around ten for a foot treatment? I'll talk to her then."

"That sounds good, Leah. We'll be there on time."

Just then, Susan Diener, whose home they were at, stopped by. "Leah," she said, "I just wanted to tell you that I haven't had any trouble with my sinuses since you worked on my feet last Friday."

"I'm glad to hear that." Leah smiled at the elderly woman, who then moved on down the table to talk with some of the other women.

Elaine hoped Grandma would have equally good results when she went to see Leah for a foot treatment. Maybe while her feet were getting massaged, Grandma would be more receptive to the idea of seeing the doctor.

For the first time all day, Elaine relaxed a bit. This was the first time since last autumn that anyone had been able to have the after-church meal outside. The Dieners' spacious backyard featured two large maple trees to sit under. The leaves were just emerging and offered little shade, but no one seemed to notice in this mild April weather. There was plenty of room in the yard for all the tables and benches to be set up as well.

Elaine smiled to herself. She could imagine Grandpa Schrock sitting among the men, as he'd done so many times over the years. Several conversations were going on at one time, each carrying a sense of excitement in the voices as they discussed various topics with friends. How Grandpa would have enjoyed being here today and taking part in the discussions.

"Are you listening to me?" Leah patted Elaine's hand gently.

Elaine shook her thoughts aside. "What was that?"

"I said, while I'm working on your grandma's feet in the basement, it might be best if you wait upstairs with my mamm. I don't want Edna to think we're ganging up on her. She may be more willing to listen to me if you're not there."

Elaine nodded, but she wasn't sure that her absence when Leah talked to Grandma would make any difference. She hadn't been around the last time Leah expressed her concerns to Grandma. Maybe this time, since Grandma had gotten dizzy again, things would be different.

Elaine had just finished eating and was heading over to see if Grandma was ready to go home when Jonah stepped up to her. "I was wondering how things are going and if there's anything I can do for you."

"You can pray for Grandma. Things didn't go well during the dinner we hosted."

"What happened?"

"For one thing, Grandma had a dizzy spell."

"Is she all right?" Jonah's expression revealed his concern.

"I'm not sure, and I'm hoping she'll agree to see the doctor."

"That would probably be a good idea. Did anything else happen at the dinner?" he questioned.

"It was a total disaster. Grandma dropped one of our pies, and that crazy parakeet, Millie, got out of her cage and created quite a stir with the tourists. I've always enjoyed helping Grandma with our dinners, but I was actually relieved when the people left." Elaine paused to massage the back of her neck. "Anyway, I'll be taking Grandma to see Leah in the morning for a foot treatment."

Jonah's forehead creased. "I have nothing against Leah's reflexology practice, but she's not able to do blood tests and some other things that the doctor would want to do. And, as I'm sure you'd agree, Leah's treatments are not a cure-all for every illness."

"I realize that." Elaine didn't know why, but Jonah's comment made her defenses rise. "The only reason I'm taking Grandma to see Leah is in the hope that while Leah works on Grandma's feet, she can talk her into seeing the doctor."

"Do you think Edna will listen to Leah?"

"I hope so, because I wasn't able to convince her." Elaine's lips compressed. "When Grandpa was alive, he could talk Grandma into almost anything. I remember once when he wanted the three of us to go camping. Grandma didn't take to the idea, because she wasn't comfortable with sleeping in a tent."

"So what happened?" Jonah asked.

"Grandpa said if Grandma went camping, then he'd wash and dry the dishes for a whole week after we got home." Elaine smiled. "That was all it took. Grandma went camping."

"Did she enjoy it?"

"For the most part, but when it came time to crawl into that little tent for the night, she let it be known that she wasn't happy about it." Elaine's smile disappeared. "If Grandpa was here now, he'd figure out some way to get Grandma to see the doctor."

"Please let me know if there's anything I can do for you or Edna. I'll drop everything to come and help if you need me." Jonah's tender brown eyes remained fixed on her face.

"Danki." While Elaine appreciated Jonah's offer, he had a thriving business to run, and the thought of asking him for help made her feel guilty.

"I don't see why you felt it necessary to come with me today," Grandma said to Elaine as they headed to Leah's on Monday morning. "I've been to her house for foot treatments many times, and you never went along unless you were getting one, too."

Elaine gripped her horse's reins a little tighter. How could she explain her concerns without Grandma getting upset? She couldn't admit that she'd talked to Leah yesterday and planned the whole thing. Nor did she intend to mention that she didn't want Grandma taking the horse and buggy out alone until her physical issues had been resolved.

Were these spells due to stress because Grandma missed Grandpa so much, or were they caused by some illness or other medical condition? If anything happened to Grandma, Elaine didn't know what she would do. More than anything, she longed for things to be as they were before, but that was just wishful thinking.

In an effort to relieve some of her own stress, Elaine tried to focus on the fruit trees growing in a nearby orchard, with some of their colorful blossoms opening while other blossoms were drifting away. The white blossoms looked like snow as they flew off the trees and floated in tiny swirls across the road in front of them.

"Did you hear what I said?" Grandma asked, lightly bumping Elaine's arm.

"Jah, I heard. Just thinking about how to respond, is all."

"It seems rather simple to me." Grandma's brows furrowed. "I just want to know why you felt it necessary to accompany me today."

"Well," Elaine began hesitantly, "I know how tired you've been, and I thought you might not feel up to driving the horse by yourself."

Grandma folded her arms and huffed. "I may be old and tired, but I'm not too feeble to handle a horse and buggy."

"Okay." Elaine paused, searching for the right words. "I also thought it would be nice for me to visit with Leah's mamm while you have your foot treatment. Dianna and I haven't had a chance to talk since Grandpa's funeral, and I wanted to personally thank her for helping out during the funeral dinner."

"She was very helpful," Grandma agreed, "just as so many others from our community were that day. I'm thankful for the kindness of our Amish friends and neighbors."

Elaine nodded as she clicked her tongue and gave her horse, Daisy, the freedom to trot. The mare seemed eager to go, and Elaine was equally anxious to get to Leah's. She hoped and prayed that everything would go well once they got there.

"It's good to see you," Leah said when Edna and Elaine entered her parents' house. "How are you today?"

"We're both fine, but I'll probably be better once I've had a foot bath—I mean massage," Edna quickly corrected. Her cheeks colored and she fanned her face with both hands. "My, my, it's sure a warm day. Soon it'll be hot and humid."

Leah glanced at Elaine and gave her a brief smile. Then, taking Edna's arm, she said, "Why don't we head down to the basement now? Or if you'd rather not have to deal with the stairs, we can do the treatment up here in the living room."

"I've never had a problem going up and down stairs, and I'm sure I'll be just fine with them now," Edna huffed.

"Okay." Leah looked at Elaine again. "My mamm's outside in her garden. You may have seen her there when you pulled in."

Elaine shook her head. "Actually, I didn't, but I was focused on the front door. I'll go out and see if I can find Dianna now."

"Elaine wouldn't let me drive over here by myself this morning," Edna complained as Leah led the way to the basement. "She was afraid I might get woozy again, but I feel fine today." She moved across the room where the recliner sat and grunted as she lowered herself into it. "Elaine said she wanted to visit with your mamm, but I think she only came along because she's being overprotective."

"I know that Elaine is concerned, but then, shouldn't we appreciate it when someone we love cares about us?" Leah asked.

"Um. . .what was that?"

"I said, Elaine's concerned, and shouldn't we appreciate it when someone we love cares about us?" Leah repeated.

"You're right." Edna removed her shoes and stockings and reclined the chair, giving Leah better access to her feet.

As Leah started pressure-pointing the balls of Edna's feet, she found several sore spots that caused her patient to flinch. One area in particular, on the inside of the foot, signaled that there was a problem with Edna's pancreas. "That's really tender there, isn't it?"

Edna nodded. "I'll say. It feels like I've been walking barefoot and stepped on a sharp rock."

"I believe it's sore because there's a problem with your pancreas," Leah explained.

"What does that mean?"

"Well, I'm not a doctor, so I can't give you a diagnosis, but if you want my opinion, I think you should see your doctor so he can run some tests." Leah pulled her hands away from Edna's feet. "It's possible that you might have either diabetes or low blood sugar."

"Isn't there something you can do about that?" Edna asked with a hopeful expression.

"I might be able to help some, but not until you've had blood work done and know exactly what you're dealing with. If it is your blood sugar, the doctor will have special instructions for you and perhaps prescribe medicine to take."

Edna sighed. "Oh, all right; I'll see if I can get in to see the doctor sometime this week."

"Good. I'm glad you're willing to go." Leah handed Edna her socks and shoes. She hoped Edna kept her word, because she was truly worried about her. Not just because there might be a problem with her pancreas, but because of her lack of concentration and failing memory.

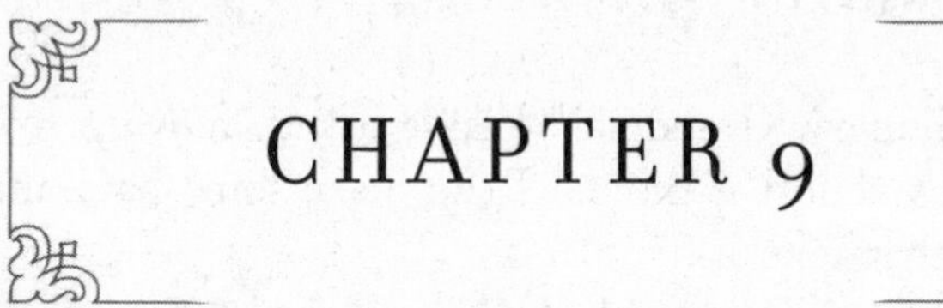

CHAPTER 9

When Edna returned home after her doctor's appointment on Thursday, she was so tired she could barely put one foot in front of the other. Elaine had hired a driver to take them since her horse had thrown a shoe. After a long wait, they were finally taken into the examining room, and then more waiting, until the doctor came in. Edna had never liked waiting, not even when she was a girl. After Dr. Larkens had examined Edna, he'd asked her so many questions it made her head hurt. Then he'd given her the paperwork needed to get some blood work. Since the lab work could only be done following an overnight fast, Edna would have to wait until tomorrow morning to go to the lab. That meant hiring their driver again.

Edna looked at the calendar on the kitchen wall and frowned. They had no more dinners scheduled for the rest of April, and just one so far for May. Now that the weather was warming up, she hoped more tourists would come to the area and book a dinner in her home. With today's doctor's appointment, and now lab work to get done, she could use some extra money to pay the bills. "The Lord will provide," she murmured.

"What was that, Grandma?" Elaine asked, entering the kitchen.

Edna turned and smiled at Elaine. "What was what?"

"What were you saying when I came into the room?"

"Just that. . . Oh, never mind, it wasn't important." No way was Edna going to admit that she'd forgotten what she'd said. It had bothered her today when Elaine told the doctor that she was concerned because Edna seemed forgetful lately.

I don't know why she even mentioned that, Edna thought. *What's forgetting a few little things got to do with the wooziness I've felt a few times?*

"Are you hungry, Grandma?" Elaine asked, moving toward the refrigerator. "It's almost noon and I can make some ham-and-cheese sandwiches, if that appeals."

"That'll be fine," Edna replied. "No *moschdept* for me, though. It makes my teeth burn."

"You mean mustard burns your tongue?"

Edna's cheeks warmed. "Jah, that's right." She was relieved when Elaine didn't make an issue out of her having said the wrong word.

"No problem. I don't particularly like mustard on my sandwich, either." Elaine took the ham, cheese, and a jar of mayonnaise from the refrigerator. Then she placed them on the counter near the sink.

Wanting to help, Edna got out the bread and a knife. "I'll make the sandwiches while you set the table."

Elaine shrugged. "Whatever you want to do is fine with me."

While Edna put the sandwiches together, Elaine set the table and poured them each a glass of iced tea with a slice of lemon. When the sandwiches were done, they took seats at the table and bowed their heads for silent prayer.

As Edna thanked God for the food, she thought about Lloyd and how, whenever he'd finished praying, he would rustle his napkin so that she and Elaine would know he was done. Oh, how she missed that sound. Even more, she missed him sitting at the head of their table. It was hard to think of her dear husband never coming back, but somehow she had to press on. Elaine needed her, and as much as she hated to admit it, she needed Elaine, too.

Heavenly Father, Elaine prayed, *I thank You for this meal and for the hands that prepared it. Lord, You know how much I love my grandma and how worried I am about her. I pray the outcome of her blood tests will let the doctor know what's wrong, and if it should turn out to be something serious, then please give us the grace to deal with it.*

Upon hearing a rustling noise, Elaine opened her eyes. When she looked over at Grandma, she noticed that her hand was on a napkin near the place where Grandpa used to sit. A lump formed in Elaine's throat. Hearing that familiar sound had almost been her undoing, but she held herself together in order to be strong for Grandma's sake. *Jah, Grandma, I miss him, too.*

Except for the muffled crying Elaine heard coming from behind Grandma's closed door each night, she hadn't witnessed Grandma openly grieving much. Elaine figured it was because Grandma was trying to put on a brave front for her sake. Maybe keeping busy and attempting to be strong for each other was what they both needed in order to deal with their grief and move forward.

Grandma pointed to her plate. "Shall we eat?"

Elaine nodded and picked up her sandwich. She really wasn't that hungry, but Grandma needed to eat, so she would do the same.

"Will you be going with me tomorrow for the blood tests?" Grandma asked, reaching for her glass of iced tea.

"I thought I would. When we're done, maybe we can stop somewhere for breakfast, since you'll have been fasting and will need to eat."

Grandma picked up her glass and took a drink. "Don't like it much when I prick my finger with a sewing needle, so I'm not looking forward to getting my arm stuck."

"I understand, but the blood draw is the only way to monitor your blood sugar in the morning, and I'm sure the doctor will be checking for other things as well."

Grandma frowned while fingering the edge of her plate. "Sure hope there's nothing seriously wrong. As much as I'd like to join your grossdaadi in heaven, I don't like the idea of leaving you alone."

"I wouldn't like that, either," Elaine said sincerely. "But let's not put the buggy before the horse. We need to wait till the tests are all in and we've talked to the doctor again next week. Now, why don't we change our topic of conversation to something cool and tasty?"

Grandma quirked an eyebrow. "Like what?"

"Well, we have some lemon sherbet in the freezer that we can have after lunch, if that appeals."

"That sounds good, but first there's something I need to say."

"Oh, what's that?"

Grandma looked directly at Elaine. "I think you need to think about the future, not just today."

"What do you mean?"

"Maybe you should marry Jonah right away, so you won't be alone after I'm gone."

Elaine nearly choked on the cold tea she was drinking. "For goodness' sakes, Grandma, I can't get married right now. I need to be here to take care of you. Besides, Jonah hasn't even asked me to marry him, and even if he did—"

Their conversation was interrupted by a knock on the door. "I'll see who it is," Elaine said, rising from the table.

When she opened the back door, she was surprised to see Jonah on the porch. She hadn't heard his horse and buggy pull in. She hoped he hadn't heard through the open kitchen window what Grandma had said to her. "Hello, Jonah. I—I didn't expect to see you today," Elaine stammered. "I figured you'd be hard at work in your buggy shop."

"I was, but I needed some bread at the bakery down the road, so figured it'd be a chance to drop by and see how things went at Edna's appointment this morning." Jonah smiled, and when he removed his straw hat, his curly dark hair stood straight up.

Elaine resisted the temptation to laugh, or worse yet, to reach out and flatten his hair in place. Instead, she asked him to come in. He either hadn't heard what Grandma had said or chose not to mention it.

When Jonah entered the house, he hung his hat over a wall peg and smoothed the top of his head. Elaine was glad, because she figured her outspoken grandma surely would have said something about Jonah's unruly hair if he went into the kitchen with it sticking up like that.

"Well, Jonah, now isn't this a coincidence?" Grandma grinned at Jonah. "We were just talking about you."

Oh no, Elaine groaned inwardly. *Please, Grandma, don't tell Jonah what was said.*

Jonah smiled. "Is that a fact? And what, might I ask, were you saying?"

"Oh, nothing much," Elaine was quick to say. She motioned to the sandwich makings on the counter. "Have you had lunch yet? I'd be happy to make you a sandwich."

"Sure, that'd be great. I'll head to the bathroom and wash up."

As soon as Jonah left the room, Elaine whispered to Grandma, "Please don't say anything to Jonah about marrying me, okay?"

Grandma shook her head. "I would never do that."

"That's good. Let's just keep the conversation on anything other than that topic."

"No problem."

Hoping Grandma kept her word, Elaine set about making a sandwich for Jonah. By the time he returned, it was ready and sitting on the table.

"Would you like iced tea or something else to drink?" Elaine asked after Jonah took his seat.

"Iced tea is fine, since that's what you're having," he replied.

Elaine poured Jonah a glass and then sat quietly while he said his silent prayer. "The ham-and-cheese sandwich has only mayonnaise on it, but I can get the mustard if you want some of that," she said once he'd lifted his head.

"No, that's okay. This is just how I like it."

"How about some potato chips?" Grandma asked. "I think we still have some in the pantry."

"The sandwich and tea are plenty for me," he responded. "Fact is, it's more than I expected to have for lunch today."

"If you had a wife, she'd make sure you were fed properly." Grandma glanced briefly at Elaine; then, looking away, she grabbed her iced tea and took a drink.

"This is sure nice spring weather we're having, isn't it?" Elaine asked Jonah, attempting to change the subject.

He nodded. "Always did like spring. It's not too hot and not too cold. Perfect weather for fishing and taking buggy rides."

They finished their meal with a bit of light conversation. Then Jonah turned to Elaine's grandma and said, "Did you see the doctor today?"

"Jah. He said he won't know why I've been feeling a bit puny lately until he gets the results of my blood tests." Grandma frowned. "I can't eat any breakfast in the morning because I'll be getting my blood drawn at the lab."

"We'll return to the doctor's next week," Elaine put in. "He should have the results of her blood work by then."

"It's good that you went. Please keep me posted when you know something definite." Jonah scooted his chair away from the table. "Danki for the lunch, but I probably should be on my way, unless there's something you need me to do first."

"How about doing the dishes?" Grandma asked in a teasing tone. "Since you're a bachelor, I'm sure you've learned how to wash them quite well."

A trickle of perspiration ran down Elaine's forehead. She hoped, once again, that Grandma wasn't on the verge of bringing up the topic of marriage.

"I'm sure Grandma's only kidding," Elaine was quick to say. "I'm perfectly capable of doing the dishes, and I'm sure you have better things to do with your time."

Jonah grinned and winked at Grandma. "I do know how to wash and dry the dishes, and maybe I'll prove that to you the next time I'm invited here for a meal. I hope you both have a good rest of the day," he added, moving toward the door.

Grandma leaned toward Elaine and whispered, "Aren't you going to see him out?"

"Certainly." Elaine followed Jonah to the door and handed him his hat. "Danki for stopping by, Jonah."

"No problem." He opened the door, but paused and turned to face her. "Say, I was wondering if you'd like to go for a buggy ride with me tomorrow evening. There's supposed to be a full moon, and I thought it would be a chance for us to spend a little time together."

"That sounds like fun, but with Grandma not feeling well, I'd better stay close to home in case she needs me."

"I'll be fine," Grandma called from the kitchen in a bubbly voice. "You two need to get out and enjoy this beautiful weather, and Elaine, I insist that you go for that ride."

Feeling that she had little choice in the matter, Elaine smiled at Jonah and said, "Unless something comes up to prevent it, I'll see you tomorrow night." Truth was, it would be nice to spend some time alone with Jonah, and hopefully it would lift her spirits.

CHAPTER 10

"If you don't need me for anything else right now, I think I'll get supper started," Sara told her mother-in-law.

"No, I'm fine," Betty said, leaning against the pillows Sara had placed under her head after she'd reclined on the sofa. Sara had also put an extra pillow under her broken leg. "I only wish I didn't have to lay here staring at the ceiling while you do all the work. I feel so *nixnutzich* right now."

"You're not worthless. I'm glad I can be here to help out." Sara patted her mother-in-law's arm affectionately. "I believe I'll get started on supper now. If you need anything, just holler."

"Carolyn can set the table," Betty called as Sara started for the kitchen. "And if the older boys aren't doing anything, they can mash potatoes or do whatever else you need."

"I'll keep that in mind," Sara said before disappearing into the other room. While she had planned on asking for Carolyn's help, it would be better if the boys stayed out of the kitchen. She remembered all too well how whenever Harley had helped get a meal on, he'd ended up either burning something or making a mess that Sara later had to clean up. *Even with the messes, I'd give anything to have Harley here right now, helping me in the kitchen.*

"Let's go, boy!" Jonah snapped the reins. "You're bein' a slowpoke again."

Ignoring Jonah's command, his temperamental horse just plodded.

Jonah grimaced. At this rate, he'd never get to Elaine's for their buggy ride. It had been too long since he and Elaine had spent some quality time alone, and he looked forward to a relaxing Friday evening, just the two of them. He wouldn't keep her out long, because she'd be worried about her grandmother.

Sure hope everything's gonna be okay with Edna, Jonah thought. *She and Elaine have been through enough.* Jonah hoped that someday he and Elaine would be as blessed as his parents. Mom and Dad had been through some rough times over the years, but nothing had kept them down or driven them apart. They worked together, prayed together, had fun together. There was no doubt in Jonah's mind—his folks made a great team.

Jonah had only seen his parents once since he left Pennsylvania and hoped they would come visit him and Jean soon. Dad's buggy business was even busier than Jonah's, so it was hard for him to set work aside and travel.

Maybe Mom and Dad will come here for Jean's and my birthday in July, Jonah thought. *That would sure be nice.*

As Edna's place came into view, Jonah guided his horse and buggy up the driveway. Just as he was securing Sassy to the hitching rack, a sleek-looking black cat streaked out of the barn and darted under the buggy. Sassy spooked and nearly pulled the reins from Jonah's hand. He didn't recognize the cat as one of Edna's and figured it was either a stray or had come from one of the neighboring farms. *Probably went into the barn to steal some of Patches' food,* he mused. *Or maybe the cat was looking for mice.*

Jonah secured Sassy to the rack and sprinted up to the house.

"Jonah's here," Grandma said as she and Elaine stood at the sink doing the last of the supper dishes. "I just saw a horse and buggy come into the yard. I'll bet he's anxious to take you for a buggy ride."

"I heard the *clippety-clop* of his horse's hooves, too." Elaine finished drying the plate she held and went to the back door.

"How are things going?" Jonah asked when he stepped onto the porch. "Is your *grossmudder* doing okay?"

"She's still quite tired, but at least she didn't have any dizzy spells today. But then, I made sure she took it easy and ate regular meals, with a few healthy snacks in between."

Jonah smiled. "That's good to hear. I'm sure you're anxious to get the results of her blood tests."

"Jah." Elaine opened the door wider. "Would you like to come in while I finish drying the dishes? There are just a few left to do."

"No problem. I don't mind waiting." Jonah removed his straw hat and smoothed the top of his hair. "I wanted to come in and say hi to Edna anyway."

Elaine smiled. She was glad Jonah was so considerate and thoughtful. In many ways, he reminded Elaine of her grandfather—a hard worker who was always conscious of others and their needs.

Elaine led the way to the kitchen, where Grandma stood at the sink, washing the last of the dishes.

"*Guder owed*, Edna," Jonah said.

Grandma glanced over her shoulder and smiled. "Good evening, Jonah. How are you?"

"I'm doin' well. How about yourself?"

"Can't complain, although I'd be doing much better if Lloyd was still here."

"I'm sure you must miss him," Jonah said. "I didn't know Lloyd as well as you and Elaine, of course, but from the first time I met him, I knew he was a good man."

Tears welled in Elaine's eyes. Knowing she needed to get her mind on something else, lest she start blubbering, she picked up the dish towel to dry the remaining dishes.

"Would you like a cup of coffee, or maybe some tea?" Grandma asked. "Lloyd used to enjoy having tea around this time every night, because coffee kept him awake."

Jonah glanced at the clock. "If it's not too late when Elaine and I get back from our buggy ride, I'll have a cup of tea."

"We should probably go now," Elaine said, placing the last of the dishes she'd dried into the cupboard. "I don't want to leave Grandma alone too long, so it's best if we're not out real late." Truth was, Elaine felt apprehensive about leaving Grandma alone at all, but if she didn't go on the ride with Jonah, Grandma would insist.

"That's fine," Jonah said. "We can go whenever you're ready."

"Just give me a minute to get my shawl and outer bonnet." Elaine hung up the dish towel and hurried from the room. When she returned, she was surprised to see Jonah sitting at the table, alone.

"Where'd my grandma go?" Elaine asked.

"Said she was tired and went to her room."

"I'd better go check on her." Elaine started in that direction but paused. "Maybe it would be best if we didn't go for a ride tonight."

Jonah dropped his gaze to the floor. He was obviously disappointed.

"Well, maybe it would be okay," Elaine said, quickly changing her mind. "Let me just go check on Grandma first."

While Elaine left the kitchen, Jonah remained in his chair. Elaine was concerned about Edna, but he wondered if she was being overly protective. Still, if Edna wasn't feeling well, they probably should put off the buggy ride until a better time.

"Grandma's resting, but she's not asleep," Elaine said when she returned. "I asked again if she'd prefer that I stay home with her this evening, but she insisted on us going for a buggy ride."

Jonah rose from his seat. "Okay, if you're sure, then I guess we'd better get going."

When they left the house and started across the yard, Jonah's horse snorted and stamped his hooves impatiently. "We'll be heading out soon, Sassy, so don't be so impatient," Jonah called before helping Elaine into his buggy. "That horse of mine is either raring to go or doesn't want to go at all. Here lately, he wants to move at a snail's pace."

Elaine smiled. "Sometimes I feel that way myself. There are days when it's an effort just to get out of bed."

"Makes sense that you'd feel that way when you have so much to do and are worried about your grandma besides." Jonah untied Sassy and had barely taken his place in the driver's seat when the horse started backing up. Any other time he would have had to coax the animal to back away from the hitch rack. "Talk about unpredictable!" Jonah chuckled and shook his head.

After Jonah guided the horse and buggy down the driveway and out onto the road, Sassy fell into a nice, easy trot. He glanced over at Elaine and smiled, noticing her peaceful expression, which he hoped meant she was beginning to relax. A romantic ride on a nice evening such as this could be good therapy for both of them.

Going past a small wetland area not far down the road, Jonah's ears perked up when the sound of nature's chorus greeted him. "Just listen to those peepers," he said, pulling back on the reins to slow Sassy. "That sounds like music to my ears every time I hear it this time of the year."

"I know what you mean," Elaine agreed. "Grandpa used to say that when the tree frogs started singing, it meant winter was over." Her voice cracked. "I wish he was still with us. Things could be much easier on my grandma. He was so good to her, and every day I miss him."

Jonah reached for her hand. "It's hard losing a loved one."

"Jah."

Feeling the need to talk about something a little lighter, Jonah said, "The other evening, when I was in the backyard picking up some twigs, I heard the peepers out behind my house by the pond. I've been opening my window every night since, 'cause that sound is like a lullaby singing me to sleep."

Elaine giggled, which was a confirmation to Jonah that she was having a good time. For Jonah, this evening would be another memorable time. He thought Elaine was one of the sweetest women he'd ever known. The fact that she was staying true to her responsibilities to take care of Edna was proof of Elaine's caring attitude, and he respected her for it. *What a great girl I have chosen. She's just right for me.*

They approached a row of sugar maples growing near the edge of the road. In autumn, the trees would be all aglow in their brilliant colors of gold, orange, and red. This area had become a popular spot for picture taking by many tourists who visited Douglas County. Jonah couldn't blame them. They were his favorite trees as well.

Although fading in the distance, Jonah could still hear the peepers behind them. That, plus the steady *clip-clop* of Sassy's hooves, was enough to put anyone into a peaceful state of mind.

"Have you done any rock painting lately?" Jonah asked, breaking the silence.

"No, I haven't had much time for that since Grandpa died." Elaine sighed. "I miss it, though. It's a relaxing hobby, and it's always fun to see what kind of rocks I can find that look similar to some animal."

"Speaking of rocks, I thought it might be fun if we went over to Rockome Gardens some Saturday afternoon. We could make a day of it."

She smiled. "That sounds nice, Jonah, but I wouldn't be comfortable leaving Grandma that long."

"She could come with us."

Elaine shook her head. "Grandma gets tired when she does a lot of walking. Maybe we could go some other time, once Grandma's doing better."

"Okay, I guess that would work."

Elaine touched Jonah's arm. "How are things going with your house? Are you getting it fixed up the way you'd wanted?"

Jonah nodded. "There are still some things I'd like to have done, and I'm trying to do a little something to each of the rooms every chance I get. It's slow going at times, because making and repairing buggies can be pretty demanding. Finding a few hours to work on my house gets a little difficult." He leaned in close to Elaine and smiled. "If you get some time in the future, I could use your thoughts on the type of cabinets to put in the kitchen. I'm not too sure what would look presentable or would accommodate someone using the space."

"Maybe I could do that sometime when Grandma has company. That way she won't feel like I've left her alone. Owning a home is a lot of responsibility, but I'm sure it's rewarding."

"Jah." *It would be even more rewarding if you agreed to marry me.* Jonah resisted the temptation to pull his buggy to the side of the road, take Elaine into his arms, and ask her to marry him right then. *"Patience is a virtue,"* his mother had reminded him many times over the years. Mom was right, but that didn't make it any easier to deal with impatience—especially when it came to his desire to marry Elaine. *I'll give her a few months, until Edna's doing better physically and has gotten over Lloyd's death sufficiently so she can be by herself.* Jonah's jaw clenched. *It wouldn't be fair to expect Elaine to leave her grandmother all alone in that big house if she marries me and moves to my place. The only logical thing is to suggest that Edna come live with us, too.*

As Jonah's horse picked up speed, he made a decision. When he felt the time was right to propose marriage, he would make sure Elaine knew that he intended to provide for her grandmother and that Edna was welcome to live with them.

CHAPTER 11

"Now, don't look so *naerfich*, dear one," Grandma said as she and Elaine entered the clinic on Thursday of the following week. "I'm sure everything's going to be fine."

"I'm not really nervous—just anxious to get the results of your blood test." Elaine took a seat in the waiting room. *Does my apprehension show that much?* she wondered.

Grandma sat down next to Elaine and picked up a gardening magazine. She began thumbing through it as though she hadn't a care in the world. Was she putting on a brave front for Elaine's benefit, or was this Grandma's way of dealing with her own trepidation?

Guess I'm having enough anxious thoughts for both of us. I hope we don't have to wait too long to see the doctor today. Elaine twisted the handles on her purse while glancing at the stack of magazines on the table in front of them. *No point in trying to read a magazine. I wouldn't be able to focus on any of the articles, interesting or not.*

Elaine was tempted to get up and start pacing but didn't want to draw attention to herself. Instead, she sat rigidly in her chair, picking at a bothersome hangnail. She couldn't help wondering how a little thing like that could be so sore. Fortunately, she didn't have to think about it long, for the nurse came out and asked them to follow her into the examining room.

Grandma took the magazine she'd been reading with her. Elaine figured Grandma may have thought they'd have to wait awhile for the doctor, or perhaps she'd found an interesting article she wanted to finish reading.

Once they were seated in the examining room and Grandma's vitals had been taken, Grandma continued to look at the magazine while Elaine's thoughts wandered. She looked around the room at all the charts on the wall. Some showed the heart and different valves and arteries leading in and out of the chambers. Other charts listed symptoms of certain health issues.

Elaine was glad she could be here for Grandma today and remembered back to a time when she'd had the flu and Grandma had sat up with her most of the night, doing all she could to bring down the fever and settle her upset stomach.

Elaine's thoughts switched to her first day of school, when Grandpa had given her a ride with his horse and buggy. He'd told Grandma that he didn't want Elaine walking to school by herself, and until she found a friend to walk with, he'd see that she got there safely each morning. Grandma and Grandpa had both taken an interest in the things Elaine had learned throughout her eight years of attending the Amish one-room schoolhouse—helping with her homework and listening intently as she shared some of the things she'd learned in class. Along with all the other parents, Elaine's grandparents had always attended Elaine's school programs. Just seeing their smiling faces as they sat on a bench in the schoolhouse had given Elaine a sense of joy. She'd never once felt like she didn't belong.

Grandma rustled the magazine, drawing Elaine's attention back to her. "What are you doing?" she asked when Grandma began tearing out a page.

Grandma smiled. "I found a recipe that sounds really good, and I'd like to try it sometime."

"But someone else may want to try that recipe, too." Elaine pulled a pen and notebook from her purse. "If you want, I'll write it down for you."

"I guess that would be the best thing to do. I don't know why I didn't think of it myself." Grandma handed the magazine to Elaine.

Elaine had just finished copying the recipe when Dr. Larkens entered the room.

"Good morning, ladies. I'm sorry to keep you waiting."

"Oh, that's all right." Grandma smiled up at him. "It didn't seem like we were waiting that long, and we know how busy you are."

He pulled up a chair in front of Grandma and motioned to the lab report he held. "All the results from your blood tests are back, Edna, and it appears that your symptoms are caused by high blood sugar."

"Does that mean my grandmother has diabetes?" Elaine asked before Grandma could offer any kind of response.

The doctor nodded. "It's Type 2 diabetes, and from the results of her tests, in addition to her symptoms, I'm guessing she's had it for a while."

"What should I do about it?" Grandma asked, calmly laying her magazine down.

"Most people can usually manage their diabetes with meal planning, physical activity, and, if needed, medications," he responded. "In your case, I want to begin by prescribing an oral form of insulin, and if that doesn't bring your blood sugar down, you may eventually need insulin shots."

Grandma's eyebrows shot straight up. "I don't like needles, and I'm sure I could never give myself an injection. If Lloyd was here, he could do it, because he always doctored our horses." She shook her head vigorously. "But no, not me. I just couldn't do it."

"It's okay, Grandma." Elaine reached over and clasped Grandma's hand. "Should it become necessary for you to take insulin shots, I'll do it for you." *I won't like it, but I'll do whatever I have to do,* she mentally added.

"Elaine, if it comes to that, my nurse, Annie, will give you the proper instructions." Dr. Larkens looked back at Grandma. "Edna, you'll also need a kit to test your blood sugar every day, and Annie will show Elaine how to use that as well."

Grandma groaned. "I'll take the pill, eat right, and exercise. I'd do anything to avoid getting an insulin shot."

Elaine took the prescription the doctor had written, as well as a list of foods Grandma should and shouldn't eat, and put them in her purse. They would stop at the pharmacy for her medicine before heading home. She hoped Grandma would do everything the doctor suggested, because even though she'd volunteered to give Grandma her insulin shots, just the idea of it made her feel nervous.

"I'll walk over to the pharmacy to get your prescription," Elaine told Edna after she'd pulled her horse and buggy up to one of several hitching racks in downtown Arthur. Typical of late April, the weather had been pleasant and comfortably dry. No doubt humid weather would be coming soon. But for now, the sun shone brightly in a clear azure sky, and a pleasant breeze had come up from the south. It was a near-perfect day.

"I can go with you." Grandma opened her mouth wide and yawned, then quickly covered it with her hand. "That way I can tell the pharmacist what I need."

"He will know what you need as soon as I show him this." Elaine reached into her purse and took out the prescription. "You look tired, Grandma, so it might be best if you stay here and rest." While that was true, the real reason Elaine didn't want Grandma to go into the pharmacy was because she'd be tempted to buy something sweet. In addition to prescriptions and other medical-related products, the pharmacy on Vine Street had an old-fashioned soda fountain where a person could sit and enjoy a tasty cold treat. Grandma had never been able to resist the root beer floats that were sold there.

Grandma frowned, making Elaine wonder if she might insist on getting out of the buggy, but to her relief, she finally nodded and said, "I am kind of tired. Maybe I'll just sit here and close my eyes for a bit."

"I shouldn't be gone long, so try to relax." Elaine patted Grandma's arm gently, then climbed out of the buggy and headed down the street.

When she entered the pharmacy a short time later, Elaine went straight to the drop-off area and turned in Grandma's prescription, since it might take awhile for it to be filled. After she was told that it would be about fifteen minutes, she headed toward the discount aisle, where things were usually marked down. On her way, she passed the candy and gum aisle. Normally, Elaine would have bought some candy, but knowing Grandma shouldn't have any, she thought better of it.

I'm going to have to think twice before I bring sugary treats into our home anymore. Since Grandma had always enjoyed sweets, it would be hard for her to give up some of the things she liked to eat. Elaine didn't like the idea of giving up sweet things, either, but if it would help Grandma, she would do whatever it took to keep her from being tempted. *It's probably best for me, too,* she told herself, *since diabetes can be hereditary.*

Elaine looked at a few of the discounted items but didn't see anything that interested her. She was about to head back to the prescription area and wait for her name to be called when she noticed Priscilla standing in the checkout line at the other end of the store. Elaine hurried to catch up with her and got there just as Priscilla finished paying for her purchases.

"I'm glad I ran into you today," Elaine said to her friend. "I thought you might like to know that we got the results of Grandma's blood work today."

"How did it go?" Priscilla asked.

Looking for a better place to talk, Elaine led the way to the greeting-cards aisle, since no one else was there at the moment.

"Grandma has Type 2 diabetes." Elaine cringed at the thought of what may lay ahead for Grandma—and her as Grandma's caregiver. "That's why she hasn't been feeling well lately."

"I'm sorry to hear that." Priscilla's tone was as sincere as her expression. "Can it be controlled by altering her diet, or will she have to be on insulin?"

"The doctor said Grandma will have to change her eating habits and exercise, but he also gave us a prescription for medicine, which she'll have to take every day." Elaine sighed deeply. "I hope Grandma does everything she's supposed to, because if her diabetes worsens, she may have to take insulin shots. Unfortunately, I'll be the one giving them to her, and just the thought of that makes me naerfich."

"Try not to worry about it." Priscilla gave Elaine's shoulder a tender squeeze. "I'm sure with you there to remind Edna to eat right and take her medicine, everything will be fine."

Edna had been in a deep sleep, but the nap hadn't lasted long. The sound of her own snoring suddenly woke her. Waiting for Elaine, she grew more restless. It was getting stuffy inside the buggy, and she could really use something to drink. Whatever breeze had been moving through the open buggy door when they'd first arrived was suddenly at a standstill. *Think I'll get out and walk over to the pharmacy,* she decided, taking a hankie and wiping the back of her neck where perspiration had collected. One of Edna's legs was on the verge of getting a charley horse, and no matter how much she wiggled and rubbed it, her toes started cramping, too.

The idea of treating herself to a frosty chocolate malt, root beer float, or dish of hand-dipped ice cream sounded pretty good to Edna. The pharmacy in Arthur had been making milk shakes, malts, and sodas in a variety of flavors for a good many years, and for as long as she and Lloyd were married, they'd made a trip into town once a week to indulge in one of the icy cold treats. Edna's mouth watered just thinking about it.

With the decision made, she grabbed her purse, stepped down from the buggy, and headed toward the pharmacy. It felt good to get the kinks out of her legs, although her dress clung tightly against the front of her legs as she walked head-on into a sudden, refreshing breeze.

She'd only gone a short distance when she spotted the Stitch and Sew, which was also on Vine Street. *Maybe I'll pop in and buy some white thread,* she decided. *It won't take long, and I'm sure I'll be done before Elaine leaves the pharmacy.*

CHAPTER 12

When Elaine left the pharmacy and returned to the buggy, she was surprised to discover that Grandma wasn't there. It was much warmer than when she'd gone into the drugstore, so perhaps in order to cool off, Grandma had taken a walk. *But where can she be?* Elaine felt a sense of panic. *She didn't come into the pharmacy—I'm sure I would have seen her there.*

Elaine looked up and down the street, but there was no sign of Grandma. She figured she only had two choices: wait at the buggy and hope Grandma returned soon from wherever she'd gone, or start looking for Grandma in some of the stores. Deciding on the latter, Elaine headed back down the street.

After checking a few places along Vine Street with no success, Elaine decided to stop by the Stitch and Sew. When she entered the building, the smell of material hit her nostrils and made her sneeze. Her eyes also began to water. *It must be my allergies to chemical odors kicking in.*

Stepping up to the counter, Elaine was about to ask the clerk if she'd seen her grandmother when she spotted Grandma talking to Priscilla's mother, Iva, near the notions aisle.

"Oh, what are you doing in here?" Grandma asked when Elaine walked up to her. "I thought you'd gone to the pharmacy to get my prescription filled."

"I did go there, but when I got back to the buggy you were gone."

"It was getting stuffy, so I went for a walk, and when I saw the Stitch and Sew, I realized that I needed some thread." Grandma gestured to Priscilla's mother. "Then when I spotted Iva, we got to talking." She stared at Elaine and pursed her lips. "Is everything okay? You look like you're about ready to cry."

"I'm all right," Elaine said when Grandma handed her a tissue. "Sometimes the smell of so much material in one place makes my eyes tear up and causes me to sneeze." She smiled at Priscilla's mother. "It's nice to see you, Iva."

"You, too, Elaine."

Feeling a sneeze coming on, Elaine held the tissue up to her nose. "Achoo!"

"Bless you," Grandma said, patting Elaine's back.

Elaine giggled self-consciously, feeling heat creep up the back of her neck and spread quickly to her cheeks. "How are you, Iva?"

"I'm doing pretty well. By the way, Priscilla was going to the pharmacy. Did you happen to see her there?"

"As a matter of fact, I did." Elaine placed her fingers against her nose to stifle another sneeze. "We visited awhile, and then I think Priscilla said she was going over to Yoder's Lamp Shop. She's probably there now."

Iva turned toward the door. "I'd better go see if I can catch her. It was nice seeing you both, and don't hesitate to let us know if you need anything at all."

"Danki." Elaine waved as Iva went out the door, but Grandma just stood there with a peculiar expression.

"What's wrong, Grandma?" Elaine asked. "Are you pondering something?"

"I—I know I came in here for a reason, but for the life of me, I can't think of what it is."

"You said you needed some thread."

"Oh, that's right." Grandma made her way to the notions aisle and picked out her thread.

"Let's go get something cold and frosty." She pointed toward the door. "I'll have a root beer float."

"That sounds good, but remember what the doctor said. You're supposed to be careful of what you eat now that you've been diagnosed with diabetes."

Grandma's chin dropped slightly. "I'll feel deprived if I can never indulge in anything sweet."

"You can have fruit in moderation, and we'll learn to make some desserts using sugar substitutes."

Grandma sighed. "If I can't get a root beer float, then as soon as I pay for my thread, we may as well head for home, because I'm hungerich."

Elaine felt bad as she watched Grandma shuffle over to the checkout counter with slumped shoulders. With all that had happened in the last couple of weeks, it would be hard to see Grandma deprived of something as simple as enjoying ice cream. Once she got started on her insulin, and with the doctor's approval, maybe it would be okay if she cheated on her diet once in a while.

"We'll stop at the market before going home and pick up some fresh fruit," Elaine said after they'd left the store.

Jonah had just pulled up to one of the hitching racks in Arthur when he noticed Elaine's horse and buggy parked at the other end.

"How are ya doin' there, Daisy girl?" Jonah asked the horse, walking up to her and petting her velvety soft nose.

Daisy nickered in return, stomping her foot and swishing her tail to keep the bothersome flies at bay.

"Good thing you're in the shade over here. The sun's warming things up real quick today." Jonah glanced down the street as he reached up to scratch behind Daisy's ears.

Daisy shook her mane as if in agreement, then nudged her head closer. "Ah, I see that you like your ears scratched, too." Jonah smiled and watched as Daisy's head lowered and she closed her eyes. He even thought he heard the horse heave a sigh.

Jonah felt silly standing here, talking to a horse, but he was actually biding time. *Should I wait till Elaine comes back to her buggy, or would I have a better chance of seeing her if I went looking in some of the shops?* As always, Jonah was anxious to see Elaine, if only for a few minutes. But knowing he needed to get back to his shop soon, he decided to poke his head into some of the stores on his way to Yoder's Lamp Shop, where he needed to pick up a gas lamp he'd taken in for repairs a week ago.

One last scratch behind Daisy's ear and Jonah began to whistle as he headed toward Yoder's. He checked a few of the other stores as he went by but didn't see any sign of Elaine. When he reached his destination, he collided with Priscilla, who was just coming out the door.

"Sorry about that," Jonah apologized, propping the door open with his foot. "Sure hope you're not hurt. I should have been watching where I was going."

Priscilla's face flushed as she quickly shook her head. "You just startled me, is all. I didn't expect anyone would be coming in the door at the same time I was going out."

"Me neither." Jonah stepped to one side. "Say, you haven't by any chance seen Elaine around town? I spotted her horse and buggy at one of the hitching racks, so I figured she must be here someplace."

"I met up with her at Dick's Pharmacy awhile ago," Priscilla replied. "She was getting a prescription filled for her grandma."

Jonah's forehead wrinkled. "Is Edna grank?"

"She saw the doctor today and got the results of her blood tests." Priscilla pursed her lips. "I should probably let her tell you this, but Edna has diabetes and needs to take insulin for it."

"Wow, that's too bad. Will she have to give herself shots?"

"Not at this time, but she will have to take a pill that will hopefully balance her blood sugar. She'll also need to be on a special diet."

"Hopefully between the medicine and eating right, she'll be okay."

Priscilla nodded. "I know Edna likes sweets, so it'll probably be hard for her to stay on the diet."

"I'm sure Elaine will see that she does," Jonah said. "Speaking of Elaine, do you know where she went after she left the pharmacy?"

"No, I don't. If her horse and buggy's still at the hitching rack, she's obviously in town somewhere."

"Guess I'll pick up my lamp and then check for her in some of the other stores. See you around, Priscilla."

After Jonah left Yoder's, he stopped at several stores, but there was no sign of Elaine. Hoping he might catch her before she left town, he headed back to his horse and buggy. When he got there, Elaine's rig was gone. He was warm and sweaty and couldn't help thinking how refreshing a dip in his pond would feel. That would have to wait for some other time, because he had plenty of work waiting for him once he got home.

"Guess I should have come back here as soon as I left the lamp shop," Jonah mumbled, placing the box with his lamp in it inside his warm buggy. He would have headed over to Edna's place to see Elaine right now, but he needed to get back to the shop and finish upholstering the seat he'd started this morning for the buggy he was making for their bishop. *Maybe I'll go see her this evening after supper,* Jonah decided. *I need to ask her something important.*

When they arrived home that afternoon, after stopping for lunch, Grandma went into the house while Elaine tended to Daisy, rubbing the mare down and giving her fresh water. Following that, she took a few minutes to play with the cats. Patches, as usual, demanded the most attention, purring and rubbing against Elaine's ankles. This was the second cat she'd named Patches, and like the first one, whom her grandparents had given to her shortly after her parents died, Patches had always been a good mouser, even when she was a kitten.

"Oh, I know what you want." Elaine knelt on the barn floor and smiled when Patches rolled over on her back with all four paws in the air. "Does that feel good?" Elaine rubbed the cat's belly and laughed when Boots, one of their other cats, got into the act, batting at Patches' tail. Patches jumped up, and the two felines ran off. "That's okay," she murmured. "I need to quit lollygagging and go into the house."

As Elaine rose to her feet, she realized how nice it had been to take a bit of time and enjoy something as simple as petting the cat. As busy as she was, she needed to take time once in a while to do little things like that.

When Elaine entered the kitchen, she was surprised to see several things cooking on the stove, and from the wonderful aroma, something was baking in the oven. Grandma was busily setting out the good dinnerware they used when hosting tourist guests.

"Oh, I'm glad you came in." Grandma turned to smile at Elaine. "I didn't realize it was so late, and there's so much to do before the tour group arrives."

"Oh no, Grandma, I think you're confused about—"

"Elaine, could you please check on the potatoes?" Grandma gestured to the stove. "I don't want anything to boil over while I'm in the other room, setting the table. Oh, and the cake I have in the oven needs to be tested to see how close it is to being done."

Elaine couldn't believe Grandma thought they were hosting a dinner. *Could she have booked it without telling me?* She hurried over to the desk in the kitchen to check the reservation book, but nothing was scheduled.

"We aren't hosting a dinner tonight, Grandma," Elaine explained. "The tour director said she would give us at least a month before she called to schedule another one."

Grandma's face blanched. "What?"

Elaine repeated herself and added with emphasis, "There are no tourists coming here this evening."

Grandma blinked rapidly. "Oh, how silly of me. Don't know why I thought that." She motioned to the food on the stove. "Looks like we'll have plenty to eat for our supper tonight, with lots of leftovers for tomorrow. And oh, won't it be nice to have a piece of that chocolate cake for dessert?"

"Sorry, Grandma," Elaine said, slowly shaking her head, "but that cake in the oven will have to go to someone else, because it's not going to stay here to tempt you."

CHAPTER 13

Jonah had just finished a tuna sandwich when a knock on the door startled him. Setting his empty plate on the kitchen counter, he went to answer it. Jonah hadn't heard a horse and buggy pull into the yard, or he would have looked out the window to see who it was.

When Jonah opened the door, he was surprised to see his twin sister, Jean, standing on the porch.

"From the look of shock on your face, I'm guessing you're surprised to see me," Jean said, smiling up at him.

He nodded. "It's suppertime. Figured you'd be home fixing your family's meal."

"We've already had our supper, and my thoughtful husband not only offered to watch the kinner while I went for a bike ride, but he also volunteered to do the dishes."

"Well, that was sure nice of him." Jonah opened the door wider. "Come in. I'll fix you a cup of tea."

"I'd like that."

Once Jean was seated at the kitchen table, Jonah poured them both tea and took the chair across from her.

"What's new with you?" she asked.

"I finished upholstering the seat on a new buggy for our bishop today."

"That's interesting, but I was thinking more along the lines of what's new with you and Elaine."

He folded his arms. "Oh, that."

"Jah, that." She winked at him. "Have you gotten up the nerve to ask her to marry you yet?"

Jonah's face heated. After hearing about Edna's diagnosis, he'd made a decision. Did his sister know what he was planning to do this evening when he went to see Elaine? Well, he wouldn't tell her now—not until he'd proposed and Elaine had said yes. Then Jean would be the first to know.

"Carolyn and Marla, you two need to help Sara with the dishes," Sara's father-in-law, Herschel, said after the family had finished eating supper on Thursday evening.

"That's okay; I can manage," Sara was quick to say. Truth was, she'd been dealing with the energetic children all afternoon and needed some time by herself. She'd never met two little girls who got on her nerves as much as her two young sisters-in-law, and it seemed that she had so little patience these days. Caring for Mark didn't bother her so much, because he had no siblings and wasn't looking to pick on a little brother or sister. But since coming here to take care of Betty and oversee the children, Sara's ability to cope seemed to diminish a little more each day.

"All right then," Herschel said, "Carolyn and Marla can keep little Mark occupied in the living room while you're in here getting the dishes done." He smiled at his wife. "Isn't it nice to have Sara here to manage things for us?"

Betty gave an agreeable nod. "I appreciate everything you've done, Sara, but I'll be glad when my leg is healed. Then I'll be able to resume my household duties and take care of my kinner again. It's hard to sit around all the time and watch you do most of the work, Sara."

"I don't mind, really," Sara responded, filling the sink with soapy water. "Now why don't you go into the other room and rest your leg? When I'm finished with the dishes, I'll bring in some coffee for the adults and milk for the kinner, along with some peanut butter cookies I made earlier today."

"Kichlin! Yum!" Marla exclaimed.

Sara couldn't help but smile. She remembered how much she had enjoyed the treat of cookies and milk when she was girl. For that matter, she still enjoyed eating them.

As Betty rose from her chair, Herschel handed the crutches to her. Then he removed his and Betty's dishes from the table and took them to the sink. "Now I want all of you kinner to clear away your *schissele* and then scoot on outa here and let Sara have some peace and quiet. Ya hear?"

All heads bobbed, and the children quickly did as their father said.

An hour later, after Sara had cleaned up the kitchen and finished doing the dishes, she set out the coffee, milk, and cookies. Then she took a seat at the table to rest a minute, because a sense of exhaustion had settled over her like a heavy blanket of fog. Of course, feeling this way was nothing new; she'd felt weary ever since her husband died. The tiredness Sara felt now was different, though; it was the kind of fatigue that stayed with her no matter how many hours of sleep she got every night. It often came on in the afternoon, and sometimes her muscles felt weak. The other day, when she was dealing with a senseless squabble between Carolyn and Marla about who would get to feed the cats, Sara's lips had felt sort of tingly, and her limbs became weak and shaky. Figuring it was caused from the stress of it all, Sara had shooed the children outside, fixed herself a cup of chamomile tea, and gone to the room where little Mark was napping. There, she'd taken a seat on the bed and tried to relax. *"Too much stress can make your body react in strange ways,"* she remembered her mother saying.

I wonder how much longer I can continue taking care of Betty and her family, feeling the way that I do. Truth was, Sara felt like she needed someone to take care of her right now.

Sara drew in a deep breath and closed her eyes. *Heavenly Father, please give me the strength I need for each new day, and help me to be a blessing to Betty, Herschel, and their children.*

Elaine had just turned out the gas lamp that hung over the kitchen table when she heard the whinny of a horse. Going to the window, she glanced out and saw Jonah getting down from his buggy. She hurried to the back door, anxious as always to see him. She didn't have to wait long, for Jonah was already sprinting across the lawn toward the house. Elaine smiled, watching Patches get out of his way. By the time Jonah stepped onto the porch, Elaine had opened the door.

"Good evening, Jonah," she said, smiling up at him. "It's nice to see you."

"Same here." Jonah shifted from one foot to the other and raked his fingers through the ends of his thick, curly hair. "I ran into Priscilla today at Yoder's Lamp Shop. She told me about Edna having diabetes."

Elaine nodded. "It was a surprise to both me and Grandma—especially when the doctor said her diabetes is so bad that she needs to be on insulin. Now, in addition to her taking the medicine, we'll have to start cooking differently, since her intake of sweets will need to be limited. By the way, I have a cake here that Grandma baked today, and I don't want it to tempt her. Would you like to take it home?"

"That'd be great, but I'm sure sorry to hear about her diagnosis. If she does everything the doctor says, hopefully her diabetes won't get any worse."

"That's what I'm hoping for, too." Elaine was on the verge of telling Jonah about Grandma cooking a big meal for tourists who weren't coming but changed her mind. If Grandma's forgetfulness was a symptom of her diabetes, then Elaine needed to inform the doctor about it rather than telling Jonah. Besides, she was embarrassed for Grandma.

"It's a nice evening. Would you like to sit out here and talk, or would you rather go inside?" she asked, motioning to the wicker chairs on the porch.

"Out here's fine with me," Jonah replied. "That way we can talk in private."

Elaine couldn't imagine what he might have to say that couldn't be said in front of Grandma, but she nodded and took a seat.

After Jonah seated himself in the chair beside Elaine, he looked over at her and smiled. "I was going to wait awhile longer to ask you this question, but I've decided not to wait any longer."

"Wait for what, Jonah?" she questioned.

"I'm in love with you, Elaine, and if you'll have me, I'd like you to be my wife."

Elaine's heart hammered so hard, she wondered if Jonah could hear it pounding in her chest. She had been hoping for this day and would have answered yes immediately if things had been different. But not now. It just wasn't possible for them to get married anytime soon.

As Jonah watched her with an anxious expression, Elaine turned her head toward the setting sun. As she gazed at the sky, it took on a beauty of its own. Various shades of orange and pink blended with the fading blue. Farther back, the sky looked almost purple, which added to what should have been the most romantic and memorable evening of Elaine's life. Jonah's proposal was supposed to be her dream come true, but now, even on this ideal evening with nature flawlessly cooperating, things were different. Her heart screamed, *"I love you, too, and nothing would make me happier than to be your wife!"* If only she felt free to say those words.

Jonah reached over and touched her arm. "Your silence makes me wonder if you have no desire to marry me."

Tears sprang to Elaine's eyes as she looked back at Jonah. "It—it's not that. I do care for you, Jonah, but. . ." Her words trailed off, and she dropped her gaze, staring down at her shoes. *Why now, Jonah?*

Elaine had imagined what the first time would be like when she declared to Jonah how much she loved him. But now her mouth went dry, and the words seemed to stick in her throat. Common sense made Elaine hold her tongue, but it was the hardest thing she'd ever had to do.

"Do you care about me enough to become my wife?" he asked.

"I—I can't, Jonah."

"How come?"

"Grandma's ill, and she needs me. Not to mention that both of us are still trying to come to grips with Grandpa's death. There's no way I can leave her now."

"I'm not asking you to leave her, Elaine." Jonah lifted his hand from Elaine's arm and took hold of her hand. "I was thinking that Edna could move in with us. My home is big enough for the three of us, and if she wants an area all to herself, I could add on to the house so she would have her own *daadihaus*."

"I don't think Grandma would be happy moving from her own place here, or living in a grandparent house somewhere else. This has been my grandma's home for a good many years, and she enjoys doing the dinners here for tourists." Elaine blinked as Jonah's face became a blur through her tears. "I can't take that away from her, Jonah. She's going through a difficult time getting used to Grandpa being gone, and now finding out that she has diabetes. . . Well, it just wouldn't be fair to expect her to deal with yet another change." Elaine looked toward the horizon again, noticing that the sun had faded. The moment had passed, just like her hopes and dreams.

Jonah sat quietly with his head down, as though studying something on the porch floor. Elaine figured he was trying to process everything. After several minutes, he lifted his head and turned in his seat to face her. "I understand all that you've said, and as anxious as I am to make you my wife, maybe it would be best if we wait awhile longer to get married."

"Danki for understanding, Jonah."

"When you feel the time is right, will you please let me know?" he asked, swiping at a pesky mosquito that had picked a poor time to buzz past his ear.

She smiled and nodded. "Jah, I surely will."

CHAPTER 14

It had been a month since Elaine rejected Jonah's marriage proposal. *Well, maybe not rejected, exactly,* Jonah told himself as he entered his shop on the last Thursday of May. Elaine had just put her decision on hold for a while, which to him was somewhat reassuring, and better than Elaine saying no to his proposal. He wondered, though, how long it would be before she felt ready to make a commitment to him. Would it be a year from now, when her grandmother's time of mourning was up, or would Elaine feel ready for marriage sooner? While Jonah waited, he would continue to fix up his place, and maybe it would be more than ready by the time Elaine agreed to marry him. Keeping busy always helped time pass quickly, and there were certainly several projects at home, as well as in his shop, to keep Jonah busy.

The waiting wouldn't be easy, though. Jonah could still picture that night when he'd proposed marriage, with the sunset glowing on Elaine's beautiful face. Jonah couldn't take his eyes off her as he watched for a clue, anticipating the answer he'd hoped to hear. Everything about that moment would have been perfect if she'd only said yes. Afterward, like a craving that couldn't be satisfied, Elaine's image was all he could think about, for she'd never looked more radiant.

Aside from seeing Elaine at their biweekly church services, Jonah hadn't spent much time with her, and he truly missed that. Just being near Elaine stirred his heart. It was pure agony standing around after services, talking with the other men and trying to seem interested in what they were saying. On one occasion, Jonah had only heard about half of the conversations going on around him when he'd caught a glimpse of Elaine walking with her grandma to their buggy. Jonah had excused himself and hurried in that direction, but then he got waylaid when one of his friends stopped to ask him a question. By the time Jonah got away, Elaine's horse and buggy were heading down the road toward home. He'd planned to go over there that evening, but Jean had invited him to her place for supper, and Jonah felt obligated to go.

Jonah had hoped that one day soon he could take Elaine to Rockome Gardens. Now he wasn't sure he would bring the subject up again. He doubted that she would leave Edna alone for that long.

Jonah paused at his workbench and drew in a deep breath. *What if Elaine never feels ready to leave her grandma? What if Edna isn't willing to leave her home and move in with us?*

Jonah's thoughts were halted when Adam Beachy entered his shop. Jonah didn't know the Amish man very well, but from what he'd heard, Adam was in his late twenties and preferred to keep to himself as much as possible.

"Guder mariye. What can I do for you, Adam?" Jonah asked.

"Mornin'," Adam mumbled, barely making eye contact with Jonah. "I came to see about getting a new buggy. My old one's seen better days."

"I have several orders ahead of you. How soon do you need it?"

Adam shrugged and lifted his straw hat, swishing his fingers through the sides of his thick blond hair. "There's no real rush, I guess, but I was hoping to have it before my sister and her family come to visit me."

"When will that be?" Jonah questioned.

"They live in Indiana and will be here for Christmas."

"It shouldn't be a problem to get it done before then. Starting today, Herschel Stutzman's son Timothy will be helping me in the shop. Once I get him trained, I'll be able to get more done." Jonah glanced at the battery-operated clock on the far wall. "In fact, Timothy ought to be here most any time."

Adam's pale eyebrows lifted. "So the boy wants to learn the buggy-making trade, huh?"

Jonah nodded. "He's sixteen, and now that he's done with school, his folks want him to learn a trade that will always be in demand—at least among us Amish folks. Since I need help here in the shop, I'm hoping it'll work out well for both of us." He reached for an order blank and took a seat at the desk. "Now, if you'll tell me what specifics you'd like in your new buggy, I'll write it all down."

"I'd like a dark gray color for the seat upholstery." Adam leaned on one corner of the desk. Then he went on to tell Jonah all the other things he wanted, including his need for the new buggy to be large enough to carry six people. "I want the buggy to accommodate my sister, her husband, and their three girls, even though they don't come here often," he explained.

"Okay, that shouldn't be a problem."

Jonah had just finished writing up Adam's order and taken his deposit of half down on the new buggy when Timothy showed up. "Sorry I'm late," the lanky teenager said. "One of our frisky goats got out of its pen, and I had to help my *bruder* Paul get him put back in."

"That's okay," Jonah said. "Things happen sometimes."

"Danki for understanding." The boy's worried expression quickly disappeared, and he moved across the room to hang his straw hat on one of the wall pegs.

Jonah had made a carbon copy of the buggy order, so he handed that to Adam. "I'll give you a call as soon as the buggy is ready, but feel free to drop by anytime to see how things are progressing. That way, if there's anything you want to add or change, there'll be time for me to do it. I'll probably get started on it in the next few weeks."

"All right then. I'll be in touch." With a brief "Good-bye," Adam headed out the door.

That fellow never smiled once while he was here, Jonah mused. *I wonder what soured fruit he had for breakfast. No wonder he's not married. Guess he's destined to be a bachelor.*

"Ouch, that hurts!" Sara winced when Leah pressed a certain area on her left foot. She'd come here for a treatment this morning because her feet were sore from standing so much, not to mention running after Betty's children and doing what seemed like an abundance of chores every day.

"You're not feeling well, are you?" Leah asked, continuing to massage and probe Sara's foot. "I can tell by how you're reacting to some of the pressure points I've touched so far."

"I'm not sick." Sara sighed. "Just tired and feeling quite stressed."

"That's understandable. It can't be easy for you taking care of Betty, her children, and little Mark and, on top of that, doing all the household chores."

"I don't mind, really, but it has taken a toll. Besides the fatigue, my limbs sometimes feel kind of tingly." Sara squeezed her eyes shut and clenched her fingers when Leah hit another tender spot. "It's most likely my nerves, and it's probably terrible of me to say this, but I'll be glad once Betty is back on her feet, and Mark and I can return home where it's quiet."

"How much longer till Betty's cast comes off?" Leah asked.

"Another week or so, but then she'll need physical therapy."

"Maybe once that happens you can go back to your own place and just go over to help out at Betty's during the day."

"Guess I'll have to wait and see how it goes."

"In the meantime, it might be good if you tried to get more rest." Leah reached for her bottle of massage lotion and put some on Sara's other foot. "And if possible, you may want to come back here more often for treatments, at least until you're feeling better."

"That might be a good idea." Sara smiled. "I appreciate your mamm keeping an eye on Mark while I'm down here in the basement with you. Betty's not up to watching him yet, and I sure couldn't ask Carolyn or Marla. Neither one of them is responsible enough to take care of an active toddler."

"I'm sure Mom doesn't mind spending time with your boy," Leah said. "She loves kinner and has a special way with them, too."

As Leah continued to work on Sara's feet, the pain subsided, and she found herself beginning to relax. It felt good to do something for herself for a change, and hopefully after the treatment, she would have a bit more energy and be able to cope better with things.

As Elaine left the phone shanty and started walking toward the house, she paused to pick a few flowers. "So pretty." Elaine smiled, inhaling their fragrance.

Millie seemed to be enjoying the moment. The weather was nice, so Elaine had decided to bring the parakeet's cage outside on the porch. Of course, the little bird had been jabbering ever since. *"Purdy, purdy, purdy,"* Millie repeated several times.

"Jah, you silly bird, the flowers are pretty." Elaine thought the colorful irises would make a nice bouquet to put on the table, and it might help lift Grandma's spirits. After learning that she had diabetes, Grandma had become negative, complaining about having to give up her favorite desserts. Even though Elaine had found some sugar-free recipes in a diabetic cookbook she'd bought at the health food store, Grandma said they didn't taste as good as desserts made with real sugar.

Hoping Leah could convince Grandma that she needed to follow the diet her doctor had suggested, Elaine had scheduled several more reflexology appointments for Grandma. In fact, Grandma had seen Leah yesterday, but apparently it hadn't helped much, because everything she'd talked about on the way home was negative. Was her attitude because of her diabetes, or did she miss Grandpa so much that she couldn't focus on anything positive?

Maybe Grandma needs something to look forward to, Elaine thought. Well, the phone message Elaine had found on their answering machine might put some sparkle back in Grandma's eyes. It was from Sharon Sullivan, asking if Grandma was ready to host another dinner for a group of tourists Friday evening. It had been over a month since the last one, so maybe it was time to try again.

Elaine had talked with their doctor's nurse about Grandma and been told that depression could be the cause of Grandma's memory issues, which was logical, given that she was still grieving for Grandpa and now had diabetes to worry about.

Elaine frowned, thinking back on the dinner they'd hosted soon after Grandpa's death. After everything that happened that evening, it had been obvious to her that Grandma wasn't up to cooking a big meal or serving guests. She'd had some time to rest, though, and since Grandma was taking her medicine and watching what she ate, maybe things would go better with this dinner. Elaine hoped so, because if

Grandma kept making mistakes and forgetting things, they might have to give up the dinners and find some other way to supplement their income. But what could it be?

CHAPTER 15

"Oh, Grandma, what are you doing with that?" Elaine asked, watching in surprise as Grandma poured sugar into one of their saltshakers.

"I'm filling the saltshakers to set on the tables," Grandma replied.

"But you've got *zucker* not *salse*."

Grandma set the bag of sugar on the counter and stared at it with a peculiar expression. "Ach, my! You're right about that. I think I may need to clean my glasses." Grandma went to the sink and turned on the water. After she'd rinsed off her glasses and dried them with a soft towel, she put them back on. "There, that's better. I can see everything more clearly now."

"That's good," Elaine said, smiling with relief. Grandma had been so forgetful lately, and Elaine was worried that she may have confused the sugar for salt. Apparently it was just that she hadn't seen the label clearly.

While Grandma poured the sugar back into the bag, Elaine glanced out the window, wondering what the noise was that had caught her attention. A woodpecker was making quite a racket as it worked to get insects out of the old maple tree in their yard. This particular tree had been struck by lightning last year, which ended up scorching the leaves. In the spring when no new growth emerged, it became evident that the tree had not survived. It had become quite the meeting place for woodpeckers, though. Even from inside the house, Elaine could hear the bird as it chiseled its way around the tree, leaving holes at each place it searched.

Seeing the bird gave Elaine an idea. The next time she went to town, she would check at the hardware store about purchasing a few bird feeders. Grandma would probably enjoy watching all the birds in their yard, and it might help her mind stay active, trying to identify each one. Elaine would find a good spot for the feeders so she and Grandma could see them while they were either porch-sitting or seated in the kitchen near the window. Actually, observing the birds' antics would be fun for both of them.

Elaine thought more about the dead tree. It would probably be good to find someone to cut it down. Otherwise the tree would eventually become brittle, and as much as the birds enjoyed looking for insects inside the bark, Elaine wanted to make sure the tree was no threat to the house. She would add it to her ever-growing to-do list. But like Grandpa had told her one time, "It's better to have a full in-bin instead of an empty one."

Elaine smirked. Right now an empty bin would be just fine.

Physically, Grandma seemed to be feeling a little better since she'd been eating right and taking her medicine, but her emotions were up and down. One minute she'd be laughing and talking about the future, and the next minute she seemed sullen and almost out of touch with what was going on. Elaine felt sure it was part of the grieving process, but she would let the doctor know if things didn't improve. In the meantime, she'd keep reminding Grandma to take her medicine, exercise, and eat the right foods.

"Shall we get busy cooking for our guests now?" Grandma asked. "It won't be long and the evening will be upon us."

Jonah had been working in the buggy shop with his apprentice all morning and was getting ready to take a break when the boy asked him a question.

"Say, Jonah, I've been meaning to ask. How long have ya been makin' buggies?"

"I started working in my daed's buggy shop when I graduated eighth grade." Jonah chuckled. "But sometimes it seems like forever."

"What makes ya say that?" Timothy asked, looking curiously at Jonah.

Jonah shrugged. "Guess it's because I've had an interest in buggies since I was a boy. When I was a little guy, my daed made me a wooden buggy that I could sit inside and pretend I was driving a horse. I had more interest in thinking up things to do with that little buggy than I did in pretending there was a horse at the front of it." Jonah rubbed his chin thoughtfully, thinking back on those carefree days, when all he had to worry about was doing the few chores his dad had assigned him and finding new things to do with his wooden buggy. One day, he'd removed all the dark blue material Dad had used on the buggy seat and replaced it with one of Mom's good tablecloths. Mom had been none too pleased about that.

"Are you enjoying the work here?" Jonah asked, pulling his thoughts back to the present.

Timothy nodded enthusiastically. "It's interesting to see how a buggy is put together, and I'm anxious to learn all I can."

"Think you might want to own your own buggy shop someday?"

The boy shook his head. "There's a lot of stress that comes with ownin' your own business. I've seen how frustrated my daed gets sometimes when things don't go right in his leather shop. Even my brothers Andy and Paul, who work with Dad, have mentioned how Dad gets upset about certain things."

"There can be some stressful times when you have a business," Jonah agreed, "but if you like something well enough and you want to be your own boss, then the stressful things don't bother you quite so much. Of course, being your own boss is not all stress, and I do have to remember to treat all of my customers right and get their orders done in a timely manner. Another advantage of having my own business is that I can take a long lunch or run errands whenever I need to."

Timothy scratched the side of his head. "Think I'll just be happy workin' for you right now and not think too hard about the future."

Jonah smiled. "That's probably a good idea." *I'd better take Timothy's advice,* he thought. *I need to quit worrying about my future with Elaine and leave it in God's hands. When the time is right for Elaine to accept my marriage proposal, it'll happen. I just need to be patient and keep offering her support as she helps Edna deal with Lloyd's death and her health issues.*

❧

As the six o'clock hour approached, Elaine checked everything twice to be sure they were ready for the tour group that would be arriving soon. Both tables had been set with their best dishes, and the food they'd be serving was keeping warm on the stove. Elaine had even checked the door on Millie's cage to be sure it was latched. She'd also covered Millie's cage so the bird would think it was nighttime and wouldn't chatter away, like she often did. Elaine did not want the noisy little parakeet to swoop into the dining room, creating a stir, as she had done during the last dinner they'd hosted. What an embarrassment that had been for both her and Grandma.

An hour ago, Elaine had made a light supper for the two of them so that Grandma could take her medicine. That would be better than waiting to eat until after the tourists all left. By then Grandma could become weak and shaky.

"Is my head covering on straight?" Grandma asked, stepping out of the kitchen and joining Elaine in the dining room.

Elaine smiled and nodded. "Jah, Grandma. You look just fine."

"That's good, because the last time these people came, I don't think I left a very good impression."

Elaine's eyebrows squeezed together. "No, Grandma, it won't be the same people we served dinner to several weeks ago. It'll be a new group of tourists coming here this evening."

Grandma pulled back slightly but then gave a quick nod. "Of course. How silly of me. I don't know what I was thinking."

Elaine didn't know what Grandma had been thinking, either, but she chose not to make an issue of it. Perhaps it had just been a slip of the tongue. Maybe Grandma hadn't really thought the people coming tonight were the same ones who'd been there before. At least, Elaine hoped that was the case.

"Oh, look, they're here," Grandma said, motioning out the window to a van.

As Elaine went to the door to greet their guests, she sent up a silent prayer. *Dear Lord, please help everything to go well this evening.*

❧

"It's so good to see you again," a tall, dark-haired woman said when she entered the house and gave Edna a hug. "I couldn't believe it when Sharon, our tour guide, told us your name and said you'd been hosting tourist dinners for several years."

Confusion settled over Edna like a heavy quilt on the bed. She had absolutely no idea who this woman was and found it to be quite unsettling. If she were a previous dinner guest, she probably would have said so, not acted surprised that Edna was hosting meals for tourists. *Think, Edna. Think. Have I ever met this woman before, and if so, where? Maybe she has me confused with someone else.*

"Sorry, but I'm not sure. . . Have we met before?" Edna asked, looking beyond this lady as the rest of the tour group lined up to come in. She felt uneasy, making people wait while she tried to figure out who the woman standing in front of her actually was.

"I'm Cindy Hawthorne." She gestured to the older, gray-haired woman beside her. "I've been visiting my friend Dawn, who lives in Chicago, and she signed us up for this tour, not realizing that I used to live in Arthur."

Edna stared at Cindy, trying to recall her face. She felt foolish not being able to recognize someone she'd apparently known in the past.

"My husband, Rick, and I used to be your neighbors before we moved to Nevada." Cindy's dimples deepened when she smiled. "But then, that was twenty years ago, so I can understand why you might not have recognized me. Unfortunately, time has a way of changing how people look." She touched her face, moving her fingers around. "A few wrinkles here, and several gray hairs there. Oh, and I've probably put on a couple of pounds from when you knew me, too."

"Ah, yes," Edna said, relieved that she now remembered Cindy. She just hadn't recognized her at first. "And of course, I've changed a good deal since then, too."

"Not that much." Cindy shook her head. "You've still got that nice smile I remember so well."

"Thank you," Edna said. "Did your husband make the trip to Chicago with you?"

Cindy shook her head. "He's working as a computer analyst and couldn't get away from work."

"Ah, I see." Of course, Edna didn't really see. She had no idea what a computer analyst did, and the truth was, she barely remembered Rick.

"So how is Lloyd?" Cindy asked. "Will I get to see him, too, or is he off doing something else this evening?"

Edna swallowed hard, hoping she wouldn't give in to the tears that so often seemed near the surface. "Lloyd passed away a little over a month ago. He had a heart attack."

"I'm sorry to hear that." Cindy gave Edna another hug. "I'm sure it must be difficult for you to be without him."

"Yes, it is. I miss Lloyd so much, but I'm thankful that I have my granddaughter living with me. She's such a comfort." Edna motioned to Elaine. "This is Elaine. She came to live with Lloyd and me after her parents were killed in a buggy accident. She was just a little girl then, and it was after you'd moved, so you never got the chance to meet her."

"You mean, Milton was killed?" Cindy's eyes widened.

"Yes, Milton. You remember my son, I'm sure," Edna added.

Cindy nodded and then she looked at Elaine. "Since Rick and I lived next door to your grandparents, we knew your father when he was a boy. He was a fine young man."

Edna thought Cindy would simply shake Elaine's hand. Instead, she gave her a hug. "I wish we'd had the chance to know you, because I'm sure that any granddaughter of Edna's must be as kind and sweet as she is."

Elaine's cheeks colored. "It's nice to meet you as well."

"Well, I'd better move aside and let the others in the door," Cindy said, stepping farther into the room. "I'm sorry. I didn't mean to hold things up."

"We'll talk more later." Edna bobbed her head. "Maybe when dessert is served."

Soon everyone was inside and seated at the tables. After the tour guide introduced Edna and Elaine to everyone, the two of them headed for the kitchen to bring in the food.

"I feel so *narrisch* not remembering Cindy," Edna remarked as she removed the chicken from the oven.

"It's okay, Grandma. You're not foolish. As the woman said, it's been some time since you last saw her."

"I know, but it's just another reminder of how my memory seems to be slipping these days. Makes me wonder if I'm losing my *glicker*."

"You're not losing your marbles, either." Elaine patted Edna's arm. "We all forget things sometimes, and you've been under a lot of stress since Grandpa died."

"Jah, but that's no excuse. My mind used to be sharp as a sewing needle. Guess maybe it's just old age catching up with me." Edna sighed and turned toward the door. "Well, I can't fret about that now. We have a meal to serve."

As Edna headed into the other room, a terrible thought hit her. *What if I am losing my glicker? That would be baremlich. Jah, absolutely terrible.*

CHAPTER 16

When Sara stepped into her house with Mark, she breathed a sigh of relief. It was good to be home again, with the peace and quiet of just her and her son. It wasn't that Sara didn't love her husband's family; she just wasn't used to so much commotion on a daily basis. And those petty squabbles that had gone on between her two young sisters-in-law had really grated on her nerves. She and Mark could never move into Harley's parents' home on a permanent basis. If she chose to remain in Arthur, it would be right here, in her own house.

When my sister, Marijane, and I were children, we never fussed at each other like that, Sara thought, placing Mark in his high chair before offering him a cheese-and-cracker snack. *But then, our folks would never have tolerated it if we had.*

Nevertheless, Sara couldn't help but observe that Carolyn and Marla's disagreements seemed to go unnoticed by Herschel and Betty. Could be that they were just more tolerant than some parents. Or perhaps her in-laws may have been allowing their children to work out their differences. Of course, Herschel wasn't home that much due to his business, so he probably had no idea how often the girls argued about things. And Betty may not have had the energy to deal with it.

"Well, I'm home now, and taking care of my nieces and nephews is no longer my problem," Sara said aloud. She leaned over and kissed Mark's forehead. "All I have to worry about is taking care of you, my sweet little boy."

Mark looked up at her and grinned; then he popped a piece of cheddar cheese into his mouth and smacked his lips. "Yum. . .*gut kaes.*"

Sara smiled. "Jah, cheese is always good to eat." Watching her son, Sara's love for him swelled to overflowing. According to Betty, Mark was a mirror image of what Harley had looked like when he was that age. Sara had to admit that Mark certainly took after his daddy, with the same deep blue eyes and dark hair. He even had a dimple in the middle of his chin—a feature Sara had thought was so cute about her husband when they'd first met, before he'd started growing his beard.

The love Sara felt for Mark couldn't be measured, for there was nothing she cherished more on this earth. Even with the bumps along the way that everyone encountered in life, Sara would do all that was humanly possible to make sure Mark grew into a fine man like his father had been.

Taking a seat near Mark's high chair, Sara let her head rest on the table. She felt so tired this morning that she could almost fall asleep right now. Hopefully after Mark's snack he would go down for a nap, and then maybe she could rest awhile, too. After spending the last eight weeks at her in-laws', it felt wonderful to finally be home, where everything was familiar. There were so many things she wanted to do once she caught up on her rest, however.

Earlier, Sara had looked around and seen all the dust she wanted to tackle. It was so thick, she could actually write her name on some pieces of furniture. Sara didn't know how a house could get so dusty when no one was around, but somehow it had. She didn't mind, though. She was anxious to start doing her own household chores and get back into a routine of some sort.

Sighing, and unable to keep her eyes open any longer, Sara let them close and soon succumbed to sleep.

"*Mammi!* Mammi!" *Bang! Bang! Bang!*

Sara's head came up and her eyes shot open. Poor little Mark, tears rolling down his flushed cheeks, pounded his fists on the high-chair tray with a look of desperation. How long had she been sleeping, with her poor little guy crying like this? Sara certainly didn't enjoy upsetting her son and figured from the appearance of his aggravated red face that it must have been long enough to frustrate him.

"Mamma's sorry." Sara rose to her feet, and after lifting her son from his chair, she patted his back, soothing him the best that she could. Glancing at the clock on the far wall, she grimaced, realizing that she'd been asleep for thirty minutes. It was a wonder Mark hadn't woken her sooner, but either he'd remained quiet for most of that time, or she'd been in such a deep sleep that she hadn't heard him.

"Let's get you cleaned up, and then you and Mamma can take a nap," Sara murmured, holding her son tightly to her chest. Mark squeezed his arms around Sara's neck, burrowing his face into her shoulder.

Sara's limbs felt weak, and her hands tingled as she made her way to the bedroom. Hopefully after sufficient rest, she would feel better.

"Where are you going, Grandma?" Elaine asked when Edna put her black outer bonnet on and opened the back door.

"I'm gonna head into town to run a few errands," Edna replied, turning around.

"Do you have to go right now?" Elaine asked. "I need to get the rest of the clothes washed and hung on the line, but I can go with you after that's done."

Edna shook her head. "There's no need for that. I'm perfectly capable of going to town on my own."

"But I thought—"

"If you're worried about me going out alone, please don't. I'll be fine." Edna motioned to their wringer washer. "You go ahead and finish the laundry. When I get back, we can fix lunch and spend the rest of the day working in our vegetable garden."

Elaine hesitated a moment but finally nodded. "If that's what you want to do, Grandma, but I'm willing to run errands with you."

"We'll go shopping together some other time." Edna smiled and stepped out the door. She didn't want to hurt her granddaughter's feelings, but the truth was, she was eager to spend some time alone. Ever since Lloyd had passed away, and particularly after she'd been diagnosed with diabetes, Elaine had been acting like a mother hen, always reminding Edna to take her medicine, check her blood sugar, eat this and not eat that. Even though it was a bit irritating, Edna realized her granddaughter meant well.

Edna's thoughts took her back to the past. In all the time she and Lloyd had been raising Elaine, it had been them telling her what to do, but now the tables were turned. It made Edna feel almost like a child again. Well, their roles seemed to be reversing, but for a few hours today she would be free as a bird, and she planned to enjoy this time to herself. She'd been feeling better these past few weeks and hadn't had any dizzy spells or memory lapses, so she felt perfectly capable of running a few errands by herself.

Elaine hummed as she hung the last batch of clothes on the line. It was such a beautiful June morning, and she was trying not to worry about Grandma but to keep her focus on positive things. The birds chirped joyfully in the trees nearby, and she watched with interest as a robin pulled a worm from the lawn. It was amazing how God provided for the birds with insects and seeds, and how their continual singing made it seem as if they were nearly always at peace.

She glanced at the dying maple and felt sorry for the tree, knowing that next week it would be gone, for their closest neighbor had agreed to cut it down. The birds sure loved that old tree, even without its leaves. Maybe after it was gone, the stump could be left for a birdbath to sit on, or perhaps one of their feeders. Elaine and Grandma could plant some wildflowers around the bottom of the stump and finish it with some pretty-shaped rocks scattered among the flowers. That way, a section of the tree that held so many memories would still be a part of the landscape.

Maybe I'll even get a bit of painting done, making some of the rocks I've found look like different animals. Elaine sighed. She surely did miss painting. It was so relaxing, not to mention fun. Right now, she could use a good dose of that. It would be better than any medicine she could take.

Elaine thought of the words of Matthew 6:26: *"Behold the fowls of the air: for they sow not, neither do they reap, nor gather into barns; yet your heavenly Father feedeth them. Are ye not much better than they?*" It was a timely reminder that, despite any hardships she or Grandma might face in the future, God would take care of them.

Elaine's thoughts switched gears as she reflected on the fact that Jonah hadn't come around much lately. Was he avoiding her, or had his visits lessened because he was too busy in his shop? "But if he is staying away on purpose, what could be the reason?" she wondered aloud. *I hope because I haven't given Jonah an answer about marrying him yet, he doesn't think I'm not interested.* Elaine remembered, not too long ago, when she'd seen Jonah watching her after church one Sunday. But Grandma had been in a hurry to get home, so unfortunately, Elaine hadn't been able to talk with him.

Elaine loved Jonah and was eager to become his wife, but she couldn't say yes until she was sure that Grandma would be willing to move to Jonah's house with her. "If only I could tell him how much I love him," Elaine grumbled out loud. But the right time never seemed to happen. Elaine knew it was more than that, but it was easier not to admit how the words stuck in her throat every time she tried to tell Jonah the way she truly felt about him.

Anyway, I couldn't move and leave Grandma here by herself, she thought. *I'd be worried every minute, wondering if she was taking her medicine and eating the right foods. If only Grandma wasn't so determined to keep hosting the tourist dinners, I might be more apt to ask her to move. But is it too soon for another major change in Grandma's life? Or am I justifying things because I'm afraid to make a change?*

Elaine picked up a towel and pinned it to the line. *No, I can't take the tourist dinners away from Grandma. She enjoys doing them. Besides, I'm not sure Grandma would be willing to move from this place, and I can't expect Jonah to sell his home, which is close to the buggy shop—especially since he purchased his house not long ago and has been fixing it up for our future together.* She frowned. *Do we still have a future together? Maybe it would be best if I didn't marry Jonah. He deserves to have a wife and family, and as much as it hurts to even think about it, I'm not sure I'll ever be able to give him that.*

❧

Things went well for Edna as she made her purchases in several stores, and she'd even run into her long-ago friend, Cindy, who'd been shopping in one of the stores. Edna invited Cindy to come over in a few days so they could get caught up on each other's lives, but when Cindy said she'd be going home later today, the women said good-bye and parted ways.

Edna's morning had been fun, but when she entered the Stitch and Sew and glanced at the clock, she realized it was way past noon and she should have been home already, eating lunch. She'd planned to bring a snack along, in case she got hungry. But she'd been in such a hurry to leave, she had forgotten about packing a snack.

Maybe I'll go across the street to the Country Cheese and More and get something to eat, she told herself. *Then I'll come back here and finish my shopping before heading home.*

Edna left the store and made her way across the street. When she entered the store, she spotted Leah and her mother, Dianna, sitting at one of the tables. They smiled and waved her over.

"Is Elaine with you?" Leah asked.

Edna shook her head. "She's at home doing the laundry, and I came into town to do some shopping. It's taken me a little longer than I thought, so I decided to come over here and get some lunch."

"Why don't you join us?" Dianna suggested. "We've just barely started on our sandwiches, and it'll give us a chance to visit."

"I'd like that." As Edna started for the counter to place her order, a feeling of wooziness came over her. *I probably feel this way because I need to eat,* she told herself.

After she'd ordered a sandwich and some iced tea, Edna took a seat across from Leah. Then she reached into her purse to get her medicine, which she was supposed to take before her meal. "Oh, oh," she muttered, rifling through her purse.

"Is something wrong?" Dianna asked.

"I can't find my medicine." Edna's hands trembled and perspiration beaded on her forehead. "I—I must have forgotten to put it in my purse before I left home this morning."

"Are you feeling all right?" Leah asked. "You look pale, and. . ."

Leah's face blurred, and her words faded. A wave of dizziness descended on Edna, and she spiraled into darkness.

CHAPTER 17

Elaine glanced at the kitchen clock and frowned. It was an hour past lunchtime and Grandma should have been here by now. *What in the world could be keeping her?* she worried, pacing the floor. *I wonder if she stopped somewhere to eat lunch.*

Elaine looked at the shelf where Grandma kept her medicine and gasped. There sat the bottle. *Oh dear,* Elaine fretted as she reached for the medicine. *Grandma forgot to take it with her this morning.*

If I knew all of the places Grandma was planning to shop, I'd go looking for her right now. Elaine went to the door, hoping to see Grandma pull in. *But I might not find her, and what if Grandma came home while I was out searching for her?*

Elaine drew in a deep breath and tried to relax, realizing that fretting about this was getting her nowhere. What she needed to do was stay right here and hope that Grandma was okay and would be home soon.

Taking a seat at the table, Elaine bowed her head. *Heavenly Father, I'm worried about Grandma because she's been gone so long and didn't take her medicine. Please be with her, wherever she is, and bring her safely home.*

Elaine heard a car pull into the yard, and her eyes snapped open. Thinking it might be someone who had seen the sign at the end of their driveway advertising the dinners they hosted, Elaine hurried to the door. When she opened it, she was surprised to see Leah get out of her driver's car. She only lived a few miles away and always came over by horse and buggy or on her bicycle.

Leah hurried to the house and approached Elaine with a worried expression. "I came to tell you that your grandma's in the hospital."

Elaine's heart pounded and her mouth went dry. "Wh–what happened?"

"Mom and I were at Country Cheese and More, having lunch, and your grandma came in. She ordered something to eat and sat down at our table. A few seconds later, she blacked out."

Elaine covered her mouth to stifle a gasp. "I just discovered a few minutes ago that she forgot to take her medicine along when she left home this morning, so I'm sure her blood sugar was probably out of whack."

"We called 911, and the paramedics came soon after," Leah explained. "As soon as they put her in the ambulance, I called our driver to bring me here. I knew you'd want to get to the hospital right away."

"I certainly do. Danki, Leah, for coming to tell me. I'll get my purse and be right with you."

Sara had been avoiding the picnic area where she and Harley used to relax under the trees at the back of their property, but this afternoon she'd felt the need to go there. She had felt better after sleeping awhile and soon after started doing housework. Mark played contently after his nap and seemed well rested, but eventually he lost interest in amusing himself. Sara was more than ready to get some fresh air and figured Mark was, too. So she packed a picnic lunch, set her work aside, and decided to take a break. After being at Betty and Herschel's, she needed a little downtime with her son.

As they sat together on the blanket she'd brought along, eating the last of their peanut butter and jelly sandwiches, Sara felt her body relax for the first time in many weeks. It did her heart good to see her little boy's contented expression. She hoped he was enjoying this time with her as much as she was with him. Being in this area, near where Harley had been killed, didn't bother Sara as much as she'd expected it to. In fact, she felt a sense of peace. Although she didn't understand the reason her husband had been taken from them, she'd finally come to terms with his death, accepting it as God's will. *For His ways are not our ways,* she reminded herself.

When they'd finished eating and Sara had washed Mark's face and hands with some wet paper towels she'd packed, she decided that it might be nice to take a walk. "Should we go walking awhile?" Sara asked Mark in their traditional Pennsylvania-Dutch language.

He bobbed his head.

Sara clasped the boy's hand as they strolled along their property line, stopping every once in a while to listen to the birds, look up at the lofty trees, and pick a few wildflowers. June was such a beautiful month. Adult birds were busy feeding their young, crickets had begun chirping, and the tiger lilies bordering her land were just beginning to bloom.

After a while, Mark stopped walking and said he wanted Sara to pick him up. So she lifted him into her arms and headed back to the blanket. She'd no more than laid him down when his eyes closed and he fell asleep.

The warm sun shining down on them made Sara feel sleepy, too, so she curled up on the blanket beside her precious little boy and closed her eyes. Lying there, she felt the gentle breeze as it blew across her face. That, along with the sweet melodies the birds sang, made her relax even more. Sara opened her eyes and watched as a flock of quacking ducks flew over. She glanced at her son and could tell by his even breathing that he was sleeping soundly.

Sara smiled and closed her eyes once more. The last thing she remembered before falling asleep was an image of her husband's face the final time they'd come here together.

"Can you hear me? Can you open your eyes?" From a faraway distance, Edna heard a stranger's voice.

Where am I? she wondered, trying hard to open her eyes. People were talking. A child cried. A strange beeping noise kept going in the background. *Nothing seems familiar to me. I don't think I'm at home in my bed.*

Slowly, Edna's eyes opened. She blinked at the middle-aged woman dressed in white, standing beside her bed. "Who are you?" she murmured through parched lips.

The woman offered Edna a drink of water. "I'm a nurse. Do you know where you are?"

"I—I'm not sure." Edna moistened her lips after drinking some water. It helped to quench her thirst.

"You're in the hospital."

Edna's head ached, and she reached up to touch the lump on her forehead. "Wh–what happened to me? Why am I here?"

"Some of your friends followed the ambulance to the hospital," the nurse explained. "They said you passed out, and they alerted us to the fact that you're diabetic."

"Oh, yes, I am." Edna remembered going into the restaurant and ordering something to eat, but that was all.

"I'm going to leave you for a few minutes," the nurse said, touching Edna's hand. "The doctor will be in to see you soon, and your granddaughter will come once she gets here and has finished filling out the necessary paperwork."

"Okay." Edna took another sip of water and closed her eyes, trying to remember the events that led up to her being taken to the hospital. It was frustrating not to be able to recall the details of passing out, much less to be brought to the hospital and not know it until now. *I must have bumped my head when I fainted,* she told herself, touching the knot on her head. *That must be why I can't remember much of anything right now.*

"Sara, wake up!"

Sara's eyes opened suddenly, and she sat up with a start. *Harley?* She'd been dreaming about her husband, and then she'd heard his voice. That must have been part of the dream, she realized, rubbing her eyes as she became more fully awake. It had been such a nice dream until she'd heard his alarming voice.

Remembering that she'd lain down beside her sleeping son, Sara glanced at the spot where he lay. "Ach, Mark! Where are you?" she cried, seeing that her little boy was gone.

Sara looked this way and that. Mark was nowhere to be seen. Fear enveloped her, and she shivered involuntarily. Had he woken up and wandered off, or. . .God forbid, had someone come along and taken her child? She couldn't believe that she'd fallen into such a deep sleep and hadn't heard her son wake up.

Heart pounding and perspiration rolling down her forehead, Sara scrambled to her feet and cupped her hands around her mouth. "Mark, where are you? Please, answer me, Mark!"

No reply. As if life was normal, the only sounds were the wind whispering gently through the tops of the trees and several birds calling to their mates. But for Sara, life was far from normal.

She called her son's name over and over, running up and down the length of the property line as she did so. There was still no sign of the boy. To add to her mounting fear, thunder rumbled loudly in the distance, and the sky turned darker toward the west. "Help me, Lord," Sara prayed aloud, her panic mounting as she headed toward the house, hoping her little boy had gone there. "Please help me find my son. I lost Harley; I can't lose Mark, too."

CHAPTER 18

"Come on, Sassy, I know you can go faster than that," Jonah called to his temperamental horse. He was heading over to see Elaine this afternoon and was anxious to get there. They hadn't visited in a while, and he wanted to see how she and Edna were doing. Despite the fact that marrying Elaine was all he'd been thinking about, Jonah wouldn't bring up the topic and had come to accept the fact that Elaine might not be ready until next year perhaps. Well, Jonah was a patient man, and he would wait for as long as necessary. After all, what other choice did he have?

As Jonah continued on down the road, he noticed the sky was darkening in the distance. Then he heard a far-off rumble of thunder. Jonah liked listening to thunderstorms, especially the gentler ones. When he was a boy, he'd enjoyed lying on the floor upstairs in his room and listening to the pouring rain pelt down on the tin roof of their home in Ohio. He remembered a few wicked storms, where the lightning was actually pink, and the air felt like it was charged with electricity. Constant lightning with claps of thunder, one right after the other, caused him to hide under the covers back then. Those kinds of storms, Jonah could do without.

This afternoon, Jonah could smell rain in the air, but fortunately, this approaching storm didn't sound violent, and hopefully he would arrive at Edna's place before the skies opened up.

Jonah's thoughts came to a halt when he caught sight of a young Amish boy chasing a butterfly in a field near the road. The child looked like Sara Stutzman's little boy. But if that were the case, where was Sara, and why would Mark be out here by himself?

Jonah guided his horse to the side of the road, secured him to a tree, and sprinted into the field, calling the boy's name. He hadn't seen any lightning yet. Only the sound of thunder in the distance, and for that, Jonah was grateful. He felt confident time was on his side.

When the butterfly landed on the stem of a wildflower, the child stopped chasing it. Then, turning to Jonah with a grin, he pointed and said, *"Die fleddermaus."*

Jonah nodded and said in Pennsylvania-Dutch, "Jah, Mark, that's a butterfly, but where is your mamm?"

"*Schlaeferich*," Mark replied, grinning up at him.

Jonah frowned. If the boy thought his mom was a sleepyhead, was Sara at home in bed? Could she be sick, and had Mark been wandering around her place unattended? Jonah hoped not. While Sara had been at her in-laws, taking care of Betty after she'd broken her leg, he'd heard that Betty was better now, so Sara had gone home. And this field bordered Sara's place, so if Mark had meandered off by himself, he easily could have ended up here. With no hesitation, Jonah decided to get Mark home right away, especially in light of the approaching storm. The wind had started to pick up, and dark clouds nearly blocked out the sun.

"*Kumme*," Jonah said, urging the boy to come to him. "Come now, I need to take you home."

When Mark didn't resist, Jonah bent down and picked him up. He was almost to his buggy when he heard Sara screaming in the distance, calling her son's name.

"That sounds like your mamm." Jonah smiled as little Mark pointed in the direction of Sara's voice.

"He's here, in the field!" Jonah shouted. "Stay where you are, and I'll bring him to you."

Sara's heart pounded as she stood near the edge of her property. Had she imagined it, or had someone shouted that he'd found Mark in a field and was bringing him home?

With heart pounding and legs trembling, she waited. *Dear Lord, please let it be that I heard someone*, she prayed as a few drops of rain mixed with her tears.

Several minutes went by, and then she heard the distinctive sound of a horse and buggy approaching. When it drew within sight, she knew immediately that it belonged to Jonah, and she could see inside the buggy that Mark was with him.

"Oh, thank the Lord," Sara cried as the buggy pulled up alongside of her. Happy tears welled in her eyes as Jonah handed Sara her son. "Where did you find him?" she asked, clinging tightly to Mark. It felt so good to have her son back where he belonged, held in the safety of her arms.

"In the field on the other side of the wooded area that borders your property," Jonah replied. "He was chasing a fleddermaus. When I asked where his mamm was, he said you were a sleepyhead, so I was worried that you might be sick in bed."

Sara shook her head, pointing. "I took Mark for a picnic out there by the trees, and after we'd eaten and taken a short walk, he fell asleep on the blanket. I foolishly laid down beside him and went to sleep." She paused and kissed her son's head. "When I woke up, he was gone. I was so afraid. I called Mark's name over and over, with no response, and of course, I prayed and asked God to help me find my son. Danki, Jonah, for bringing my precious boy back to me." Sara grabbed Jonah's hand and squeezed his fingers; she was ever so grateful.

"No thanks is needed." Jonah smiled. "I'm sure God must have directed me to head down this road on my way to see Elaine at just the right time so your prayers would be answered.

"Come on," he suggested. "Hop in the buggy and I'll take you and Mark back to your house before the rain really lets loose."

Sara nodded in agreement, appreciative of his offer.

Because they had a little time yet to beat the storm, Jonah asked Sara where her picnic things were so she could take them home. As they headed to the grove of trees to retrieve the blanket and picnic basket, she was tempted to tell Jonah about hearing Harley's voice in a dream, telling her to wake up, but she didn't say anything, thinking he might not understand. Truth was, she didn't understand it, either, but was thankful that it happened. If she hadn't woken up when she had, there was no telling what might have happened to Mark. Of course, Jonah most likely still would have found him, but from now on, Sara would try to keep a closer watch on her boy and make sure she never fell asleep unless they were inside the house with the doors closed and locked.

Elaine sat beside Grandma's hospital bed, thanking God that she was all right. They'd given her the insulin she needed and gotten her blood sugar stabilized, but they wanted to keep Grandma overnight for observation, since she'd hit her head on the floor when she'd passed out. Outside the window, Elaine could see a downpour from a thunderstorm. *What if Grandma had been trying to get home in the buggy during this storm?* Elaine thought. She was thankful that Grandma was safe at the hospital, although she wished Grandma had remembered to take her medicine and hadn't gotten ill to begin with.

"How are you feeling?" Elaine asked, taking Grandma's hand.

"Other than feeling foolish for passing out at the restaurant this morning, I'm fine." Grandma offered Elaine a weak smile.

"What about your head? Does it hurt?"

Grandma reached up and touched her head. "Jah, just a bit. I don't see why I can't go home with you right now. Didn't you say Leah and her driver are still in the waiting room?"

"They are, but the doctor wants to keep you overnight, just to make sure your blood sugar remains stable and there are no problems from your head injury. There may be a few more tests to run as well."

Grandma wrinkled her nose. "I don't like all the prodding and poking they've already done to me."

Elaine gently patted Grandma's arm. "I know, but I'm sure you'll be able to come home tomorrow morning."

"I hope so, because I don't like hospitals one bit. Your grandpa didn't like them, either."

"I understand, but this is where you need to be right now." Elaine sat quietly with Grandma until a nurse came in to take vitals.

"I think I'd better tell Leah and her driver they can go now," Elaine said, rising from her chair. She was relieved when Leah had said that her brother had gone and taken Grandma's horse and buggy back to their house.

"You should go with them," Grandma said. "There's nothing you can do here but sit and hold my hand."

"Which is exactly what I want to do."

"But really, there's no need—"

Grandma's words were cut off by the nurse placing a thermometer under her tongue.

"I'll be back soon," Elaine called over her shoulder as she hurried from the room. No way was she going home until she knew the results of all Grandma's tests.

CHAPTER 19

When Jonah headed back down the road in the direction of Elaine and Edna's place, he thought about Sara and her grief at losing her husband. It was a shame little Mark would never know his father. Life could sure be hard sometimes. But Jonah knew firsthand that when faced with adversity, with the strength, help, and guidance of the Lord, a person had to pick themselves up and move on, rather than giving in to grief and despair. It appeared that Sara had done that, although Jonah was sure it hadn't been easy. Probably the support she'd received from her husband's parents had a lot to do with her being able to cope. He wondered once more why she hadn't moved back to Indiana to be close to her own parents. *Must be a good reason,* he rationalized. *Besides, it's really none of my business.*

Jonah held on tight as a car sped past, spraying water on his horse and buggy. "It's okay, boy," Jonah said softly to Sassy, trying to calm him down after the inconsiderate driver flew farther down the road.

Sassy nickered as if he understood.

"What's wrong with that guy, driving like there's no tomorrow?" Jonah shook his head, muttering under his breath. "If he's not careful, he's likely to hurt someone, and it could be himself or some innocent victim." How people could drive like that, when it was raining so hard, was beyond Jonah's comprehension. Didn't that fellow have a family or worry about hurting someone else's family? Families were important, which was why Jonah was thankful he lived near his twin sister. If anything were to happen to Jonah's parents, his sister, or anyone in her family, he didn't know what he would do.

Jonah really wished his folks would move to Arthur so they'd all be in the same area. Now that he'd gotten busier with his buggy business, it would be nice if he and Dad could be partners again. Jonah had always worked well with Dad, and if things had turned out differently for Jonah back in Pennsylvania, they would most likely still be working together in Dad's buggy shop.

Maybe I can talk Dad into moving, Jonah thought as he turned his horse and buggy up the Schrocks' driveway. He hadn't spoken to his parents in a while and decided he needed to call them soon. *In the meantime, I'll keep training Timothy and be thankful for the help he's giving me.*

Jonah guided Sassy up to the hitching rack and secured him. Then he sprinted through the wet grass, which he noticed was getting a bit too long, and stepped onto the porch, making a mental note to see about cutting the grass for Edna. The rain had lingered, falling steadily after the initial storm had passed, but Jonah was grateful to have gotten Sara and Mark home before it really cut loose.

As Jonah waited, a siren wailed in the distance; then the sound grew louder as the rescue vehicle raced down the road. Jonah couldn't help wondering if the car that had passed him moments ago might have been in an accident. Of course, with the slick roads, it could have been some other vehicle in an accident.

Quickly, Jonah offered up a prayer. *Thank You, Lord, for being with me and Sassy and for getting us here safely. Please be with the driver of the rescue vehicle, and also with whoever was involved in an accident.*

After several knocks on the door, with no response, Jonah determined that Elaine and Edna must not be home. Since he had a pen and tablet in his pocket, he wrote a quick note and placed it inside the screen door, letting them know that he would be back sometime tomorrow, at which time he would cut the grass. Hopefully the lawn would have a chance to dry out by then.

Whistling, Jonah hurried back to his horse and buggy and headed for home, where his own chores awaited.

Sara gently stroked her son's silky head as she sat in the living room, rocking him to sleep. She was ever so thankful that Jonah had come along when he did. What if Mark had gotten out in the road? He could have been hit by a car, especially with that storm making visibility difficult for drivers. *Heavenly Father, You were surely watching over my boy,* she prayed. *Thank You.*

"Mama will never be so careless again," Sara murmured as Mark's eyelids grew heavy and he closed his eyes.

The sound of the rain gently falling against the window was soothing. Once she was sure that Mark was sleeping soundly, Sara rose to her feet and carried him down the hall toward his room. *Maybe I should move Mark's crib into my room,* she thought. *Think I'd feel better if he slept closer to me.*

First, Sara entered her room and placed Mark in the middle of the bed. Then she rolled the crib across the hall and into her room. Once she had it in place against the wall adjacent to her bed, she picked up her son and laid him in the crib. "Sleep well, precious boy," Sara whispered, covering him with a sheet.

The rain was coming straight down, so she could lower the top window a little, allowing some fresh air to drift in and clear the stuffiness in the room.

Sara yawned, and after she'd changed into her nightgown and brushed her hair, she stretched out on the bed. The sound of rain made her feel relaxed and sleepy. Not only did she love hearing rain, but Sara liked the smell of it, and how clean everything looked afterward. Even though it was only eight o'clock, she was exhausted and more than ready for bed. She'd left their supper dishes soaking in the sink, but they could wait until morning. Right now, all she wanted to do was sleep. Tomorrow was another day, and maybe when she awoke she would have more energy.

Sara's last thought before falling to sleep was a prayer that Jonah had arrived safely at the Schrocks'.

Elaine's frustration mounted as she sat beside Grandma's hospital bed waiting for all the test results. *What in the world could be taking so long? It's getting late, and if we don't hear something soon, we probably won't know anything until tomorrow morning.*

She glanced at Grandma, sleeping peacefully after she'd been given something for the pain in her head. The doctor had determined that there was no concussion, so there wasn't any danger in Grandma going to sleep now. Several tests had been run before Elaine had gotten to the hospital, and more were done while she'd gone to the hospital cafeteria to eat supper. What Elaine couldn't figure out was what the other tests were about. They knew Grandma had diabetes, her blood sugar had been stabilized, and her head injury wasn't serious, so what else could there be?

She stood and began to pace the floor. Waiting had never come easily for her, and especially now, when she was worried about Grandma and wanted to take her home. When they'd said Grandma should be kept overnight, Elaine had decided that she would stay at the hospital and sleep in the reclining chair beside Grandma's bed. Leah had offered to stay with her, but Elaine had insisted she would be fine by herself. As she became more frustrated, however, she wished she'd agreed to let Leah stay. She could have used the company, not to mention some moral support.

Elaine jumped when the door to Grandma's room opened and a middle-age doctor with thinning blond hair stepped in. "I'm glad you're still here. I'd like to speak to you, if I may," he said, glancing briefly at Grandma, then back at Elaine.

"Yes, of course. My grandma's sleeping right now. Should I wake her?" Elaine questioned.

He shook his head. "There's no one in the waiting room right now. Let's go in there so we can talk privately."

Elaine didn't like the sound of that. Seeing the doctor's furrowed brows, she feared he might have bad news, but she nodded and said, "The waiting room will be fine." She followed the doctor down the hall.

Once they were seated in the waiting room, he cleared his throat and got right to the point. "When you first got here, you were asked some basic questions about your grandmother's health history. Is that correct?"

Elaine nodded.

"Well, besides needing to know that, we tested Edna's cognitive skills."

"Why did you feel that was necessary?" Elaine asked, feeling a bit agitated. Did they, like some other people she'd met, think Grandma was uneducated because the Amish only go through eight years of schooling?

"Because when one of the nurses asked your grandma some questions during her initial examination, she gave many unclear answers."

Elaine leaned slightly forward in her chair. "What do you mean?"

"She couldn't remember certain things. Things that were important. Answers to questions that most people would know right away. Edna also kept asking some of the nurses the same question about why she was here."

"Grandma was probably confused and scared. She doesn't care much for hospitals."

He shook his head. "We thought it was more than that, so we did a few more tests."

"What other tests?" Elaine clutched her arms to her chest.

"For one thing, we did some reasoning and perceptive tests, where Edna was asked several questions, for which she either had no answers or the ones she gave didn't make sense."

Elaine opened her mouth to say something more, but the doctor rushed on. "We also did some blood work, and after your grandmother gave us her written permission, we did advanced brain imaging."

Elaine sat in stunned silence as the doctor gave her the worst possible news. Grandma was in the early stages of dementia, and there was no cure for the disease.

"Dementia is a progressive illness, and each person experiences it in their own way," the doctor said. "Your grandmother's ability to remember, understand, communicate, and reason will decline as time goes on. It will probably be gradual at first, but in some cases, a person may lose their memory very quickly. Now, if you are caring for someone with dementia, there is a lot you can do in the early stages to help that person maintain their independence and be able to cope for as long as possible. I will go over all of that with you before Edna is released from the hospital tomorrow, as well as a list of things to watch for as she progresses to the middle and final stages of the disease."

He paused for a few minutes, as though knowing Elaine had a lot to digest. "And I think it would be good if you would attend a support group we have here at the hospital for caregivers of patients with dementia," he added, lightly touching her arm.

Speechless, Elaine slumped in her chair. Diabetes they could deal with, but this? No, the news the doctor had just given her was impossible to accept. If there was no cure for dementia, then Grandma would need Elaine more than ever. They faced some tough decisions.

Elaine gripped the arms of her chair. *Oh, Lord, what am I going to do? How will I ever tell Grandma this horrible news?*

A still, small voice seemed to say, *Trust Me. I will see you through.*

CHAPTER 20

It's good to be home," Grandma said, smiling at Elaine as they settled themselves on the sofa the following day. "No more poking and prodding, with doctors and nurses asking me a bunch of silly questions when they wouldn't answer any of mine. Now we can get busy working in the garden and planning the menu for the dinner we'll be hosting tonight."

"No, Grandma, that's not tonight," Elaine corrected. "Our next big dinner isn't scheduled until two weeks from this Friday."

Grandma blinked rapidly and tapped her fingers against her chin. "Are you sure? I was certain it was tonight."

"No, Grandma. I can show you our appointment book if you like."

Grandma shook her head. "That's okay. I believe you."

Elaine drew in a deep breath and released it slowly. She hadn't told Grandma what the doctor had said about dementia and wanted to put it off as long as she could. Grandma would be terribly upset by this news. Then again, maybe she wouldn't believe Elaine at all.

Instead of me telling the doctor last night that I would explain things to Grandma, it might have been best if I'd asked him to give Grandma the devastating news, Elaine thought. *But then, Grandma may have become upset with him and gone into denial. Or maybe I should ask Leah to help me tell Grandma. Well, however it's done, I'm not ready just yet.*

Elaine leaned her head against the back of the sofa and rubbed her temples, reflecting on everything the doctor had told her last night before she'd returned to Grandma's room. Some of the common signs of dementia included memory loss, impaired judgment, faulty reasoning, disorientation of time and place, and even the loss of some motor skills or balance problems. As much as Elaine hated to admit it, Grandma had already experienced several of those things. Some she'd noticed before Grandpa's passing, such as repeatedly asking the same questions, having difficulty paying bills, and forgetting people's names.

Elaine closed her eyes, fearful that if she didn't, the tears that had gathered might splash onto her cheeks. *So some of the symptoms Grandma's been having lately may not be related to her diabetes at all. Now we are dealing with two different diseases, both with similar symptoms that could overlap, such as loss of balance.*

"Elaine, are you listening, or have you fallen asleep?"

Grandma's question brought Elaine's eyes open, and she blinked several times. "No, I'm not sleeping. What was it you were saying?"

"I asked if you wanted to get started on the garden right away, or should we wait till after supper to do it?"

"Supper's several hours away, Grandma," Elaine reminded. "Maybe we should eat lunch first, and then if you're feeling up to it, we can work in the garden awhile. Otherwise, the weeding can wait until another day."

Grandma shook her head with a determined expression. "It can't wait. The weeds will choke out the garden if we don't get 'em pulled today. Especially after that rain we had yesterday." She rose from her seat. "And I'm feeling perfectly fine, so there's no reason not to do it right away. The weeds will pull easy since the ground is still damp."

"You're right," Elaine admitted. "All right then, I'll make our lunch now while you rest here in the living room."

"I'm not tired," Grandma argued. "When they weren't poking me with needles at the hospital, I slept."

Elaine could see by the fixed set of Grandma's jaw that she was not going to stay here and rest. "Okay. I'll make a tossed green salad, and you can fix some iced tea. How's that sound?"

"Sounds good." Grandma headed straight for the kitchen. Based on what the doctor had said, Elaine figured the symptoms of dementia would probably come and go until Grandma moved into the next phase of the disease, at which time her memory loss would worsen. He'd also said the changes could occur quickly or slowly over time. Elaine hoped in Grandma's case that her memory loss and other symptoms came slowly, for she wanted as much time with her as possible. Once

Grandma no longer recognized Elaine, it would be unbearable, but she couldn't allow herself to dwell on that. One day at a time. That was the only way to deal with something like this.

Following Grandma into the other room, Elaine's gaze came to rest on the note she'd found tucked inside the screen door when they'd returned from the hospital this morning. It was from Jonah, saying he was sorry he'd missed her and that he would be by again sometime today.

Oh, how she dreaded having to tell Jonah that she couldn't marry him, but there was no point in putting off the inevitable. Jonah needed the freedom to plan for his future—a future that didn't include her. As much as it hurt, Elaine had concluded that it must not be God's will for her and Jonah to marry.

Elaine and Grandma had just finished eating lunch when Grandma yawned and said, *"Ich bin mied wie en hund."*

Elaine chuckled, despite her dark mood. "Well, if you're tired as a dog, maybe you ought to take a nap. I'll wash and dry the dishes."

"What about the garden? I thought we were going to do some weeding."

"We can do it after you wake up, Grandma. Getting some much-needed rest is more important than weeding."

Grandma yawned again, covering her mouth with her hand. "You're probably right. I'll have more energy to work in the garden after I've rested a bit."

Elaine watched with pity as Grandma ambled out of the room. If only she could do something to make Grandma better.

She couldn't solve Grandma's problem by bemoaning her fate, so Elaine poured dishwashing liquid into the sink and filled it with warm water. Methodically, she washed and rinsed each dish while staring out the kitchen window. A robin landed in the grass and quickly sought out a worm, while one of the barn cats chased an unsuspecting mouse. For the worm and the mouse, their lives were over, but the cat and the bird had been fed, so some good had come from the insect's and rodent's deaths.

"But what good comes from people dying?" Elaine murmured aloud, spiraling deeper into depression. Eventually, Grandma's body would shut down from the dementia, but worse yet, by then she wouldn't know who she was or that she'd ever had a granddaughter who loved her so much.

Tears trickled down Elaine's cheeks and splashed in the soapy water. Crying wouldn't change the situation, but she desperately needed the emotional release, so she let the tears fall.

Sniffling her way through the chore, Elaine managed to finish washing, drying, and putting away the dishes. Then, deciding that she needed to work off her frustration, she went to the utility room and grabbed a pair of gardening gloves and a small shovel. Then she stepped out the back door, closing it quietly so as not to wake Grandma.

As Elaine worked silently in the garden, she tried to keep her focus on the weeds and not the situation with Grandma. It was difficult, with the doctor's words still playing over and over in her head. If only there was some way they could stop the dementia in its tracks, or at least keep it from becoming any worse.

May Your will be done, Elaine prayed. *But if it's Your will for Grandma to get better, then please show us the way. And help me to know when and how I should tell her about the doctor's diagnosis.*

Elaine had been attacking the weeds for nearly an hour when Leah and Priscilla rode into the yard on their bikes.

"I'm glad you're home," Leah called. "We're anxious to find out how Edna's doing."

Elaine swallowed hard. Did she dare tell Priscilla and Leah what the doctor had said? She really needed to unburden her soul and talk to someone about this. And who better than her two best friends?

"You look *umgerennt*," Leah said as she and Priscilla parked their bikes and approached Elaine. "Weren't you able to bring Edna home this morning, like you said when you called and left me a message last night?"

"I did call our driver, and we brought Grandma home. She's inside taking a nap." Elaine groaned, rubbing the bridge of her nose. "And you're right. I'm upset."

Priscilla touched Elaine's arm. "What's wrong? Is your grandma's diabetes worse than you thought?"

Elaine shook her head. "Grandma has something else, and it's much worse than diabetes."

Leah's eyes widened. "What is it, Elaine?"

"Grandma has dementia." Elaine's voice faltered, and she gulped on the sob rising in her throat.

Immediately, Elaine's two special friends gathered her into their arms, and they wept bitterly. Elaine was certain that Priscilla and Leah understood and even felt her pain.

CHAPTER 21

Danki for that delicious meal," Jonah said, patting his stomach as he pushed away from the table and stood. He'd been invited to his sister's house for supper again and had enjoyed some of Jean's crispy fried chicken, creamy mashed potatoes, a tasty fruit salad, and steamed peas, fresh from her garden.

"You're welcome, but don't rush off," Jean said. "I made strawberry-rhubarb pie for dessert."

Jean's husband, Nathan, smacked his lips. "That sounds *wunderbaar*."

"It does sound wonderful," Jonah agreed, giving his stomach another pat. "But as full as my belly is, I'm not sure I could eat any pie right now. Guess that's what I get for takin' two helpings of chicken and potatoes." He looked over at Jean's daughter, Rebecca, and grinned. "If I'm not careful, your mamm's good cooking is gonna fatten me up," he said in Pennsylvania-Dutch.

The little girl snickered and poked Jonah's stomach. "You're not *fett*, Uncle Jonah."

"Jah, well, I could end up being fat if I keep eating like I did tonight." Jonah smiled at Jean. "I want to stop over and see Elaine this evening, so if you don't mind, I think I'd better get going. If I hang around here till my stomach's ready for pie, it'll be too late to make a call on Elaine, not to mention mowing her lawn, as I'd planned."

"No problem," Jean said. "I'll put a few pieces of pie in a plastic container, and you can take it along to share with Elaine and her grandma."

"None for Edna," Jonah said with a shake of his head. "She has diabetes, remember?"

Jean touched her flushed cheeks. "Oh, that's right, I'd forgotten about that. How would it be if I send some fresh strawberries for Edna?"

"I'll bet she'd like that," Jonah said.

While Jean put the pieces of pie and a container of berries into a box for Jonah, he took a seat at the table again and visited with Nathan, while Rebecca and her little brother, Stephen, scampered into the living room to play. Baby Zeke snuggled contently in his father's arms.

Jonah couldn't help feeling a bit envious, watching Nathan and his son. It made him wish, once again, that he and Elaine were already married and had at least one child of their own. Hopefully, one day soon, she would accept his marriage proposal.

"From the way the weather's been lately, looks like we're in for a nice summer," Nathan said, pulling Jonah's thoughts aside.

"Jah," Jonah agreed. "Seems like everyone's crops and gardens are doing real well."

"How's that new apprentice of yours workin' out in the buggy shop?" Nathan questioned, patting little Zeke's back.

"Real well. Timothy's a quick learner and seems eager to please. Not only that, but so far, he's never questioned anything I've said or asked him to do."

"That's good to hear. Glad things are working out."

"How's it going with your job at the bulk foods store?" Jonah asked.

"Pretty well. Seems like everyone came shopping there today. We were busy from the time we first opened till right before closing."

"It's always good to be busy." Jonah rubbed his chin, wishing he had the beard of a married man, like Nathan.

"Here you go, Brother." Jean placed a small cardboard box on the table. "Tell Elaine and Edna I said hello."

"I sure will." Jonah stood and tousled little Zeke's hair, which was dark and curly, just like his and Jean's. He gave Jean a hug, shook hands with Nathan, and picked up the box. "I'm going to the living room to say good-bye to the kinner, and then I'll be on my way."

Elaine had just finished the supper dishes and decided to sit outside on the porch awhile to enjoy the fresh evening air. Grandma had already gone to bed, saying she was tired and couldn't keep her eyes open any longer.

Grandma needs all the rest she can get, Elaine thought, taking a seat on the porch swing. Trying to sleep in the chair beside Grandma's hospital bed last night hadn't given Elaine much quality rest, either. She hoped she would sleep better tonight in her own bed, but with so much on her mind, she wasn't sure that was even possible. Between concern over Grandma and the dread she felt about telling Jonah she couldn't marry him, Elaine was a ball of nerves.

Oh, Grandpa, I wish you were still here to help us during this difficult time. You were so smart and patient; I'm sure you would know just what to do.

But the reality was, Grandpa wasn't here, and a lot of responsibility rested on Elaine's shoulders. She'd made a promise to Grandpa that she would take care of Grandma, and that's exactly what she planned to do, no matter how exhausting or difficult it might prove to be.

I have Leah and Priscilla to lean on, Elaine reminded herself. The three of them had been there for one another since they were young girls, and they'd never let each other down. While her friends couldn't make her problems go away, Elaine felt certain that they would offer her support and help in any way they could. Like today, when they'd mowed the lawn for her. Leah had gone around picking up small branches from the trees that had fallen, while Priscilla did the mowing.

Elaine lifted her gaze toward the sky, which was just beginning to darken. *Please guide and direct me through this, Lord,* she prayed. *And help Grandma to deal with all the challenges she'll be faced with as her memory worsens. Give us what we need for each day, and show me what to do about our financial situation.*

She watched as the first fireflies came up out of the grass and began lighting up the trees. Smiling, Elaine continued to gaze as some of the insects soared high above the trees. It was almost as if they'd become part of the twinkling stars overhead. She was tempted to get a jar and catch a few, like she'd done when she was a child. Grandpa had shown her how to cut holes in the lid to give the bugs some air once they'd been caught. He'd also told her to put a few blades of grass inside the jar so the lightning bugs, as they were sometimes called, would have something to crawl onto. What fun it had been, taking the jar of fireflies up to her room when it was time for bed. After Grandma and Grandpa kissed her good night, Elaine would lie in bed for a long time, watching the lightning bugs blink rapidly, until they put her to sleep. The next day, as Grandpa had also taught her, she released the bugs back into the air.

Elaine put that happy memory aside and thought about her current situation. She and Grandma couldn't keep hosting dinners for tourists once Grandma's memory had severely declined. However, they would do it for as long as possible, which would not only help financially, but hopefully give Grandma a purpose in life and keep her focused on something positive.

Elaine smiled when Patches, who'd been lying at the edge of the porch, meowed as if understanding the anguish Elaine had been facing since Grandma took ill.

Elaine's musings halted when a horse and buggy turned up the lane. She recognized Jonah's horse, Sassy, plodding along at a snail's pace.

Tempted to rush out to meet Jonah, Elaine remained on the porch swing, waiting for him to join her. Patches lay watching, and her tail swished back and forth.

After Jonah secured his horse, he stepped onto the porch, carrying a small box.

"Guder owed," he said, smiling at Elaine as he took a seat beside her. "Did you get the note I left for you yesterday?"

She nodded but was barely able to tell him good evening because her throat felt so swollen. Just the sight of him caused her to feel so many regrets.

"I came from Jean's place, and since I was too full to eat dessert, she sent over two slices of strawberry-rhubarb pie for us and some fresh strawberries for your grandma. Thought maybe we could enjoy them together after I mow your lawn."

Elaine's forehead wrinkled as she pointed to the yard full of fireflies. "I think it's getting too dark for that, Jonah. Besides, Priscilla took care of mowing it when she and Leah were here earlier today. Leah got all the sticks in the yard cleaned up, too. With all that rain we had, a lot of twigs and leaves had come down from the trees."

"That was nice of them. Guess I should have come by sooner, but I was kept busy all day in the shop, and then after promising Jean I'd come for supper, the day got away from me."

"It's not a problem." Elaine looked at the box of goodies. "A piece of pie sounds good. I haven't eaten many sweets since Grandma was diagnosed with diabetes."

"Guess that must be kinda hard for both of you."

She nodded. "It's harder on Grandma than it is me. She's always enjoyed eating most anything that's sweet. Should I take the box inside and put the pie on some plates for us?"

"Jah, that'd be great. Think now I have room for dessert."

Jonah remained on the porch while Elaine went to the kitchen, where she placed the berries for Grandma on the counter and made some tea. As she was putting the slices of pie on the plates, Grandma walked into the kitchen. "Ach, my, that looks so good!" She rubbed her hands together, smiling eagerly. "I'm more than ready for dessert."

Elaine jumped at the sound of Grandma's voice. "You startled me! I thought you had gone to bed."

"Thought I was tired, but I couldn't sleep." Grandma stared hungrily at the pie. "I heard you moving around in the kitchen and decided to come see what you were up to."

Elaine felt bad having to disappoint Grandma, but she needed to be reminded that she shouldn't eat such things. "Jonah's out on the porch, Grandma," she said. "He brought the pie for him and me, and his sister sent fresh strawberries for you." She motioned to the container.

"Oh, I see." Grandma didn't argue, but took the bowl of berries and ambled out of the kitchen with her head down. She was clearly disappointed.

"Are you all right, Grandma?" Elaine called after her.

"I'll be fine. Just want to find a good book to read while I'm eating these berries."

"Okay, then. I'm heading out to the porch to be with Jonah. If you need anything, just give a holler." Elaine went out the back door, closing it behind her so Grandma wouldn't hear her conversation with Jonah. She dreaded telling him what was on her mind, but it had to be said before she lost her nerve.

"Here you go." Elaine handed Jonah the plate, then placed the tray with two cups of tea on the small table between their chairs.

They sat in silence for a while as they ate. "The pie was delicious," Elaine said after she'd finished eating. "Your sister's a good cook."

"Jah, Jean's always been an excellent baker. Our mamm taught her well."

Elaine handed Jonah his cup of tea. It was all she could do not to burst into tears as she reflected on all the other times she and Jonah had sat on this porch together. *A year ago, who would have thought things would be so different now?*

"Is something wrong?" he questioned. "You look umgerennt."

"I am upset," she admitted.

"What's wrong? Are you still worried about your grandma's health?"

"Jah, and things are even worse now."

"In what way?"

"Yesterday, Grandma went shopping by herself, and she forgot to take her medicine along. Since she was gone longer than she'd planned, she decided to get some lunch while she was in town."

Jonah sat quietly as Elaine told him how Grandma had blacked out and been taken to the hospital and kept overnight.

"I'm sorry to hear that," he said. "Is she doing better now?"

"They managed to get her blood sugar stabilized with the proper dose of medicine, but since she'd hit her head, the doctor wanted her to be kept overnight for observation and more tests." Elaine paused, struggling not to break down. "At the hospital last night, one of the doctors took me aside and gave me some very distressing news."

"What was it?"

"Grandma has dementia."

Jonah's head jerked back. "What made them reach that conclusion?"

"They ran several tests, including an oral cognitive." Elaine's fingers curled around her cup of tea. "The results helped them determine that she has dementia."

"But a loss of memory can be typical for a person her age," Jonah said. "Some folks much younger than Edna become forgetful. Even I forget certain things—especially when I get busy or am under too much stress. That's pretty normal, don't you think?"

"It's more than that, Jonah," Elaine explained. "The results of Grandma's tests showed that she does have dementia, and sorry to say, it's only going to get worse in the years ahead."

Jonah sat several seconds, head down, as though studying something on the porch floor. Slowly raising his head, he reached for Elaine's hand and gave her fingers a gentle squeeze. "I know how upset you must be by this news, but I want you to know that I'll be here to help you through it."

Elaine moistened her lips with the tip of her tongue, barely able to make eye contact with Jonah. "I appreciate that, but Grandma's my responsibility, and—"

"And you're going to need all the support you can get."

Elaine couldn't argue with that, but it wasn't going to come from Jonah. She had to make him understand. "I'm not free to marry you, Jonah."

"Why not?"

"I just told you. I need to take care of Grandma."

"I can help you with that."

"You have enough to do with your buggy business."

"My business is important, but I would still take time to help out where Edna's concerned."

Elaine shook her head forcefully. Apparently, Jonah did not understand. "If we were to get married, I'd want to be a full-time wife, and since I'll be acting as grandma's caregiver, for what could be several more years, I need to concentrate fully on that."

Jonah slipped his fingers under Elaine's chin and tilted her face so she was looking directly into his eyes. "I'm in love with you, Elaine."

She swallowed hard and lowered her gaze, unable to look at him. "It's not meant for us to be together, Jonah. You need to move on with your life because there is no future for us. Oh, and please don't say anything about this to Grandma. I haven't told her yet that she has dementia." Before Jonah could offer a response, Elaine rushed into the house. Leaning her full weight on the back of the door, she let the tears flow. It was all she could do not to run back outside and tell Jonah she'd changed her mind and would marry him, despite all the hardships they would endure. But as Elaine grappled with her emotions, she heard Jonah's horse and buggy pull away. Jonah was hurt, but the decision she'd made was final. For Jonah's sake, as well as Grandma's, it had to be.

CHAPTER 22

Two weeks had passed since Elaine told Jonah she couldn't marry him, but to Jonah the pain was as intense as the moment she'd given him her reasons. Thinking about it gave Jonah a headache and made it difficult to concentrate on his work.

There has to be something I can say or do to make Elaine change her mind, he thought, reaching for a piece of upholstery that would cover the seat of the buggy he was working on. *Maybe after some time goes by, Elaine will reconsider. She's most likely overwhelmed by all that happened with Edna.*

Jonah stopped for a minute, hearing a squirrel chattering in the elm tree outside his shop. "I wonder what's got that critter so worked up," he muttered, walking to the open door.

"Could be most anything, I guess," Timothy called from across the room. "I can hear him carrying on clean over here."

Jonah stood by the doorway and watched as the squirrel clung to the side of the tree, repeatedly shaking its tail. Then Jonah saw another movement, on a branch higher up. It was partially concealed by all the leaves, but he could see there was a hawk sitting quietly, watching the squirrel as if it was just waiting for the right opportunity to have a meal. The squirrel kept climbing, closer and closer to the hawk. Jonah thought if the squirrel moved any closer to the bird of prey, it would be a goner. At one point, the bushy-tailed critter got on the same branch as the hawk, and they sat watching each other. The whole time, the squirrel never relented and seemed to bark out warnings of the hawk's trespassing. Soon after that, a bunch of crows flew in, giving the hawk a piece of their minds. The crows' scolding, plus the squirrel's chattering, went on for several minutes. Quick as a wink, the squirrel hopped to another branch. The hawk flew away, with the crows following close behind.

That's one lucky squirrel, Jonah thought, watching the tree limbs bob as the squirrel jumped from branch to branch. *Guess even God's creatures have their own frustrations, same as me.*

Jonah hadn't told anyone, not even Jean, that Elaine wouldn't marry him. Since he was hopeful that he could get Elaine to change her mind, he'd decided not to say anything about it, unless he was put on the spot.

He needed to think about something else before he gave in to self-pity, so Jonah decided to check for mail. "I'll be right back," he called to Timothy, who was busy sanding some wood for another buggy. A week ago, Jonah had started on Adam Beachy's new rig, and it was progressing nicely.

The boy gave a nod. "Okay. I'll just keep workin' on this while you're gone."

As Jonah headed down the driveway to the mailbox, he thought about how grateful he was that he'd hired Timothy as his apprentice. There was little doubt that the boy would keep working while he was gone. At the age of sixteen, Timothy was already a responsible young man.

When Jonah opened the mailbox, he was pleased to find a letter from his folks. Grabbing it, along with the rest of his mail, he stepped into the phone shanty and took a seat. This would be a good place to read Mom and Dad's letter in quiet and without any interruptions. Jonah needed to relax a bit before he went back to work, so he settled into the fold-up chair and kept the door open to let in some fresh air.

Tearing open the letter, Jonah was pleased to learn that Mom and Dad were both doing well and were anxious to come for a visit soon. It seemed like forever since he'd last seen his folks, and it would sure be good to see them again. Jean would be pleased with this news, too, and he figured she'd probably gotten a letter from their folks as well.

As Jonah read on, he was surprised to learn that Luke and Meredith were expecting another baby. He was happy for them, of course, but it made him long all the more for a wife and children. As much as Jonah hated to admit it, maybe that was not meant to be.

That morning when Elaine went out to the phone shanty to check for messages, she discovered one from Priscilla, suggesting that she, Elaine, and Leah get together soon for a girl's day out. Priscilla said she figured Elaine probably needed some time away to do something just for fun, and that her mother had agreed to stay with Elaine's grandma while they were gone.

Elaine stared at the answering machine. *Should I take Priscilla up on that offer? It would be nice to spend some time with my two best friends. We haven't done anything together for quite some time.*

With no further hesitation, Elaine picked up the phone and dialed Priscilla's number. When she left the phone shanty a few minutes later, there was a new spring to her step. She looked forward to spending a few hours with her friends and felt confident that Grandma would be in good company with Priscilla's mother, Iva.

"It's good to see you," Sara said when Jean Mast stopped by shortly before noon. "It's been awhile since we've had a visit. Can you stay for lunch?"

"That would be nice. Nathan's mamm volunteered to watch the kinner for me today so I could run some errands, and since she said I could take all day if I needed to, I have plenty of time to stay for lunch." Jean smiled and bent to ruffle Mark's hair. He'd been sitting on the throw rug in front of the kitchen sink, playing with some of Sara's pots and pans while she was making sandwiches. "He's sure growing, and such nice thick hair."

"It's like his *daadi's*," Sara said.

Jean smiled. "Is there anything I can do to help with lunch?"

"The sandwiches are almost finished, but you can pour some iced tea for us if you don't mind." Sara gestured to the refrigerator. "I made sun tea yesterday and it should be nice and cold."

"No problem. I'll get the tea and glasses."

While Sara put the finishing touches on the roast beef sandwiches and Jean poured the tea, Sara told her how she'd fallen asleep a few weeks ago and Mark had wandered off. "I was ever so grateful that your brother spotted Mark in the field near my property," she said. "It was right before a storm hit, and I'm thankful that no harm came to my boy."

"I heard about that from Jonah." Jean placed their glasses on the table. "You must have been really scared when you woke up and discovered that Mark had wandered off."

"I really was. Thankfully, God was watching over my boy. And when I saw him with Jonah, I knew that my prayers had been answered. Jonah got us back to the house in the nick of time, before the rain let loose." Sara picked Mark up and put him in the high chair. "I was surprised that Mark took to Jonah right away. Even though my little guy doesn't know Jonah very well, he didn't cry or seem to be afraid at all."

"Jonah has a way with children," Jean said, taking a seat at the table. "All three of my kinner adore their uncle Jonah."

"If he's as kind and gentle with them as he was with Mark, I can understand why."

"Jonah will make a good daed someday," Jean commented. "He plans to marry Elaine, and I hope it will be soon, because I want my brother to be happy, and I'm anxious to become an aunt."

"When will they be getting married?" Sara had known Jonah and Elaine were courting but hadn't heard there was a wedding in their future. Of course, she should have assumed that would be the case. Couples who'd been courting awhile usually ended up getting married.

"It probably won't be until Elaine is sure her grandma can live on her own," Jean replied. "Edna was recently diagnosed with diabetes, so between that and losing Lloyd, I'm sure it's been quite an adjustment."

Sara nodded in understanding. "I've never had a serious illness, but losing Harley and facing all the responsibilities of raising our son, plus everything there is to do around here, has been a difficult adjustment for me. Some days I think I can do it. Other days, I don't know how I will manage."

"I understand. After I lost my first husband, Silas, I felt as if my whole world had fallen apart. With two small kinner to raise, I was sure I'd never make it. But then Nathan came along, and my life took on new meaning. He's such a kind, loving man, and a wonderful stepfather to my two older children. I'm grateful that God has given me a second chance at love." Jean touched Sara's arm. "Perhaps someday you'll have the opportunity to fall in love and marry again, too."

"I doubt that, because I'm not looking for love. Besides, my heart belonged to Harley, and no one will ever take his place."

"I felt the same way about Silas. But eventually I came to realize that I could love again. Even though I will never forget what Silas and I had, my love for Nathan is strong."

Sara smiled. "I'll keep an open mind and trust God with the future. In the meantime, though, I think we ought to pray so we can eat. *Heavenly Father,* she silently prayed, *thank You for good friends like Jean, and if it's Your will for me to ever marry again, please give me wisdom in choosing the right man.*

CHAPTER 23

Elaine took a sip of iced tea as she opened the book she'd picked up at the library the other day. She'd received some information from the doctor on dementia, but this book was more detailed and provided a lot of information about the disease, as well as things that caregivers could do. Elaine felt better knowing all the facts. Understanding the disease was important, but so was knowing what she could do to help Grandma through the agonizing process that lay ahead. Elaine would have to be strong. She was committed to taking care of Grandma the best way she could, and since that meant making some sacrifices, she wouldn't have a lot of free time to spend with her friends.

But I don't have to worry about that today, she thought with anticipation. *Grandma is still doing well enough for me to leave her awhile. Besides, Priscilla's mamm will be with Grandma while I go to lunch and do some shopping with Leah and Priscilla, and I'm sure we'll all enjoy the day.*

Elaine's thoughts turned to Jonah. He had dropped by again yesterday to see how she and Grandma were doing. Elaine appreciated that but hoped he wouldn't come over on a regular basis. It was difficult seeing him and knowing they couldn't get married. She was also concerned that if they saw each other too often, Jonah might try to pressure her into accepting his proposal. She couldn't marry him now, and she wouldn't ask him to wait.

If it becomes necessary, I may ask him not to come around anymore, Elaine decided. Oh, how she dreaded having to tell him that. She would miss Jonah so much.

Elaine had cried herself to sleep so many nights recently, and it had only made her more miserable, knowing her dreams of a life with Jonah were no longer possible. She was exhausted, holding her emotions in throughout the day and then letting them loose after she'd gone to bed.

Crying was good; Grandma had often said that when Elaine was a girl, but Elaine couldn't allow herself to give in to tears too often, for it would do no good. She needed to pull herself together and take one day at a time.

A squirrel chattered from a tree nearby, as if to scold Elaine. "I know. . .I know," she said. "I need to perk up."

It was a beautiful morning—the kind of day that made a person feel energetic. Elaine had always been appreciative of the simple things, but life's challenges had overwhelmed her, and she wondered if she'd ever be truly happy again.

She glanced over at the stump where the old maple tree once stood. The yard looked almost bare without it, even though a few other trees stood nearby. It just added to the emptiness that consumed Elaine. She truly needed to be with her friends today, and maybe, if only for a little while, some of that emptiness she felt would be replaced.

"What are you doing out here?" Grandma asked a bit harshly, stepping out the back door. "I thought you were going to clean Millie's cage."

"I did that yesterday, Grandma." Taken aback, Elaine quickly closed her book. It wasn't like Grandma to speak to her in such a severe tone. Elaine took a deep breath, allowing her heartbeat to slow to a normal rate again. "I've been sitting out here waiting for Leah and Priscilla to arrive."

"Oh, are they coming to visit?" Grandma's tone softened as she took a seat beside Elaine, folding her hands in her lap.

Elaine had told Grandma during breakfast that her friends would be coming by to pick her up shortly before noon, but apparently she'd forgotten about that. "I'm going out to lunch with Priscilla and Leah," Elaine said patiently. "Priscilla's mamm will stay here with you to visit."

Grandma smiled. "Oh, that'll be nice. I haven't seen Iva Herschberger for a long time."

"We just saw her on Sunday, Grandma," Elaine reminded. It had only been three days, yet Grandma couldn't remember? *Is she one of those dementia patients I read about in the book who goes downhill quickly? Oh, I hope not.*

Grandma looked out into the yard and pointed. "Would you look at those pretty birds drinking from the birdbath? I wish Millie could join them." She sighed. "But then, I guess if we brought her cage out here and let her out, she'd probably fly away and we might never get her back."

"You're right," Elaine agreed. "Even if we bring her cage outdoors for some fresh air, we must never open the latch on her door."

"When Iva gets here, I'll see if I can get Millie to talk for her." Grandma snickered. "I like it when she says, 'Pretty bird. . .pretty bird.' "

"It's fun to listen to your parakeet mimic the things she hears." Elaine was glad Grandma had a pet. The little bird gave her such pleasure and, quite often, a good laugh.

"Millie can be quite the chatterbox sometimes." Grandma yawned and covered her mouth as she leaned back in her chair. "I don't know why I feel so tired today. Guess maybe I didn't get enough sleep last night."

"Would you like a glass of iced tea?" Elaine asked, pleased that she and Grandma were having a nice conversation and that Grandma seemed to be thinking more clearly right now. These were the moments Elaine would always cherish.

"No thank you, dear. I'm not thirsty just now, but you go ahead and enjoy yours." Grandma pointed to Elaine's glass of iced tea on the small table between them. It was a piece of outdoor furniture Grandpa had made several years ago, and except for a few water stains, the table was still in good shape. Some folks might try to get rid of those stains, but Elaine saw them as memories from the days when Grandpa was still with them. He'd enjoyed relaxing on the porch after a hard day's work, and the three of them had spent many an evening out here together, drinking iced tea and having dessert.

Elaine reached for her glass and took a drink. She'd just placed it back on the table when she spotted Priscilla's horse and buggy coming up the driveway.

"Looks like your friends are here," Grandma said, rising to her feet. "Should we walk out to the hitching rack to meet them?"

"We can," Elaine responded, "but it might be better if we wait here on the porch."

Grandma tipped her head and looked at Elaine curiously while rubbing the tiny mole on the left side of her nose. "How come?"

"Some horses can get a bit spooky while they're being tied to the rack. At least that's how mine is sometimes."

"My horse is never spooky," Grandma said. "Misty is gentle as a sweet little lamb."

It was true. While Misty was calm, Grandpa's horse, Dusty, acted up sometimes. When Grandpa was alive, he'd always been able to handle the gelding. Since they didn't use his horse for pulling a buggy anymore, Elaine thought they ought to sell him. She hadn't mentioned that to Grandma, though, knowing she probably wasn't ready to part with Grandpa's horse. Grandma often went out to the barn to talk to Dusty and had even told Elaine that being near Grandpa's horse made her feel closer to him. Elaine wasn't about to take that pleasure from her—not yet, at least. Besides, Grandma needed as much familiarity around her as possible right now.

Knowing his folks would be arriving early next week, Jonah decided to take some time away from the buggy shop and shop for groceries as well as a few cleaning supplies. He'd left Timothy in the buggy shop to work by himself, knowing he'd only be gone a couple of hours. Sassy must have wanted to make a trip to town, too, for he seemed to be quite frisky this morning, trotting down the road without Jonah having to flick the reins or holler at him to get moving.

Jonah couldn't blame his horse for feeling energetic. It looked to be a glorious day, one that could win first place if there was a weather contest. He'd been up early, and standing in the door of his buggy shop, he'd watched the sun slowly rise. Jonah wasn't sure what the temperature had been, but after exhaling a few times, he thought he could actually see his breath. Of course, that was probably his imagination, since it was still summer. Today was so cool and crisp, though, that it felt like fall.

Jonah looked up at the bluest of skies and breathed deeply, filling his lungs with fresh, clean air. On a day like today, he didn't feel weighed down by the humidity. There was not a cloud in the sky, which made being outdoors pure pleasure.

As far as I'm concerned, this kind of weather could stick around for the rest of summer, Jonah mused. *Bet it'll be a good night for stargazing, too.*

When Jonah guided his horse and buggy to the hitching rack outside the bulk foods store, he spotted his friend Melvin Gingerich getting out of his buggy.

"How's it going?" Melvin called, lifting his hand in a friendly wave.

"Fair enough, I guess." Jonah stepped down from his buggy and secured his horse. "How are things with you, Melvin?"

"With weather like this, I can't complain. My crops are doing well, and oh, you may not have heard, but Sharon Otto and I will be getting married this fall, so I have much to be thankful for."

"Glad to hear it." Jonah gave Melvin's shoulder a squeeze.

"How are things going with you and Elaine?" Melvin questioned. "Will you two be setting a wedding date soon?"

Jonah shook his head. "Afraid not. Elaine hasn't agreed to marry me. At least, not yet," he quickly added.

"How come? I thought you two were getting along well."

"We were, but Elaine's grandmother isn't well, so Elaine doesn't want to commit to marriage right now." Jonah's forehead wrinkled. "I told her I'm willing to help out, but she refused my offer."

"That's ridiculous. You'd think she'd want your support."

"That's what I thought, too, but apparently Elaine thinks taking care of Edna is something she has to do alone, and she doesn't want to burden me with it."

"What's wrong with Edna?" Melvin asked.

"For one thing, she has diabetes."

"That can usually be controlled with medication, exercise, and eating right."

"I know, but there's more." Jonah paused, wondering if he should be telling Melvin this. But he really needed someone to share his burden with, and who better than his good friend? "You see, Elaine found out recently that her grandma has dementia."

"You mean, Edna's losing her memory?" Melvin's forehead creased.

Jonah gave a slow nod. "I'm afraid so."

"That's baremlich."

"I agree; it's terrible, and short of a miracle, Edna's condition will deteriorate."

Melvin rubbed his chin, wearing a thoughtful expression. "That's a pretty heavy burden for Elaine to carry by herself. She really needs someone to share in Edna's care."

"I know that, and I'd like it to be me, but if I can't convince Elaine, then there's little I can do. I'm not sure Elaine has told Edna about her condition yet, either, so please don't mention this to anyone."

"The only one I'll talk to about this is the Lord, and I'll surely keep you and Elaine in my prayers." Melvin's dark eyes revealed his concern as he placed his hand on Jonah's shoulder and gave it an encouraging squeeze. "Maybe something will happen that'll open Elaine's eyes, and then she'll realize just how much she needs you."

"That would truly be an answer to prayer," Jonah agreed. "Jah, a God-given answer to the prayers I've been sending up ever since Elaine turned down my marriage proposal."

"Well, don't give up," Melvin said sincerely. "With God all things are possible."

CHAPTER 24

"You're not eating much today," Priscilla said, gently bumping Elaine's arm.

Elaine looked at her half-eaten salad and sighed. "Guess I'm just not all that hungry right now."

"You're worried about your grandma, aren't you?" Leah questioned from across their table at Yoder's restaurant.

Elaine nodded slowly. "I'm trying not to worry, but I can't help feeling apprehensive when I'm not with her. What if she doesn't take her medicine? What if she doesn't eat what she's supposed to?"

"My mamm's there with her," Priscilla said. "I'm sure she'll remind Edna of those things."

"That's right," Leah agreed. "So just try to relax and have a good time. After all, it's not very often that the three of us can get together for lunch like this anymore."

"And don't forget, we're going shopping afterward." Priscilla flashed Elaine a cheery smile. "I wish we could have more days like this. I know we're getting older, but I still miss how things used to be with the three of us."

"That would be nice." Elaine took a drink of water. "But we all have responsibilities, and life is full of changes. I've certainly been reminded of that recently."

Leah reached for the bottle of ketchup and poured some on her french fries. "It's true, but we should still take time out to be together. Even if it's just to sit on the porch and talk, it's good for all of us." She grinned and pointed at her plate. "These fries are sure good. Would you like to try some, Elaine? Maybe they'll pique your appetite."

"No thanks."

"Maybe we should set one night a week aside so we can get together and talk," Leah suggested.

Priscilla bobbed her head. "I agree with that."

"We'll have to see how it goes." Her friends meant well, but she had a feeling that in the not-too-distant future times like today would be few and far between. She shivered as a blast of cold air from the air-conditioning vent above her blew down across her shoulders. She almost asked the waitress if the air-conditioning could be turned off, but maybe she was the only one who minded the chill. While it was nice to be indoors away from the summer heat, especially on days when it was unbearable, too much time spent in a room with air-conditioning sometimes made her throat feel sore. Hopefully that wouldn't be the case today.

"I appreciate you coming over to clean my house, but I didn't expect you to bring lunch for me, too," Jonah told his sister when she entered the buggy shop with a basket of food.

Jean smiled and set the basket on the counter. "What else is a little sister for if not to help her older bruder?"

He chuckled. "I'm not that much older. According to Mom, I was born just ten minutes before you." He gave Jean a hug. "Are you excited about our folks coming to see us next week?"

"Definitely. It's been too long since we've seen them, and I'm sure they'll be surprised to see how much my kinner have grown."

"You've got that right," Jonah agreed. "Every time I see 'em it seems like they've grown another inch or two."

She swatted his arm playfully. "You're such a kidder."

"Can you join me for lunch?" Jonah asked. "Timothy left early today because he had a dental appointment. And since there are no customers right now, it's a good chance for us to talk."

"Sure I can, but I don't want to sit too long or your house will never get cleaned."

Jean took a seat at the metal table near the window. Jonah followed with the wicker basket. After their silent prayer, she opened the basket and handed Jonah a sandwich.

"Danki," Jonah said, thankful for his sister's thoughtfulness. "Ham and cheese is one of my favorites."

"There's a thermos of coffee, some peanut butter cookies, and a few apples in there, too." Jean gestured to the basket.

Jonah thumped his stomach. "If I'm not careful, you're gonna fatten me up."

She smiled. "It would take a lot more than one of my lunches to make you fat, Jonah. You work hard out here in the shop, and once I go back up to your house to finish cleaning, you'll probably burn off most of the calories you're about to take in."

"That could be." Truth was, Jonah had never had a problem with his weight, and at twenty-four, he wasn't worried about his metabolism slowing down.

They ate in companionable silence, until Jean posed a question. "Have you seen Elaine lately?"

"Not since last Sunday at church," Jonah replied. "Why do you ask?"

Jean tilted her head. "I thought since you two are courting that you'd see her as often as possible."

Jonah swallowed the last bite of his sandwich and washed it down with some coffee. "To be honest, Elaine and I aren't courting anymore."

Jean's eyebrows lifted, and her mouth formed an O. "You're kidding, right?"

"No, unfortunately I'm not. Elaine broke things off with me." It was hard admitting this to Jean, especially when Jonah had been hoping that Elaine would change her mind. But now, with his sister's question about him seeing Elaine, he figured he may as well tell her the truth.

"But why would she do that?" Jean questioned. "I thought you two would be planning a wedding soon."

"That's what I'd hoped for." Jonah groaned. "But with her grandma ill, Elaine thinks it would be a burden on me if we got married and she was caring for Edna. I think Elaine also believes that under those circumstances, she couldn't be the kind of wife I need."

"She's not thinking straight." Jean placed her hand on Jonah's arm, giving it a supporting pat. "I'll bet Elaine changes her mind when she realizes how difficult it will be to take care of Edna on her own. Besides, from what I can tell, Elaine loves you, Jonah. I'm sure if you just wait patiently, she will agree to marry you. In the meantime, you ought to keep going over there, offering your support and letting her know that you're there for her."

Jonah nodded. "You're right, Jean. Think I'll go on over there tonight."

"Your garden is doing so nicely," Iva said as Edna sat beside her on the porch swing. "Have you had much trouble with bugs this year?"

"I—I don't think so." Edna glanced briefly at Iva, then turned her attention to a big black beetle that had found its way to the porch.

A few seconds later, Patches leaped onto the porch, spotted the bug, and nudged it with her nose. That was clearly a bad idea, for the beetle latched right onto the cat's nose and hung on with its pinchers. Screeching, Patches leaped into the air, then tumbled off the porch, landing on her back in the flower bed.

"Oh dear!" Iva gasped. "That poor cat!"

Edna chuckled. "Patches seems to be all right; she just had an encounter with a very determined beetle."

By this time, the creature had let go of the cat's nose and disappeared among the foliage of a miniature rosebush. Patches got up, shook her head a couple of times, and hissed all the way to the barn.

"Sometimes I forget how silly Elaine's *katze* can be," Edna said.

"I know what you mean," Iva agreed. "The other day one of our cats ran up a tree and sat there meowing for most of the day."

"Did it ever come down?" Edna asked.

"Oh jah, but not till Daniel got the buggy out of the shed so we could get ready to go to the bulk foods store." Iva laughed, flapping her hand. "That crazy cat leaped out of the tree and landed in the back of the buggy. Guess it wanted to take a ride to town with us."

Edna smiled and got the swing moving faster. It felt good to sit here, laughing and chatting. She hadn't found much to laugh about since Lloyd died. "You know, cats aren't the only pets that do silly things," she said. Then she went on to tell about some of the silly words her parakeet often repeated, and how whenever she let Millie out of her cage, she would fly around the house and sometimes land on Edna's head.

"My mamm used to raise canaries when I was a girl," Iva said. "They sang beautifully, but I think it would have been more fun if they'd mimicked some of the things our family said."

Edna sat quietly for a bit, thinking about how Lloyd had been able to get Millie to say so many different words. She squeezed her eyes shut, hoping she wouldn't give in to the tears she felt pushing against her eyelids. *It feels a lot better to laugh than cry,* she thought.

"Are you all right?" Iva asked.

Edna quickly opened her eyes. "Oh, I'm fine. Just thinking, is all."

Several minutes went by. Iva touched Edna's arm. "I was sorry to hear about the physical problems you've been having."

"Oh, you mean my diabetes?"

Iva gave a nod. "That, as well as your dementia diagnosis."

Edna blinked several times, sitting straight in her chair. "Wh–who told you that?"

"Priscilla. She said Elaine told her about your memory loss."

Edna's spine went rigid, and she halted the porch swing abruptly. "I may be a bit forgetful at times, but I don't have dementia! If I did, don't you think the doctor or Elaine would have told me about it?"

Iva's face blanched. "Perhaps I've spoken out of turn. I just thought—"

"Well, you thought wrong! If I had dementia, I'm sure I would know it, and I can't understand why Elaine would tell anyone such a horrible thing. I'm certainly going to ask her about it when she gets home." With her hands shaking and her mouth suddenly dry, Edna got up from the swing and tromped into the house. She knew Iva had brought lunch, but right now, Edna didn't think she could eat a thing!

CHAPTER 25

Edna felt bad leaving Iva on the porch by herself, but she couldn't face the look of pity on her friend's face. All Edna wanted was to be left alone so she could think and try to sort things out.

She took a seat in her rocking chair, staring at the clock Lloyd had given her when they'd first gotten married. What Iva had said was such a shock. If it was true, then why hadn't Elaine or someone at the hospital told her?

A knot formed in Edna's stomach as she thought about a woman in their church district, Lizzie Bontrager, who'd died a few years ago after suffering through the agony of dementia. The poor woman had ended up not knowing anyone, even her own family members.

She folded her arms and held them tightly against her chest. *Is that what's going to happen to me?* Just the thought made Edna feel sick to her stomach. How could she ever forget her dear husband or all the years of raising Elaine? Would the memories from her own childhood be gone? Her parents, her friends, and everyone in their community—would she forget them all? And what about this farm, the animals, and all the simple joys she'd known over the years? Was it really possible that the chapters of her life could be completely erased by this terrible disease, as though they had never been there at all?

Edna got the rocking chair moving faster, her fear of the unknown changing to anger. This was not going to happen to her—not if she could help it. She'd keep herself busy and her mind alert so the disease wouldn't get the best of her. *I will not allow it to rob me of a life's worth of memories!*

"Where's Grandma?" Elaine asked when she returned home with Priscilla, after they'd taken Leah to her home. Iva was sitting on the porch by herself.

Iva's cheeks turned pink. "She's inside. I'm afraid I said something to upset her."

"What'd you say, Mom?" Priscilla asked, joining them on the porch.

"I said something I shouldn't have, but I didn't realize it was a mistake until it was too late."

"Too late for what?" Elaine moved closer to the chair were Iva sat. "What was it that you said?"

"I told Edna that I was sorry to hear that she'd been diagnosed with dementia." Iva stared down at the floor. "It didn't take me long to realize that she hadn't been told."

"Ach, no!" Elaine covered her mouth with both hands. She'd been fearful that something like this might happen and blamed herself for not telling Grandma the truth right away. "I was planning to tell her but was waiting for the right time."

"Is there ever a 'right' time to tell someone they have serious memory issues?" Priscilla interjected.

Elaine's chin quivered as she slowly shook her head. "No, I suppose not, but I didn't think Grandma was ready to hear such distressing news yet."

"I—I wouldn't have said anything, but I thought Edna already knew." Iva's voice cracked. "I'm very sorry about this. I just had no idea." She folded her hands as though she was praying.

"It's okay. How could you have known? What's done is done." Elaine drew in a shaky breath. "Guess I'd better go inside and speak to Grandma about this now."

Priscilla nodded. "We understand, and we should be going anyway—unless you'd like us to stay."

"I appreciate your offer," Elaine said, "but this is something I should handle by myself." Elaine wondered, though, how much longer she'd be able to cope with situations concerning Grandma on her own.

"Please let us know if there's anything we can do to help," Iva said, standing up and gathering the basket she'd brought with lunch for her and Grandma. "We were having such a nice visit until—"

"Don't think any more about it." Elaine patted Iva's arm. "It really is my fault for not telling Grandma right up front, and I will let you know if I need anything." She opened the door and hurried inside.

Grandma was in the living room, sitting in the rocking chair, staring at the clock on the far side of the room.

Elaine knelt on the floor in front of Grandma and clasped her hands. "I—I'm so sorry for not telling you about your illness, Grandma." Tears welled in her eyes, and she nearly choked on the sob rising in her throat. "I didn't think you were ready to hear it just yet."

"I could never be ready to hear something like that." Grandma slowly shook her head, sniffing, as though trying to hold back tears. "I believe I had the right to know, and I shouldn't have heard it from Iva Herschberger." She paused a moment, as if to gain control of her emotions. "Now I know why I haven't been able to remember some things. I thought it was just ordinary forgetfulness, but I. . .I guess I was wrong."

Elaine rubbed her fingers gently over Grandma's hand. It nearly broke her heart to see Grandma's pained expression.

"The one thing that saddens me the most is knowing that one of these days I won't be able to remember much of anything. I still can hardly believe it." Tears trickled down Grandma's cheeks as she rose from her chair.

Elaine wrapped her arms around Grandma and held her tight. "Oh, Grandma, there was no easy way I could tell you. I just couldn't seem to find the right words." She was repeating herself, but she wanted to make sure Grandma understood how truly sorry she was.

Elaine felt even worse when Grandma started rubbing her back, just like she'd done when Elaine was a child and needed to be comforted. "I promise I'll be here for you, Grandma, and we'll fight this together for as long as we possibly can."

Sara winced as Leah probed several sore spots on her left foot. "I don't understand why my feet are always so sore," she complained.

"Some people's feet are more tender than others," Leah said. "And of course, when there's inflammation anywhere in the body, it's usually indicated by the sensitive areas of certain meridian zones on a person's feet."

"Does that mean there's inflammation somewhere in my body?" Sara questioned.

Leah nodded, continuing to rub the places on Sara's feet that were the most painful.

"Do you know what's wrong with me—why my arms and legs sometimes feel numb or tingly?"

"I can't be sure," Leah responded. "But as I've mentioned before, I think it would be a good idea for you to see your doctor."

"Doctors are expensive, and I'd much rather come here to see you and just make a donation." Sara wiggled her toes. "Besides, I always feel better after I've had a foot treatment."

Leah smiled. "I'm glad to hear that, but there are some things reflexology can't help, so you need to use good judgment in deciding when to see a doctor and when to visit me."

"I understand, and if my problem gets worse, I'll make an appointment with the doctor."

Hoping his mission this evening would be successful, Jonah directed his horse and buggy up the lane leading to Edna and Elaine's house. After tying Sassy to the hitching rack, he started for the house, but had only made it halfway there when a sleek black cat darted out of the barn and ran in front of Jonah. *Sure am glad I'm not a superstitious man,* he thought, sidestepping the cat as it zipped this way and that, in hot pursuit of a little gray mouse. *Otherwise, I might think something bad is about to happen.*

Jonah's hands grew sweaty as he stepped onto the porch and knocked on the door. He didn't know why he felt so nervous; it wasn't like he'd never come to call on Elaine before. A few seconds went by, and then Elaine, wearing an apron decorated with splotches of flour, answered the door.

"Jonah, I—I didn't expect to see you this evening," she stammered, brushing at the front of her apron. "I was just making some biscuits to go with the stew I'm preparing for supper."

Jonah couldn't help noticing that the rims of Elaine's eyes looked red, and so did her cheeks, indicating that she may have been crying earlier. "Is everything all right?" he asked, feeling concern.

She nodded.

"I came over to see how you were doing, and I. . ." Jonah paused, groping for the right words to say what was on his mind. "I was wondering if you've changed your mind about us."

Elaine stepped out to the porch. "No, Jonah, I'm not able to marry you. My obligation is to Grandma right now."

"I realize that, but I really want to help, and I'm going to keep coming over until you accept that fact." It was all Jonah could do not to reach up and wipe away the tiny streak of flour clinging to Elaine's cheek.

Elaine lowered her gaze. "We really don't need any help right now, and I'd feel better if you'd just move on with your life."

"But I don't want to move on, Elaine. I want to be with you." Frustration welled in Jonah's chest. "The only way I'll ever give up on us is if the day comes that you stop loving me."

She lifted her gaze to meet his. "That day has already come, Jonah."

He jerked his head, feeling as though he'd been slapped. "What are you saying, Elaine?"

She looked him straight in the eye and said, "After thinking about it these last few weeks, I have come to the conclusion that what I felt for you before was never love; it was infatuation."

"I don't believe you," he said with a shake of his head. "You're just saying that because you're too proud and stubborn to let me help with your grandma's care."

"That's not true. I just don't love you, Jonah, and I'm not sure I ever did. Now please go home, and don't stop over here anymore. What we had is over." Elaine's lips quivered slightly, but she held his steady gaze.

Jonah stared into Elaine's beautiful blue eyes, and still her expression did not waver. On most things, Jonah was pretty easygoing, accepting people's decisions without question. Not this. But even though arguing the point was what he really wanted to do, he held back. Emotions that had taken him a long time to bury came rising to the surface again. Jonah felt just as bad as, if not worse than, when his plans back in Pennsylvania with Meredith had been crushed. Could he handle another rejection?

Staring across the yard, Jonah noticed the black cat he'd seen earlier gripping a dead mouse between its teeth and disappearing slowly into the barn. *Superstitions, huh?* he thought, feeling as if his world had just been turned upside down. Looking back at Elaine, Jonah said. "Tell me the truth, Elaine. Is that the way you really feel?"

She nodded.

Jonah could see by the set of Elaine's jaw that her mind was made up. Suddenly, he realized that even if he stayed here all night, he wouldn't get Elaine to change her mind or say she loved him. "Then I guess I have no other choice but to accept your decision."

With shoulders slumped and head down, Jonah turned and stepped off the porch, feeling like a rambunctious horse had just kicked him in the stomach. Never in a million years had he expected Elaine to say she didn't love him or that what she'd felt before was just infatuation. Of course, looking back on it, she'd never really said she did love him—just things like she enjoyed his company and she cared for him. *Have I been fooling myself all this time?* he wondered. *Maybe our relationship was one-sided, and I was just too blind to see it.*

CHAPTER 26

Elaine woke up the following morning with a sore throat. "Oh, great," she said, grimacing as she swallowed. *Could my throat hurt from all the talking I did yesterday with Leah and Priscilla?*

She sat up and swung her legs over the side of the bed. She swallowed again, just to make sure. She might expect to have a sore throat during the winter months, but not in July. Maybe it was from sitting under the air-conditioning vent at the restaurant during lunch.

"I sure don't need this right now," she grumbled, ambling across the room to her closet. This evening, Elaine and Grandma would be hosting another sit-down dinner, and there was still a lot that needed to be done before their guests arrived.

Elaine hoped Grandma was feeling up to it. After yesterday's discovery that she had dementia, Grandma might not want to host any more dinners.

What had made things worse was that after Elaine had apologized for not telling the truth right away, Grandma had tried to reassure her. Elaine felt helpless but reminded herself once again that Grandma wouldn't have to go through this alone.

Swallowing again while rubbing her throat, Elaine was convinced her glands weren't swollen. *I can't let a little thing like a sore throat keep me from doing what needs to be done.*

For so early in the morning, it was already warm, in sharp contrast to yesterday's cooler temperatures. That's how July could be on the plains as weather systems moved through.

Elaine hurried to get dressed and then went to the kitchen to start breakfast. She found Grandma mixing a batch of pancake batter. A slight breeze from the shady side of the house drifted through the open kitchen window.

"Don't go to any trouble for me this morning, Grandma," Elaine said. "My throat hurts, and I don't feel like eating much right now."

The wrinkles in Grandma's forehead deepened. "Are you grank? Do we need to call the doctor?"

Elaine shook her head. "I don't feel sick, and my glands aren't swollen. Think I either did too much talking yesterday, or my sore throat is from sitting under an air-conditioning vent at the restaurant where I went with Priscilla and Leah yesterday."

Grandma went to the cupboard and took down a jar of honey. "I'd better fix you a lemon-and-honey drink. That'll make your throat feel better," she said, after taking a lemon from the refrigerator.

Once the lemon had been squeezed and the juice poured into a glass, Grandma added a spoonful of honey and stirred it well. Then she handed the glass to Elaine. "We have to get you better so you don't miss too much school. Sure don't want you falling behind on your studies or ending up with a lot of homework to do in order to catch up." Grandma touched Elaine's forehead with her cold hands. "I don't think you have a fever, but it might be best if you skip school today and go back to bed."

Elaine drank the lemon/honey mixture and grimaced; not from the taste of it, but because of what Grandma had just said. "Grandma, I've been out of school for several years now, so you don't have to worry about me missing school or having any homework to do."

Grandma's eyebrows squished together as she stared at Elaine for several seconds. Then a light seemed to dawn, and she snickered, giving a quick nod. "Well, of course you're not still in school. Silly me. Guess it was just wishful thinking."

As Grandma resumed making pancakes, Elaine placed her empty glass in the sink and stared out the window. If only she could turn back the hands of time, she'd go back to when she was a little girl. Her life had been carefree, and Grandma's memory had been just fine. Was this what she could expect in the days ahead—Grandma acting okay one minute and living in the past the next?

Elaine closed her eyes. *Dear Lord, please give me the wisdom and strength I need in order to care for Grandma.*

Jonah reached for the thermos of coffee he'd brought to his shop that morning and opened the lid. Overnight, a warm front had moved in, and he hadn't slept well. It was going to take more than one cup of coffee to get through the day, much less get the house ready for his folks' arrival in a few days. Jonah wished the cooler weather had lasted a bit longer, but it wasn't the temperature that had given him a restless night. Thoughts of Elaine and her announcement that she didn't love him had kept him awake. He'd tossed and turned for hours, trying to come to grips with everything. He still couldn't believe she didn't love him. All these months they'd been courting, and even though she'd never actually said the words, she'd never given any indication that she didn't love him.

Why now? he wondered. *Maybe I need to talk with one of Elaine's friends about this. I'm sure either Leah or Priscilla would know if Elaine has ever loved me or not. Think I'll stop by and see Priscilla after I'm done working today.*

"Wow, it's sure gettin' warm out there." Timothy wiped his brow as he entered the shop. "Where should I put the bolt of upholstery that just came in?"

"I don't care. Put it anywhere!" Jonah snapped.

Timothy flinched, and he silently hauled the material to the table on the other side of the room.

Jonah knew immediately that he'd spoken too harshly. "Sorry for snappin' at you, Timothy. I didn't get much sleep last night. Guess it put me in a bad mood, but then, that's no excuse." He poured coffee into his cup and took a drink. "Hopefully this will help me wake up and be more civilized."

Timothy shrugged. "That's okay. My daed isn't worth much till he's had a few cups of coffee in the morning. He doesn't snap, though. Just doesn't say a lot till he's fully awake."

"Jah, well, my being tired is not a good reason for barking at you, and I'll try not to do it again."

"Would you please load that up and take it over to Rockome Garden Foods at Rockome?" Priscilla's mother asked, motioning to a box filled with raspberry jam that sat on the counter in their small shop.

Priscilla nodded. "Sure, Mom. Is there anything else you want me to take over there?"

Mom shook her head. "Just the jam for today. Oh, and when you're out and about, maybe you could drop by Edna's place and see how she's doing. I still feel terrible about blurting out that she has dementia."

"It wasn't like you did it on purpose." Priscilla gave her mother's shoulder a gentle pat.

Mom sighed. "I wish there was something I could do to help Edna deal with the terrible disease."

"I feel the same way about Elaine. It's going to be difficult for her, too."

"We can pray for them and be there to help out whenever possible."

"You're right about that." Priscilla picked up the box. "Guess I'd better get going. I'd like to be home before it gets too hot. This weather isn't good for me or my horse. See you later, Mom."

"Mammi! Mammi!"

Feeling as though she'd been drugged, Sara groaned and forced her eyes open. Mark stood at the side of her bed, red-faced, with tears running down his cheeks.

"Oh, my poor baby." Sara rolled out of bed and scooped Mark into her arms. Feeling a bit light-headed, she sank back to the bed and cuddled him close. She glanced at the clock on her nightstand and grimaced when she saw that it was nine o'clock. She couldn't believe she'd slept so long, even after a restless night. It had been so warm in her room that she'd lain awake for several hours before finally dozing off. Apparently, she'd been sleeping so hard that she hadn't heard Mark climb out of his crib and walk to the side of her bed, tugging on the quilt as he continued to fuss. She wondered how long he'd been calling to her.

When Sara stood up again, her head felt fuzzy and the room seemed to tilt at an odd angle.

I wonder if I'm coming down with something. Maybe it's just the stuffy heat in this room making me feel so off-kilter.

Going to the window, Sara opened it to let in some fresh air. After taking in several deep breaths, she felt a bit better, so she took Mark by the hand and headed down the hall to the kitchen.

Moving slowly so as not to upset her equilibrium, Sara managed to scramble some eggs for breakfast. When they finished eating, she ran water in the sink to wash their dishes. By the time she had them washed, dried, and put away in the cupboard, Sara had little strength left in her arms.

Something is terribly wrong, she thought, taking a seat at the table while Mark sat on the floor, playing with a few pots and pans. *Maybe I overdid it yesterday when I was cleaning house.*

Sara sat with her head down, massaging her temples, until she heard the *clip-clop* of horse hooves coming up her driveway. She groaned. "Now is not a good time for company."

Rising to her feet, Sara peered out the kitchen window, watching her friend Jean climb out of her buggy and secure her horse at the hitching rack near the barn. Then Jean went around and helped her three children out of the buggy.

Mark would be excited to have someone to play with this morning, but Sara wasn't sure she could take all the activity. Well, she couldn't be impolite and tell them not to come in, so she forced herself to go to the door.

"Guder mariye," Jean said cheerfully when she and her children entered the house. "We've been out doing some shopping, plus I wanted to show you the progress I've made on the quilt I've been making for our upcoming charity event."

Sara knew how much Jean liked to quilt. Her current project was going to be auctioned off to benefit a local family in need.

"Morning," Sara said, forcing a smile. "I'm interested in seeing the quilt, but first, why don't we have a cup of tea?"

"That sounds nice. The kinner can play while we visit awhile."

Another wave of dizziness came over Sara, and she grabbed the back of her chair to steady herself.

"Are you all right?" Jean took hold of Sara's arm and guided her into a seat.

"I had trouble sleeping last night, and when I finally dozed off, I slept later than I'd planned," Sara explained. "I think I'm still kind of drowsy and a bit light-headed."

Jean eyed Sara curiously. "This isn't the first time you've felt like this. I really think you ought to see a doctor, at least to rule out any kind of problem."

"Maybe another foot treatment with Leah will help. In fact, I'll make an appointment with her right away."

"That's up to you, but please don't put off seeing the doctor."

Sara nodded slowly. Until she saw some money coming in from the aprons she'd been making for one of the gift shops in town, she really couldn't afford to see the doctor. Still, she had to be well in order to care for Mark, so if another treatment with Leah didn't help, she would call the doctor.

Jonah was about to tell Timothy they were done for the day when Priscilla entered the buggy shop.

"What can I do for you?" Jonah asked, pleased to see her, since he'd planned to ask her about Elaine.

"I'm on my way to Rockome Garden Foods and discovered that there's a problem with one of my buggy wheels," she replied. "It's kind of wobbly, and I'm worried that it might fall off."

"Want me to go take a look at it?" Timothy offered, rolling up his shirtsleeves.

Jonah nodded. This would give him a few minutes to talk to Priscilla privately, which was exactly what he needed.

As soon as Timothy went out the door, Jonah turned to Priscilla and said, "I'll see what I can do about your wheel in a minute, but first, there's something I'd like to discuss with you. In fact, I was planning to stop by your place later today to talk about it."

She tipped her head back to look up at him, and he noticed that her cheeks were flushed, probably from the warm weather. "Oh, what's that? Is something wrong?"

He cleared his throat a few times, feeling suddenly unsure of himself. "Uh. . .well, it's about Elaine."

"What about her?"

"She says she doesn't love me and that what she felt for me before was just infatuation." Jonah paused and moistened his parched lips with the tip of his tongue. "Do you think that's true, Priscilla, or did Elaine only say that so I'd quit coming around?"

Priscilla's gaze dropped to the floor. "Well, I can't speak for Elaine, and it's really not my place to give my opinion."

"But you have an opinion, right?" he prompted.

She lifted her shoulders in a brief shrug but continued to stare at the floor.

Jonah took a step closer to Priscilla. "Please tell me what you think. Does Elaine love me or not?"

CHAPTER 27

"Priscilla, did you hear what I asked?"

"Jah, Jonah, I heard," Priscilla murmured, refusing to look into his eyes.

"Does Elaine love me or not?"

Perspiration beaded on Priscilla's forehead, and not just from the heat. She didn't like being put on the spot, but Jonah was expecting an answer. It made her feel like a go-between, and the truth was, she couldn't be sure how Elaine really felt about Jonah.

"I think that question should be answered by Elaine," Priscilla said, forcing herself to look at Jonah again.

A muscle on the side of his neck twitched. "She already has, but now I'm asking you."

"I've always thought Elaine loved you, but maybe I was wrong. No one but Elaine really knows how she feels."

"Would you ask her how she feels about me? And also find out if I've said or done something to cause her to pull away?"

Priscilla clutched the folds of her apron, feeling like a helpless fly trapped in a spider's web.

"Please, Priscilla. I really need to know."

Jonah's pleading tone and his look of desperation made Priscilla reconsider. "Okay, I'll speak to Elaine."

Jonah's face relaxed a bit. "Danki, Priscilla. I'm grateful." He motioned to the door with his head. "Guess I'd better take a look at that buggy wheel now."

As Edna moved around her kitchen, preparing food for tonight's tourist dinner, she couldn't stop thinking about the book she'd found earlier today, tucked inside one of the drawers inside the desk in their kitchen. Elaine had been reading that book yesterday while she sat on the porch, waiting for her friends. It was about the various types and symptoms of dementia. What a rude awakening it had been for Edna when she read a few pages of information about the different stages of the disease and what could be expected in the months ahead. From the little she'd read, dementia was incurable, and there wasn't much that could be done to stop the loss of her memory. Oh, there were some medicines she could try, but they all had side effects and offered no promise of a cure. *Well, I won't be taking any of those,* she determined.

Edna had slammed the book shut, unwilling to accept her plight and praying that none of the things she'd read about would happen to her.

Maybe it was an old book and by now there are new treatments, she consoled herself. But even as the thought flitted through her mind, Edna knew her future looked bleak. *Wish it was me who'd died instead of Lloyd. At least he had a healthy mind and would have been here for Elaine.*

While Edna stirred the filling for her special sour-cream peach pie, she continued to fret. She wasn't about to forget her dear husband or any of the wonderful memories they'd made together. How could she forget about raising their son, Milton, and the joy of seeing him and his wife get married and later become happy new parents? And what about Elaine? There was no way Edna would let some disease keep her from remembering who her granddaughter was. Elaine had brought new meaning to her and Lloyd's existence after the tragic accident that took their son and his wife. Surely those were memories that would never slip away.

Edna placed the crust into the pie pan, added the peach filling, and placed it into the oven. Leaning against the counter, she thought about the last time she'd talked with her older sister, Margaret. How long had it been since she'd seen Margaret or their younger brothers, Irvin and Caleb? As Edna recalled, it had been a few years, but that was because they lived in some other state. Her brothers had farms to tend, and even though Edna's sister still taught sewing classes, she was in her eighties and didn't travel much anymore. All these things made it difficult to visit, but they'd managed to keep in touch through letters and phone calls.

Maybe I should call and tell them about this terrible disease. No, I'm going to wait. What if it's all a mistake?

Edna hadn't told Elaine that she'd seen the book on dementia, and she thought it might be better not to mention it. Elaine had probably checked the book out from the library, looking for information that might enlighten her as to what to expect if Edna's memory loss worsened.

If it's true, then I wish there was something I could do to spare my granddaughter this experience, Edna thought with regret. *It's not fair to expect Elaine to take care of me and put her own life on hold. Like other young women her age, she should be allowed the freedom of getting married and raising a family, instead of caring for an old woman who will one day not even know who she is.*

With conflicting thoughts swirling through her head, Edna left the kitchen and went out the back door. She wandered around the yard for a while, until she became bored.

Returning to the kitchen, she stared vacantly out the window, barely noticing the birds flitting back and forth to their feeders. *Maybe the doctor who told Elaine I have dementia was mistaken. The tests could have been wrong. Oh, I just need to stop worrying about this.*

"How's it going in here?" Elaine asked, stepping into the kitchen from the dining room, where she'd gone to set the tables for their dinner guests.

Edna watched as Elaine glanced around the room, sniffing the air. "It smells like something is burning."

Edna turned and looked at the stove, suddenly remembering her pie. When she opened the oven door and smoke poured out, she gasped. "Ach, my peach pie is burned. It's burned to a crisp!"

"Burned. Burned," Millie screeched from her cage across the room.

Elaine grabbed a pot holder and quickly removed the pie, placing it on a cooling rack. Then she opened the kitchen window to let out the smoke.

Edna stood nearby, slowly shaking her head. "I'm sorry about this.

Guess I got preoccupied and forgot to set the timer."

"It's all right, Grandma." Elaine slipped her arm around Edna's waist. "I'll put another pie together, and it should be done in plenty of time. Remember, we also have two coconut cream pies to serve to our guests this evening, and there will only be twenty people this time."

Edna's throat constricted. Forgetting to check on her pie was just one more reminder of how forgetful she'd become. All these years, cooking and baking had been second nature to her. She'd made countless meals without giving it much thought. Ruining the peach pie might be a small thing, but it made her wonder with dread what else she might forget. Next time she baked a pie, she'd be sure to set the timer and stay right here in the kitchen until it was done.

Elaine felt bad as she watched Grandma staring at the burned pie. *Will something like this be a regular occurrence? How much longer will we be able to keep doing dinners for tourists? If we have to give it up, then I'll need to think of something else Grandma can do so she won't become bored. And of course, I'll have to look for some other way to make extra money—something I can do from home.*

A knock sounded on the back door, halting Elaine's musings. "I'll get it," she said, but Grandma gave no reply, just moved away from the pie and walked over to Millie's cage.

When Elaine opened the door, she found Priscilla on the porch. "How's your grandma?" Priscilla whispered. "Is she still upset about what my mamm blurted out yesterday?"

Elaine stepped onto the porch and shut the door. "Grandma took it hard, and I still feel guilty for not telling her myself, but she seems to have forgiven me."

"Mom feels badly about it, too." Priscilla motioned to the chairs. "Do you have time to sit awhile? I'd like to ask you something."

Elaine glanced toward the house, massaging her throat. "I can sit a few minutes, but I need to get back inside soon and bake a pie because we're hosting another dinner tonight." She decided not to mention the pie Grandma had burned. After all, most people had burned something in their kitchen at one time or another.

"How come you're rubbing your throat? Does it hurt?" Priscilla asked, taking a seat.

"A little, but it was worse when I first woke up. I think it may be from yesterday, when I sat under that air-conditioning vent at the restaurant." Elaine took the chair next to Priscilla.

"I felt a little chilled from the AC as well, but at least I didn't wake up with a sore throat." Priscilla paused, crossing her leg and bouncing it up and down. "Um. . .I saw Jonah earlier today."

"Oh?"

"I stopped by his buggy shop so he could take a look at my wobbly buggy wheel."

"Is everything okay?"

"It is now, since he fixed it." Another pause. Leaning closer to Elaine, Priscilla said, "Jonah wanted me to ask you a question."

"What's that?"

"He said you told him that you're not in love with him, and he wants to know if it's true or not."

Elaine squeezed her hands tightly together in her lap. "So he sent you here to ask me?"

"Jah. Is it true?"

Elaine bit the side of her cheek. She'd lied to Jonah; did she dare lie to Priscilla, too?

Priscilla touched Elaine's arm. "You've told me before that you care for Jonah, and I thought you were looking forward to him asking you to be his wife. Have you changed your mind about that?"

"I do care about Jonah," Elaine murmured, "but not in the way I once did. When you speak to Jonah again, would you please tell him that?"

"Are you sure? I mean—"

"I'm very sure. This is the way it's meant to be, Priscilla." Elaine rose from her seat. "I appreciate you stopping by, but I need to get back inside now. I'll see you at church on Sunday." She turned and slipped into the house, feeling even guiltier for lying to Priscilla, while trying to convince herself that breaking up with Jonah had really been the best thing to do.

⁂

After Jean left with her children, Sara, feeling somewhat better, decided to see Leah for a reflexology treatment. She'd tried calling first but had gotten Leah's voice mail. If Leah was at home today, Sara hoped she wouldn't be too busy to see her.

As Sara headed to Leah's with her horse and buggy, she began to feel a bit woozy again. Perspiration beaded on her forehead and dripped onto her face. Reaching for the bottle of water she'd placed on the seat between her and Mark, she took a drink and offered him one as well.

By the time Sara arrived at her destination, she felt even worse, and the heat of the day had become almost unbearable. After taking another drink of water, Sara secured her horse and took Mark out of the buggy. When she knocked on the door, Leah's mother, Dianna, greeted her on the porch.

"Is Leah here?" Sara asked. "I was hoping to get a foot treatment today."

"Jah, she is at home, but unfortunately, she's not feeling well right now. When Leah got up this morning, she complained of a sore throat, so I suggested that she go back to bed." Dianna sighed. "I think sometimes my daughter tries to do too much and then she ends up wearing herself out. Her immune system is probably weak, and I'll bet she got the sore throat from being around someone who came to her for a treatment."

"I'm sorry to hear that." Sara lifted one hand to wipe the perspiration from her forehead, while clutching Mark's hand with her other.

"You look flushed. Why don't you and Mark come inside for a cold drink?" Dianna suggested.

Sara shook her head. "Danki for the offer, but I have some water in the buggy, and I'm not feeling the best right now, so I think we need to go home."

"You could be coming down with whatever bug might be going around."

"Maybe, so I'd best be going home."

Dianna reached out and tousled Mark's hair. "Take care, Sara, and I hope this little guy doesn't get sick, too. Oh, and let us know if there's anything we can do for you."

"Danki, I will."

As Sara headed for home, Mark became fussy, and she noticed that his face was flushed. She hoped it was just from the heat and that he wasn't coming down with something. As eager as Sara was to get home, she didn't want to push Lilly to go any faster than necessary, so she kept the horse at a slow, steady pace. She'd have to rub the horse down once she got there, and she dreaded it. She wished she could take Mark up to the house, curl up on the bed beside him, and take a long nap.

By the time they'd made it home, Mark had cried himself to sleep. After securing Lilly to the hitching rack, Sara took her boy inside and tucked him safely in his crib. Then she went back outside to take care of her horse.

As Sara began brushing Lilly, her arms started to tingle, and they didn't seem to want to work. Her shoulders tightened as she breathed slowly in and out. *What's happening here?* she asked herself. *Could I be having a stroke?*

CHAPTER 28

On Saturday morning when Sara woke up, she felt some better. *Guess all I needed was a good night's sleep,* she thought as she fixed breakfast for Mark. It didn't make sense how one day she could feel so bad, and the next day she felt better.

"*Melke!*" Mark hollered, smacking his palms on the tray of his high chair.

"Okay, little man, Mama will get you some more milk, but can you say please?" Sara asked in Pennsylvania-Dutch.

Mark extended his hands. "*Sei so gut.*"

Sara smiled. "That's better, Son."

After she poured milk into Mark's sippy cup, she took a seat at the table and bowed her head. *Heavenly Father, I thank You for the food You've provided for us and for the blessings You give every day. Thank You for helping me to feel better, and please give me the strength I need for this day. Amen.*

As Sara began eating her toast and eggs, she thought about her visit with Jean the other day, and how, just before Jean went home, she'd invited Sara and Mark to join her family at Yoder's Restaurant this evening. It had been awhile since Sara had gone out to eat and would be a nice change from having to cook supper. Mark would no doubt enjoy being with Jean's children. It was good for him to be around kids close to his age—especially since it seemed unlikely he'd ever have any siblings.

Is it God's will that I should marry again someday? Sara wondered. *How will I know if the right man comes along? One thing's for sure. He'd have to love Mark as if he were his own son.*

Elaine stood at the kitchen sink washing the breakfast dishes. The room was quite warm, so she'd opened the window, hoping for a breeze, but there was none. From what she'd read in yesterday's newspaper, a round of thunderstorms was predicted for later today that would push the humid air eastward, bringing in more comfortable temperatures like they'd had earlier in the week.

Yesterday had been a stifling day, and even with the battery-operated fans, the dining room, where they'd hosted their dinner last night, had been much too warm. Most of the tourists didn't complain, except for one of the teenagers in the group. The girl acted rather spoiled, fanning her face with a napkin and making rude remarks about the lack of air-conditioning, asking how the Amish could stand the heat. Sometimes, Elaine had actually wondered that, too, but just like the pioneer women from long ago, the Amish were used to it, and better acclimated to the heat than those having the comfort of an air conditioner at the touch of a button.

Elaine had been pleased at how well Grandma had done throughout most of the evening, until someone asked her what kind of pie they'd been served. With a blank expression, Grandma looked at Elaine and said, "What kind of pies did we make?"

Elaine could still picture Grandma's red face when she'd replied, "Sour-cream peach and coconut cream."

How many times had Grandma made those pies and served them to their guests, without ever forgetting their names?

This morning when Elaine had looked for some honey to put on her toast, she'd finally discovered it under the sink where all their kitchen cleaning supplies were kept. Grandma must have put it there, since she was the last one to use the honey. There was no doubt Grandma's memory was failing, and it seemed to be happening fast.

Think I'll go to the health food store and look for something that might help Grandma's memory. Surely there has to be a remedy that would at least slow the progression of her illness, Elaine decided.

She glanced to her right, noticing the calendar on the wall. It was then that she was struck with the realization that today was Jonah's birthday. Last year, when he'd turned twenty-four, Elaine had invited Jonah over for supper and baked him a birthday cake. She had been full of dreams for the future—dreams for her and Jonah that she'd thought by now would be coming true. But those dreams had dissolved like ice cubes on a hot summer day. This year Elaine wouldn't even see Jonah on his birthday. As much as that hurt, she had to sever all ties with him. She needed to keep her focus on Grandma's care; that was the only way.

After Jonah sent Timothy on an errand to pick up a few supplies, he stood in front of the window of his shop, watching for his folks to arrive. Mom had said they were hiring a driver to bring them to Arthur and should arrive sometime this afternoon. They would stay at Jonah's house for the week they'd be here, since he had more room than Jean. Tonight, Jean had made plans for them all to go to Yoder's restaurant to celebrate her and Jonah's birthday. It would be great to have their parents here for the occasion, although Jonah had mixed emotions. Last year Elaine fixed him a nice birthday supper and even baked him a cake. But much to his disappointment, she wouldn't be helping him celebrate his birthday this year.

It's not fair, he fumed inwardly. *Some men meet the woman of their dreams, get married, and raise a family, but not me. Seems like the women I fall in love with are always out of reach. Maybe I'm just unlucky at love. It took me a long time to get over Meredith, and now I have to do it all over again with Elaine.*

Jonah's thoughts halted when he saw a silver van coming up his driveway. It must be his folks. He hurried outside as his parents stepped down from the van.

"It's just wonderful to see you," Mom said, giving Jonah a big hug. Her hair was the same light brown color as when Jonah had left home, only now he noticed a few gray hairs mixed in, too. Jonah's mother was a tiny woman, with a narrow waist and flat stomach. Even at the age of fifty-seven, she almost looked like a teenage girl.

Jonah hugged Dad. "It's sure good to see you both. How was your trip?"

"It went well; no problems at all." Dad smiled and lifted the straw hat from his head, revealing dark, curly hair with a few streaks of gray. "We stopped by Jean's place for a few minutes before coming here, and we're sure glad to be able to spend some time with both of you. Happy birthday, Son." He gave Jonah's back a few thumps.

"Danki. Jean and I are getting the best present ever, having you and Mom here to celebrate our special day with us. We've both been lookin' forward to your visit." Jonah motioned to the van. "Does your driver need a place to stay? I've got plenty of room in my house if he'd like to stay here."

Mom shook her head. "Al has a cousin in Arcola, so he'll be at his place till we're ready to go home. Before we got out of the van, he said he wanted to get going, since he heard there's supposed to be a storm moving in later this afternoon or evening."

"He's right about that, but after the storm blows over, the weather's supposed to be more comfortable." Jonah moved toward the back of the van and opened the hatch. "Now, let's get your suitcases hauled into the house. Once you two are settled, we can sit and visit awhile."

"Don't feel that you have to entertain us if you're busy in the buggy shop," Mom said. "We can unpack our suitcases and fend for ourselves until it's time to meet Jean and her family for supper."

Jonah pulled out his pocket watch to check the time. "I'm just about done with the work I planned to do today, so as soon as my helper gets back, I'll close up the shop."

"I'm anxious to see your new place of business," Dad commented as their driver pulled out and they began walking toward the house.

"It's not as big as the shop you have in Lancaster County," Jonah said, "but it's working out okay."

"How about your helper?" Mom asked as they entered the house. "Is he working out for you, too?"

Jonah nodded. "Timothy still has a ways to go, but he's a hard worker and eager to learn. How's your helper doing, Dad?"

"Aaron already knew the buggy business when he came to me, and we work well together, so I'm sure things will be fine there while I'm gone." Dad thumped Jonah's back. "I still miss working with you, though."

"I miss that, too," Jonah said, "but it would have been too hard for me to stay in Pennsylvania after Luke returned to Meredith and their son."

"We understand." Mom slipped her hand through the crook of Jonah's arm. "I'm glad you've found someone else, and your daed and I are anxious to meet her."

"That's right," Dad agreed. "Will Elaine be joining us for supper this evening?"

"Elaine won't be there, Dad. We aren't seeing each other anymore," Jonah muttered.

"What?" Mom's eyebrows lifted as she removed her hand from the inside of Jonah's arm. "But I thought you were on the verge of marrying her."

Jonah's shoulders slumped, and he held his elbows tightly against his sides. "I thought so, too, but I was wrong. Elaine broke things off with me."

"Why would she do that?" Mom asked. "I thought you two were in love."

"I do love Elaine, but I guess the feeling was never mutual." Jonah touched the base of his neck, where a muscle had knotted. "Elaine's grandma was diagnosed with dementia, and Elaine has to care for her now."

"Aren't you willing to help her with that?" Mom questioned.

"Of course I am, but Elaine seems determined to do it all on her own."

"Maybe she'll change her mind when she sees how hard it's going to be," Dad put in.

Jonah shrugged. "I was hoping for that, but the truth is, Elaine said she never really loved me, so as hard as it is, I've come to the conclusion that I may need to accept her decision."

"Maybe there's some other available woman in this area who might be better suited to you," Dad said.

Jonah shook his head. "I doubt it, but even if there was, it's too soon for me to be thinking about that."

Jonah had just begun showing his dad around the buggy shop when Timothy showed up. "Did you get all the supplies I needed?" Jonah asked.

Timothy shoved his hands into his trouser pockets. "Jah, they're in the trailer behind your buggy. Should I bring everything inside?"

"That'd be good, but first I want you to meet my daed."

After Jonah made the introductions, Dad smiled at Timothy and said, "So how do you like the buggy-making business?"

"Like it just fine." Timothy grinned at Dad. "I was glad when Jonah offered me the job."

"And I'll bet Jonah's happy to have you." Dad looked at Jonah and winked.

"I'll go out and give you a hand bringing in the supplies," Jonah said. "Dad, you can stay here and look around the rest of the shop if you like."

"Once we get everything hauled inside, you're free to go," Jonah told Timothy as they walked toward the buggy trailer.

"Are ya sure?" the boy questioned. "It's still kinda early yet."

"That's okay. I've decided to close the shop earlier today so I can visit with my folks before we head out to supper. After all, it's Jean's and my birthday."

"All right, that sounds good to me. Maybe I'll stop at your fishin' hole on my way home. Oh, happy birthday, and I hope you have a good birthday meal tonight."

Jonah smiled. Timothy had been bringing his fishing pole with him to work every day, and often fished in Jonah's pond before going home.

"Better keep an eye on the sky this afternoon while you're fishing," Jonah cautioned the boy. "Just in case the storm they're predicting rolls in."

"I'll do that," Timothy said with a nod. "And if it starts rainin', I'll head straight for home."

After Jonah and Timothy made a few trips into the shop with supplies, Timothy headed for the pond. A few minutes later, Jonah caught sight of Priscilla riding in on her bike. Was she here on business, or had she spoken to Elaine?

She pulled her bike alongside of him near the empty trailer. "I came by to tell you that I talked to Elaine," she said, getting right to the point. Her grim expression told Jonah that it wasn't good news. "There's no easy way to say this, Jonah, but Elaine said she doesn't love you."

Jonah's stomach twisted. "Do you believe her?"

"I don't know, but Elaine's never lied to me."

"I see. Well then, I guess I have no choice but to accept her answer." Jonah felt like someone had punched him in the stomach. It was just as he feared—what he thought he had with Elaine was over.

"I'm really sorry, Jonah," Priscilla said sincerely. "With the way things are for her grandma right now, I think Elaine may have shut herself off from love."

Or maybe, Jonah thought with deep regret, *Elaine made her decision because she really never cared for me at all. It might be that until recently, she was just too afraid to say it.*

CHAPTER 29

"Are you all right, Jonah?" Jean asked as they entered Yoder's restaurant with their family. "You look like you're not feeling well this evening."

"I'm okay," Jonah said. "Guess I'm just tired, is all." There was no way he would spoil the evening by talking about his woes. Besides, discussing the situation with Elaine wouldn't change a single thing. He needed to move on with his life, but it wouldn't be easy. Although Jonah was uncertain of his future, he had to trust God and wait to see what the plan was for him from here on out.

"Looks like there's quite a crowd here tonight," Dad commented, glancing around the restaurant. "The place must have good food."

"They sure do," Jonah and Jean said in unison.

Jean's husband, Nathan, chuckled. "You two may not be identical twins, but I think it's kind of funny the way you often speak at the same time, and sometimes even say the exact thing."

"We've been doing that since we were kinner." Jean giggled and nudged Jonah's arm. "Haven't we, big brother?"

Jonah chuckled. "Jah, we sure have."

The hostess came then and led them to the back of the room where two tables had been set up for eleven people. Since only eight were in their group, Jonah didn't know why there were three extra seats. He was about to ask when Jean spoke up.

"I invited your friend Melvin to join us this evening, and also Sara and little Mark, since Sara's my best friend," Jean explained. "They should all be here soon, I expect."

"The more, the merrier." Jonah helped Jean and Nathan situate their children on booster seats before taking a chair himself. Try as he might, he couldn't help but wonder what Elaine was doing tonight.

"*Hallich gebottsdaag*," Jonah's four-year-old niece, Rebecca, said, grinning over at Jonah from where she sat in a booster seat.

Jonah smiled, reaching over to tweak the little girl's nose. "Danki, Becca." It was amazing how the simple smile of a child could lift one's spirits.

A waitress came to take their beverage orders, and just as Jonah asked for a glass of lemonade, his friend Melvin showed up.

"Sorry I'm late." Melvin seated himself in the chair on the other side of Jonah. "There seems to be a lot of traffic on the road this evening."

"Not a problem," Jonah replied. "We're still waiting for Sara and her son, Mark, so we wouldn't have ordered our food without you."

"I appreciate that, and oh, by the way, Hallich gebottsdaag, Jonah. You, too, Jean." Melvin handed Jonah a paper sack. "Here's a little something for your birthday, my friend."

"You didn't have to get me anything."

"I know, but I wanted to." Melvin bumped Jonah's arm. "Go ahead, open it. I'm hopin' you'll like what's inside."

"Okay, but first let me introduce you to my mom and dad, Raymond and Sarah Miller."

After Melvin shook hands with Jonah's folks and had told them a little about himself, they got to talking as if they'd known each other for a good many years. Then Melvin looked over at Jonah and said, "I think your little niece is anxious for you to open the gift I brought ya."

Jean laughed. "That's right. Rebecca's been sitting there quietly, staring at it, since you first arrived."

"Do you want to see what's in the sack?" Jonah asked Rebecca after seeing the anxious look on her face.

"Jah, open it, please." With an eager expression, she clapped her hands.

"Naw. Think I'll wait till after we eat." Jonah winked at Rebecca. "Just kidding." When he opened the sack and withdrew an ornate pen with a buggy carved on the wooden base, he grinned. "Wow, this is sure nice. Danki, Melvin."

"You're welcome."

"Where'd ya find something like this?" Jonah asked.

"Had it special-ordered. If you turn the pen over, you'll see that the name of your buggy shop is engraved there. Thought if you liked it well enough, you might want to order more of the pens to give out to your customers."

"That's a good idea." Jonah bobbed his head. "I never thought of doing something like that."

"Can I take a look at that?" Dad asked, peering over at Jonah.

Jonah handed the pen to his dad, and after Dad studied it for a bit, he passed it around the table so the rest of the family could see.

"Think I might have to get some of those made up to hand out to my buggy-shop customers, too," Dad said. "I really haven't done much advertising in that way; just mostly through word of mouth."

"Sometimes word of mouth is the best form of advertising," Nathan put in. "But then, handing out the pens to customers could also be beneficial. It's useful to them and good advertising."

"Oh good. Sara and Mark made it," Jean said, motioning toward the front of the restaurant. "Now we can all order our meals."

When Sara entered the restaurant, holding tightly to Mark's hand, she struggled with her balance. Pausing to take in a deep breath, Sara started walking again toward the tables where Jean and her family sat. She didn't know why, but she felt out of place tonight. It wasn't that she didn't want to spend time with Jean. She just would rather have gotten together with Jean on her own—maybe gone out to lunch or had Jean over to her house for a meal. They would have had a better chance to visit that way.

A few days ago, Sara and Jean had gotten together, but Sara couldn't count that as much of a visit. She hadn't been feeling well, and Jean had ended up entertaining Mark, along with her own children, while Sara rested. She hoped she and Jean could get together again, maybe sometime next week, after Jean's parents went home.

"I'm glad you and Mark could join us," Jean said as Sara and Mark neared the table. She quickly introduced Sara to her and Jonah's parents, noting her mother had the same first name as Sara, only spelled differently.

"It's nice to meet you." Sara shook hands with them both and placed Mark in a booster seat. She sat in the chair between him and Jonah.

"Have you met Jonah's friend Melvin?" Jean asked.

Sara nodded and smiled at Melvin. "I heard you and Sharon are getting married this fall."

Melvin grinned. "Jah, and we're gettin' pretty excited about it."

"Are you okay, Sara?" Jean touched Sara's arm. "Your face is pasty white and you appear to be shaken."

"I had a little problem with my horse on the way to the restaurant," Sara replied, "but it was nothing serious, and I'll be okay once my nerves settle down."

"Was it due to all the traffic?" Melvin questioned. "It was pretty bad for me tonight."

Sara shook her head. "Lilly kept tossing her head, and at one point I lost my grip on the reins. I guess my horse figured that meant she had the freedom to gallop." Sara shivered, remembering how hard she'd had to pull on the reins in order to get Lilly to slow to a trot. It made her wish she had the strength of a man. For some reason, her hands and arms seemed to have less strength these days.

"I'm glad you and Mark are okay," Jonah said. "And it's nice that you both could join us tonight."

"*Der gaul laafe*," little Mark exclaimed, his eyes shining brightly.

"Jah, the horse ran, didn't he?" Sara smiled, while the others chuckled at the boy's innocent remark. She tried to remember how wonderful it was to see everything through a child's eyes.

Sara relaxed a bit. Just those few kind words from Jonah made her glad she'd come to the restaurant to join them this evening. Jean was fortunate to have a brother who cared about people the way Jonah did. She still felt grateful that he'd found Mark when he did. The day they'd had their picnic by the woods could have ended tragically if her little boy had gotten out on the road. God was surely watching out for them, just as He had been this evening when she'd had trouble with her horse. She just needed to relax more and put her trust in Him.

A huge clap of thunder sounded, and the lights in the restaurant flickered. Sara nearly jumped out of her seat, and she grabbed Mark's little hand, thinking he must be frightened, too. But her brave little boy seemed not to notice the storm brewing outside as he played with his spoon. Sara glanced out the closest window and shuddered. The rain was coming down in sheets, and soon it became a torrential downpour.

"I hope this storm passes by the time we leave here," Sara said. "It'll only spook Lilly if it's still storming like this on the way home."

"Don't worry," Jonah reassured her. "I'm sure that none of us are in a hurry to go. If the storm continues for a while, we can just sit here enjoying ourselves and hang out till the storm passes by."

"My guess is that it'll be over quickly," Melvin put in as another crash of thunder boomed from above.

Sara was glad to be with everyone instead of being home alone with Mark. It made the storm less menacing. She glanced around and noticed that everyone else in the restaurant seemed to be paying little attention to what was going on outside. She decided to try to forget about the storm and concentrate on having a nice evening.

Remembering that she'd brought a gift for Jean and had tucked it in her tote bag, Sara wished she'd thought to bring something for Jonah as well. After all, today was his birthday, too.

Maybe it's just as well that I didn't, she decided. *It might have seemed out of place for me to give him a gift since Jonah is courting another woman.*

A new thought leaped into Sara's head. *If Elaine and Jonah are courting, then why isn't she here tonight? I guess it wouldn't be polite to ask.*

Several minutes went by, and when Sara next glanced out the window, the rain had stopped. That was a relief. At least she wouldn't have to drive home in the midst of a storm this evening.

CHAPTER 30

Two months later

Edna stepped outside with a basket of laundry and shivered, wondering why it felt so chilly this morning. During breakfast, Elaine had said something about it being the first day of autumn, but Edna didn't know what had happened to summer. Had it really gone by that quickly, as each day blended into another?

Sighing, Edna set the basket on the ground under the clothesline. She was about to hang one of the towels when she heard a horse whinny from the barn. She ignored it at first, but the whinnying continued, so she decided to check on things.

When Edna entered the barn, she walked to the back and discovered that the door to the stall where Lloyd's horse, Dusty, was stabled hung open. She gasped, seeing that his horse was gone.

Panicked, Edna dashed outside, calling for Dusty and looking all around. When she saw no sign of the horse in their yard or the field bordering her home, she headed down the driveway, hoping Dusty hadn't gotten out on the road.

Making sure to stay on the shoulder of the road, Edna walked for a distance, until she spotted a horse in a field to her right. It had to be Dusty. Its coat was a deep brown.

Several times she hollered for Dusty to come, but he merely kept eating with his head down.

Now, why is Dusty ignoring me? Edna fumed. *He's always come to me before, whenever I've called. Of course, I usually have a lump of sugar for him. Guess I should have gotten a piece before I came looking for Lloyd's horse.*

Disgusted, Edna tromped up the driveway toward the house next to the field and knocked on the door. Several minutes passed before a middle-aged English woman, whom Edna didn't recognize, opened the door. "May I help you?"

Edna nodded. "My husband's horse, Dusty, got out, and he's in your field."

The woman stepped out of the house to take a look. She peered at Edna strangely over the top of her metal-framed glasses. "Sorry, but that horse belongs to my son, and his name is Chester, not Dusty."

Edna pursed her lips and stared at the horse. He sure looked like Dusty. Despite what the woman said, Edna was certain that was Lloyd's horse in the field.

"I'll go home and get my husband," Edna said determinedly. "He'll come and tell you that Dusty's his horse." She whirled around and started back down the driveway, but when she reached the road, Edna couldn't remember which direction she'd come from, or even how to get home. *Do I turn right or left?* she wondered, feeling a sense of panic.

Having just finished washing another batch of clothes, Elaine piled them in the laundry basket. She'd help Grandma hang them on the line and then do some baking for the dinner they'd be hosting tomorrow evening.

As she took the clothes from the wringer washing machine, Elaine reflected on how Grandma had been these past two months. Some days were good, and others were bad.

Elaine had purchased a natural remedy from the health food store that was supposed to help with memory problems. Grandma usually forgot to take it, even when Elaine set it out with her other breakfast pills. Sometimes Grandma became argumentative, stating that she didn't need any pills and wasn't going to take them, no matter what Elaine said.

At times, Grandma wandered around the house as though looking for something, but when Elaine asked about it, Grandma would say she couldn't remember what it was. All of these things concerned Elaine deeply, because in addition to Grandma's forgetfulness and mood swings, her diabetes seemed to be getting worse. It was getting harder to monitor her numbers because Grandma snuck food she shouldn't eat and sometimes refused to take her insulin pills.

The doctor had recently put Grandma on insulin shots, but she wouldn't always allow Elaine to give them to her. On a few occasions, Grandma had phased out all of a sudden, until her insulin kicked in, and the struggle of getting her stabilized was hard on Elaine. It was difficult to know when she might have another spell, and Elaine simply couldn't be with Grandma every minute of the day. Leah, Priscilla, and a few other women from their community came by each week to help with things, but most of the responsibility for Grandma's care fell on Elaine's shoulders.

Oh, Lord, I need Your help and guidance, because I'm getting so tired. Please show me the best way to take care of Grandma.

A few weeks ago, Elaine and Grandma had gone to a quilting bee, and when refreshments were offered, Grandma helped herself to several cookies and a hefty piece of pie. Elaine scolded her for it, but Grandma got snippy and said she was not a little girl and didn't need anyone telling her what to do.

Grandma had also begun losing things. To make matters worse, she'd get huffy and accuse Elaine of taking missing items, or moving them to some other place. Just yesterday, Grandma had let Millie out of her cage and accidentally left the back door open when she went outside to sit on the porch. Of course, Millie took the opportunity and flew right out. Grandma got upset and accused Elaine of leaving the door open and letting Millie out on purpose because she didn't like the parakeet.

Sadly, Elaine had later found the remains of a bird near the barn. She figured it had fallen prey to one of their cats. She'd buried poor Millie but hadn't said anything to Grandma about it, not wanting to upset her more than she was. Grandma had asked about the bird several times but seemed to accept the fact that Millie flew away and might never come back.

Grandma's personality change was the hardest thing for Elaine to deal with. Before, Grandma had always been so easygoing, rarely saying a harsh word to anyone, especially Elaine. But Elaine kept reminding herself that it was the disease making Grandma this way and that she wasn't being mean on purpose. That didn't make it any easier to deal with, though. Some nights, after a difficult day of trying to reason with Grandma, Elaine would fall into bed in a state of exhaustion, but often, sleep wouldn't come. She'd sometimes lay there for hours before her mind and body relaxed enough so that she could finally doze off.

Knowing she needed to get busy and think of something else, Elaine took the clothes outside to be hung on the line. Glancing over at her swing, Elaine wished she had time for a little fun, or even just a few minutes to clear her head. Unfortunately, that would have to wait.

As Elaine approached the clothesline, she was surprised to see the basket Grandma had taken out awhile ago sitting on the ground with most of the towels still inside.

Elaine's brows furrowed. Grandma was nowhere in sight.

"Where are you, Grandma?" she called.

No response.

She called Grandma's name once more, but still, no reply.

Grandma hadn't gone back inside, for she would have come through the back door and into the utility room, and Elaine would have seen her right away.

Maybe she went to the barn. Elaine hurried inside and looked throughout the barn, but Grandma wasn't there.

A sense of panic welled in Elaine's chest, and she wasn't sure what to do. She hated to even consider it, but one section of the book on dementia talked about a person wandering away from home in a state of confusion. *Could Grandma have become confused and wandered away from our property? Should I get my bike and go looking for her, or wait here, hoping Grandma comes back from wherever she went?*

Mark had spent the night at his grandparents' house, and they wouldn't bring him home until after supper. Deciding to take advantage of this free time, Sara went to do a few chores in the barn. Cobwebs were everywhere, and her horse's stall was a mess.

Sara hadn't had any more dizzy spells lately, and thankfully, she felt a bit stronger than she had this summer. She figured that was probably because she'd been seeing Leah for weekly foot treatments, which she would continue doing whenever possible. In addition to the benefits she experienced from reflexology, Sara enjoyed every opportunity to visit with Leah. While Jean was still Sara's best friend, Sara and Leah were quickly establishing a strong relationship, too.

Think I'll begin by cleaning the cobwebs. Sara got a broom and knocked down all the webs around the windows. Then she moved on to take care of those in less obvious places. It was dark in the back of the barn, so she lit a gas lantern. As the area became illuminated, more cobwebs came into view. *How did I let things get so bad?* The barn had never looked this way when Harley was alive. He'd kept it nearly as clean as Sara kept the house.

All of Harley's tools were in the barn, just as he'd left them, neatly hanging on the wall or placed on a shelf. Sara wondered if she should continue to keep them. Harley had taken good care of his tools, and any other equipment that he used. Her husband had always said, "If you take good care of your things, they'll last a long time."

At times like this, Sara missed Harley so much: not just for the things he did around the place, but for his companionship and the love they shared. It would be hard to get rid of the items she remembered him using, but then, didn't everyone go through this when they lost their spouse?

Sara remembered Harley saying something else to her one evening as they were getting ready for bed: "If anything ever happens to me, please move on with your life and do whatever is necessary in order to make things easier for you and Mark."

Sara didn't like having that kind of conversation, but Harley had always been the practical one who liked to be prepared. She'd felt so loved by her husband, and now, even in death, she could almost hear him encouraging her to do what needed to be done.

It did no good to dwell on the past or wish for things that could never be, but thinking about the man she'd loved so dearly caused tears to fill her eyes, making everything look fuzzy.

"Just keep working," she said aloud. "If I work hard enough, I won't have time to think about all that I've lost."

Swiping the broom toward yet another cobweb, Sara missed, and hit the lantern instead. It fell on a bale of straw and quickly ignited. As the flame grew, she stood staring at it, disbelieving that it had happened.

"Oh no!" Sara gasped, coming to her senses. "I need to put the fire out before it burns out of control!"

CHAPTER 31

Sara's eyes stung and her lungs felt like they were going to burst as she battled the flames with her garden hose. It did little good. The fire was burning out of control.

A loud whinny from the back of the barn reminded Sara that Lilly was still in her stall.

"Ach, I need to get her outside before anything happens to her!"

Sara skirted around the flames and by the grace of God made her way to Lilly's stall. Releasing the latch, she swung the stall gate open and slapped the horse's rear. "Go on, girl!" she shouted. "Get out of the barn!"

Lilly didn't hesitate as she raced out of her stall. Sara followed, barely able to breathe or stay on her feet. Suddenly, she halted and looked back at Harley's tools. *Should I try to save some of his things?* For a split second, Sara almost turned around. But the heat from the fire had grown more intense, and she only had seconds to save herself. The barn could not be saved. Thank the Lord, her son was safe with his grandparents and Lilly was unharmed and out of the barn. Did anything else really matter?

Gasping for breath, Sara prayed for the strength to make it safely outside.

"Giddyup there, Sassy," Jonah called to his horse, shaking the reins. As he quite often did, the lazy horse was poking along. Jonah was anxious to get home from his dental appointment, since work orders had been piling up again. If he knew for sure that business would continue to grow as it was and if he had a bit more money saved up, he'd be tempted to hire on another man. Of course, unless he could find someone with experience in buggy making, he'd have to train him, like he was doing with Timothy, and he really didn't have time for that. So Jonah would continue to do his best and hope that business remained steady, but not more than he and Timothy could handle.

It would be so nice if he could convince his folks to move to Arthur. Then he and his dad could work together again. But Dad seemed pretty set on staying in Pennsylvania.

Jonah couldn't believe how well things had gone at the dentist's today. Once the hygienist had cleaned Jonah's teeth and he'd seen the dentist, Jonah nearly fell out of the chair when the dentist said, "All is well; you have no cavities. I'll see you next year, Jonah."

Not only was he enjoying that good news, but he was glad it was the first day of autumn. Something in the air when he took a deep breath made Jonah glad to be alive. The rich, earthy scent that only fall could bring was one he welcomed every year.

Jonah looked up at the sky and couldn't believe its color. Like the blush of a ripened blueberry, it was so beautifully clear. On a day like today, he had to admit it would have been easy just to keep on riding, letting his horse take him wherever he wanted to go.

Jonah remembered how pretty it was in Pennsylvania, but he was glad to be here, where there were fewer people and not as many tourists. Illinois was already in his blood. Some folks living in the area still farmed for a living: some grew wheat and oats, and others planted corn and clover. Jonah loved seeing the farms and knew how important they were for one's existence. But as times had changed, many people began using other skills to make their way in life, like Jonah had chosen to do with his buggy shop. Some of the men created fine cabinetry and beautiful oak furniture. Still other Amish men and women had jobs in various businesses around the Arthur area.

As Jonah went a bit farther, he took another deep breath. His nose twitched, and he sniffed again. Was that the odor of smoke? It wasn't the aroma of burning leaves or someone's barbecue; it smelled like a building was on fire. As Jonah rounded the next bend, smoke and flames colored the horizon. He realized with alarm that they were coming from Sara Stutzman's place. Immediately, he turned into her lane, urging Sassy to hurry up the driveway.

Sassy didn't want to move at first, but the normally lazy horse must have sensed the urgency in Jonah's voice, because he trotted quickly up the driveway leading to Sara's house.

When Jonah spotted Sara lying on the ground, several feet from the barn, he hopped out of the buggy, haphazardly secured Sassy to the fence post, and dashed across the yard.

"Sara!" he yelled. "Sara!"

She lay unresponsive, and that worried him even more. Jonah dropped to his knees beside her and felt relief when he discovered that she was breathing. He couldn't see any evidence of burns on Sara's body; just a few streaks of ash across her forehead and cheeks. If she had been in the barn, which Jonah suspected, then she may have breathed in a lot of smoke, as the structure was now burning out of control.

Jonah could feel the heat from the fire and thought it best to move back away from the sparks that were floating through the air. Gently he picked Sara up and laid her on the cool, thick grass a safe distance away.

Seeing water seeping out of a hose a few feet away, Jonah wet his hanky and wiped Sara's face, tenderly removing the smudges. "Can you hear me, Sara?"

A few seconds passed, and then Sara opened her eyes. "Jonah?" she croaked after a series of coughs.

"Jah, it's me. What happened here? How'd your barn catch on fire?"

"I was doing some cleaning and accidentally knocked a gas lamp over. Before I knew it, the whole barn was in flames."

Sara tried to sit up, but Jonah told her to lie still a bit longer. "Is anyone in the barn right now?" he asked.

"No. I got Lilly out, and then. . ." Another round of spasmodic coughing came from Sara's mouth. "My barn is surely lost, and all of Harley's tools are in there."

Jonah could see that Sara was visibly shaken and needed comforting, so he gathered her into his arms, gently patting her back. "It's okay, Sara. The barn can be replaced, and so can any items that were inside. I'm glad you don't seem to be seriously hurt, but I think you oughta see a doctor. If you inhaled a lot of smoke, it could harm your lungs."

Sara shook her head. "I—I don't think I took in that much smoke, and I'd rather not go to the hospital. What I really need most is just to be with my son."

With deep concern, Jonah glanced around. "Where is Mark? Is he in the house?" He hoped the little boy wasn't running around the yard someplace or, God forbid, had somehow gotten into the barn.

"No, no. My boy's okay. He spent last night with my in-laws, so he's safe. I just need to be with him right now." Tears streamed down Sara's face, and she gulped on a sob.

Sighing with relief that Mark was safe, Jonah nodded in understanding. "I hear sirens coming this way. Someone must have seen the smoke and called the fire department." He helped Sara to her feet and held on to her, since she seemed a bit wobbly. "Are you okay to go into the house and wash up and change your clothes?" he asked.

"Jah, I'm all right," she reassured him.

"Okay. While you're doing that, I'll talk to the firemen, and afterwards take you over to Herschel and Betty's place to get your boy."

As Elaine pedaled her bike quickly along, she spotted Grandma plodding along the shoulder of the road, away from their home. *Where in the world is she going, and why did she leave the yard without telling me?*

Elaine sped up until she was alongside of Grandma. She stopped the bike right in front of her, halting Grandma in her tracks.

Grandma blinked and touched her fingers to her lips. "Nancy, I'm so glad to see you. Can you help me find my way home? I think I'm lost."

"It's me, Grandma. . .Elaine. Mama is. . .well, she's not here anymore." Elaine figured it would be best if she didn't mention that her mother was dead. No point in confusing or upsetting Grandma any more than she was.

Grandma tipped her head, staring intently at Elaine. After a few seconds, a slow smile spread across her face. "You're my *grossdochder*, aren't you?"

"That's right, Grandma. I'm your granddaughter. What are you doing out here on the road by yourself? I've been worried about you."

Grandma's cheeks flushed a bight pink. "I went looking for Dusty because he wasn't in his stall. Thought I saw him in someone's field, but the lady there said the horse was her grandson's." Her forehead creased. "That horse was brown, and it sure looked like Dusty."

Elaine got off her bike, set the kickstand, and gave Grandma a hug, realizing that she needed a little reassurance right now. "We sold Dusty a few weeks ago. Remember?"

Grandma squinted while rubbing the bridge of her nose. "Why would we sell your grossdaadi's *gaul*?"

"Because we have no need for three horses now that Grandpa's gone."

"Gone? Where did he go?" Grandma glanced around as though looking for answers. She was clearly quite confused.

Oh great, Elaine thought. *Grandma must think Grandpa is still alive.*

Undecided as to what else she should say, Elaine patted Grandma's arm tenderly, hoping to reassure her that everything was okay. "We need to go home now. I'll ride my bike slowly, and you can follow me there."

Grandma looked uncertain at first, but finally nodded. "That's good, because I need to talk to Lloyd about his horse. He'll be upset knowing Dusty got out of the barn."

Elaine hoped by the time they got home, Grandma might remember that Grandpa had died. She didn't want to shock her with that news.

Climbing back on her bike, Elaine noticed some smoke in the distance. *I hope that's just from someone burning something and that no one's house has caught fire.*

While Elaine pedaled slowly toward home, glancing back every few seconds to see if Grandma was following, she made a decision. Tomorrow she would call the doctor and ask why Grandma's memory was failing so fast. According to that book on dementia, Grandma was losing her memory quicker than she should be and heading toward the more advanced stages of the disease. Elaine wished with all her heart that there was something she could do to slow the progression. She could hardly stand seeing her grandma like this.

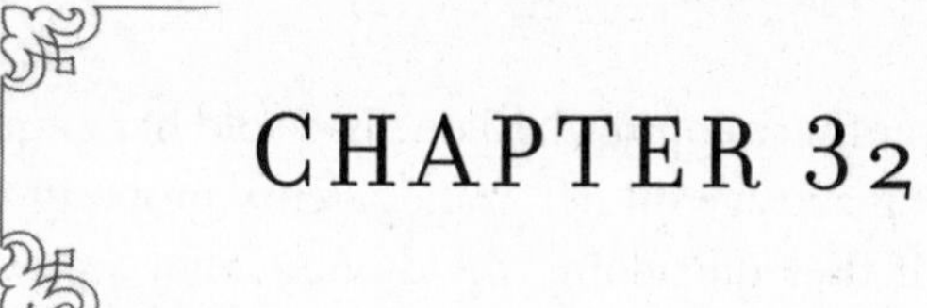

CHAPTER 32

The following day after Jonah finished working, he decided to drop by Sara's and see how she was doing. He took a quick shower, put on clean clothes, and headed outside to get his horse and buggy ready. Hopefully Sassy, having rested all day, would move a little faster this time.

Going down the road, Jonah remembered another time when he'd come to someone else's rescue. Memories took him back to Pennsylvania, when he'd first arrived in Bird-in-Hand. He'd just gotten settled in at Mom and Dad's house when he'd learned about the tragedy concerning Meredith's husband, Luke. Jonah had decided to visit Meredith and offer his condolences. It was good that he got there when he did, because shortly after his arrival, Meredith collapsed and could have gone into labor and lost her baby if she hadn't gotten to the hospital in time.

Was it divine intervention that Jonah had come to Sara's aid when her barn caught fire? *Maybe it's my responsibility to rescue people in distress by showing up at just the right time,* Jonah decided, pulling his thoughts back to the present.

Jonah was halfway to Sara's when he saw Elaine's friend Leah riding her bike. She must have seen him, too, for they both waved at the same time.

Jonah was tempted to stop and ask Leah how Elaine was doing, but decided against it. He wanted to get to Sara's before she started cooking her supper. Besides, he'd talked to Leah's dad, Alton, the other day when he'd stopped by the buggy shop. Elaine's name had come up when Alton mentioned that Leah and her mother had been helping Elaine do some canning a few weeks ago. Alton said that Edna wasn't doing well and if things didn't improve, she and Elaine might not do the sit-down dinners for tourists anymore. Jonah had also learned that with her grandmother's approval, Elaine had sold her grandfather's horse and was renting acreage on her grandparents' property to one of their neighbors, so if they quit doing the dinners, they would at least have enough money to live on. But would it be enough?

Jonah wished he was free to help out, but Elaine had made it clear that she didn't want that.

"Did she ever really feel anything for me?" Jonah muttered as he continued on down the road. "Or was I always just a passing fancy for her?"

Sassy's ears perked up and he neighed as if in response.

"Was that a yes or a no?" Jonah asked with a snicker. At least he wouldn't be showing up at Sara's house with a sour expression.

Jonah thought about how he'd been one of the witnesses at Melvin and Sharon's wedding last week. Seeing their smiling faces after they'd said their vows had made Jonah wish all the more that he, too, was happily married.

Sara wasn't sure what to fix for supper this evening. Nothing appealed, and she'd worked hard cleaning house most of the day, so she had no energy for cooking. Of course, some of her fatigue could be related to the ordeal she'd gone through yesterday when the barn caught fire. She still couldn't believe it was gone or that she'd been so careless when she was attacking all those cobwebs. Each time Sara glanced out the window, it made her sick to see what little was left of Harley's barn. What would he think of her being so careless?

I should have been watching what I was doing, Sara berated herself as she sat on the living-room floor next to her son while he played with some of his toys. She was glad Mark was young and wouldn't remember any of this as he got older.

Sara thought about Jonah and how thankful she was that he'd come along when he did. In addition to talking with the firemen after they'd arrived, he'd helped Sara calm down and reassured her that if she decided to rebuild the barn, he would come to help out. Jonah had also made sure that Sara's horse was put out in the field. After the fire was extinguished, Sara was checked over by the paramedics, who had followed in an ambulance behind the fire trucks. Once it was determined that Sara was okay, Jonah had taken her over to Herschel and Betty's, where she and Mark had spent the night.

Turning her attention back to Mark, Sara realized that she couldn't sit here all evening; she needed to feed him something. Maybe she would make them sandwiches for supper. That wouldn't be much trouble.

Since Mark seemed content to play with his toys, Sara made her way to the kitchen. She'd just opened the bread box and taken out a loaf of bread when she looked out the window and saw a horse and buggy pull in. Pleased to see that it was Jonah, Sara set the loaf of bread on the counter and opened the back door.

When Jonah stepped onto the porch, he smiled and said, "I came by to see how you're doing. That was quite an ordeal you went through yesterday."

She nodded, appreciating his concern. "It was, and I'm thankful you were there to help me through it."

"Are you doing okay?" Jonah moved closer to Sara.

"I'm fine now. Still coughing a bit from the smoke I inhaled, but otherwise doing okay. However, I fear all of Harley's tools have been lost."

"You can worry about that later." Much to Sara's surprise, Jonah slipped his arm around her shoulder and gave it a gentle squeeze. "I can even come over once the area has cooled and see what things might be salvageable."

"You would do that for me after all you've already done?" she asked in disbelief.

"Sure, why not?" A blush of pink spread across Jonah's cheeks. "That's what friends are for, right?"

Sara nodded in agreement.

He shifted his weight from one foot to the other, as though nervous about something. "Um. . .I know it's short notice, Sara, but if you haven't started supper yet, I thought maybe you and Mark would like to go out someplace to eat."

"I haven't started supper and going out does sound nice, but I'm worried that with us being seen together at a restaurant, it might cause some people to talk."

"Talk about what?"

"Well, it might not seem right for you to be seen with me when you're courting Elaine."

"That won't be an issue, because Elaine and I broke up a few months ago," Jonah said. "With the way information travels around here, I thought you would have heard by now."

"No, I hadn't heard." No wonder Elaine hadn't been at Jonah and Jean's birthday dinner. Sara wondered if Jonah had broken things off with Elaine, or if it was the other way around. Even though she was curious, she wouldn't ask, because it just wouldn't be polite. If Jonah wanted her to know the details, he would share them with her.

"So, how about it, Sara? Will you and Mark go out to supper with me?"

Barely giving it a second thought, Sara nodded. She looked forward to spending the evening with Jonah.

"I'm glad you were free to have supper with me," Elam Gingerich said as he and Priscilla took seats at Yoder's restaurant.

"It was nice of you to invite me." Priscilla had known Elam since they were children and had attended the same school together. Her family worshipped in a different church district than his, but they'd spent time together during several young people's gatherings. Priscilla had known for some time that Elam was interested in her, but he was kind of shy and hadn't made his intentions known until last week, when he'd invited her to have supper with him tonight. Elam was twenty-five and had never had a serious girlfriend that Priscilla knew of. He had medium-brown hair, hazel eyes, an average nose, and ears that were a bit larger than most. But Elam wasn't ugly; there was actually a handsomeness about him, and Priscilla found his quiet way and genuine smile appealing.

Elam worked part-time at his parents' bulk foods store and also helped an English man in their area who was a roofer. Elam seemed to be highly motivated and had joined the church last year, so Priscilla figured he was secure in his faith and had no plans to leave his Amish heritage. He would probably make someone a good husband. But if

Elam decided to pursue a serious relationship with her, could she see him as more than a friend?

"Did ya hear what our waitress said?" Elam's question pulled Priscilla's thoughts aside.

"Oh, sorry, I didn't realize you'd come to our table," Priscilla stammered, feeling foolish as she looked at Barbara Yoder, their Amish waitress.

Barbara smiled. "Would you like something to drink besides water?"

"I'd like a glass of iced tea," Priscilla responded.

"And I'll have a root beer, please," Elam added.

"I'll get those now and be back to take your order." Barbara smiled and walked away.

"Sure is nice weather we've been having," Priscilla commented after several minutes of awkward silence.

Elam glanced out the window. "Jah, and I'm glad for it, 'cause my boss has a couple of roofing jobs that need to be done next week, and we sure don't need any rain."

"Do you enjoy roofing more than working in your folks' store?" Priscilla asked.

He nodded. " 'Course when the weather's bad and we can't roof, it's nice to have a second job to fall back on."

Barbara returned with their drinks and asked what they'd like to eat. Elam ordered a burger and fries, and Priscilla said she'd like some fried chicken, mashed potatoes, and a small garden salad.

While they waited for their food, they talked about some of the things they'd read in the paper lately, like the accident that had taken place in the town of Sullivan, not too far away.

"At least that collision didn't involve a horse and buggy." Elam drew in a deep breath and exhaled quickly. "As bad as it was, if one of our people had been in a buggy and gotten hit by that truck, they probably would have been killed."

Priscilla was about to comment when she glanced toward the door and saw Jonah enter the restaurant with Sara and her son, Mark. Priscilla was so surprised to see them together that she choked on the iced tea she'd just sipped.

"You okay?" Elam asked, leaning toward her with a look of concern.

Priscilla nodded, blotting her lips with a napkin. "I'm fine. Guess I must have swallowed the wrong way." She watched with curiosity as the hostess seated Jonah, Sara, and Mark on the opposite side of the room. Had they seen her? Should she go over and talk to them? Maybe not. It might be best just to keep her focus on Elam and pretend she hadn't seen Jonah with Sara and her little boy.

"How come you're frying so much chicken?" Edna asked, peering over Elaine's shoulder as she stood at the stove. "There's just the two of us, and we can't eat that much chicken for supper tonight."

"This isn't just for us, Grandma," Elaine said. "We're hosting another dinner tonight for a small group of tourists."

Edna rubbed her forehead as she pondered this information. "Really? Did I know about that?"

"The tour director set things up with us a few weeks ago. Do you remember?"

Edna continued to rub her forehead. It was upsetting not to be able to recall something like this. "I can't say that I do, but if it's true, then we need to get busy, because there's a lot yet to be done."

"Not so much." Elaine motioned to the hefty-size kettle on the back burner. "The potatoes are cooked, mashed, and keeping warm on the stove, and the salad is in the refrigerator."

Still puzzled, Edna squinted. "Oh, really? I don't remember making those."

"Actually, you didn't. I made them while you were napping earlier this afternoon."

Edna slid one finger down the side of her nose, stopping at the tiny mole. "That's right; I was kind of sleepy." She smiled at Elaine, removing her finger. "Danki for doing all of that, Nancy. You've always been a hard worker. My son picked well when he married you."

"No, Grandma, I'm not Nancy. I'm your granddaughter, Elaine."

Edna's cheeks warmed. "Of course. How silly of me to say such a thing. You look so much like your mamm; it's easy to get you mixed up sometimes."

Elaine nodded as she continued to fry the chicken.

Edna turned and moved slowly across the room. "Think I'll go to the dining room and make sure the tables have been set." *Sure wish I didn't feel so confused. Makes me feel like I'm losing my glicker.*

Things went okay during the first half of the dinner, but when it was time to serve dessert, Grandma started talking to Elaine like she was a child, saying things like, "If you can't be a little faster serving that pie, I'll send you to bed without any dessert."

Elaine merely smiled and tried to shrug it off, hoping none of their guests had heard what Grandma said. But when Grandma started talking about Grandpa and said someone had stolen his horse, Elaine became concerned.

"Grandma, could I speak to you in the kitchen for a minute?"

"Whatever you want to talk about can be said right here with my friends." Grandma turned and smiled at their guests.

Feeling a sense of panic, Elaine gave Grandma's arm a little tug and whispered, "Would you please come with me for just a minute? It's important that I talk to you alone."

"Well, okay, if you must, but we can't be gone too long." Grandma followed Elaine into the kitchen and pulled out a chair at the table. "What did you want to talk to me about, Nancy?"

"I'm not Nancy, I'm Elaine, and—"

"Are you jealous because I have friends here and you don't?"

"No, it's not that. You look tired, Grandma, and I think it might be better if you went to your room now and rested, while I serve dessert to our guests."

"Well, if that's the way you feel about it, then fine!" Glaring at Elaine, Grandma stood up and then tromped out of the room.

It nearly broke Elaine's heart to see Grandma responding to her in such a negative, almost hostile, way. She wasn't acting like the grandmother she'd always known.

Breathing deeply as she tried to calm her racing heart, Elaine returned to the dining room.

"Is there a problem?" the tour guide asked as Elaine approached the table.

"No, everything's under control." Elaine placed two pies on the first table and was about to set the other ones on the opposite table when she heard Grandma loudly mumbling while stomping around in her room. *This will be the last dinner Grandma and I host,* Elaine thought regrettably. *Tonight has been too difficult for us.*

CHAPTER 33

The following day, Priscilla decided to stop and see Elaine. Rather than taking the time to hitch Tinker to her buggy, she rode over on her bike. Along the way, she rehearsed what she was going to say.

Last night at the restaurant, Priscilla had chosen not to speak with Jonah or Sara. They'd seemed to be preoccupied and didn't appear to notice her, so she had simply concentrated on visiting with Elam.

Jonah couldn't be in love with Sara; it hasn't been that long since he was courting Elaine, and I know he was crazy about her, Priscilla told herself as she pedaled along, keeping her bicycle on the shoulder of the road. The more she thought about it, the more concerned she became. *If Jonah and Sara are courting, will Elaine be upset?* Jonah had been good friends with Sara's husband, so maybe he and Sara were just friends, too. But if Jonah was courting Sara, there was nothing she could do about it, so it did no good to fret.

Priscilla turned up the Schrocks' driveway. After she'd parked her bike, she hurried up to the house. She was about to knock on the door when Elaine stepped out, quickly shutting the door behind her.

"I'm glad you're here; I need some moral support right now."

"Oh, what's wrong?" Seeing the stress lines on Elaine's face had Priscilla concerned.

Elaine signaled to the chairs on the porch. "Let's take a seat."

Noting that Elaine wasn't wearing a sweater, Priscilla suggested they go inside. "It's chilly this morning."

Elaine shook her head. "I'd rather talk with you here. Grandma's in the kitchen, and I don't want her to hear our conversation."

"Okay, but maybe you should get a sweater."

"No, I'm fine." Elaine took a seat, and Priscilla did the same.

Priscilla couldn't help but notice the dark circles beneath her friend's eyes. *I'll bet she hasn't slept well in weeks.*

Tears sprang to Elaine's eyes, and she clasped Priscilla's hand. "Grandma's getting worse, Priscilla. Much worse than I expected, and it's happening so quickly."

Priscilla sat quietly as Elaine told how her grandma thought she'd seen her husband's horse and that she often believed Elaine was her mother, Nancy. "And you should have seen how Grandma acted during the dinner we hosted last night." Elaine shook her head as more tears came. "I can barely cope with things anymore, Priscilla. It's overwhelming."

"Have you spoken to her doctor about this?" Priscilla questioned.

"Not directly, but I called his office and talked with the nurse."

"What'd she say?"

"Just that some dementia patients' memory loss is gradual and can take place over several years. But with some who have advanced dementia, like Grandma apparently does, their memory goes quickly. Trouble is, I already knew all of that." Elaine paused and blew her nose on the tissue Priscilla had just given her. "To make all this worse, since Grandpa died, Grandma seems to have lost her zest for living. At first she was a fighter and said she'd go down kicking. Now it makes me wonder if she's just given up on life."

"Have you tried giving her that remedy you found at the health food store?"

"I have, but she usually won't take it. It's hard to get her to cooperate when it's time for her insulin shots, too." Elaine's chin quivered. "It's difficult to take care of her when she doesn't cooperate. And it's even more so when she gets upset with me and says harsh things."

Priscilla gave an understanding nod while gently patting her friend's hand. "I feel so bad for what you're going through, but I'm sure you must know that your grandma would never treat you that way intentionally."

Elaine sniffed. "I—I know, but it still hurts."

"I'm sure it does, and I wish there was more I could do to ease your burden."

"You, Leah, and so many others have helped out as often as you can, and I appreciate it so much. But you have busy lives of your own, and I don't expect someone to be here all of the time." Elaine sighed, leaning back in her chair. "Besides, even if you could be here on a regular basis, it wouldn't make any difference in how things are going with Grandma right now. No one but God can stop or even slow this horrible illness that is taking the grandma I've always known from me."

"It's a terrible disease, and sometimes it can be harder on family members than on the patient when their loved one becomes like a stranger to them."

"You're right, Priscilla, but I can only imagine the struggle going on inside Grandma's head with all this." Elaine paused and swiped at the tears that had fallen onto her cheeks. "Just talking to you about this has been helpful. Danki for listening."

"Oh, you're welcome. It's the least I can do for a special friend like you."

"You and Leah are such good friends, and I don't know what I'd do without your love and support." Elaine sniffled. "Something else happened the other day, too. On Thursday, Grandma's parakeet got out, and later on, I found her remains over by the barn. I haven't the heart to tell Grandma that one of the cats probably got her pet bird. Even though I took Millie's cage out of the house and put it in the back of the barn, I don't think Grandma realizes that the bird is gone. If she does, she hasn't said anything about it."

"Oh, that's such a shame." Priscilla blinked against her own tears. *I'm definitely not going to tell Elaine about seeing Jonah and Sara at the restaurant last night. She has enough to deal with right now.*

"After all that happened at the dinner we hosted last night, I've made a difficult decision." Elaine shivered, crossing her arms in front of her chest.

"What's that?"

"There will be no more sit-down dinners for tourists in this house. In fact, after everyone left, I spoke with the tour guide and explained my decision."

"How'd she respond to that?"

"Said she understood, but was sorry to lose our business. She also stated that if things should ever change, and I decide to start doing the dinners again, to let her know." Elaine stared out across the yard. "It's not likely that I'll ever host dinners for tourists again. Those days are behind us now."

"If you want to keep doing them, I'd be happy to come over and help out," Priscilla offered.

"Danki for your willingness, but I don't want to invite strangers into our house for dinners anymore, never knowing what Grandma might say or do."

"How will you support yourselves?" Priscilla questioned. She wished again that there was more she could do for her dear friend.

"We have the rent money from the land we're leasing, and there's still some money left in our bank account." Elaine shifted in her chair. "I could take in some sewing or maybe try selling some of my rock paintings at one of the gift stores in town. I'm going to take one day at a time and keep trusting the Lord to provide for our needs."

Priscilla nodded. "And remember the words of Psalm 125:1: 'They that trust in the Lord shall be as mount Zion, which cannot be removed, but abideth for ever.' " She gave Elaine's arm a reassuring squeeze. "Please don't forget to ask for help whenever you have a need."

More tears fell as Priscilla stood and gave Elaine a hug.

Jonah stepped out of his house and paused a minute before heading to the shop. His mind was full of scattered thoughts as he reflected on the enjoyable evening he'd had with Sara and Mark. It had been fun, being with Sara, and that little boy of hers had just about stolen Jonah's heart. Jonah looked forward to spending more time with them.

What would it be like to have a son like Mark and be able to pass on to the child the same values as my parents taught me? Jonah was beginning to think his desire for a wife and children was just a dream—a dream that had twice been broken.

Lifting the apple he'd taken from the house, he took a bite. Some of the juice sprayed out and dribbled down his chin. Apples always tasted best this time of year. Jonah munched on it while his thoughts kept spinning. Some of the leaves in his yard were slowly turning, with just a hint of color, but for the most part they were still green. Birds had begun flying in larger groups as they started migrating. Acorns were falling, and the apple harvest was in full swing. Soon the trees would be bare, and then the upcoming holidays would swoop in.

Jonah reflected on how Jean had told him the other day that Mom and Dad might be making another trip to Illinois to be with them for Thanksgiving. At first, Jonah and Jean, along with her family, had talked about going to Pennsylvania, but Mom and Dad said they thought it would be easier for them to come to Illinois, since it was only the two of them. Jean had already begun planning a festive dinner with all the trimmings.

Jonah wished Dad was here right now so he could talk to him about Sara. Jonah wasn't sure how he really felt about her, or if he was ready to establish another relationship, especially so soon. The last two had ended up emotionally draining, so maybe it was best just to remain friends with Sara. Although he had to admit, he did have a good time, and little Mark took to him so easily. Jonah loved kids. Even when he was out and about and saw children he didn't know, as soon as he made eye contact, the child would smile at him.

The subject of the holidays didn't come up last evening, but I guess I could ask Sara if she and Mark would like to join us for Thanksgiving this year. But then, she might be planning to go to Indiana to spend the holiday with her parents.

Jonah didn't know why he was thinking about all of this right now. Thanksgiving was still a ways off. Not only that, but there was work to be done in his shop, so he'd better quit thinking and get busy.

As Sara sat at her sewing machine, making another apron to sell, she thought about last night and how much she'd enjoyed being with Jonah. He reminded her of Harley—not in the way he looked, but with his caring attitude and gentle spirit. Jonah had been so attentive to Mark during the evening and kept the boy occupied when he'd become restless, waiting for his meal. When Jonah brought them home afterward, Mark had fallen asleep, so Jonah carried him inside for Sara. Before he left,

Jonah had told Sara that he'd had a good time and hoped they could go out for supper again sometime soon.

Does Jonah want to court me? she wondered. *Is he over Elaine, and could he possibly be interested in beginning a relationship with me?*

Sara looked out the living-room window and focused on the swirling leaves. The wind had picked up, and the few leaves that had fallen from the trees in her yard were being carried away on the breeze. It wouldn't be long before Thanksgiving would be upon them.

Sara's thoughts turned to Harley again and how much he'd loved this time of the year. He had enjoyed seeing the leaves turn color, and after a heavy frost, Harley had mentioned how much he liked those see-your-breath-in-the-air mornings. Many times, when their chores were done early, he'd say, "Let's go for a ride, Sara." They'd hop in the buggy and drive through the farmlands, enjoying the stunning colors of autumn. Fields would be turning a rich golden tan, with hay cut for a second time. The mums were brilliant colors, blooming by fence posts and throughout flower beds in many backyards. Sara, too, enjoyed fall days, with less humidity and crystal-clear skies.

She closed her eyes, not wanting to let go of the past. Was it only a year and a half ago that Harley had died? Sometimes it seemed like just yesterday. Other times, memories of Harley felt like such a long time ago.

Sara had never known any man who loved the holiday season like her husband did. Harley became almost childlike when the first white flakes of snow started falling. He loved the smell of wood burning in their fireplace, and many times during a snowy afternoon, they'd get out one of their board games, make a batch of buttery popcorn, and relax in front of a cozy fire. She missed those times so much.

Sara would stay home for Thanksgiving this year but had been considering going to see her parents for Christmas. But traveling that far with a two-year-old might prove to be stressful, so she'd invited her folks to come here. Mom and Dad had agreed, and Sara looked forward to their coming. She couldn't help wondering, though, what Jonah would do for the holidays. Would he stay here in Arthur and celebrate with his sister and her family, or return to Pennsylvania to be with his parents?

If he stays, she thought, *maybe I'll get the chance to see him during that time. I'm sure Mark would enjoy it, and truth be told, so would I.*

CHAPTER 34

"Danki for agreeing to stay with my grandma while I do some shopping today," Elaine said when Iva came over on the first Monday of October. "I'd take her with me, but she seems to be afraid of riding in the buggy lately."

"That's too bad. Where's Edna now?" Iva lowered her voice to a whisper as she took a seat at the kitchen table.

Elaine gestured toward the door leading to their dining room. "She does have some good days, and she's working on a puzzle. It was something I thought might help to stimulate her brain. Even though Grandma probably won't be able to get many of the pieces to fit, she seems content at the moment."

Iva sat quietly and then slowly shook her head. "I feel so bad for Edna—and you, too, Elaine. I never expected your grandma would go downhill so quickly."

"Neither did I," Elaine admitted. "It's unbelievable."

"I have an aunt who was diagnosed with dementia, and it took several years for the disease to progress to the stage Edna appears to be in now."

"I've taken Grandma back to see the doctor several times, but he always says the same thing: she apparently has an aggressive form of dementia, and. . ." Elaine's voice trailed off as tears sprang to her eyes. She was tired of crying, and just plain tired. "I've tried everything I know of to help her, but nothing seems to make much difference. All I can do is to watch Grandma's memory fail a little more each day. My greatest fear is that soon she won't recognize me at all."

"It's a shame. I wish there was something more I could do to help you, Elaine." Iva's tone was comforting.

"You have helped, just by coming to sit with Grandma while I'm gone." Elaine looked down at her hands, red and chapped from all the work she'd been doing. "I still have some moments with Grandma when everything seems somewhat normal, and believe me, I cling to those times."

"That's what you have to do, Elaine." Iva gave Elaine's arm a tender pat. "As I've said before, please don't hesitate to call on me or any of your friends during this difficult time. You need time for yourself and deserve to get out whenever you can."

"It helps, knowing that." Sighing, Elaine rose from her seat. "Guess I'd better get going. I should be back before lunch, but if you and Grandma get hungry, there's a container of vegetable soup in the refrigerator that you can reheat."

"That's fine. Just take your time. I'm free for the rest of the day. Oh, and if it helps even a little, someone told me awhile back that, while every day may not be good, there's something good in every day."

Elaine entered the bulk foods store and started down the aisle where the spices were shelved. She'd just started filling her basket when she heard voices she recognized in the next aisle over.

"Did you know that Jonah Miller might be courting Sara Stutzman?"

"I figured as much. Saw them eating a meal together at Yoder's restaurant awhile back. Of course, Sara's son was with them, but to me it looked like they were on a date."

"I've heard that he goes over to her place quite often these days."

Elaine gripped the basket she held so tightly that her fingers ached. She could hardly believe the conversation Leah and Priscilla were having, or that Jonah had begun courting someone else so soon after she'd broken up with him. *Of course,* she reasoned, *it has been a few months.* She couldn't expect Jonah to remain unattached, especially when she'd made it clear that there was no hope for the two of them to be together.

Elaine squeezed her eyes shut, trying to come to grips with all of this and remembering how difficult it had been to tell Jonah that she didn't love him. *Will Jonah end up marrying Sara?* Since Sara was a widow and her little boy needed a father, it was quite likely she would marry again. *I wonder if Sara is in love with Jonah. Could he love her, too?*

Jonah deserved to be happy, but it hurt to hear that he and Sara might be courting. Elaine hoped Sara realized how fortunate she was, because as far as Elaine was concerned, there was no finer man than Jonah.

Elaine couldn't help feeling betrayed, hearing her friends talking about this. If they thought Jonah and Sara were courting, why hadn't they said something to her about it?

Placing the spices back on the shelf, Elaine turned and rushed out the door. She'd return some other time. Right now, she just wanted to go home.

"You're awfully quiet," Iva said as she sat across the table from Edna, eating lunch.

Edna shrugged. "Don't have much to say, really. My husband's dead; people don't want to come here for dinners anymore, and I'm just sittin' around waiting to die, so that doesn't give me much to say."

Iva frowned. "I wish you wouldn't talk like that."

"Why not? It's the truth."

"None of us knows when we are going to die, and we need to see each day as precious." Iva handed Edna some crackers to go with the soup. "From what I understand, you and Elaine aren't doing the dinners anymore."

Edna placed both hands against her temples, trying ever so hard to recall. Had they really decided that? Could she have forgotten such a thing? "My granddaughter is precious to me, but sometimes I can't even remember her name. Do you know how frightening and frustrating that is?"

"I'm sure it must be devastating, but I'm equally certain that Elaine understands. She loves you so very much, Edna."

"I love her, too." Edna broke some crackers into her bowl of soup and took a bite. "Sometimes Elaine takes things that are mine and puts 'em in strange places. The other day, she took my glasses." She blinked rapidly, pointing across the room. "I found them in the kichlin jar, of all things."

Iva looked at Edna strangely at first; then she chuckled and said, "Were they full of cookie crumbs?"

"No, there weren't any kichlin in there right then." Edna laughed, too. She was glad Iva had come to visit. It was nice to relax, share a meal with a friend, and find something to laugh about. Things almost felt normal. If only they could remain so.

"Wasn't that Elaine who just went out the door?" Priscilla asked Leah.

Leah nodded. "I think it was. I wonder why she dashed out of here in such a hurry. Think I'll go outside and see if I can catch her before she leaves."

"I'll come, too." Priscilla set her shopping aside and followed Leah out the door.

When they came to the area where the horses were tied, they found Elaine getting ready to leave.

"Elaine, wait up! We saw you rush out of the store. It looked like you were in a hurry, but we wanted to say hi." Priscilla put her hand on the side of Elaine's buggy.

"I was in the aisle next to where you two were talking and left the store after hearing what you said." Elaine's lips quivered slightly. She was clearly upset.

Priscilla shifted uncomfortably. "Was it about Jonah and Sara?"

"Jah. All this time has gone by, and you've never said a word to me about this. Why, Priscilla? I thought we were friends."

"We are friends, and the reason I didn't say anything is because you have enough to deal with taking care of your grandma, and I didn't want to upset you with information that might not mean a thing."

"You must have thought it did, or you wouldn't have discussed it with Leah." Elaine's shoulders drooped as she picked up the reins.

Leah reached into the buggy to touch Elaine's arm. "Please don't go yet. Like Priscilla said, we didn't want to upset you. Besides, we don't know for sure if Jonah and Sara are actually courting. They just went out for supper together, and from what I hear, Jonah's been over to Sara's a few times." Leah paused a few seconds and then continued. "You know, Sara went through a horrible experience awhile back, narrowly escaping from her burning barn, so maybe Jonah was just doing a kind deed when he took her and Mark out for supper."

"I heard about the fire. It's a shame Sara lost her barn."

"Then you probably know that Jonah was the one who saw the smoke, and when he went to investigate, he found Sara collapsed on the ground." Leah hesitated another moment. "Jonah may have been checking on Sara the other day, and then they decided to go out to eat someplace. Friends sometimes do that, you know, and Jonah was good friends with Sara's husband."

"That's right," Priscilla interjected. "He may feel a sense of obligation to Sara, and that might be all there is to it."

Elaine shrugged.

"Are you in love with Jonah? Is that why you're upset?"

"I'm upset because you kept it from me," Elaine responded, instead of answering Priscilla's question about her loving Jonah. "Friends aren't supposed to have secrets from one another. Now, if you two will excuse me, I need to go home." Before either Leah or Priscilla could respond, Elaine backed her horse up and headed down the road.

"We need to do something to make things better." Leah's tone was full of the regret she obviously felt over this misunderstanding.

"I agree, Leah, but I'm not sure what it could be."

"Well, for one thing, we need to start by apologizing to her."

Priscilla bobbed her head. "Jah, and the sooner the better."

Elaine pulled Daisy into the driveway, unhooked her from the buggy, and put her in the corral, where there was a trough full of water. She'd have to rub her down later and put her in the stall before dark. Right now, she wanted to go inside and relieve Iva. Besides, she was hungry and needed something to eat. Even though Iva had said she didn't mind staying all day, Elaine thought it would be better if she sent Iva home.

Elaine had chores she needed to get done, and after hearing the news about Jonah and Sara, she had to get her mind on something else and quit feeling sorry for herself. Working around the house had always helped before, and it kept her from dwelling on the negative when something was really bothering her, like it was now. While it was true that Elaine wanted Jonah to get on with his life, it hurt to know he'd moved on so quickly and seemed to have forgotten about her. Elaine's heart ached from letting him go. After their breakup, she figured that Jonah would be miserable from her rejection. But that didn't seem to be the case. Maybe he hadn't cared about her as much as he'd said. Well, none of that mattered now. She and Jonah were no longer together, and he really did have the right to move on with his life.

Taking a deep breath before walking in the door, Elaine heard laughter coming from the dining room. She found Iva and Grandma working on the puzzle together while carrying on what almost sounded like a normal conversation.

"Oh, you're back so soon." Iva looked up with a surprised expression when Elaine entered the room.

"Did you get all the items on the list?" Grandma asked as she tried to make an unmatched piece fit in the puzzle.

"I didn't go shopping, after all. Decided what I had on my list could wait for another day. Maybe I'll go again tomorrow, or the day after." It was wrong to fib, but she didn't want to admit the real reason she'd left the store. Besides, looking back on it now, she had overreacted. She should have just done her shopping rather than running out of the store. It seemed like Elaine's emotions ruled her actions these days, but that was no excuse.

Elaine remembered when the doctor at the hospital first told her about Grandma's dementia and had suggested that Elaine attend a support group. She hadn't felt it was necessary at first, and then later, when she really needed more support, she made the excuse not to go because it would mean asking someone to sit with Grandma while she was gone. Besides, Elaine didn't relish the idea of talking about her situation with strangers. She felt more comfortable discussing things with close friends, like Leah and Priscilla. *I'll bet they're upset with me right now. I need to apologize for my behavior.*

Grandma tugged on Elaine's arm. "I was hoping you'd get me that sugar-free angel food cake mix. Can't you go back to the store and get everything now? It's still early, and you know what? I'd like to go with you."

"Not today, Grandma. We'll go tomorrow." Elaine really didn't feel up to going back to the bulk foods store right now and hoped Grandma would just drop the subject.

Grandma stared at Elaine, and Elaine held her breath. *Please, Grandma, let it go for now.*

For the moment, Grandma just sat staring at the puzzle pieces in front of her. This was one time Elaine hoped Grandma had forgotten what had been said. There were times when Grandma would get upset about something and start whining, and then she'd suddenly get distracted and forget all about what she had wanted. Maybe this was one of those times.

Elaine glanced at Iva, who appeared to be busy snapping in another piece of the puzzle. "You're free to go on home now, Iva. I can handle things from here."

"Are you sure? I can hang around longer and assist you with anything you need to have done."

"I appreciate it, but everything's fine, and now that I'm home, I can take over," Elaine assured her. "I may need to call on you again soon, though, and I'm grateful that you came here today, short as the time was."

"Not a problem at all." Iva smiled as she rose from her chair. "Guess I'll be going, then." She paused and placed her hand on Grandma's shoulder. "Oh, and Edna, you keep working on that puzzle, 'cause you're doing a good job. Why, I'll bet you will probably have a lot more done on it when I come by again."

Grandma grunted in reply as she studied the puzzle intently.

Elaine walked Iva to the door. "Thank you again for taking the time to be here today, Iva."

"It was no problem at all. Edna and I had a good time visiting while we worked on the puzzle." Iva gave Elaine a hug. "Remember, now, to let me know when you need me again. I really don't have anything going on that's all that pressing these days."

"I'll keep that in mind." Elaine couldn't help thinking how lucky Priscilla was that her mother was still with her. Elaine would give anything to have either one of her parents here to lean on right now.

She stood in the doorway and watched as Iva's horse and buggy went down the driveway and turned onto the main road, thanking God, once again, for people like Iva who truly cared about others and wanted to help out in their time of need.

When Elaine returned to the dining room, feeling just a bit better, she was greeted with an angry scowl.

"I want to go to the store today." Grandma's tone was defiant, and she looked at Elaine in such a cold way that it caused her to shiver. "I want that cake mix, Nancy, and I want it now!"

"We can go later on." Elaine would never win this argument, so she might as well give in. There was no point in correcting Grandma about her name, either. Whenever Grandma referred to her as Nancy these days, Elaine chose to ignore it. "First, I need to eat some lunch and get a few things done around here. We'll go after that. Okay, Grandma?"

Grandma's expression softened some, and appearing to be satisfied, she gave a quick nod.

While Elaine did some cleaning around the house, wiping several small blood spots off the wall, she tried not to get too frustrated. It wasn't Grandma's fault that she had to have her finger pricked to test her blood, but Elaine wished Grandma would at least wait until the bleeding stopped before she touched anything. *Grandma probably doesn't realize what she's doing,* Elaine reasoned, blowing a straggly piece of hair off her forehead while she scrubbed. She walked slowly back toward the kitchen and used her sponge to wipe another red spot off the wall.

As Elaine continued to clean, she remembered a story that Grandma had read to her a long time ago. The tale involved a young girl who had been exploring a forest, and in order to keep from getting lost, she would drop a piece of popcorn along the path every few feet. That way, if the girl got confused, she could find her way home by following the popcorn trail.

Grandma could do something similar. Only for her, she would have specks of blood on everything she'd touched.

"That should do it," Elaine murmured after she'd finished cleaning. She collapsed into a chair at the table, then jumped back up when

Grandma tromped into the kitchen.

"Can we go now?" Grandma asked, sounding kind of huffy again.

"Okay. Just let me get Daisy hitched to the buggy again."

"Let's take Misty instead. She hasn't been out for a while and could use the exercise."

Elaine was hesitant about taking Misty, but Grandma was right. It had been a few weeks since they'd used Misty to pull their buggy. The animal probably needed to stretch her legs. Elaine hoped the ride to town would be without incident and that Misty wouldn't be too full of pent-up energy.

Everything went well at first, but all of a sudden, Misty became rambunctious. It took Elaine several minutes to get the horse under control, but fortunately, Misty started behaving rather well for not having been out on the road in a while.

Grandma's contented smile told Elaine that she was enjoying the fresh air and, at least for today, had forgotten about her recent fear of riding in the buggy. Elaine had relaxed a bit, too, after getting Misty to settle down.

October was a beautiful month, and this afternoon was no exception. Elaine noticed how beautiful the landscape was, with the glorious colors of autumn all around. The crimson red maples and bright yellow birch with the orange of sumac mixed in would have made a lovely scene for a painting, mingling with the earth tones of freshly cut fields. Elaine had never painted anything on canvas, but if she ever found the time, she might give it a try sometime. Meanwhile, she'd been able to squeeze in a few minutes each evening after Grandma went to bed to paint more of the rocks she'd found near the creek not far from their home.

Last Monday, when their bishop's wife, Stella, had come by to visit Grandma, Elaine had been able to slip away for a short time. She'd gone to the creek and picked up several nice rocks. Visits from others in their community were the only times when Elaine could get away, as she wasn't about to leave Grandma alone, for fear of her wandering off or burning something on the stove.

"Are you warm enough, Grandma?" Elaine pulled the blanket over Grandma's legs.

"I'm fine. Quit fussing all the time. You're acting like a mother hen." Grandma frowned, but then she reached over and patted Elaine's arm.

Elaine relaxed a little, taking in a deep breath. This was one of those rare times when things seemed almost normal. If only it could last. Even Misty seemed to enjoy the crisp autumn air, having no pesky bugs to swish away with her tail.

Big puffy white clouds billowed on the horizon as they continued toward town. Elaine remembered how, a long time ago, she and Grandpa had put an old blanket on the grass and, lying there together, watched the clouds roll by. One time, Grandpa had looked over at Elaine and said, "Someday, Lainie, I'll be sittin' on one of those beautiful clouds, watching over you and your grandma." Did Grandpa know back then that he'd be the first to die? Was he looking down on them today from one of those puffy clouds?

Maybe it's just wishful thinking, Elaine thought. *At least I can be sure of one thing—our heavenly Father's watching over us.*

Elaine was thankful that even through the darkest of times God was only a prayer away, and He knew what they were going through and cared about all their troubles.

Riding farther along, Elaine looked into an open field and spotted a doe watching as they approached. Elaine was about to point it out to Grandma when a smaller deer shot out from the opposite side and ran right in front of Misty. How the two animals kept from colliding was beyond Elaine's reasoning, but unfortunately the horse spooked. Misty took off like a bullet, and Elaine held on to the reins with all the strength she could muster. To make matters worse, Grandma seemed to enjoy the adventure, hollering for Misty to go faster.

"It's like being in a race!" Grandma clapped her hands like an excited child. "This is fun. Go! Go faster, Misty!"

Elaine didn't have time to look at Grandma, but from her shouts of delight, it was obvious that she had no idea of the danger they were in. At this speed even the slightest bump in the road could send them crashing into a tree, someone's fence, or worse—a car.

"Whoa there, Misty! Slow down, girl!" Elaine shouted. But Grandma's exuberant horse had a mind of her own. All Elaine could do was cling tightly to the reins and hope that Misty would tire out soon.

"Sit back, Grandma, and hang on to your seat!" she instructed.

Grandma seemed oblivious to everything as she continued to clap, shout, and giggle.

Elaine should have slowed down when she first saw the doe standing by the road. Again, she could almost hear Grandpa's words when he'd told her another time: *"If a deer runs across the road, slow down, because there will most likely be another."* This doe had obviously been waiting for her fawn to catch up before going any farther. Elaine had only gotten a glimpse of the young deer before Misty went haywire.

After what seemed like forever, Misty finally slowed to a trot, snorting and shaking her mane. Elaine's arms felt as though they were coming out of their sockets as she let up on the tension of the reins. She was relieved that no cars had passed during Misty's wild romp and that they were now out of immediate danger.

The rest of the trip was uneventful, and it gave Elaine time to calm down. By the time she guided Misty to the hitching rack, Elaine was breathing normally again.

Once in the store, Elaine hurried to get everything on her list, and then she stopped to look in the aisle where the baking supplies were kept.

"There's no angel food cake mixes here," Grandma mumbled, pouting like a child as she pointed to one of the shelves. "It's your fault, Nancy. You shoulda got it for me this morning. I'll bet they had plenty of cake mixes then."

"I can make a sugar-free cake from scratch after we get home," Elaine said, hoping that would appease Grandma.

"That'll take too long." Grandma shuffled toward the checkout counter, muttering under her breath.

Elaine placed the things in her basket on the counter and waited for everything to be rung up by the cashier.

"Is that a wig you're wearing?" Grandma asked the clerk while pointing to her hair.

Elaine was about to apologize for Grandma's impolite behavior, but the clerk just smiled and said, "Yes, it is a wig. You see, I have cancer, and my treatments have caused most of my hair to fall out."

Elaine hoped that Grandma would respond properly, or better yet, just drop the subject. To her surprise, Grandma looked at the cashier with a sympathetic expression and said in a tone of sincerity, "I'm very sorry. I didn't realize that."

"I'm sorry, too," Elaine put in. "And I hope you'll be better soon."

"Thank you."

After Elaine had paid for her purchases, she gathered up the packages, took hold of Grandma's arm, and led her out the door. She was relieved that this shopping trip was over.

CHAPTER 35

"I hope Elaine is at home," Leah said to Priscilla as she guided her horse and buggy down the road the following day. It was another beautiful autumn morning, but there was a definite bite in the air—the kind of nip that warns of winter coming soon. "Maybe we should have called and left a message yesterday to let her know we were coming."

"Well, if she isn't home, we can visit with Edna," Priscilla responded. "I'm sure she would appreciate some company, too."

"I doubt that Elaine would leave her grandma at home unless someone is there with her." Leah shivered as the cold air seeped into the buggy. "Let's hope Edna knows who we are today. Sometimes when I've dropped by, Edna didn't have a clue who I was. Elaine's even mentioned that some days her grandma thinks she's Elaine's mother, Nancy."

"That's so sad. Dementia is such a cruel disease for the person who has it, as well as for their family. I wish this had never happened and that Edna could be healthy again."

Leah shook the reins to get her horse moving faster. "I guess that won't happen till she's in heaven with Jesus. Only then will God's children be completely healed of their diseases."

Elaine gathered up the living-room throw rugs and was on her way to take them outside when she smelled something burning. *Oh no, not this again.* Had Grandma decided to bake another pie or some cookies and left them in the oven?

Elaine dropped the rugs on the floor and hurried to the kitchen. No sign of Grandma in there. She opened the oven door and was relieved to see that it was cold and nothing was inside.

When she sniffed again, she suddenly realized that the odor she'd smelled was drifting down the hall. As she headed in that direction, it became clear that something in Grandma's bedroom was burning.

Alarmed, Elaine jerked the door open. When she stepped into the room, she gasped. Grandma stood near the ironing board, staring across the room with a faraway look, as though completely out of touch with what was going on. One of her dresses lay on the ironing board, with the iron resting on top of the bodice. Smoke from the burning material drifted in front of Grandma's face, but she didn't seem to notice.

Elaine rushed over, snatched the iron up, and grimaced when she saw a nasty hole with the telltale signs of brown where the iron had scorched the material.

"Oh, Grandma, just look at your dress!"

No response. Grandma kept staring across the room.

Elaine tried again, this time giving Grandma's arm a little shake and hoping to get through to her. "What happened here? Didn't you see that your dress was burning, or even smell the smoke?"

Slowly, Grandma turned to look at Elaine and blinked her eyes several times, as though coming out of a daze. "I've been thinking about Lloyd and wondering if he fed the katze this morning."

Elaine groaned inwardly, placing the iron upright on the end of the ironing board. Today was starting off on a bad note. "Well, your *frack* is ruined now, and you should have asked me to iron it for you." Annoyed, Elaine gestured to the hole. Sometimes she felt like she was dealing with a child instead of a seventy-five-year-old woman. But then, she had to remind herself that Grandma was ill and couldn't help the things she said and did. *"Be kinder than necessary, for everyone you meet is fighting some kind of a battle,"* she'd heard Grandma say. Now it was Grandma's turn. She was fighting the battle of dementia, and Elaine needed to be as kind as possible. She touched Grandma's arm. "I'm not mad at you, Grandma. Just concerned. Next time you need to have something ironed, would you please ask me?"

Grandma pointed at the hole in her dress. "What happened to that? It's disgusting!"

"You were ironing and must have forgotten to lift the iron from your dress." Elaine talked calmly, trying to keep her patience and not upset Grandma.

"Why would I do that?" Tears welled in Grandma's eyes and dribbled down her wrinkled cheeks. "Lloyd won't like this one little bit. He always liked it when I wore that dress."

Elaine made no comment. She picked up the dress, as well as the iron, and left the room. She would need to find a better place to store the iron so that Grandma couldn't find it, because she couldn't take the chance of her burning another dress—or worse yet, catching the house on fire. From now on, she would need to keep a closer watch on Grandma.

Sara hummed to herself as she buttered a piece of toast for Mark. He'd already eaten breakfast, but around ten this morning he'd said he was hungry again, so some toast with peanut butter would get him by until she fixed their noon meal. It wouldn't be a big lunch, however, because this evening Jonah would be coming to take them out for pizza. Sara looked forward to going. Not just for the taste of tangy pepperoni pizza, but because it was another opportunity to be with Jonah. The more time she spent with him, the more she found herself enjoying his company. And the more she got to know Jonah, the more he reminded her of Harley. Of course, he had been Harley's friend, so they must have had some things in common. Something seemed to be happening between Sara and Jonah—something she hadn't expected. Was it possible that after just a few short months of spending time together, she could be falling in love? Or could it be that she still missed Harley and being with Jonah filled a void in her life? And how did Jonah feel about her? Was he still in love with Elaine, or had he begun to see Sara in some other way than just Harley's widow who needed a friend? She remembered her mother saying, *"When God wants to bless you, He brings certain people into your life."* Sara certainly felt blessed to have Jonah in her life right now—even if it turned out that he was only a friend.

Sara's musings halted when Mark meandered into the room, asking for his toast. She lifted him into the high chair, placed the toast on his tray, and then filled his sippy cup with milk and gave him that, too.

While Mark ate his snack, Sara busied herself at the sink, cutting vegetables for the soup they would have for lunch. She was glad Mark liked most kinds of soup and wasn't a picky eater, like some children his age. That made it easier to prepare meals they could both enjoy.

Once the veggies had been cut, Sara placed them in the kettle, added water and some beef broth, then set it on the stove to simmer. By the time the noon hour rolled around, it should be ready to eat.

The *clip-clop* of horse hooves drew Sara's attention to the window. She was pleased when Jean got out of the buggy, along with her three children. It had been a few weeks since they'd visited, and Sara was eager to find out what was new with her friend.

When Jean and the children entered the house, Sara asked if they would like to have some toast. The children eagerly agreed, and after Sara fixed their snack, she and Jean sat at the table so they could visit.

"Would you like a cup of peppermint tea?" Sara asked.

Jean nodded. "That sounds nice."

"You're welcome to have toast, too, if you like."

"No thanks. I had a big breakfast."

"Will you and the kinner stay and have lunch with us?" Sara motioned to the stove, where her soup simmered in the pot. "I have more than enough soup for all of us."

"That sounds good, but not today. We were on our way to town to do some shopping, and I decided to stop in here first and see how you're doing. Maybe you and Mark can come over to our place soon, so he can play with our new beagle pup, Chubby." Jean smiled. "That little beagle loves to play with the kinner, and he seems to be full of boundless energy. I don't know who gets played out first, Chubby or Rebecca and Stephen, but they sure do have a good time together."

"Mark likes puppies, too. I've even thought about getting him one but haven't done it yet, since training a pup and taking care of its needs requires a lot of work."

"That's true," Jean agreed. "But I think it's worth all the trouble. Chubby is just the right size for our kinner, too. He's a miniature beagle and won't grow to be a whole lot bigger than he is right now." Jean's expression turned serious. "I've been meaning to ask. Have you had any more dizzy spells or other unusual symptoms lately?"

Sara hated to admit it, but she told Jean how, just last night, when she was heading upstairs to get ready for bed, she'd had trouble making her left leg work.

"That does not sound good. Now, when are you going to see the doctor about this, Sara?" Jean released her breath in a huff. "You could be dealing with something serious, and if that's the case, then you need to know what it is so you can handle it."

Sara nodded, and as she looked up at Jean, a lump formed in her throat, making it difficult to swallow. "You're right. Tomorrow morning I'll call the doctor's office and make an appointment."

Jean placed her hand on Sara's arm. "Promise?"

"Jah. I won't forget." Sara sat quietly for several seconds; then, gathering up her courage, she decided to ask a question that had been on her mind for some time. "I know that Jonah isn't seeing Elaine anymore, but I was wondering if you know the reason."

Looking a bit uncomfortable, Jean quietly said, "Elaine told Jonah that she doesn't love him and never did. He didn't admit that to me at first, but several weeks after they broke up, I questioned him about it, and he told me what Elaine had said."

"I see. Danki for sharing that with me." Now that Sara knew the truth about why Elaine and Jonah had broken up, she felt a little more hopeful that there might be a possibility of her and Jonah developing a serious relationship. But she couldn't understand how Elaine, after being courted by Jonah for nearly a year, could not have fallen in love with him.

When Elaine stepped onto the porch to shake out a few more throw rugs, she spotted Leah and Priscilla riding in on their bikes. She knew without asking why they were here. No doubt they wanted to talk to her about what had happened yesterday. Elaine wished she hadn't overheard their conversation, and more than that, she still wished one or both of them had told her about Jonah and Sara. She guessed it was better hearing it that way than if she'd seen Jonah with Sara in town or noticed them leaving together after church.

"Wie geht's?" Leah asked after she and Priscilla parked their bikes and joined Elaine on the porch.

"I'm doing okay, but Grandma isn't." Elaine went on to explain how Grandma had burned a hole in her dress.

"That's baremlich," Priscilla said. "I'll bet it really upset her."

Elaine shook her head. "Not really. I was the one who was upset. Grandma seemed more concerned about how Grandpa would respond, saying she'd ruined his favorite dress."

"Sounds like she's getting worse."

Elaine nodded, her shoulders sagging from the weight of the day. "When we went to the kitchen for coffee awhile ago, Grandma pointed to the coffeepot and called it a 'putalator.' I was about to correct her when she squinted and pointed again, saying this time that it was a 'purfalatore.' I can't stand to see her like this. I've done everything I know to do, but it's just not enough, and I feel like I'm at the end of my. . ." A slight sigh punctuated her unfinished sentence, and she let her head fall forward into her hands.

"I'm sorry, Elaine; I know how difficult this is for you, but remember that when you've done all you can, God will do what you can't." Leah touched Elaine's shoulder gently. "Priscilla and I came over here today, not just to check on you and Edna, but to say how sorry we are for not telling you about Sara and Jonah. You were right to be upset when you heard us talking at the store."

"That's right, and we hope you'll find it in your heart to forgive us," Priscilla put in.

Elaine had to move past her feelings of betrayal and had already come to realize that she'd overreacted. Priscilla and Leah were her best friends, and she wanted to keep it that way. "I accept your apology," she said sincerely. "I'm sorry, too, for responding in such a negative way. It was just such a shock to hear it like that. But to be truthful, I would have been stunned no matter how I found out."

Leah and Priscilla slipped their arms around Elaine's waist, and they shared a group hug. Then, at Elaine's suggestion, they all took a seat on the porch.

"It concerns me," Elaine said slowly, "that at the rate Grandma's memory is failing, any day now she could completely forget me, her sister, or her two brothers and never remember any of us again."

"Say, here's a thought," Leah spoke up. "Why don't you invite your Grandma's relatives here for a get-together? It will give them all the chance to spend time with her now, before her memory is completely gone."

"That's a good idea." Elaine nodded. "I don't know why I didn't think of that myself. Grandma's birthday is in three weeks, so maybe I could plan a party in her honor and invite her sister and brothers, as well as any of their families who might be able to come. Hopefully it will be a good day for everyone—especially Grandma."

CHAPTER 36

Oblivious to the scenery as they went down the road, Sara stared blindly out the window of her driver's van, struggling not to cry. She'd just come from seeing the doctor, and the news wasn't good. It was so dreadful she could hardly believe it. After a series of tests she'd been given the week before and based on her symptoms, the doctor had determined that Sara had multiple sclerosis. She should have gone to see the doctor much sooner. No wonder she'd been having such unusual symptoms.

The doctor had explained that Sara's blurred vision, extreme fatigue, loss of balance, numbness, tingling, and weakness in her arms and legs were all symptoms of the disease. He'd also told Sara that MS was a complex illness, and it could affect people differently. A person with MS might have a single symptom and then go for months, or even years, without any other indications of the disease. For some people, however, their symptoms could be varied and become worse within months or even weeks.

For Sara, the worst part of learning all of this was in knowing that there was no cure for MS. Some medications had been developed that helped control symptoms, but all of them had side effects. Sara didn't want that. The disease alone was enough to cope with. She thought she might be better off trying a more natural approach, which would include getting plenty of rest, exercising regularly, eating a healthy, well-balanced diet, finding ways to relax, and keeping herself as cool as possible, since the symptoms of MS often worsened when a person's body temperature increased.

The worst thing Sara's doctor had told her was that some MS patients' symptoms got so bad they eventually ended up in a wheelchair. Of course, some people with the disease never reached that point, but Sara couldn't help worrying that she would be severely disabled. If she decided to stay in Arthur, her barn could be rebuilt. While the fire was an unfortunate event, her MS diagnosis was far worse. Unlike a barn that could be built again, there was nothing that would cure her body. It seemed like any chance of hope and happiness was out of Sara's reach.

As the scenery rolled by, Sara thought of the night Jonah had taken her and Mark out for pizza. It had turned out to be a wonderful, relaxing evening. She'd felt pretty good that entire day, almost normal, and for that she'd been thankful. It was one of those rare times lately when she hardly knew she had any health issues at all. Mark had enjoyed himself, too, especially when Jonah surprised him with a wooden horse he had carved. Ever since then, Mark wouldn't let that toy out of his sight.

After their meal, Jonah had brought them home, and he and Sara had visited awhile. When it was time for Mark to go to bed, he wanted Jonah to tuck him in. Smiling, Sara remembered how she'd stood in the doorway watching and how the scene had tugged at her heart. Harley would never be able to do these simple little acts of love for their son. But Sara was glad Jonah was there and had taken such a liking to Mark. Watching the two of them together, she'd felt something that, until that moment, had been buried for too long. She felt hope.

Dared she even dream of living a normal life now that she'd been diagnosed with MS? There were so many things Sara wanted to do. She had yet to go through the barn to see what items could be salvaged, and several projects around the house needed work, too.

Her eyes brimmed with tears, and Sara tried to hold them back. *What if I'm one of those people who will become hampered by my symptoms? I won't be able to take care of Mark if I end up in a wheelchair. Should I move back home with my folks, so they can help me raise my boy? That would be the sensible thing to do, but I need to pray about this before I make a decision.*

"Have you seen my *aageglesser*?" Grandma asked, shuffling into the living room where Elaine was dusting.

"No, I haven't, Grandma. You usually put your glasses on top of your dresser when you're not wearing them. Have you looked there?"

Grandma gritted her teeth while twisting the end of her apron. "Of course I looked there. Do I look dumm?"

"Of course you're not dumb. I just thought—"

"Never mind. I'll just have to keep looking." Grandma turned and plodded out of the room, but not before Elaine heard her mumble, "She's always hiding my things."

It was then that Elaine noticed Grandma was wearing two different shoes. On her left foot, she wore one of her black dress shoes. On Grandma's right foot was a navy blue clog that she wore when she worked in the garden. Elaine debated about whether to say anything or just let it go. She decided on the latter for now but would make sure Grandma wore her dress shoes for her birthday party tonight.

It would be good to see Grandma's older sister, Margaret, and her two brothers, Irvin and Caleb, who all lived in Iowa, where Grandma had been born. Grandma would probably be living there still if she hadn't met Grandpa at a friend's wedding when they were teenagers. In addition to Elaine's great-aunt and great-uncles, some of their children and grandchildren would also be visiting to celebrate Grandma's birthday. Elaine hoped the festivities not only would be a fun time for all, but also would give Grandma a chance to reconnect with her family before she lost her memory of them forever.

Elaine had the house almost cleaned, and she'd made plans to cook Grandma's favorite meal—baked chicken, mashed potatoes, coleslaw, and creamed corn. For dessert she'd baked a chocolate cake for everyone else, and a sugar-free apple pie for Grandma; although she would make sure that Grandma didn't eat too big of a piece, since the pie did have some natural sugar in the apples, as well as in the apple juice concentrate that was added for flavor and sweetening.

Elaine went to the sink to get a glass of water and glanced out the window as she raised the cup to her lips. She stopped abruptly, her hand in midair. "Now when did she go outside?" Elaine watched as Grandma walked through the backyard and over toward the swing, hanging from the big maple tree in their yard. Her first thought was to go out there and bring Grandma back inside, but something compelled her to remain where she was and watch.

Grandma sat down on the swing and started moving it slowly back and forth, then a few minutes later, she got it going a little bit higher.

Seeing the contented look on Grandma's face took Elaine back in time. Grandma appeared to be so happy, and it made Elaine want to cry. How long had it been since she'd seen that peaceful expression on her beloved grandma's face? Oh, how Elaine could relate to that carefree feeling of swooping down, then up again, over and over. She could almost feel the butterflies and the tickly feeling that being on a swing could bring.

Grandma's face turned almost childlike as she continued swinging back and forth. Elaine had to restrain herself from joining her. Grandma wasn't going too high and wasn't likely to fall off, so Elaine just kept on watching.

Before Grandpa died, Elaine had gone out to that old swing many times. Sometimes, just to be outside, especially after the days they'd hosted dinners. Other times, swinging helped her think more clearly about life or make plans for her future. It didn't happen often anymore, but a few times when Grandma was napping, Elaine had gone out to that old swing just for the pure joy of it and to reclaim how it felt during those untroubled years as a young child when she'd had no real worries to drag her down. Elaine longed for that feeling again.

Everything was happening too fast. With Grandma going downhill quickly, then hearing about Jonah courting again so soon, Elaine didn't know how much more she could take. But she couldn't run away from the problems or the fact that Jonah was moving on with his life. She was the one who had prompted their breakup, and if Jonah and Sara ended up getting married, she'd have to face it, no matter how difficult it might be.

One thing at a time, Elaine told herself, upending her thoughts and hoping once more that tonight would be special for Grandma.

She closed her eyes and whispered a prayer. "Dear Lord, please help everything to go well this evening and make this one of Grandma's best birthdays ever."

"Look who's here, Grandma!" Elaine gestured to her great-uncles, Irvin and Caleb, who'd just entered the house.

Grandma tipped her head and stared at the men a few seconds. Then she turned and shook her finger at Elaine. "Why didn't you tell me the tourists were coming here tonight? We don't even have our dinner started yet."

"Oh no, Grandma. We're not hosting a dinner for tourists. Some of our family has come to celebrate your birthday."

Grandma stared at her brothers a bit longer, looking as though she was seeing them for the very first time. She looked over at Elaine and said, "Is today really my birthday?"

Elaine nodded. "Yes, it is, and your brothers, Irvin and Caleb, have come to help you celebrate it."

"How old am I?"

"You're seventy-six," Irvin answered, pulling his fingers through the ends of his mostly gray beard.

Grandma moved a little closer to the men, squinting as she looked first at Irvin, then at Caleb. "You sure don't look like my *brieder*."

"We are your brothers," Uncle Caleb said with a decisive nod. The poor man looked quite flustered. "It's been a few years since we've seen you, Edna, and we're all getting older, so maybe that's why you don't recognize us."

Grandma bobbed her head, but Elaine wasn't sure she'd identified the men even yet.

"*Ich ab mic him busch verlore*," Grandma said, moving closer to Irvin.

His bushy gray eyebrows lifted. "You got lost in the woods? When did that happen?"

Grandma shrugged in response.

"I think she may be referring to a time when she wandered off our property and couldn't find her way home," Elaine quietly explained. She didn't bother to go into all the details, figuring it was best not to discuss this right now. Maybe later, after Grandma went to bed, she would talk about the situation with Grandma's brothers and the rest of the family. For now, Elaine just wanted to try to make this day as pleasant as she could.

A short time later, Great-Aunt Margaret showed up with her daughter and son-in-law. Margaret was in her eighties and used a cane to walk, but after talking to her just a few minutes, Elaine knew her aunt was sharp as a tack.

"How are things going?" Aunt Margaret whispered, giving Elaine a hug after she'd first greeted her sister, Edna. "Are you getting by all right?"

"Some days are more difficult than others," Elaine admitted, "but Grandma and I are getting by the best we can."

Aunt Margaret clasped Elaine's hands and gave them a little squeeze. "What about that young man you've been seeing? I'll bet he's a big help to you right now."

Elaine grimaced. She disliked having to tell her aunt that she and Jonah had broken up but figured it was best just to get it said. "Jonah and I aren't seeing each other anymore. We broke up some time ago."

"Oh dear, I'm sorry to hear that. I never got the chance to meet him, but from the things Edna said in her letters, he seemed like a nice man."

"He is, but with the way things are with Grandma right now, I thought it best if Jonah and I went our separate ways." Elaine lifted her hands and let them fall to her sides. "Anyhow, I'm not sure what we felt for each other was strong enough to continue with our relationship."

"That's a shame, but I'm sure you'll find someone else when the time is right."

Elaine made no comment because there really was no point in talking about this anymore. Besides, she wanted to get Grandma's sister and brothers' things taken upstairs to their rooms so they could get settled in.

Soon other family members from Iowa arrived, including Grandma's niece, Doris, and her six-year-old twins, Mary and Melinda. Grandma said she had no memory of the girls at all, but then, she'd only seen them once, a few weeks after they were born.

After everyone greeted Grandma, they gathered in the living room, where Grandma proceeded to open her gifts. While she did that, Melinda took out a tablet and began drawing Grandma's picture.

Grandma had just opened her sister's gift, a small bird feeder, when she stopped what she was doing, looked at Melinda, and said, "Are you cooking me?"

"Cooking you?" The girl's eyes widened. "What are you talkin' about, Aunt Edna?"

Embarrassed for Grandma, Elaine quickly said, "Melinda is drawing your picture, Grandma."

Grandma glanced around, as though expecting something to happen, or maybe someone to say something. Then she grinned at Elaine and said, "I can explain more when they get here. They said they weren't ready?"

"Who else is coming, and what is it they're not ready for, Edna?" Aunt Margaret asked.

Grandma snickered. Then she leaned back against the sofa cushions and closed her eyes. "I'm tired."

Oh dear, Elaine thought. *If this is how the evening is going to be, I wish I'd never invited any of these people.*

CHAPTER 37

By the time Elaine went to her room to get ready for bed, she was exhausted. Not only did they have a house full of relatives sleeping in the bedrooms upstairs, but she'd had a hard time getting Grandma settled into her room downstairs. While it had been good for Grandma to connect with her family from Iowa, Elaine had spent most of the evening reminding Grandma who everyone was or trying to make light of the strange things Grandma said. One minute she'd be talking to her sister, Margaret, about old times, and the next minute she'd confuse her with someone else.

At one point, Grandma thought she was at Aunt Margaret's house and had even complimented her sister on how nice everything was. She'd asked Aunt Margaret to show her around the place, until Elaine stepped in and said, "Maybe later."

Poor Aunt Margaret had teared up more than once. Grandma's brothers hadn't shown quite so much emotion, but it had been obvious from their furrowed brows and exchanged glances that they were concerned about their sister's declining memory.

To make the evening more tense, Grandma had taken not one, but two pieces of chocolate cake when Elaine wasn't looking, in addition to a piece of no-sugar apple pie. It was so difficult to stabilize Grandma's blood sugar when she kept sneaking sweets, and that, too, caused Elaine to worry about the days ahead and how she would manage Grandma's declining health on her own. At times, Elaine couldn't help wondering, *Would it really hurt if once in a while I let Grandma enjoy some sweets? Why not let her take pleasure in what little time she has left doing something as simple as eating a piece of cake?*

Elaine stood at her bedroom window staring out at the bright, full moon. She didn't know what was more difficult: watching Grandma's condition deteriorate, or seeing others react when they tried to communicate with her.

A knot formed in Elaine's stomach. *I never expected something like this would happen to my dear, sweet grandma. Growing up, I could always count on her. Now, she needs me, even if she doesn't realize it.*

Focusing again on the October moon, Elaine marveled at how it was so bright that it lit everything up, casting shadows on the ground. She glanced toward the barn and caught sight of something moving across the yard. After watching a few seconds, she realized that a raccoon was heading to the area where a bird feeder hung. She assumed the raccoon was looking for sunflower seeds that had dropped to the ground from the birds feeding all day. Slowly, it searched the grass, picking its way as it went along. What a treat it was to observe something so ordinary and simple.

Moving away from the window, Elaine removed her head covering and loosened her hair. After brushing it thoroughly, she undressed and slipped into her nightgown. Then, turning off the gas lamp, she slipped into bed. The freshly laundered sheets smelled clean and felt cool against her skin. Soon she'd be adding another blanket to the bed as cold weather swept across their state.

She closed her eyes and conjured up a mental picture of Grandma tucking her in, just as she'd done when Elaine was a girl. "Snug as a bug in a rug," Grandma would say. *Oh, those were such special days.*

Elaine smiled, remembering fondly how it had felt to be secure and warm in her bed and to be loved that much by her grandparents. *Oh Grandpa, I miss you so much, but I'm glad you're not here to see Grandma the way she is now.* It would have been especially hard on Grandpa, seeing Grandma struggling with dementia and not being able to do anything to stop it.

Tears seeped out from under Elaine's lashes and dribbled down her cheeks. She loved Grandma so much and would do anything for her, but at times she resented the sacrifices she'd been forced to make in order to act as Grandma's caregiver. Some days, she felt depleted, physically and mentally. Guilt consumed her whenever bitterness crept in. She often had to remind herself of all the sacrifices Grandma and Grandpa had made for her over the years.

As she readjusted her covers and plumped up her pillow, Elaine's thoughts turned to Jonah. If not for Grandma's diagnosis of dementia, she and Jonah might be married by now—or at least planning a spring wedding. He would have been at Grandma's birthday party tonight, too, and everything would have seemed normal and right.

At awkward moments, like tonight when Aunt Margaret had asked if Elaine was still seeing Jonah, she wondered if her decision to break things off with him had been the right thing to do. Aunt Margaret brought the subject up again later, and Elaine was surprised that her aunt thought she'd been a little hasty in making such a decision.

In hindsight, Elaine couldn't deny that it would be comforting to have Jonah's support through all of this, but taking care of Grandma was Elaine's duty, not his. If they were married, they'd most likely have children, and that would have stretched Elaine's responsibilities even further. No, Jonah deserved to be happy with someone else, and Elaine loved him enough to make that sacrifice and give Jonah his freedom—although guilt still plagued her for lying about her feelings for him. It was wrong to be deceitful, but she simply saw no other way. If she had admitted to Jonah that she loved him, he'd probably still be coming around and may have insisted they get married so he could share in the responsibility of Grandma's care.

Maybe I should have considered it; God does intend for couples to see each other through the tough times. And when you get married, you never know what the future holds. Elaine clutched the edge of her quilt. *Lord, did I mess up? If I did, well, it's too late now. Jonah's moved on with his life, and I have responsibilities.*

But the fact that Jonah and Sara might get more serious was difficult to accept. What if they did get married? How would Elaine be able to face them at church or anywhere else she might see them? She would have to put on a happy face and pretend everything was okay and as it should be.

"I'll never get married," Elaine whispered, turning her head into the pillow as more tears came, "but I'll always love Jonah."

Sara's throat constricted as she stood at the foot of Mark's crib, watching her son suck his thumb as he slept contently, with slow, even breathing.In his other hand, he clutched the wooden horse Jonah had crafted.

The moon shone into the bedroom, illuminating the crib and Sara's precious son. He looked so angelic and peaceful. *If only the light could protect my boy. Of course, only God can do that.*

Sara had prayed often throughout this day, hoping for clear direction on whether she should move home with her folks or stay in Arthur, close to Harley's family—and to Jonah. Her parents, as well as Harley's, still had children living at home, and neither couple needed the burden of caring for her and Mark. Yet Sara didn't see how she could manage on her own if her MS symptoms increased. It was a no-win situation, and she dreaded having to tell her family.

Moving slowly across the room toward her own bed, Sara decided not to say anything just yet. She needed more time to pray about things and wrap her mind around the whole situation. Until a clear answer came, she would leave things as they were. And while waiting for God's will to be revealed to her, she would make a concentrated effort to do all the things the doctor had mentioned and hope that her symptoms improved.

A pounding on her bedroom door roused Elaine from a deep sleep. It was dark in her room, and except for the moon's brightness, no other light shone in from the window. Rolling over, she fumbled for her flashlight, switched it on, and shined it at the clock on her nightstand. It was two o'clock, and that meant whoever was at her door must have an urgent need.

"I'm coming," she called, crawling out of bed and slipping into her robe.

When Elaine opened the door, she was surprised to see Grandma standing in the hall, fully dressed and holding a flashlight.

"It's time to go, and my driver's not here." Grandma's shrill voice was a bit too loud.

Elaine put her finger to her lips. "Time to go where?" she whispered, hoping Grandma's knocking hadn't wakened anyone upstairs.

"I have an appointment with the doctor, and if I don't leave now, I'm gonna be late."

Elaine shook her head. "No, Grandma. It's two o'clock in the morning, and you don't have a doctor's appointment till next week." She slipped her arm around Grandma's waist. "I'll walk you back to your room so you can get undressed and back into bed."

Grandma folded her arms and refused to budge. "I am not going to bed, and you can't make me!"

With a sigh of exasperation, Elaine motioned Grandma into her own room. The last thing she needed was for Grandma to wake everyone upstairs and perhaps create a scene.

Grandma balked at first, but then she finally relented and stepped into Elaine's bedroom. "If my driver isn't here in the next five minutes, I'm gonna hitch up my horse and buggy and go see the doctor myself."

Please, Lord, Elaine prayed. *Help me get through to her.*

Talking softly in an effort to calm Grandma, Elaine shined her flashlight on the clock near her bed. "See, there? It's only two o'clock, so it's way too early to be up. And just look out the window. It's still dark outside."

Grandma tapped her foot as she stared at the clock and then toward the window, as though trying to decide if Elaine was telling the truth. "What about the doctor? Won't he be waiting? Looks like daylight out there to me."

"No, Grandma. It's only the full moon making it look so bright. Your appointment isn't until next week, and it's in the afternoon, not the middle of the night."

Grandma stood silently for several seconds. Then she pointed to Elaine's bed. "Can I sleep here?"

At first Elaine was going to tell Grandma that she'd be more comfortable in her own bed, but she didn't want to provoke her. Besides, if Grandma slept here for the rest of the night, Elaine could keep an eye on her, and there'd be less chance of Grandma sneaking outside to the barn and buggy shed.

"Sure, you can sleep in my room." Elaine gently patted Grandma's arm. "Oh, and since you're here, there's something special I want to give you. Now, close your eyes and hold out your hands."

As Grandma sat on the edge of the bed with her eyes shut and hands extended, Elaine moved to her dresser, where she'd set the rock she had painted for Grandma yesterday morning. She had planned to give it as a birthday present, but it wasn't dry by the time Grandma had opened her other gifts. The rock was oblong and actually stood on end. Elaine had painted the rock to look like a parakeet, using the same color green that Millie had been. "Happy birthday, Grandma," she said, placing the rock in Grandma's outstretched hands.

Grandma opened her eyes and squealed, "Millie! You've come home!"

Elaine was tempted to explain that it wasn't really Millie but decided it would be better to let Grandma think whatever she wanted.

"Why don't you take off your dress so it doesn't get wrinkled, and then you can sleep in your underskirt?"

With a brief nod, Grandma did as she was told. A few minutes later, holding Millie in one hand, she was tucked under the covers in Elaine's bed. With a peaceful smile on her face, Grandma fell asleep soon after.

"Thank you, heavenly Father," Elaine whispered as she slipped under the covers on the other side of Grandma.

A frightening thought occurred to her. *What if Grandma had actually gone outside, hitched her horse to the buggy, and headed down the road? In her state of confusion, she'd surely have gotten lost.*

Elaine clutched the edge of her quilt. *I need to do something to prevent that from happening. I'm just not sure what.*

CHAPTER 38

Elaine smiled as she watched the birds flit from feeder to feeder as though in search of the best seeds. She'd just finished filling each of the bird feeders and had left Grandma in the house, where she'd been relaxing in the living room with a magazine. Elaine wasn't sure if Grandma had actually been reading or just looking at the pictures, but at least she seemed content. So far today, she hadn't accused Elaine of taking or hiding any of her things.

Deciding to take a few extra minutes to enjoy the fresh fall air, Elaine stood in the yard and took it all in. Fallen leaves lay scattered about, and she caught sight of a squirrel taking its share of the seeds that had dropped on the ground under one of the feeders.

Suddenly, the loft doors of the barn opened. Grandma, sitting in the hay on the second story, smiled down at Elaine in the yard.

"Look at me!" Grandma called, waving her hands. "I'm a bird, high up in a nest."

Elaine's heart pounded. "Grandma, stay right there. Don't move!" She ran into the barn and hurried up the ladder to the loft. "What are you doing up here?" she asked, taking a seat beside Grandma.

"I was looking at Millie and saw that she couldn't fly, so I brought her up here to the loft."

It was then that she noticed Grandma was holding the parakeet rock Elaine had painted for her. She cringed. Even though Grandma had never mentioned that her parakeet had flown out of the house, never to return, here she was now, convinced that the parakeet on the rock was real. If that wasn't bad enough, poor Grandma thought the bird would be able to fly. *Should I tell her that Millie got attacked by one of the cats? No, that would probably upset her too much.*

She patted Grandma's hand ever so gently. "You know, sitting up here like this brings back memories from a time long ago when I used to climb into the loft and pretend I was a bird."

Grandma sat without saying a word. Then she looked over at Elaine and grinned. "I remember when you did that. Used to scare me half to death seeing you way up so high, but your grandpa said I shouldn't worry so much and that every child had the right to pretend and explore." She chuckled. "Of course, you didn't know it, but he kept a close watch to make sure you were safe."

Elaine smiled. "And I remember how he'd sometimes climb the ladder and sit beside me. We'd watch the birds in the yard below as they flew back and forth between the trees."

They sat quietly for a while, and then Elaine managed to take the rock from Grandma and coax her back down the ladder, coming down each rung behind her. When they reached the bottom, Elaine paused to thank God for keeping Grandma safe and for giving them those few moments when Grandma could remember a special time from the past. Elaine could only hope there would be more days like this. Oh, how she longed for things to be as they once were, with her and Grandma simply enjoying each other's company, without any worries about the horrible disease that was taking Grandma from her.

Sara fiddled with the ties on her head covering as she waited for Jonah to arrive. He'd invited her and Mark to go out for supper with him again, but Mark had the tail end of a cold, so Sara thought it would be better to fix supper here, rather than taking her son out on this chilly November evening. Besides, it would be easier to talk to Jonah here than in a restaurant, where others might hear what she had to say.

It had been two weeks since Sara received her MS diagnosis, and she'd finally made a decision. She was going to put her house up for sale and move home to live with her folks. It had been a difficult decision, but she felt it was the best thing for both her and Mark. She really had little choice. Sara had also decided not to do anything with the barn, although she had asked some of the men from her district to haul the remains of it away. Maybe whoever bought her place could build a barn of his choosing. She planned to go to her folks' for Thanksgiving, at which time she would tell them about her MS and ask if she and Mark could move in with them.

Sara went to check on the roast she had cooking in the oven. The potatoes and carrots surrounding the meat poked tender, and the thermometer showed that the roast was done. She turned down the temperature, closed the oven door, and went to the counter to slice some pickled beets. In addition to the meat and vegetables, she'd also made coleslaw, mixing mayonnaise and vinegar into the shredded cabbage, just like her mother always did. Some people preferred a sweeter-tasting coleslaw, to which a bit of sugar had been added, but she'd always liked it on the tangy side. She hoped Jonah would enjoy it that way, too.

Certain that everything was ready to be put on the table once Jonah arrived, Sara went to the living room to check on Mark. She'd left him happily sitting on the floor with the wooden horse Jonah had made.

When Sara entered the room, Mark looked up at her and grinned. "*Scheme gaul*," he said, pointing to the horse that had been painted brown with a white patch on its head.

Sara nodded. "Jah, Mark. It's a pretty horse."

Jonah had already won her son's heart. Not just with the little gifts he often brought Mark, but with the attention and quality time he gave the boy. That would be something she'd be taking from Mark if she moved back with her parents, although she was sure that Dad, busy as he was, would show Mark some attention. Still, it wouldn't be the same as time spent with Jonah, for Mark had bonded with him in a special way. *It's almost like how Mark would have been with his dad if he were still alive.* Sara reached out to touch her son's soft cheeks. Remembering how tender the scene had been when Jonah had tucked Mark into bed one night, she grieved to realize there would never be a man in Mark's life whom he could call *Daadi*.

❧

"Come on now, Sassy, let's get a move on it," Jonah called to his horse, snapping the reins. "I'm gettin' hungry, and I don't want to be late for supper."

Jonah had to admit it was more than appeasing his hunger that made him anxious to get to Sara's house this evening. He looked forward to visiting with Sara again and, most of all, spending time with Mark. It was hard not to spoil the little guy, but Jonah figured he could get away with it, since he wasn't the boy's father.

But I wish I was, Jonah admitted to himself as he approached Sara's driveway. *I'd give anything to have a son like Mark—to love and cherish, and to have carry on my name.* Once again, his thoughts turned to Elaine. *If only she hadn't shut me out. I really believed she was the woman for me. Could I have been that wrong?*

Pulling up to the hitching rack, Jonah stepped out of his buggy and secured his horse. *I need to quit thinking about Elaine and enjoy this evening with Sara and Mark.*

Stepping onto the porch, he knocked on the door, glancing over at the burned-out barn and wondering if Sara ever planned to see about having a new one built. It seemed odd that she'd let it go this long, but perhaps she had her reasons.

Sara answered the door, wearing a dark blue dress with matching apron and cape. She smiled, but there was no sparkle in her eyes.

"Is everything all right?" Jonah asked, feeling concern. "You look mied."

She released a ragged sigh and pushed a wayward lock of hair back under her head covering. "I guess I am a bit tired tonight."

"If having me here for supper is too much, then I can come some other time," he was quick to say.

Sara shook her head. "I'm not that tired. Besides, I made too much food for me and Mark to eat by ourselves. And Mark would be very disappointed if he didn't get to see you this evening. I told him you were coming, and he's been saying your name over and over all day." Sara laughed. "Onah. That's what he says instead of Jonah."

Jonah grinned as he walked into the house. "For a little guy who's not even three yet, even saying 'Onah' seems pretty smart to me. A lot of kinner his age don't say near as many words as Mark does already."

"That's true. He can be quite the little chatterbox at times." Sara motioned to the living room. "Mark's in there, if you'd like to keep him entertained while I put supper on the dining-room table."

"Is there anything I can do to help?" Jonah asked.

Sara shook her head once more. "I think I can manage on my own, but danki for asking."

"Okay. Call me if you need anything, though."

When Jonah entered the living room, he found Mark sitting on a braided rug in the middle of the floor with some wooden blocks, which he'd placed in a large square. The wooden horse Jonah had given him was inside the square. As soon as Mark saw Jonah, he held out his hands and shouted, "Onah!"

Jonah knelt on the floor beside Mark, and the little boy crawled right into his lap. "*Der gaul is darichgange.*"

"Jah, that's right," Jonah said, laughing. "The horse ran away." Then he picked up the horse and made it prance around the wooden-block corral, smiling as Mark laughed and clapped his hands.

A short time later, Sara entered the room and announced that supper was ready. Jonah stood and, lifting Mark onto his shoulders, followed Sara into the dining room.

"Yum. . .something sure smells good in here." Jonah surveyed the food she had set on the table before placing Mark in his high chair. "Makes my mouth water just looking at all that food."

"Well, I hope it tastes as good as it looks." Sara motioned for Jonah to take his seat. Then they bowed their heads for silent prayer. When the prayer was over, Sara passed the platter of roast beef to Jonah, followed by the potatoes, carrots, and other items she'd set on the table. Then she gave Mark what she knew he would eat.

"Aren't you going to eat anything?" Jonah asked, gesturing to Sara's empty plate.

Her cheeks colored. "Oh, jah, of course."

"This is a great meal, Sara. The meat is so tender, and I like how you cooked the vegetables with the beef. That's how my mamm's always made it, too."

"Danki, Jonah." Sara's cheeks darkened further.

After Sara dished up some food for herself, they ate their meal and visited. Every once in a while, Mark looked over at Jonah and said, "Onah."

Jonah had to admit it felt pretty good sitting here with Sara and Mark, enjoying some of her delicious cooking. It almost seemed as if they were a family. *But of course,* he reminded himself, *Sara's not my wife and Mark's not my son.*

"I've been wondering what you plan to do about your barn," Jonah said. "Are you going to have a barn-raising before winter sets in, or wait till spring?"

"I won't be putting up a new barn," Sara said with a shake of her head. "You may have noticed when you arrived that I had the remains of the old barn hauled away."

"What about your horse? Won't she need a warm, dry place this winter?"

"She's doing well in a three-sided lean-to, so I think she'll be fine for now."

"Oh, I see." Jonah could hardly believe that Sara wouldn't want a new barn to replace the one that had been burned or provide a warmer place for her horse, but it was her decision.

They visited about other things, and by the time they'd finished dinner and enjoyed apple pie and coffee for dessert, Jonah was full to the point of being drowsy. In an effort to keep awake, he pushed away from the table and began clearing the dishes.

"You don't have to do that." Sara shook her head. "Why don't you and Mark go back to the living room, and I'll do the dishes?"

"I wouldn't hear of it," Jonah said. "You worked hard fixing this meal, and the least I can do is help with the dishes."

"Okay, if you insist. I'll wash, and you can dry."

Sara took Mark out of his high chair, and he followed them into the kitchen. While they did the dishes, Mark sat on a throw rug nearby, playing with his wooden horse. Every once in a while, the child would call out, "Onah!"

Jonah smiled and hollered in reply, "Mark!"

"He sure has taken a liking to you," Sara said, placing a few clean plates into the dish drainer for Jonah to dry.

"The feeling's mutual." Jonah smiled. "I'm hoping we can enjoy a lot more times like this. Maybe during the holidays, if we get some good snow on the ground, I'll get out my sleigh and take you and Mark for a ride. Does that sound like fun to you, Sara?"

She lifted her hand from the soapy water and opened her mouth as if to comment, but then, almost as though she was moving in slow motion, she closed her mouth and began scrubbing the roasting pan.

"Sara, what's wrong? Did I say something I shouldn't have?" Jonah questioned.

She drew in a quick breath. "It's not that. It's just that. . .well, Mark and I won't be here for the holidays."

"Oh, I see. Are you planning to go home to spend Thanksgiving and Christmas with your family?"

Sara nodded but avoided making eye contact with him. "The truth is, Mark and I will be moving to Indiana permanently—as soon as I can find a buyer for my house."

Jonah's mouth dropped open. "Really? I had no idea you were planning to move. Do you mind if I ask what caused you to make that decision?" Jonah felt like he'd been kicked in the stomach by an unruly horse. He would miss Sara, and the idea of never seeing little Mark again was the worst part of all.

"Why would you do that, Sara?" he asked again. "I thought you liked living here in Illinois."

Still refusing to meet his gaze, she said in a shaky voice, "I—I'm not well, Jonah. I recently found out that I have MS."

Jonah silently let what she'd said sink into his brain, while searching for the right words in response. Once he'd collected his thoughts, he looked at her and said, "I'm sorry to hear that, Sara. I didn't have an inkling that you were ill."

"Neither did I." Sara continued to scrub at the pan. "Well, I knew there might be something wrong because at certain times I've had some strange symptoms. Although some days I feel perfectly fine, at other times I'm dizzy, exhausted, or my arms and legs tingle and won't work as they should." She paused and looked down at her son. "If my disease progresses, I may not be able to take care of myself as I should, much less do everything I need to for Mark. So moving home with my parents is the only logical solution."

"I see." Jonah dried a few more dishes as he mulled things over. "You know, you really wouldn't have to move if you didn't want to, Sara."

"Jah, I do. Didn't you hear what I just said about the possibility of me not being able to take care of myself and Mark?"

He gave a slow nod. "I heard, and I understand why you feel the need to move, but. . ." Jonah swiped his tongue over his lips and swallowed a couple of times. "You could marry me and stay right here."

Sara's eyes widened. "Oh, Jonah, it's nice of you to make such an offer, but I know you're not in love with me, and—"

Jonah touched his fingers gently to her lips. "I care for you and Mark, and I wouldn't have suggested that you marry me if I didn't mean it, Sara. Will you at least consider becoming my wife?"

Sara's eyes filled with tears. "I don't think something like this should be entered into lightly, Jonah. Why don't we both take some time to think and pray about the matter?"

"All right, then how about this: for the next seven days, you can pray about the matter, and then a week from today I'll come back here, and you can give me your answer. How's that sound?"

"I—I suppose that would be okay, but you need to be praying about it, too."

"Jah, I sure will." Jonah glanced down at Mark, and a lump formed in his throat. *But I've already made up my mind.*

CHAPTER 39

As Elaine sat in church next to Grandma the following Sunday, she was pleased to see that Grandma was singing along with everyone else. Many times during the last month, Grandma had sat through church with a blank expression. Today was obviously a good day for her, and for that Elaine felt relief. To add to her joy, just a few minutes ago, Grandma had looked over at her and smiled sweetly. It was the kind of smile Elaine remembered from her childhood, when Grandma would give Elaine a quick nod and a pleasant smile, letting her know that she was loved.

She knew Grandma still loved her, but there were days, such as yesterday, when Grandma's frustration with not being able to remember something had caused her to be irritable and out of sorts.

When Grandma got up this morning, she'd put her everyday dress on over her Sunday dress and come into the kitchen saying she was ready for church. Elaine had thought this would turn out to be a difficult day, but to her surprise, Grandma had agreeably taken off her regular dress when Elaine asked her to. She'd also helped do the breakfast dishes and waited patiently in the buggy while Elaine brought her horse out of the barn. On the trip to church, Grandma had actually carried on a fairly normal conversation with Elaine, although she had mentioned Grandpa a few times, referring to him as though he were still alive. Grandma hadn't mentioned Millie needing to fly again, but Elaine often saw her holding and talking to the rock parakeet. Apparently, Grandma truly believed that the rock was Millie. Well, if it made Grandma happy to believe that, then Elaine wouldn't tell her otherwise. It was easier just to let Grandma think whatever she wanted in that regard.

I'm thankful for the good days, Elaine thought, returning Grandma's smile. *And as for the not-so-good days, I'll just keep asking God for more patience.*

Pulling her gaze away from Grandma, Elaine glanced at the men's side of the room and caught sight of Jonah. He sat straight and tall on his bench, looking attentively at their song leader. Unexpectedly, he glanced Elaine's way, and she quickly averted his gaze, fearful that her true feelings for him might show.

Always on her guard whenever Jonah was around, Elaine had to make sure he never found out that she hadn't stopped loving him.

Jonah didn't know who he was the most worried about this morning—Sara, who hadn't come to church with Mark, or Elaine, who appeared to be tired and strained. He planned to head over to Sara's house to check on her as soon as church was over, even skipping the noon meal, but he didn't know what he could do about Elaine's situation, for she'd made it clear that she didn't want his help or attention. Still, he couldn't get rid of the feeling of wanting to protect Elaine.

Even yet, Jonah had a hard time accepting the fact that Elaine had never loved him, but if she'd told one of her best friends that, it must be true. Elaine's decision was one of the reasons he'd begun courting Sara—that and his connection with Sara's son. Then three nights ago when he'd learned of Sara's illness, Jonah knew what he had to do. By marrying Sara, he'd not only gain a wife, but he'd have the son he'd always wanted. *Sara needs a husband,* Jonah reminded himself. *And if she says yes to my proposal, I'm going to be the best husband and father I can possibly be.*

As soon as church was over, Jonah headed straight for his horse and buggy.

"Where are ya going?" Jean's husband, Nathan, called.

"Over to Sara Stutzman's to see why she wasn't in church today," Jonah said after Nathan caught up to him.

"Aren't you gonna stay long enough to eat?" Nathan questioned.

Jonah shook his head. "I had a big breakfast this morning, and I'm not all that hungry right now."

Nathan eyed Jonah curiously. "According to Jean, you've been seeing a lot of Sara lately."

Jonah nodded.

"Maybe it's none of my business, but are you two getting serious about each other?"

Jonah felt like telling Nathan that he was right, it was none of his business, but that would be rude. So he gave a simple one-word reply: "Jah."

Nathan blinked rapidly. "Wow, that was sure quick."

"What? My reply, or the fact that I haven't been courting Sara very long?"

"Both." Nathan drew his fingers through the ends of his beard. "You're not thinking of marrying her already, I hope."

Jonah's jaw clenched. He didn't like the way his brother-in-law was giving him the third degree. "Would there be anything wrong with it if I was?"

Nathan shrugged. "Well, no, I guess not, but as you said, you haven't been courting her very long."

"That's true, but when a man knows what he wants, why should he have to wait?" Jonah grabbed Sassy's rope and led the horse over to his buggy.

Nathan followed. "When are you planning to ask her to marry you?"

"I already have. Just waitin' for Sara's answer." Jonah saw no purpose at this point in telling Nathan about Sara's MS. He figured Nathan might already know, since his wife was Sara's best friend. But if that was the case, why hadn't he mentioned it?

Nathan placed his hand on Jonah's arm. "Uh, listen, before you go, there's one thing more I'd like to say."

"What's that?"

"If you decide to marry Sara, you'll have Jean's and my blessing, but I think you oughta give it a little more time—maybe wait till spring to get married."

Jonah rolled his shoulders, trying to release some of the tension he felt. "I appreciate your advice, but Sara hasn't said yes yet, and if she does, then I doubt we'll wait till spring." With that, Jonah finished hitching his horse, said good-bye to Nathan, and climbed into the buggy. As he rode away, he pondered Nathan's words. Had he reacted too soon where Sara was concerned? Should he have thought it through a bit more before asking her to marry him? Well, it was too late for that. He wouldn't feel right about un-asking her now, and if she said yes to his proposal, then he would take that as a sign from God that he'd done the right thing. And if she said no, he would let her move back to Indiana with his blessing.

Curling up on one end of the sofa, with her sleeping son on the other end, Sara yawned and closed her eyes. In addition to the fact that she felt more tired than usual today, Mark's cold seemed to have gotten worse than it had been earlier in the week. So Sara decided it would be best for them to stay home from church and rest. Since the doctor had said she needed plenty of rest, she felt her decision was justified.

As Sara lay there, covered with the quilt she was sharing with Mark, she thought about Jonah and his marriage proposal. There was no doubt that he'd make a good husband and father, but was she ready to marry again and start a new life with another man? Did she care enough for Jonah to become his wife? Would it be fair for him to be faced with the challenges of her illness?

I need to make a decision soon, she told herself. *Jonah will be coming by in a few days, and he'll expect an answer.*

Sara had been praying about this ever since Jonah had asked her to marry him, yet she hadn't received an answer from God. If she went home to live with her folks, she would place a burden on them. But wouldn't becoming Jonah's wife be a burden for him, too?

Why can't life be simple? Why's it so hard to know what God wants me to do? she wondered. Ever since Harley's death, it seemed like she had been faced with one challenge after the next. Some days, when she didn't think she had the strength to go on, she would turn to the Bible and find comfort in God's Word. *That's what I should do right now.*

Sara slipped out from under the quilt, being careful not to disturb Mark, and tiptoed across the room to where she kept her Bible on the end table near the rocking chair. Taking a seat, she opened the Bible to the book of James and read chapter 1, verse 5 out loud. "If any of you lack wisdom, let him ask of God, that giveth to all men liberally, and upbraideth not; and it shall be given him."

She bowed her head and closed her eyes. *I'm asking You, Lord, for wisdom in deciding what to do about Jonah's proposal. If I'm supposed to say yes, then please give me a sign.*

Sara had just finished her prayer when she heard the *clip-clop* of horse hooves coming up her driveway. Figuring it was probably Harley's parents stopping by to check on her, Sara rose from her chair and went to the door. When she opened it, she was surprised to see Jonah securing his horse to the hitching rack.

"Hi, Sara. Are you okay?" Jonah asked when he joined her on the porch. "When I realized you weren't at church, I became worried about you."

Sara smiled. "It was nice of you to come by, Jonah. I'm more tired than usual today, and Mark's cold seems to have gotten worse, so I decided it would be best if we stayed home and rested today."

"That makes good sense." Jonah moved closer to Sara. "Is there anything I can do for you—maybe spend some time with Mark so you can rest?"

"It's kind of you to offer, but Mark's sleeping right now."

"Oh, I see."

Sara couldn't help but notice the look of disappointment in Jonah's dark eyes. He'd obviously been hoping to enjoy her son's company for a while, and she couldn't blame him for that. Mark was such a sweet boy, and Sara relished every moment she had with him.

"Sure is chilly out today," Jonah said when a harsh wind blew under the porch eaves. "Bet it won't be long till we see our first snowfall. Could even happen before Thanksgiving."

Sara nodded as Jonah briskly rubbed his arms. Thinking Jonah might like to get in out of the cold for a bit, she invited him inside for a cup of coffee.

"That sounds real good," Jonah said, following Sara into the house.

She was about to suggest that they go to the kitchen for coffee, when Mark woke up. Seeing Jonah, he bounded off the sofa and darted into the utility room, where Sara and Jonah stood, shouting, "Onah! Onah!"

Jonah bent down and scooped the boy into his arms. "Hey, little buddy, it's sure good to see you."

"Don't get too close or you might catch his cold," Sara cautioned, handing Jonah a tissue.

Jonah shook his head as he wiped Mark's nose. "Aw, I'm not worried about that. I've never been one to catch many colds. Even if I did, it'd be worth it just to spend some time with this special boy."

Sara's heart nearly melted as she watched the tender way Jonah looked at Mark. And her son looked equally enchanted with Jonah as he clasped his hands around Jonah's neck and held on tight. Drowsy from just waking up, Mark laid his head on Jonah's shoulder and closed his eyes, while Jonah gently rubbed Mark's back. Suddenly, as Sara's heartbeat thudded in her chest, she felt as if she'd been given her answer.

"Jonah," she said, pausing to take in a quick breath. "I know we agreed that we'd both take a week to decide, but if you still want to marry me, then my answer is yes."

Jonah's face broke into a wide smile, and he reached for Sara's hand. "I still want to marry you, and the sooner the better."

CHAPTER 40

"I'm sorry to hear you have MS but glad you finally went to see the doctor," Leah said as she worked on Sara's feet. "Most of the symptoms you were having weren't responding to reflexology, but I think my treatments should at least help you relax."

Sara nodded. "I always feel calmer after you've worked on my feet, and according to the doctor, feeling less stressed can help decrease the symptoms of MS."

"So where is that cute little boy of yours today?" Leah questioned.

"I left him with my mother-in-law. She'll be keeping him most of the day so I can get some shopping done after I leave here."

"It's nice that Betty and Herschel live close to you and are willing to help out with Mark." Leah pressed on an area of Sara's foot that appeared to be inflamed.

Sara flinched.

"Sorry if that hurts."

"It's okay. You're just doing your job."

As Leah continued to massage and pressure-point Sara's feet, they talked about the upcoming holidays.

"Will your folks be coming here for Thanksgiving or Christmas?" Leah asked.

"I was planning to go there for both holidays, but since Jonah and I are planning to be married the first week of December, they'll probably come here for Thanksgiving and then stay on for the wedding."

Leah's eyes widened. "You're getting married?"

"Jah. I thought you might have heard." Sara gave a nervous laugh. "You know how quick news travels in our community."

"No, I hadn't heard, and I'll admit, I am a bit surprised, since he hasn't been courting you very long."

Sara's cheeks darkened with a pinkish blush. "That's true, but we've known each other for some time—since Jonah moved here and he and Harley became friends."

Leah wasn't quite sure how to respond. Sara and Jonah may have known each other for a reasonable amount of time, but most of that had been while Sara was married to Harley and Jonah was courting Elaine. While Jonah and Harley had been friends, it wouldn't have been possible for Jonah and Sara to establish a close relationship—at least not in a romantic sort of way. The fact that they hadn't been courting very long concerned Leah. She'd always felt that a long courtship was the best for most couples, in order to know if they were truly compatible. Leah would certainly never marry a man unless they'd been seriously courting for a while.

"Jonah's a wonderful man, and my son adores him," Sara went on to say.

Leah slowly nodded. "I hope you and Jonah will be happy, and I wish you all of God's best." She reached for the bottle of massage lotion and poured some into her hand. *I wonder if Elaine knows about this. If so, what does she think?*

"It's nice to see you," Elaine said when Priscilla pedaled her bike into the yard on Wednesday of the following week.

Priscilla smiled. "It's good to see you, too. I was out checking some of the stores that sell our jams to see if they're running low and decided to come by here before I went home." Priscilla parked her bike and moved toward the line where Elaine was hanging clothes. "Um. . .there's something I think you need to know."

Holding a clothespin in her mouth, Elaine tipped her head. "What's that?"

"I was talking with Leah the other day, and she said Jonah's asked Sara to be his wife and they're planning to get married the first week of December.

Elaine's whole body trembled, and she let the clothespin fall to the ground. She'd suspected this could happen but hadn't thought it would be so soon. Had Jonah gotten over her so quickly?

Priscilla slipped her arm around Elaine. "Are you okay?"

"It just took me by surprise." Elaine picked up the clothespin, reached into the basket, and clipped a towel on the line. She hoped Priscilla wouldn't notice how badly her hands were shaking.

"You love him, don't you?"

"It doesn't matter how I feel about Jonah. He's made his choice, and there's nothing I can do about it."

Priscilla stepped in front of Elaine, looking directly into her eyes. "Jah, there is, Elaine. You can go to Jonah right now and tell him you love him. If you did that, I'm sure he would break things off with Sara."

Elaine shook her head vigorously. "I can't, and I won't say anything to Jonah about this. My responsibility to Grandma hasn't changed, and if Jonah's asked Sara to marry him, then he must be in love with her now." She shrugged. "Jonah deserves to be happy, and I would never think of coming between them. Besides, even if Jonah wasn't with Sara, with everything going on in my life, where would we find time for each other?"

Priscilla looked like she might say more on the subject, but she reached into the basket and picked up a towel instead. "You look tired, Elaine. Think I'll stay here awhile and help out."

"You don't need to do that. I'm fine." *But you're not fine,* Elaine's conscience told her. She wished she could just go to her room, have a good cry, and sleep the rest of the day. But she couldn't do that. Chores still waited, and in a little while, it would be time to test Grandma's blood sugar and fix them both some lunch.

"I'm sure you have plenty to do today, so I am staying to help," Priscilla insisted. "If I was in your situation, I'm sure you'd do the same thing for me."

Elaine couldn't argue with that. If either of her best friends had a need, she would do whatever she could to help out. "Okay," she said, appreciating Priscilla's offer. "You can help me finish the laundry, and after that, we'll have lunch."

Priscilla smiled. "That sounds good to me, and if you have the ingredients, I'll make some chicken noodle soup for our noon meal."

"Leah's mamm came by yesterday to sit with Grandma, and I

was able to do some shopping," Elaine replied. "The cupboards and refrigerator are full, so I'm sure I have everything you'll need to make soup."

"This soup is sure good," Elaine said after taking her first bite. "Don't you think so, Grandma?"

Grandma sat across the table from Elaine and Priscilla, her lips compressed as she stared at her bowl.

"Grandma, did you hear what I said?" Elaine asked, speaking a little louder.

As though coming out of a daze, Grandma looked over at Elaine and blinked. "Did you say something to me?"

"I said the soup is good and asked if you like it, too."

Grandma spooned some into her mouth and smacked her lips. "It tastes pretty good, but I think it needs more salse." She picked up the saltshaker and sprinkled some into her soup. Then she pointed at Priscilla. *"Sie is en gudi Koch."*

Elaine nodded. "You're right, Grandma, she is a good cook."

Elaine glanced at Priscilla to see her reaction, but Priscilla just smiled and handed her the basket of crackers.

They ate in silence for a while. Then Priscilla asked Elaine if she'd made any special plans for Thanksgiving.

Elaine shook her head. "Not really. I'll probably fix a small turkey, along with some potatoes and a vegetable for Grandma and me. Then we'll have some no-sugar apple pie for dessert."

"You two are welcome to join my family for Thanksgiving," Priscilla offered.

"That's nice of you, but I think it would be better if we stay here and have a quiet day by ourselves." Elaine would have enjoyed spending the holiday with Priscilla's family, but it would be too stressful taking Grandma there and not knowing what she might say or do that could be embarrassing.

"Hot eier nei haus viel geld gekoscht?" Grandma asked, looking at Priscilla again.

Elaine grimaced. She had no idea why Grandma had just asked

Priscilla if her new house cost a great deal of money.

"No, Edna," Priscilla said, shaking her head. "I don't have a new house. I'm still living at home with my parents."

Grandma's brows furrowed as she pursed her lips. "Really? I thought I'd come to visit you there."

"You've been to the home of Priscilla's parents many times," Elaine said, handing the crackers to Grandma.

Grandma nodded and set the basket down. "I know, and I. . ." She stopped talking and looked absently across the room.

"What were you going to say, Edna?" Priscilla prompted.

Grandma sighed. "I forgot."

"That's okay." Priscilla gave a nod of understanding. "Sometimes we all forget things."

Grandma picked up her bowl of soup and began slurping it, like a child might do. Elaine was on the verge of telling her to eat the soup with a spoon, but hearing a horse and buggy coming up the driveway, she went to see who it was.

Struggling with the desire to flee, Jonah secured his horse to the hitching rack and started for Edna's house. After praying about it, he'd decided to tell Elaine about his plans to marry Sara, before she heard it from someone else. But now that he was here, he'd begun to have second thoughts. Jonah hated to admit it, but somewhere deep inside, he hoped Elaine might say that she still loved him. Of course, that wasn't likely, but as close as he and Elaine had once been, he thought she had the right to know of his plans.

As Jonah walked across the yard, he noticed a bicycle sitting near the clothesline and figured Elaine or Edna might have company. Maybe this wasn't the best time for him to be here.

Jonah was about to return to his horse when Elaine stepped out of the house. "I thought that was you, Jonah. What brings you by here today?"

Jonah shuffled his feet and cleared his throat. "Well, first of all, I've been wondering how your grandma is doing. I haven't seen her for quite a while."

"Grandma's memory is failing fast," Elaine replied, refusing to look directly at him. "Her diabetes seems to be getting worse, too."

"I'm sorry to hear that." Jonah cleared his throat again. "I. . .uh. . . wanted to also tell you that I'm planning to. . ."

"Marry Sara?"

"Jah. How'd you know?"

Elaine pointed to the bicycle. "Priscilla's here, and she told me." She turned to face him directly. "I appreciate you coming by, and I wish you and Sara the best." Elaine didn't smile, but her expression was sincere.

Jonah kicked at a clump of dead grass with the toe of his boot. "Well, uh. . .guess I'd better head back to my shop. Tell Edna I'm praying for her." He started to go but turned back around. "I'm praying for you, too, Elaine."

"Danki. Good-bye, Jonah." Elaine opened the door and went back in the house.

When the door clicked shut behind her, Jonah headed back to his horse and buggy, full of mixed emotions. He was relieved that Elaine didn't object to him marrying Sara. But on the other hand, he was disappointed that she hadn't challenged his decision. It was confirmation that Elaine didn't love him. *Maybe this is how it's meant to be,* he told himself. *Sara and Mark need me, and apparently Elaine does not.*

CHAPTER 41

It was the week after Thanksgiving, and as Jonah sat at his kitchen table, his shoulders tightened. He remembered a March day much like this morning, when the weather had been nearly the same. Only back then his marriage to Meredith had been only hours away. A cold rain had fallen overnight, but by morning the clouds had broken up, with the promise of a clear blue sky for his wedding. So far, the weather was turning out to be the same today.

As Jonah continued to reflect on the day he and Meredith were to marry, a nervous flutter went through his stomach. What if something happened and Sara changed her mind? He'd been jilted before. Could it happen again?

"Come on, get ahold of yourself," Jonah murmured. The weather might be similar, but Jonah could think of no reason his marriage to Sara would not take place. The circumstances that led to the halt of his and Meredith's wedding were quite understandable after finding out that Luke was still alive. *So why am I worrying now?* Jonah took a deep breath to calm himself.

Jonah's parents had come for Thanksgiving, and Sara's mom and dad had done the same. They'd been staying at Sara's house and would be there until after the wedding. On Thanksgiving, Jonah and his parents had been invited to Sara's. Jonah had been relieved that from the moment the two sets of parents met, it was as if they'd known each other all their lives.

Sara had moved some of her and Mark's belongings into Jonah's place, but after the wedding, they'd get the rest of their things.

Getting up from the kitchen table, Jonah took one last look out the window. He was glad all seemed normal and no buggies were coming up his lane with distressing news. Sparkling drops of rain left over from last night's showers glistened like diamonds as the sun warmed the earth. Today was a new beginning, and it would be the start of the rest of his life with Sara and Mark. Jonah could hardly wait for that.

As Sara stood beside Jonah in front of their bishop, responding to their marriage vows, joy and hope flooded her soul. Even though she'd been married once before, her heart swelled with emotion and a sense of excitement over becoming Jonah's wife.

"Can you confess, brother, that you accept our sister as your wife, and that you will not leave her until death separates you?" Bishop Levi asked Jonah.

"Yes," Jonah replied with a nod.

"And do you believe that this is from the Lord and that you have come thus far because of your faith and prayers?"

Jonah, glancing quickly at Sara, answered, "Yes."

The bishop then turned to Sara. "Can you confess, sister, that you accept our brother as your husband, and that you will not leave him until death separates you?"

Barely able to speak around the constriction in her throat, Sara nodded and said, "Yes."

"And do you believe that this is from the Lord and that you have come this far because of your faith and prayers?"

"Yes," Sara replied, struggling not to let the tears slip out.

Bishop Levi looked at Jonah again. "Because you have confessed that you want to take Sara for your wife, do you promise to remain loyal to her and care for her if she may have any adversity, sickness, or weakness, as is appropriate for a Christian husband?"

"Yes, I will."

The bishop asked Sara the same question, and she also replied, "Yes, I will."

Then Bishop Levi took Sara's right hand and placed it in Jonah's right hand, putting his hands above and beneath their hands. "May the God of Abraham, the God of Isaac, and the God of Jacob be with you together and give His blessings upon you and be merciful to you. And may you hold out until the blessed end. This all in, and through, Jesus Christ. Amen."

At this point, Bishop Levi, Jonah, and Sara went down on their knees for prayer. When they rose, the bishop said, "Go forth now in the name of the Lord. You are now man and wife."

As Sara and Jonah returned to their seats, she almost felt like she was floating. It was as if all of her burdens had suddenly been removed. Her illness would still present challenges, but with Jonah at her side, Sara was sure she could get through them.

Glancing at the women's side of the room, she smiled when she saw that Mark had fallen asleep on Grandma Stutzman's lap. How grateful she was that Harley's parents hadn't objected to her marrying Jonah. They'd given Sara their blessing, as had Sara's parents, who were also here for the wedding. Jonah's sister and his parents were here, too, along with several others from Sara and Jonah's church district, including Leah. Because it was a smaller wedding than most, and since this was Sara's second marriage, she hadn't invited many people. But she didn't mind the smaller group. The people she was closest to were here, and that's what mattered.

As Jonah listened to the words of testimony from one of their ministers, he reflected on the vows he and Sara had just agreed upon. He was relieved that his silly fears from this morning had been for nothing. Jonah cared deeply for Sara and would take those vows seriously as they made a new life together. He would be a loving husband to Sara and a good father to her son. Hopefully someday, if the Lord allowed, they would be blessed with more children. It would be nice for Mark to have a little brother or sister to grow up with.

In the meantime, though, Jonah would enjoy his time with Mark, setting a godly example and creating pleasant memories for their family of three. At last, Jonah's desire to be a husband and father had come true, all in the same day, and he was convinced that God had brought him and Sara together. Christmas was just around the corner, and for the first time, he would enjoy the holiday with a wife and son.

After the other ministers in attendance spoke, Bishop Levi offered a few closing remarks. Then he asked the congregation to kneel in prayer. When that was over, everyone rose and sang a closing hymn. The church service was over, and the wedding meal could begin.

Elaine sat on the sofa in the living room, trying to focus on the article she'd been reading in *The Budget*, but she couldn't seem to keep her mind on it. All she could think about was that today Jonah and Sara were getting married and had probably become husband and wife by now. All those months during Elaine and Jonah's courting days, Elaine had thought she would be the woman who'd become Jonah's wife. Instead, Sara had ended up with the man Elaine loved. How ironic was that?

There's no point in having regrets or even thinking about this, Elaine reminded herself. *I'm doing what's best for Grandma, and Jonah's doing what is best for him. He obviously loves Sara and her little boy, and I need to set my regrets aside and try to be happy for them.*

She glanced at the clock, wondering if Grandma was still asleep. She'd gone to her room shortly after breakfast, saying she was tired and needed more sleep. But that was almost two hours ago. Surely she ought to be awake by now.

Elaine was about to check on Grandma when a knock sounded on the door. *That's strange,* she thought, rising from the sofa. *I didn't hear a horse and buggy pull in.*

Elaine opened the door and was surprised to see Priscilla on the porch. "What are you doing here?" she asked. "I thought you'd be at Jonah and Sara's wedding this morning."

"I decided not to go. Figured you would need me today."

Overcome with emotion, Elaine hugged Priscilla and invited her in.

"How's your grandma doing?" Priscilla asked after following Elaine to the living room.

"She's about the same. Still has a few good days, but mostly bad." Elaine frowned.

"I'm truly sorry, and I wish there was more I could do to help you through all this."

"It helps every time you or Leah drop by." Elaine motioned to the sofa. "Why don't you have a seat while I go check on Grandma? I won't be gone long. Just want to see if she's awake or needs anything."

"No problem. Should I make us some tea?"

"Jah, that'd be nice." Elaine hurried from the room, thankful for friends like Priscilla.

When Elaine entered Grandma's bedroom, her body tensed. Grandma wasn't in her bed. *That's strange. Could she have gone to the bathroom without me hearing her walk down the hall? Oh, I hope she didn't make her way outside somehow.*

Elaine was about to leave the room and investigate, but she decided to go to the window and look out first. As she started around the foot of Grandma's bed, she froze. There lay Grandma on the other side of her bed, stretched out on the floor.

Elaine dropped to her knees and reached out to touch Grandma's hand. It felt cold. Grandma's eyes were open, as if she were staring at the ceiling.

"Grandma! Can you hear me, Grandma?" Elaine shouted, vaguely hearing Priscilla's footsteps in the background, running toward the room.

No response.

Elaine's muscles jumped under her skin as she felt Grandma's wrist for a pulse. She found none. There was no movement in Grandma's chest or breath coming from her mouth. This seemed like a dream—a horrible nightmare.

Elaine's thoughts became fuzzy. She couldn't think—could barely breathe. It wasn't possible. Grandma couldn't be dead.

CHAPTER 42

Jonah stood at the side of the bed, looking down at his new bride, who'd taken sick with the flu during the night. "Is there anything I can bring you right now? Maybe some soda crackers or a cup of mint tea?" he asked, pulling the covers up to her chin.

Shivering, Sara shook her head. "I don't think I could keep it down, Jonah."

"Maybe later then." He felt her forehead and was thankful that it wasn't as hot as it had been earlier this morning.

Sara's eyes fluttered. "I'm sorry we couldn't go to Edna Schrock's funeral today."

"It's okay," Jonah replied. "I'm sure there will be plenty of people from our community to offer Elaine support."

"Now that Edna's gone, Elaine is free to marry," Sara said, her voice barely above a whisper. "Are you sorry you didn't wait for her instead of marrying me?"

Jonah reached under the covers and clasped Sara's hand. "No, Sara, I made the right decision and have no regrets about marrying you." He squeezed her fingers gently. "I'm looking forward to the days ahead and seeing what God has planned for our lives."

"Me, too. And Jonah, I have no regrets about marrying you."

"Onah! Onah!" Mark hollered from across the hall.

"I'd better go see what our little guy wants, but I'll be back to check on you soon. Oh, and there's a glass of water on the nightstand for you. You need to sip it so you don't get dehydrated."

"Okay, but please keep Mark out of our bedroom. I don't want him to get sick, too," Sara called as Jonah exited the room.

"I'll make sure he doesn't come in." Jonah hurried into Mark's room and lifted him from the crib. "Let's get you some breakfast, little buddy."

After Jonah had Mark settled in his high chair with a bowl of cereal, he made a pot of coffee and took a seat at the table. He, too, felt bad about missing Edna Schrock's funeral, but his first obligation was to Sara. He sure couldn't leave her alone when she was this sick.

Jonah had gone to Edna's viewing the other day, and it tugged at his heartstrings to see the look of despair on Elaine's face. As difficult as it had been for her to be Edna's caregiver, it would be even harder for Elaine to cope with the loss of her grandmother. It had been a rough year for Elaine, losing both of her grandparents.

Jonah wished once more that she would have allowed him to help her through it. Of course, that was out of the question now. He was a married man, and it wouldn't look right for him to go over to Elaine's by himself to help with chores or anything else she may need to have done. But Elaine's friends would be there for her, helping in whatever way they could. Eventually, Elaine would meet someone special, fall in love, and get married.

"Onah! Onah!"

Jonah jumped at the sound of Mark's voice. He looked over at the boy and laughed when he saw that Mark had turned his empty bowl upside-down and put it on top of his head.

Jonah was glad for this lighthearted moment. It wasn't good to think too deeply about things that were out of his control.

Removing the bowl from Mark's head, Jonah cleaned Mark's face and hands with a wet paper towel. Then he lifted Mark out of the high chair, returned to his seat at the table, and held the boy in his lap while he waited for the coffee to perk.

Mark burrowed his face into Jonah's chest, and Jonah's throat constricted. The love he felt for the boy was beyond measure, and Jonah had no doubt he would love and nurture this child as if he were his own flesh and blood.

Elaine's throat burned as she struggled not to break down. She, along with several others from their church district, had arrived at the cemetery a few minutes ago. It had been determined that Grandma's death was caused by a heart attack, just as Grandpa's had been. Her somber funeral had taken place inside the Otto Center earlier this morning, and afterward, the mourners had come to the cemetery to lay her body to rest.

If I'd found her sooner, could she have been saved? Elaine winced. Hadn't she thought the very same thing when Grandpa died? All the wishing for what she might have done would do her no good now. Grandma was gone, and Elaine was alone. Now she needed to find the strength to go on.

"We're here for you," Leah whispered as she and Priscilla slipped their arms around Elaine's waist.

Elaine's forehead broke out in a sweat, even though it was a chilly day. Oh, how she needed their friendship—more now than ever before. The anguish she felt over losing Grandma shook Elaine to her very core.

She shivered as Grandma's simple coffin was placed inside the rough pine box that had been set in the opening of the grave. Elaine felt certain that Grandma was with Jesus and Grandpa now. Her dear grandmother was no longer bound by any illness, and in that, Elaine found some measure of comfort. She really wouldn't wish Grandma back with her, suffering and confused. But someday she would see her grandparents again, when it was her turn to be called to heaven. What a joyous reunion they would have—the three of them.

A group of men from their church district began to sing as the grave was filled in by the pallbearers. With each shovelful of dirt, the heavy feeling in the pit of Elaine's stomach increased. At one point, she felt as if she might faint, but the support of Priscilla and Leah kept her standing firm. As the last shovelful of dirt was placed over the coffin, she remembered the promise she'd made to Grandpa before he'd died—to take care of Grandma.

I did the best I could, Elaine thought. *I only wish I could have done more.*

Bishop Levi asked the congregation to pray the Lord's Prayer silently and concluded the graveside service. It was time to head back to Grandma's house for the funeral meal her friends and neighbors had prepared. Eating at their table wouldn't seem right without Grandma to share in the meal. Elaine would miss all the times she and Grandma had together—even on Grandma's bad days—but somehow she must learn to cope.

As all the people turned from the grave site and began walking back to their buggies, Elaine made a decision. She would try to make the best of her situation and look to God for answers concerning her future. She would claim and cling to His promises to help get her through the grieving process. And she would call upon her special friends, Priscilla and Leah, whenever she had a need. No more trying to do everything in her own strength, for she had tried that and failed. Elaine could count on her dear friends—not just for today, but in the days ahead. And someday, if the Lord willed it, she might meet someone special, fall in love, and get married. But until then, she would put her trust in the Lord.

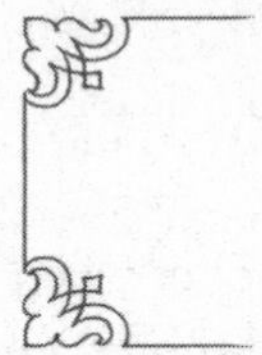
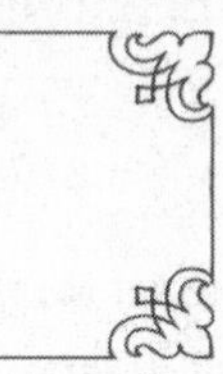

EPILOGUE

Six months later

"How are you feeling today?" Jonah asked, stepping behind Sara as she stood at the sink, washing their breakfast dishes.

"I'm good. In fact, I feel better than I have in a long time."

"Glad to hear it."

"And remember, the doctor said there is no evidence that MS is linked to any problems with pregnancy." Sara leaned her head against Jonah's chest. "He also said that most women experience relief from many or even all of their MS symptoms during pregnancy, and I'm happy to say that I seem to be one of those women."

Jonah slipped his arms around Sara's waist and gently patted her slightly protruding stomach. They had only been married two months when Sara became pregnant. At first, Jonah had been concerned for Sara's health because of her MS, but Sara had been feeling quite well, for which he was thankful. Their child would be born in November, and Jonah could hardly wait to introduce Mark, who was now three, to his baby brother or sister. Life was good for Jonah, and he was happier than he'd been in a long time.

To add to his joy, the last time Mom and Dad came to visit, Dad had informed Jonah that he was going to sell his buggy shop in Pennsylvania and move to Illinois to be partners with Jonah. Mom and Dad were even going to buy Sara's old house. They would also see that the barn was rebuilt once they'd moved in, but other than that, not much else needed to be done. Having his parents living closer would make Jonah's life complete. Without question, he'd made the right decision when he'd moved to Arthur. At first, he'd thought his future would be with Elaine, but the Lord had other plans for Jonah, and every day he thanked God for bringing him and Sara together.

As Elaine sat on the old swing Grandpa had hung for her when she was a girl, she looked up at the crystal-clear June sky and thought of all the changes that had taken place during the past year. She'd lost both of her grandparents, inherited their house, and with the help of her friends, had learned how to cope with the changes.

In addition to hosting dinners for tourists again with the help of a neighbor girl, Elaine now had a suitor, Ben Otto, who was a cousin of Melvin's wife, Sharon. Ben and his family had moved from Sullivan to Arthur a few months ago. Elaine wasn't sure what she felt for Ben was strong enough to develop into anything serious, but she enjoyed his company, and it was nice to go out to supper with him once in a while.

Hearing a bird chirp overhead, Elaine looked up and saw a bright yellow finch sitting on one of the feeders. She didn't know why, but the beautiful golden bird made her think of Grandma's parakeet, Millie. Grandma had been so upset after the bird had first disappeared. But after Elaine had given Grandma the painted parakeet rock, Grandma became convinced that Millie had come back. It was nice to know that a simple little thing like that rock could have brought Grandma happiness during her last days on earth.

Elaine still missed her grandparents, but she had learned to take one day at a time and be content. Life was full of disappointments, but there were lots of good things, too. Elaine looked forward to seeing what the future held for her, and as she continued to watch the finch, she whispered a prayer. "Heavenly Father, may Your will be done in my life. Please give me the wisdom to make good decisions in all things."

RECIPES

ELAINE'S SUGAR-FREE APPLE PIE

Ingredients:

8 cups peeled and sliced Yellow Delicious apples (or other sweet variety)
1 (12 ounce) can frozen apple juice concentrate
2 tablespoons butter
1 teaspoon cinnamon
½ teaspoon nutmeg
4 tablespoons tapioca
1 (9 inch) pie shell, baked

In a saucepan, cook apples with frozen apple juice concentrate. Add butter, cinnamon, nutmeg, and tapioca. When apples are tender, pour into baked pie shell. Cool and serve with whipped topping or ice cream.

GRANDMA'S SOUR-CREAM PEACH PIE

INGREDIENTS:
1 egg, beaten
½ teaspoon salt
½ teaspoon vanilla
1 cup sour cream
¾ cup sugar
2 tablespoons flour
2½ cups sliced fresh peaches
1 (9 inch) pie shell, unbaked

TOPPING:
½ cup butter
⅓ cup sugar
⅓ cup flour
1 teaspoon cinnamon

Preheat oven to 375 degrees. In a saucepan, combine egg, salt, vanilla, sour cream, sugar, and flour; add peaches and stir. Pour into unbaked pie shell and bake for 30 minutes or until pie is slightly brown. Remove pie from oven. Combine topping ingredients and spread on top of pie. Bake for 15 minutes.

DISCUSSION QUESTIONS

1. Elaine felt that the care of her grandmother was her responsibility, so she had trouble accepting help from others at first. Have you ever been in a situation where you needed help but tried to do everything on your own? How did you feel when someone stepped in to help?

2. When Edna first learned that she had dementia, she was in denial. Have you or someone you know ever been told by a doctor that something was seriously wrong? If so, how did you deal with it?

3. Elaine told Jonah a lie when she said she didn't love him. Is there ever a time when it's okay to lie?

4. When Sara began having health issues, she put off going to the doctor, using the cost as an excuse. Have you or someone you know ever avoided going to the doctor due to lack of money? Was Sara right in neglecting her health, or should she have asked someone for the money she needed? By not going to the doctor sooner, was Sara putting her son at risk?

5. Edna knew she was losing her memory, and her biggest concern was that she wouldn't remember any of her family or friends. If you suffered from memory loss, what would you do to help remember those who are closest to you?

6. Elaine's closest friends, Leah and Priscilla, helped her deal with the sorrowful events that came her way. What are some ways we can help a friend who is going through a difficult time?

7. Jonah had been hurt by two women and was afraid to take another chance. Have you or someone you know ever been fearful of entering a new relationship because of past failures? If so, how did you or your friend deal with those fears?

8. Elaine's friends often gave her advice. When should we listen to a friend's recommendations, and when should we choose to ignore them?

9. Elaine waited too long to tell her grandma about her illness, and Grandma ended up hearing it from someone else. If you knew someone in your family had been diagnosed with a serious illness, would you tell them right away, or would it be better to keep it from them?

10. Do you think Jonah gave up too quickly on Elaine, even though she said she didn't love him? Should Jonah have tried harder to assure Elaine of his love for her and his willingness to help during her time of need?

11. Do you think Elaine was being overprotective of her grandmother? As a caregiver to a relative with dementia, how would you handle things?

12. While reading this story, what did you learn about the Amish community of Arthur, Illinois?

13. Did any passages of scripture mentioned in the book specifically speak to you? If so, in what way?

14. Does reading about the Amish influence you to simplify your life? What are some ways we can simplify?

The GIFT

To my dear friend Irene Miller, who has
helped many people with her special gift.

In quietness and in confidence shall be your strength.
Isaiah 30:15

CHAPTER 1

Arthur, Illinois

As clouds, black and boiling, filled the darkening sky, Leah Mast pedaled her bicycle harder, knowing that if she didn't get home soon, she'd be caught in a downpour. The muscles in her calves felt as if they could give out at any moment, but she ignored the pain, concentrating on just getting home. Leah had noticed the sky darkening before she left the house. So much for thinking she could outsmart the weather.

"Guess this is what I get for taking my bike instead of the horse and buggy," she muttered, moving to the shoulder of the road as a car sped past. *Too bad I can't pedal as fast as that car.*

Right after eating breakfast and helping her mother with the dishes, Leah had bicycled to Family Health Foods, a mile south of Arthur, to buy some massage lotion. She'd scheduled a few people for foot treatments this afternoon and needed to restock her supply.

With determination, Leah continued her trek toward home. Attempting to keep her mind off the leg cramps that threatened with each downward push, she thought about the special relationship she'd had with her maternal grandmother, who had taught her reflexology. During her lifetime, Grandma Yoder had helped a good many people with her gift of healing.

Leah had the gift, too. At least that's what Grandma had always told her. Many Amish people in Leah's community, as well as some Englishers, came to her for foot treatments. Of course she couldn't charge a set fee for her services, since she didn't have a license to practice reflexology. But the people who came to Leah always gave her a donation. She treated back and shoulder pain, sinus congestion, sore throats, headaches, and insomnia. She also used reflexology to help folks relax, balance their body, and increase blood circulation. When people came to her with more serious illnesses, she always suggested that they see a doctor, because some things she simply could not help.

A clap of thunder sounded, bringing Leah's thoughts to a halt. Big drops of rain pelted her body and stung her face. This was a cloudburst, not an ordinary gentle rainfall. If it kept up, she'd be drenched by the time she made it home—that is, if she could see well enough to get there. The rain came down sideways, and Leah could hardly keep her eyes open. She hoped this was just a freak storm that would move out as quickly as possible. Well, there was nothing she could do about the weather except keep pedaling as fast as she could.

The *clip-clop* of a horse's hooves caused Leah to look over her shoulder. She guided her bike farther off the road and was surprised when the horse and buggy stopped behind her. The driver's side door opened, and Adam Beachy called, "Do you need a ride?"

Astonished by his invitation, Leah quit pedaling. "What about my bike?" she asked as the rain dribbled over her face.

"Not a problem." Adam stuck his blond head out and pointed to the rear of his buggy. It was then that Leah realized he was driving his market buggy. Partially enclosed, it had an open wooden bed that extended from the back. If it was empty, there would be plenty of room for her bicycle in the bed.

Leah climbed off and was about to push the bike around back, when Adam shouted, "If you'll get in my buggy and hold the reins, I'll put your bicycle in and snug it in place."

Shivering from the drenching rain, Leah climbed into Adam's buggy and grabbed the reins, while Adam stepped out and picked up her bicycle.

Leah felt soaked clear through to her skin, and her muscles continued to cramp. It would be a miracle if she ever warmed up. Even though it was the middle of June, a storm like this could chill a person to the bone.

"*Danki*," Leah said when Adam climbed back into the buggy. Her breathing was getting back to normal, but her wet clothing clinging to her drenched skin made her feel icy cold.

Leah handed the reins back to Adam, and using the sleeve of her dress, she wiped rainwater from her face. "I appreciate you stopping, because I need to get home and change out of these wet clothes before Sara Miller comes for a reflexology treatment this afternoon."

With water dripping off his chin, Adam's brown eyes squinted as he wrinkled his nose like some foul odor had permeated the buggy. "So you're still foot doctoring, huh?" He reached behind his seat and handed Leah a small blanket.

She gave a quick nod, wrapping the cover around her shoulders. Even though the blanket pressed her soggy dress against her skin, Leah was grateful for its warmth.

"Humph! I can't believe there are still people who believe in all that hocus-pocus."

Gritting her teeth, Leah pulled the blanket tighter. "Reflexology is not hocus-pocus; it's a form of bodywork that focuses on the feet, and—"

"And nobody's ever been cured of anything by having their feet massaged." Adam snapped the reins and directed his horse onto the road. "You oughtta quit taking people's money for something that's fake and get a real job, Leah."

Fuming, Leah nearly had to bite her tongue to keep from shouting at him. In all her twenty-five years, she'd never met such an opinionated, rude man! Adam had only said a few words to her whenever she'd visited his hardware store, and he had never made eye contact until now. Leah had also observed how, after their biweekly church services, Adam often hurried off, sometimes not even staying for the meal that followed. She'd always thought it was strange that he didn't linger to visit with the men after church, like most others did. Apparently he wasn't much for socializing. *No wonder he isn't married*, she thought. *No woman looking for a husband would put up with being talked to like that. And what does he know about reflexology, anyway?*

Unable to hold her tongue, Leah snapped her head in Adam's direction. "For your information, Mr. Beachy, there are reflex areas on people's feet that correspond to specific organs, glands, and other parts of the body. Those who practice reflexology believe that applying pressure to these reflex areas can promote health in the corresponding organs through energetic pathways."

"Puh! Is that so? Just what illnesses have you helped cure, Leah?"

"Many, in fact." Leah held up one finger. "Some people who come to me get relief from headaches and stress."

Adam flapped his hand in her direction, which only fueled her irritation. "Any kind of massage can make a person relax and feel less tension. Besides, I wouldn't call stress an illness."

"Maybe not in itself, but stress can lead to many different ailments, including headaches." Leah held up a second finger. "Some folks who get reflexology treatments have found relief from back pain." Before Adam could respond, a third finger came up. "And some with digestive disorders or insomnia have felt better after I've worked on their feet. I believe my ability to help them is a gift."

Adam shook his head. "I'm not interested in hearing a bunch of mumbo jumbo. If people are willing to pay whatever fee you're charging and believe they'll get well, that's up to them, but I'm not a believer in that sort of thing."

His tone cut like glass. Leah crossed her arms and glared at him. "The people who come to me for treatments believe in what I'm doing, and I don't have a set fee. I work on anyone's feet for a donation, which means whatever they can afford."

Adam glowered at her. At least Leah thought it was a glower. To give him the benefit of the doubt, she supposed he could have a case of indigestion. "Well," he said with a huff, "you'll never catch me taking off my shoes and socks so someone like you can press on my feet."

Someone like me? Leah's face burned. *Oh, you don't have to worry about that, Adam Beachy. Even if you gave me a hundred-dollar donation, I would never touch your smelly feet!*

"You have a right to your opinion," she muttered.

"That's right, I sure do."

"And I have a right to mine." Refusing to look at Adam, Leah focused on the road ahead. Her folks' house wasn't too far from here, so she should be able to make it that far without saying anything more. She would have liked to give Adam some specific details on reflexology, but what would be the point? He had obviously made up his mind, so she probably wouldn't get very far defending her skill.

I wish now I'd never accepted a ride from him, she fumed. *I'd have been better off riding my bike the rest of the way home, even in the drenching rain.*

"Where have you been that you got caught in this storm?" Adam's deep voice penetrated Leah's angry thoughts.

She looked down at the plastic sack in her hands, unwilling to tell him that she'd bought massage lotion to use on Sara's feet. He'd probably have something negative to say about that, too. "I just needed something at the health food store," she murmured, wiping a drop of water as it trickled down her nose.

Adam clucked to his horse to get him moving a bit faster. He was probably as anxious to drop Leah off at her house as she was to get there.

Leah watched Adam pull back on the reins, guiding his horse through a waterlogged area. The small creek, which normally flowed through a pipe under the road, now splashed across the asphalt pavement. As the horse walked slowly through the fast-flooding creek, she noticed the cause of the rising water. The pipe was clogged with debris that had washed down from farther up. Small branches and clumps of dead leaves had caused the creek to detour from its natural flow. The water was still shallow, but if the rain kept coming down like it was, the road might become impassable. Thankfully, they'd made it this far and would hopefully make it home before the storm got any worse.

They rode in silence the rest of the way, and Leah felt relief when Adam directed his horse and buggy up her folks' driveway. Except for that one small area of flooding, the drive had been without incident.

"I'll get your bicycle." Adam guided his horse up to the hitching rack. Before Leah could respond, he jumped out of the buggy, secured the animal, and went around back.

Leah climbed out, too. "Danki for the ride," she said when Adam pushed her bike around the side of the buggy. She noticed how the rain poured from the top of his hat.

"Sure, no problem." Adam speedily untied his horse, stepped back into the buggy, and as he backed the horse away from the wooden rail, he gave a quick wave.

Leah waved in response then, dodging puddles, made a dash for the house. If Adam hadn't acted so negatively toward her reflexology, in appreciation of him bringing her home, she might have invited him in for a cup of hot tea and the chance to dry off a little while waiting for the storm to subside. But after that conversation, Leah hoped she would never again be put in a position where she'd have to be alone with Adam Beachy. He might be the most attractive single Amish man in Arthur, but as far as she was concerned, he had the personality of a donkey!

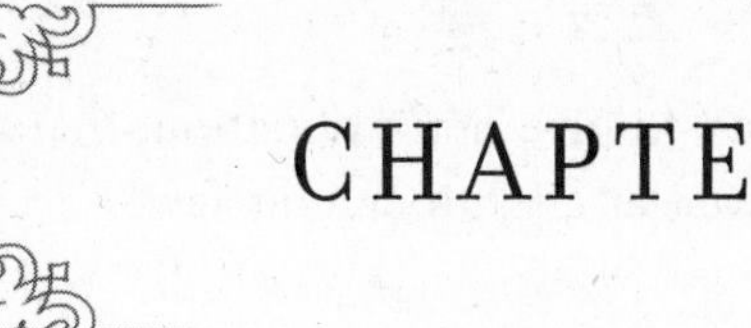
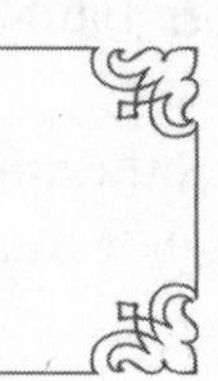

CHAPTER 2

Leah Mast may be pretty, but she's sure opinionated," Adam muttered as he headed for home. "No wonder she's not married."

Adam had never met a woman as independently determined as Leah. Of course, he hadn't known that many women personally, since he kept to himself as much as possible when it came to socializing. At a young age, Adam had reached the conclusion that he would never marry. It wasn't that he had no interest in the opposite sex—he just didn't trust them.

Bringing his thoughts to a halt, lest he start feeling sorry for himself, Adam concentrated on the road ahead. It was still raining hard, making it difficult to see. If he didn't pay close attention, he could end up off the road. So far, his horse, Flash, was behaving himself and didn't seem to mind the driving rain. Unfortunately, Adam couldn't say the same about his own demeanor. Thanks to his generosity in giving Leah a ride home and then getting out in this horrible weather to transport her bike, he was wet and cold. Drips of rainwater still hung on the brim of his hat, and his shirt and trousers felt like a second skin. He couldn't wait to get home and out of the soaking wet clothes. First and most importantly, though, Adam knew he had to keep his mind on the road, or he might not make it home at all.

Maybe I should have kept going when I saw Leah riding her bike. She was already soaking wet by the time I came upon her. If I hadn't picked her up, we'd never have had that conversation about foot doctoring.

The more Adam thought about it, the more upset he became. Leah reminded him of someone he'd rather forget—not in looks, but in that sure-of-herself attitude. Well, the pretty woman with blue-green eyes and golden brown hair could practice reflexology all she wanted, but it wouldn't change the fact that it was a waste of time. If certain people thought otherwise and wanted to give her a donation, that was their business, but Adam would never let Leah touch his feet!

"*Ach*, my, you're sopping wet!" Mom exclaimed when Leah found her in the utility room, washing clothes.

"I got caught in the downpour," Leah replied.

"I wish you would have taken the buggy instead of your bike. I'm guessing by now you probably wish that, too."

Leah nodded. "Where's Sparky?"

"Last time I looked he was lying just inside the barn."

"Guess he doesn't want to get wet, either." Leah chuckled, wiping another drop of rainwater rolling down the middle of her forehead. "*Schmaert* dog."

"Until I closed the window, the rain was actually blowing into this room, even with the large overhang on the porch to protect it." Mom handed Leah a clean towel. "You'd better dry off some before you head to your room to change, or you'll be leaving a trail of water."

"Danki, Mom." Leah removed her saturated head covering and hung it on a wall peg; then she blotted her hair with the towel. "I'd probably look even worse if Adam Beachy hadn't come along and offered me a ride home."

A wide smile stretched across Mom's face, and her thinning eyelashes fluttered above her dark brown eyes. "That was sure nice of him. Did it give you a chance to get better acquainted?"

A jolt of heat traveled from Leah's neck to her face, despite the chill she felt on the rest of her body. "Oh, we got better acquainted, all right. I found out that Adam doesn't believe in reflexology, and he really didn't have much of anything nice to say."

Mom's lips compressed. "I'm sorry to hear that. I was hoping. . ."

"What were you hoping. . .that Adam might be interested in courting me?"

Mom pulled a towel free from the wringer washer and placed it in the wicker basket at her feet. "Now that you brought up the subject, it would be nice if you had a suitor, don't you think?"

Leah shook her head. "I don't need a man in my life right now. What I do need is to get out of these wet clothes so I'm ready when Sara Miller shows up for her reflexology appointment."

Mom glanced at the battery-operated clock on the wall to her left. "Oh that's right. You did mention before you left that you had a few appointments this afternoon."

Leah nodded and turned toward the stairs but paused when she smelled a delicious aroma coming from the kitchen. "Do you have something on the stove, Mom?"

"*Jah.* It may be the middle of summer, but on a rainy day such as this, I thought a pot of vegetable soup would taste good for our supper tonight. I also made a loaf of homemade bread." Mom gestured to the adjoining room. "Would you mind checking on the soup before you go upstairs?"

"Sure, Mom, no problem. Oh, and if Sara gets here before I've changed, please tell her to go on down to the basement, and that I'll meet her there."

"Okay, I'll let her know."

Leah blotted her arms and legs with the towel then went to the kitchen to check on the soup. Taking a sip of the broth, she smacked her lips. "Yum. I can't wait till suppertime." Turning the burner down so the soup could simmer, she left the room.

As Leah made her way up the stairs, she thought about her mother's comment about a suitor. Although Leah acted like she didn't care, she longed to be a wife and mother. But so far, the right man had not come along. No one, that is, who had swept Leah off her feet. It was probably wishful thinking, but she wanted to fall in love with a man who made her heart beat like a thundering herd of horses. Leah's friends Elaine Schrock and Priscilla Hershberger both had boyfriends. Priscilla was being courted by Elam Gingerich, and Elaine had recently started seeing Ben Otto, who was fairly new to the area. She figured they'd both be married with children long before she had a suitor.

Leah entered her room, removed her wet clothes, and changed into a clean, dry dress. *Here I am, twenty-five years old already, and I don't even have a boyfriend, much less the prospect of marriage. Maybe it's not meant for me to get married.* Leah wasn't going to marry just anyone merely because time was running out before she'd be considered an old maid. *I must leave things in God's hands and remember Isaiah 30:15, the verse I read last night: "In quietness and in confidence shall be your strength."* Leah sighed. *I am certainly not quiet by nature. Adam sure got under my skin today, and I probably said more than I should have in defense of myself. Well, he said more than he should have, too.*

When Leah entered the basement a short time later, Sara was sitting in the recliner with her shoes and stockings off. Her normally slender legs and feet looked a bit swollen, and several strands of her medium brown hair peeked out from under her head covering. Sara's shoulders were slumped, and Leah noticed dark circles beneath her friend's brown eyes.

"Sorry for making you wait," Leah apologized. "I rode my bike to the health food store earlier and got caught in that downpour, so I had to change out of my wet clothes."

"It's not a problem; I haven't been here that long." Sara motioned to a plastic container on the small table to her right. "I brought you some chocolate-chip cookies that I baked this morning."

"Danki. That was nice of you. Except for bread, neither Mom nor I have done much baking lately. We've been too busy picking strawberries from our garden and making them into jelly." Leah smiled. "Last night, I was going to make a strawberry cheeseball but decided to make a chocolate-chip one instead."

Sara smacked her lips. "I'll bet that was good."

Leah nodded and took a seat on the stool in front of the recliner to begin working on Sara's feet. "I enjoy making cheeseballs, and it's always fun to try out new combinations." She picked up the bottle of lotion, poured some into her hands, and rubbed it gently into Sara's feet. "How have you been feeling lately? Are you having any unusual symptoms with your pregnancy?"

"No, not really. In fact, my symptoms have actually diminished, which the doctor said often happens to pregnant women who have MS."

"That's good to hear. So you're not having any problems at all?"

"Not with my MS, but my lower back has begun to hurt, and it's hard to sleep." Sara frowned. "I'm only four-and-a-half-months pregnant, so I wasn't expecting back pain this early. I didn't experience it at all when I was carrying Mark, but I know that many women have trouble with their back—especially toward the end of their third trimester."

Leah began to work on the heel of Sara's right foot. After a while, she moved to the other foot. "Is that tender?" she asked when Sara winced.

Sara nodded. "Jah, a little."

Leah worked on Sara's left foot for several minutes, then she asked her to stand and walk around for a bit.

"My back feels much better. Danki, Leah." The dimples in Sara's cheeks deepened when she smiled.

"You're welcome. Let me know if it flares up again or if you need another foot treatment just to help you relax."

"I will." Sara put on her shoes and stockings.

"Now let me rub your neck a bit before you go." Leah usually did that for most of her patients. It helped them relax and finished the treatment on a positive note.

As Leah massaged Sara's neck, they talked about the weather.

"How were the roads when you came here?" Leah asked. "Were any sections flooded?"

"At one place," Sara said as Leah worked the knots out of her neck, "but my horse cooperated well and walked right through it without a problem."

"That's good. Some horses get spooky over things like water in the road."

"You're right about that." Sara slipped some money into the jar Leah had set on the small table near the chair. "Guess I'd better go. Jonah took some time away from his buggy shop to watch Mark so I could come here, and I'm sure he's anxious to get back to work."

Leah hugged Sara, and as the young woman headed up the stairs, Leah thought about her friend Elaine, who had once been courted by Jonah. Listening to Elaine talk about Ben, Leah wondered if she cared for him as much as she had Jonah.

Since she had a few minutes until Margaret Kauffman, their bishop's wife, arrived for her treatment, Leah washed her hands and tasted one of the cookies Sara had brought. It was soft and chewy, and she relished the taste of chocolate along with the little bits of nuts inside. Tempted to eat a second cookie, she put the lid back on the container and took a seat in the recliner to wait for Margaret. Maybe later this evening, she'd have another cookie with a cup of hot tea.

Drawing in a deep breath, Leah closed her eyes. If she wasn't careful, it would be easy to succumb to sleep. A vision of Adam Beachy flashed into Leah's mind, and her eyes snapped open. *Now why was I thinking about him again?*

Leah stood and opened the lid on the plastic container. She was on the verge of taking another cookie, despite her resolve, when she heard footsteps coming down the stairs. Closing the lid, she turned and smiled at Margaret. "Did your husband bring you here today, or did you come alone?"

"I brought my own horse and buggy." Margaret placed her black umbrella on the floor near the chair. "It's stopped raining, but it sure came down hard for a while there." She removed her cape and black outer bonnet, revealing her white head covering, perched on top of her salt-and-pepper hair.

"I know. I got caught in the downpour when I was riding my bike earlier." Leah motioned to the recliner. "If you're ready, why don't you take a seat? Oh, and if you're hungry, there's some chocolate-chip *kichlin* there on the table. Sara Miller made them."

Margaret's pale blue eyes twinkled when she smiled and took two cookies. "Anything with chocolate in it appeals to me." She took a seat in the recliner and ate both cookies before removing her shoes and socks. Suddenly, a strange look came over her face and she started wheezing, as though she was having trouble catching her breath. "I—I think I'm having a reaction to what I just ate. I feel a strange tightness in my throat and chest—it's like I can't breathe."

Leah's shoulders tightened as perspiration beaded on her forehead. She'd heard about allergic reactions to certain foods, but she'd never dealt with one before. "Have you ever had an attack like this?"

Margaret shook her head.

Knowing she needed to get help for their bishop's wife, she told Margaret to lie back in the chair and try to stay calm. Then Leah rushed upstairs, quickly told Mom what had happened and asked her to go downstairs and keep an eye on Margaret, while she ran outside. Her heart hammering, she raced for the phone shack to call 911.

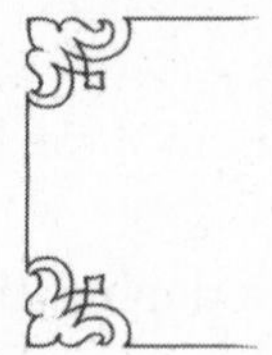

CHAPTER 3

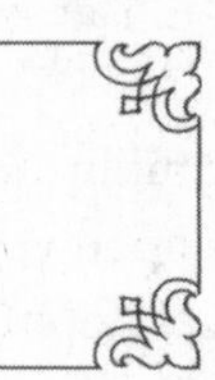

"I heard that Margaret Kauffman had an allergic reaction while you were working on her feet yesterday," Leah's friend Priscilla said as they ate supper together at Yoder's Kitchen the following day.

Leah nodded and reached for her glass of lemonade. "I never even got started on her feet, because it came on after she'd eaten a couple of the cookies Sara Miller had brought earlier. When Margaret said she was having trouble breathing, I knew I needed to get help for her right away."

"Did you know it was a reaction to what she ate, or did you think it might be something else?" Priscilla's coffee-colored eyes revealed the depth of her concern.

"I wasn't sure what to think at first, but then Margaret said she thought she was having an allergic reaction. So I asked my *mamm* to stay with her, while I rushed out to the phone shack and called 911." Leah paused to take a drink. "When the paramedics got there, they knew what to do, and at the hospital, they ran tests that revealed Margaret's allergic to walnuts, which were in the chocolate-chip cookies."

"It's good she found that out so she can be careful not to eat anything else with nuts," Priscilla said before taking a bite of salad. "If she's allergic to walnuts, she might have that same reaction to other kinds of nuts as well."

"The doctor wrote Margaret a prescription for an EpiPen, which she will keep with her in case an incident like that ever happens again," Leah explained.

"That must have been frightening, not only for Margaret, but for you as well."

"Jah, it was." Leah sipped more lemonade. "You know, it's too bad

Elaine couldn't join us this evening. It's been awhile since the three of us had a good visit."

"I was hoping she could come, too, but she has a dinner scheduled this evening for a large tour group."

"That's right; I do remember her saying that." Leah paused to eat some of her salad. "Oh, I forgot to mention that Mom sent a container of vegetable soup for you and your parents. It's in a cooler out in my buggy. I'll get it for you after we eat. It might be something you can enjoy for lunch tomorrow."

Priscilla smiled. "Please tell your mamm I said danki."

"I will. She made enough soup to feed a small barn-raising crew, so she was more than happy to share."

"We enjoy anything your mamm makes because she is such a good cook."

"You're right about that. I do all right in the kitchen, but my cooking skills aren't nearly as good as hers." Glancing to her left, Leah cringed when she noticed Adam enter the restaurant. Trying to suppress a cough, she almost choked on the little tomato she was chewing. She was relieved when the hostess handed Adam a takeout box, which meant he wasn't planning to stay.

Before Leah had a chance to look away, Adam glanced in her direction and gave a brief nod. She smiled in return then quickly focused on her salad.

Priscilla bumped Leah's foot under the table. "Your face is red. Are you okay?"

"I'm fine," Leah muttered. She glanced back at Adam and was relieved when she saw him go out the door.

Priscilla tipped her head, looking curiously at Leah. "Are you interested in Adam Beachy? Is that why your cheeks are so pink?"

Leah touched her hot cheeks. "No, of course not!"

"Is he interested in you?"

"The only person Adam's interested in is himself and his biased opinions."

"What makes you say that?"

Leah proceeded to tell Priscilla about the ride Adam had given her and his attitude toward reflexology. "He thinks it's hocus-pocus."

Priscilla's eyes narrowed. "That's *lecherich*."

"You're right, it is ridiculous."

"How would Adam know anything about reflexology?"

Leah shrugged. "All I know is that man is unsociable and too sharp with his words. Makes me wonder how he can run a business and keep customers coming back to his store. Guess it's a good thing he has Ben Otto and Henry Raber working there, because they're both friendly and quite pleasant."

"You're right," Priscilla agreed. "The last time I went there to get some nails for my *daed*, Adam was behind the counter, and he barely said two words to me. What do you think his problem is, anyway?"

Leah shrugged again. "I have no idea. The only thing I do know is that I'll never accept another ride from him, no matter how hard it's raining. I'd rather be waterlogged than listen to him say negative things about the very thing I feel called to do."

"I can't blame you for that. Personally, I see your foot doctoring as a gift from God." Priscilla smiled. "Not everyone has the ability to help people the way you do, Leah. Maybe someday Adam will have a sinus headache or some other type of problem and come to you for help."

Leah shook her head. "I doubt that. I'm sure he'd be the last person in our community who'd ask me for help. For that matter, I have no desire to work on Adam's feet."

When Adam entered his house that evening, a deep sense of loneliness encompassed him. He should be used to coming home every evening to an empty house, but he'd never quite adjusted to it. He missed his dad and the conversations they used to have, and he missed his sister, Mary, whom he'd been close to during their childhood. But Mary lived in Nappanee, Indiana, with her husband and three girls. Two years ago, Adam's dad had passed away after a freak accident when he'd been helping a neighbor in his field. After six months of grieving his loss, Adam had left Indiana and moved to Arthur, Illinois, seeking a new start with the hardware store he'd purchased. He didn't have any relatives in the area, but that was okay. Adam was used to moving and starting over. Dad had uprooted them several times after Adam's mother walked out on them when they lived in Pennsylvania. Adam didn't know why they'd moved, but he'd later found out that Dad didn't want Adam and Mary's mother to have anything to do with them if she ever came back. He'd said she was a wicked woman and didn't deserve to spend any time with her children. Well, that was fine with Adam, because he wanted nothing to do with her. When she'd left the Amish faith and divorced his dad, Adam had been five years old and Mary had been eight. How any woman could walk out on a man as great as Dad and leave her children behind was a mystery to Adam, and he'd never come to grips with it. He had struggled the last twenty-five years to keep from hating her for what she'd done. It was wrong to dislike anyone that much, but Adam's anger festered like a splinter that wouldn't come out. It had kept him from getting close to anyone except for Mary and her family. Adam loved his sister and would do anything for her. He cared about her husband, Amos, and their daughters, Carrie, Linda, and Amy, too, although he didn't see them as often as he would like.

Adam hung his straw hat on a wall peg in the kitchen and, after pouring himself a glass of milk, took a seat at the table. He'd put in a long day, and it felt good to be off his feet.

As he sipped some milk, his gaze came to rest on the coloring book lying on top of the desk across the room. He'd purchased it so his nieces would have something to do when they came here for Christmas last year, but the girls had forgotten to take it home with them. Several months before the holiday, Adam had asked Jonah Miller, the local buggy maker, to build him a buggy that would accommodate six people so all his guests could ride together. Having his sister and her family with him to celebrate the Christmas season had been nice, but he hadn't gotten much use out of the larger buggy since they went back to Indiana. He hated to admit it, since he'd paid Jonah Miller a good price for making the buggy, but it seemed like a waste to have the larger rig sitting out in the buggy shed. At least he would have it for the next time Mary and her family came to visit.

Sure wish Dad could have celebrated Christmas with us, Adam thought with regret. *If his life hadn't been snuffed out that way, we'd be together right now.*

"We never know what's coming in life," Adam mumbled, setting his empty glass on the table. "Never know what the future holds."

CHAPTER 4

Elaine Schrock had never been one to give in to self-pity, and tonight was no exception. She'd just told her helper, Karen Yoder, good-bye and had put the last of the dishes away from the tourists' dinner she'd hosted. Every time Elaine hosted another dinner, she pictured Grandma working beside her, wearing a cheerful-looking smile. Oh, how she missed their conversations and the humorous stories Grandma often shared from her childhood, but the memories of Grandma were also what motivated Elaine to continue providing these dinners. Knowing how much her grandmother had loved doing them, wasn't she, in a way, helping to keep Grandma's memory alive by continuing this tradition?

When Grandma died, Elaine had considered selling the house and moving away, but this had been her home since she was a girl, and she couldn't bring herself to leave the old house where so many memories lived. Perhaps if Elaine ever got married, she would raise her own children in this place where so much love had abounded when Grandpa and Grandma were alive. The swing in the yard, the big back porch, and even the bedrooms upstairs with their creaky floorboards needed children to fill them.

If only Grandma and Grandpa could have lived long enough to see great-grandchildren, she thought, moving over to her desk on the other side of the room to get the book on gardening she wanted to read. *I know they would have loved my* kinner *as much as they loved me—if I ever have any children, that is.*

Bringing her thoughts back to the dinner she'd just hosted, Elaine chuckled over the group's reaction to one of the guests. An Asian man, Mr. Lee, burped out loud after eating his salad. Then he did the same thing after finishing his mashed potatoes. At that point, the whole dining area grew silent, and the other guests stared at the man. An uncomfortable hush settled over the room. Mr. Lee must have noticed it, for he stood up and explained that in the part of China he came from, it was customary to show appreciation for the food by burping out loud. He even offered to stop doing it if anyone was offended, but the other guests seemed to be satisfied with his explanation. Everyone continued eating, accepting the fact that Mr. Lee was going to burp during the whole meal. Bethany, a young college student, even thanked Mr. Lee, saying she had signed up for the dinner to learn about Amish customs but had learned something about another country's customs, as well. She went on to say that she could use this information for her thesis. Everyone clapped, and the group seemed to relax even more.

Later Elaine served strawberry pies for dessert. After they were done eating, everyone burped. One of the ladies said that it was the best pie she'd ever eaten, and if burping was a way to show her appreciation, then she was glad she had. More clapping and laughter followed.

Elaine joined in, feeling almost weightless in her joy. She wasn't sure how Grandma would have reacted to the burping that went on around the dinner table, but to Elaine, it felt good to see the whole group get along so well.

Pushing those memories aside, she started toward the living room. She thought she heard a horse and buggy coming up the lane. Wondering who would be calling at this time of night, she peered out the window into the darkened yard. Lights on the buggy revealed little, and she couldn't make out whose rig it was. Thinking it might be Ben Otto making a surprise call, Elaine left the kitchen and hurried to the back door. Moments later, Leah stepped onto the porch, holding a flashlight in one hand. "*Wie geht's?*" she asked.

"I'm doing fine," Elaine answered, "but I'm surprised to see you. I didn't expect you'd be coming by tonight."

Leah smiled. "I wanted to see how things went with your dinner. Were there lots of people? Was Karen Yoder a big help to you?"

Elaine opened the door wider. "Come in. I'll tell you about it." She led the way to the kitchen and asked her friend, "Would you like a cup of tea?"

"That'd be nice."

Elaine gestured to a chair. "Take a seat, and I'll join you as soon as I get the water heating."

"Is there anything I can do to help?" Leah offered.

"That's okay. It'll only take me a minute." Elaine filled the teakettle and turned on the propane stove. "Now in answer to your earlier questions, things went quite well tonight. But I couldn't have done it all without Karen's help."

"I'm glad to hear that. When I was having supper with Priscilla tonight, I kept thinking I ought to be here, helping you."

"No need to worry about that. Karen and I managed just fine." Elaine took a seat beside Leah. "I did miss Grandma, though."

Leah reached over and clasped Elaine's hand. "That's understandable. You helped her with the dinners for several years. It's only natural that you'd miss her when you were doing something you knew she enjoyed."

"Hosting dinners for tourists brought Grandma much happiness," Elaine agreed. "I only wish we hadn't been forced to quit doing them because of her dementia."

"You did what you had to do." Leah's sincere smile conveyed heartfelt sympathy. "There was no way you could keep hosting the meals with Edna going downhill so quickly."

Elaine sighed. "I know, but I missed doing the dinners, and Grandma did, too—at least until her memory got so bad that she forgot about the tour groups."

"Now you're carrying on her legacy. I'm sure she would be pleased."

When the teakettle whistled, Elaine fixed their tea and got out the leftover strawberry pie. "Would you like a piece?"

"Sure. That looks good."

Elaine cut them each a piece and returned to her seat. "How are things going with you? Have you given many foot treatments lately?"

Leah nodded. "I saw Sara Miller yesterday, and our bishop's wife came after that. Unfortunately, Margaret had an allergic reaction to the walnuts that were in the cookies Sara had given me. The poor woman ended up at the hospital."

"That's *baremlich*. Is she doing okay?"

"It was terrible, but she's much better. Now she'll have to carry an EpiPen at all times in case something like that should happen again."

Elaine sipped some tea. "I'm sensitive to some chemical odors, but I've never had difficulty breathing."

Leah leaned her elbows on the table. "I hope you never do."

As they ate their pie and finished the tea, Leah told Elaine about her encounter with Adam Beachy. "I'm not sure why, but he's against reflexology."

"Maybe he ought to give it a try." Elaine got up to clear their dishes. "Personally, I find your foot treatments to be very relaxing. Since Adam seems to be so uptight, maybe reflexology would help him unwind."

Leah's forehead wrinkled. "I doubt that he'd ever come to see me. Even if he did, I wouldn't want to work on his feet."

"How come?"

"I just wouldn't, that's all."

"Adam is a handsome man. As far as I know, he's not courting anyone."

"He may be handsome, but his personality leaves a lot to be desired." Leah carried the teakettle back to the stove. "Can we talk about something other than Adam Beachy?"

"We can talk about anything you like, but let's go in the living room where the chairs are more comfortable."

Elaine followed Leah out of the kitchen, and they took seats on the sofa. "How are things going with you and Ben these days?" Leah asked.

Elaine shrugged. "Okay, I guess. He drops by fairly often to see how I'm doing, and we went out for supper a few times last month."

"I don't mean to pry, but are you two getting serious?" Leah questioned.

"I'm not sure how Ben feels, but right now, I see our relationship as more of a close friendship than romance. I'm comfortable when I'm with him, but the feelings I have for Ben aren't the same as what I felt for. . ." Elaine's voice trailed off. "Sorry, I didn't mean to go there."

"As what you felt for Jonah?" Leah prompted. "Is that what you were going to say?"

"Jah. Jonah was my first love, and the feelings I had for him will probably remain in my heart. But he's married to Sara now, and they seem to be happy. I wish them well."

Leah squeezed Elaine's arm tenderly. "You're one of the nicest people I know. Despite what you told Jonah about not loving him, I know you ended your relationship so you'd be free to take care of your grandma. When he married Sara, you were gracious. I'm not sure I could have been that understanding. It seems like he rushed into it, if you ask me."

Elaine leaned heavily against the sofa cushions. "Jonah did what he wanted to do, and I did what I had to do. I loved him enough to let him go so he could find the happiness he deserved with someone else. Now he has Sara and little Mark to fill up his life, and they have a new *boppli* on the way."

Leah rubbed the bridge of her nose, the way she often did when deep in thought. "Have you ever wondered if Jonah married Sara just so he could be Mark's father?"

Elaine leaned slightly forward. "It's not my place to wonder things like that, and it doesn't matter what Jonah's reason was for marrying Sara. They're husband and wife now, and I'm no longer a part of Jonah's life. I'm determined to move on and leave my regrets in the past. Someday, if the Lord wills it, I'll fall in love, get married, and fill this house with enough kinner to take up all the empty places. In the meantime, I'm going to take one day at a time and keep hosting tourist dinners."

Leah smiled. "Everyone should learn to take one day at time, but I do hope that someday we'll both find the man of our dreams."

When Leah arrived home, she found her parents in the living room playing a game of checkers. "Where have you been all this time, Leah?" Mom asked. "It's after ten, and we were starting to worry."

"More to the point, your mamm was worried." Dad chuckled as he jumped one of Mom's checkers.

"We knew you were meeting Priscilla for supper, but I thought you'd be home before this," Mom said.

"I'm sorry. I did meet Priscilla for supper, but I decided to stop by and see Elaine on my way home," Leah explained. "I wanted to see how things went with the dinner she hosted this evening."

"Did things go well?" Mom asked.

"Jah. Elaine seemed quite happy and relaxed."

Mom removed her glasses, blew on them, and wiped the smudges with the edge of her apron. "It was nice of you to stop and see your friend, and it's good to hear that Elaine's evening went well. But Eli and Kathryn Byler were here earlier with their son, Abe, who wasn't feeling well. They wanted you to work on his feet. When I told them you weren't here, they were disappointed."

Leah felt bad, but at the same time, the Bylers hadn't made an appointment, so she'd had no idea they were coming. And she couldn't stay home all the time in case someone might need a reflexology treatment.

"Did you tell Eli and Kathryn to take Abe to the clinic for help?" Leah questioned.

Mom gave a nod. "I did, but they asked if you'd be here in the morning."

Leah sighed, wondering if the Bylers had found help for Abe or if she would see them in the morning. If that turned out to be the case, she hoped a foot treatment would be all that Abe needed. If there was something seriously wrong with the boy that was beyond the scope of her abilities, she would certainly tell them so.

CHAPTER 5

Leah smiled as a male hummingbird hovered directly above her head while she filled one of their numerous feeders in the backyard. To describe these little birds as curious was an understatement. The hummer was so close to Leah that she could actually feel the breeze from its fast-moving wings, which buzzed like a bee.

Leah loved watching the beautiful flying jewels. It never ceased to amaze her how quickly the hummingbirds could get from one place to another. She'd even observed them flying backward a few times. Occasionally, after she had the feeders cleaned and refilled before hanging them back on their hooks, Leah would hold a feeder and watch the hummingbirds close up when they flew in to feed. One time she held a feeder with one hand at the top then opened her other hand real wide, holding it directly under the feeding perches. Leah could hardly believe it when one of the little hummers landed on her finger and drank from the flowered portal. Although her arm grew tired, she didn't move a muscle, wanting to make the experience last as long as possible.

This year, they seemed to have a lot more hummers than usual, and every other day she had to refill their five feeders. Leah was glad she'd stocked up on sugar in early spring, because it wouldn't be long before the feeders would need to be filled every day—especially in mid-July, when the birds started migrating to their area from the north. It wasn't unusual for Leah to go through ten pounds of sugar in a week's time while the hummingbirds stayed over for a few weeks before heading to the Gulf of Mexico. From morning until just before dark, the hummers chattered nonstop as they flitted from one feeder to another. Sometimes they dive-bombed one another in a fierce battle to get to the feeders. Other times, the tiny birds took turns at the feeders and everything seemed quite peaceful.

Leah was excited that Alissa Cramer, one of their English neighbors, would be coming over during the active time in August to band the hummingbirds. She couldn't imagine a metal band being small enough to fit on their little legs but big enough to have a number inscribed on it for tracking future behavior. It would be interesting to see the process.

Leah had just filled the last feeder when a horse and buggy pulled in. Sparky raised his head from where he laid on the porch, but he didn't bother to bark.

Leah recognized the Bylers' rig as it pulled up to the hitching rack. Kathryn got out and helped three-year-old Abe down while Eli secured their horse.

"I'm so glad you're here," Kathryn said, carrying her son as she rushed over to Leah. "Our boy has a nasty cold, and with his asthma, I think it's gone into his chest." Dark circles stood out beneath the young woman's pale blue eyes, and Leah figured Abe's mother hadn't gotten much sleep.

"I'm sorry to hear that, and I feel bad that I wasn't home when you stopped by last night." Leah motioned to the house. "Come inside, and I'll see what I can do for Abe."

Leah led the way, stepping around Sparky. Once inside, she suggested that Eli wait upstairs with her dad. Since this was Saturday and Dad wasn't working, the two men could visit while Leah worked on Abe's feet in the basement. The boy's mother would want to be with him, so she didn't ask her to wait upstairs, even though Kathryn could have visited with Mom.

When they entered the basement, Leah asked Kathryn to place Abe in the recliner, and then Leah took a seat on the footstool in front of him while his mother seated herself rigidly on a nearby chair.

"How long has Abe been feeling *grank*?" Leah asked.

"He's been ill almost a week." Kathryn sighed. "We thought he'd be better by now, but when his wheezing seemed worse, we decided it was time to bring him to you."

"Did you take him to the clinic?"

Kathryn shook her head. "It's expensive to go to the doctor, and we were hoping you could help."

"I'll do what I can." Leah picked up the little boy's left foot. "But I'm not a doctor and make no promises."

"I understand. Please, just do what you can."

As Leah began working on the little guy's feet, she discovered that the areas representing his adrenal glands were tender and inflamed. "I have never found a case of asthma where the reflexes to the adrenal glands weren't tender," she told Kathryn. "It may take awhile, but I believe with a little persistence, stimulating the adrenals will help."

Kathryn's face seemed to relax a bit, and she leaned back slightly in her chair. Meanwhile, Leah kept applying pressure to the two spots on Abe's small feet that needed the most attention.

After she'd been working on him nearly half an hour, his color improved and he seemed to be breathing better. "I'd like to see Abe again in a few days," Leah said. "But do keep an eye on him, and if he gets any worse, please don't hesitate to take him to the doctor. I'm sure your church district will help financially."

"Danki, Leah. I appreciate what you've done." Tears welled in Kathryn's eyes as she placed a few dollars in the jar on Leah's table.

Leah touched the woman's hand. "You're welcome."

When the Bylers left, Leah went to the kitchen to see if her mother needed help with anything.

"If you have time, would you mind running an errand for me?" Mom asked.

"Sure. I don't have anyone scheduled for a foot treatment until this afternoon. Where did you want me to go?"

"I need a few things from Rockome Garden Foods." Mom handed Leah a list. "I'd go myself, but I'm in the middle of making bread and don't want to leave it."

Leah thought about offering to finish the bread but decided it would be more enjoyable to take a buggy ride. Besides, she usually found a few things to buy at the store, and it would be fun to browse. "No problem, Mom. I'll go there right now."

Arcola

As Adam headed down the road in the direction of Rockome Garden Foods, he made sure to keep a tight rein on his horse, because for some reason the normally docile animal wanted to run at full speed. Maybe it was the smell and feel of summer that caused Flash to be so frisky. Sunny days like today certainly put a spring in Adam's step, so why wouldn't they have the same effect on his horse? The way Flash was acting, his name truly fit.

Since both of Adam's employees were working at the hardware store, he had decided it would be a good time to do some grocery shopping. His cupboards were getting bare, and there wasn't much in the refrigerator. If he didn't restock, he would either have to eat supper at one of the local restaurants this evening or get by on crackers and cheese. Of course, Adam could have gone to one of the other stores closer to his home, but he liked going to Rockome because they had a good selection of canned goods, butter, cheese, pastas, and bulk foods—not to mention all the baked goods and homemade candy. Adam's mouth watered just thinking about the cookies and sweet breads he planned to buy.

"If you had a wife, she'd cook and bake for you." Adam shook his head, thinking about what his sister had said the last time they'd talked on the phone. Mary was determined to see Adam married, and he was just as determined to remain single.

Who needs a wife? Adam thought. *I'm perfectly capable of washing my own clothes, cooking, and cleaning.* If he were completely honest with himself, he'd have to admit that he wasn't the best cook or the tidiest housekeeper. He got by, though, and he was fine with that. Of course, no wife meant having no children or future grandchildren. It also meant he'd be a lonely bachelor for the rest of his life, without the warmth, companionship, or love of a woman. But even if he found someone and fell in love, how could Adam trust her not to break his heart the way his mother had broken his dad's? Adam never wanted his children to go through life feeling like they were unwanted. No child deserved that.

No, Adam told himself, *even if I have to spend the rest of my life in solitude, I'll be better off alone.*

When Rockome Garden Foods came into view, Adam directed Flash into the parking lot and up to the hitching rack. After he'd made sure the horse was secure, he headed into the store.

It took awhile to get everything on his list, and as he was heading to the checkout counter, he remembered he still needed some honey.

Hurriedly, he headed back to the aisle where several varieties of honey were located and picked one off the shelf. It slipped out of his hand and smashed on the floor. "Oh no!" he groaned. "This is not what I need today."

Using the toe of his boot, Adam pushed the broken glass aside and rushed to the front counter, where he told the clerk what had happened. "Do you have something I can put the broken glass in?" he asked.

"Don't worry about that," she said, smiling. "I'll get one of the other clerks to take care of it."

Just then, Adam spotted Leah entering the store.

Leah was looking over her mother's list when she glanced up and saw Adam standing near the checkout counter. *Oh, great. I hope he doesn't say anything to me.*

Hurrying, she zipped down the pasta aisle, grabbing a bag of noodles, the first item on Mom's list. She turned and was about to head down the canned-goods aisle when she stepped in something gooey. Her feet slipped out from under her, and down she went.

"Ach, my!" Leah gasped, seeing that she had sticky honey on her hands, knees, and the lower part of her dress. Then she noticed the broken glass pushed off to one side, nearly hidden under the bottom shelf. Someone must have either knocked the jar off the shelf or picked the honey up and dropped it.

As Leah attempted to get back on her feet, she heard Adam's voice.

"Are you all right?"

She looked up and grimaced when she saw him staring down at her. "I–I'm not hurt. I just slipped in some honey."

"That's my fault," he mumbled, extending his hand to Leah. "I dropped a jar a few minutes ago. The clerk said she would ask someone to clean it up, but I guess you got here first."

Despite her best efforts, Leah couldn't seem to stand on her own, so she reached up and clasped Adam's hand. It was surprisingly warm, and as he helped her stand, she noticed his look of concern.

"Are you sure you're not hurt?" Adam's tone seemed sincere.

"I'm fine. Just a sticky mess." Leah let go of Adam's hand and noticed that she'd transferred some of the honey onto his hand, too.

"I'm really sorry." He took off his hat and ran his fingers through his hair. "Oh, now look what I've done."

Leah held her breath, gazing at the sticky goo that had shifted from Adam's fingers to his hair, making it clump in several places. He stood several seconds with a peculiar expression; then he burst out laughing. It was the first time Leah had heard him laugh, and she couldn't keep from giggling herself.

"We're a mess, aren't we?" Leah grew serious, trying to contain her laughter. "Anyway, it's not your fault. If someone said they'd clean it up, they should have followed through."

"I'm sure they were planning to," Adam said. "This just happened right before you got here."

"Well, I'm glad it was me who fell and not some elderly person. Besides, I didn't get cut by the broken glass, and that's a good thing." Leah looked down at her hands and groaned. She really was a sticky mess, and wondered how she would ever get all that honey off her shoes, not to mention her dress. "I'd better head to the restroom and get cleaned up," she said.

"Jah, me, too."

"Danki for your help, Adam."

When Adam nodded, Leah noticed that he was smiling, as though trying to hold back more laughter. Was that smirking because he thought she looked funny, or was it just a friendly smile? Maybe Adam had an agreeable side that she hadn't seen before. Well, there was no time to figure it out now. After she got cleaned up, she needed to get her shopping done quickly, because she had two more people coming for foot treatments this afternoon. Her shoes sticking to the floor with each step she took, Leah tiptoed her way to the restroom. She hoped someone would get the mess cleaned up soon, because she was making sticky spots all the way to the bathroom. *I hope Adam doesn't have any trouble washing that honey out of his hair*, she thought, suppressing another giggle.

CHAPTER 6

Arthur

Adam glanced out the window of his store and grimaced. Several soda pop cans were strewn about the parking lot, as if someone had just pitched them out the window of their vehicle. Most likely some thoughtless Englisher's action, but then it could have been done by one of the local Amish youth. The litter made his business look scruffy, so he needed to dispose of it right away.

"I'm going outside to pick up some aluminum cans," he told Ben Otto, his newest employee.

Ben looked up from behind the counter where he'd been waiting on an elderly Amish woman. "Want me to get 'em?"

"No, that's okay; I'll take care of it." It was getting hot and stuffy inside the store, even with the overhead ceiling fans that were run by a diesel air compressor, so this was a good excuse for Adam to get some fresh air.

"I'll keep an eye on things in here." Ben ran his fingers through his wavy brown hair. "I enjoy working in your store, Adam, and I appreciate you giving me this job."

"And I appreciate everything you do." Adam was glad he'd hired Ben. The twenty-three-year-old Amish man had a good work ethic. Adam had quickly discovered that he could depend on Ben, who aimed to please.

When Adam stepped outside, the heat and humidity almost took his breath away. Not even a hint of a breeze was blowing. So much for the fresh air he was hoping to find. No wonder it had gotten so hot and stuffy inside the store. It was the middle of July, so warm temperatures could be expected. But this extraordinary heat surprised him.

Gathering up the empty cans, Adam tossed them into the recycle bin. Then he headed around to the back of the store to make sure his and Ben's horses had plenty of water. He'd built a lean-to for the animals so they had enough shade inside the small corral. Adam's other employee, Henry Raber, usually rode his bike to work, but today Henry hadn't come in because he'd pulled a muscle in his shoulder yesterday while picking up a heavy sack of cement at the close of work. Adam had suggested that Henry take today off and see one of their local chiropractors. Hopefully he'd done that and would find relief. Adam figured they could get by without Henry for a few days, but so far this summer, business had been brisk. He couldn't afford to be shorthanded for any length of time.

Try not to worry about it, he told himself. *As Dad used to say, "Just take one day at a time." What was that verse Dad always quoted? Oh, yeah, Matthew 6:34: "Take therefore no thought for the morrow: for the morrow shall take thought for the things of itself."*

Adam glanced around the parking lot once more to be sure he hadn't missed any cans or other litter. A few weeks ago, he'd discovered that someone had emptied their car's ashtray in the planter box by the entrance door of the store. The planter had colorful petunias growing in it, so surely the person knew it wasn't a container for waste. He wondered what would make someone get out of their car, walk up to the entrance door where the planter sat, and empty their cigarette butts. Adam didn't know if he was being overly critical because of the way things were these days, but he sure wished folks would be more considerate.

Satisfied that the parking lot looked clean and inviting, he returned to the store. He found Ben waiting on their bishop, Levi Kauffman. Since Ben seemed to have everything under control, Adam started toward the other side of the store to see if he was getting low on any gardening tools. First though, he needed to make sure the dolly was readily available, because anytime now, the delivery truck should be pulling in with his most recent order. Various-sized bags of thistle and sunflower seed were due in today, which was good, since there wasn't much left of either in the store right now.

Adam went to the storage room, which was in the rear of the building and led to the back door where deliveries were usually dropped off. He always liked to help the driver unload supplies, so he pushed the dolly over and left it sitting close to the back door. That would be one less thing to look for when the truck arrived.

As Leah headed to the health food store to buy some vitamins, she found herself panting for breath. The road was perfectly flat, so pedaling the bike wasn't causing a problem. What had zapped her strength was the unrelenting heat. Summer was nice, but when it was humid and hot like this, Leah longed for the cooler days of fall, but they hadn't even reached the dog days of August yet. What she wouldn't give for a gentle breeze right now. Up ahead, she was glad to see a huge maple tree that provided some shade along the road.

Leah stopped to catch her breath, and took a drink from the Thermos of iced tea she carried in her basket. The next time she made the trip to town this summer she would take the horse and buggy. At least then the horse, who was trained to pull and could withstand the heat, would be doing all the work and not her.

She watched as a delivery truck approached. It wasn't unusual to see trucks on this road making deliveries into Arthur or to businesses just outside of town. As the truck whizzed by, it created a breeze that felt really good for the few seconds it lasted, even though it smelled of exhaust. All too soon the air grew still again.

Leah looked up into the tree. The thick cover of maple leaves hung motionless. She wiped her forehead with the back of her hand, standing there just a bit longer. She took the cap off the Thermos and guzzled more of the iced tea, grabbing a small ice cube with her teeth to let it melt in her mouth. When she peeked into the Thermos and saw only a few ice cubes left in the remaining tea, she snapped the lid back on, knowing if she stayed any longer, the humidity would get worse and her tea would no longer be cold. Taking one more look around, she watched a butterfly slowly flitter past and land on some chicory weed that was growing in clusters along the road. Even the butterfly's wings looked bogged down from the clammy, moisture-laden air as it sat on the blue, daisylike flower.

Leah moved on, trying to keep her focus on the scenery instead of how miserable she felt. Sweat ran down her back as the sun beat relentlessly on her body. The creek, running from one side of the road and through a pipe to the other side, looked inviting as Leah pedaled over it and continued onward.

She knew how good the cool water would feel, but there was no time for such a childlike venture. She giggled, thinking how silly it would look if she showed up at the health food store soaking wet.

As Leah proceeded, her bicycle pedals kept slipping. Something must be wrong. When they quit working altogether, she had to stop and get off.

Looking down at her bike, Leah groaned. The chain was loose, and she had nothing to tighten it with. "At this rate, I'll never get to the health food store," she mumbled, making sure her bike was on the shoulder of the road as she began to push. Even when she did get there, she'd either have to walk the bike home or find some way to fix the chain.

While Adam waited for his delivery to arrive, he went back to the main part of the store and headed to the first aisle, where the garden tools were kept. There he caught sight of a freckle-faced English boy who appeared to be in his early teens. The kid had his hands in the pocket of his jeans, and a worn-looking baseball cap covered most of his red hair, which was pulled back into a ponytail. He stood staring at the shelf full of gardening gloves and hand shovels and didn't seem to notice Adam standing nearby. Adam thought it was strange that the boy was wearing a denim jacket, buttoned up to his neck. On a day as warm as this, he didn't think anyone would feel the need for a jacket.

Just as Adam was going to ask the boy if he needed any help, the kid grabbed two pairs of gloves off the shelf, along with two of the small shovels, and stuffed them inside his jacket. Then he turned, caught sight of Adam, and froze.

Adam didn't say anything at first, hoping the boy would take the items to the checkout counter to pay. Of course, that wasn't likely. Most people who planned to buy something didn't stuff the articles inside their jacket.

Time seemed to stand still as they stared at each other. Adam didn't back down, and the kid nervously broke eye contact, glancing toward the front doors. Adam didn't have time to blink before the boy ran past him, headed for the exit.

"Stop where you are!" Adam shouted, convinced the boy was shoplifting. He raced after him. "You'd better give me those items you took!"

Glancing to her right, Leah saw Adam's hardware store come into view. Thinking she might find some type of tool there to fix her chain, Leah pushed the bike into the parking lot and set the kickstand. She noticed the delivery truck that had passed her earlier was parked along the side of the store. The driver, talking on a cell phone, stood by the rear of the truck.

Leah went up the front steps and reached for the door handle. The door flew open, and—*wham!*—a teenaged boy crashed into her, knocking her down. As she tried to clamber to her feet, Adam barreled out the open door, shouting for the boy to stop. In his haste, Adam plowed into Leah, and they both landed on the porch in a heap.

CHAPTER 7

"Are you okay?" Adam and Leah asked at the same time.

Leah looked at Adam and bobbed her head. "When I reached for the door to your store, I never expected to get plowed down by that boy. He didn't even look back or apologize." She looked at her hands and noticed that they were a bit scraped. Nervously brushing them together, she added, "The least he could have done was to ask if I was all right."

"I'm sorry about that." Adam stood and reached for her hand. "And I never expected to catch someone shoplifting in my store." He grimaced. "I didn't actually catch the fellow, now did I? Thanks to me tripping over you and falling, that young thief got away."

Leah scrunched up her face, realizing the hand Adam held in his stung more than she'd first thought it did.

"Let me look at those hands," Adam said, his voice filled with concern. Before she could react, he took her other hand and examined it as well. "I have some witch hazel in the store. We'd better get your hands cleaned off."

Leah quickly pulled back from Adam's grip. Confusion mixed with a bit of irritation bubbled in her soul as she gazed up at him. Wiping her hands on her dress, she asked, "Are you suggesting that it's my fault you didn't capture the boy?"

He shook his head. "You were just in the wrong place at the wrong time."

"So if I hadn't come to the hardware store, you'd have your merchandise back by now?"

Adam shrugged. "Can't say for sure, but there's a pretty good chance I would have caught the kid."

"Maybe you should go after him now. Did you see what direction he took?"

"No. Did you?"

Leah's hands went straight to her hips. "Of course not. How could I see anything with you lying in a heap beside me, blocking my view?" She bit back a chuckle, thinking how silly Adam had looked when he fell down. His thick blond hair was in a disarray, and she resisted the urge to reach up and comb it with her fingers.

Adam stared at Leah. Then, in a surprise gesture, he reached out and touched her head covering.

She pulled back slightly. "Wh–what are you doing?"

"Your *kapp* is crooked. Looks like it's about to come off." Adam's voice seemed deeper than usual, and Leah swallowed hard as she stood, letting him readjust her covering.

"Are you going to call the authorities about the shoplifter?" Leah questioned, hoping the change of topic would get her mind off his dreamy brown eyes.

"I'm not sure what I'm going to do." Adam grunted, rubbing his chin. "If I call the sheriff, I should do it soon, but if I wait, maybe I'll see the boy in Arthur or somewhere else in our area and approach him myself."

"That could be dangerous, don't you think?"

"He's just a kid, Leah. Maybe there's a reason he stole from my store."

"I can't understand why anyone would steal. Even if a person is poor, they should ask for help. Our community is always willing to help out when Amish or English have a need." Leah reached up and felt her head covering, noting that it seemed to be in place. "Danki for fixing my kapp." Feeling a bit tongue-tied, she could feel her cheeks warm. Why was Adam staring at her like that again? Was something else off-kilter? Should she ask?

After what seemed like forever, Adam blinked and looked away. "So, uh. . .what brings you to my store today?" he asked, looking down and brushing at the dust on his trousers.

"The chain on my bike came loose. I was hoping you might have something here that would help me fix it."

Adam chuckled. "I'm not a bike shop, Leah."

The heat she felt on her face intensified. "I know that, but I thought maybe—"

"Come to think of it, I do have a tool in the back of my buggy that's exactly what you need."

"Would you mind if I borrow it?" she asked.

His eyes narrowed. "You really think you can fix the chain?"

Leah's defenses rose. "Despite what you might think, Adam, I'm not *dumm*."

"I never said you were dumb. Just didn't know if you'd ever tightened a bicycle chain."

She relaxed a little. "I've never done it before, but I think I can figure it out."

"Okay." Adam shrugged. "If you'll wait right here, I'll get it."

That young woman is sure hard to figure out, Adam thought as he made his way around the back of the store to his buggy. *One minute she's sweet as date pudding, and the next minute she acts like she has a bee under her kapp. Sure wish she hadn't come along when she did; I'd have my shoplifter by now. Who knows where he ran off to, or why he took those things from my store.*

Adam picked up his pace, noticing that the delivery truck was already there. Luckily, the driver was talking on his cell phone, so that would give Adam a few extra minutes before he'd need to help the guy unload his order. *Sure wish Leah wasn't so pretty. Makes it hard for me to look at her and not long for a wife. I wonder how well she cooks.*

He slapped the side of his head. *Now where did that foolish notion come from? I'm just not thinking straight today. Must be all the excitement.*

When Adam reached the buggy, he opened his toolbox and took out what he needed. Then he went back to where he'd left Leah but discovered she wasn't there. He glanced at her bike, parked in one of the bicycle racks. No sign of Leah over there, either.

Adam crouched down to examine the chain and realized that it needed to be shortened. Thinking Leah may have gone into the store, he went inside, where he discovered Leah near the checkout counter, talking to Ben.

"Here you go, Leah." Adam handed her the tool.

She stared at the object. "What's that?"

"It's called a 'chain tool,' and it's used to push the pin out of the chain so you can take out links to make it the right length. I took a look at your bike before I came inside, and it appears that the chain has stretched. That's why it's loose."

Leah stared at the small metal tool with a curious expression. "Are you sure this will work on my chain?"

"Course it will. If you know what you're doing, that is. Since there aren't any common tools you would find in my store that can do a decent job of removing and reinserting chain pins, you really do need this tool."

"Oh, okay." Leah hesitated, glancing at the chain tool then back at Adam. "Umm. . . I'm really not sure how to use this."

"Figured as much. Want me to do it for you?" he asked.

"I appreciate the offer, but you have a store to run, and I noticed a delivery truck out back when I entered the parking lot, so you'll probably be busy with that."

"It's not a problem." Adam looked at Ben. "Since there are no customers in the store at the moment, would you open the back door and help the driver bring in those bags of seed? The dolly is inside the door, and you can just stack them anywhere in the back room. I'll get to them as soon as I help Leah."

Ben nodded. "Sure, no problem."

Adam followed Leah out the door. While he knelt next to her bike, Leah stood off to one side, watching. "I've done this a good many times," he said, looking up at her. "My daed owned a bike shop when I was a boy, so I've had lots of practice fixing chains and a whole lot of other things related to bikes. Fact is, I've repaired my own bike chain several times."

Her eyebrows lifted. "Really? I didn't know you owned a bike. I've never seen you riding one."

"Jah, well, there are a lot of things about me you don't know."

CHAPTER 8

Ich hab's im rick," Priscilla complained to her mother as they pulled weeds from their garden. Mom straightened, rubbing an area on her lower back. "I can understand why you have a backache. My back's about to give out, too." She gestured to the wicker chairs sitting under the gazebo Dad had built a few years ago. "Let's take a break. I'll go get us some lemonade, and we can sit out there in the shade and rest awhile before we finish up for the day."

Priscilla smiled. "That sounds good to me, only why don't you sit and let me get the lemonade?"

"That's okay," Mom said. "I need to go inside anyhow. While we've been weeding, I thought of a few things I want to put on the grocery list. If I don't do it now, I'll probably get busy doing something else and forget." She frowned. "I've been kind of forgetful lately."

"That's fine, Mom, but if you need me for anything, just give a holler."

Watching her mother go toward the house, holding her lower back as she walked, Priscilla sauntered around the yard for a bit, hoping to get the kinks out of her own back. All that bending, stooping, and pulling of weeds had really done a number on her this morning. She glanced at the small store connected to their home, where she and Mom sold homemade jelly and several kinds of home-canned fruits. It was closed today. Otherwise, she would have been working there instead of in the garden. Priscilla helped her mother process all of their fruits, vegetables, and berries, which she found somewhat rewarding, but weeding was not one of her favorite things to do. Mom's either, for that matter, but it needed to be done.

Priscilla looked up at the house, thinking about how Mom had said she'd been forgetful lately. She hoped it was just a case of having too much to do, and that Mom wouldn't end up with dementia someday, like what Elaine's grandma had gone through. It had saddened Priscilla to watch her good friend deal with the heartache of losing her grandma to such a horrible disease. Priscilla, as well as Leah, had offered Elaine their support. Priscilla knew if she were ever faced with an adversity that her two best friends would be there for her, too.

Rubbing at the knot in her lower back, Priscilla glanced toward the road and was surprised to see Leah pedaling up the driveway.

"I was just thinking about you," Priscilla said when Leah rode up.

Leah grinned. "I hope they were good thoughts."

"Of course. I was thinking how fortunate I am to have good friends like you and Elaine, and how we've always been there for one another."

"That's true, and I feel blessed because of it." Leah climbed off her bike and set the kickstand. "I'm on my way home from the health food store and decided to stop here and ask for a cold drink of water." She fanned her face with one hand while holding up her Thermos with the other. "All the ice cubes melted, and what little tea I have left is now warm. When I left home, I didn't realize it was going to be such a hot day. After all I've been through, I'm drenched with perspiration."

Priscilla felt concern. "What do you mean, all you've 'been through'? Did something happen on the way to or from the health food store?"

"It was on the way. My bicycle chain became loose, so I stopped by Adam Beachy's hardware store to see if I could find something to fix it, and then. . ." Leah paused and blotted her damp forehead with her dress sleeve. "Whew, the air is so humid today. My clothes are actually sticking to me."

Priscilla motioned to the wicker chairs under the shade of the gazebo. "Take a seat. I'll run in the house and get you something cold to drink. You look miserable, and I'm worried that you may have been in the sun too long."

"Danki," Leah said. "I really do need to rest awhile. When you come back, I'll tell you what happened after I got to Adam's store."

" 'Here you go; I brought lemonade, and it's nice and cold," Priscilla said when she returned from the house carrying two glasses.

"Danki." Leah took a big drink then held the cool glass against her hot cheek. "This is so refreshing. It's just what I needed right now."

"I know what you mean." Priscilla took the seat beside Leah and drank from her own glass. "Mom and I have spent most of our morning weeding, and it didn't take long till we were both hot and sweaty; not to mention that our backs are hurting."

"I'm sorry to hear that. By the way, where is your mamm?"

"She's in the house, adding things to her grocery list."

"I have a couple appointments early this afternoon, but I'm free around four o'clock, if you'd like to come by for a foot treatment and neck massage. You can bring your mamm along, and I'll work on her, too."

"That sounds nice, and if Mom doesn't have anything important she needs to do, we both may take you up on that offer." Priscilla sipped her drink and set her glass on the wicker table between them. "Before you leave, I'll refill your Thermos with cold water and lots of ice cubes. That way you'll have something to drink on your trip home."

"That'd be great. Danki."

"So tell me now; what happened at Adam's store this morning?"

Leah fiddled with the ties on her head covering, remembering how flustered she'd felt when Adam fell beside her on the porch.

"Your cheeks are bright red." Priscilla's voice was edged with concern. "Maybe you need to drink more lemonade."

Leah shook her head. "No, I'm fine. Just thinking about what happened is all."

"Please tell me. I'm anxious to hear."

Leah recounted the events, from when the teenage boy rushed out the door and knocked her to the porch to when Adam had nearly fallen on top of her.

Priscilla giggled. "I'm sure it wasn't funny, but I can just picture you and Adam lying there beside each other."

"You're right, falling wasn't funny, but if you'd seen the look on Adam's face, you would have laughed." Leah suppressed a giggle. "I seem to be falling a lot lately whenever Adam's around."

"What do you mean?"

"I saw him at Rockome Garden Foods the other day and managed to slip in some honey that got on the floor when he dropped a jar of the stuff."

"Oh no! Maybe it's a sign that you're meant to *stick* together." Priscilla snickered.

Leah shook her head. "No way! Adam's not my type, and I'm sure the feeling is mutual."

"I didn't think Elam was my type when he first seemed interested in me, but look at us now—we're courting."

"That's different. You've known Elam since we were kinner, and he was your friend before he asked if he could court you." Leah took another drink. The tangy, cool lemonade felt good on her parched throat. "Adam and I don't even like each other, so there's no chance of him ever courting me."

"Who let this mutt in my store?" Adam asked Ben. A bedraggled-looking black Lab was sniffing around the garden rakes.

Ben shrugged his broad shoulders. "Beats me. I didn't even notice him till now."

Adam inhaled a long breath. "Well, he needs to go out. No dogs are allowed in here, unless they're service animals." He pointed at the Lab. "And that mangy critter definitely doesn't qualify!"

"Want me to get him out?"

"No, I'll take care of it." Adam opened the front door, pointed at the dog, and hollered, "Go on outside where you belong!"

The dog looked up at Adam as if he had no idea what he wanted.

Adam wasn't keen on touching the dirty animal, so he grabbed a broom and shooed the dog out the door, quickly shutting it behind him. Hopefully, by the time the next customer came in, the dog would have gone back to wherever it came from. In the meantime, Adam had a box of paintbrushes to unpack, as well as the bags of birdseed to unwrap and stock on the shelves. He decided to work on the seed bags first. The bags weighed from ten pounds all the way up to fifty pounds, so that would keep him busy for a while.

"I'll be in the back room if you need me," he called to Ben.

"No problem. I'll take care of any customers who come in," Ben responded.

Adam finally got the bags off the pallets and used the dolly to wheel them out to the shelves. First he put the smaller bags on the higher shelves, then the forty-and fifty-pound bags went on the lower shelves. In the same aisle, opposite the seed, were various-sized bird feeders, along with boxes of suet cakes.

After several trips, Adam brought out the last two fifty-pound bags of seeds. His shoulders had started hurting. *I wonder if Leah could help my shoulders.* Pausing, Adam thumped his head. *Now what made me think that?*

Making sure there was room for the last bag, Adam picked it up and felt his fingers poke through the middle of the bag. As if watching it in slow motion, he saw the birdseed pour out, spreading all over the floor.

"Oh, great! What more could go wrong today?" Adam moaned as he inspected the almost-empty bag. Apparently there'd been a tear in the bag, which his fingers had made bigger when he'd lifted it. "Now how did I not see that before?" He looked down at the seed-covered floor, slowly shaking his head.

"Do you need some help here?" Ben offered, joining Adam in the aisle.

Adam looked at him and rolled his eyes.

"I'll go get a container, and we can put the seed in there." Ben left quickly. When he returned, he held a garbage can, two brooms, and two dustpans. As they worked together to clean up the mess, Adam decided to question Ben.

"I don't know if you realized what happened a little bit ago, but we had a shoplifter in the store. That's who I was chasing when I ran out the door and bumped into Leah Mast."

"No, I didn't realize that." Ben's dark eyebrows squished together. "Guess I must have been busy with a customer at the time."

"Did you notice a teen enter the store before that? He had on a denim jacket and a baseball cap. Oh, and he had red hair, which he wore in a ponytail."

"I was up at the front of the store, but I didn't see anyone like that come in." Ben scratched his head with a quizzical look. "Course, I may have been helping a customer and just didn't notice the boy. What are you going to do about this, Adam? Will you call the sheriff?"

"Think I'll wait on that." Adam shoveled another dustpan full of seed and poured it into the can. "He only took some garden gloves and two hand shovels, so I'm really not out that much."

"Okay, whatever you think is best," Ben responded with a shrug.

"Would you mind finishing this up while I take care of the paintbrushes that need to be put out?" Adam asked.

"Sure, no problem."

Adam headed to the back of the store, tore open the box, and had begun sorting the paintbrushes but had to stop. "Guess I overdid it with all those seed bags," he mumbled, rolling his shoulders, hoping to get the kinks out. "Well, this isn't going to get done by itself." Reaching inside the box, he stopped again when he heard a whimper. Standing a few feet away was that same black Lab.

"You again? What are you doing back in here, boy? Are you lost or just looking for trouble?"

The scraggly-looking dog walked timidly over and pawed at Adam's pant leg. It looked as if the mutt had something in his mouth. At Adam's command, the Lab dropped it and backed up when Adam's voice grew stern. "I don't know what you want, but whatever it is, you won't find it here." Adam opened the back door this time and practically pushed the dog outside. "Go home!"

With his tail between his legs, the Lab slunk off, but before Adam saw which direction the dog took, he quickly shut the door. *I wonder how that* hund *got in here again.*

Massaging his shoulder, Adam walked back toward the box of supplies but stopped short when he kicked something with his shoe. Bending down to pick up the article, he realized it was a pair of garden gloves, still packaged together and unopened. It looked to be the same type, or perhaps even one of the pairs the shoplifting kid had snatched earlier today. But that couldn't be—he'd seen the boy run out the door with the gloves. Could he have dropped one of them as he was running away, and had the dog picked it up? Adam would probably never know the answer to that, and right now, it didn't seem that important.

Scratching his head, Adam groaned. If the rest of this day didn't turn out any better than the first part had, tomorrow he might decide to let Ben run the store by himself and stay home in bed.

Of course, Adam told himself, *that's really not an option.*

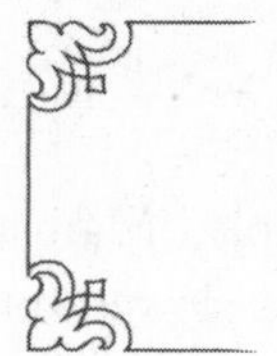

CHAPTER 9

How are you doing today?" Leah asked when Margaret entered the basement for another foot treatment.

"I've recovered from my reaction to the walnuts, but since I never got a foot treatment that day, my back is still hurting." Margaret reached around and touched a spot on her lower back. "Seems like the older I get, the more aches and pains I seem to have. Even when I do the simplest chores, some part of my body ends up hurting."

"Well, have a seat in my chair, and I'll see what I can do to ease some of that." Leah motioned to the recliner.

Margaret did as Leah told her. "When I was walking up to your house, I noticed all the hummingbird feeders you have. I paused a few minutes to watch them flitter around. Now that was kind of fun."

"They are fun to watch." Leah took a seat on the stool in front of Margaret. "We have so many hummers this year that I've had to add a few extra feeders to accommodate them all."

"I've only seen a couple at our place," Margaret said as Leah applied lotion to her left foot. "I don't have any feeders out, but they seem to like our honeysuckle bush."

Leah nodded. "Several bushes and flowering plants attract the hummers, but with so many coming into our yard, keeping the feeders filled seems to work best."

"That makes sense," Margaret agreed.

"Isn't it amazing how watching something that simple can help a person relax and forget all their troubles, even if only for a few minutes?"

"Jah. My husband often says it's a shame more people don't take the time to stop and look at a pretty sunset or observe God's creatures that are here for our enjoyment."

Leah smiled. "He's right about that. A lot of times the beauty God's given us goes unnoticed."

"It's good to know you're not one of those people," Margaret said. "The world would be a lot better place if folks just slowed down and uncomplicated life a bit."

"It could certainly be good therapy. I know it is for me."

As Leah began working, she found several sore spots on Margaret's left foot. Moving to the right foot, she uncovered more tender areas, which she pressure-pointed and massaged. "The areas I worked on that were so tender are related to your back," Leah explained, "so I'm hoping I was able to open the pathways and offer you some relief."

When Leah finished, Margaret put her shoes on and stood. Walking around the room for a bit, she smiled and said, "Danki, Leah. My back feels much better than it did when I first got here."

Leah smiled. "I'm glad it helped, but you may want to take it easy for the rest of the day, and if your back begins to hurt again, be sure to ice it for a while."

Margaret placed some money in the jar and gave Leah a hug. "What you do here in this room is a good thing, and I hope you won't ever quit, because you've helped many people."

Leah was pleased to hear that. It was a reminder that she was using the ability God had given her to help others, and that was reward enough. Too bad people like Adam didn't appreciate or believe in reflexology.

Well, to each his own, Leah thought after Margaret said good-bye and went upstairs. *I don't know why I'm thinking about Adam right now, because I certainly don't need his approval.*

Leah glanced at her appointment book and realized that she didn't have anyone else scheduled for the rest of the day. Maybe this would be a good time to sit outside, enjoy the sunshine, and get a little reading done. She'd started a new novel set in the Old West the other day but had only read the first two chapters. Most days she was too busy to read, and by the time she went to bed at night, Leah was so tired she couldn't keep her eyes open.

After putting away her massage lotion and washing up, Leah went upstairs. She found Mom in the kitchen, peeling potatoes at the sink. "It's only four o'clock," Leah said, glancing at the clock on the far wall.

"Are you starting supper already?"

"Just thought I'd get the potatoes peeled and cut; then I'll put them in a kettle with cold water till it's time to start cooking." Mom smiled at Leah. "How'd it go with Margaret? She looked quite relaxed when she came upstairs."

"She said her back felt better after I worked on her feet, so with less pain to deal with, I'm sure that's why she was relaxed." Leah took a pitcher of iced tea from the refrigerator and opened the cupboard where the glasses were kept. "Would you like some iced tea, Mom?"

"Maybe later," Mom replied. "Right now I just want to finish this."

"I was going outside to read awhile," Leah said, "but if you need my help with supper, it can wait."

Mom shook her head. "You go ahead. I can manage. Besides, there aren't many potatoes left to peel."

"Okay then, call me if you need anything." Leah poured herself some tea and put the container back in the refrigerator. Taking her book from the drawer where she'd put it the other day, she went out the back door.

Leah had just seated herself on the porch when a hummingbird zoomed in. At first it hovered above the book she held. Then it flew right over her head and found its way to the nearest feeder hanging from one of the shepherd's hooks near the house.

Glancing down at the book, Leah realized that the hummingbird had probably been attracted to the red in the cover. She grinned, watching the tiny bird at the feeder dip its beak in and out to get the sweet nectar. Leah never tired of watching the hummers and wished they could stay all year. Since that wasn't possible, she would enjoy them for the few months they were in the area. And next month, when Alissa came to band the birds, Leah would make sure she was available not only to watch the procedure but also to offer Alissa assistance if needed.

Pulling her gaze from the hummingbird, Leah set her drink on the table and opened the book. She'd only read a few pages when Priscilla rode up on her bike. Leah figured she was probably here for the foot treatment they had talked about working in.

So much for getting any reading done, Leah thought. But then, she quickly corrected herself. Priscilla had complained of back pain, and if Leah could help, she would gladly set aside her free time to accommodate a friend.

Sparky ran out to greet Priscilla, although he didn't bark.

"Hey, pup. How are you doing?" Priscilla bent down and scratched behind the dog's ears.

"Mom and I did some more weeding after lunch, and now my back hurts even worse than it did before," she said, joining Leah on the porch. "Would you have time to give me a treatment?"

Leah bobbed her head. "Of course; I told you I would."

"Jah, but I don't want to take you away from your book. It looks like you've been enjoying having some time to relax."

"It's fine, really." Leah set the book aside. "Where's your mamm? When you mentioned earlier that she was also sore from weeding, I figured she'd want a treatment, too."

"That's what I thought, but Mom said that she had some other things she wanted to get done today. If she's still hurting tomorrow, I'm sure she'll make an appointment to come see you."

"Okay, let's go down to the basement."

After Leah finished working on Priscilla's feet, she asked her to sit in the straight-backed chair so she could massage her neck and relieve some tension. "Oh my, you have some knots in there, too."

"After all that yard work, I'm not surprised, but I'm feeling better already."

Leah smiled. She didn't always get immediate results with those who came to her for help, but when she did, it gave her a sense of satisfaction. But the ability to help others was her gift, and she reminded herself once more that it came from God.

"When we were outside, I couldn't help noticing all the hummingbirds in your yard. They seemed to be flitting around everywhere. Some even went to the bee balm flowers you have near the porch," Priscilla commented.

"They do love that bee balm." Leah laughed. "But I think the main reason we have so many hummers is because of all the feeders we have out. It's a lot of fun to watch them chirping at one another as they zoom in and out all day. You should hear all the commotion they make."

"Makes me wish we had some feeders in our yard," Priscilla said. "Is it too late in the season to hang them out?"

"I don't think so, but the peak of the season for hummers in our area is just a month away, so if you're going to try luring them into your yard, I'd suggest you get some feeders hung out soon. When I was talking to my neighbor the other day, she explained how the hummingbirds start migrating down here around mid-July, and that's why it gets extra busy at the feeders. With our local hummers sticking around, as well as the migrating ones from up north, it's like watching a swarm of bees."

"Think I'm gonna get a feeder or two right away."

As Leah started massaging the other side of Priscilla's neck, Priscilla screamed and jumped onto the seat of her chair.

"What's wrong, Priscilla? Was I massaging your neck too hard?"

"No, it wasn't that." Priscilla pointed. "Look, there's a *maus*! It's nibbling on the laces of my sneaker!"

Leah grabbed a broom and chased after the mouse. It zipped across the room and disappeared behind a stack of boxes.

"You can come down now. The maus is gone." Leah extended her hand to Priscilla.

Priscilla looked a bit hesitant but finally stepped down. Quickly grabbing up her shoes, she took a seat in the chair and slipped them on her feet.

"I wonder why that little mouse was so interested in your shoelace." Leah snickered. "It's certainly not covered in peanut butter or cheese."

Priscilla's fingers touched her parted lips. "No, but I spilled some chicken soup during lunch, and a little of it ended up on my shoes. Guess I didn't get it all cleaned off."

Leah looked at Priscilla's shoes and giggled. Priscilla did the same. Soon, Leah was laughing so hard she had to sit down. It felt good to find some humor in such a small thing. With all the horrible things that went on in the world, a little bit of laughter was good medicine.

❧

When Adam secured his horse to the hitching rack outside his house that afternoon, he was surprised to see the black Lab that had come into his store, prancing up the driveway. "Oh no," he moaned. "Not you again! What'd you do, boy, follow me home?"

Woof! Woof! The dog raced up to Adam and pawed at the leg of his pants.

"I can't believe this. Why me, of all people? I don't even like dogs that well." Adam clapped his hands and pointed toward the road. "Go home, boy! Go back to where you belong!"

After Adam brushed his horse down, he went into the kitchen so he could get his Thermos and lunch pail ready for the next day. Cleaning the Thermos, Adam watched out the window and rolled his eyes. The dog had made himself comfortable lying near the wheel of Adam's buggy.

"That crazy mutt has a mind of his own," Adam muttered. "Maybe if I stay inside awhile longer, he'll leave." Adam took a few celery stalks from the refrigerator and snipped off the ends. After rinsing the pieces, he got the peanut butter and spread it on the celery. He munched on one and wrapped the others to put in his lunch pail for the following day. After placing the rest of the celery back in the fridge, he paused a minute, making sure he had enough bread, lunch meat, and cheese to make a sandwich in the morning to take to work. Satisfied that there was plenty, he shut the refrigerator door. He looked out the window but didn't see the dog.

"Oh, good." Adam grabbed the peanut butter and went to the pantry. After putting the jar away, he took out a pack of crackers and a few cookies to add to his lunch box. Now all he'd have to do in the morning before heading to work was make a sandwich.

"Guess it's safe to go back outside." Grabbing his hat, Adam went out the door but halted when he approached the barn and saw the mutt lying there, looking up at him.

"Are you still here?"

The dog wagged his tail but didn't budge.

Adam wondered if the critter might be lost or abandoned. He'd heard of people driving to an area outside their neighborhood and dropping off their unwanted pet. Even though Adam didn't care much for dogs, he thought it was terrible if someone had deserted the Lab.

Flash nickered when Adam drew near and ran a hand down the horse's neck. "What do you think of that pesky dog?"

Flash snorted and shook his head.

"I feel the same way." Adam chuckled as he unhooked the horse, leading him past the dog and into the barn.

Before leaving for work, Adam had raked out the stall and put fresh bedding inside for his horse. At least that was one chore he wouldn't have to do this evening. Adam led Flash into the stall and started brushing him down. When that was done, he gave the horse fresh water and put oats in the feeding bin. While Flash ate, Adam ran a curry comb through the horse's mane. Taking care of Flash was relaxing, especially after the way today had turned out.

When Adam finished combing Flash's mane, he noticed that his shoulders actually felt somewhat better. He put the brush and comb away then came back to scratch Flash's ears. "You're good therapy for me, you know that Flash? Who needs reflexology anyways?"

Flash nuzzled his nose into Adam's hand and nickered softly.

Adam brushed off some wet oats from his horse's mouth that had stuck to his hands. Glancing over his shoulder, he saw that the dog was still there, watching from the barn's entrance. Closing the door to the stall, he hung the horse's bridle, along with the blinders, on the hook next to the stall door.

Suddenly, Flash started snorting and blowing air through his nostrils. Because he knew his horse so well, Adam was sure something was wrong. He looked around but didn't see anything unusual. Then he noticed that Flash appeared to be looking toward the back corner of the barn. Adam moved cautiously in that direction. Backed into the corner was a portly groundhog, baring his teeth and snarling. The groundhog ran past Adam's feet, toward the open barn door.

Adam ran outside in time to see the barking Lab disappear as he chased the varmint behind the barn. "Good, let him take care of the groundhog." Adam closed the barn door. "I don't need any more hassles today."

Just as he reached the porch steps, Adam heard a distressed-sounding *yip*! Groundhogs had large front teeth and could probably deliver a nasty bite. Without thinking twice, he ran to the back of the barn, but all was quiet, and neither the dog nor the groundhog was anywhere to be seen. Looking closer, Adam noticed a chewed-out hole that went through the wall of the barn. In the dirt in front of the hole was a spot of blood. Adam scanned the area again but saw no sign of the dog or groundhog. Taking off his hat, he ran his fingers through his hair. *Did that groundhog bite him? Or did the Lab bite the groundhog?* Either way, he'd have to get rid of the pest, because he couldn't have a groundhog getting into the barn again, alarming, or even biting his horse.

He hoped the mutt was okay and would find his family, because that dog would never have a home with Adam.

CHAPTER 10

Entering the kitchen, Adam paused to yawn and stretch his arms over his head. Then he rolled his head from side to side, hoping to get the kinks out. For some reason, he'd had a hard time sleeping last night, and now he had a stiff neck. *Probably from all that went on yesterday*, he decided. *Well, today is bound to be better.*

Before leaving for work, Adam fixed himself a cup of coffee, ate a banana, and then headed outside to the phone shack to check for messages, which he'd neglected to do last night. Opening the back door and stepping onto the porch, he nearly tripped over something. Looking down, he realized that the determined mutt was lying on his porch.

Disgusted, he stepped around the dog and sprinted down the driveway. *Maybe if I ignore the critter he'll go away. Guess that's wishful thinking, 'cause it hasn't worked yet.*

Inside the phone shack Adam took a seat and checked his messages. The first one was from his neighbor, Clarence Lambright, saying they had some extra eggs and asking if Adam wanted a dozen. Adam dialed Clarence's number and left a message, thanking him for the offer and letting him know that he would pick up the eggs on his way home from work.

The next message was from Adam's sister telling him that she and her family planned to hire a driver next week and come to Arthur to celebrate Adam's birthday. As much as Adam looked forward to their visit, he didn't really care about celebrating his birthday. Turning thirty was no big deal. Adam wouldn't discourage her from coming, though. He hadn't seen Mary, Amos, and their girls since Christmas, and it would be good to see them again.

After returning Mary's call and leaving a message saying he looked forward to their visit, Adam stepped out of the phone shack.

Woof! Woof! The Lab looked up at Adam with sorrowful brown eyes.

Adam gritted his teeth. He couldn't believe the mutt had followed him here. Didn't this dog ever give up?

Adam headed back to the house, and as he opened the door, the dog leaped forward. Adam grabbed the Lab's collar to pull him back, stepped inside, and quickly shut the door. The persistent animal remained on the porch and whined. Adam remembered the dog's encounter with the groundhog and figured he'd better check to see if he had been bitten.

"The critter's probably hungry and thirsty, too," Adam mumbled under his breath. "Guess it wouldn't hurt if I gave him a little something to eat and drink."

Adam found a plastic bowl and filled it with water. Then he went to the refrigerator and grabbed a couple leftover hot dogs. While the dog ate hungrily and lapped up the water, Adam checked for wounds. Seeing none, he figured the Lab must have been the victor or at least chased the groundhog off.

Adam patted the dog's matted coat. "What you need is a good bath and thorough combing." He thumped the side of his head. *I must be getting soft in the noggin. If I do all that, I'll never get rid of the mutt.*

"I'm heading to Elaine's now," Leah called to her mother after she'd finished drying the breakfast dishes.

Mom had been gathering up the living-room throw rugs to shake outside, and she poked her head into the kitchen. "Oh, that's right. I had forgotten you were going over there to help her clean. Will you be back in time for lunch, or will you stay and eat with Elaine?"

"I'll stay there. Priscilla is coming over around noon to eat lunch with us. We three haven't gotten together in a while, and it'll give us a chance to catch up with one another's lives."

"Well, have a good time, and don't work too hard."

"Same goes for you, Mom. I know you said during breakfast that your back feels better, but try not to overdo it."

Mom smiled. "I'm not going to do any heavy cleaning—just touch things up a bit."

"I'd stay and help if I hadn't already promised Elaine."

Mom waved her hand. "That's okay. Go and enjoy your day."

Leah took her black outer bonnet down from the wall peg and put it on over her white head covering. "See you later, Mom."

As Leah headed down the road on her bike, she passed Adam's house and noticed a black Lab sitting at the end of his driveway.

I wonder where that dog came from. As far as Leah knew, Adam didn't have a dog. *Well, it's none of my business*, she told herself. *If it's a stray or one of his neighbor's dogs, it probably wandered onto his property looking for food, or maybe it was chasing a cat or some other critter.*

Thinking about Adam, Leah reflected on how he'd fixed her bicycle chain. She'd definitely seen a kinder side of him yesterday. Maybe they could set their differences aside and be friends. Of course, Adam might not be interested in being Leah's friend. He seemed content to be by himself when he wasn't working in his store, so she wouldn't pursue a friendship with him. If Adam wanted to be Leah's friend, he'd have to do the pursuing.

When Adam arrived at his store a few minutes later than usual, he was glad to see Ben already waiting on a customer, Leah's father. There was no sign of his other employee, so Adam figured Henry's shoulder was still giving him problems. He probably wouldn't be in again today, but hopefully by Monday, Henry would be back to work.

Adam stepped up to the counter. "*Guder mariye*, Ben. Same to you, Alton."

Ben nodded, but Alton barely squeaked out a "good morning" in response. Wrinkling his nose, he turned from the counter. "Guess I'll go look again for that blade I need," he called over his shoulder.

"Whew. . .what's that spicy smell?" Ben asked, leaning away from Adam.

Adam's face flushed. "Well, I did use some new aftershave lotion this morning. Guess that could be what you smell."

"What'd ya do, take a bath in it?" Ben plugged his nose.

"Course not." Adam grunted. "Thanks to the time I took to take care of the mutt that followed me home yesterday, I was in a hurry this morning. Guess I must've put on a little too much balm after I shaved."

"What mutt was that?" Ben asked.

"The black Lab that was hanging around here yesterday. The critter followed me home, and I couldn't get rid of him." Adam turned toward the back room. "I'll fill you in later. Right now I need to go to the washroom and try to get some of this lotion off my face so I don't chase away all our customers today. After that, I'll be in my office, going over some paperwork. If you need me, just give a holler."

"No problem. It doesn't look like Henry will be working again today, but I'm sure I can manage on my own unless it gets really busy."

Adam nodded, thankful once again that he'd hired Ben.

A bit later, as Adam was heading toward his office, a teenage boy wearing a baseball cap stepped up to him. It was the shoplifter.

"Came back to return this stuff to you." The boy handed Adam a pair of gloves and the two small shovels he'd taken. "I know what I did was wrong, and I. . .I just wanted to say that I'm sorry."

Stunned, Adam hardly knew how to respond. He'd never expected to get the stuff back, much less receive an apology from the boy. "Why'd you do it?" Adam asked. "Was it just for the sport of it, or to prove that you could take those things and get away with it?"

The boy shook his head. "My dad's out of work, and my folks are short on money right now. So my mom's been trying to sell some produce from her garden." He frowned. "She's been pulling weeds with no garden gloves, and the handle on the shovel she uses broke yesterday morning."

"So you came into my store and took what wasn't yours." A muscle on the side of Adam's neck quivered. He felt bad about the boy's father being out of work, but stealing was wrong, and the kid ought to learn a lesson.

The boy dropped his gaze to the floor. "The stuff I took hasn't been used. When my folks found out what I did, they said I had to bring everything back this morning." His voice cracked. "Dad's making me do extra chores around the place now, and he said I should do some work for you, too, to make up for what I did."

Adam stood with his arms folded, trying to decide what to do. If he let the kid go without making him do any work, would he really learn a lesson? "I'll tell you what," he said, clasping the boy's shoulder. "You can do some cleaning in the store for me this morning, and when you're done and ready to go home, you can take these with you." He motioned to the gloves and shovel. "Not before you tell me your name, though."

The boy's eyes widened. "You mean it, mister? You won't turn me in?"

Adam gave a hesitant nod, wondering if he was doing the right thing. "But you've got to promise that you'll never steal anything from me or anyone else again."

"No, I won't. I've learned my lesson." The boy grabbed Adam's hand and shook it. "My name's Scott Ramsey. I'm pleased to meet you."

"Likewise, I think," Adam mumbled, handing the boy a broom. "You can start by sweeping the floor."

"No problem. I'll do a good job."

"Oh, before you do that," Adam said, "I was wondering if you own a black Lab."

The boy shook his head. "Nope, just a beagle hound. Why do you ask?"

"One was hanging around the store yesterday, and the mutt followed me home. He also brought a package of gardening gloves into the store. I figured it might be one of the pairs you took."

"I did take two pairs, but I dropped one on my way out." The boy shrugged. "The dog ain't mine, and I don't know anyone who has a Lab."

After Scott moved down the aisle, pushing the broom, Adam went to his office and took a seat at the desk. This had been an interesting morning so far. Not only had he fed a dog he didn't want hanging around, but he'd agreed to give the shoplifting kid the very things he'd stolen from him. He really must be getting soft in the head.

Adam wondered if the dog would be waiting for him when he got home. When he'd checked the animal over this morning, he'd looked at the dog's collar for a name tag or license, but there was nothing to indicate who the Lab belonged to. Adam hated to admit it, but deep down, he almost hoped the dog would still be there. He had to stop at his neighbor's first, to pick up the eggs they had for him, but after that, he would be anxious to get home. Even though it meant extra work, having a pet to care for might relieve some of the lonesomeness and tension he often felt.

CHAPTER 11

Adam spent the next week getting ready for his sister's arrival, making sure there was plenty of food in the house, the beds were all made, and the house was cleaned. He'd hired a couple young Amish women to do the cleaning, since he had little free time after work each day.

As he sat on the front porch, watching for his family to arrive, Adam wondered what was taking them so long. They'd hired a driver and were coming in a van, but since it was Friday, the traffic might be heavier than usual, with people heading places for the weekend. Mary had said she and the family would arrive before supper and that she would fix the meal. But when Adam checked his pocket watch and saw that it was five o'clock, he figured they might not get here in time for that. Maybe he would take them out to eat, which would probably be better anyway. Since they'd been traveling all day, Mary was bound to be tired.

Feeling a wet nose nudge his hand, Adam looked down. The Lab was still with him, lying on top of his feet. Adam had resigned himself to the fact that the dog had adopted him. He'd asked around to see if anyone had lost a Lab, but no one knew anything about the dog. Adam had even hung several "Lost Dog" flyers around town but had gotten no response. He didn't have the heart to let the dog roam around, neglected, and since the mutt seemed to have claimed Adam as his new master, he'd finally given in. He had named the dog Coal because of the color of the animal's thick coat of hair. Adam knew that naming the Lab was just as significant as if he'd signed adoption papers.

"Guess you and me are stuck with each other now." Adam smiled, moving his feet while Coal let out a low moan. The dog felt like a sack of potatoes and was cutting off the circulation in Adam's ankles. But it was kind of nice, having the dog around. He'd actually caught himself looking for Coal every day when he got home from work. Faithfully, the dog was there, either on the porch wagging his tail or sitting at the end of the driveway, barking when Adam's horse and buggy came into view.

Even in the little bit of time Coal had been around, he'd proven his worth. On Wednesday, Adam had noticed the disgusting smell of a dead animal permeating the barn. After finding a hole coming up through the floor where he kept bales of straw, Adam realized that the groundhog had actually made a tunnel under the barn and was probably the source of the stench. Adam wasn't sure how to get the critter out but hoped that after a while the odor would fade. The next morning, when he walked out onto the porch, Coal sat with the dead groundhog, smelling even worse than the day before. Adam had no idea how Coal managed to get the carcass out from under the barn, and he wasn't even going to try and figure it out, but he was glad the dog had.

Adam snickered, thinking that if his sister had been visiting and found a smelly old carcass right by the door, she would have probably fainted. At any rate, that evening, Coal had gotten a bath, and his coat still shone like a piece of blue-black coal. No more did the Lab have that mangy mongrel look. Now Coal had the appearance of a sleek purebred black Labrador retriever. Not only would Adam have a dog to introduce to his nieces, but he'd have a clean dog at that.

The groundhog wasn't the only thing the dog had surprised Adam with this week. Last evening, Coal had walked into the barn, where Adam had gone to feed his horse, and dropped a ripe tomato at his feet. Adam recognized it right away, being the first to ripen on the vine. He'd been watching it for the last week, and now the plump tomato was perfect. Adam had intended to pick that tomato this morning, to have with dinner tonight, but Coal had beaten him to it. Amazingly enough, the tomato was intact, with no teeth marks on it—just dog slobber. Luckily, that could be washed off.

"How'd you like to play a game of fetch?" Adam asked, as the dog's tail thumped the ground.

"I'll take that as a yes." Adam headed for the barn, and like a shot, Coal followed. Once inside, Adam pulled the plastic lid off an old coffee can. "This oughtta work fine for what I have in mind."

With Coal at his heels, Adam left the barn and stood in the middle of the lawn. "If you can fetch a tomato, then this makeshift Frisbee should be easy for you." Adam flung the lid high and hard, and it flew across the yard.

The dog watched it go, and just before it hit the ground, he chased after it. Returning the lid to Adam, Coal looked up in anticipation. *Woof! Woof!*

Adam chuckled. "Okay, okay, don't get so impatient." He threw the lid again and smiled, watching the dog race across the yard, leap into the air, and catch the object with his teeth.

They continued playing for a while until Adam called a halt to the game. "Enough is enough, boy. We both need to relax."

Coal flopped onto the grass, and Adam stood staring at the trees lining his property, appreciating the fact that this place was his.

Several minutes went by until Coal grunted, drawing Adam out of his musings. He squatted down and rubbed the dog's ears. "You're a fair enough pooch, but don't get any ideas about sleeping in the house. Even though you are nice and clean, a dog's place is outside, so you can just keep sleeping in the barn till I find the time to build a doghouse with a fence around it."

As if in response, Coal put his head on Adam's knee and closed his eyes.

Adam smiled. When Carrie, Linda, and Amy got here, they'd probably be excited to discover that Adam now owned a dog.

As Leah removed a pair of her father's trousers from the clothesline, she thought, once again, about Elaine and Priscilla and their boyfriends. Elaine had been seeing Ben, and Priscilla had Elam. Leah had no one, and even though her reflexology was meaningful, she secretly longed to be a wife and mother. But Leah had never had a serious suitor. Was there something about her that turned men away? Was it her looks, or didn't they care for her personality? While Leah had never considered herself beautiful, she didn't think she was homely, either.

Her father always said Leah had pretty blue-green eyes, and Mom often commented on Leah's lovely golden brown hair.

There must be something about my personality that repels any would-be suitors. Leah sighed, shaking out another pair of dry trousers. *Well, what does it matter? If I'm meant to be married, then it will happen, in God's time.*

Arf! Arf! Arf! Leah's Jack Russell terrier darted across the lawn and skidded to a stop in front of her laundry basket. Before Leah could say one word, the dog stuck its snout into the basket, grabbed one of Dad's clean shirts, and raced back across the yard.

Leah chased after the dog, shouting, "Come back here right now, Sparky, and give me Dad's shirt!" Of all things, it was one of Dad's good Sunday shirts. If Leah didn't get the shirt from Sparky soon, she'd have to wash it again and hope it would dry before the sun went down.

To her annoyance, the dog kept running without looking back. As Leah bore down on him, he darted around the side of the barn, slipped under the fence, and disappeared into the field of corn.

Leah groaned. "Oh, great! Guess Dad won't be wearing that shirt on Sunday." After she took the clothes inside, she was supposed to set the table, because her brother, Nathan, and his family were coming for supper. Well, she'd have to go after Sparky and get Dad's shirt back before heading up to the house. She hoped by the time she caught the dog that the shirt would still be in one piece.

Adam was about to head out to the phone shack to check for messages, thinking his sister might have called to let him know they were going to be late, when the sheriff's car pulled into his driveway. Adam swatted at the annoying little bugs hovering in a cloud around his head. Humid weather seemed to make them worse, and they appeared as soon as one walked outdoors. Those gnats could be so aggravating, especially when they went right for one's eyes or ears.

The sheriff got out of his vehicle, and from the man's serious expression, Adam had a feeling this wasn't a social call. He glanced over at Coal, who moments ago had been rambunctious but was now sitting quietly by the porch steps.

"What can I do for you?" Adam asked. He knew the man because he'd come into his hardware store a few times.

The sheriff cleared his throat. "Brace yourself. I'm sorry to say that I've come with bad news."

Adam's heart started to pound as he waited to hear what the man had to say. *Dear God, please don't let it be about Mary or anyone else in her family.*

"I'm sorry, Mr. Beachy, but there's been an accident. The van your sister and her family were traveling in was hit by a truck just outside of Arcola."

Adam's mouth went dry. "Are. . .are any of them hurt?"

The sheriff nodded. "But I don't know how badly. Everyone, including their driver, has been taken to the hospital. If you'd like to go there now, I'll give you a ride."

Fear such as Adam hadn't known since he was boy rose in his chest. He had no idea what to expect once he got to the hospital; he just knew he had to get there as quickly as possible. Grabbing his straw hat from the porch, he followed the sheriff to his car, not even stopping to put Coal away. All Adam could think about was his beloved sister and her dear family. *Dear Lord, please let them be okay.*

CHAPTER 12

Leah had just captured Sparky when a black Lab wandered into the yard. She thought it was the same dog she'd seen at the end of Adam's driveway. Figuring the dog must be a stray, she waved her hands and shouted, hoping to chase it off. Instead, it sniffed around, as though looking for something. The dog looked a bit different from when Leah had seen it before. Its coat was black as night, and there was an almost bluish tint to its fur. This clean animal was not the shabby, dingy-looking mutt from before.

"Go home!" Leah hollered.

The Lab wagged its tail and let out a loud bark. That brought Sparky from the barn, where he'd gone with his tail between his legs after Leah had finally rescued Dad's shirt.

Arf! Arf! Arf! Sparky chased after the black dog, barking and nipping at its heels.

Woof! Woof! The Lab zipped around the yard twice then turned and chased Sparky.

Panting for breath, Leah ran after Sparky, who was now chasing the Lab. After calling several times, her ornery little dog would not stop. The overwrought animal either didn't hear her or chose to ignore her commands, for he wouldn't give up the chase. Desperate to find a way to bring it to an end, Leah picked up the garden hose. Turning it on full force, she sprayed both dogs with a blast of water.

Yip! Yip! Yip! Arf! Arf! Sparky and the black Lab took off like a shot for the field of corn.

"Go ahead and run, you crazy critters!" Leah called, shaking her head. She sure wasn't going to chase them into the field; she'd already gone there after Sparky, and once was enough. Leah pulled her dad's shirt from around her neck, where she'd draped it before chasing the dogs. She wasn't sure how, but Dad's Sunday shirt was still in one piece. But it would need to be washed again.

Turning toward the house, Leah halted when a horse and buggy pulled in. Behind them, the sky was turning a brilliant orange as the sun began to set. Her brother and his family had arrived, and she was a hot, sticky mess. Not only that, but she hadn't done a thing to help Mom get supper on. Because Nathan worked in the bulk food store and had to close it up for the evening, Leah was glad Mom had planned to serve supper later than usual—especially with this dog episode.

"What happened to you?" Nathan asked when he got off the buggy. "Your dress is dirty, and your face is flushed."

Leah could see little Zeke's arms going up and down on his mother's lap. Holding out her own arms to greet Rebecca and Stephen, who were trying to get to her first, Leah smiled. "It's a long story, and I'll tell you all about it when we go inside."

Adam sat in the hospital waiting room with his eyes closed and head bowed, praying fervently and waiting for news on the condition of Mary and her family. All he'd been told was that Mary and Amos were in serious condition and that the girls and their driver had minor injuries. He clenched his fists until his fingers dug into his palms. Mary and Amos had to make it. Their girls were so young and needed their parents. For that matter, Adam needed Mary, too, for she was his only sibling and his closest living relative. Adam's father was dead, and for all he knew, his mother was, too. Not that he'd ever want to see her again. Even if she was still alive, in every sense of the word, his mother was dead to him. All Adam wanted right now was to see his sister and know that she would be all right.

How could something like this have happened? he asked himself. *And whose fault was it, anyway? Was it the driver of the van they'd hired, or was the person in the other vehicle responsible for the accident? Oh, Lord, I can't lose Mary, too.*

Adam's thoughts came to a halt when a young doctor entered the room and took a seat beside him. "Are you Mr. Beachy?" he asked.

Adam nodded. "Do you have word on my sister and her husband? Are they going to be okay?"

The grave look on the doctor's face told Adam all he needed to know. "I'm sorry, Mr. Beachy, but Amos has died, and Mary is seriously injured. She's lost a lot of blood. I'm afraid she doesn't have long to live."

Barely able to believe the doctor's words, Adam sat in stunned silence. His chin quivered as he closed his eyes. It wasn't possible. He felt as though he was in the middle of a horrible dream—a nightmare.

"Is. . .is she awake? Can I see her?" Adam asked when he finally found his voice.

"Yes. She's been asking for you." The doctor stood. "If you'll follow me, I'll take you to see Mary now."

Numbly, Adam followed the doctor down the hallway, which bustled with normal activity. Adam barely noticed.

"She's in here," the doctor said, leading the way into a dimly lit room, where a nurse stood beside a hospital bed.

The window blinds were tilted, allowing pink light from the sunset to flow between the slats onto Mary's bed. How could something so beautiful be happening outside when inside this room everything was horrible? The silence at Mary's bedside was broken only by the slow, erratic beep of the heart monitor.

Adam swallowed around the lump in his throat as he looked down at his sister's battered body. "Mary," he whispered, touching her hand.

She opened her eyes and blinked, tears trickling down her swollen, bruised cheeks. "Adam?"

"Jah, Mary, it's me."

"Amos is gone, and I. . .I think I'll be joining him soon." Mary's voice was barely above a whisper, but Adam understood every word.

A chill ran through him as he leaned closer to Mary's face. "Don't talk like that, Mary. You're going to be fine."

"No, Adam, listen. I. . .I need you to promise me something."

"Anything, Mary. Anything at all." Adam's throat felt so swollen, he could barely talk.

"Please, take care of my girls." Mary drew in a shuddering breath.

"Promise me, Adam. Please say that you will. I'll not be at peace till I know."

Tears pricked Adam's eyes as he slowly nodded. "I promise, Mary. Don't you worry. I'll take care of your girls."

A faint smile played on Mary's lips while Adam gazed at her, knowing it would be the last time. Then her mouth opened as she shuddered her last breath.

The monitor changed from a sporadic beep to an eerie flat-lined tone, and a sob rose in Adam's throat. When the doctor announced that Mary was gone, Adam closed his eyes in grief. Mary's hand was still warm in his, and even though the nurse had switched off the heart monitor, Adam looked down at his dear sister, barely able to accept the fact that she was truly gone. They would never again share precious moments on this earth.

Several minutes passed. As the truth sank in, Adam felt as though a part of him had died with Mary. How brave and thoughtful his sister had been, thinking only of her girls' well-being, while facing her own death. His stomach clenched as the reality of the situation hit him. Mary and Amos were dead, and he had just agreed to be responsible for their children. Who would tell those sweet little girls that their mom and dad had died? Amy was ten years old, but even at that age, would she understand why her folks had been taken? How could she? Adam sure didn't. The younger ones—Linda, who was seven, and Carrie, who'd recently turned four—how would they grasp this tragic news?

And what about me? Adam swiped at the tears running down his cheeks. He loved his sister and would honor her wishes, but he knew nothing about raising children. Adam bowed his head and closed his eyes. *Lord, how can I keep my promise to Mary? I'm scared. Please, show me what I need to do.*

CHAPTER 13

Adam placed four plates, knives, and forks on the table and sighed. Two weeks had passed since Amos and Mary's deaths, and Adam's world had been turned upside down. In addition to seeing that his sister and brother-in-law received proper burials at the Amish cemetery back in Nappanee, he'd brought Mary's three girls and their belongings to his house last night and didn't have a clue how to properly care for them. Carrie, who was small for her age, seemed timid and whined a lot. Linda was full of nervous energy and had a bit of a temper. Then there was stubborn Amy. Because she was the oldest, she liked to take charge and tell her sisters what to do.

When they'd arrived last evening, Amy had made it clear that she didn't want to live with Adam. Even when he'd been with them in Nappanee, it seemed nothing he said or did was good enough. The girl's belligerent attitude didn't help at all. Of course, who could really blame her? She'd not only lost both parents, but she'd also been uprooted from her Amish community and the only home she and her sisters had ever known. He understood how lost they must feel, because he felt bewildered and misplaced, too. Adam was sure the girls would miss their paternal grandparents, who lived in Nappanee, but since Amos's father had become disabled after a fall from his barn roof, there was no way their grandmother could be responsible for the care of three young girls. Amos's brother, Devon, who wasn't married, would see that Mary and Adam's home and other things were sold, but he was in no position financially to take the girls in.

Adam knew from personal experience how difficult moving could be for a child. Even though he had only been five when his mother had left, he could still remember the shock and confusion over her leaving. A few months later, Adam's dad had packed up and moved Adam and Mary from their home in Lancaster, Pennsylvania, to Ohio. After several more moves, they eventually settled in Nappanee, Indiana. Adam had not only struggled with resentment toward his mother, but he'd been angry at Dad for taking him and Mary to places where they didn't know anyone and had to start over at new schools. Mary, being the outgoing one, had made new friends right away, but Adam held back and never allowed himself to get close to any of the other children. Mary was not only his sister but his best friend, so he'd never felt the need to develop any other friendships. Besides, with everything that had happened to him at such a young age, Adam wasn't sure who he could trust. It wasn't hard for him to understand what the girls were going through right now, even though he'd lost only one parent when he was child, not both at the same time.

Putting his thoughts aside, Adam concentrated on getting the girls' breakfast made, knowing they would be waking soon and no doubt be hungry. He'd decided to fix pancakes this morning, so he set out a bottle of maple syrup. Adam was glad the girls wouldn't have to start school for several more weeks. It would give them time to adjust to their new surroundings and hopefully help them get to know him better. Having the children home all day was a problem, since Adam needed to be at the hardware store. He certainly couldn't take them to work with him every day, but he couldn't leave them at home alone, either. After the girls had been released from the hospital and he'd taken them to Nappanee for their parents' funeral, Adam had left Ben and Henry in charge of the store. But now that he was home, he needed to get back to work as soon as possible. At the very least, he planned to drop by the store sometime today to check on things.

Adam hated to admit it, but he didn't want to be cooped up in the house on another rainy day with three nieces he didn't know how to entertain. The girls would have to go with him to the store whether they liked it or not. Adam might not know much about parenting, but he wasn't about to leave them home alone. He would need to ask around and see who might be available to watch the girls while he was at work. Once school started toward the end of August, they would only have to be watched for a few hours in the afternoon, until Adam came home from work. His evenings would certainly be different. The freedom he'd enjoyed to do whatever he pleased would now be replaced with the responsibility of caring for the girls' needs. The only way to get through this was to take one day at a time and trust God to see him through.

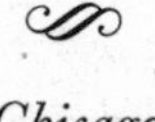

Chicago

Cora Finley had never liked the rain, and today was no exception. She'd had trouble sleeping last night, thanks to the incessant raindrops beating on the roof of her house. She had finally succumbed to sleep well after midnight, and now it was six o'clock, and she needed to get ready for work. Glancing out her bedroom window, she grimaced. It was such a gloomy day. They'd had too much rain already this summer, and she was tired of it. Unlike some people, Cora didn't find the continuous pelting sound relaxing at all.

In addition to that irritation, she was concerned about her fourteen-year-old son, Jared. He'd become a rebellious teen ever since the divorce, often trying Cora's patience until she was at her wit's end. He'd become friends with a couple boys from broken homes, and they seemed to find trouble at every turn. With Cora's nursing job, she couldn't be with Jared every minute, and since he was too old to leave with a sitter, he often hung out with his friends.

Cora punched her pillow and moaned. It was bad enough that her husband had left her for another woman. Did he have to abandon his only son, too? At least it felt like abandonment, since Evan spent so little time with their son these days. Didn't he care how much Jared missed him? Didn't it bother him that their son was without his father's guidance much of the time? *I was a fool to believe I'd met my Prince Charming and that my future held nothing but good things. Now I have to try and be both mother and father to Jared, and so far, I'm failing miserably.*

When Cora had first met Evan during his residency at the hospital, she'd been convinced that they were meant to be together because they had many things in common. They both had careers in the medical field and were dedicated to their jobs. They enjoyed traveling and had taken trips to several places around the country whenever they could. Once Evan got established in his own private practice, he'd bought them an upscale condo, with all the benefits of high-class living. When Jared was born, they'd sold the condo and bought a house. Evan was thrilled when he found out Cora was having a boy—said he couldn't wait to build a relationship with his son.

"Yeah, right! Where's Jared's father now, when Jared needs him the most?" Cora grumbled. At this stage in their son's life, he needed his father more than ever—especially when Cora didn't have a clue what a teenage boy really wanted or needed. All she knew was that Jared hadn't been happy since Evan walked out of their life, and she had no idea what to do about it. Apparently, Dr. Evan Finley wasn't the dedicated father she'd thought him to be. Emily, the pretty blond nurse who'd stolen him from Cora, seemed to be all he could focus on these days. What kind of power did a woman like her have over a man? Was it because "Miss Blondie" was younger than Cora? Or did she have a personality that meshed better with Evan's?

Sighing, Cora pushed the covers aside and rose from the bed, stretching her arms over her head. *Maybe I should sell this place and move somewhere else—someplace where there aren't so many temptations for Jared. Perhaps a rural area would be better than living here in the big city. Jared might find a better class of friends if he lived in a more wholesome environment. If we moved, I wouldn't be the focus of the hospital gossip mill, either.*

Cora moved over to the window and stared out at the drizzling rain. She and Jared were still living in the house Evan had bought for them several years ago. It had been their dream home, even though it needed some improvements. Over the years, they'd remodeled it nicely, choosing one project each summer, the last one being a new roof. Not thinking anything of it when they chose the type of roof, it was beyond Cora why she'd ever agreed to the fancy roofing tile. It just added to her annoyance this morning, with every *ping* of raindrops hitting the roof reminding her of what used to be. Looking out the window, Cora felt irked by how agreeable she'd always been with Evan—not just concerning the roof he'd chosen but about practically everything else he'd wanted.

We should have chosen regular shingles like most of the other homes in this area have, she fumed, folding her arms. *But no, Evan had to have the best of everything. Humph! Guess that's why he went for someone younger than me.*

It still amazed Cora that Evan had let her keep the house. He was so selfish, she figured he'd not only want his new wife but the house he'd once shared with Cora, too.

Even though Cora's home was lovely, her anger toward Evan made it difficult to look at his favorite chair or the bed they'd once shared. The death of a spouse, whom one loved so dearly, would be difficult for anyone, but divorce was a bitter path, filled with many regrets. Every time Cora saw Evan and Emily together, her slow-healing wounds reopened. A clean break might be the only way for her and Jared to get through this ordeal.

Think I'll call a Realtor after I get off work today and see how much he thinks I can get for the house. Then I'll put my résumé out to a few of the hospitals and clinics in some of the rural areas here in Illinois and see what happens.

Arthur

"What's on your agenda for the day?" Leah's mother asked as they prepared breakfast that morning.

Leah shrugged while stirring cinnamon-dusted apple slices in a frying pan. "Not much, really. I don't have anyone coming for a reflexology treatment today, so I thought I might stop over at Adam's and see how he's doing since his sister's death. I'm sure it must have been a terrible shock for him to lose his sister and brother-in-law."

Stirring a batch of oatmeal, Mom turned her head toward Leah. "I didn't realize he was back from Indiana. I thought Adam would stay there a few more weeks in order to take care of his sister's estate."

"I heard he was coming back last night, and I don't know why he didn't stay longer. I ran into Elaine yesterday, and she said that Ben told her Adam was bringing his nieces home to live with him."

Mom's mouth formed an O. "A bachelor raising three small girls? I don't see how that's going to work."

"I'm sure he will hire someone to help out." Leah removed the frying pan, took three bowls down from the cupboard, and placed them on the table. "Thought maybe I'd take some cookies for the children, because I doubt that Adam does any baking."

Mom raised her eyebrows, giving Leah a questioning gaze. "Are you sure that's the only reason you're going over there?"

Leah's face heated. "Of course that's the only reason. What other motive would I have for going to Adam's house?"

"Well, he is an attractive man."

Leah held up her hand. "Don't get any ideas about me and Adam, Mom. He may be good looking, but he's definitely not my type."

"Exactly what type of man are you looking for, Leah?"

"One who will love me for the person I am. Someone who respects my opinion. Of course, I'm not looking for a man, so there's no point in discussing this." Leah opened the silverware drawer and took out three spoons. She should have known better than to mention Adam, and maybe she shouldn't go over there today. But she loved children and wanted to meet his nieces and see how they were all doing. They'd been through quite an ordeal and needed some reassurance. She was almost certain that Adam didn't have a clue how to care for his nieces. The children needed nurturing, and with Adam working all day, how could he offer them that?

But if she ever decided to go over to his place again, she'd just go without mentioning it to Mom. No point in giving her false hope. Leah was not interested in Adam. *And he's certainly not interested in me.*

CHAPTER 14

"What's that supposed to be?" Ten-year-old Amy squinted her brown eyes and pointed to the plate of pancakes Adam had placed on the table.

"It's *pannekuche*." Adam gestured to the maple syrup beside the plate. "You girls like pancakes, don't you?"

"Jah, but these are burned." Linda, who was seven and also had brown eyes, plugged her nose, backing away from the table. "They smell awful, too."

"Aw, they aren't so bad." Adam absently rubbed his arms. "They're just a little brown around the edges."

Amy thrust out her chin and folded her arms. "Our mamm wouldn't have burned the pannekuche, and we're not gonna eat 'em. Besides, they don't even look like pancakes. They're too *flach*."

Before Adam could respond to Amy's comment about the flat pancakes, four-year-old Carrie looked up at Adam, her blue eyes brimming with tears. "I'm *hungerich*."

Carrie reminded Adam of his sister—shiny brown hair and ice-blue eyes. He had to turn away so the girls wouldn't see his tears.

Feeling more helpless by the moment, Adam was tempted to tell the children that the pancakes were all he had for breakfast, but then he remembered there was a box of cold cereal in the pantry. "If you three will take a seat, I'll get some cereal," he said, moving in that direction. "You like cereal, don't you?"

Adam sighed with relief when they all nodded. "Okay, that's good."

When Adam returned with the cereal and milk, the girls were seated at the table. Three innocent faces guardedly watched him, as if to see what he would do next.

He then poured himself a cup of coffee and sat down across from

Amy. "Let's bow our heads for silent prayer."

"Don't you think we need some bowls and spoons? I mean, how do you expect us to eat cereal without 'em?" Amy questioned.

His face heating up, Adam got up and took three bowls down from the cupboard, then he grabbed some spoons from the silverware drawer. After placing them on the table, he sat back down. "There. How's that?"

"Aren't you gonna eat?" Linda wanted to know.

He shook his head. "I'm not that hungry this morning. A cup of coffee's good enough for me." The truth was, Adam's stomach was so knotted he didn't think he could eat a thing.

Amy grunted and pushed a lock of blond hair out of her eyes. She'd obviously made an attempt to braid her hair, as well as her sisters', when they'd gotten up. But Adam could see that the braids were loose and probably wouldn't hold up all day.

"I'm gonna pray that Mama and Papa come and get us soon," Carrie announced.

"They're not coming to get us 'cause they're in heaven with Jesus." Linda's brown eyes filled with tears. "Don't you remember when we put Papa and Mama in the ground at the cemetery?"

Carrie shook her head vigorously. "No! They'd never go in the ground. It's cold and dirty down there."

Adam's throat constricted. Carrie either hadn't realized it was her parents they'd buried, or else the little girl was in denial. Then again, perhaps she was too young to grasp the concept of what death really meant. He tried to think of the best way to explain, but once again her older sister spoke up.

"There's no point talking about this right now 'cause it won't bring Mama and Papa back." Amy took a drink from her glass of milk.

Carrie's eyes widened, and she started to cry. "They're gone for good?"

Amy nodded then grabbed the cereal box and poured some into their bowls, adding some milk. Pushing two of the bowls in front of her sisters, she said in a bossy tone, "Just eat now, and quit talking."

"We can't eat till we've prayed. God wouldn't like it, and neither would Mama and Papa if they were here." Linda looked over at Adam, as if waiting for him to comment.

"That's right," he agreed. "We always need to pray and thank God for the food."

Amy wrinkled her nose. "It's a good thing we don't have to eat those pannekuche 'cause I'm sure they'd taste baremlich. I could never be thankful for that."

The constant rain outside could be heard hitting the roof, and Adam lifted his gaze toward the ceiling. What was he going to do with his nieces today? They wouldn't be able to go outside and play—not in this nasty weather. He had a few games but no puzzles or anything exciting to keep them entertained other than a coloring book and a box of crayons. If there was one thing he knew with certainty, taking care of three little girls was not going to be easy. Short of a miracle, he didn't see how he could manage the task alone. "As soon as we've finished our prayer, I'll take the pancakes outside for the dog."

Amy rolled her eyes. "I'll bet even Coal won't eat 'em."

Adam was tempted to argue the point because so far the dog had eaten anything set before him. But instead of trying to explain that, he bowed his head and closed his eyes. *Heavenly Father*, he prayed silently, *please give me the wisdom and strength to see that Mary and Amos's girls are raised properly.*

Adam's place was less than a mile from Leah's, and had it not been for the steady rain and the food she was bringing, Leah would have ridden her bike. Instead, she'd gotten out the horse and buggy.

In addition to the peanut butter cookies Leah had baked, Mom had sent along a chicken casserole Adam could heat for supper this evening. She hoped he and the girls would like it.

Leah had only met Adam's nieces briefly when their parents had attended church during one of their visits last year. She couldn't imagine how difficult it must be for the girls, losing both of their parents and then having to leave their home and move in with their uncle in another state.

She thought about Elaine, who had lost her parents when she was a girl and had been raised by her grandparents. But there'd been two adults to nurture and guide Elaine throughout her childhood. Adam wasn't married and lived alone. Surely he had no idea how to care for his nieces.

I guess it's none of my business, Leah told herself. *If Adam needs any help with the girls, I'm sure he'll ask for it.*

When Leah pulled into Adam's yard, she spotted the black Lab sitting on the porch. *Guess I was right about the hund*, she told herself. *That dog must belong to Adam.*

She climbed down from the buggy, secured her horse, and picked up the cardboard box she'd placed on the floor of the passenger's side. Dodging puddles and the relentless raindrops, she hurried toward the house, trying not to lose her balance.

When Leah stepped onto the porch, the Lab ambled up to her, let out a pathetic whine, and then flopped down on the porch again. That's when she noticed a plate sitting near the dog, full of what looked like burned pancakes. She could only assume that was Adam's attempt at making the girls' breakfast, which seemed to have not gone so well. Even the dog wouldn't eat the burnt-looking, flat pancakes. The poor pooch didn't look too happy, either.

Leah knocked on the door. A few seconds later, Adam opened it. "Oh, it's you," he said, mouth open wide. "I. . .I wasn't expecting company right now." Leah couldn't help noticing that his shirt was not tucked into his trousers, his hair looked like he hadn't taken the time to comb it this morning, and his eyes were bloodshot, probably from lack of sleep. The poor man looked so disheveled her heart went out to him.

Leah looked down at the box. "I brought a casserole dish and some kichlin," she said.

Adam rubbed his forehead. "Actually, the girls are just having breakfast."

"I didn't mean to interrupt," she apologized, watching as the dog, nose in the air, sauntered over to her, trying to get a whiff of the food she held. "I brought the cookies for the girls, and my mamm made the chicken casserole. She thought you might like to reheat it for supper this evening."

"Danki, that was thoughtful of you both." He took the box and stepped outside. "Coal, go lay down. You have food in your dish."

"I think he's trying to tell you something." Leah grinned, looking from the dog to Adam. "Perhaps he doesn't like pancakes. They are pancakes, right?"

Adam looked at her, showing no emotion, then shrugged his shoulders.

I shouldn't have said that, Leah scolded herself. "I didn't know you had a dog," she said, trying to lighten the conversation.

"Didn't. Until recently, that is," Adam responded.

"He's a beautiful Lab. How long have you had him?"

"Not long. The mutt came into my store one day and followed me home. I tried to shoo him away several times, but he kept coming back. When I had no luck finding his owner, I took the critter in."

"I've seen the Lab at the end of your driveway, and he wandered over to our place once, but I wasn't sure whose dog he was. If I'd have known he was yours, I would have brought something over for him to eat, too." Leah was relieved when a hint of a smile formed on Adam's lips.

"Truth is, I'm not much of a cook, which even the dog can attest to." His voice lowered as he leaned closer to Leah. "I just never expected it would be this hard to have three little girls in my house. They miss their mamm and daed something awful, and I'm grieving myself. I don't know what to do to help them through this."

"I know it must be difficult, but remember, Adam, those in our church district, as well as others in the community, will help out wherever and whenever it's needed. All you have to do is ask, and I'm sure that many will help without being asked."

"Jah, I know." Adam's eyes brightened a little. "Since you're here, if you're not busy the rest of the morning, I do have a favor to ask."

"What is it?"

"Would you be able to keep an eye on the girls so I can go to the hardware store and check on things? I'll only be gone a few hours."

Leah smiled. "I'd be happy to do that."

Adam blew out his breath. "Danki. I sure do appreciate it." He leaned against the door. "Say, you wouldn't be available to watch the girls while I'm at work every day, would you? I'd pay you, of course."

Leah shook her head. "I might be able to on some days, but not every day, since I often have people scheduled for reflexology treatments."

Adam frowned. "Oh yeah, that."

"I could ask my mamm if she'd be free to watch the girls," Leah was quick to say.

Adam's face relaxed a bit. "That'd be great. If she's agreeable, make sure you tell her that she'll be paid for her services." He opened the door. "Come in. I'll introduce you to the girls and let 'em know that you'll be with them for a few hours while I'm at the store."

I hope I didn't overstep my bounds when I mentioned that Mom might be willing to watch Adam's nieces, Leah thought. *What if she doesn't want to?*

CHAPTER 15

After Adam left, Leah took a seat at the kitchen table to watch the girls eat their breakfast. Even though Adam had introduced her, Leah was at a loss for words. It was obvious from the girls' grim expressions that they were in pain. Leah wished there was something she could say or do to make them feel better.

Maybe if I find something fun for them to do, it'll help break the ice, she decided, looking toward the window. The rain had finally subsided, and partial blue sky was visible among the slowly departing clouds.

"How would you all like to go for a walk after I wash the dishes?" Leah asked. "We'll take Coal along. He could probably use the exercise, and I'm sure he would enjoy spending time with you." Leah paused and waited for the girls' response.

Amy, the oldest, shook her head. "We can't go for a walk."

"Why not?" Leah asked.

"Uncle Adam will be worried if he comes home and we're not here."

"We wouldn't go far," Leah assured her. "Just down the road a ways, where I saw some pretty wildflowers growing in a field."

Amy's nose twitched. "Can't do that; Linda's allergic to some flowers. She might start sneezing or wheezing."

"Does she have asthma?"

Amy shrugged. "Don't know. She just sneezes and can't breathe well when she's near some flowers."

Leah glanced at Linda, wondering why the child didn't speak for herself. Was she always this quiet, letting her older sister speak on her behalf?

Linda's chin trembled. "Mama likes flowers, but she never brings 'em inside 'cause she knows they make me sneeze."

"Mama's gone," Amy stated in a matter-of-fact tone. "So quit talking about her like she's still here."

Linda glared at her sister as a few tears escaped and rolled down her cheeks.

In an effort to smooth things over between the girls, Leah said, "Would anyone like to dry the dishes after they're washed?"

No one responded.

"I know it's a bit early to have a snack, but I brought some peanut butter kichlin with me today. After the dishes are done, I thought maybe we could all have a few cookies with milk."

Carrie, the youngest, who hadn't said a word so far, climbed down from her chair and pushed it toward the sink.

"What do you think you're doing?" Amy called.

"I'm gonna dry dishes," Carrie replied.

"You can't dry the dishes," Amy argued. "You're too little for that."

Carrie shook her head determinedly. "Mama lets me dry the plastic things, so why can't I here?"

"Let's give Carrie a chance," Leah spoke up. "She can dry a few of the dishes, and then you and Linda can dry the rest."

"I don't wanna dry the dishes." Linda pushed her cereal bowl aside.

"Then how about this," Leah said patiently. "After we do the dishes, why don't we all go outside and pick up those branches that have fallen from the trees in your uncle's yard? I'm sure he would appreciate that."

"The grass is wet, and we'll get dirty picking up sticks." Amy lifted her chin, looking right into Leah's eyes.

Leah clenched her teeth. *Oh, boy. Looks like I have my work cut out for me this morning. I sure hope Adam won't be gone too long.*

When Adam entered his store, he noticed Henry behind the counter, waiting on a customer. Then he spotted Ben, standing off to one side, talking to Elaine.

Irritation welled in Adam's soul. He was still frustrated from this morning's happenings, and now this? Well, at least the rain had finally quit.

With no regard for who might hear, or how it could look to anyone who was in the store, he stepped up to Ben and said, "I'm paying you to work, not take time out from your duties to visit with your *aldi*."

Ben jumped back, as though startled, and blinked a couple times. "I wasn't shirking my duties, Adam. Henry only has one customer at the checkout, and Elaine came here to get some fertilizer for her garden. She was just asking me what kind I thought was best for her roses."

Elaine nodded. "That's right; Ben's telling the truth."

Adam's face heated; he felt like a fool. "I–I'm sorry for snapping at you, Ben. I've been under a lot a stress since Mary and Amos died, but I realize that's no excuse."

"It's all right." Ben clasped Adam's shoulder. "I understand. It's not an easy time for you right now."

"That's partly right; having lost Mary, and now having the responsibility of raising her children makes it hard for me to cope. But it's not all right that I barked at you like that." Adam shook his head. "I appreciate you and Henry taking charge of things at the store during my absence. Don't know what I'd do without you both."

Ben smiled. "We're glad to do it."

"Did you bring your nieces home with you?" Elaine asked.

Adam nodded. "I almost brought them to the store this morning, but Leah dropped by and agreed to stay with 'em till I get home."

Elaine smiled. "That was nice of her. Will she be watching the girls every day while you're here at the store?"

"Afraid not. Since she has her 'patients' to treat, she's tied up most days. She did say she would talk to her mamm, and see if she might be willing to watch the girls."

"I hope it works out," Elaine said. "Leah's mamm has such a sweet personality. I'm sure your nieces will take right to her."

"That'd be good if Dianna can help." Adam groaned. "Because they're sure not taking to me very well."

"I know how hard it is to lose both parents at a young age. If there's anything I can do to help, please let me know."

"Danki, I will."

❧

Leah's suggestion of picking up sticks in the yard must have appealed to Carrie and Linda, for without complaint, they walked around the yard with her, gathering the smaller branches that had fallen. For the time being, at least the two younger ones had something to keep them occupied. Amy, however, would have no part of it as she sat on the porch steps, watching. The sun shone through the clouds, and a gentle, warm breeze wafted around them. With each drift of air that stirred, it almost sounded like rain falling again, as water dripped from the still-wet leaves."I'll pick up the bigger branches." Leah pointed to the pile she'd started.

With all the rain recently, nature had a way of trimming the trees, bringing down dead branches and waterlogged limbs that could no longer hold on. Leah had always found that whenever she felt sad, working outside or even watching the hummingbirds that came into her yard helped to lift her spirits. She hoped it would do the same for Adam's nieces, especially Amy, who seemed to be carrying the weight of the world on her small shoulders. Leah figured that if Amy watched her sisters, she would see how much fun they were having and take part. But so far, she kept to the porch, staring absently at her bare feet.

"Look how many I got." Carrie smiled, taking her small bundle over to the stack of branches. "This is *schpass*."

"You're right," Leah agreed. "It is fun."

"I got a lot, too." Linda joined in, looking pleased with what she'd collected.

"That's wonderful, girls." Leah was glad they were both cooperating. "Keep up the good work. I'm sure your uncle will be pleased when he sees what you have accomplished. He'll probably wonder where that stack of branches came from."

Both girls bobbed their heads in agreement.

Leah looked back at Amy and wished once more that she would join them. But Amy just sat staring off into space. Hopefully in her own good time, the girl would come around.

"Look! Look!" Carrie squealed, pointing at the woodpile as Leah ran over to see what had excited her.

"It's a little chipmunk." Linda smiled, standing next to her sister. "Ain't it cute?"

Carrie nodded and grinned back at her.

Leah was tempted to correct Linda's English but decided not to make a big deal out of it. Glancing back at the woodpile, she figured the chipmunk must have discovered the stack of wood and come out to investigate as more sticks were being added to the top. The cute little critter sat quietly, watching them, then quickly scampered under the pile.

"Okay girls, we don't want to disturb the chipmunk, so we'll have to be gentle when we place the rest of the sticks we gather on the top," Leah said. "When we're done, we'll go inside and see if we can find something to feed to the chipmunk. How's that sound?"

"I can't wait!" Carrie clapped her hands and jumped up and down. "Let's name the critter, 'Chippy.'"

"That's a good name for the chipmunk." Leah breathed a sigh of relief. This little critter might be just what the girls needed to bring a little happiness into their lives. She watched as Carrie and Linda quickly went about to get the rest of the sticks. Leah had to admit Adam's yard looked a lot better. Adam had seemed so preoccupied earlier, she wondered if he really would notice.

Leah glanced back at the porch and spotted Coal sitting beside Amy. She was stroking the dog's back. Coal closed his eyes and leaned against the child's knee. It was amazing how Coal seemed to have honed in on Amy's feelings, as though he were trying to make her feel loved and comforted.

Chicago

"What do you mean you don't have time to talk? This is your day off, isn't it?" Cora's voice rose as she sank to the couch, clenching her cell phone.

"You're right, it's my day off, and Emily and I are about to head out."

There was an edge of impatience to Evan's voice that Cora recognized all too well. If she was going to say what was on her mind, she'd better do it quickly.

"I won't take up much of your precious time." She shifted the phone to her other ear. "I just wanted you to know that I'm thinking of moving, and—"

"Why do you want to move? Is the house too big for you to handle?"

"It's not that." Cora fanned her face. "For that matter, it's much easier to keep clean with just Jared and me," she added dryly. "Not so much clutter lying about."

"Well, what's the problem then?" Evan asked, ignoring her sarcasm. "I think you ought to forget about selling and stay put."

Cora plucked at a piece of white lint that had stuck to her dark skirt. "You don't understand, Evan. My wanting to move has nothing to do with this house." After being married to Evan almost twenty years before he dumped her for another woman, Cora figured he ought to know her well enough to figure things out.

"What does it have to do with then?"

Cora heard him take a deep breath and exhale in irritation. She felt like making this phone call last as long as she could, just to make his precious new wife wait for him.

"As I've mentioned before, our son has become rebellious, and I think he needs a better environment," she continued.

"You're being ridiculous, Cora. Jared's just going through a phase. He'll come out of it sooner or later."

"It's not a phase." Cora clenched her teeth. What did Evan know? He hardly came around anymore. "Jared hasn't handled the divorce very well. Now he's running around with some boys who are leading him astray."

"You worry too much. Just cut our son some slack. Give him a chance, Cora. You shouldn't have to feel pressured to move." Evan paused. "Now, if that's all you have to say, I really do need to go."

"Wait, Evan. I need to ask you something."

"For heaven's sake, Cora, what is it?"

Cora cringed. "If we did move, would you be okay with it?"

"I guess so; just don't move out of the country. I'd like to see my boy once in a while."

"Really, Evan! Of course we won't leave the country," she snapped. "I just want to move to some rural area where Jared won't be faced with so many temptations."

"Yeah, okay. Do whatever you want. Just make sure you let me know where you are so I can keep in touch with Jared." Evan hung up.

Cora's eyes burned as she clicked off her phone. Slapping her forehead, she scolded herself. Why did she need Evan's approval? It was obvious that all he cared about was being with Emily and pleasing her. Cora didn't know why she let Evan's indifference bother her so much. *Was I hoping he'd beg us to stay?* she wondered. *Since Evan obviously doesn't care, I'm going to take that as a sign that it's meant for Jared and me to move. Maybe someday he'll realize what he lost.* She picked up her phone. *I'm definitely calling my Realtor. Then I'll go online to look for a job.*

CHAPTER 16

Arthur

Adam sank into his recliner with a groan. The day had been exceptionally busy, and he was exhausted. He'd been relieved when, half an hour ago, the girls had gone willingly to bed themselves, because right now, he didn't have the energy to climb the stairs to their bedroom. It had been a week since Dianna had begun watching the girls during the day, and he was grateful for that.

Yesterday had been an off-Sunday for their church district, which had given both him and the girls a little more time to rest and get better acquainted. Many Amish in the area visited another church district on their in-between Sundays, but Adam rarely did. In addition to the fact that he wasn't much for socializing, he needed that every-other-Sunday as a time to rest and reflect on things.

Hearing voices coming from upstairs, Adam gritted his teeth. His nerves were on edge this evening. "You three need to go to sleep," he called, cupping his hands around his mouth. Adam valued his peace and quiet and hoped this kind of thing would not go on every night, because he didn't have the patience for it.

"I'm not sleepy!" Linda's high-pitched voice floated down the stairs.

"You'll never feel sleepy if you don't quit talking! Just lie down now, and please be quiet."

"Why?" Amy chimed in.

"Because I said so." Adam hoped that would put an end their idle chitchat.

When no one responded, he reached for the glass of milk he'd placed on the coffee table and took a drink. He wished he had some cookies to go with it, but the girls had eaten the last of the ones Dianna had brought over when she'd come to watch the kids last Friday. Adam knew he should limit their sweets, but while trying to make them happy, he didn't always do the right thing.

Adam reminded himself that at least the girls were functioning better in the new life they'd been forced to accept. At night no more muffled crying came from behind closed doors, as it had during the first few weeks they'd been here. Adam had wanted to rush into the girls' room and gather them into his arms, but they had been keeping him at arm's length and he feared their rejection. So when he'd heard his nieces crying themselves to sleep, he just stood there, with his forehead pressed against the side of their door, letting his own tears fall along with theirs. Other times, he'd stand there, barely able to breathe, until the girls' whimpers were replaced with even breathing, letting him know they'd fallen asleep. Then he would quietly enter and tuck them in before heading downstairs to his room in the hopes that he could sleep. Linda and Carrie shared a room and slept in the same bed. Adam had set up a cot in their room for Amy so they could all be together. He figured that later, if Amy wanted her own room, she could sleep in the one across the hall from her sisters.

Last night he'd gone into the girls' room after they'd fallen asleep. When he'd pulled the blanket up to cover Carrie and Linda, Carrie had mumbled sleepily, "Good night, Papa." The poor little thing still didn't seem to understand that her parents weren't coming back.

At the supper table this evening, Adam had felt like his head was going to explode. Linda and Carrie talked nonstop about the chipmunk they'd discovered that lived in the brush pile out back. Dianna had apparently brought some popcorn with her today, and they'd placed the popped kernels on the ground in front of the branches. Linda was excited that Chippy, as she'd named the critter, had peeked out a short time later and filled his pouch with as much popcorn as possible before storing it back underneath the branches. Adam had to admit, it was kind of cute when Carrie puffed out her cheeks, trying to show him how Chippy had looked. After hearing their stories, Adam had joined the conversation long enough to suggest that they save some apple peels for their newfound friend.

It was good to see Linda and Carrie smiling once in a while, but

Amy was another story. While her younger sisters jabbered on and on about Chippy, Amy sat quietly, toying with her food. Adam continued to hope that something would bring Amy around and give her a reason to smile, but he'd begun to think that might never happen.

He rubbed his forehead, making little circles above his brows. *Mary should have picked someone else to raise her children, not me. I don't know how to relate to them, and I'll never be able to take their mamm and daed's place.*

"Uncle Adam, Carrie's hogging the covers." Linda's shrill voice scattered Adam's thoughts. A few seconds later, she padded into the room.

Adam grimaced, wondering if he was ever going to have any peace. There was another empty bedroom upstairs, and he thought about suggesting that Linda move into that room, so she'd have her own bed, but the girls had indicated they didn't want to be separated. "Come on, Linda," he said, rising from his chair. "I'll walk you back up to your room and tuck you into bed."

"Will you tell Carrie she can't have all the covers?"

He nodded. "Jah, sure."

As Adam followed Linda up the stairs, he thought about the challenges that lay ahead for him. The only way to deal with the situation was to take things as they came, because if he looked too far ahead, he'd feel even more overwhelmed. He thought once again how grateful he was that Leah's mother had agreed to watch the children while he was at work. Having a woman's influence to help guide them in areas where Adam couldn't was a huge relief. At least that was one phase of this challenge he didn't have to worry about right now.

"How did things go over at Adam's today?" Leah asked her mother.

Mom's lips compressed as she set the magazine she'd been reading aside. "Adam's nieces are well behaved, and they do whatever I ask, but they're having a hard time adjusting. Losing one's parents at any age is difficult, but when a child loses both parents at the same time, I believe they may feel a sense of abandonment."

"Do you think the girls are angry at their mamm and daed for dying?" Leah questioned, seating herself beside Mom on the couch.

Mom gave a slow nod. "That's possible—especially Amy. And the fact that their uncle is gone so much due to his job isn't helping things any."

"But you're there for them during the day, and Adam's with them in the evenings and on weekends."

"True, but it's not the same as having two parents, and a mother who's at home with them during the day. That little chipmunk is about the only thing that seems to have made those two younger girls happy." Mom smiled. "This morning we put some of that old popcorn I took over in front of the pile of branches. Then we all stood back and watched until Chippy came to investigate. He must have liked it, because back and forth he went, storing the kernels underneath there somewhere, where he'll no doubt eat them later."

"Sounds like a positive distraction that gives the children some joy," Leah said. "At least they have you to share it with them."

"True, and while I like the girls, I'll never have the bond with them that their mother had. And Adam. . .well, he's their uncle, and a bachelor at that, so unless he gets married someday, the girls might never feel as if they're part of a complete family."

"I doubt that Adam will ever find a woman who'd be willing to marry him."

"Why do you think that?"

"He's too set in his ways." Leah popped a piece of gum into her mouth. "No woman I know would want to marry a man who thinks he's right about everything."

Just then Leah's father entered the room with a grim expression.

"What's wrong, Alton?" Mom asked. "Was there a problem in the barn when you were feeding the horses?"

"It's not the horses." He took a seat on the other side of Mom. "I just came from the phone shack. There was a message from your brother-in-law James. Guess your sister is having a hard time with her pregnancy, and the doctor's worried she may lose the boppli, so he put her on bed rest."

"That's going to be difficult." Mom looked at Dad and then touched Leah's arm. "Since James and Grace moved to Wisconsin and have no family close by, I should go there and help out."

Leah nodded. "I understand. And don't worry about things here. Dad and I will get along just fine while you're gone." Grace was Mom's youngest sibling, and this was her fifth child. The other children, all boys, were all less than ten years old and had been born every two years. The boys were quite active, and none would be that much help to their mother, so Leah knew Mom's assistance would be greatly appreciated.

"There's just one thing." Frowning, Mom rubbed the bridge of her nose. "If I go to help Grace, Adam won't have a sitter for his nieces. Would you consider taking over that responsibility, Leah?"

"Oh, I don't know, Mom—"

"The girls will be starting school in a few weeks, and you wouldn't need to be at Adam's house all day."

"Adam doesn't get home until close to suppertime," Leah reminded. "That would mean the girls would be alone after they get out of school until Adam gets home. Besides, Carrie's not in school yet, so she'll need someone with her during the day."

"You're right about that."

"But it won't work for my schedule, Mom, because I need to be available for people who need a reflexology treatment."

"Maybe you could schedule appointments during the evening hours," Dad suggested.

"Or perhaps Adam could bring the girls over here every day," Mom interjected.

Leah shook her head. "They'd be by themselves while I was in the basement working on people's feet. I wouldn't be able to concentrate, knowing they were upstairs, unattended." Leah grabbed the throw pillow and pushed it behind her back. "Besides, I'm sure Adam would never go for that."

"If you're willing to watch them, at least we could ask," Mom said with a hopeful expression.

Leah sucked her bottom lip as she mulled things over. "I suppose I could do that, but Adam may want to ask someone else to watch the girls."

"You won't know that till you talk to him about it." Mom rose from her seat. "I'm going out to the phone shack and leave a message for James, letting him know that I'll be coming to help out."

Leah leaned her head against the back of the sofa and closed her eyes. Adam needed someone to care for his nieces during the day, and for some strange reason, she hoped it would be her. Not to see Adam, of course, but to spend time with those precious girls.

Chicago

Cora sat at her desk in the kitchen, searching for nursing jobs on the Internet. For Jared's sake, she'd been keeping her search to the more rural areas in Illinois, not wanting to move too far from Chicago. She wanted him out of the big city but figured she'd have to deal with Evan if she and Jared moved too far away. Besides, it was only fair to her son to live close enough so that he could spend some time with his father—what precious little time Evan gave.

So far, Cora hadn't found any jobs that met her criteria, but she would keep looking. Yesterday, she'd made contact with a Realtor, who'd be coming by tomorrow morning to take a look at the house. Cora was anxious to find out how much he thought she could get for it. Hopefully, it would sell quickly and bring in enough that she'd be able to put a good share of the money into Jared's college fund. Of course, she had to convince him that he needed more schooling once he graduated from high school. The last time the subject of his education came up, Jared had insisted that he didn't need college and wanted to find a job doing something with his hands. Cora couldn't imagine what that would be. Jared didn't seem to have much interest in anything other than running around with his friends and playing video games on their large-screen TV.

Maybe things will change once we're out of the city and away from his friends, Cora told herself, turning off the computer. Tomorrow was another day, and hopefully things would go well with the Realtor. Her one big concern, however, was what she would do if the house sold before she found a job someplace else. She sure couldn't move without suitable employment.

"*You worry too much,*" Cora's mother had often said during Cora's childhood. *"Just take each day as it comes, and trust God for the rest."*

"That was easy enough for you to say, Mom," Cora muttered under her breath. Cora hadn't trusted God for anything in a long time; not since she was a young girl.

"Who you talking to, Mom?" Jared asked, stepping into the room.

Cora jumped. "Oh, you startled me. I thought you'd gone to bed."

"Nope. I ain't sleepy. Thought I'd fix myself something to eat." Jared marched across the room and flung the refrigerator door open. "Is there any of that pepperoni pizza left from yesterday?"

"There probably is, but do you really want to stuff yourself at this hour of the night?"

He lifted his shoulders in a brief shrug. "Don't really matter to me what time it is. When I'm hungry, I eat. So there!"

Cora cringed. When had her son gotten so mouthy? As far as Cora was concerned, she and Jared really needed to move, and the sooner the better. She might have to take the first job that came along, regardless of how much it paid.

CHAPTER 17

Arthur

The next morning before leaving for work, Adam peeled an apple then wrapped the peelings in a paper towel and wrote a note to the girls. He hoped they'd be happy that he'd left a little something for their chipmunk friend.

As Adam began fixing a sandwich to take to work, he heard Coal barking outside. Glancing out the kitchen window, he was surprised to see Leah riding up on her bicycle. It was a beautiful morning, so he could understand why she'd be on her bike. What he couldn't figure out was why she had come here.

Going to the door, he met her on the porch, with Coal wagging his tail and nudging her hand to pet him.

"Guder mariye," Leah said, looking up at Adam.

"Good morning," he replied. "Out for a morning ride?"

"No, actually, I came to let you know that my mamm can't watch the kinner today," Leah said. "Her sister's expecting a baby and the doctor ordered bed rest for her, so Mom is going there to help out with her four children and will probably stay till the boppli's born."

Adam groaned. This was not the kind of news he needed this morning. "I can understand why she'd want to help her sister, but it kind of puts me in a bind right now. I can't very well take the girls to work with me today. There's nothing for them to do at the store, and they'd either be bored or get into things I don't want them to touch."

Leah held up her hand. "I have the answer to that—at least for today."

"What do you mean?"

"I also came here to say that since my mamm will not be available to watch the girls, I can take over that responsibility today and even until Mom returns home. Unless, of course, you have someone else in mind to be here with the girls."

Adam shook his head. "I don't know of anyone right now, but didn't you say before that you wouldn't be available to watch my nieces?"

"Jah, I did say that, but I've decided that I can give reflexology treatments during the evening hours, which will leave me free to watch the girls until you get home from work each day." She paused. "That is, if you think the arrangement will work for you."

"Sounds good to me, and I'll pay you the same as I was giving your mamm," he said, feeling both grateful and relieved. He figured Leah would do as well with the girls as her mother had and certainly better than he could.

"Are you feeling all right this morning?" Jonah asked, coming up behind Sara and placing his hands against her growing stomach. "I heard you get up several times during the night."

"I'm fine," Sara said. "My back hurts a bit, and I had a hard time finding a comfortable position."

"Sorry to hear that. Would you like me to make you an appointment with our chiropractor?"

Turning to face Jonah, Sara shook her head. "I thought I'd see Leah first and see if she can help me."

"Are you sure about that?"

Sara nodded. "When Leah works on my feet, it always helps me relax. I think stress plays a role in causing my back to flare up."

"Why are you feeling stressed?" Jonah's face was a mask of concern. "Is it your MS? Have you been having more symptoms?"

Sara leaned into him. "Now don't look so concerned. My MS symptoms have actually been better since I got pregnant. I'm feeling stressed because Mark is demanding more of my attention lately. He clings to me a lot when he should be happily playing."

"I think that's partially my fault because I haven't been giving him enough attention."

"You've been busy in the buggy shop, Jonah."

"That's true, but it's no excuse. When I'm done working for the day, I'll try to spend more time with him."

Sara smiled. "I know Mark would like that. He thinks the world of you."

"Maybe I'll close the shop early one day this week, and the three of us can go on a picnic," Jonah said.

"That'd be nice." Sara reached around and massaged her back. "I think I'll go out to the phone shack and call Leah. Hopefully she can see me sometime today."

"What about Mark? Will you need me to come up to the house and watch him while you're gone?"

She shook her head. "I can take him with me. Leah's mamm will probably be there, and I'm sure she'd be glad to keep Mark occupied while I'm getting my feet massaged."

Jonah kissed her cheek. "Okay, but if you need me for anything, just let me know."

"I will." Sara was grateful to be married to such a thoughtful man. Her first husband, Harley, had been that way, too, and she felt doubly blessed to have found such a caring man the second time around. After Harley's death, Sara had struggled trying to raise Mark on her own. Then when she'd been diagnosed with MS, everything had become a challenge. How grateful she was for Jonah's friendship during that time and even more so once they had fallen in love.

Turning from the refrigerator, Leah was holding a chocolate-chip cheeseball when Amy entered the kitchen, rubbing her forehead, followed by the other two girls.

"What's wrong, Amy?" Leah asked, feeling concern.

Amy frowned. "When my sisters and I were playing tag, Carrie kept yelling real loud, and now I have a *koppweh*."

"Carrie didn't give you a headache on purpose," Linda said in her younger sister's defense. "She always hollers when we play that game."

Leah figured it did the children good to run and play. Even Carrie's shouting wasn't a bad thing. It meant they were beginning to relax and have a little fun, despite missing their parents. "The chocolate-chip cheeseball I made this morning is ready to eat," she said, placing it on the table. "Why don't you three go wash up while I get out some graham crackers and milk to go with our snack?" Leah gave Amy's shoulder a gentle squeeze. "Maybe after you've had something to eat you'll feel better."

"Okay." Amy followed her sisters down the hall. When they returned to the kitchen, Leah had everything set on the table.

"*Is gut*," Carrie announced, after she'd eaten a graham cracker Leah had spread with some of the cheeseball.

Leah smiled. "I'm glad you like it. I've made lots of different cheeseballs, but chocolate-chip's my favorite."

"Bet Uncle Adam would like it," Linda said. "We should save him some."

"Jah, we'll do that." Leah looked over at Amy. The child sat with her head down, rubbing her temples. "Aren't you going to try some, Amy?"

Amy moaned. "My head hurts too bad to eat anything, and I feel sick to my stomach. Sure hope I don't throw up."

Remembering how she'd helped several people with sick headaches, Leah touched Amy's arm gently and said, "Would you like me to rub your feet?"

"My head hurts, not my feet."

"I've helped many people get rid of their headaches by rubbing certain spots on their feet," Leah explained. "What I do is called 'reflexology,' and it can be quite effective. Would you like me to try it on you?"

Linda came alongside her sister. "I think you oughtta let her do it, Amy. I wanna see Leah work on your feet."

"Me, too!" Carrie shouted, then she quickly covered her mouth. "Sorry for yelling in the house."

Amy looked up at Leah and shrugged her slim shoulders. "I. . .I guess so. Suppose it can't hurt to let you rub my feet."

"I wanna watch." Linda bounced on her toes.

"Since it's such a nice day, let's all go outside and sit in the yard," Leah suggested. "The fresh air might help Amy's headache, too. I'll take an old quilt out that we can sit on while I work on her feet."

Leah grabbed the quilt from the back of the couch, and the girls followed her outside. After Leah spread the quilt on the grass, they all plopped down on it. Even Coal ambled over and lay down between Amy and Linda. Then Amy took off her shoes, leaned back on her elbows, and closed her eyes.

"Who taught you how to do that?" Linda asked as Leah began to pressure-point Amy's feet.

"My grandma taught me," Leah replied. "I've been doing it since I was a teenager."

"Don't you mind touching strangers' feet all the time?"

"No, it doesn't bother me at all." Leah smiled. "In fact, it makes me feel good to use the gift God gave me to help others."

Carrie wrinkled her nose. "Eww. . . *Schtinkich fiess.*"

Leah bit back a chuckle. "Not everyone's feet smell stinky, Carrie."

"But some people's do," Linda put in. "And you must like touching their feet to do them."

Leah nodded, and as Amy's younger sisters looked on, she continued to massage Amy's feet. Several more minutes passed, then Amy opened her eyes. "My head quit hurting," she announced.

Leah smiled. "I'm so glad."

"Will you do my feet next?" Linda took off her shoes and stuck her feet out toward Leah.

"Sure, I'd be happy to." Leah massaged Linda's feet, and when she was done, Carrie scooted in front of her. "Me, too, Leah."

"Okay, little one." Leah began to rub the little girl's feet, while the other girls, and even the dog, moved aside.

Carrie giggled, looking up at Leah with such a sweet expression. *"Ich bin ewe kitzlich."*

Leah smiled. "So you're ticklish, huh?" It gave her such pleasure to see the child laugh.

"What's going on here, Leah? What do you think you're doing?"

Startled, Leah looked up. Adam stood a few feet away, looking down at her with a scowl. She'd been so engrossed in what she was doing that she hadn't heard Adam's rig pull in. Even Coal hadn't budged from the edge of the quilt.

"Amy had a koppweh, and Leah made it better," Linda spoke up. "Then she worked on my feet. After that, Carrie wanted hers done, too."

Adam's eyebrows drew together as he continued to stare at Leah. "So you were poking around on the girls' feet?"

Linda shook her head. "Leah weren't poking. She was doing 'flexology."

"Is that so?" Adam's eyes narrowed, looking sternly at Leah. "You can do whatever you want with the people who come to you for foot treatments, but I'll have none of that hocus-pocus here at my place. Is that clear?"

Carrie started to cry, and Leah's head snapped back, feeling as though she'd been slapped. Didn't Adam care that she'd been able to relieve Amy's headache? Wasn't he willing to at least give reflexology a chance?

"It's okay," Amy said, as though she understood Leah's embarrassment. "My koppweh's gone now, so Leah did a good thing." Before Adam could say anything more, the child jumped up and raced into the house. Carrie and Linda followed, both sniffling as they went. Didn't Adam realize how sensitive these girls were? Hadn't he even heard what Amy said?

Leah scrambled to her feet. "You know something, Adam?" she said through clenched teeth.

He tipped his head. "What's that?"

"You have a lot to learn about children, and unless you've had a reflexology treatment yourself, then you shouldn't be so narrow minded."

"I am not narrow minded. Since this is *my* house, and these girls are *my* nieces, I have every right to say what I will and won't tolerate concerning their welfare."

Leah could see by the determined set of Adam's jaw that he wasn't going to back down. "Since you're here now, I'm sure you can manage things on your own for the rest of the evening, so I'll be on my way home. I have some hummingbird feeders that need to be cleaned, and I need to start supper for my daed." She went into the house and grabbed her purse. When she stepped back outside, she met Adam on the porch. "Please tell the girls I said good-bye and that I'll see them in the morning."

As Leah walked away, she heard Adam mumble something but couldn't make out what he'd said. She wasn't about to go back and find out!

With arms folded and lips pressed tightly together, Adam watched out the kitchen window as Leah hopped on her bicycle and rode off.

Dropping into a seat at the table, he groaned. He hated the fact that he was physically attracted to Leah, yet at the same time, she got under his skin. "I probably should have called her back and apologized," Adam muttered. "But then, why should I? Leah shouldn't be introducing my nieces to reflexology." He tapped his foot in agitation. *Maybe I should look for someone else to watch the girls. Someone less appealing and easier to communicate with. But the girls seem to like her, and I need to focus on their needs and making their transition as smooth as possible. Too many changes will only make it more difficult for my nieces right now.*

Linda stomped into the kitchen, her cheeks still damp with tears. "You know what, Uncle Adam?"

"Say what you have to say," he said, trying to hide his irritation.

"You're mean!" With that, Linda plodded out of the room and tramped noisily up the stairs.

Spotting the cheeseball and graham crackers sitting out, Adam helped himself to some. Maybe it would make him feel better if he ate something. *Linda's right*, he decided. *I was rather harsh. Guess I owe everyone an apology.*

After spreading some of the cheeseball on a cracker, Adam ate it and smacked his lips. *This isn't bad. In fact, it's real tasty. I bet Leah made it.* He fixed another one. *If she promises not to practice her hocus-pocus on Carrie, Linda, or Amy, guess I'll let her keep watching the girls. I hate to admit it, but they seem to like her better than they do me.*

CHAPTER 18

Chicago

Cora sat in the living room, holding her laptop on her knees. For the last hour she'd been looking once again for nursing positions in various areas across Illinois. The few openings she found didn't pay well enough. In addition to her wages, the child support Evan paid for Jared would help with expenses, but it didn't come close to what he used to contribute when they were married. Cora had to hold out for a better-paying job, or she and Jared would be getting by on a lot less than they were used to.

On the plus side, she had met with her Realtor a few days ago, and he'd scheduled an open house, hoping to generate some interest in her home. Cora knew it might take awhile, and once it was sold, she'd have plenty of money, but she wanted to move as soon as possible. In addition to her struggles with Jared, seeing Evan whenever he came to check on patients at the hospital, not to mention bumping into his new bride, was taking a toll. If she only had the support of family right now to help her through this difficult time in her life. But Cora's parents were dead, and she'd lost touch with her four brothers years ago—not that they would have offered much support. They'd never been close to Cora. Of course, that was probably her fault, since they had differing opinions on certain things. Cora had several friends in Chicago, including Ellie and Shannon, both nurses. But they were both too busy for her these days. Perhaps once she and Jared relocated, they'd find a new set of friends.

Cora glanced at her watch. It was almost five. Jared should have been home an hour ago. When she'd arrived home from work this afternoon, she'd found a scribbled note from him on the table, saying he'd gone to a friend's house and would be home by four o'clock. Something, or someone, must have detained him.

Rubbing her eyes, Cora set her laptop aside and began to pace. Last week, Jared had gotten into a fight when some kid made a wisecrack about Jared's father cheating on his mother. While Cora appreciated Jared's anger over what Evan had done, she didn't condone fighting and knew nothing good could come from her son beating someone up. Maybe Jared had run into that same boy today and been involved in another skirmish. But if that were the case, why hadn't Jared come home right away, like he had the last time, when he'd been left with a split lip and bloody nose?

She glanced out the front window. No sign of Jared coming up the walk. Should she start calling some of his friends?

Reaching for the phone, Cora was about to make the first call, when the front door flew open and Jared stepped in.

"Where have you been?" Cora moved quickly toward him, relieved that he showed no signs of having been beaten up. "I've been worried about you."

He sauntered across the room, dropped his backpack on the floor, and flopped onto the couch. "Chill out, Mom. I hung out with my friend Chad all day, like I said in my note."

Jared plunked his feet on the coffee table and clasped his hands behind his head. "What are we having for supper? I only had a candy bar for lunch, so I'm starving!"

"I have a meat loaf in the oven," she replied. "And please take your feet off the table."

He dropped his feet to the floor and wrinkled his nose. "I hate meat loaf."

"If you're hungry, you'll eat it."

"Guess I shoulda stayed over at Chad's. His mom works nights, so Chad's on his own all evening. I coulda ate whatever I wanted to over there."

Cora frowned. "Chad being on his own is exactly why he gets into so much trouble." She took a seat on the end of the couch beside Jared and grasped the throw pillow, hugging it to her chest. "I don't like you hanging around him so much. He's a bad influence."

Jared jumped up. "Since you're gonna give me a lecture now, I'm going to my room." He raced up the stairs before Cora could say another word.

Flinching as her son slammed his bedroom door, Cora's jaw clenched. She felt her relationship with Jared slipping further every day. Things weren't like this when she and Evan were married. Jared had been easier to deal with then.

Maybe I should consider one of those jobs I was looking at earlier, even though they don't pay as much as I make now. I really need to get Jared out of here before school starts.

Arthur

"I'm glad you were able to see me this evening," Sara said as Leah worked on her feet. "I've been having trouble with my back again."

"I'm sorry I wasn't able to see you yesterday," Leah apologized. "I was watching Adam's nieces all day and didn't check phone messages till this morning. Otherwise, I could have seen you last evening."

Sara winced when Leah pressed on a particular spot that Leah knew must be tender.

"It's all right. Jonah worked late in his shop last night, but tonight he's home with Mark, so everything worked out." Sara leaned her head against the back of the recliner and drew in a deep breath, which let Leah know she was beginning to relax.

"I haven't had the chance to get to know Adam's nieces," Sara said. "Losing both of their parents has to be difficult for them."

Leah slowly nodded.

"How are they adjusting?"

"Each of them seems to be dealing with it in her own way, but they all have insecurities and behavioral issues."

"Such as?"

"Carrie, the youngest, clings to me most of the day. When Mom was watching them, she said Carrie did that with her, as well."

"It's understandable. Carrie's still very young and misses her mamm."

Leah probed another spot on Sara's foot. "Linda's the middle child, and she's full of nervous energy. She also has a bit of a temper."

Sara's forehead creased. "That can be difficult to deal with. I get stressed out whenever Mark throws a temper tantrum."

"Then there's the oldest, Amy. She tries to act grown up and tends to boss her sisters around, but she's still a little girl and needs to be loved and nurtured as much as the other two. I know she's still hurting, but she holds it in. I figure she uses her bossiness to cover up her pain. Even though Amy trusted me enough to use reflexology to get rid of her headache, she keeps her distance." Leah saw no point in mentioning Adam's reaction to her working on the girls' feet.

"Maybe Amy just needs a little more attention. Jonah and I have recently come to realize that we need to spend more time with Mark. Once the boppli comes, he will require it even more, so he doesn't feel left out."

"I agree. In fact, I think all three of Adam's nieces need more love and attention. I've actually been thinking of a fun thing I might do that could help them focus on something other than their grief," Leah said.

"What's that?" Sara murmured, now appearing to be even more relaxed.

"As you know, we have a lot of hummingbirds in our yard. Watching them around the feeders each day has made me think that the girls might enjoy having a feeder in Adam's backyard."

"That's a good idea." Sara yawned. "It would certainly give them something to look forward to."

"That's what I was thinking. You'd be surprised to see what a little chipmunk has done to give Linda and Carrie some enjoyment. Adam told me that he heard them talking about it the other day." Leah smiled. "Think I'll take one of my unused feeders over there, and if he has no objections, I'll find a place to hang it where the girls can easily watch the hummers feed."

"Next time I come here I'll be anxious to hear how it worked out."

Leah's excitement mounted. "When my neighbor comes over to band the hummingbirds in my yard, I might see if Adam's okay with me bringing the girls over so they get to see how the procedure is done. It might be one more thing to bring a little joy into their lives."

"That sounds interesting," Sara said. "I'll bet Mark would enjoy watching that, too."

"Feel free to bring him. The girls would probably have fun getting acquainted with your cute little guy."

Sara smiled. "You know, I think we will come over that day. Just let me know when."

"Jah, I will." Leah looked forward to seeing the girls tomorrow and hopefully setting up the feeder. She had so much love to give Adam's nieces and wanted to share the enjoyment she got out of something as simple as watching the tiny birds that had brought her so much pleasure over the years. If she ever had any children of her own, she would try to instill in them a love for all things found in nature. But until that time came, if it did, she would enjoy spending time with Adam's nieces, for they clearly needed her love and attention. She just wished Adam wasn't so against her practicing reflexology on the girls. He ought to at least give her the chance to prove that it wasn't hocus-pocus.

Adam yawned as he stood in front of the stove, trying to make supper. He'd been tempted to ask Leah if she could stay awhile longer and fix the meal for him and the girls but figured she'd be anxious to get home and prepare supper for herself and her dad. Besides, things had been strained between them since Tuesday, when he'd forbidden her to massage the girls' feet, even though he had apologized to everyone for being so harsh.

He reached for a package of macaroni and added the contents to the kettle of boiling water on the stove. *Leah may think I'm being impossible, but she doesn't understand the reason behind my opposition to reflexology.* Adam shook his head. *And what's the point of telling her? What happened in my past doesn't concern her, and it's really none of her business.*

Adam grimaced when he glanced at Amy, whom he'd asked to set the table. She ambled from the silverware drawer to the table, dragging her feet as she carried one item at a time and then placed it haphazardly on the table. It was as though she were moving in slow motion. Was she doing it on purpose, just to irritate him, or did Amy's placid expression and lack of interest mean that her heart wasn't in this chore because of her sadness? She was certainly detached, and Adam wished there was something that would bring her out of it.

He had considered setting the girls down and having a talk with them about their folks—maybe try to get them to open up and express their feelings. *Would it help for them to know I'm hurting, too?* he wondered. But Adam hadn't followed through on that, because he wasn't sure what to say. The simple truth was that the girls didn't relate well to him, and frankly, the feeling was mutual. It wasn't that Adam didn't love his nieces; he just didn't feel comfortable in his new role as their guardian. If he were married and had children of his own, he'd have experience as a father and would understand the girls' needs a little better.

Well, I can learn, he told himself. *It would just be nice if I had a wife to help me through this process.* Adam slapped the side of his head. *What am I thinking? I don't want a wife. And even if I did, who would it be? Certainly not Leah—although I find myself fighting an attraction to her.*

Pushing the conflicting thoughts to the back of his mind, Adam concentrated on getting the macaroni and cheese finished. Maybe he'd toss in some cut-up hot dogs with it. The girls would probably like that. Then after they ate their meal and cleaned up the dishes, he'd suggest they all go outside and look at the bright, full moon. Maybe that would have a calming effect on everyone and let the girls know that he was trying a little harder to take an interest in them.

CHAPTER 19

The following day, as Adam watched the girls eat their cereal and toast, he reflected on how things had gone last night when he'd showed them the beautiful full moon. The two younger ones had seemed quite interested, especially when Adam gave them the binoculars to get a closer look. They'd gasped at how big and orange it was when it first crested the horizon. Then as the moon went higher, it turned its typical white color, with the craters becoming more visible.

But Amy acted bored with it all. She'd said that she didn't see what was so special about the moon. It was just a big round ball of nighttime light.

Later, Amy had asked if she could sleep in her own room, across the hall from her sisters. Adam could tell she wanted to be more independent and keep to herself, so he agreed that she could have her own room. He hoped Amy's indifference wouldn't affect her ability to do well in school, which would be starting in two weeks. Both Amy and Linda would be attending, which meant Carrie might be lonely without her sisters all day.

I hope Leah will continue to watch Carrie. The other girls will need someone here with them when they get home from school, too. Adam supposed he could offer to bring Carrie over to Leah's house each morning, after he'd taken Linda and Amy to school, but having her come here was much more convenient. Besides, his home was more familiar, and right now, Adam thought that was important for the girls.

Guess I'd better talk to Leah about this, he decided. *I'll mention it as soon as she gets here this morning.*

Adam finished his bowl of cereal and was putting his dishes in the sink when Leah showed up. This time she arrived by horse and buggy.

He watched out the kitchen window as she unhitched her horse,

Sugar. He could see she was talking to the mare, while gently rubbing Sugar's neck. She was as gentle with animals as she was with children. He'd noticed this when Coal ran out to greet her every morning. The dog would sit patiently, after running circles around her, accustomed to the special treat she often brought him.

Adam continued to watch Leah as she put Sugar in the corral and took a small box out of the buggy. He waited until she reached the porch, then he opened the back door.

"Guder mariye," they said in unison.

"What have you got in there?" he asked, looking curiously at the box Leah held as she stepped into the utility room.

"It's a hummingbird feeder." Leah smiled. "Unless you have some objection, I thought I'd fill it with nectar and hang it somewhere in your yard. The hummers won't be around too many more weeks, but I think the girls would enjoy watching them drink from the feeder until the hummers head south for the winter. Right now, the little birds are quite active, migrating down from the northern states, so I'm sure it won't be long before they discover this new feeder."

"I don't object at all, and I think the girls might like that. At least Linda and Carrie will." Adam lowered his voice. "I'm not sure about Amy. She doesn't seem to be interested in much of anything other than telling her sisters what to do."

"Well, you never know; watching the hummers might catch Amy's attention. She also might find it fascinating to see how those little birds are just as curious about us as we are about them." Leah paused, pushing the sleeves on her dress up a little. "You know, Adam, I'm surprised you haven't figured it out yet."

He tipped his head. "Figured what out?"

"I think Amy is bossy because she's covering up her true feelings. She's trying to be strong for her sisters and doesn't want to appear weak in front of them. Since Amy is the oldest, she probably feels that she's the only mother her sisters have now, even though she's only ten.

Adam nodded slowly. What Leah had said made sense.

"Oh, and there's one more thing I wanted to talk to you about," Leah said.

"What's that?"

"Next Wednesday morning one of my neighbors will be coming over to our place to band the hummingbirds that flock around my feeders every day. Would it be all right if I take the girls over there so they can watch the procedure?"

Adam shrugged. "Sure. It sounds interesting. Maybe I'll go into work a little later that day so I can watch the banding, too."

Leah blinked, and her mouth opened slightly. "Oh, I didn't realize that would be something you'd be interested in."

He nodded. "I may be tied up with my store a good deal of the time, but I do enjoy all things related to nature. I find watching God's critters to be relaxing."

"Same here; and you're more than welcome to join us that day. I'm sure it'll be a learning experience for all of us."

Adam hadn't been sure how Leah would feel about him inviting himself to the banding session, but he was glad he'd mentioned it. Right now, he couldn't seem to take his eyes away from Leah's as he noticed how easily she blushed.

When Leah broke eye contact and started for the kitchen, he touched her shoulder. "Now there's something I need to ask you."

She halted and turned to face him. "What is it, Adam?"

"As I'm sure you're aware, school will be starting the week after next, and even though Amy and Linda will be in school most of the day, Carrie will still need a sitter. So I was wondering. . ."

"If I would continue watching her?"

"Jah."

"Of course, I will, Adam. I enjoy being with the girls, and since I'm seeing people for foot treatments in the evening hours, that leaves me free during the daytime."

"Are you sure? I could ask around and see if there's someone else willing to watch Carrie and be here after Linda and Amy get home from school."

Leah shook her head. "No, really, I'm fine with the way things are now. The schedule I'm on has been going fairly well for me."

Adam breathed in a sigh of relief. "That's good to hear. Jah, real good."

"So, girls, how would you like to help me with something?" Leah asked after Adam left for work.

"What do you want us to do?" Linda looked up at Leah inquisitively.

Leah went to the box she'd placed on the kitchen counter and removed the feeder. "This is a special kind of feeder for hummingbirds. Do you girls know what a hummingbird is?"

"Course we do," Amy spoke up. "They're little birds with long beaks."

"And they fly real fast, too," Linda added.

"That's right," Leah agreed. "And hummers, as they're sometimes called, don't eat birdseed like most other birds do. They drink sweet nectar instead."

"What's sweet nectar?" Linda asked.

"It's sugar water." Amy poked her sister's arm. "I'll bet even Carrie knows that."

Linda poked her back. "Bet she doesn't."

"Let's go ask her then." Amy tromped across the room to where Carrie sat, stirring the milk around in her cereal bowl. "What's sweet nectar, sister?"

Carrie grinned at Amy and said, "It's *zucker wasser*."

"That's right!" Amy patted Carrie's back.

Linda rolled her eyes. "I'll bet she was listening to what we said. That's how she knew."

"Let's mix some of that sugar water right now," Leah was quick to say. "First, we need to rinse the feeder real good, to make sure it's nice and clean. Then we can all go outside and get the feeder hung."

"Do you know how much to mix?" Amy questioned.

"I sure do. The general rule is four cups of water and one cup of sugar. At home, I prepare the mixture every night and keep it in a container in the refrigerator. So if your uncle has something in his kitchen to store it in, we'll do the same thing here." Leah watched as all three girls listened intently. "So what do you say? Are you ready to find a good spot for the feeder?"

Carrie and Linda bobbed their heads agreeably. Amy merely shrugged her shoulders, but she did get a bag of sugar from the pantry while Linda found a plastic container and got the cup to measure water in. Leah had a feeling that Amy was more interested in feeding the hummers than she let on.

"I wonder how things have been going for Leah since she started watching Adam's nieces," Elaine commented as she and Priscilla headed down the road in Priscilla's horse and buggy. They'd gone out for breakfast and were on their way back to Elaine's.

"I don't know. It's been awhile since I've talked to her," Priscilla said. "Maybe we should stop by Adam's and say hello."

Elaine smiled. "That's a good idea. If you have the time, that is."

Priscilla nodded. "Mom closed our store for the day so Dad can paint it. When I left this morning, she said not to hurry back and to take the rest of the day for myself. I can't think of a better way to spend it than with my two best friends."

"I would have invited Leah to join us for breakfast," Elaine said, "but I knew she'd have to be at Adam's early to watch the girls."

Priscilla pulled back on the reins a little to slow her horse some. "I wonder how much longer Leah will keep watching Adam's nieces."

"I would think at least till her mamm comes home. And who knows, she might even keep on after that."

"I guess that's possible, but being at Adam's all day is probably affecting Leah's ability to practice reflexology."

Elaine shook her head. "From what Leah said when I saw her at church the last time, she's been working on people's feet during the evening hours."

Priscilla drew in a sharp breath and released it slowly. "Wow, that makes for a long day. I wonder how long she'll be able to keep up with that schedule."

"We do what we have to at times when it's needed." Elaine reflected on her own situation when her grandmother was alive. She'd put in long hours caring for Grandma, in addition to doing whatever she could to make a little extra money. But she had no regrets. She had made a commitment to Grandma and kept her promise to Grandpa before he died. As tiring and stressful as those days had been, she would do it all again if it meant having Grandma with her right now.

Life keeps moving on, she thought, *and I've had to learn to live by myself and carry on.* The pain of losing both her grandparents was still with Elaine, but she'd learned to trust God and look to the future. The question was, would Elaine's future be with Ben Otto, or did he only see her as a good friend? An easy friendship was all she wanted from Ben for now, but perhaps someday it could turn into something more.

Elaine closed her eyes, and an image of Jonah Miller popped into her head. She'd never loved anyone the way she had him. But that was in the past, and she'd forced herself to let go. Their relationship had ended the day Elaine had learned that Grandma had dementia. She reminded herself once more that her love for Jonah had prompted her to break things off with him. Setting him free to live a life with Sara and her son had been the best thing for Jonah. He and Sara were happy. Every time Elaine saw the couple together, their love and devotion to each other was more evident.

"We're here. Wake up, sleepyhead."

Elaine's eyes opened. "I wasn't really sleeping—just thinking is all."

Priscilla smiled. "I hope they were good thoughts."

Elaine nodded.

Once Priscilla had the horse secured at the rail near Adam's barn, she and Elaine headed across the yard, where they found Leah and the girls sitting in chairs on the porch.

"It's good to see you," Leah said. "Look what I put up for the girls." She pointed to a hummingbird feeder hanging from a hook under the porch eaves.

"How nice." Elaine looked at Amy and smiled. "Have you seen any hummers yet?"

The child shook her head. "Probably won't, neither."

"What makes you think that?" Priscilla asked.

"Nothing good ever happens for me."

Leah put her arm around Amy. "Good things come to those who

wait. It's going to take a bit of time for the hummingbirds to find our feeder, but when they do, more hummers will come. Who knows? We may even need another feeder or two. Oh, and let's not forget that next Wednesday morning we'll be going over to my place to watch my neighbor put little bands on the hummingbirds." Leah looked at Elaine and Priscilla. "If you two aren't busy that day, you're welcome to come and watch, too."

"I wish I could," Elaine said, "but I have a dental appointment that day."

"I'll try to make it," Priscilla said. "I'm sure it'll be fun. Don't you think so, girls?"

Linda nodded, and Amy said nothing, but Carrie moved closer to Leah and climbed into her lap. "I'm gonna sit right here and wait for the hummers to come."

Elaine looked over at Priscilla and smiled. It was obvious that Leah had won Adam's youngest niece over. Elaine figured it wouldn't be long and her friend would have them all coming to her for the love they surely needed.

That night, Adam read Carrie and Linda a bedtime story in their room. According to Amy, it was Carrie's favorite story. Carrie had closed her eyes after he'd only read halfway through the book. Thinking she had fallen asleep so he wouldn't have to read the whole story, he'd skipped to the last page to finish it quicker. When he was about to close the book, Carrie sat up and announced that he'd skipped the most important part. Linda agreed. Sheepishly, Adam went back and finished reading the rest of the story.

He smiled as he came downstairs and headed to the kitchen to get a drink. At least he was making some progress with Carrie, although she still preferred Leah over him. As he stepped into the kitchen, he realized that the moon was very bright. He could see everything he needed by its glow shining in through the window.

"Let's see now, what do we have in here to drink?" He opened the refrigerator door. There was a carton of milk and some orange juice, but he wasn't in the mood for either. Then Adam spied another container he assumed Leah had made for the girls—probably lemonade, he decided. After pouring himself a glass, he stood by the window and took a big gulp. "Ugh! What is this sweet stuff?" Then he realized he'd forgotten all about the nectar the girls had helped Leah mix for the hummingbirds that day. During supper, Linda hadn't been able to stop talking about the feeder Leah had brought them and how they'd waited patiently for the first hummer to arrive.

Adam had to admit he was happy to see Linda's enthusiasm. If only Amy would come out of her shell and try to find some interests. He was glad that Leah was so good with his nieces. Carrie had especially warmed up to her. This evening, she'd started crying when Leah was getting ready to go home. It was hard watching Carrie cling to Leah's dress, pleading with her not to go. Leah had even teared up, assuring the child that she'd be back bright and early the next day. It seemed to satisfy Carrie when Leah said they would have lunch out on the porch tomorrow so they could watch for any hummingbirds that might come to the new feeder.

Adam missed his sister but hadn't had time to mourn her death since his nieces had come to live with him. Although it hadn't been easy at first, he'd begun to think that the girls were there for a reason, and he couldn't help but wonder if Leah might be, too.

CHAPTER 20

The next Wednesday found Leah scurrying about the kitchen, getting the breakfast dishes washed, dried, and put away. Normally, she would have been over at Adam's by now, but since he'd be bringing the girls over to see the hummingbirds get banded, she wouldn't go there until the banding was done. Last evening, Leah had prepared a few snacks to share with everyone after the process was finished. She'd cleaned and cut fresh vegetables, made some creamy ranch dip, and fixed her favorite chocolate-chip cheeseball. She had also found a cake recipe named, of all things, Hummingbird Ring. It was easy to make and the perfect dessert to serve for this occasion.

Leah looked forward to watching this exciting event and was sure the girls, and maybe even Adam, would enjoy it, too. She hoped Sara and Mark would be able to join them, as well as Priscilla.

It's too bad Elaine can't make it, Leah thought as she put the silverware away. *I'm sure she would find it interesting.*

Leah glanced out the window, and when she saw Adam's horse and buggy coming up the driveway, she hurried to the door. When Leah had first started watching the girls, she'd hoped Adam would find someone else, but now she couldn't think of anything she'd rather do than be with Adam's nieces. She didn't even mind having to schedule her reflexology appointments during the evening. In some ways, it was more convenient for those who came to her, since many of them had day jobs and couldn't take time off from work to get a treatment. So it had worked out best for all.

"Look at all the hummers!" Linda exclaimed when she and her sisters looked around the backyard, where Leah's feeders hung, before stepping onto the porch. "Wish we had that many at Uncle Adam's place instead of just a few."

"It took awhile before so many hummingbirds showed up here," Leah explained, patting the top of the little girl's head. "But since I started feeding them, they've become quite active. In fact, I mark the calendar every year on the day that I first see them, and it's pretty much around the same time when they start arriving each April."

"Maybe that's something we can start doing." Linda's eyes sparkled with enthusiasm.

"That's a good idea." Leah leaned down to give Carrie a hug while Amy's gaze remained fixed on the hummingbirds.

"Are we here too early?" Adam asked when he joined Leah and the girls after taking care of his horse.

"No, it's fine," Leah replied. "My neighbor Alissa, who does the banding, should be here soon, along with the others I invited to watch." She gestured to the chairs on the porch. "Why don't we all take a seat, and we can watch the hummers eat at the feeders until Alissa shows up."

The girls scampered over to the porch swing and sat together while Adam took a seat in the chair beside Leah's.

"Sure is a nice day," Adam commented. "There's not a cloud in sight."

Leah nodded. "I was hoping it wouldn't rain today. That would have put a damper on things."

Adam removed his straw hat, placing it on his knee. "I think getting the girls a hummingbird feeder was a good idea, Leah. Even Amy showed some interest in it this morning. She seemed eager to come over here as well." He paused and grinned at Leah. "Course, it may be less about the hummers and more about spending time with you."

Leah smiled in return. "I enjoy being with all three of the girls. They've become very special to me."

They visited a few more minutes, and then Sara and little Mark showed up. They'd just gotten seated on the porch when Priscilla arrived.

"Where's the woman who'll be doing the banding?" Priscilla asked. "She didn't come and go already, I hope."

Leah shook her head. "Alissa must be running late, but hopefully she'll be here soon." She gestured to the one empty chair. "Why don't you take a seat? We can all visit while we wait for Alissa to get here."

Fifteen minutes later, Leah decided to walk out to the phone shack to see if Alissa may have called and left a message. She'd just opened the door to the small wooden building, when Alissa's car pulled in. Leah waved and followed the vehicle up the driveway.

"Sorry I'm late," Alissa said, her auburn-colored ponytail bouncing as she stepped out of her car and joined Leah on the lawn. "I had a few interruptions this morning and it put me a little behind."

"That's okay. Everyone I invited is here, so we're ready and eager for you to get started."

"Perhaps one of the girls can help me bring some of my things to the banding area," Alissa suggested.

"I'll help," Amy volunteered.

"Alissa, this is Amy. She's the oldest of Adam's nieces." Leah then introduced the other two girls, as well as Adam and her other guests.

"It's nice to meet all of you. Amy, would you mind getting my canvas bag? That has all my instruments in it. Leah, if you'll carry the birdcage, I'll get the tables." Alissa reached into the trunk of her car to get the rest of her things. "I think that's everything I'll need." She put the birdcage on a small table near the hummingbird feeders. That way, while everything else was being set up, the hummers would have some time to get used to the cage and fly in and out of it to get to the feeder she'd hung inside.

Alissa laid out all her instruments and rechecked the bands she'd brought, saying she needed to make sure they were in consecutive order. "Amy, how would you like to be my helper today?" Alissa asked. "That is, if it's okay with your uncle and Leah."

Instantly, Leah nodded her approval. Glancing over at Adam for his reaction, she was glad when he also nodded.

"I'd like to help, but I'm not sure what to do," Amy said hesitantly.

"I'll explain everything as we go along." Alissa smiled as she explained how the hummingbirds would be caught. "The door to the birdcage will be left open, but it's operated by a remote control, which Amy will be using. Once a hummingbird flies into the cage to the feeder, Amy will hit the button on the remote to quickly close the door."

Alissa went on to explain how the doorway was lined with soft material, in case a hummer tried to fly out while the door was going down. "In all the years I've been banding hummingbirds, that's never happened," she added. "But we want to do everything possible to ensure the safety of the birds. My husband usually accompanies me when I do bird banding, but he isn't feeling well this morning. He's the one who actually set up this remote to close the door."

Alissa looked at Amy. "Now, once a hummingbird is caught, you will need to carefully take it out of the cage and put it in one of the soft cloth bags I brought, and then bring it up to me."

Amy's eyes widened. "You. . .you mean I get to hold the little birds?"

"That's right, but your hands are small, and I'm sure you'll be very gentle."

Eyes now bright with anticipation, Amy nodded. "I'll do my best not to hurt any of 'em."

Leah was pleased that Alissa had asked for Amy's help rather than one of the adults. The child seemed eager, and Leah hoped everything would go as it should. If Amy were to injure one of the delicate birds, she would no doubt be extremely upset.

"Try not to worry," Adam whispered, leaning close to Leah, as though he could read her thoughts. "I think this is good for Amy."

Leah, feeling almost breathless from the nearness of him, nodded. "Jah, so do I."

Pulling her gaze from Adam, Leah focused on the little white bag that resembled an onion sack, with tiny holes through it. This was the bag that safely held the hummingbird until Alissa was ready to band it.

"The first thing I will do is band the hummingbird," Alissa told them. "After that, I'll determine if it is a hatch-year or after-hatch-year hummer."

"What does that mean?" Adam asked, looking at Leah's neighbor curiously.

"After-hatch-year means the hummingbird is an adult, and hatch-year means it was hatched out that year, so it's an immature hummingbird," Alissa replied.

"That certainly makes sense." Adam's ears turned pink. "Guess it was a silly question."

Alissa shook her head. "Hey, no question is silly. That's how we learn."

"How do you determine if it's an adult hummingbird?" Sara asked, bouncing Mark on her lap.

"I actually use a jeweler's loupe, which is a small round magnifying glass that I hook onto my glasses. It gives me a close-up look at the hummingbird's beak. The beak is also referred to as the *culmen*." Alissa picked up the eyepiece and showed it to everyone. "Grooving on the culmen tells me it is an immature bird. No grooving and a smooth beak indicate it's an adult."

Leah looked around, noticing how interested everyone seemed to be. The girls, especially, were intently watching and listening to every word Alissa said, leaning forward as though anxious to learn more. Leah was pleased that this day was working out so well. Hopefully all the little hummingbirds would cooperate, too.

Alissa then showed them the other instruments she would be using to gather information on each hummingbird. One was the small tool especially made to put the band on the hummingbird's leg. Each band had a number engraved on it, all in sequence.

"Each band gets put on the bird's right leg," Alissa explained. "All bird banders follow that rule."

"Does it hurt the bird?" Linda questioned.

"I was going to ask that, too," Priscilla put in.

"There is no harm to the bird. These bands are especially made for the hummingbird species, and they won't even know it's on them," Alissa assured everyone.

"I've been watching, and several hummingbirds have flown into the cage to get a drink. Then they flew right back out again," Amy stated.

"That's good." Alissa smiled. "It means they're getting used to the cage. We shouldn't have any trouble at all banding a good number of them this morning."

Alissa explained about the rest of the instruments. The small scales were to weigh the bird, and she also described the instrument that measured its culmen, wings, and tail. She told them that the ruby-throated was the most common species of hummingbirds in the state of Illinois. "But it's not unusual for another type of hummingbird to venture into our state," she added. "When that happens, it causes a bit of excitement among the licensed banders and the bird-watching community, especially if it's a rare hummingbird not common to our area."

Leah was amazed at all the things Alissa told them. She had no idea so much was involved with banding a hummingbird. Amy sat forward, as if grasping every word her neighbor said. It was a far cry from the disinterest she had shown about other things since she and her sisters had come to live with Adam.

"I will also check for the gorget feathers, which are the bright red feathers on the hummingbird's throat. Only the male hummingbirds have those types of feathers, and this is why they are called ruby-throated," Alissa said.

"I see another hummingbird just flew out of the cage." Priscilla pointed in that direction.

"Leah, you certainly weren't kidding when you said you had a lot of hummingbirds at your feeders," Sara commented. "They're like a swarm of bees buzzing around."

"How much sugar do you go through each summer?" Adam asked.

"Believe it or not, last year at this time during migration, I almost went through ten pounds of sugar each week. This extreme activity goes on for about three weeks. Then as more hummers head south of here, it slows up a bit." Leah gestured to her feeders. "As you can see, I have six feeders hanging out to accommodate all the hummingbirds I get. By the end of the day, those feeders will be empty."

Adam's eyebrows lifted. "That must really keep you busy."

"It does, but it's a nice kind of busy. I always refill the feeders in the evening so that in the morning when the hummers really need to juice up, the feeders will be full for them."

"I can see this is a good place to band hummingbirds," Alissa said to Leah. "I only have one other place in this area that I go to each year for banding. Maybe I can talk to you later about having a session here next year as well." She looked at Linda. "How would you like to write the information down on the chart as I do each hummingbird? And Leah, maybe you can help her with that."

Linda nodded enthusiastically.

Both Leah and Linda listened as Alissa explained the chart and where all the information should go. After that, everyone watched and waited for the next hummingbird to enter the cage. They didn't have to wait long before one zipped in and landed on the feeder for a drink. This would be their first one to band.

"Okay, Amy, hit the remote button," Alissa advised.

Amy did as she was told, and the door to the cage quickly closed.

Leah couldn't help smiling as she watched Amy follow Alissa to the cage. She could see that Alissa was explaining to her how to gently take the bird and put it in the small sack.

"We caught our first hummingbird." With a look of sheer joy, Amy held up the bag as they returned to the porch.

The first thing Alissa did was call out the number on the band so Linda could write it on the chart. Then all eyes were on the hummingbird as Alissa gently removed it from the cloth bag and put the bird into the small cut-out end of a nylon sock. "This," she explained, "makes it easier to handle the hummer and also helps keep the bird calm."

Everyone watched closely as she carefully crimped the band around the hummer's right leg and then took the rest of the measurements. This hummingbird was an immature male with only two little gorget feathers on its throat. The feathers resembled two red dots. After that, Alissa called each measurement out so that Linda, with Leah's help, could document the information.

"Carrie, now that I'm all done, how would you like to hold a hummingbird?" Alissa smiled as Carrie grinned shyly and nodded her head. "Just hold out your hand and be very still."

Leah had tears in her eyes when she saw the look of joy on Carrie's face as Alissa put the little bird into the palm of her hand. It seemed as if everyone held their breath, watching to see what the hummingbird would do. It sat there quietly for a bit, looking around; then all of a sudden, it flew into the trees where the little birds liked to perch.

Sara clapped her hands, and little Mark did, too, prompting the rest of them to do the same.

"And that, my friends, is how the process is done," Alissa announced. "I think it went very well. Sometimes," she added, "a hummingbird will get away from me before I can get all the information about it. So that's why I band the hummer first. That way, if it gets away, at least we have it banded and can log the number into our data center."

"Data center?" Amy asked. "What's that?"

Alissa told them that all the information they compiled on the chart would be put into a large data system through an Internet site. "This system is assessable to all licensed bird banders, so if a bird is captured that has already been banded, they can check the computer for its information," she explained. "They can find out where that bird was originally banded and compare all the other information. It's exciting to capture a hummingbird and find out that it had been banded in another state."

Little Mark eventually fell asleep on Sara's lap, but everyone else watched the entire procedure; especially the girls.

After about two hours, more hummingbirds had been caught and banded—thirty-seven of them to be exact. Everyone got the chance to hold a hummingbird before it was released. Alissa further explained that she always tried not to have the hummingbirds in her possession for longer than three minutes, in order not to stress the birds.

Leah couldn't believe how fast the morning had gone. It was good to see Amy smiling as she helped Alissa pack up everything and take it to her car.

"Thank you so much for inviting me." Priscilla gave Leah a hug. "It was amazing. I'll never forget this exciting event."

"You're welcome, but aren't you going to stay long enough to have some refreshments?"

"I'd love to, but I need to run to the grocery store for a few things." Priscilla thanked Alissa for a great experience and headed down the driveway on her bike.

"Unfortunately, I need to leave, too, and get this little guy home," Sara added. "Thank you so much for inviting me and Mark. Like

Priscilla said, it was a great experience."

After that, Leah, the girls, Alissa, and Adam enjoyed talking and discussing the hummingbirds as they ate fresh vegetables with dip, crackers, and the homemade cheeseball Leah had made. They also enjoyed the Hummingbird Ring cake.

"Did you put hummingbirds in this cake?" Carrie asked, pointing to a maraschino cherry.

Leah smiled. "No, dear one. Those are cherries. The cake is just called a hummingbird ring."

"Oh, that's good." Carrie giggled, and so did everyone else. But all too soon, the morning ended.

Leah glanced back at Adam, who was waiting on the porch with his nieces as she walked with Alissa to her car. It had been nice to see him relax and enjoy something so much. He actually seemed like a different person today. "I don't know how I will ever thank you for giving us all such a wonderful experience," Leah told Alissa. "The knowledge you have is incredible, and it was so interesting to learn the banding process. Next year if you'd like to come again, you'd be more than welcome." After giving her neighbor a hug, Leah joined Adam and the girls on the porch, and they all waved until Alissa's car was out of sight.

"I also have to get going, but I thank you for including us today." Adam smiled—a genuine smile that showed in his eyes. "I sure enjoyed it. I know the girls did, too."

"You're welcome. It certainly was a wonderful learning experience, and I had fun, as well."

"You girls help Leah clean up after I go," Adam said before he walked to his buggy then turned to wave. "I'll see you all this evening."

"Wait, Uncle Adam. Wait!" Linda yelled, running to his buggy.

Leah watched as Adam jumped out to see what was wrong. Her heart swelled as Linda hugged her uncle and Adam squeezed her right back.

"Danki, Uncle Adam, for bringing us today. It was fun."

Leah thought she saw Adam wiping his eyes before climbing back into the buggy. That one small gesture from his niece had touched him deeply. Leah couldn't have been happier when all three girls gave her a hug once their uncle had gone. A lump formed in her throat when Amy said how much she appreciated Leah inviting them. Leah's only regret was that her mother couldn't have been here to watch the banding, for she was certain that she would have enjoyed it, too. But Mom was still helping out at her sister's and would remain there a few weeks after the baby came, so Leah didn't expect to see her anytime soon.

Chicago

Cora's skirt swished as she hurried down the hospital corridor. She'd just had an encounter in the elevator with Evan, who'd said he was on his way to see a patient. Cora had made the mistake of telling him that she'd put the house on the market, and it hadn't gone over well. Fortunately, no one else had been in the elevator when Evan glared at her and said, "If you didn't want the house, then you shouldn't have fought so hard to get it, Cora. I would have been happy to keep it and give you the money for a smaller place where you and Jared could be comfortable."

"I fought to get it so you couldn't bring your pretty little wife into what used to be our home," Cora shot back. "You knew I wanted to move and planned to sell the house. If you wanted it so badly, then you should have been satisfied with me and not gone looking for someone you thought was better." It angered her that she let Evan get to her like that, and she'd begun to wonder lately if she'd done something to deserve his unfaithfulness.

Maybe I'm being punished for something I did in the past, Cora fumed. *Or maybe Evan never really loved me at all.*

Continuing down the hall, Cora halted when she nearly bumped into Dr. Rogers going in the opposite direction.

"Oops. Sorry about that," she mumbled. "Guess I wasn't watching where I was going."

He paused and touched her arm. "You look upset. Is something wrong?"

Of course there's something wrong. My husband left me for another woman, and now I feel forced to move. Cora swallowed against the lump in her throat. "I–I'm just in a hurry, that's all," she mumbled.

"Okay. Well, no harm was done." Dr. Rogers started to walk away but turned back around. "I heard from one of the other nurses that you're planning to move."

She nodded. "I haven't found another job yet, though, so I'll continue on here until I do."

"You're well liked here, by the staff and also the patients, so you'll surely be missed." The sincerity in the middle-aged doctor's brown eyes was nearly Cora's undoing. Until this mess with Evan had erupted, she'd always enjoyed her job at this hospital. It wouldn't be easy to leave and start over again, but for her sake, as well as Jared's, that's what she needed to do. From the time Cora was a little girl, her life had been full of changes and complications. Leaving Chicago and the painful memories behind would be just one more hurdle to jump.

CHAPTER 21

We'll be moving in two weeks, so you'd better start packing," Cora told her son the next Monday.

Jared's eyebrows shot up. "Moving? To where, Mom?"

"The town of Arthur." She dished some scrambled eggs onto a plate and handed it to him. "I poured you a glass of orange juice, and there's some toast on the table."

"But we can't move. School starts two weeks from Monday, and. . ." He grabbed his chair with force and sat down abruptly.

"And we'll be moved by then, so you'll be going to a new school," Cora said in a smooth, calm tone. "Also Jared, I'd really like it if you'd go to the barber and get your hair cut. It's getting a bit unruly, and as you start a new school, it'll be nice for you to make a good impression. Your appearance is what people see first."

Jared grunted and slunk down in his seat, pushing back his uncombed hair. "I don't wanna move. I told you that before. And I'm not getting my hair cut. I like it this way, and I don't really care what people think of me. If they don't like what they see, that's their problem."

"I know what you said, and I also know how you feel about your hair, Jared. I was young once, too. If you had it styled a little better, or washed it every day, that would make a difference."

"Yeah. Yeah. Whatever." Jared rolled his shoulders, while tilting his head.

"I also know that this move will be the best thing for both of us." Cora placed her plate on the table and took a seat next to him. "Meeting new people and living in different surroundings could be a good thing for both of us."

"What's in Arthur, anyways? I've never even heard of the place."

"If you want to know more about Arthur, check it out on the

Internet. There's an interesting website all about the town. There's also a nursing position at the clinic there, and I applied for the job yesterday afternoon."

Jared's mouth formed an O. "You went to Arthur?"

"No. I applied online and they interviewed me over the phone."

"You're kidding, right?"

Cora shook her head. "I offered to drive down, but the woman conducting the interview said my résumé and work experience spoke for itself, and so did the information they received from the hospital about me."

Jared folded his arms and frowned. "So you found a job, even though our house hasn't sold?"

"That's right, but I'm confident that it will sell in good time." Cora paused and drank some coffee. "Arthur's only a few hours from here, so it won't be hard for your dad to come visit, or for me to take you there."

"Humph! Dad doesn't see me that much anyway, and I doubt he'd go there. I can't believe you waited till now to let me know about this."

"Jared, it just happened," Cora explained. "Don't worry; it won't be a problem when you want to see your dad."

"Yeah, right. Bet I'll never get to see Dad at all." His voice faltered. "What have I done wrong, Mom, that Dad would just leave me out of his new life since he got remarried?"

"You haven't done anything wrong." Cora placed her hands on his shoulders.

Jared's forehead creased as he shrugged her hands away. "Don't see why you and Dad couldn't have worked things out between you, instead of getting a divorce."

"I wanted to work them out, but some things aren't meant to be."

"Well, you'll never get back with Dad if we move."

Cora blew out her breath in a puff of air that lifted her bangs. "You don't understand, Jared. Your dad has moved on with his life, and we need to do the same." She pointed to Jared's plate. "Now please eat your breakfast so you can start packing while I'm at the hospital. I'll be putting in my two weeks' notice today."

Arthur

"You look *mied* this morning," Sara said as she, Jonah, and Mark sat down to eat breakfast. "You've been working late hours again and aren't getting enough sleep."

Jonah yawned. "You're right, Sara, I am tired, and I apologize for that—especially after promising to spend more time with Mark. But as you know, Dad hasn't been able to work since he cut two fingers last week. Even with Timothy's help, I'm getting behind again, and it could be awhile before Dad's able to work with that hand."

"Have you considered hiring another man?"

Jonah shook his head. "No one else in the area is experienced at making and repairing buggies. Even if someone was, it wouldn't be fair to hire him for just a few weeks and then let him go. Timothy and I will just have to manage till Dad's on the job again."

Sara nodded. "I see what you mean." She turned to Mark and handed him a cup of milk.

Jonah reached over and took her hand. "Let's pray about this—that the Lord will get our business through this rough patch."

They bowed their heads and prayed silently. When Jonah finished, he lifted his head. Seeing that Sara had, too, he smiled and said, "As soon as Dad's able to work in the shop again, and we get caught up, things will be back to normal." He tweaked the end of Mark's nose. "We'll do something fun together soon."

Mark giggled. *"Riggel reide?"*

"Sorry, but I can't play on the see-saw with you today, little buddy." Jonah ruffled the boy's hair. "I'll read you a bedtime story tonight, though. How's that sound?"

Mark bobbed his head, grinning widely.

Sara hoped her husband would be able to keep that promise. Last night when Jonah had finally left his shop and came up to the house, Mark was already sleeping. She dreaded seeing the look of disappointment on her son's face if he had to go to sleep without that bedtime story tonight.

Jonah reached for the bottle of syrup and poured some on his pancakes. "Since I've been so busy these past few days, I forgot to ask how things went at Leah's when you and Mark went to watch the hummingbirds get banded."

"Everything went well. It was fascinating to watch the whole procedure." Without going into too much detail, Sara described the process.

"Sounds like it must have been something special to see," Jonah said. "Wish I could have joined you and Mark that day."

"I think Mark is a little too young to understand what was actually going on, but he got very excited when Alissa placed a hummingbird in his hand for a few seconds. Later, though, he got tired and fell asleep."

"Wish you'd had a camera and had taken a picture of those hummers. That would have been a great memory to capture."

"The memory is up here." Sara touched her forehead. "I even got to hold a few hummingbirds after Alissa had them banded. She explained the proper way to hold them. You can't imagine how fragile those little birds feel, yet they didn't seem alarmed that we were holding them. It was so cute."

"That's incredible, when you think about it." Jonah grinned. "I remember one time when I was a boy. I was carrying a box of ripe tomatoes from Mom's garden, and a hummingbird hovered over the box a few seconds before it flew off. It seemed like it thought I had something there for it to eat."

Sara laughed. "From what Alissa explained, the hummingbirds are attracted to red. She said when her husband wears his red ball cap every year at least one hummingbird flies up and hovers in front of his hat."

"When I first saw a hummer, back when I was a kid, I thought it was a big bumble bee." Jonah chuckled. "Their wings go so fast, they make a buzzing sound."

"I'm hoping that maybe next year we can all go there and watch the banding," Sara said. "I believe that Leah's neighbor will be doing it again."

"That would be fun. When the time comes, I'll try to take that morning off."

"Speaking of hummingbirds, I think maybe next spring I'll get a few feeders to hang up in our yard. It'll be fun for us, as well as Mark, to watch the hummers zip back and forth as they drink the sweet nectar." Sara placed her hands against her growing stomach. "It'll be awhile before our boppli's old enough to enjoy watching the little birds, but by the time he or she is ready, I'm sure those tiny hummers will get lots of attention."

"Who let the mutt in?" Adam grumbled, when he discovered Coal sleeping under the kitchen table.

Carrie, Amy, and Linda looked up at him with guilty expressions, but no one said a word.

Adam frowned. "You know the rules about bringing the dog inside. He's to stay out at all times."

"But Uncle Adam, Coal gets lonely out there by himself," Linda spoke up. "Besides, we like him."

Carrie and Amy nodded in agreement.

"I like the mutt, too, but he's a dog, and he belongs outside." Adam opened the back door, clapped his hands and hollered, "Come on, Coal! Outside you go!"

The dog crawled out from under the table, but instead of heading out the door, he ran past Adam and darted up the stairs.

"Come back here right now, you stubborn animal!" Adam's face heated as he tromped up the steps after the dog. At this rate, he'd never get the girls' breakfast served, and he might be late for work.

All the bedroom doors were open, so Adam figured Coal could have gone into any one of them. Choosing the first room, he stepped inside. "Coal, are you in here, boy?"

No response.

Adam squatted down and peered under the bed. No sign of the dog. The closet door was open, so he looked in there as well, but Coal wasn't inside.

Moving on to the second bedroom, Adam checked all the obvious places, but there was no dog. That meant he either had to be in the third bedroom or the bathroom.

Exasperated with all the time this was taking, Adam entered the last bedroom and spotted a long black tail sticking out from under Amy's bed.

"I know you're under there," Adam muttered. "So you may as well come out."

Coal whined pathetically and moved farther under the bed, turning in the opposite direction so that Adam could only see the dog's head.

Adam groaned. This was not a good way to start the day.

Dropping to his knees, he reached under the bed, hoping he could grab hold of the dog's collar, but the mutt was just out of his reach. "Oh, great."

Adam figured he had two choices: he could either crawl under the bed and try to grab Coal, or go back downstairs and let the dog stay where he was. The second idea really wasn't an option.

Crawling on his belly, Adam inched along until he was nose-to-nose with Coal. The next thing Adam knew, the dog's tongue shot out and slurped Adam's mouth.

"Yuck!" Adam jerked his head, bumping it on the slats holding the box spring. "Ouch!"

Arf! Arf! Coal backed out quickly, and by the time Adam crawled out from under the bed, the dog was gone.

Disgusted, Adam tromped down the stairs. "Where is that mutt?" he bellowed, storming into the kitchen. "Did he come back in here?"

Carrie started to howl, Linda whimpered, and Amy's eyes widened. "You don't have to holler like that, Uncle Adam," Amy said. "You oughtta be nicer to Coal. And you're scaring my sisters, too."

Sweating profusely, Adam drew in a deep breath. "I wouldn't have had to holler or run around upstairs if one of you hadn't let the dog in. We'd have all had our breakfast by now." He looked back at the girls, his frustration mounting. "Have you seen Coal or not?"

Amy pointed to the utility room. "He went in there."

As Adam started in that direction, he heard Amy mutter that their dad never yelled at them like that. Pretending he didn't hear, Adam was almost to the utility room, when a knock sounded on the back door. When he opened it, he discovered Leah on the porch. He was about to invite her in, when Coal darted between his legs and zipped out the door, nearly knocking Leah over.

Instinctively, Adam reached out to grab her, and she fell into his arms.

"Ach, my!" she exclaimed, her face turning red as she pulled slowly away and stepped into the house. "What's going on with your hund?"

"It's a long story, but the shortened version is this: Coal was where he doesn't belong, and I would appreciate it if you'd have a talk with the girls about making sure that he stays outside from now on."

Leah looked at him strangely but then gave a quick nod. "Where are the girls?" she asked.

"They're in the kitchen, waiting for their breakfast, which I was going to make till I ended up chasing after the hund." Adam pulled out his pocket watch and grimaced when he saw the time. "At this rate, I'll never make it to work on time."

"Don't worry about breakfast," Leah said sweetly. "I'll fix the girls whatever they want. If you have time to eat, you're welcome to join us at the breakfast table."

He shook his head. "If I don't leave now, I'll be late, so maybe I'll stop by the bakery on my way to the store and grab a doughnut."

"That's not the healthiest breakfast, Adam. Wouldn't you rather take some fruit or a piece of toast along?"

At first, Adam's defenses rose. Who did Leah think she was, telling him what to do? But after he thought it through, he realized she was concerned for his welfare.

"Maybe I will grab an apple," he mumbled, moving into the kitchen and reaching into the bowl of fruit on the counter. With a quick good-bye to everyone, he picked up his Thermos full of coffee and headed out the door. He shouldn't have lost his temper or made such a big deal about the dog. From the way Coal had responded to Leah in the past, she'd probably have better luck taking control over the mutt than Adam did. It was too bad Leah couldn't be here all the time. But in order for that to happen, he and Leah would have to get married.

Adam thumped the side of his head. *I'd better get that idea out of my head. Even if I did propose to Leah, I'm sure she'd say no.*

CHAPTER 22

"Amy and Linda, are you two ready to go to school today?" Adam asked. Though this was the first day of school for Amish children in the area, most English kids wouldn't start back to their schools until next week.

The girls, who had just entered the kitchen, both shook their heads. "I don't wanna go to *schul*," Linda said in a whiny voice.

"Why not?" Adam asked. "It shouldn't be much different than the school you used to go to." As soon as Adam mentioned their other school, he immediately regretted it. *What was I thinking, bringing that up?*

"I'll miss Leah."

"Me, too," Amy put in. "And we hardly know anybody who'll be going to this school. Carrie's lucky 'cause she gets to stay here all day with Leah. She's our only friend right now."

Adam flinched. They obviously didn't think of him as their friend, but then did he really want them to? He was their guardian—a father figure of sorts—so it probably wouldn't be good if they saw him as a friend. The only time any of the girls had shown him affection was after the hummingbird banding, when Linda rushed up to give him a hug. That simple act had kept him whistling all afternoon. He wasn't quite sure how to respond to Amy's statement just now but was glad the girls hadn't gotten upset at the mention of their other school. He was also pleased that his nieces liked Leah.

Even so, they had to go to school, and he wanted them to enjoy it. Leah had said she would take Linda and Amy to school today, which meant Adam could leave for the store on time. He was having second thoughts about that now, knowing that if he took them it would give him a chance to speak with their teacher, Barbara Yoder. But maybe that wasn't necessary, since he had introduced the girls to her at church a few weeks ago.

Adam moved over to the refrigerator and took out a carton of eggs. *Maybe I shouldn't expect Leah to take Linda and Amy to school. I'm their uncle, and it's really my job, after all.*

Adam didn't know why he was going back and forth like this, but as he cracked open several eggs into a bowl, he made his decision. It would be him taking the girls to school this morning, not Leah.

"I hope I'm not late," Leah said breathlessly when she entered Adam's house. "For some reason, Sugar didn't want to do anything but plod along on the trip over here this morning."

Adam glanced at the clock on the kitchen wall. "You're not late, but I do need to head out pretty soon. I'll be taking Amy and Linda to school on my way to work."

Leah smiled at the girls, who sat beside each other at the table. "I'll come pick you up after school, so you won't have to walk." Truthfully, Leah felt that Linda and Amy were both too young to walk home alone. She felt protective of them—almost as if they were her own daughters.

"That's nice of you," Adam spoke up. "Maybe after the girls make some friends who walk this way, you won't have to pick them up anymore."

She smiled. "I don't mind, really, but if the time comes that they want to walk home, I'll be fine with that, too."

Linda's chin trembled as she looked up at Leah. "I don't wanna go to school; I'd rather stay here with you."

Amy nodded in agreement. "It's not fair that Carrie gets to be with you all day. Me and Linda are gonna miss out on all the fun."

"You'll have fun at school," Adam interjected.

Linda shook her head vigorously. "Uh-uh, we'll have to work."

"It won't all be work," Leah corrected. "Barbara Yoder is a wonderful teacher. You'll get to play games and have fun during recess, and learning about new things can be fun, too."

"Leah is right," Adam agreed. "And I'm sure you'll make some new friends quickly. I can almost guarantee that you will like your teacher, too." Picking up his lunch pail and Thermos, he added, "Now get the lunches I fixed for you, and let's be on our way."

Linda jumped up from the table and gave Leah a hug. Amy did the same. Leah felt sorry for the girls, and she would miss them. She was glad she would have Carrie to watch during the day and looked forward to when Linda and Amy came home after school.

"Remember now," she told the girls, "I'll be there to pick you up when school lets out this afternoon, and then you can tell me all about your first day."

That seemed to satisfy the girls, and with a wave, they followed their uncle out the door. Holding Carrie's hand, Leah stood watching as Adam helped the children into the buggy and backed his horse away from the hitching rack. At that moment, she knew exactly how her mother must have felt when she'd sent Leah and her brother, Nathan, off at the beginning of each new school year.

"Well, little one," she said, smiling at Carrie, "it's just you and me now. Should we find something fun to do?"

Carrie's eyes shone as she nodded. "Let's look for Chippy!"

It had been awhile since they'd seen the chipmunk, but maybe it was because all their attention had been on the hummingbird feeder. Once the hummingbirds had found the feeder, poor Chippy had soon been forgotten.

Leah patted the child's head then glanced at the kitchen sink, full of dirty dishes. Apparently Adam hadn't had time to do them before she'd arrived. "Maybe after a while we can go outside. Right now, though, you can color a picture while I wash and dry the dishes."

Cora looked around the small house she had rented just a mile outside of Arthur. Since it was fully furnished, she'd only brought the basic things they would need, plus their clothes and personal items. Once the house in Chicago sold, she would see about purchasing a home here, and then all of their furniture could be moved.

"I'll be heading to the clinic soon," Cora told Jared, taking a seat across from him at the breakfast table. She didn't realize that moving could be so tiresome, but then when she and Evan had moved into their house they'd hired movers, so everything had been done for them.

Pushing a piece of hair behind her ears, Cora closed her eyes for a minute. She was exhausted, not just from the move but from worrying about Jared.

"You're starting work already?" Jared asked.

She opened her eyes and nodded, noticing how much her son had changed since the divorce. His droopy jeans somehow stayed up without a belt. He wore them for days on end, until Cora insisted that he wear something else so she could launder his clothes. Then there was his hair. Jared was lucky to have a thick head of jet-black hair like his father's. When his hair was cut and styled, he was a handsome young man. But now he didn't seem to care how it looked, and it had become a shaggy mess. Jared's eyes were a vivid deep blue, like Cora's. These days though, Cora hardly recognized her son. Hopefully, once he got used to his new surroundings and made a few friends, that would change and he'd pay attention to his appearance.

"What am I supposed to do all day?" Jared mumbled around his piece of toast.

"For one thing, you can get your things unpacked." Cora reached for her cup of coffee and took a drink. "Since you'll be starting school next week, now's a good chance to get your room organized."

Jared wrinkled his nose, as though some putrid odor had made its way into the kitchen. "We've only been here a couple days, and I hate it already, Mom."

"A few days isn't long enough to judge whether you like it or not. I'm sure that once you start school, you'll make some friends and things will seem better."

"I ain't interested in making any friends—not in this backwater town where there's nothing to do."

"The correct word is *isn't*, and I'm quite sure there are fun things in the area for a boy your age to do. I saw a pizza place when we drove into town the other day, and your school will no doubt have activities after classes and in the evenings. Oh, and I saw a barber shop, too." She tapped his shoulder. "Hint, hint."

Jared grunted. "Whatever they have in this dinky town, I'm sure it's boring."

The *clip-clop* of horse's hooves could be heard on the road out front, and Jared glanced out the window. "Oh, I know, Mom. Maybe I could befriend some Amish kid, and we could ride around in a horse-drawn buggy. Now that would be a lot of fun, wouldn't it?"

Cora's jaw clenched. "You're being sarcastic."

"You never told me we'd be moving to Amish country," he said, ignoring her comment.

Living among the Amish wasn't what Cora had planned, either, but the pace would be much slower than it was back home, and she figured there'd be less chance of Jared getting into trouble out here in the country. And though they didn't know anyone here yet, Cora thought it wouldn't take long for both her and Jared to make new friends.

Leah hummed as she clipped one of Amy's dresses to the clothesline. Today had turned out to be quite nice—a good time to be outside in the fresh air. As part of her duties at Adam's house, she'd agreed to do the laundry for the girls. When she'd asked if he wanted her to wash his clothes, too, Adam's face had colored. "Don't worry about that," he'd said. "I've been washing my clothes for a good many years. Of course, if you'd like to wash the sheets and towels, I'd be okay with that."

Leah smiled, thinking how easily Adam blushed. Just the slightest word or look from her, and his face, and sometimes ears, would turn crimson. She wondered if he reacted like that to things other people said. But then, she was one to talk about blushing. Her face heated quite often these days, especially when she was around Adam.

Hearing Carrie calling for Chippy, Leah turned her head. She figured he was probably hiding under the woodpile or had left the yard and found a new home someplace else.

Woof! Woof! Leah smiled, seeing Coal run out to join Carrie on the lawn. But the child didn't seem interested in playing with the dog right now. She gave Coal a pat on the head then continued to call for Chippy, while poking around in the pile of wood.

Turning back to her job at hand, Leah concentrated on getting the rest of the clothes hung on the line. She was getting ready to clip the last towel in place when Coal started barking frantically. A few seconds later, Leah heard a blood-curdling scream.

Whirling around, she saw Carrie running across the lawn, waving her arms while she hollered, "*Ieme!* Ieme! They stung me bad!"

Instinctively, Leah dropped the towel and raced toward Carrie, knowing that if a person was allergic, even one bee sting could have serious consequences.

CHAPTER 23

As Cora headed for work that morning, she realized the drive would take longer than she'd anticipated. In addition to other cars on the road, there were several horses and buggies. She would have to pass them at the first opportunity, or she'd be late for work. Cora had never understood why anyone would be content with such a slow mode of transportation.

Well, it doesn't concern me, and I can't think about that, she told herself. *I just need to make sure I'm not late for work.*

Moving her minivan toward the center lane and seeing that it was clear, Cora pulled out and passed two Amish buggies. Pulling back into the right lane, she sped up a little and was relieved when the clinic came into view. She'd actually made it with a few moments to spare.

Turning into the parking lot, she couldn't help but compare the small size of the building to the enormous hospital she'd left behind in Chicago. *Of course*, she rationalized, *this is a clinic, not a hospital.* It was adequate for this rural area and serviced the needs of the people who required medical assistance but weren't in need of a hospital.

Continuing to observe the building, while applying some lip balm, Cora had a feeling she'd made the right decision. Something about this small clinic appealed to her simple side.

Outside the clinic stood a few mature trees, and a rustic-looking picnic table had been placed under one of them. It would be a peaceful place to eat lunch every day—at least before the weather turned cold. Brightly colored mums in various shades were beginning to bloom among the shrubbery near the building, and two planters were positioned on either side of the entrance door. The building seemed unusually quiet, with no hustle and bustle of nurses, doctors, and visitors coming and going. If it weren't for the four cars in the parking lot,

Cora would have thought the place was closed.

Pulling down the visor for one last look in the mirror, she tucked her short brunette hair behind her ears. *Oh my, look at those eyes. I hope no one thinks I've been crying.* Cora's eyes were a bit bloodshot from not getting enough rest, so she quickly applied some drops from the bottle she kept in her purse. Stepping out of the car and taking a deep breath, Cora headed toward the doors that would open to a new beginning for her.

Once inside, Cora introduced herself to the office manager and was taken to the back of the clinic, where she met two doctors, as well as another nurse. Everyone seemed friendly and said they looked forward to working with her. Dr. Franklin, the older of the two doctors said that if she had questions or needed anything, to let him know. Already she felt at ease with everyone's relaxed attitude. It was a far cry from the constant buzz of activity Cora had become used to at the hospital in Chicago.

A short time later, a young Amish woman with a small child entered the clinic. Cora knew her day was about to begin.

Leah was relieved when she and Carrie were taken to an examining room right away. Even though Carrie hadn't exhibited any life-threatening symptoms from her bee stings, her little arms and legs were covered with raised welts, which she said itched and burned something awful. She'd also received a few stings on her neck and face.

"My name is Cora." The middle-aged nurse with short brown hair who had brought them into the room looked at Leah and said, "Do you know what kind of bees stung your daughter?"

Leah decided now wasn't the time to explain she wasn't Carrie's mother. All that mattered was getting Carrie the treatment she needed.

"They were yellow jackets," Leah replied. "Apparently they had built a nest under a woodpile, and when Carrie was poking around in there, she must have disturbed them."

"Has she been short of breath or had trouble swallowing?" Nurse Cora questioned as she took Carrie's vitals.

Leah shook her head. "Just itching and burning where she was stung. I gave her half a dose of an antihistamine while we were waiting for our driver to pick us up. I also applied ice packs that I'd wrapped in a towel to help with the swelling. If she'd had any trouble breathing or swallowing, I would have called 911 instead of bringing her here in a neighbor's car."

"Bringing her by car was better than horse and buggy," the nurse said before asking Carrie to open her mouth. "I don't see any sign of stings in there, so that's a good thing. Even a single sting in the mouth or throat could cause swelling and obstruction of the airway." She patted Carrie's shoulder. "Children are at increased risk for these types of breathing problems from a sting."

Leah nodded. "Yes, I know. That's why I brought her here to be checked out."

Leah was impressed at how well the nurse handled Carrie. The child seemed to relax because of the nurse's calming manner. Leah couldn't help but notice that Nurse Cora's complexion was flawless. But behind those blue eyes was a sadness similar to the sorrow Leah had seen in Amy all these weeks. *I wonder what might be going on in this woman's life.*

The doctor came in then, so the nurse stepped aside as he began to examine Carrie. When he told Leah that Carrie wasn't in serious danger, she felt relieved. But she was worried about what Adam would say when he came home from work and saw Carrie's arms and legs. She hoped he wouldn't think she'd been neglectful in watching the child.

Leah glanced at the clock on the far wall. Her other concern was that she might be late picking Amy and Linda up from school.

As Adam worked at the back of his store, putting new inventory on the shelves, he thought about Leah and how the girls had reacted to her this morning. They were clearly becoming attached to her, and he couldn't blame them. With no mother to nurture them and with him making a weak attempt at filling their father's role, the children were starved for attention and in need of a parent's guidance and love.

Taking the girls to school this morning had been difficult. Riding in silence, he hadn't been able to find the right words to ease their apprehension about going to a new school. Bravely, though, they had walked beside him while he took them inside to meet the teacher. Linda had even reached up to take his hand. At that moment, he'd felt more like a father than the uncle he truly was. Being a father figure was harder than Adam had ever imagined. He never quite knew if he was saying or doing the right things. *If Mary could see how things are going with me and the girls, would she regret having asked me to take care of them?*

Adam pushed a box of hammers closer to the shelf where he was working. *I wonder what Leah would say if I asked her to marry me. It would be a marriage of convenience of course, because I'm sure she doesn't love me.* Weighing the idea further, he pursed his lips. *Would she think I've lost my mind if I brought up the subject? It would be in the girls' best interest if they had a substitute mother. Having Leah there full-time to cook, clean, do laundry, and take care of the girls would take a lot of pressure off me.*

As Adam continued to stock the shelves, he let the idea of marriage roll around in his head. He'd been opposed to finding a wife all these years because of his mother's abandonment, but Leah seemed grounded in her faith. He was fairly certain that if she had any plans of leaving their Amish community, she would have done so by now.

Maybe I should talk to someone about this—see if they think Leah might be willing to marry me. But who? Adam's mind raced, searching for answers. He could speak to Ben about this, since they'd gotten to know each other fairly well, but then Ben wasn't that well acquainted with Leah. *I might talk to Ben about my mother, though. It would feel good to share the feelings I've kept bottled up all these years with someone I can trust.*

Finished with his task, Adam rose to his feet and took the empty boxes to the storage room. When he stepped out again, he nearly bumped into Elaine Schrock, one of Leah's closest friends. If he could talk to anyone about Leah, it would be Elaine.

"I'm glad you're here, Elaine," Adam said. "If you have a few minutes, could I talk to you?"

She smiled up at him. "Sure, Adam. I came in to get some birdseed, but I'm not in a hurry."

Adam gestured to his office. "Could we talk in there? I don't want anyone to hear our conversation."

"I guess that would be okay." Elaine glanced around before taking a few hesitant steps in that direction.

Adam entered his office and motioned for her to take a seat at his desk.

"Don't you want to sit there?" she asked, barely meeting his gaze.

"No, that's okay; I'll just stand." While Elaine took a seat, Adam positioned himself in front of the desk, where he could look directly at her. He wanted to see the expression on her face when he asked his question.

Moistening his lips, Adam spoke quickly, before he lost his nerve. "I need to ask you something. It's about Leah."

"If it's about Leah, then shouldn't you be talking to her?"

He shook his head. "I'd rather not talk to her until I know how she might respond."

Elaine leaned forward, resting her arms on Adam's desk. "I can't really speak for Leah, but what is it you want to know?"

"Do you think she would agree to marry me?"

Elaine touched her fingers against her parted lips. "I knew Leah had been watching your nieces, but I didn't realize you two had been courting."

A tingling sensation crept up the back of Adam's neck. How was he going to explain this to Elaine? It was so embarrassing.

"Well, uh. . .we're not exactly courting." He paused and swallowed a couple times. "Actually, we're not courting at all."

"Then why would you be thinking of marriage?"

Adam shifted nervously, giving his shirt collar a tug. "Well, umm. . .the thing is. . ."

"Oh, wait! I think I get it." Elaine pushed her chair aside and stood. "You want Leah to marry you so she can take care of the girls all the time; not just when you're here working. Am I right?"

Adam nodded. "I know it may seem selfish, but I'm really thinking of Carrie, Linda, and Amy. In the short time Leah's been caring for them, they've grown attached to her."

Elaine's eyes blinked rapidly. "So if Leah agreed to marry you, your marriage would be based on need, rather than love?"

"Jah, but I do have a high regard for Leah. She's been good with the girls, and I believe she cares for them as much as they do her."

"Do you want my opinion, Adam?"

He nodded once more.

"You ought to talk to Leah about this, because I have no idea whether she'd be willing to marry you or not. I just know that if it were me, I wouldn't marry a man I didn't love."

When Elaine left Adam's office, he sat down at his desk and wiped his forehead with a hankie. This evening, when he got home from work, he would do as Elaine suggested.

CHAPTER 24

When Cora arrived home from work that afternoon, she went straight to the kitchen to fix herself a glass of iced tea. As she'd pulled into the driveway, she'd noticed that Jared's bike wasn't on the porch, and she figured he might have gone out for a ride. Looking out the kitchen window, Cora gazed into the backyard. She was lucky to have found this house to rent, even though it was rather small. Across the road was a cornfield that belonged to the farm sitting farther back. The rental agent had told Cora that the land this house was built on was once a part of that farm, but a good many years ago the owner sold off a section of the property and kept only what was on the other side of the road. It was peaceful, and even with the road out front, the meager traffic was made up mostly of horses and buggies.

I hope Jared gets home soon, because I'm hungry and would like to start supper, Cora thought, moving to the living room and plopping down on the couch. She took a sip of iced tea then set her glass on the coffee table. Yawning, she removed her shoes and stretched out on the couch. Even though there were no long corridors to walk at the clinic, she'd been on her feet most of the day, and they'd begun to ache. With one last peek at the cozy living room, Cora closed her eyes, letting her mind wander.

Things had gone fairly well with her first day on the job. The doctors seemed nice and weren't demanding, like a few of the physicians at the hospital in Chicago had been. The other nurse, Sandy, had been helpful, too. Compared to the hospital routine, the amount of patients that came to the clinic today had been few.

She thought of the little Amish girl she'd seen first thing this morning. For some reason, Cora couldn't seem to get that child off her mind. She hoped Carrie would be able to sleep tonight. Just one bee sting could be miserable, but Carrie had so many of them. It was good that she hadn't had a severe reaction. While the child's mother had shown concern, she'd seemed quite calm about it. Cora figured that was probably why Carrie hadn't overreacted, as she'd seen some children do when they were frightened or in pain.

Several other Amish people had come to the clinic today, in addition to a few people who weren't Amish. Living and working in this rural area would take some getting used to, but Cora felt that she'd made the right decision by moving here. Evan and his pretty new wife weren't about to leave Chicago and the private practice he'd worked so hard to establish. Cora couldn't live with the painful reminder that she'd been jilted by the man she still loved.

When the front door opened and slammed shut, Cora opened her eyes. "Jared, I'm glad you're finally home. Where have you been anyway?" she asked, stretching as she sat up.

He sauntered across the room and flopped into the recliner. "I rode around on my bike for a while, checking things out in town. Then I went to the pizza place for lunch."

"Do they have good pizza there?"

"It was okay."

"I'll have to try it sometime. Did you do anything else today?"

"Met this kid named Scott Ramsey. He's my age, and guess I'll be going to the same school as him."

Cora smiled. "That's good. I'm glad you've made a friend already. I'm anxious to meet him."

Jared shrugged. "Didn't say he was my friend. Just said I met the guy."

"Do you like him?"

"He's okay, I guess." Jared rose from his chair.

"Where are you going?" she asked in irritation. "I'm going to be starting supper soon."

"I'm going outside for some fresh air." As Jared shuffled toward the door, the hem of his jeans dragged on the floor. "It's hot and stuffy in here."

"That's fine. I'll call you when supper's ready. Oh, and you need to throw those jeans you're wearing in the laundry basket tonight. After they've been washed, I can hem them up a bit."

"No way, Mom! I like these jeans just the way they are," Jared called as he went out the door.

Cora rose from the couch with an exasperated sigh. *Whatever happened to the darling little boy Jared used to be?*

Walking back to the kitchen to start supper, she had to admit her son was right. It was a bit warm in here. Fanning her face, she opened the kitchen window then went back to the living room to open the front door. Thankfully, there was a screen door to keep the bugs out. Cora hoped this good country air would cool things off soon.

This little two-bedroom house was a far cry from the spacious home they'd left in Chicago. It didn't even have an air conditioner. Cora thought about buying a portable one and putting it in one of the windows, but fall was just around the corner and the weather should be turning cooler soon. For now, they'd get by with what they had.

Leah scurried about the kitchen, getting a snack for the girls. She'd been late picking Linda and Amy up from school and wanted to make sure their treat wouldn't be eaten too close to suppertime.

"Are you doing okay?" Amy asked, gently patting Carrie's arm.

Tears welled in Carrie's eyes. "Jah, but Chippy's gone."

"I'll bet he's hiding out in that pile of wood," Linda spoke up.

Carrie sniffed deeply, as more tears fell. "*Die* ieme will get him."

"I'm sure that Chippy won't be bothered by the bees," Leah said, placing a platter of cheese and crackers on the table for the girls. "He may even have left the woodpile and found another home by now."

"I don't think so," Linda said with a shake of her head. "Chippy liked our woodpile."

"If he is in there, he'll come out when he's ready." Leah poured each of the girls a glass of milk and joined them at the table. "How was school today? Did you make some new friends?"

"I did," Linda said around a mouthful of cracker. "Her name is Carolyn. She's the same age as me."

"I'm glad you made a friend." Leah looked over at Amy. So far, the child hadn't eaten a thing. "How was your day, Amy? Did you make a new friend?"

Amy slowly shook her head, as she fingered her napkin. "I miss my friend Mandy back in Nappanee."

"I understand," Leah said. "Good friends are special, and some friends we keep for the rest of our lives."

Amy heaved a sigh, dropping her gaze to the table. "Don't think Mandy and I will be friends for life, 'cause we live too far away now. I'll probably never see her again."

"Maybe Mandy and her family will come here to visit sometime. Or maybe you'll get to go visit her there," Leah gave Amy's arm a light tap. "In the meantime, it would be good if you made some new friends here."

Amy frowned. "Don't want any new friends. Never wanted to move here, neither. I wish things could be like they were when Mama and Papa were alive."

Leah's heart went out to Amy. The girl still grieved the loss of her parents. Amy's sisters did, too. Leah was sure that being here in a strange place with no special friends probably made it seem even worse.

"Who would like to help me make a tossed green salad for supper?" Leah asked, hoping a new topic might help.

"I will!" Carrie's hand shot up.

"Are you staying for supper?" The question came from Linda.

"No, but I thought a tossed salad might go well with whatever your uncle decides to prepare."

"He usually just fixes sandwiches or soup," Amy mumbled.

"Oh. Well a tossed salad would go with soup, don't you think?"

The two younger ones nodded their heads, but Amy sat staring at her glass of milk.

Leah left the table and was about to get the lettuce from the refrigerator, when Coal started barking from the porch. Leah liked it when the dog alerted her that someone was coming. She presumed it was Adam. She watched from the window as the girls' uncle stooped down to pet the black Lab. Although she'd never heard him say so,

Leah knew Adam liked the dog.

Soon after, Adam entered the kitchen. His cheeks were pink, and perspiration gathered on his upper lip. "Hello everyone." Deep wrinkles formed across Adam's forehead as he stared at Carrie. "What happened to you?"

"She got stung by bees," Linda spoke up before Leah or Carrie could offer an explanation.

Adam stiffened. "How did that happen?"

Leah explained how Carrie had gone looking for Chippy in the woodpile and disturbed a yellow jackets' nest. "Even though she didn't appear to have a serious reaction, since she had so many stings, I took her to the clinic to be checked out."

Concerned for his niece's welfare, Adam bent to take a closer look at the welts on Carrie's arms and legs. Then he looked back at Leah. "What did they say at the clinic?"

"Carrie was seen by a new nurse there first, and then the doctor came in," Leah replied. "He gave us some medicine for Carrie to take that will help with the swelling and said I should continue to put ice on the places where she'd been stung."

"You said the hive is under the woodpile, right?" Adam asked.

Leah nodded.

"I'll take care of this problem, once and for all!" Adam opened one of the kitchen drawers and took out a package of matches. Then he grabbed a can of kerosene and headed out the back door.

"Where're you going, Uncle Adam?" Linda called.

Adam glanced over his shoulder and saw that the girls and Leah were following in quick pursuit.

"I'm doing what needs to be done. Something I should probably have done long before now." Adam dashed into the yard, doused the woodpile with kerosene, and threw in a match. In an instant, the wood went up in flames.

"No! No!" Carrie shouted, running toward Adam before Leah could pull her back. "You're gonna kill Chippy!"

Adam's brows pulled together. "Chippy?"

"The little chipmunk that's been living in the woodpile. Remember when the girls told you about it?" Leah stepped up to Adam. "We haven't seen him for a while, so I think he may have found another home."

Adam gave a nod. "Guess I'd forgotten about him."

"Chippy! Oh, poor Chippy!" Carrie sobbed. Then Linda started crying, and soon Amy joined them.

Adam was flustered and didn't know how to make things right. In his state of confusion, he turned to Leah and said, "I. . .I really need your help with the girls. Will you marry me, Leah?"

CHAPTER 25

Leah stood in stunned silence, staring at Adam and wondering if he'd lost his mind. Surely he couldn't have meant what he had just said. Until now, he'd given no indication that he wanted to marry her. They weren't even courting, for goodness' sake.

She glanced at the children and noticed their wide-eyed expressions, as their tears were brushed quickly away. They were obviously as surprised by Adam's proposal as she was. Except for Carrie's hiccups after she'd stopped crying, not a sound could be heard. At this moment, the chipmunk was obviously far from their minds, but what were Adam's nieces thinking right now?

"Uncle Adam, are you and Leah getting married?" Linda finally asked, looking at him with astonishment.

Adam shuffled his feet a few times. "Well. . .umm. . . We are, if Leah agrees to it."

Rubbing the back of her neck, Leah looked at Adam and said, "I. . .I think we need to talk about this in private, don't you?" She couldn't imagine why Adam had suddenly asked her to marry him—especially in front of the girls. He certainly wasn't in love with her.

Adam's face turned a brighter shade of red as he nodded. "But I want to stay here with this fire a little longer to make sure it goes out. Why don't you go into the house with the girls? I'll come in when I'm finished out here."

"I have a better idea," Leah responded. "The girls can go inside and finish their snack, while you and I talk out here in the yard."

"Guess that would be okay."

Leah opened the back door and gestured for the girls to go in. They hesitated a minute before stepping inside. Then Leah joined Adam on the lawn and stood watching the fire. When the branches burned to glowing embers, Adam stirred through them with a garden rake.

"Let's sit in my buggy so we can talk without our conversation being heard," he suggested. "I can still watch the embers from there."

Leah nodded but turned her attention to the small pond at the far end of Adam's property. He'd told her once that the water was always cold, no matter what time of year it was. The pond was spring fed, and at the lower end, the water emptied into a small stream. Adam had said that even during the drought they'd had last year, the pond stayed full of water.

Right now, Leah wished she were a little girl again, because as warm as she felt, she'd like nothing better than to kick off her shoes, run down to the pond, and jump in. Suddenly, the air seemed so heavy, she could hardly breathe. *Those lucky ducks*, Leah thought when she noticed a pair of mallards swimming in the center of the pond.

"Leah, are you coming?"

Startled, Leah looked back at Adam. "I'll be right there." Her palms grew sweaty as she followed Adam across the yard. When they reached his buggy, she took a seat in the passenger's side, and he went around to the driver's side.

"Leah, I. . ." Adam paused and cleared his throat. "I'm sorry for blurting that out in front of the girls. It was stupid."

Leah tipped her head. "Which part was stupid—asking me to marry you or saying it when the girls were present?"

"The second one. . .or maybe both." Adam gave his earlobe a tug. "I mean, you might think I'm dumb for proposing marriage when we haven't even courted." Adam paused again, as though waiting for her response.

"I'll admit, you took me by surprise," Leah said. "I assume the reason you suggested we get married is because you're concerned about the girls and want them to have a full-time caregiver."

"It's true, but it's more than that."

Leah held her breath, waiting for Adam to continue. Part of her hoped, even wished Adam had asked her to marry him because he felt something for her. The truth was, she'd begun to have feelings for him. While she might not be in love with Adam, a friendship was forming, and if given the chance, she was sure it could turn into love.

"What else were you going to say, Adam?" Leah prompted, trying to control her uneven breathing.

"It's just that. . . Well, the girls have developed a fondness for you, and I've seen the way you are with them. I believe you must care a lot for my nieces."

"You're right. I've come to love Carrie, Linda, and Amy very much."

"As do I," he said. "That's why I want what's best for those girls. I believe having you as their substitute mother would be a good thing for all of them."

"What about you, Adam? What's best for you?"

He glanced at Leah, looked quickly away, and turned to face her again. "Clearly, you can see that I need help with the girls."

Leah released an exasperated sigh. "I know that already, which is why I've been coming over to help every day while you're at the store."

Adam undid the top button of his shirt then pulled the collar away from his throat. "You're making this hard for me, Leah."

"I'm not trying to be difficult. I'm just trying to understand how us getting married would be the best thing for me."

"Does the idea of marrying me repulse you?" His unreadable expression made Leah even more confused.

She shook her head slowly, unable to look away. "Of course not. But since we're not marrying for love, I have to wonder what kind of life we would have."

He paused, tapping his chin. "It would be a marriage of convenience, Leah. You can sleep in the guest room, because I wouldn't expect you to share my room."

"I see. And you would be fine with that?"

"Jah. Unless there comes a time that we both felt differently."

Holding her hands tightly in her lap, Leah forced a smile that she didn't really feel. This truly wasn't the type of proposal she'd romanticized about. Glancing over at the embers that had nearly gone out, she murmured, "For the sake of the girls, I will marry you, Adam."

"R–really?" he stammered. "How soon?"

"I think the soonest I could plan and get ready for a wedding would be the second week of November. That's less than three months from now, and I don't think our church leaders would approve of us getting married any sooner than that."

Adam drew in a deep breath, pressing his palms against his chest. "Danki, Leah. I promise to be a good provider for you and the girls."

Provider? Leah swallowed hard, as the reality of the situation hit her like a bale of hay falling from the loft in the barn. She had just agreed to become Mrs. Adam Beachy, but they would be married in name only. *What in the world have I agreed to? I've thought many times that I would never marry a man unless we had been seriously courting and were deeply in love. Oh my. I wonder what Mom and Dad are going to say about this—especially when I haven't even taken the time to pray about my decision.*

"Can we go tell the girls our news?" Adam asked, feeling like a sudden weight had been lifted from his shoulders. He could hardly believe that Leah had said yes to his proposal.

"I think that's a good idea," she responded. "Since they heard you ask if I would marry you, I'm sure they're anxious to learn whether I agreed to become your wife."

My wife. Adam let the words play over and over in his head. All these years he'd sworn that he would never marry, yet in a split second, here he was an engaged man. Could a marriage of convenience such as theirs really work, or was it wishful thinking on his part? For Carrie, Linda, and Amy's sake, he needed it to work, and he would do his best to make everyone happy and see that Leah had everything she needed.

She'd have to give up doing reflexology, of course, because she would be too busy for that once they were married. Adam wouldn't mention anything about that to Leah yet—not until after they were married. She may not be willing to give up something she thought was helping people. If he said anything now, it could be a bone of contention, and it might keep Leah from marrying him.

Adam stepped down from his buggy and went around to help Leah get out, but by the time he got there, she was already on the ground. "If you'll wait a minute, I want to pour a bucket of water on the ashes. I think the fire's almost out, but I want to make sure before we go inside."

"Sure, that's fine."

As Adam put water into the pail, he glanced at Leah. She was looking toward the pond again. *What is she thinking about? Is she watching those ducks, or wondering what she's agreed to? What was I thinking with a proposal like that? Shouldn't I have prayed about this first? Well, I can't take back my proposal now.*

Adam poured water where the branch pile had been. White smoke wafted through the air as the last of the embers sizzled out. "I think that about does it." He motioned to Leah, and they headed for the house. "Would you like to tell the girls, or would you prefer that I make the announcement?"

Leah stepped onto the porch and turned to face him. "Since it was your idea, I think you ought to be the one who tells them."

"You're right." Adam opened the door for Leah and then followed her into the house. Thinking the girls might be in their rooms by now, he cupped his hands around his mouth and shouted up the stairs, "Amy! Linda! Carrie! Would you please come down here? I have something I need to tell you."

"Adam, look at me a minute," Leah said, brushing his arm with her hand.

When he turned his head, she wiped her thumb over a spot on his cheek. "You had something smeared on your face. I think it was a piece of ash from the fire."

Adam ran a finger over the spot where Leah had made contact. Was the sudden flush he felt from her gentle touch?

"It's gone now." Leah lowered her gaze.

A few minutes later, the girls appeared. "We were watching out the living-room window," Linda said. "Saw you and Leah sitting in your buggy."

Carrie bobbed her head in agreement, rubbing one of the spots where she'd been stung.

Adam bit back a chuckle. When he glanced Leah's way, he noticed a smile tugging at her lips. Did she think it was funny that the girls had been spying on them?

"Why don't we all go into the living room so we can talk?" Leah suggested, ushering the girls into the other room.

"Good idea," Adam agreed, wondering why he hadn't thought of it.

After everyone had taken a seat, Adam got right to the point. "Well, girls, as you know from what I said earlier, I've asked Leah to marry me." He paused and waited, hoping at least one of them would say something, but they just looked at him with curious expressions.

Adam rubbed his sweaty palms along the sides of his trousers. "Leah said jah, so unless you object, we're going to be married in November."

"Do you have to wait that long?" Linda asked.

Adam glanced at Leah and noticed her look of relief. He was glad, too, that none of the girls had objected.

"It's not really that far off," Leah said, slipping her arm around Linda, as she sat beside her on the couch. "I'll need time to make my dress and complete some preparations for the wedding."

"Can I help?" Amy asked.

Leah nodded. "I'm sure there will be plenty that all three of you can do to help me get ready for the wedding."

Carrie climbed into Leah's lap. "Are you gonna be our new mamm?"

Tears welled in Leah's eyes. "I could never take the place of your mother, but I won't have to go home every evening once your uncle and I are married, and I'll love you like you were my very own kinner."

The girls seemed satisfied with that as they clustered around Leah, expressing their happiness at this news. Even Amy, although looking guarded, seemed okay with the idea.

Adam leaned back in his chair, suddenly exhausted. Maybe he'd made the right decision, asking Leah to marry him. Of course, he might feel differently in the morning.

CHAPTER 26

Leah could hardly believe Adam had suggested they invite their friends over for a bonfire on Saturday night. But here they were gathered around the fire by the pond, roasting hot dogs. The girls sat between them, and on the other side of the fire sat Priscilla with her boyfriend, Elam, and Elaine with Ben.

It was a cool evening, perfect for sitting around the fire pit. The end of August had a way of giving little hints of the fast-approaching autumn weather. One day it could be sweltering and uncomfortably humid, and the next, it could be the exact opposite.

The girls seemed to be having a good time, and after getting stung by all those bees, Carrie seemed to be healing well. Leah didn't think she'd ever forget the sound of little Carrie's screams that day. Thankfully, as with most children, Adam's youngest niece had recovered rather quickly.

Earlier, while Adam was gathering wood for the bonfire, Leah had stood watching the girls trying to catch frogs near the pond's edge. Their laughter, as well as the excitement they still exuded after learning about the upcoming marriage, put a smile on Leah's face. Already she felt as if they were a family. *How could this be wrong? Surely God would not object to me helping raise Adam's nieces, whom I already love so much.*

Leah had always enjoyed cookouts, especially roasting hot dogs over an open fire. But as the evening wore on, she found that with each bite she took, it was getting harder to swallow. Even with the hot dog on the verge of being burned and smeared with lots of mustard and relish, just the way she liked it, Leah couldn't seem to enjoy it. Somehow she managed to take the last bite. That little bit of happiness she'd felt earlier had been replaced with apprehension. Was it too soon to be announcing their news? How would her friends react when Adam told them that he and Leah were planning to be married?

Elaine sputtered as smoke wafted from the fire in her direction then lifted into the air. "Oh my!" She coughed. "I thought I might have to move my seat, but it seems to be better now."

Ben grabbed hold of her hand. "You know what I've always heard? 'Smoke follows beauty.'"

"Behave yourself." Elaine blushed while the others laughed.

Spending time with her two best friends had always been fun, and when times got tough, they'd been there for one another. But this evening, knowing the reason she and Adam were having this gathering, Leah felt tense and ill at ease. She couldn't stop wondering what Elaine and Priscilla would think of her sudden plans to marry Adam. She swallowed hard, getting the last mouthful of her hot dog down as she watched Adam stand up to make his announcement.

"I'm glad you could all be here this evening," he said, shifting his weight, as though unsure of himself. "Leah and I have an important announcement to make, and except for the girls and Leah's parents, you are the first ones to know."

With the glow of the fire, Leah could see that all eyes were focused on Adam as everyone got quiet. The only thing that could be heard was the croaking of a frog and the crackling wood in the flames of the fire. She held her breath, waiting for him to continue.

"Leah and I have decided to get married," Adam proclaimed. "The wedding will take place the second Thursday in November, and we would like the four of you to be our witnesses."

No one said anything at first, making Leah wonder if they all disapproved. Maybe the frogs approved, though, because now there was a chorus of them singing.

Finally, Ben left his seat and came around to shake first Adam's and then Leah's hand. "Congratulations."

Elaine joined him, and after shaking Adam's hand, she gave Leah a hug. But Leah suspected from the look on her friend's face that she had some misgivings.

Priscilla and Elam came next, offering handshakes and hugs as well. Priscilla's smile appeared to be forced, and Leah figured Priscilla wasn't happy to hear this news, either. Since she couldn't come right out and ask in front of the others, Leah decided to wait until she had a chance to speak with Elaine and Priscilla alone.

"Sure wish Leah could move in with us right now," Linda said after Adam handed her another hot dog to roast. "November's a long way off."

Leah reached over and touched the child's arm. "It'll be here before we know it."

"The girls are pleased that Leah and I getting married," Adam spoke up.

"I imagine they would be, especially since Leah's such a good cook." Elam bumped Priscilla's arm with his elbow. "Don't you think Leah's a good cook?"

Priscilla responded with a brief nod. Something was wrong, and Leah planned to find out what it was before the evening was out. Watching the tips of the flames as sparks disappeared into the air, Leah prayed that her friends would understand and be happy for her.

After everyone had eaten and the girls began roasting marshmallows, Leah gathered up the rest of the food and took it into the house. She was glad when Elaine and Priscilla came along, carrying some of the items.

"Are you in love with Adam?" Elaine asked the minute they entered the kitchen.

Placing the tray of food on the counter, Leah smiled and said, "Adam has many good qualities. I think he'll be a good husband."

"But do you love him?" Elaine repeated, setting her items on the table.

"Well, I. . ." Leah's face heated. "Adam and I are not in love, if that's what you mean, but we do respect each other."

Priscilla's gaze flicked upward. "Then you shouldn't have agreed to marry him."

"I agree with Priscilla," Elaine interjected. "I've always felt that a person should marry for love."

"I love Adam's nieces. That ought to count for something."

"Is that the reason you've agreed to marry Adam—because of the girls?" Priscilla crossed her arms in front of her chest.

"That's mostly the reason," Leah admitted. "He needs someone to be with the girls full-time. Even when Adam's at home, he has a hard time managing things."

"Have you prayed about this?" Elaine questioned.

"Well, not exactly, but I feel confident that—"

"So you're going to make the ultimate sacrifice and marry Adam in order to make his life easier because he can't take proper care of his nieces?" Priscilla uncrossed her arms and tapped her foot. "Look what happened when Elaine sacrificed her needs to take care of her grandma. She ended up losing the man she loved to another woman, who was more than happy to marry him, I might add." Priscilla's hands shook as she held them close to her sides.

Elaine's chin quivered and her eyes filled with tears. "I thought you understood why I broke up with Jonah. I thought you supported my decision to put Grandma's needs ahead of my own."

"I did, but. . ." Priscilla turned and fled the room.

Leah watched as her friend dashed down the hallway and into the bathroom, slamming the door shut behind her. Stunned by Priscilla's outburst and feeling sorry about what had been said, Leah slipped her arm around Elaine's waist. "I'm sure Priscilla didn't mean to hurt you. She's just concerned about me marrying Adam and doesn't want me to sacrifice my own needs."

Elaine sniffed. "I don't regret caring for Grandma. Jonah is happy being married to Sara, and I'm glad for them. Someday, Lord willing, I'll find the right man and know the kind of joy Sara feels when she's with Jonah."

"What about Ben? He's been courting you for a while now. He seems quite attentive tonight, so I assumed you two might be getting serious."

Elaine twisted her finger around her head covering ties. "I enjoy being with Ben, but right now we're just friends."

"Friendship should always come first," Leah said. "Perhaps it will blossom into love." She cringed, thinking about her own situation. *Are Adam and I really friends?*

Priscilla leaned against the bathroom door, sobbing and berating herself for the hurtful things she'd said to Elaine and Leah. She didn't know what had come over her to spout off like that. Elaine and Leah were both good friends, and she'd never intentionally hurt either of them before. Yet that's just what she'd done.

Pressing her hands against her forehead, Priscilla tried to figure out what had just happened. *When Elaine broke up with Jonah, I tried to be understanding and supportive. So what made me say what I did just now? I should have just congratulated Leah on her engagement to Adam and shown support, even if I'm concerned about her reason for marrying him. And I never should have brought up the topic of Jonah to Elaine. She didn't deserve that.*

More tears fell as Priscilla came to grips with her feelings. As much as she hated to admit it, she was jealous because Leah would soon be getting married. All these months Elam had been courting her and he'd never said a word about marriage. Yet Adam hadn't courted Leah at all, and he'd asked her to marry him.

Of course, she reasoned, *he only asked her because he needs a wife—someone to take care of his nieces and cook and clean.* If Adam and Leah were deeply in love, she'd be even more envious. And it hadn't helped to hear Ben make that remark to Elaine about her beauty and then tenderly hold her hand. Priscilla felt even sorrier for herself. Elam had never said such sweet things to her, although he did sometimes hold her hand.

It wasn't right to envy her friends, and she should never have taken her disappointment and frustration out on them. Grabbing a tissue from the vanity, she wiped her eyes and blew her nose. She owed Leah and Elaine a heartfelt apology.

When Priscilla stepped into the kitchen, she found Leah and Elaine sitting at the table. "I'm sorry for the way I acted and the horrible things I said." She placed her hands on Elaine's shoulders. "I do understand why you broke up with Jonah, and I shouldn't have brought that up. I hope you will forgive me."

Elaine reached back and patted Priscilla's hand. "You're forgiven."

Priscilla touched Leah's shoulder. "If you feel that marrying Adam is the right thing to do, then I'm happy for you."

Leah smiled. "Danki. I appreciate that."

"It's hard for me to admit this," Priscilla said, taking a seat across from them, "but the truth is, I'm jealous."

Elaine's forehead wrinkled. "About what?"

"I've known Elam since we were kinner, and we've been courting for several months, yet he hasn't said a word about marriage. Makes me wonder if he's stringing me along until someone better catches his eye. Or maybe Elam only sees me as a friend."

"I've seen the dreamy way he looks at you," Leah said. "No man looks at a woman like that unless he cares deeply for her."

"Then why hasn't he asked me to marry him?"

"Perhaps he's afraid you'll say no," Elaine suggested.

Priscilla shook her head, gripping the tissue she held tightly in her fingers. "I wouldn't say no."

"Does Elam know that you love him?" Leah questioned.

"Well, he ought to. I think my actions have proved that. Surely he must realize that I would have broken things off with him by now if I didn't love him."

Elaine nodded. "But have you actually said the words?"

"Course not. That would be embarrassing. Besides, I think he should be the one to say it first, don't you?"

Leah shrugged. "I suppose so, but then I'm no expert on love."

"If my grandma were still alive, I'll bet she'd say, 'If you love someone, you ought to let them know; if not in word, then by your actions,'" Elaine put in.

"Is there something you could do to let Elam know you love him?" Leah asked.

"I'm not sure."

"Maybe you could cook a tasty meal and invite him over for supper," Elaine suggested. "You know what they say about the way to a man's heart being through his stomach."

Priscilla snickered. "I don't think that would get a marriage proposal from Elam. He's sampled my cooking several times, and even though he said what I fixed was good, he didn't mention marriage."

"You could let him know that you think he's handsome and strong," Elaine said. "His love language might be words of affirmation."

Priscilla's eyebrows lifted. "Love language?"

Elaine nodded. "There's a book about it. According to the author, certain things cause a person to feel loved. One is words of affirmation, and then there's—"

Linda tromped into the kitchen with her hands on her hips. Turning to Leah, she said, "Uncle Adam wants to know if you three are coming outside to roast marshmallows with us. He said if you're not, then he's gonna eat the whole bag himself."

Laughing, Leah pushed back her chair and stood. Elaine and Priscilla did the same.

"Guess we'd better get out there," Leah said, still chuckling, "because we sure wouldn't want Adam to eat all the marshmallows and end up with a *bauchweh*."

Linda shook her head. "No one likes to have a stomachache."

Feeling a little better about things, Priscilla followed the rest of them out the door and headed toward the fire burning brightly in the yard. She wasn't planning to tell Elam that he was handsome, but maybe there was something she could say that would let him know she thought highly of him. If words of affirmation really was his love language, maybe they would give him what he needed to finally pop the big question.

CHAPTER 27

Cora stood in front of the living-room window, staring out at the darkened sky. It was the last Friday of September, and Jared was spending the night with his friend Scott again. She had met the boy, as well as his parents, but wasn't sure if he would make a good friend for Jared. While Scott seemed nice enough, he wore his hair too long, dressed sloppily, and had so much dirt under his fingernails she wondered if he ever washed his hands. Of course, Cora realized that she shouldn't judge the boy by his looks. As long as Jared didn't get into any trouble when he was hanging out with Scott, she had no objections to their friendship.

Shivering, Cora pulled the collar of her pink velvet bathrobe tightly around her neck. It was a bit chilly this evening. She wished she'd thought to ask Jared to bring in some wood before he'd left so she could build a cozy fire in the fireplace. A small house had its advantages, for it didn't take long to warm things up with a roaring fire. But that wouldn't happen tonight, because Cora wasn't about to go outside and haul in wood. That would risk ruining the beautiful robe Evan had given her for Christmas last year. She fingered the silky ribbon decorating the sleeves. Evan had chosen pink because it was Cora's favorite color.

Tears trickled down Cora's cheeks as she reflected on that beautiful morning. If she'd only known then that it would be the last Christmas she, Evan, and Jared would spend as a family, she might have said or done things differently. Of course, looking back on it now, she wasn't sure what she could have done differently. If Evan wanted to cheat on her, she probably couldn't have done anything to prevent it.

Pulling her thoughts back to the present, Cora left the window and turned on several of her decorative battery-operated candles. She preferred them not only because they created the ambience of real candles, but they also were handy in case the lights went out and were safer than regular candles. A few of the battery-operated ones were also scented, which released a nice aroma into the room.

Taking a seat in the rocking chair, Cora leaned back and set the chair in motion. She and Jared had been here almost a month now, but she hadn't made any real friends. She couldn't count on Jared for companionship, either. After school when she got home from work, he was either in his room doing homework or making some excuse to be outside by himself. While he hadn't actually said the words, Cora knew he was still angry at her for moving to Arthur.

Thankfully, Cora's job at the clinic kept her busy during weekdays, but the weekends were the worst. She hadn't even made any close connections with the people she worked with at the clinic. During the day, as expected, most of the conversations were on a professional level; then after work, everyone went home to their own lives. Cora hoped that as she got to know everyone better, maybe some close friendships would form. In the meantime, she had suggested several things she and Jared could do together, including a trip to one of the nearby lakes, but he'd said he wasn't interested. Cora was convinced that her son didn't want to spend any more time with her than he had to.

Cora had tried to set things up with Evan so he could have Jared over the weekend, but Evan had said he had something else going on and he'd have Jared some other time.

"I'll bet you will," Cora muttered, clenching her teeth until her jaw ached. "When you walked out on me, you apparently deserted our son, as well." She stared into the flame of the flickering candle she had placed on a doily in the center of the coffee table. She loved the feel of velvet, and while rubbing her hand over the sleeve of her robe, she continued to think about Evan. They'd been so happy during the first several years of their marriage. At least, she'd thought they were. Evidently, she'd been too blind to see that he'd lost interest in her and had started seeing the other woman. *Maybe I'm just too naive*, Cora thought, remembering how her mother used to call her that. *I should have seen the warning signs when Evan lost interest in me.*

Because it signified happier times, Cora had almost gotten rid of the robe she wore this evening. But as she looked around at the few things she'd unpacked, just about everything Cora owned reminded her of the marriage she thought had been made in heaven.

Leaning her head against the back of the rocker and enjoying its soothing motion, Cora closed her eyes and allowed her mind to take her on a trip down memory lane. Back to when she and Evan were newlyweds. . . .

"Have I told you lately how much I love you?" Evan asked, caressing Cora's cheek with his thumb.

Her eyelids fluttered as her lips curved into a smile. "I think you told me an hour ago, but I never get tired of hearing it." She leaned into his embrace. "I love you, too, Evan."

"I can't imagine us being any happier than we are right now, but I think as the years go by, our love will grow even stronger." He kissed Cora's cheeks and her nose, and then his lips settled on hers, in a kiss so tender and sweet, Cora felt that it would stay with her forever. Nothing and no one could ever come between her and Evan. He was her soul mate—the man she was destined to marry. And this was the life she was meant to live.

Cora's cell phone rang, jolting her eyes open and bringing her memories to a halt. The phone lay on the small table beside her, and she quickly reached for it. Looking at the caller ID, she realized that it was her Realtor, so Cora answered the call. "Hello, Mr. Sherman. I hope you're calling with good news."

"No, not really," he said. "No offers have come in on your house yet."

"Then why are you calling me?" she asked a bit too sharply. This was not what she wanted to hear.

"The house has been on the market for a month now without even a nibble, so I think it might be time to lower the price."

"Lower the price?" Cora nearly jumped out of her chair. "Are you kidding me? That house is in top-notch condition, and it's worth every penny I'm asking for it."

"It may be worth that much to you, Mrs. Finley, but during the last open house I conducted, several people said they thought it was overpriced." There was a pause. "If you really want to sell your home, then I think we ought to drop the price by ten thousand dollars."

Cora's face felt like it was on fire. She needed every penny she could get. "Ten thousand dollars is a lot of money, Mr. Sherman!"

"Do you want to sell it or not?"

Cora could hear the impatience in his voice and knew she'd better give him an answer quickly. Drawing in a deep breath, she said, "Okay, you can lower the price by eight thousand, but I won't go down any more than that." Even as she spouted the words, Cora knew if the house didn't sell at the lower price, she might have to relent and let it go for even less. If it meant getting out of this dinky rental, it might be worth the sacrifice.

"Sounds good, Mrs. Finley. I'll keep you posted."

Feeling defeated, Cora clicked off the phone, turned the candle switches off, and headed down the hall toward her bedroom. Maybe things would look better tomorrow.

The next morning, as Cora sat at the kitchen table drinking a second cup of coffee, she stared at the tablet and pen in front of her. She needed to make out a grocery list, as well as record a few things she needed at the health food store. She glanced at the clock. It was a few minutes past ten. If she waited to leave the house until closer to noon, she could stop somewhere for lunch before doing her shopping.

Maybe I'll try out that pizza place where Jared met Scott awhile back. Since he found a new friend there, maybe luck will be on my side and I'll meet someone, too.

Cora knew that probably wouldn't happen, but the thought of a Canadian bacon with pineapple pizza sounded pretty good to her. If she bought a large size, she could bring the leftovers home for her and Jared's supper this evening. She'd told him to be home by three, so that meant he planned to be here for the evening meal.

Cora hurried to finish her lists and then gulped down the last of her coffee. She would take a shower, get dressed, and head out the door by eleven.

A chilly wind blew under the eaves of the porch as Leah stepped out to shake some throw rugs. Since Adam let his employees run the store most Saturdays, it gave her a chance to get some cleaning done at home. She'd been at it since early this morning and was almost done.

Arf! Arf! Arf!

"What's the matter, Sparky?" Leah looked toward the screen door, where the dog stood, peering out.

Sparky turned and ran through the house, barking. Then he came back to the door again.

"I know, boy, I miss her, too." Leah felt sorry for Sparky. Ever since Mom had gone to Wisconsin to help Aunt Grace, the little terrier had been watching for her return. He whined like a child crying on their first day of school, not wanting to be separated from their parents. If a dog could mope, Sparky had certainly been doing a lot of that lately. The other night Dad had laughed and said, "That dog's gonna wear a path to the door, watching for your mamm."

Leah glanced at the single feeder she had left hanging near the porch. It had been almost two weeks since they'd seen the last hummingbird. She smiled, remembering how just yesterday she'd mistaken a dragonfly for a hummingbird. She was surprised to have seen even that.

Alissa had suggested leaving at least one feeder out until closer to December. That way, she'd explained, any late-migrating hummers would have a place to stop and juice up before heading southward to warmer climates.

I'm sure going to miss those flying jewels, Leah thought as she scanned the yard, just in case. *Think maybe I'll treat myself to lunch in town. Then I need to make a visit to the Stitch & Sew to choose the material I want for my wedding dress.*

Leah knew she should have done that already, since the wedding was only two months away, but she'd been so busy taking care of Adam's nieces and trying to keep up with everything that needed to be done at home. With Mom still gone, Leah had taken on more responsibilities, although Dad helped out as much as he could when he wasn't working. Hopefully Mom would be home by the first week of November, so she would not only be able to attend Leah and Adam's wedding but could take over her household chores again, too.

Leah smiled, thinking about her folks' reaction to Leah's acceptance of Adam's proposal. Dad had simply said he thought Adam was a good man and that he hoped they would be happy. When Leah had called Mom and told her the news, she'd chuckled and said, "I'm not a bit surprised, Leah. Remember when I told you that I thought Adam was a handsome man? I figured it was just a matter of time before you saw that about him, too."

Leah shook the last rug and stepped back inside. *Surely Mom has to know I'm not marrying Adam just because he's good looking.*

Leah had actually been surprised when neither Mom nor Dad had questioned the reason behind Leah's hasty decision. *Maybe they're so relieved that I won't be living at home the rest of my life as an old maid that they don't care what made me decide to marry Adam.*

Leah placed the rugs on the living-room floor and headed to the bathroom to wash up. "I wonder if Adam thinks I'm pretty," she mused, glancing in the mirror. "I guess it doesn't really matter, but I'd kind of like to know."

After washing her face and hands and changing into a clean dress, Leah slipped her black outer bonnet on her head, grabbed her purse and shawl, and headed out the door. She would stop at the pizza place in Arthur for a quick lunch and afterward go straight to the fabric store.

CHAPTER 28

Cora tapped her fingers impatiently on the table as she waited for the pizza she'd ordered. It seemed like it was taking a long time. Maybe that was because she was so hungry. Her stomach growled noisily, and taking a quick scan of those sitting closest to her, Cora was glad that no one seemed to notice. The pizza shop was busy this afternoon, typical of the ones back in Chicago. Some folks came and went, picking up takeout orders, while others like her were eating in the restaurant.

A few teenagers sat at a booth in the corner. Cora noticed Jared wasn't among them. *I wonder what he and Scott are doing today.* Jared rarely talked about the things he and Scott did. As a matter of fact, Cora's son didn't share much of anything with her these days. But at least she knew who he was with, and having spoken to Scott's mother on the phone the other evening, Cora felt once again that Scott was a nice enough kid. His mother had mentioned that her husband had been out of work for a while but had found another job recently. It was one more reminder of how grateful Cora felt for her position at the clinic.

Turning her attention to a young Amish couple with two small children, Cora watched as they bowed their heads before eating. *How long has it been since I said a prayer?*

Cora smiled when one of the little boys, who couldn't have been much older than three or four, closed his eyes like his parents. Taking a closer look, Cora realized the boys were twins with the blondest hair she'd ever seen. When their prayer was over, one of the boys looked at her and grinned. She returned his smile and gave a discreet wave. *I wish Jared was still that young and innocent. Things were much easier when he was a small child.*

Looking toward the counter where the pizzas were made, Cora's nose twitched. The aroma of pepperoni, onions, peppers, and sauces made her stomach rumble again. *What in the world could be taking so long to make my pizza?*

Cora glanced toward the door and saw a young Amish woman with golden brown hair enter the restaurant. Even though it had been several weeks, Cora remembered meeting her when she'd brought her little girl into the clinic.

Cora waved, and the young woman waved in response before placing her order. When she took a seat at a table near Cora's, Cora looked over at her and smiled. "Do you remember me? I'm Cora Finley—the new nurse at the clinic. We met when you brought your daughter in after she'd been stung by yellow jackets."

The woman nodded. "My name is Leah Mast, and Carrie's not my daughter. I take care of Carrie and her two older sisters while their uncle's at work."

"Oh, I see." Cora thought it was odd that Leah had said the girls' uncle, and not their parents, but she didn't think it would be proper to ask about it.

"If you're not waiting for someone, would you like to join me at my table?" Leah asked.

Cora didn't have to be asked twice. "It's no fun eating by yourself, and since I'm all alone, it would be nice to have the company." She scooped up her glass of iced tea and took a seat across from Leah. "How is Carrie doing now?"

"She's fine. We were relieved that she didn't have a serious reaction to the stings."

"Allergic reactions can be quite serious," Cora agreed.

"You're right about that. I practice reflexology, and one of the women I treat had a reaction to some walnuts awhile back, so I know how frightening things like that can be."

Cora's eyebrows lifted. "Are you a licensed reflexologist?"

Leah shook her head. "I'm not licensed, but I've been doing reflexology for several years. In fact, my grandmother taught me when I was a teenager. Since I don't charge a set fee, I'm not required to get professional training or be licensed."

"Don't you think you'd make more money if you could charge a set fee?" Cora questioned.

"I don't know. I've never really thought about it." Leah shrugged. "Besides, I don't practice reflexology just to get paid."

Cora leaned her elbows on the table and looked closely at Leah. She wanted to know what made this young woman tick. "Why do you do it, if not for the money?"

"I want to help others. I see my ability to help them feel better as a gift."

Cora reflected on that before responding. *Do I see my nursing abilities as a gift or just a way to make money?*

When Cora had finished her nurses' training, her focus had been on helping others, but she'd also needed the money she made—especially since she'd had to go into debt to pay her way through nursing school. There'd been no financial help from any of her family. Cora had been given no choice but to make it on her own—until she'd met Evan. Dr. Evan Finley had been to Cora everything that her family had never been. He'd understood her reason for wanting to be a nurse and had even paid for her to get more schooling.

Unfortunately, things were quite different these days. *Evan wouldn't lift a finger to help me now*, she thought bitterly. *All he thinks about is satisfying his own needs and catering to the whims of his pretty new wife.*

"Are you okay?"

Cora's thoughts scattered at the sound of Leah's voice. "Oh, um. . . Yes, I'm fine. Just thinking about the past—that's all. Sorry for spacing off like that."

"It's all right. I've done the same thing myself." Leah chuckled. "One little thing can get my mind wandering, and then my thoughts will start drifting."

Both of their pizzas came, and although Cora was starving, she waited patiently as Leah bowed her head for silent prayer.

How long has it been since I uttered a prayer of any kind, much less one of thanksgiving? she asked herself once more. *Well, God's never answered any of my prayers before, so why would He now?*

When Leah opened her eyes, she smiled at Cora and motioned to the personal-sized pizza she had ordered. "Feel free to have some of mine if you like."

"It's nice of you to offer, but I have plenty of my own to eat. In fact, I'll be taking the leftovers home, so if you want some of mine, please help yourself."

"This will probably be enough for me." Leah picked up a piece of her sausage and black olive pizza. "I ordered a small one because I'm not going directly home from here. As soon as I'm done eating, I'll be heading to the fabric shop to buy some material for my wedding dress."

"Oh, you're about to get married?"

Leah nodded. "In a couple months. The second week of November, to be exact. In fact, I'll be marrying Carrie's uncle."

Cora reached for her glass of iced tea and took a sip. "I'm sure Carrie will be happy about that. From what I witnessed between the two of you at the clinic, she seemed quite dependent on you."

"Yes, and since I started watching Carrie and her sisters, I've grown attached to them."

Cora heaved a sigh. "I wish my son, Jared, and I related to each other better. Seems like he's always looking for some excuse not to be around me these days. It all started when his father left me for another woman." Cora didn't know why she was telling a near stranger all of this, but it felt good to get it off her chest. "I think Jared blames me for the breakup."

Leah reached over and touched Cora's arm. "I'm sorry you had to go through that. I'll remember to say a prayer for you."

"Thank you." It was nice to know someone would be praying for her, because she sure wouldn't be praying for herself.

As Cora and Leah continued to eat, they talked more about Leah's reflexology.

"Would you mind giving me your phone number?" Cora asked. "My feet get sore sometimes from being on them all day. I'd probably benefit from a foot massage."

Leah hesitated at first, but then she reached into her purse for paper and pen. "I'll write my number down for you, but when you call, you'll have to leave a message, because our telephone is outside in a small wooden building that we call our phone shack."

"That's not a problem. I'll leave you a message, and you can return my call to let me know when you'd be available for an appointment. I'm so looking forward to having you work on my feet."

"Since I watch the girls during the day, I've been scheduling people's foot treatments during the evening hours," Leah explained.

"That's perfect for me since I'm working at the clinic on the weekdays." Cora didn't know if it was her imagination or not, but she felt as though she and Leah had made a connection today. Perhaps this young woman would turn out to be the friend she so badly needed. At the very least, Cora had found someone to massage her feet.

When Leah entered the fabric store a short time later, she spotted Sara Miller looking at some bolts of material. "Wie geht's?" Leah asked.

"I'm doing pretty well." Sara placed one hand against her protruding stomach and smiled. "In a few months the boppli should be here. Jonah and I are both getting anxious."

"I can imagine." Seeing Sara's excitement over having another baby caused Leah to feel a bit envious. She'd be getting married soon, but to a man who didn't love her. It wasn't likely that she'd ever have any children of her own. But at least she'd have Carrie, Linda, and Amy to help raise, and she looked forward to that. "Are you hoping for a *bu* or a *maedel*?" Leah asked.

"It really doesn't matter to Jonah or me whether we have a boy or a girl," Sara replied. "As long as the boppli is healthy."

Leah nodded. It did her heart good to see the joyful smile on Sara's face. She'd been through a lot and deserved every bit of happiness she could get.

"I'll bet you're excited," Sara said. "It won't be long until you and Adam will be getting married."

"That's why I'm here," Leah said. "I need to buy some material and get my wedding dress made."

"I'm pretty good with a needle and thread, so if you need any help, just let me know," Sara offered, rubbing her stomach.

Leah slipped her arm around Sara's waist. "Danki for the offer. I just might take you up on that if I can't get it done by myself."

Sara gave Leah a hug. "I hope you and Adam will be as happy as Jonah and I are."

All Leah could manage was a brief nod. *I wonder what Sara and other people in our church district would say if they knew Adam and I aren't marrying for love.*

As Leah moved on to choose her material, she thought about Cora and how sad she'd looked when she talked about her husband walking out on their marriage. It was distressing to think that anyone could get married and not keep their vows. Even if she and Adam never fell in love, divorce would never be an option for them.

CHAPTER 29

Adam rolled out of bed and glanced at the clock on his bedside table. He couldn't believe it was almost noon. He'd been awakened in the wee hours of the morning when Coal decided to go into barking mode. At one point, he'd been on the verge of getting up to check on things, but the dog had finally settled down. After Adam finally got back to sleep, he slept harder and longer than he normally did. It was one of those deep slumbers that put him in a fog once he finally woke up. Moaning, he stretched his arms above his head, trying to get the kinks out of his back from sleeping so long. "I'll most likely be paying for this all day," Adam mumbled, bending down to touch his toes. "Wonder why those girls didn't wake me up?" This was not the way he'd planned to start his Saturday.

Hurrying to get dressed, Adam noticed that the house was quiet as he ambled down the hall. Hearing nothing from the girls, he wondered if they, too, had slept in.

When Adam entered the kitchen, he halted. All three of his nieces sat at the table, eating peanut butter and jelly sandwiches.

"Uncle Adam, you missed breakfast, but you're just in time for lunch," Linda announced. She grabbed a napkin and wiped the end of Carrie's nose, where a blob of grape jelly had stuck.

Adam glanced at the clock and grunted. "Someone should've woken me up."

"I was gonna," Carrie spoke up, "but Amy said no."

Adam looked at Amy, but she barely gave him a second glance. She was too busy chewing her sandwich.

"She said you must be tired," Linda intervened, "so we just let you sleep."

"I would have gotten a good night's sleep if it hadn't been for Coal barking in the middle of the night," Adam explained. "Did any of you hear him carrying on?"

"I didn't hear anything. Did either of you?" Linda asked her sisters.

Carrie shook her head.

"Me, neither," Amy said.

"Guess it could have been something down by the pond that had him alerted." Adam figured the girls must have really been tired to be able to sleep through all that barking. He grabbed his straw hat and plunked it on his head. "I'd better get outside and tend to the animals. They probably think I'm not coming to the barn at all."

"Want me to help?" Linda asked. "I'm almost done with my lunch."

"That's okay. I can manage." Adam figured he could get the chores done quicker if he didn't have her trudging after him, asking a bunch of silly questions or stopping to play with the dog or one of the barn cats.

He watched as Amy took a napkin and wiped Carrie's hands and jelly-stained mouth. Then she cleared off the table and put water in the sink to do the dishes. Adam couldn't help thinking that someday the girl would be a good mother.

When Adam stepped out the door he nearly tripped over Coal, who lay stretched out on the porch. "Thanks for keepin' me awake last night," he mumbled, nudging the dog with the toe of his boot.

Coal lifted his head lazily and grunted. Then he stood, shook himself, and ambled into the yard with Adam.

Adam snickered when the dog yawned in a whinnylike manner. "Serves you right. Now you know how I feel when I'm tired and have to get up."

As Adam walked across the lawn, he noticed several bruised and battered apples. They were too far from the apple tree that was on the other side of the yard, so he figured the girls must have found the apples lying on the ground and tossed them onto the lawn. As soon as he finished his chores he'd go back inside and tell the girls that they needed to clean up the mess.

Nearing the barn, Adam halted, causing Coal to plow right into his leg. Adam couldn't believe it. The window closest to the door was shattered, with a good-sized hole in it.

"That's just great!" Adam jerked the barn door open and stepped inside. Going over to the broken window, he spotted a mangled looking apple on the floor. It didn't take a genius to realize what had happened. "Those girls are really in trouble now," Adam grumbled, rubbing the back of his neck. He stood, moving his head in a slow circular motion, which relieved some of his tension. "The least they could have done was told me what happened. But no, they just sat there at the table, looking wide-eyed and innocent."

Adam bent to pick up the apple, placed it on a shelf near the door, and fed the livestock. When that was done, he grabbed the apple and headed back to the house.

"Carrie! Amy! Linda!" Adam shouted when he entered the kitchen and found it empty. "I need to speak to you right now!"

A few minutes passed, then Carrie and Linda showed up. "Where's Amy?" Adam asked, struggling to keep his temper.

"In the bathroom. Want me to get her?" Linda responded.

Adam shook his head. "You and Carrie can go to the living room and take a seat. When Amy comes out, the four of us need to have a little talk."

The two girls looked at him strangely but did as they were told.

Adam followed them into the other room and seated himself in his recliner, while they sat on the sofa.

"Is something wrong, Uncle Adam?" Linda asked. "You look like you've been sucking on sour candy."

Adam folded his arms. "We'll discuss it when Amy joins us."

They all sat quietly, until Adam heard the bathroom door open. "Amy, would you please come into the living room?" he hollered. "There's something we need to talk about."

Amy shuffled into the room with a disinterested expression and flopped onto the couch next to Linda.

"I discovered a broken window in the barn, and this on the floor below it." Adam held up the apple. "There were also several apples on the lawn." He leaned slightly forward, squinting his eyes. "What I want to know is, which one of you did it?"

"Not me," said Carrie.

"Me, neither," Linda added.

Adam looked at Amy. If the younger girls didn't do it, then she had to be the guilty one.

Amy pursed her lips and shook her head determinedly. "I never threw any apples, and since Carrie and Linda said they didn't do it, you'd better ask someone else."

"There's no one else here to ask, unless you think the dog did it." Adam gripped the arms of his chair. "And none of you had better leave this room until the guilty party fesses up."

Carrie and Linda started to cry. Amy just sat, staring defiantly at Adam. "I'm not gonna say I did something when I didn't, even if you make me sit here all day. I won't say I threw those apples just to make you happy. Somebody else must've come into the yard and tossed the apples."

Adam groaned. He wished Leah were here today watching the girls. She had a better way of dealing with them than he did. Maybe he'd been too harsh accusing his nieces, but if they hadn't thrown the apples, then who?

Leah had been looking at bolts of fabric for a while when Priscilla and Elaine showed up. They'd promised to meet her and help choose the fabric for her wedding dress, as well as for the dresses they would wear as her witnesses. If Leah had planned the day better, she would have asked them to meet her at the pizza place for lunch, but that had been a last-minute decision.

"Have you found anything you like?" Priscilla asked.

"I'm thinking maybe this." Leah gestured to a bolt of olive-green material. "Green seems to go well with my hair color." She pointed to another shade of green. "I thought this might work for your two dresses."

"Whatever you think's best." Elaine smiled. "After we leave here, I'm going right home to get started on my dress."

"Same here," Priscilla said. "With the wedding less than two months away, there's no time to waste."

"You're right," Leah agreed. "Since I'm at Adam's on weekdays and have foot treatments scheduled on many evenings, I asked Adam if I can move my sewing machine to his house so I can sew during the day."

"What'd he say?" Elaine questioned.

"Said it was fine with him. After all, once we're married, I'll be moving all of my things to his place."

Priscilla bumped Leah's arm. "It's going to seem strange having one of us married and the other two still hoping."

"Don't worry. I'm sure it's just a matter of time before you and Elaine will have your wedding dates published during one of our church services."

Priscilla shook her head. "That might be true for Elaine, but I've about given up on Elam. I may look for someone else—someone who might actually be interested in marriage."

"Really?" Leah could hard believe Priscilla was giving up on Elam. "I thought you were going to give him more words of affirmation and see if that made him feel loved."

"I did, but it didn't work," Priscilla said with a huff. "Now let's pay for our material and be on our way."

Cora's head jerked when the front door opened. She'd been reclining on the couch since she got back from town and had nodded off while waiting for Jared.

"Do you know what time it is?" she asked sharply when Jared sauntered into the room, looking disheveled. His wrinkled shirt made her wonder if he'd slept in it last night.

"Sure, Mom. It's five o'clock."

Cora's jaw tightened. "What time did I ask you to be here?"

He shrugged and tossed his backpack on the floor near the door. "I can't remember."

"I said three o'clock."

He shrugged again. "So what's a measly two hours?"

Cora sat up. "It's not about the difference in time. It's about you learning to do as I say."

Jared sank into a chair. "Well, I'm home now, so that oughtta make you happy."

"It does, but I wish you had listened to what I said and come home on time." Cora studied her son, noticing that in addition to his shirt being wrinkled, it appeared to have several splotches on it. "What's that all over your shirt?"

He looked down and brushed at the smudges. "Nothing much. Scott and I had a fight with some apples. Guess I ended up with most of 'em on my shirt."

Cora frowned. "I'm sure Scott's mother didn't appreciate that."

Jared made no reply.

"Are you hungry?" she asked.

"Maybe a little."

"If you'll change out of those dirty clothes and take a shower, by the time you're done I'll have some pizza heated for our supper."

"Where'd you get pizza?"

"I ate lunch at the pizza place in Arthur today. There was a lot left over, so I brought it home."

"What kind is it?"

"Canadian bacon and pineapple."

Jared wrinkled his nose. "Not my favorite, but I guess it'll fill the hole." Scooping up his backpack, he meandered down the hall.

Cora sighed and rose from her seat. *If that boy moved any slower, he'd stop.* She was glad Jared had made a new friend since they'd moved here, but his attitude sure hadn't improved. Even his posture had an "I don't care" stance. He still hadn't gotten his hair cut, and even worse, he now wore it in a ponytail. *Think I'll give Evan a call and see if he'll have a talk with our son.*

CHAPTER 30

"Thanks for seeing me on such short notice," Cora said as she settled into the recliner in Leah's basement.

"It's not a problem." Leah smiled. "You're the only person I have scheduled for this evening, so it worked out just fine. Often Monday evenings are pretty busy. I guess that's because things happen over the weekend to cause people pain."

Cora nodded. "That's exactly what happened to me. I was unpacking some boxes from our recent move and ended up straining my back. In hindsight, I think I picked up one too many boxes, and knowing that reflexology can help with something like that, I decided to come see you before I resort to muscle relaxers or pain meds."

"Do you ever see a chiropractor?" Leah asked as Cora removed her shoes and socks.

"I had a good chiropractor when we lived in Chicago, but I haven't found one here yet."

"I can give you the name of the one I go to," Leah offered. "Before you leave, remind me."

"Thanks, I will."

Cora reclined her chair, and Leah put some massage lotion on Cora's right foot and began massaging and probing, searching for sensitive areas. "You said you knew that reflexology can help with some back issues. Does that mean you've had foot treatments before?"

Cora nodded.

Leah was pleased to hear that. It meant Cora was a believer in the advantages of reflexology. *Unlike some people*, Leah thought as a vision of Adam came to mind. *Maybe after we're married I can make a believer out of him. He needs to stop being so narrow minded.*

"Is that spot sore?" Leah asked when Cora flinched after she'd touched a certain area just below her big toe.

"Jah, just a bit."

"Jah? Did you just say yes in Pennsylvania Dutch?"

Cora snickered. "Over half the patients we see at the clinic are Amish, so I've been trying to learn a few Pennsylvania Dutch words. *Jah* is one of the easier ones, right?"

Leah nodded. "Jah, it sure is."

Leah continued to work on Cora's right foot. When she finished, she moved on to the left one. "How are things with your son? Did he enjoy the leftover pizza you took home last Saturday?"

"The kind I bought isn't Jared's favorite, and it didn't do anything to help his attitude. Yesterday I gave his father a call and asked if he would have a talk with Jared." Cora sighed. "Of course, my request fell on deaf ears. Evan's only response was that he was too busy to talk right then. Oh, and then he said I needed to take a firmer hand with our son. Evan never seems to have time for Jared anymore. I guess other things are more important to him."

"It sounds like you have a lot of responsibility on your shoulders right now. Trying to be both mother and father to your boy must be difficult."

"You've got that right, and I feel like I'm failing miserably."

"I'm sure you're doing the best you can."

"I try, but it never seems to be enough." Cora closed her eyes.

As Leah continued to work on Cora's feet, she lifted a silent prayer on her behalf. Just the stress of what Cora was going through right now was reason enough for her back to have tightened.

"If this foot treatment helps, which I'm hoping it will, don't hesitate to call me again," Leah said.

"I certainly will, and danki for letting me blow off a little steam."

"Is that another word you learned from your patients at the clinic?"

Cora smiled. "Jah."

As Priscilla sat across the table from Elam at the pizza shop, a lump formed in her throat. When he'd suggested they come here tonight, she'd decided this might be a good time to break things off. Of course, if he brought up the subject of marriage, she would reconsider. The question was, what excuse should she give Elam for breaking up? She couldn't simply blurt out that she didn't want to see him anymore because he hadn't asked her to marry him.

Priscilla took a drink of root beer and stared at the pizza on her plate as she continued to mull things over.

"Aren't you hungerich? You've hardly touched your pizza." Elam gestured to her plate. "And you haven't said more than a few words since we sat down."

Priscilla set her glass down, watching the bubbles of the root beer rise. "I've been thinking." Not only was she holding back tears, but her stomach felt like it was tied up in knots. Pizza was one of her favorite foods, but tonight Priscilla could hardly eat. Since she'd known Elam so long, would she be comfortable with another suitor if one came along? After all, Elam was kind, and he'd been good to her. But Priscilla wanted more. She wanted marriage, children, and the chance to grow old with the man she loved. What if she broke up with Elam but never fell in love with anyone else?

"What are thinking about?"

Startled, Priscilla jumped. "Umm. . . I've been thinking about us."

"What about us?" Elam grabbed a slice of pizza and took a bite as melted cheese stuck to his lip. "Ouch, that's hot!"

"Are you okay?"

"I'll be fine. Just need to be more careful is all."

Satisfied that Elam hadn't been seriously burned, Priscilla continued. "We've been courting for some time now, right?"

He gave a quick nod.

"Well. . ." She moistened her lips. "Maybe it's time that we go our separate ways." There, it was out. Only trouble was, Priscilla didn't feel one bit better.

Elam's eyebrows lifted high on his forehead. "You're kidding, right?"

She shook her head, holding firm and hoping he wouldn't try to dissuade her.

"Why now, after all this time, do you wanna break up with me? I thought things were going along good between us."

"So did I, for a while, at least." Priscilla paused and cleared her throat. "But things are different now."

He plunked his elbows on the table and leaned closer to her. "How are they different, Priscilla?"

She turned her head, unable to look into his hazel eyes. This wasn't going well. She felt like she was backed into a corner.

"You care about me, don't you, Priscilla?" Elam reached across the table and took hold of her hand.

The feel of his warm skin and the sight of his tender gaze were almost her undoing. She did care about Elam, so how could she break up with him? Maybe if she stuck it out awhile longer, he would finally pop the question.

"Forget I said anything." Priscilla took a small piece of pizza. "I wasn't thinking right when I said we should break up."

A slow smile spread across Elam's face. "That's gut, Priscilla. Jah, real good."

Priscilla drew in a deep breath. *What have I done? Elam will probably never ask me to marry him, and I'll end up becoming an old maid. Maybe I should have broken up with him, but then, maybe I need to give him another chance.*

Before Adam went upstairs to say good night to his nieces, he decided to relax on the porch and watch the stars for a while. The sky was crystal clear, and the stars looked more vivid than ever. He felt like he could reach out and touch them. The Big Dipper hung low in the eastern sky and looked as if it were standing on its handle. The Milky Way stretched out overhead, with its twinkling pathway to the starry heavens.

Coal lay at Adam's feet, with his head tilted to one side and ears perked as a neighbor's dog started howling in the distance. "Don't get any ideas of running off," Adam warned. After a few seconds Coal laid his head down between his front paws and went back to sleep.

Reflecting on how his day had gone and how busy they'd been at the store, Adam was glad to be off his feet and relaxing at home. He was thankful that Scott Ramsey had come in after school to work a few hours before closing time. He'd ended up hiring the kid part-time, and Scott had turned out to be a good worker, except for the times his new friend showed up.

Adam wasn't sure who this kid was; he hadn't seen him around Arthur before. It could be that a new family had moved into the area and Adam just hadn't met them yet. Anyone new to these parts usually ended up coming into the store at some point.

Adam hadn't said anything when Scott's friend showed up the first couple times. And he really wouldn't have minded if the boy had been there to purchase something, but it soon became apparent that he only wanted to hang out. Adam didn't take kindly to the way this teenager kept Scott from doing his work. This afternoon, when the kid showed up again, it had been the last straw. Adam hated to do it, but he'd ended up saying something to Scott and his friend. The two boys had gone outside together. After twenty minutes passed, Adam went out to find them. If Scott wanted to get paid, then he had to work. Scott and the other boy, whom Scott had introduced as Jared, were pitching a football back and forth. When Adam told Scott that it wasn't the time to be fooling around and that he needed to get back to work, Scott said he was sorry and returned to the store. Jared, however, stood with a smirk on his face. A few seconds later, he finally stalked off, mumbling something under his breath.

Adam wondered if he should have said something more to the boy before he took off. He was obviously a bad influence on Scott.

Pushing his thoughts aside, Adam resumed his appraisal of the star-studded night. Looking up at the twinkling, sprawling sky, Adam thought of his sister. *Is heaven up there, somewhere?* he pondered. *Is that where Mary and Amos are? Can they see what we're doing down here? Do they approve of how I'm caring for their girls?*

Adam missed his sister and her husband so much. He hated to think that every year he would associate his birthday with their deaths. After all, they'd been coming to help celebrate his thirtieth birthday when the accident happened. Adam was never much on celebrating his birthday, and usually the day would pass like any other. Most people, except his sister and her family, didn't even know when it was.

If I had never been born, two precious lives would not have been lost, and three little girls wouldn't be without their mother and father, Adam thought with regret.

Coal got up and sat directly in front of Adam. Whimpering, the dog laid his head in Adam's lap.

"Somehow, boy, I think you can read my mind." Adam scratched behind the dog's silky ears. Wiping away a tear, he looked up at the sky. *Good night, sweet Mary. Pleasant dreams.*

Knowing he needed to make sure the girls had gotten ready for bed, Adam rose from his seat and went into the house.

He was about to head upstairs, when he remembered the letter he'd found in the mailbox this afternoon. Busy getting supper and doing evening chores, he'd forgotten about it. He hoped the letter would perk Amy up a bit.

Adam went upstairs, and seeing that Carrie and Linda were asleep already, he went across the hall to Amy's room. He knocked on her door, which was slightly ajar, and found her still awake, sitting up in bed.

"I have a letter that came today, and I thought you'd like to hear what it says." Adam sat on the edge of her bed.

"Who's it from?"

"Your friend Mandy's mother." Adam pulled the letter from his pocket. "Should I read it to you?"

Amy nodded.

" 'Dear Adam: We got your wedding invitation, and if all goes well, we should be able to attend. Mandy is excited to see Amy again, and we look forward to meeting your bride. Sincerely, the Burkholder Family.' "

Adam didn't know Mandy's family that well—he'd only met them a few times when he'd gone to Nappanee. But thinking it would be good for Amy to spend some time with her friend, he'd invited Mandy and her folks to attend the wedding.

A huge grin spread over Amy's face. It was the first time since his sister's death that Adam had seen her look so happy. He saw it as a sign that she might be on the road to healing.

At least he hoped she was.

CHAPTER 31

Over the next few weeks, Cora saw Leah regularly for foot treatments. Her back felt much better, and her feet weren't nearly as sore, even though she wasn't getting reflexology specifically for that. The real reason Cora kept returning to Leah's was because she felt so comfortable with her. Leah had become the friend Cora needed so badly.

The young Amish woman was real, not phony, like some of Cora's so-called friends in Chicago. Leah was someone she could count on and even confide in. A few of the nurses she'd worked with at the hospital had been genuine, but none of them had as caring an attitude as Leah's. Whenever Cora talked about her problems with Jared, Leah offered a listening ear and promised to pray for Cora. Despite the fact that Cora didn't put much stock in prayer these days, it was comforting to know that someone cared enough to petition God on her behalf.

Cora had grown up with Bible knowledge, but she'd never really taken it to heart. As far as Cora knew, none of her siblings had ever strayed from their faith. Not like Cora, who had always been a bit of a rebel. Cora's father used to accuse her of being selfish and self-centered, which wasn't pleasing to God.

"Maybe Dad was right," Cora murmured as she pulled her car up to Leah's house. "Maybe that's why God doesn't answer my prayers—because my selfish ambitions displease Him so much."

Tears welled in Cora's eyes, and she looked in the rearview mirror to make sure none had fallen onto her cheeks. She would rather not go in to see Leah in a tearful state; she'd already shed more tears than she should have while telling Leah her woes.

Cora remained in her car a few more minutes, watching the sun's gradual descent in the west. The sunset's glow cast a beautiful radiance on the few leaves still clinging to the trees in the Masts' front yard. Some of the maples still had their autumn color, glowing with the brilliance of a blazing fire. The reflection it cast on all that it touched was breathtaking. Cora rolled down the car window for a better look, enjoying the sight. Inhaling, she could actually smell autumn in the air—that damp, earthy scent. Breathing deeply, she inhaled its fragrance.

A slight breeze picked up, creating a whirlwind of leaves, lifting them into the air, and just that quickly, floating them slowly back down to the grass. Some ended up wedged into the corners by the house, joining others that had already accumulated there. As Cora continued to watch, she couldn't help comparing the leaves to herself. Like the leaves clinging to the tree branches, Cora sometimes felt as if she was just barely hanging on. Her life had been a whirlwind, with so many highs and lows. Just when everything seemed normal and calm, something happened to ruin it all.

Recently, though, Cora had begun to feel as if she was drifting toward some kind of normalcy in her life, something she yearned for in the worst way. Cora felt more confident every day that she'd made the right decision to move to Arthur. She had a good job and was making a few friends. Even if Jared hadn't wanted this move, something about this area made her feel that she belonged here—in a place she could call home.

Cora dabbed her eyes with a tissue and opened the car door. Walking toward the house, she enjoyed the sound she made from shuffling her feet through dried leaves. Another gust of wind brought down more leaves, falling like big golden snowflakes. The chrysanthemums planted on the side of Leah's house and those still in planters on the porch added to the beauty of this wonderful season. Their purple, yellow, rust, pink, and white created a rainbow of color so pleasing to the eyes that Cora found it hard to look away. The breeze coming in her direction brought the flowers' musky smell to her nostrils. The odor wasn't as pleasant as some other flowers, but there was something about their fragrance that Cora enjoyed. It was a smell that described autumn.

Maybe someday when I'm able to buy my own place here, I can plant pretty flowers like this, too.

❧

"It's a bit breezy out there," Cora mentioned as she went down the stairs with Leah. She quickly ran a hand over her hair to put some windblown strands back in place.

"You are so right," Leah agreed. "We usually have all the leaves raked by now, but with the wedding coming up, we haven't had time."

Cora thought about offering her son's help with the leaves. It would give him something constructive to do and hopefully make him realize how good it felt to help someone out. But she didn't suggest it to Leah, knowing Jared would probably refuse. She could barely get him to do a few simple chores at home.

"How are your wedding plans coming along?" Cora asked as she settled herself into Leah's recliner.

"Fairly well. My dress is finished, the guests have been invited, and everything we'll need for the wedding meal has either been bought or rented."

"Will it be a large wedding?"

"Just a couple hundred or so."

"Will you continue doing reflexology after you're married?" Cora questioned.

"I hope so, but it will depend on what my husband has to say." Leah put more lotion on Cora's right foot and massaged the pressure points on her toes.

"I don't know why men think they have to decide everything for us." Cora frowned. "If a woman has a career or wants to do something special, he ought to respect her wishes."

"Did your husband respect your wishes?" Leah asked.

"Which husband? I've been married twice."

Leah's eyes widened. "Oh, I didn't realize that."

"I left my first husband because he tried to control me. Now I'm the one who's been left in the lurch, since my second husband left me for another woman." Cora flinched but not from anything Leah was doing to her foot. It was from the pain she always felt when she thought about the past.

"Your tone makes me think you have many regrets," Leah said, moving on to Cora's left foot.

Cora sighed so deeply, it came out as a groan. "My whole life has been full of regrets." She closed her eyes as a wave of painful memories washed over her. "I've never told anyone else this before, not even Evan, but my parents were Amish, which is truthfully why I'm able to say some words in Pennsylvania Dutch."

Leah's jaw dropped, and she sucked in her breath. "You were born Amish?"

Cora nodded, wondering what she had been thinking, blurting that out. Well, since she'd said that much, she may as well tell Leah the rest of her story. She had been holding in the things concerning her past life so long that she couldn't seem to stop talking now. It would feel good to get it all out. "I was born and raised in Lancaster County, Pennsylvania. I joined the church when I was eighteen and married an Amish man a year later. We had two children—a girl and a boy."

"In addition to Jared, you have a daughter as well?"

Cora shook her head. "I had Jared after I married Evan."

"So you have two sons and a daughter?"

Cora nodded and swallowed hard, hoping she wouldn't fall apart. "I haven't seen my Amish children in over twenty-five years, and I'm sure they've forgotten all about me by now."

Deep wrinkles formed across Leah's forehead. She stopped working on Cora's foot and just stared at her with a strange expression. "You left your Amish husband and your children?"

"Jah," Cora murmured, unable to meet Leah's accusing gaze. *I should have known better than to blurt that out. Now Leah thinks I'm a terrible person and our friendship will be over.*

Leah sat on the stool in front of Cora as though frozen.

Tears welled in Cora's eyes as she lifted her gaze to meet Leah's. "Please don't judge me until you've heard the rest of my story."

Slowly, Leah shook her head. "I'm not judging you, Cora. God is our one true Judge, and the Bible says we are not to judge others. If you'd rather not tell me anything more, that's fine, too."

Cora pulled the lever on the recliner and sat up. "No, I really need to get this off my chest. I've kept it bottled up inside for far too long."

Leah sat silently as Cora began telling her incredible story.

"I was barely eighteen when I got married, and, like you, I practiced reflexology."

"You. . .you worked on people's feet?" Leah asked, almost disbelieving. If Cora had been a reflexologist, then why hadn't she said something until now?

Cora's eyes blinked rapidly. "I can only imagine what you're thinking. You're probably wondering why I've kept this a secret."

Leah could only nod in response.

"At first, the fact that I used to practice reflexology didn't seem important enough to mention. Then later, as we got better acquainted, I was afraid if you knew I used to work on people's feet, you might think I was critiquing as you worked on mine." Cora paused to take a breath. "As far as me having once been Amish, that's a part of my life that I've tried to forget."

"But how could you forget that you had two children, whom I assume stayed with their father when you left?"

Cora nodded. "I never forgot Mary and Adam, though. Not for one little minute."

Leah's hands went straight to her mouth, stifling a gasp. *Is it possible that. . . Oh, no, surely not. It just can't be!*

"I want you to understand why I left my husband and children," Cora continued. "I wasn't satisfied just doing reflexology. What I really wanted was to be a nurse. Of course, Andrew, my husband, thought that notion was ridiculous. He reminded me often that in order to become a nurse, I'd have to leave the Amish faith. My desire to be a nurse was something I just couldn't let go. I pleaded with Andrew to leave with me, but he said no, that the English world was not for him."

It wouldn't be for me, either, Leah thought. *Especially not without my husband and children.*

"Andrew said that if I left, it would have to be alone. He would not allow me to take our children." Cora's eyes pooled with tears, and when Leah handed her a tissue, she wiped her eyes and blew her nose.

"I thought I could stick it out, for my children's sake, but I guess my selfish desires got in the way of sensible thinking. So one day when Andrew took the children for ice cream, I packed my bags, left a note, and called our driver for a ride to the nearest bus station."

"Where did you go?" Leah asked, still reeling with shock.

"Chicago. I found a job as a waitress in a small café and saved up my money until I had enough to begin my nurse's training. Soon after that, I met Evan. When we fell in love, I divorced Andrew and married Evan." Cora grimaced. "Of course, when I left the Amish faith, I was shunned, and I knew the stand the Amish take against divorce."

"It's biblical," Leah reminded.

"I know."

"How old were the children when you left?"

"Mary was eight and Adam was five."

"Did you ever go back to see them?"

Cora's head jerked as though she'd been slapped. "I tried to, but when I returned to our home in Pennsylvania, Andrew and the children were gone. They'd packed up and moved, and no one would tell me where." Cora sniffed deeply. "I'll probably never see Mary or Adam again. I can only imagine how Andrew has poisoned them against me, and I can't really blame him. Looking back, I realize I was a terrible mother." She paused to wipe away more tears. "I've lived a life full of bitter regrets and tried to hide it by focusing on my life in the English world. But, of course, I've messed that up, too."

Leah hardly knew what to say. She'd liked Cora from their first meeting and thought she was a nice person. Now having learned all this about her past, Leah's heart was torn. She felt sorry for Cora, knowing it must have been hard not seeing her son and daughter all these years, but at the same time, wasn't that punishment well deserved for abandoning her family? Leah knew from something Elaine had shared with her that Adam had told Ben that his mother had abandoned him and his sister when they were small children. It had to be more than a coincidence that Cora's children had the same names as Adam and his sister. Surely, this woman must be Adam's mother.

Should I say something to Cora? No, I need to wait until I've talked with Adam. Tomorrow was Saturday, so she wouldn't be watching the girls. Adam planned to take them all out to supper that evening, including Leah, so she would speak to him about this then. Perhaps Adam would want to meet Cora right away, to confirm that she really was his mother.

CHAPTER 32

All day Saturday Leah had trouble concentrating, and by five o'clock that evening she was a ball of nerves. Adam and the girls would be coming by any minute to pick her up for supper. Tonight, when the opportunity arose, she would ask Adam about his mother.

Leah wished her own mother were home already so she could ask her opinion, but Mom wouldn't be coming home until early next week.

The one thing I do know, Leah told herself, *is that I shouldn't say anything about Cora in front of the children. A topic as sensitive as this must be raised to Adam alone.*

At the sound of a horse and buggy approaching, Leah peered out the kitchen window. *Maybe when Adam brings me home this evening I will get the chance. I'll let Adam know that I want to talk to him about something and suggest that the girls go inside and visit with Dad for a few minutes so we can talk privately.*

Watching as Adam's horse pulled his rig up the driveway, Leah's heart began to pound. She'd been looking forward to this evening until Cora had shared her story about abandoning her children. Now Leah looked on the evening with dread. How would everyone be affected by what she'd just learned? If Cora was Adam's mother, would a reunion be sweet, or could it go the wrong way? Would Adam accept his mother into his life again, or would he reject her? If Cora really was his mother, Adam had a stepbrother he knew nothing about. And poor Cora wasn't even aware that her daughter had been killed in a tragic accident. She also didn't know she had three precious granddaughters. And how would Jared feel, knowing he had an older brother who was Amish?

So many things hung by a thread, depending on what Adam said once she told him about Cora. Of course, it wasn't certain that Cora was his mother, but there were too many things that fit for it to be coincidental.

For the girls' sake, Leah would try to relax during supper and show them a good time. Since she and Adam would be getting married in two weeks, tonight was an opportunity for them to do something fun together as the family they would soon become.

"Leah, you're awfully quiet tonight, and you haven't eaten much of your pizza." Adam motioned to Leah's plate.

"Maybe she don't like plain sauce and cheese pizza," Linda said before Leah could respond.

Leah shook her head. "No, it's not that. Guess I'm just not real hungry."

"How come?" This question came from Amy, who'd been more talkative than usual this evening.

Leah reached over and patted Amy's hand. "I have a lot on my mind."

"I have a lot on my mind, too," Adam put in, "but it won't stop me from eating." He grabbed another piece of pizza and took a big bite, wiggling his eyebrows as he did so.

Carrie snickered and jiggled her eyebrows back at him.

"What's on your mind, Leah?" Amy prompted. "Are you thinking about the wedding?"

Leah shifted in her chair, searching for words that wouldn't be a lie. "That is one thing I've been thinking about." She picked up a slice of pizza and took a bite. "Guess maybe I should quit thinking so much and finish what's on my plate."

Carrie looked over at Leah and smiled. "I'm glad you're here."

Leah leaned over and gave Carrie a hug. "So am I." She felt so much love for Adam's nieces. That, in itself, made her look forward to becoming his wife. She just hoped things went well when Adam took her back to the house this evening and they had their little talk. If he didn't like what she said, would he call off the wedding?

∞

"How are you feeling, Sara?" Jonah asked, his face a mask of concern. "I saw you wince. Are you in pain?"

"I'm having some cramping and lower back pains." She forced a smile. "This is how it went before Mark was born, so I'm pretty sure my labor has started."

"But you still have a few weeks to go. Do you think something is wrong?"

"Everything is all right, Jonah." Sara almost felt sorry for her husband as she watched him begin to pace. "It's quite normal if a baby is born a little early, or even a few weeks late, especially if the calculations are a little bit off."

Jonah's eyes widened. "Then we'd better take Mark to my parents' house and get you to the hospital right away."

She shook her head. "Not yet, Jonah, and don't look so worried. My pains aren't close enough yet. I'll let you know when, so just try and relax." Sara had to remind herself that this was a first for Jonah. She remembered how nervous Harley had been when she was in labor with Mark.

"I think I should at least take Mark over to my mamm and daed's place so when it's time to head to the hospital, we can just go there directly."

"Okay, whatever you think is best. I'll pack the things Mark will need to spend the night, and then you can deliver him right to their door."

"Maybe I should pack his things so you can rest," Jonah was quick to say.

She waved her hand. "There's no need for me to rest, Jonah. In fact, I'm going to walk around for a bit and see if I can get things moving along a little quicker."

He slipped his arm around her waist. "Now, don't get too carried away. I don't want you having the boppli while I'm gone."

"Your folks don't live that far away, and I don't think you'll be gone that long."

His cheeks and the back of his neck colored as he grinned

sheepishly at her. "You're right. I'm feeling kind of *naerfich* right now. Guess I'm not thinking straight."

She squeezed his arm. "There's nothing to be nervous about. Women have been having babies since Eve gave birth to Cain and Abel."

Jonah bent to kiss her cheek. "Jah, I know. But you're having *our* baby."

Smiling, Sara started down the hall for Mark's room, where he'd gone to play after supper. She was sure he'd be excited to know that he would be spending the night with Jonah's folks. Since they'd moved here from Pennsylvania and been able to see them quite often, Mark had become very fond of them.

As Sara neared the door of her son's room, she paused to pray. *Dear Lord, please help me have a safe delivery, and may this little one who's about to be born be healthy and a blessing to You throughout his or her life.*

"I hope you don't mind, but I'd like to speak to you alone for a few minutes before you go home," Leah whispered to Adam when he pulled his horse up to the hitching rack near her father's barn. "The girls can go inside and visit with my daed while we sit on the porch and talk."

Adam's eyebrows squished together. "You want to sit outside and talk? Don't you think it's a little chilly for that?"

"No, not really, but if you'd rather, we can sit here in the buggy."

Adam couldn't imagine what Leah had to say that couldn't be said in front of the girls, but whatever it was he figured he ought to hear it. He hoped she hadn't changed her mind about marrying him. Besides the embarrassment of having to call off their wedding, if Leah backed out, he'd be left with the full responsibility of raising Mary's girls. He'd already tried that and hadn't done so well.

"Adam, did you hear what I said?" Leah touched his arm.

He nodded. "Jah. If you want to take the girls inside, I'll wait here in the buggy so we can talk."

Leah climbed down, helped the children out, and then led them to the house. As Adam waited for her to return, he became even more apprehensive. *The girls will be so disappointed if Leah and I don't get married. They're all excited about having her move into our house, and I'll have to admit, I'm looking forward to it, as well.*

With regret, Adam realized that with the exception of his three nieces, he wouldn't have any family members at the wedding—assuming it took place.

Adam wished his father had lived long enough to really get to know his granddaughters. He was sure they would have loved him as much as Adam had. For a man to be both father and mother to his children had been no small feat, but somehow his dad had accomplished it. Adam wondered if Dad had ever wished he could have gotten married again after Adam's mother left and filed for a divorce. But that was not to be, because unless Adam's mother had died, Adam's father would not have been free to remarry.

I wonder if my mother is still alive. If so, has she ever thought of me and Mary? Adam's jaw clenched. *If she was selfish enough to walk out on her family, she probably never gave us a second thought.*

Startled out of his musings, Adam's head jerked when Leah stepped into the buggy and took a seat beside him. "Oh, you're back."

"Jah, and the girls seemed happy to visit with my daed. He's been working on a puzzle and asked them to help."

"That's good. Now what did you want to talk to me about?"

Leah cleared her throat. "Well, I've been wondering about something."

"What's that?"

"You have talked about your daed and how much you miss him, but you've never really mentioned your mamm."

A muscle on the back of Adam's neck knotted. "I don't talk about her because there is nothing to say. She walked out on me and Mary when we were kids, and we never saw or heard from her again."

"Jah, I know about that."

He quirked an eyebrow. "You knew before I said anything?"

Leah nodded. "Elaine told me."

"Elaine? How'd she find out about it?"

"Well, I think—"

Adam held up his hand. "No, don't tell me. It had to be Ben. He's the only one I've ever told about my past." He frowned. "Guess I should have known better than to trust him to keep my secret."

"If Ben told Elaine after you'd asked him not to say anything, then that was wrong," Leah said. "But when Elaine told me, she thought I already knew."

Feeling a headache coming on, Adam rubbed his temples. He couldn't help wondering how many other people Ben had told. If he didn't nip this in the bud, it wouldn't be long before everyone in their community knew about his past.

"Do you know your mother's first name?" Leah asked.

"She was always Mom to me, but when I asked Dad what her first name was, he said it was Cora." Adam looked over at Leah and blinked. With only the light of the moon shining into the buggy, he couldn't see her expression, but he heard her gasp. "Where's this conversation leading, anyway, and why'd you inhale so sharply?"

"What is your daed's name?"

"His name was Andrew. Why do you ask?"

"I think I might know your mother."

A cold chill swept over Adam. "What do you mean? And where and when did you meet this woman you think is my mother?"

"She lives here in Arthur."

Adam shook his head vigorously. "No she doesn't. If she did, I would know."

"She moved here recently." Leah placed her hand on his trembling arm. "After all these years, I don't think you would recognize her, Adam. I'm sure she wouldn't know you, either, since you were just a boy when she left. Besides, in your memory she wore Amish clothes. Now, she's every bit English."

"How do you know her? Did she talk to you? Where did you meet?" Adam's sentences were running together, as his mind whirled.

"Her name is Cora, and she's a nurse at the clinic. We met the day I took Carrie in after she'd been stung by those yellow jackets. I found out later that it was her first day working at the clinic."

"You met this woman you think is my mother that long ago and have never said anything to me about it till now?" Adam flexed his fingers until they bit into his palms.

"I didn't know who she was then, Adam. And you have never told me anything about your mother. It wasn't until she started coming to me for foot treatments that she started to open up about her recent divorce from her husband who's a doctor and lives in Chicago." Leah paused and drew in a quick breath. "When Cora saw me last evening for a foot treatment, she blurted things out about her past. It really took me by surprise when she said she used to be Amish but had left her husband and two small children to pursue a career in nursing."

Adam moaned as he leaned forward, letting his head fall into his outstretched hands. He remembered Dad telling him that his mother used to say working on people's feet wasn't gratifying enough—that she wanted to be a nurse. But he hadn't thought about that until now. What he also remembered was his mother massaging and pressing on his and Mary's feet, which she'd done the night before she left. That memory had left Adam with a sense of bitterness toward reflexology. He'd always associated it with something bad—something that had left him and Mary motherless.

Adam lifted his head. "Does the woman know about me—that I live here in Arthur?" he asked, wanting to know the answer, yet hoping Leah would say no.

"I did not mention your name. I wanted to talk to you about this first."

He sighed with relief. "That's good to hear."

"Adam, there's more." Leah placed her hand on his tense shoulder.

He turned to face her, wanting to hear what she had to say but at the same time dreading it.

"Cora said she had two children—a girl named Mary and a boy named Adam—and that she had tried to—"

"I don't want to hear any more!" White-hot anger rolled through every part of Adam's body, nearly scorching his soul. "If you talk to this woman again, please tell her to leave, because I never want to see her. Is that clear?"

Leah remained quiet.

"Leah, is that clear?" he repeated.

"Jah," she murmured. "But, Adam, I think maybe—"

"And you are not to mention anything to that woman about Carrie, Linda, or Amy. I don't want her anywhere near my nieces!"

CHAPTER 33

Leah sat on the edge of her bed that night, looking in the Bible for answers to her dilemma. It would be difficult not to tell Cora about Adam when she saw her again. But she couldn't do that without going against Adam's wishes. And if she told Cora about Adam and he found out, he'd be furious. This was not a good way to start a marriage.

Of course, Leah reasoned, *we're not starting it out the way most Amish couples do. The people I know who've gotten married were deeply in love.*

Leah swallowed hard. She never thought she would admit this, not even to herself, but until last night when she'd heard the anger and bitterness in his voice, she'd thought she might be falling in love with Adam. But since he didn't feel that way toward her and seemed unable to get past his resentment of Cora, Leah would hold her feelings inside. Adam would never know that she'd begun to have strong feelings for him. She must learn to be content as his wife in name only. For now it was enough to be a mother figure to his precious nieces.

Turning to a verse she'd marked in her Bible some time ago, Leah read James 1:5 aloud: "If any of you lack wisdom, let him ask of God, that giveth to all men liberally, and upbraideth not; and it shall be given him."

Knowing that it wasn't her place to tell Cora about Adam, she closed her eyes and prayed. *I need Your wisdom right now, Lord. Please help me keep my promise to Adam.* Leah paused, as another thought entered her mind. *And please soften Adam's heart so that he will willingly speak to his mamm.*

Basking in the glow of motherhood, Sara gazed at the precious baby in her arms. "What shall we name her, Jonah?"

With a look of pure joy, Jonah stared at their infant daughter, born just an hour after they'd arrived at the hospital. "I don't know, Sara. What would you like to name her?"

"I was thinking we could call her Martha Jean. Her first name would be after my mamm, and her middle name in honor of my good friend Jean Mast."

Jonah grinned. "That's a good idea. I'm glad you thought of it, and I'm sure those two ladies will be pleased."

"I had thought about using your mamm's name, but it might be a bit confusing with two *Sara*s in the family already, even if your mamm's name is spelled a bit different than mine."

"You're right, and I'm sure Mom won't have a problem with you choosing your mother's name." Jonah stroked the baby's cheek with his thumb. "I can't wait to see the look on my folks' faces when they see their new granddaughter for the first time."

Sara nodded. "I'm excited for my parents to meet Martha Jean, too. But since they live in Indiana and Dad might be busy with his business right now, it could be a few weeks before they can come here."

Jonah laughed. "From what I've come to know of your mamm, I'm guessing the minute she hears the news, she'll be packing her bags. I bet she'll want to be here to help out for a while, too."

"You're probably right." Sara sighed, rubbing her cheek against their daughter's downy head. "I can't believe the way God has blessed us, Jonah. It almost seems too good to be true."

Jonah clasped Sara's hand and gave her fingers a gentle squeeze. "It is true. We are blessed beyond measure, and I am so thankful."

Sara gently kissed the baby's forehead, amazed at the infant's dark wavy hair, a trait she'd inherited from her father. Sara could hardly wait to take Martha Jean home to meet her big brother. They were now a family of four.

Adam punched his pillow, rolling this way and that, unable to find a comfortable position. He'd gone to bed over an hour ago, but sleep would not come. He couldn't stop thinking about the things Leah had told him. It didn't seem possible that his mother was living right here in Arthur or that she'd been seeing Leah for foot treatments.

Maybe it really isn't her. But Leah said the woman's husband was named Andrew, and her kids were Mary and Adam, so it must be her. Sure don't know what I'd do if I came face-to-face with that woman, Adam fumed. *Of course, like Leah said, I probably wouldn't recognize her, nor would she know me. She could have come into the hardware store already, and I'd never have known it. This lady doesn't even know her own daughter has died. Wonder how she would feel about that.*

It was hard to refer to Cora as Mom, because she surely hadn't been a mother to him and his sister. Adam was almost glad Mary was safe in heaven and didn't have to deal with this unsettling news. *If Mary were still alive, what would she do?* he wondered. *Would she want to see this woman?*

When they were growing up, that was one subject Adam and his sister never really discussed. Oh, they'd talked about their mother leaving when it first happened, but as time went on, her name was hardly ever mentioned. And Adam had never asked Mary what she would do if their mom came back.

Why'd Cora come here, anyway, and why now? He continued to stew. *I should've thought to ask Leah that question. If I get the chance, I'll talk more to Leah about this after church tomorrow morning.*

Adam sat up, throwing his legs over the side of the bed. It was no use. He wasn't going to fall asleep anytime soon. Just that quick, he flopped back down on the mattress, covering his face with his hands. Why did this have to happen now, when everything with his nieces and with Leah had been falling into place? *Would this alter their wedding plans?*

Spreading his fingers and then clutching the sheets, he stared at the ceiling. *This is going to change everything. I'll be looking over my shoulder everywhere I go, wondering if Cora is near.*

Adam's thoughts took him back to his childhood. He remembered how hard it was going to school programs and seeing the other kids who had both parents in attendance. Adam had felt left out because he didn't have a mother like the other scholars. Some mothers would bring a hot lunch to school for everyone, while others brought cookies or some special dessert at certain times. One of their neighbors who sometimes watched Mary and him while Dad was working came to school a couple times with treats, but she wasn't their mother, so that didn't count.

Knowing he wouldn't be able to sleep and sick of reliving the past, Adam pushed himself back up. After slipping into his trousers, and pulling on a shirt, he quietly left the room, using a flashlight as his guide.

When Adam entered the kitchen, he turned on the gas lamp hanging above the table. If he were here by himself, he might have gone to the store, even though it was the middle of the night. There were certainly enough things to do to keep him busy. A new shipment of winter items had arrived, including snow shovels, salt pellets for driveways, more birdseed, suet cakes, and feeders, and they needed to be set out. Working might help take his mind off Cora, but with the girls sleeping upstairs, he couldn't leave them alone.

Maybe if I eat something I'll feel better and quit thinking so much. Adam opened the refrigerator and looked around. Nothing in there really appealed, until he spotted a chocolate-chip cheeseball Leah had made the other day and left for him and the kids to enjoy. He took it out, as well as a container of milk, grabbed a box of graham crackers, and took a seat at the table.

As Adam ate his snack, he thought of Leah. She was a good cook, kept the house clean, and was great with the girls. She was also kind and had a pretty face. He'd begun to have strong feelings for her, although he'd kept them to himself. But could she be trusted to keep her word and not tell Cora about him?

"The practice of reflexology is a complete waste of time," Andrew hollered as Cora stood at the sink peeling potatoes for supper. "And your idea of becoming a nurse is just plain lecherich!"

"It's not ridiculous," she countered. "It's what I've always wanted—even when I was a girl. I need to help others, and I want to be a nurse. What's wrong with that?"

"Then you should not have joined the church or married me." Andrew's face grew redder with each word he spoke, and Cora flinched when he shook his finger at her. "You can help within our community if you have this need."

"It's not the same, Andrew," she argued. "I could do things as a nurse that I can't do here."

"I won't allow you to talk like this in my house where the kinner could hear. What kind of example are you setting for them?"

Tears flooded Cora's eyes and dribbled down her cheeks. She hated it when she and Andrew had words, and when he shouted at her like this, it made her feel like packing her bags and running away to someplace where she could never be found. She didn't understand why Andrew wouldn't give up his life here and go English so she could follow her dream. But they'd had this conversation before, and Andrew always remained firm. He was not going to back down on his vow to God and the church, and he did not want Cora to, either. She'd have to stay here and forget about nursing or leave without him. Perhaps if she left, he'd change his mind and follow. It would be a test of Andrew's love for her.

At that moment, Cora decided. Tomorrow when Andrew took the kids to town for ice cream, she would make some excuse not to go along. While they were away, she'd pack her bags, and by the time they returned home, she would be gone.

Drenched in sweat, Cora cried out as her eyes snapped open. She bolted upright in bed. She'd been trapped in a recurring dream about events that had actually happened to her. She felt as though she couldn't breathe.

Pushing the covers aside, Cora climbed out of bed and quickly opened the window. As a cool November breeze wafted in, she gulped in several deep breaths. *I should never have told Leah about having once been Amish and abandoning my husband and children. She must think I'm an awful person, and probably talking about my past has brought on this nightmare.*

Tap. Tap. Tap. "You okay over there, Mom?" Jared's muffled voice could be heard between the walls that separated their bedrooms. "I heard you scream."

"I'm fine, son," Cora muttered. "Just had a bad dream."

Holding her arms tightly against her chest, Cora gave in to the threatening tears. She'd done a terrible thing by abandoning her children, but she couldn't undo the past. Unless some twist of fate should occur, it wasn't likely that she'd ever see Adam or Mary again. But if somehow she did, she would apologize and beg their forgiveness.

CHAPTER 34

How come you're not dressed for church?" Leah's father asked when she placed a cup of coffee in his hand the following morning.

She blinked against the harsh sunlight streaming into the kitchen. "I have a pounding koppweh, so as soon as I fix your breakfast, I'm going back to bed."

Dad's forehead wrinkled as he looked at Leah with obvious concern. "Are you grank? Maybe you've come down with the flu."

She shook her head slowly, so as not to aggravate the pain. "I'm not sick. It's just a bad headache. I don't think I got enough sleep last night, either."

"Maybe you're stressed out about the wedding next week." Dad set his coffee cup down and motioned for Leah to take a seat. "Are you sure you want to go through with this, Daughter? I mean, your decision to marry Adam was awfully sudden."

"It's not about the wedding." Leah poured herself a cup of coffee and sat in the chair across from Dad. She wished she felt free to tell him about Adam's mother. If she broke her promise to Adam and told Dad, he'd probably tell Mom when she got home tomorrow evening. And if Mom knew about it, she would no doubt tell someone else, because Mom had never been one to keep a secret.

"If it's not about the wedding, then why'd you have trouble sleeping?" Dad asked.

"Some nights are like that, I guess." Leah massaged her forehead, thinking if she gave herself a foot treatment it might help. "I'm afraid if I go to church today, my koppweh will turn into a sick headache, and I may throw up. Now wouldn't that be an embarrassing thing to do in the middle of church?"

Dad gave Leah an understanding nod. "Then you'd better go back to bed and take care of yourself. And don't worry about fixing breakfast. I'm perfectly able to make something for myself."

Leah felt relieved. As much as she'd looked forward to seeing Adam and the girls this morning, she needed to return to her darkened room and try to sleep off this headache.

Adam had a hard time concentrating on the church service, knowing Leah wasn't there. Had she been so upset by what he'd said to her last night that she'd stayed home from church in order to avoid him? Or could Leah have come down with something and be sick in bed? He could hardly wait until church was over so he could talk to Leah's father and find out.

Adam glanced over at Amy, Linda, and Carrie. Usually they sat with Leah, but since she wasn't here today, Adam had asked Elaine to sit with them. They seemed to be doing fine, for which he was glad. When snacks were given out to the younger ones, Carrie appeared to be quite content. Adam was thankful that Leah had good friends like Elaine and Priscilla. She'd told him once that they would be there for her if she had any need. They'd both been willing to be Leah's witnesses at their wedding, just as Ben and Elam had agreed to be Adam's. It should work out well, since Ben had been seeing Elaine, and Elam was courting Priscilla. He figured it wouldn't be long before both couples would be getting married.

Maybe we can all be friends and do some fun things together, Adam thought, letting his mind wander even further from the sermon that was being preached. Since he and Leah would be getting married, Adam figured it would be good for him to establish a few friendships.

Thinking more about the conversation he'd had with Leah about his mother, Adam wondered just how much Leah knew about Cora. He'd been so upset by the news that she was in the area that he hadn't let Leah finish telling him everything.

Sure wish I hadn't told Ben anything about my childhood. I'll need to speak with him about that after church.

Sometime later, Adam was roused from his musings when all the men around him stood. Church was obviously over, and he'd missed nearly all of it.

Not a very upright, Christian thing to do, Adam thought as he made his way out of Marcus Gingerich's barn. *I should have been paying attention, and I probably missed out on a timely sermon.*

"I'll keep the girls with me until you're ready to go home," Elaine told Adam as the men began to set up tables for their noon meal.

"Danki. I'll probably leave as soon as we're done eating. I want to drop by Leah's and find out why she didn't make it to church today."

"I've been wondering that myself." Elaine's voice tensed. "I hope she's okay. With your wedding coming up next week, she's been working too hard to get things ready. She may have worn herself out."

"You could be right. Leah's a hard worker and sometimes doesn't know when to stop and rest," Adam agreed. "She's taken on quite a bit in these last couple months."

"Hopefully after the two of you are married, she won't have quite so much to do. It's been difficult for her to watch the girls, keep up with everything at your place as well as her folks' house, and squeeze in time for her reflexology patients."

She won't be doing people's feet once we are married, Adam thought, but he didn't say anything to Elaine, because he didn't want her to tell Leah. Surely after they were married, Leah would understand his reasons for wanting her to quit practicing reflexology.

Seeing Leah's father on the other side of the barn, Adam excused himself. "I noticed that Leah's not with you today," he said, catching up with Alton. "Is she grank?"

Alton shook his head. "Said she wasn't sick—just woke up with a koppweh and didn't get enough sleep last night."

Adam frowned. "Sorry to hear that. If it's all right with you, I think I'll stop by after we're done eating and check up on her."

"I have no problem with that." Alton smiled. "If she's awake and feeling better, I'm sure Leah would appreciate seeing you."

Adam wondered if Leah's headache had anything to do with their discussion last night. Could Leah be as upset about Cora coming to town as he was?

"Hey, Adam, how's it going?" Ben asked, stepping up to Adam and thumping his shoulder.

"I was just going to come looking for you. Could we talk privately for a minute?"

"Sure, what's on your mind?"

"Let's go outside." Adam led the way and found a place on the other side of the yard where no one was at the moment. "Remember when I told you about my mamm running out on my daed when my sister and I were kinner?"

"Jah."

"I heard that you told Elaine about it, even after I asked you not to tell anyone."

Ben averted his gaze. "I'm sorry about that, Adam. Elaine and I were discussing you and Leah getting married, and it just sort of came out. I don't think Elaine will blab it to anyone though."

Adam's muscles tensed. "She already has. I found out last night that she told Leah."

Ben sighed and rubbed his chin. "Isn't Leah supposed to know? I mean, she'll be your *fraa* soon, and—"

"I never saw the need to tell her until last night. Then I found out she already knew." Adam wasn't about to tell Ben that Leah had said his mother was in the area. If he knew that, too, he'd probably tell Elaine and maybe some others. From this point on, Adam would be careful what he told Ben, and it sure wouldn't be anything about his personal life.

"It's about time you got up," Cora snapped when Jared made an appearance at noon. "What were you planning to do—sleep all day?"

Jared yawned and stretched his arms over his head. "Cut me some slack, Mom. You're getting yourself all worked up for nothing."

Cora's jaw clenched. "Don't talk to me like that, young man. I'm your mother, not one of your friends."

"Sorry," he muttered, while sauntering over to the refrigerator. Pulling out a carton of milk, he drank right out of the container and then flopped into a seat at the table.

Cora rolled her eyes. What had happened to the manners she'd taught her son? "Jared! Don't drink from the carton. How many times have I told you that?"

"You don't have to get so bent outta shape, Mom." Jared smirked. "There was hardly any milk left. See." He turned the carton upside down, and only a few drops dripped onto the table.

"It's still an unsanitary habit, and I wish you wouldn't do that."

"Thought I was saving you a glass to wash." Jared sauntered across the room and threw the empty milk carton away.

"Would you like me to fix you a piece of toast?" she asked, lowering her voice in the hope that she and Jared could have a sensible conversation for a change.

He shook his head. "Naw, I'm not that hungry. I'll just get some more milk and head back to my room."

"Please drink it from a glass this time."

"Yeah, okay. . .whatever."

Cora bit the inside of her cheek. If Jared hid out in his room all day, she'd be sitting here alone with nothing to do but feel sorry for herself. "I thought the two of us could go for a ride. Then maybe we can stop somewhere for a bite to eat."

Jared looked at Cora as if she'd lost her mind. "What's the big deal in going for a ride? That sounds really boring."

"Well, I just thought—"

"Scott and I planned on doing something today."

"Like what?"

Jared shrugged. "We're just gonna hang out."

Cora shook her head. "I don't think so, Jared. You saw Scott yesterday, and today is going to be our family day."

"Family day?" Jared jammed his hands into his jeans pockets. "We ain't no family anymore, Mom. Not since you made Dad leave."

Anger bubbled in Cora's chest. "I did not *make* your father leave! He's the one who wanted a divorce so he could marry someone else."

Jared finished the rest of his milk and set his glass in the sink. "I don't blame Dad for leaving. Listening to you yammering away all the time would make any man leave."

Cora's hand shook as she pointed at Jared. "Now, you listen to me young man, your dad left because—"

"I don't wanna hear it, and I'm getting sick of you bad-mouthing Dad all the time!" Jared tromped across the room, opened the back door, and stepped outside, slamming the door behind him.

Tears streaming down her cheeks, Cora sank into a chair and sobbed. She was almost at the end of her rope. Would things ever be right between her and Jared again? The other night, she had felt good about the decisions she'd made. But now, Cora wasn't so sure. Had she made a huge mistake leaving Chicago? Should she give up and move back or keep trying to make a go of things here?

CHAPTER 35

"Leah, are you up?" Dad called from the hall outside Leah's bedroom.

"Jah, Dad, I'm out of bed," she responded. "Just putting my head covering in place."

"That's good, because Adam is here with the girls, and if you're feeling up to it, they'd like to visit with you awhile."

"My koppweh is better. Tell them I'll be down in a few minutes."

"Okay."

It pleased Leah that Adam cared enough to come by. Perhaps he had missed seeing her at church and stopped on his way home to check on her. She took one last look at herself in the mirror to be sure her covering was on straight and that no stray hairs stuck out. After smoothing the wrinkles from her dress, she hurried from the room.

Downstairs, she found Adam and the girls in the living room, visiting with Dad.

"We missed you at church," Adam said, rising from his seat on the couch. "Your daed said you stayed home because of a koppweh, so we decided to drop by and see how you're feeling."

As Adam moved closer to Leah, she could see such a look of concern in his eyes that it made her wonder if he might feel something more for her than friendship. *Don't be ridiculous*, she chided herself. *If Adam cared for me in a romantic sort of way, I'm sure he'd have said so by now.*

"I'm doing better," she said, smiling up at him. "A couple aspirin and a few hours' rest in a darkened room cured the headache."

"Glad to hear it." Adam motioned to the door. "Do you feel up to going for a walk? There's something I'd like to talk to you about."

Leah glanced at the girls, and seeing that they were occupied with some of her childhood books Dad had given them to look at, she said,

"That would be fine, Adam."

Leah slipped her shawl over her shoulders and followed Adam out the door. Then, taking a seat in one of the wicker chairs, she turned to him and said, "What did you wish to talk about?"

Looking more than a little nervous, Adam lowered himself into the chair beside Leah's. "Umm. . .guess here is fine for us to talk."

"Oh, I'm sorry. You wanted to take a walk, didn't you?" Leah couldn't believe she'd forgotten that. *I must be as nervous as Adam appears to be.*

"That's okay. We can talk here just as easy. It concerns my mother."

Leah waited quietly for him to continue, sensing that he was having a difficult time talking about this sensitive subject.

Adam clasped his fingers together and flexed them as he stretched his arms out. "I've been wondering why Cora came here to Arthur."

"She's recently gone through a divorce and was looking for a new start."

Adam snorted, as he tapped his foot against the floor of the porch. "Another divorce, huh? Why am I not surprised by that? If I could just find some way to get that woman to leave town, I'd feel a whole lot better."

Leah gulped. She wasn't sure how that could happen. With Cora working at the clinic, it wasn't likely that she'd quit her job and move. If she really was Adam's mother, then Leah wished Cora and Adam could meet and find healing from the past.

After Elaine finished eating at the Gingeriches', following their church service, she'd come right home and decided to rest, since she had no plans until the evening, when Ben would be coming over for a visit. Before lying down, however, she took out the rock she'd painted for Leah to see how it looked now that the paint had dried.

Painting rocks had always been a relaxing diversion for her, especially when she needed a break from her everyday routine. It was fun to see the transformation of an ordinary stone as it turned into something unique and pretty.

Elaine had found this particular stone among her collection of rocks she hoped to paint someday. It was one she hadn't really noticed before, but after looking at it closely, she realized the stone would be perfect for Leah. Along with the quilted pot holders and table runner she planned to give Leah and Adam for their wedding, the rock would be something special just for Leah—a gift from one good friend to another. It was because of her friend's interest in hummingbirds that Elaine had painted this unusually shaped rock. It was similar to the shape of a hummingbird. Even the piece that had been broken off left enough of the stone to resemble a beak. The rest of the rock was in the shape of outstretched wings, looking like most hummingbirds taking flight.

Thumbing through some magazines, Elaine had found a picture of a ruby-throated hummingbird, which she used as a guide for painting. It was nearly done, except for the hummingbird's red throat, which she would work on tomorrow.

Reclining on the living-room couch, Elaine let her thoughts drift. She thought about how busy she kept hosting dinners since Grandma died and how little time she had to herself these days. Although Elaine enjoyed having the tourists come to her home for a meal, it was nice having some time off to relax.

Elaine's thoughts continued as she reflected on all the memories she'd accumulated in this stately old house. Even the backyard, where her favorite swing still hung, held pleasant memories. Elaine had enjoyed that swing during her childhood, as well as during her teenage and young-adult years. Many times she'd dreamed there of a future with a wonderful man and children.

Her mind drifted back to a special night when she'd been sitting on the porch with Jonah, gazing at a beautiful sunset that had taken her breath away. Even after all this time, Elaine couldn't help thinking how different her life would be now if she had said yes to Jonah's proposal.

Today in church, she had overheard someone say that on Friday night Sara had given birth to a baby girl. If Elaine had said yes to Jonah that evening, perhaps she might have had Jonah's baby by now.

This isn't right, Elaine scolded herself. *I should not be thinking such thoughts. Jonah is happily married, and he's the father of a brand-new baby.*

He will never know how badly I'd wanted to say yes to his proposal that night. The timing just wasn't right.

Shaking her head to clear her thoughts, Elaine got up from the couch. *Things happen for a reason, and maybe it wasn't meant to be. Besides, now that Ben is in my life, I should be happy about that and enjoy his friendship.*

"Take it slow and easy now, Sara," Jonah cautioned when they entered the house. Sara clutched his arm as he carried their baby girl.

"I'm fine. Just feeling the need to sit while we introduce Mark and your folks to the newest addition in our family."

As soon as they stepped into the house, they were greeted by Jonah's mother. "Oh, let me have a look at that baby." Tears welled in Mom's eyes as she touched the baby's downy head. "How are you feeling, Sara?" she asked.

"I'm a little weak and shaky, but I guess that's to be expected," Sara replied.

"Go on into the living room and take a seat," Mom instructed. "Mark's in there with his grandpa, and I know they'll be excited to see you."

After Jonah saw that Sara was situated on the couch, he placed the baby in her arms and invited his dad and little Mark to come take a look.

"She's a nice-looking girl." Dad smiled down at the baby.

Sara motioned to Mark. "Come over here and meet your little sister."

With a dubious expression, he inched his way over to the couch. "Boppli?"

Sara nodded. "Her name is Martha Jean."

Mark reached out and touched the baby's small hand.

"I think he likes her." Jonah grinned.

"Of course he does. What's not to like?" Mom extended her hands. "May I hold her?"

"You sure can." After Mom took a seat in the rocker, Jonah picked up the baby and placed her in his mother's arms.

"When are your parents coming, Sara?" Mom asked as she began rocking the baby. "I'm sure they're as anxious to see this little girl as we've all been."

"I believe they'll be here by the end of the week." Sara yawned. "Excuse me. Guess I'm more tired than I thought."

"Why don't you go lie down in bed and rest awhile?" Jonah suggested. "You didn't get much sleep last night at the hospital, so a nap might be just what you need right now."

"You're right. Think I'll go rest for a bit. Bring the boppli to me if she gets fussy and needs to be fed." Sara rose from the couch and started across the room. She was almost to the door leading to the hallway when she let out a little gasp and fell to the floor.

"Sara!" Jonah shouted, dashing across the room, fear clutching his heart. Had she just gotten up too quickly, or was something else wrong?

CHAPTER 36

Sara's body was damp with perspiration, and her eyelids felt heavy, but she forced them open. "Wh–what happened?" she asked as Jonah's anxious expression came into view.

"When you were heading to our room to lie down, you fainted."

Feeling the familiar comfort of the pillow beneath her head and realizing that she was lying on her bed, Sara asked, "How did I get here?"

"I carried you." Using a damp washcloth, Jonah wiped the perspiration from her forehead. "You really gave us a scare."

"Where's the boppli?" Sara asked, rubbing her temples before trying to sit up.

Jonah put his hands on her shoulders and held her gently in place. "She's fine. My mamm's rocking her in the living room, and my daed's waiting to hear whether he should call 911 or not."

Sara shook her head. "There's no need for that. The doctor said I might feel a bit light-headed for a few days from a loss of blood, but I'm sure it's nothing to be concerned about. I probably got up too quickly and should have asked for some assistance instead of trying to walk to the bedroom by myself. I'm so thankful I wasn't holding the baby when I fell."

Jonah's mother stepped into the room just then. "How is she, Jonah? Do we need to call for help?"

"I'm fine," Sara replied before Jonah could respond. "But I'm kind of hungerich."

"Of course." Jonah's mother gave her forehead a thump. "Don't know what I was thinking. I should have offered to fix you something to eat or drink as soon as you got home. Little Martha's sleeping in Raymond's arms right now, so I'll just run into the kitchen and fix you and Jonah some lunch." She hurried from the room.

"I'd really like the boppli here with me," Sara said, looking up at Jonah. "She might wake up and need to be fed or have her *windel* changed."

"I'll get her." Jonah leaned over and kissed Sara's cheek. "Now please stay put and just rest."

When Jonah left the room, Sara closed her eyes and lifted a silent prayer. *Heavenly Father, please help me get my strength back soon so I can take good care of my family.*

An hour after Adam and the girls left, Leah heard Sparky barking. She had just let the dog out. "What in the world has that pooch so worked up?" She glanced out the living-room window and saw a car pull in. Normally, her dog was pretty docile and rarely barked when someone pulled into the driveway. Suddenly, Leah knew why Sparky was carrying on. She grinned, surprised to see her mother get out of the passenger side of the vehicle.

"Wake up, Dad! Mom's home!" Leah called.

Roused from his nap on the couch, Dad bolted upright. "Really?"

Leah nodded. "She just got out of her driver's car."

Dad clambered to his feet and hurried out the door. Leah was right behind him, struggling not to laugh at the way his hair stood up. Any other time, she was sure he would have taken the time to comb it, but he was obviously so excited to see his wife that he hadn't given a thought to the way his hair looked.

Though Mom and Dad rarely hugged in front of Leah, not to mention with Mom's driver in plain view, Leah was pleasantly surprised to see her parents embrace. She giggled, watching Sparky trying to get Mom's attention as he jumped up and down, pawing at her dress. It was as if he had springs on his feet.

"It's been too long, and it's so good to be home," Mom said, while Dad patted her back.

Leah held back until Mom pulled away and Dad went around to retrieve her luggage. She gave Mom a hug. "This is such a surprise. We didn't expect you until sometime tomorrow."

Mom smiled, giving Leah's arm a tender squeeze. "I decided to leave a day sooner than planned because I wanted to be here to help with all those last-minute things that will need to be done before your wedding."

"I appreciate that. How's Aunt Grace doing?" Leah asked.

"She and the boppli are fine. You'd hardly know she's recently had a baby. Grace was up the next day, acting like everything was normal. I'm so glad I was there for the birth and was able to stay awhile to help out," Mom said. "You should have seen the look on James's face when the midwife announced that it was a boy."

"Now they have five sons." Dad grinned, while wiggling his brows. "What'd they name the baby?"

"They chose Paul." Mom smiled. "I know James had mentioned that he'd like a little girl this time, but that was all forgotten when they put baby Paul in his arms. No father looked more pleased."

"I don't know about that." Dad chuckled. "I was pleased as fruit punch when I held Nathan and Leah for the first time."

As if in protest of Mom's lack of attention, Sparky sat down and started barking. "Come here, you sweet pooch." Mom leaned down with outstretched arms. "I missed you, too."

Dad and Leah both laughed as Sparky bounded into Mom's arms, almost knocking her down. Mom chuckled when Sparky slurped her cheek. "I'm guessing that even our hund must have missed me."

Tears sprang to Leah's eyes. "Oh, Mom, I'm really glad you're home. Dad and I have both missed you so much. And you're right, so did Sparky. We never heard so much whining going on. From the minute you left, and then every day after, he'd go to the window or sit by the door, waiting and watching for you."

Mom put Sparky down, and after sniffing her luggage for a bit, the dog sat right down on Mom's feet. "You know what they say: 'Absence makes the heart grow—'"

"My heart couldn't be any fonder of you—even if you never went anywhere without me." Leah gave Mom another hug. She couldn't help thinking about Adam's mother and how she'd abandoned her children.

What an awful thing to do. "I really appreciate having you as my mamm. You've always been so good to me and Nathan, and I want you to know that I'm grateful for everything you and Dad have ever done for us."

Sparky barked, as if agreeing with what Leah had just said.

Mom smiled. "I appreciate you saying that, Leah, but it's our responsibility, as well as privilege, to love and nurture our kinner. Your daed and I have always been thankful that God blessed us with two special children. We love you and Nathan so much and want only the best for you."

"I know, Mom," Leah said with feeling.

Mom clasped Leah's hand. "Well let's get inside so I can hear all about what's been going on around here since I've been gone."

Leah wished she felt free to tell Mom and Dad about Adam's mother, but she was sure Adam wouldn't appreciate that.

Elaine was about to doze off when she heard a horse and buggy outside. Getting up and going to the window, she was surprised to see Ben's rig coming up the lane. *He's here early. Did I misunderstand when he said he'd be coming by this evening?*

Elaine hurried to the door.

"I know I'm here a few hours earlier than planned," Ben said when she greeted him, "but I didn't want to wait till this evening to talk to you."

Ben's somber expression caused Elaine to feel concern. "Is something wrong? You look anxious."

"Nothing's wrong, really. I just need to talk to you about something."

"Let's go into the kitchen. I'll fix us some tea or a cup of coffee."

"Coffee sounds good to me."

Elaine led the way, and after Ben removed his jacket and hat and took a seat at the table, she poured them both some coffee.

"Hey, that's nice." Ben pointed to the hummingbird rock she'd placed on the counter. "Did you make it?"

"As a matter of fact, I did, and it's nearly finished. What do you think?"

"I've never seen anything like it before. That rock looks like a picture of a hummingbird I saw in a magazine once."

Elaine smiled. "Funny you should say that. I actually used a picture in a magazine as a guide to paint it. I think the colors match pretty closely to what that kind of hummingbird looks like."

"Very nice, Elaine. You've done a good job on it."

"Danki. The rock is going to be something special for Leah. She gets such enjoyment watching the hummingbirds that come into their yard every year. I thought she'd like something like this."

"I'm sure she will. That was thoughtful of you."

"So, what did you want to talk to me about?" Elaine asked, handing Ben his cup and taking a seat across from him.

Ben blew on his coffee and took a sip. "Remember when I told you what Adam had shared with me about his mother running away from home when he was a boy?"

Elaine nodded soberly. "That must have been hard on Adam, as well as his sister and their daed."

"Jah." Ben drank some more coffee. "I can't imagine living through something like that."

"Me, neither. As difficult as it was to lose both of my parents when I was a girl, at least they were taken in death and didn't leave the way Adam's mamm did."

Ben fingered the quilted placemat in front of him. "Adam and I had a conversation after church today. He found out from Leah that I'd told you what he'd shared with me about his mamm. Honestly, Elaine, I didn't think you would say anything to Leah about that."

Elaine nearly choked on the coffee she'd just started to drink. "Ach! You didn't tell me I wasn't supposed to say anything. I thought Leah already knew. I assumed Adam had told her. Is he *umgerennt* with me?"

Ben shook his head. "I think he was more upset with me."

"How are we going to fix this?" Elaine asked. "Would it help if I talked to Adam?"

Ben shook his head. "I don't think so. Just, please, don't tell anyone else what you know about Adam's past." He leaned slightly forward. "You haven't, I hope."

"No," Elaine was quick to say, "and I surely won't." She leaned back in her chair with a groan. "This isn't going to affect Adam and Leah's marriage, I hope."

"I don't think so. Before Adam headed out to check on Leah, he said he'd see me at the wedding."

Elaine sighed with relief. Now all she had to be concerned about was whether Leah had made the right decision in agreeing to marry Adam for the sake of his nieces. Above all else, she wanted her friend to be happy and blessed.

"There's one more thing I wanted to say." Ben clasped Elaine's hand. "I've fallen in love with you, and I know we haven't been courting even a year yet, but I was wondering if you would do me the honor of becoming my wife."

Feeling a bit dazed, Elaine sat there, unable to answer his question. She cared for Ben, and he'd become a good friend, but she wasn't certain that what she felt for him was love. Without a deep, abiding love, she didn't see how she could say yes to his proposal. "You've taken me by surprise," she said breathlessly. "Could I have a few weeks to think about it?"

"Jah, of course." He stroked her hand tenderly. "Take all the time you need."

CHAPTER 37

When Cora got off work Monday afternoon, she felt more tired than usual. On top of that, her lower back hurt again. It made no sense, because working at the clinic was a lot easier than trekking up and down the long corridors at the hospital in Chicago. While she'd had some trouble with her back then, it was nothing like what she'd encountered since she and Jared had moved to Arthur. She wondered if these back spasms had more to do with her stress levels than with being on her feet so much. Even though Jared had made a friend since they'd moved here, he wasn't doing well in school, and his belligerent attitude toward Cora was more than she could take.

I wonder if Leah would be free this evening to give me another reflexology treatment, Cora thought as she approached her car. She slid into the driver's seat, pulled out her cell phone, and punched in Leah's number. *Hopefully Leah will check her answering machine and return my call before the evening is out. But just in case, I think I'll stop by there after supper and see if she's free to work on my feet.*

Cora started her car and pulled out of the parking lot. Before she headed for home, she needed to stop by the hardware store she passed on her way to work and pick up some lightbulbs and an extension cord. Besides the outlets for the stove and refrigerator, the home she'd been renting had only one other outlet in the kitchen. She was getting tired of unplugging the toaster or coffeepot in order to plug in the electric can opener and blender. Maybe she should look for a power strip, too. That might work well, especially in the kitchen. Cora remembered how, in Chicago, Evan had used a power strip in his garage, and he'd said that it even protected against power surges.

"Chicago? Why am I even thinking about that place?" Cora berated herself. For some reason, that city had been on her mind lately. She had thought moving to Arthur would be the right change for her, but was she, once again, only thinking of herself?

Maybe I should have discussed it more with Jared and opened up to him about how I was feeling. But if I had, would he have even cared or understood?

Cora knew the reason she hadn't. She was sure that Jared's response would have been negative. And what good could have come from her expressing how she felt about the divorce? At the time, Cora thought she was sparing Jared the ugly details and an explanation of why she felt the need to start over at a place where she could use her nursing skills the way she'd always felt called to do. She couldn't really tell Jared that she'd wanted to move in hopes that it would solve his behavioral issues. That would have made him angry and perhaps even more belligerent. Cora had hoped that by now Jared would have adjusted to their new surroundings. She certainly felt comfortable and at home here. It was much more laid back than living in Chicago, but then, what kid would find that important? It didn't seem to matter to Jared. He complained that there was nothing exciting to do. Having too much time on his hands could get Jared into trouble. She was pleased that he'd made a new friend but wondered what the boys did and where they went when they spent time together.

In any event, Cora wondered if going back to the city would be the best thing for Jared. At least then his father wouldn't have any excuse for not spending time with him.

Although not keen on the idea, Cora figured she could probably get her old job back at the hospital or perhaps find something else in her field in the city. She could take the house off the market, and things would go back to the way they were before she'd come up with the idea of starting over in a new place. The more she thought about it, the more sense it made. She hadn't received even one offer on the house, and since Jared had become increasingly rebellious since the move, what was the point in staying here? She just wished that God, if He cared about her at all, would give her some direction as to what she should do.

When Cora entered the hardware store, she wandered up and down the aisles for a bit, curious as to what was for sale. Since there were just gas lamps overhead, it didn't take long for her to realize this was an Amish-run store. She'd just begun to browse, when a tall Amish man came up to her and asked if she needed any help.

"I'm looking for an extension cord and some lightbulbs, and also wondered if you have any power strips. But since this an Amish store, you probably don't have any of those, right?"

The young man raked his fingers through the sides of his thick blond hair, while giving Cora a quick shake of his head. "We never carried the power strips, but we did have some lightbulbs and extension cords for our English customers. Unfortunately we're out of those right now. You should be able to get all of the things at the hardware store in downtown Arthur, or even at the grocery store."

"Thanks. I'll head over to one of those places right now." Cora hesitated a moment. There was something familiar about this Amish man, making Cora wonder if she'd met him before. But that wasn't likely, since this was her first visit to this store. Of course, he could have been a patient at the clinic, she supposed.

"Is there something else I can help you with?" he asked.

"Umm. . .no. Guess I'll be on my way."

As the man walked away, Cora felt even stronger that she'd met him before. His dark eyes and striking blond hair, reminded her of someone she used to know, but who? Well, she couldn't waste time thinking about it now. She needed to finish running her errand and get home to make sure Jared was there. Then as soon as they'd had supper, she would head over to Leah's and see if she had time to give her a reflexology treatment.

"Have you ever seen that woman who was just here?" Adam asked Ben, after he'd finished waiting on one of their regular customers.

"What woman was that?" Ben asked.

"The middle-aged English woman with short brown hair. She came in looking for lightbulbs and an extension cord and mentioned something about a power strip."

"Did you tell her we were out of those things and to go to the hardware store in downtown Arthur?"

"Jah, I did. Said she could probably find what she's looking for at the grocery store, too." Adam tapped his chin thoughtfully. "It was kind of odd, though. She looked at me so strangely. Made me feel uncomfortable."

"Maybe she's new around here and has never seen an Amish man before." Ben chuckled. "Some of the tourists who stop by the store can't seem to keep from staring at us."

Adam nodded. "I've often wondered how they would like it if we stared right back at them."

"Or started asking a bunch of questions about their lifestyle," Ben added.

Adam shrugged. "Guess they can't help being curious, since we dress differently than they do, not to mention our slower-paced mode of transportation." He thought about the English woman again and wondered if she could be his mother. Adam quickly pushed that thought aside. *If she is my mother, wouldn't she have said something? Of course, how would she have recognized me? I'm not the frightened little boy she left behind twenty-five years ago.*

"Get a hold of yourself," Adam murmured after walking away from Ben. "You can't go thinking every English woman you see is Cora."

Leah had just ridden her bike up her parents' driveway, when a car pulled in behind her. Turning, she saw that it was Cora. *I wonder what she wants.* Leah parked her bike and waited for Cora to get out of the car.

"I'm sorry for just showing up like this, but I wasn't sure whether you'd check for messages this evening," Cora said, joining Leah near the barn. "My back hurts again, and I was wondering if you'd be able to give me a foot treatment."

Since she was hungry and wasn't anxious to speak with Cora again,

Leah hesitated. But she could see from Cora's pinched expression that she was truly in pain. Leah hoped during the treatment that there would be no mention of Adam. "Okay. Let's go inside. You can head on downstairs, and I'll join you there shortly."

Sparky rushed over to greet Cora, like he did whenever they had visitors. Leah watched as Cora bent down to pet the terrier. "You're sure a cute little fellow," Cora said when Sparky licked her hand. "I wouldn't mind having a dog like you." Cora gave Sparky's head a pat, and he seemed content with that, for he went back to his spot on the porch and lay down.

As Cora descended the basement stairs, Leah stopped briefly to say a few words to Mom and explain that Cora had come for a treatment. She then went over to the stove to see what was simmering, because something sure smelled delicious. Mom had made a pot of chicken-corn soup and had just taken a loaf of bread from the oven. The kitchen had such a wonderful aroma that it almost made Leah light-headed.

She smiled, glancing at Sparky, now lying by the stove. He certainly wasn't going to let Mom out of his sight for very long. Leah could understand that, for she was equally glad to have Mom back home.

"What about supper?" Mom asked, placing the bread on a cooling rack. "Surely you must be hungry, Leah."

"It's okay. I can wait awhile to eat. Cora's hurting, and I'm hoping a treatment will help. You and Dad go ahead and eat supper without me."

"All right," Mom said. "I'll keep some soup warming on the stove, and you can eat when you come up from the basement. Oh, and I made a blueberry pie this afternoon. We can have that for dessert." She chuckled. "Your daed was hinting last night about blueberry pie."

"Dad's always liked your blueberry pies." Leah smiled as she headed to the basement.

Seeing that Cora was settled in the recliner, Leah poured some massage lotion on her hands and began to pressure-point Cora's right foot. "Does this seem to be helping at all?" she asked.

"I can't tell yet if my back pain has lessened, but my feet feel better than they have all day."

"I can imagine being on your feet for so many hours would cause them to ache an awful lot." Upstairs, Leah could hear Mom talking to Sparky, and every now and then, Sparky would bark.

"That dog of yours is sure sweet." Cora smiled. "Sometimes I wonder if I should get Jared a puppy. But what if he didn't want it? I'd end up being the one taking care of the dog. And with my schedule, I just don't have the time for that. Although, on a positive note, a dog would make a good companion for me, since Jared doesn't seem to want much to do with me anymore."

"I'm sorry," Leah murmured. "Perhaps in time he will come around."

"I'm still hoping for that." Cora closed her eyes and seemed to relax a little. Leah was glad. It would be better for both of them if they didn't make idle conversation. She could concentrate more fully on finding the right pressure points, and Cora could just let everything go.

Leah had just started on Cora's left foot, when Cora surprised her with a question. "How are your wedding plans coming along?"

"We still have some last-minute things to do, but we should be ready on time for the wedding this Thursday."

"After you're married, will you continue to see people for foot treatments here, or will you have a place to do that at your new home?"

"I'm not sure," Leah replied. "I'll need to speak to Adam about that."

"Adam?"

"Yes, Adam Beachy, my soon-to-be husband."

Cora bolted upright in her chair, nearly knocking the bottle of massage lotion out of Leah's hand. "Adam Beachy? I don't know if it's a coincidence or not, but my first husband's last name was Beachy, and as I had mentioned before, my Amish son's name was Adam. Oh, Leah, if there's even a chance that it's him, I need to know where he lives, so I can go talk to him."

While Cora babbled on, Leah gulped. A wave of heat spread across her cheeks. She couldn't believe she'd been dumb enough to blurt out Adam's name like that. *Oh my, what have I done? If Adam finds out, he'll probably never speak to me again. And he might even call off the wedding. What do I say to Cora? I don't dare tell her where Adam lives, because she's bound to go there, and that wouldn't sit well with Adam at all.*

Cora touched Leah's arm. "Oh, Leah, do you think your Adam Beachy might be my son?"

Leah nodded. "Jah, I believe he is."

CHAPTER 38

Cora trembled, and her mouth felt so dry she could barely talk. "How long have you known that the man you're engaged to is my son, and when were you planning to tell me about it?"

Leah lowered her gaze as she squirmed on her footstool. Cora figured she was uncomfortable talking about this. After several awkward moments, Leah looked up at Cora and said, "I haven't known very long. After the things you told me, plus the few things I already knew, the pieces started coming together. Then, the other day, I spoke to Adam about you, and he—"

"Adam knows I'm here?" Cora was suddenly filled with hope.

Leah nodded slowly. "But he's bitter about the things that occurred in the past, and I'm sorry, but he wants nothing to do with you. In fact, he said if I saw you again, I was to tell you to move back to Chicago."

Cora shook her head determinedly. "I can't do that, Leah. I need to see my son and make things right between us. Please tell me where he lives, or maybe you could set something up so we can meet."

"I cannot go against Adam's wishes," Leah said. "It would cause dissension between us."

Cora sat, mulling things over. "What about my daughter? Does Mary live in this area, too?"

Leah clasped Cora's hand. "I'm sorry to tell you this, but Mary and her husband were killed in an accident several months ago."

Cora covered her mouth to hold back the sob rising in her throat. "Oh, no! That just can't be. It wasn't supposed to happen this way. I wanted to make things right with my children." As reality sunk in, Cora let her tears spill, while Leah sat quietly, gently patting her back.

"Oh, Leah, it's too late to make amends with my daughter. I'd hoped that someday I would see both of my children again so I could apologize to them."

Heartfelt sympathy showed on Leah's face, and Cora thought she saw tears in Leah's eyes. "It was hard for Adam to accept Mary's death, but I think having her girls to raise has been a comfort to him in many ways," Leah said.

Cora gripped the armrests on the chair as this new information penetrated her brain. "Are Adam's nieces the girls you've been caring for?"

Leah bobbed her head. "And I'll be more involved in their care after Adam and I are married."

Cora drew in a sharp breath. "Those little girls are my grandchildren." Pausing, she let out a whispered sigh. "I have granddaughters." Looking up at Leah through blurry vision, she said tearfully, "I'd like the chance to get to know them."

"Leah, Elaine's here to see you!" Leah's mother hollered from the top of the basement stairs.

"I'll be up soon. Tell her to wait for me in the living room," Leah called in response. She looked at Cora. "I'm sorry, but I need to go now. My friend probably came by to talk about last-minute details for the wedding."

"I understand, and I surely won't keep you." Cora rose to her feet. "Before I go home, can I ask a favor?"

"What is it?"

"Would you at least put in a good word for me with Adam? Ask if he'd be willing to meet with me—or, at the very least, allow me to visit my granddaughters?"

"I'll try," Leah said, "but you'll need to accept whatever Adam decides."

I'm not sure I can do that, Cora thought. If Leah couldn't get through to Adam, then Cora would decide what to do next. One thing was for sure: she wouldn't be moving back to Chicago now. Her place was here—with her son and granddaughters. Now Jared would get to know his stepbrother.

~

Elaine had been waiting in the living room for twenty minutes before Leah showed up, and when she did, she appeared to be quite upset.

"What's wrong, Leah?" Elaine asked. "Have you received some bad news?"

Groaning, Leah flopped onto the couch next to Elaine. "I have, in fact."

"What is it?" Elaine clasped Leah's arm. "Has someone you know been injured or taken sick?"

Leah shook her head. "Remember the talk we had about Adam's mother leaving when he was a boy?"

"Jah."

"Well, that woman who was here getting a foot treatment is Adam's mother, and she wants me to set something up so she and Adam can meet."

Elaine's eyes widened. "What did you tell her?"

"Said I'd see what I could do but made no promises." Leah folded her arms in front of her chest, rocking slowly back and forth. "I'm the reason Cora made the request. I stupidly blurted out that the man I will be marrying is Adam Beachy." She sniffed. "Worse than that, I broke my promise to Adam by telling his mother about him and the girls."

"Are you going to tell him what happened?"

Leah nodded. "And I'd better do it before this day is over, because if I don't talk to him about it now, Cora may decide to seek Adam out on her own. That could make things even worse."

"I'll pray for you, and for Adam, too."

"We surely do need some extra prayers."

Elaine picked up the cardboard box she'd placed on the coffee table when she'd first arrived. "I doubt this will make you feel any better, but I made you a pre-wedding gift."

"What is it?" Leah asked, taking the box from Elaine.

"Open it and see."

Elaine held her breath as Leah opened the lid and removed the rock.

"Oh, how beautiful! It looks like a ruby-throated hummingbird."

Elaine smiled. "When I found that rock the other day among my collection and realized it resembled a hummer, I knew I had to paint it for you."

Leah set the rock down and gave Elaine a hug. "Danki. Your timing was perfect. I miss the hummingbirds when they leave for the south. Now I'll have this cute little rock to look at all year long. This special gift has brightened my day."

Elaine was on the verge of telling Leah about Ben's marriage proposal but thought better of it. *Leah has enough on her mind right now, and it wouldn't be fair to ask her to help me decide whether I should marry Ben. Besides, that's something I need to decide for myself, after I've prayed about it. If I agree to marry Ben, then I'll tell Leah.*

As Cora drove down the road, her hands shook so badly she could hardly steer. It was completely dark, and the tears she tried holding back blurred her vision. Adam, her son, lived right here in Arthur. Oh, how she had missed him all these years, but thinking there was no chance of her ever seeing him again, she'd kept it all bottled up inside. And to have found out about Mary. . .

"Oh my sweet daughter, how can you be gone?" Cora cried out as more tears spilled down her cheeks. "I wanted so badly to make things right with you. Please forgive me, Mary. I'm so sorry I put you and your brother through all that." Cora continued to sob, hoping against hope that somehow Mary could hear her pleas.

Even though she wasn't far from home, Cora was so upset she had to pull over, unable to go on any farther. Sobs came over and over from deep within. It was hard to breathe. She turned the car off and screamed out more pain. Sounding like a wounded animal, her throat constricted and started to hurt, but she didn't care as she howled even louder. Leaning her head against the window, she cried, "Oh, what have I done?" Her punishment had come, and she deserved it. "I was wrong to think of only myself. How could I have thought being a nurse was so important that I heartlessly left my husband and two small children like that?"

Cora let her forehead fall against the steering wheel and grieved over the fact that she would never see Mary again. She'd never get to meet the man her daughter had married or have the chance to make things right with her. Life could be so cruel, and she had no one to blame but herself.

Slowly, her sobs subsided, but the hiccups that followed remained. Fishing into her purse for a tissue, Cora wiped her eyes and blew her nose. She jumped when she heard someone knocking on her car window. When Cora saw the sheriff standing outside with a flashlight, she rolled the window down.

"You all right, ma'am?" he asked, leaning in to look at her.

"Yes, yes. . .*hic*. . .I'm fine," she stammered. "I'm on my way home and needed to pull over for a bit. *Hic! Hic!*"

"Well, if you have to pull over again, remember to put your blinkers on. It's dark out, and you don't want someone to accidentally hit you."

"Thank you, Officer. I'll remember that."

Relieved that her hiccups had finally subsided, Cora watched in the rearview mirror as the sheriff got back in his vehicle and pulled away. Sighing, she turned on the ignition and headed for home.

When she walked into her home sometime later, she was greeted by Jared, who stood with his hands on his hips. "Where you been all this time?" he demanded. "I'm hungry!"

"Then you'd better fix yourself a sandwich," Cora mumbled on the way to her room. "I have a headache, and I'm going to bed." She fled past Jared straight to her room, not wanting him to see her puffy eyes. There was no way Cora could discuss with Jared all that she'd just learned. Not tonight anyway. She had too much information to digest. Somehow, Cora had to come to grips with the knowledge that her daughter had died, her son lived here in Arthur, and she had three granddaughters. To top that off, Leah would soon be married to Cora's son and, technically, would be her daughter-in-law.

Cora undressed, slipped a nightgown over her head, and climbed into bed, pulling the blankets up to her chin, as if to wrap herself in a safe cocoon. "Sleep is what I need," she whimpered. "Maybe things will make more sense in the morning and I can figure out what I need to do."

Adam had just finished tucking the girls into bed, when he heard a knock on the back door. He made sure the girls' doors were shut then went quickly down the stairs.

When he opened the door, he was surprised to see Leah on the porch, her black outer bonnet slightly askew.

"Leah, what are you doing here at this time of night? Is everything all right?"

"I need to talk to you," she said breathlessly.

Concerned for her welfare, he opened the door wider and invited her in. "Let's go into the kitchen."

Once they were seated at the kitchen table, Adam said, "You look umgerennt."

"You're right. I'm very upset."

"What's wrong?"

"Cora came to see me for another foot treatment earlier this evening, and I. . .I accidentally mentioned your name."

Adam's head fell back. He felt like he'd been kicked by a mule. "You told her about me?" He could hardly believe Leah would betray him like that.

Tears gathered in Leah's eyes. "I'm sorry, Adam. I didn't mean to blurt it out. We were having a casual conversation, and she asked me about the wedding. It was just a slip of the tongue."

Adam sucked in air between his teeth. *Why did this woman have to come here now? She'll ruin everything.*

"Adam." Leah touched his arm. "She asked about Mary, too. I had to tell her. I had no choice."

"I bet that was a jolt to hear. Serves her right!" He thumped his knuckles on the edge of the table. "I suppose she wants to see me now?"

Leah gave a quick nod. "And the girls, too. She's anxious to meet her granddaughters."

His back muscles tightened. "You told her about them? Leah, how could you?"

"I didn't mean to, Adam. It just slipped out. Besides, she sort of figured that out for herself."

Adam's hand came down hard on the table. "It'll be a snowy day in sunny Florida before I allow her to see those girls!" His lips compressed. "You'd better talk her into leaving Arthur, Leah, because if she comes anywhere near me or the girls, I'll do just like my daed after that woman left us. I'll pack up our things and move so far from here that she'll never find us!"

CHAPTER 39

I'm tired. It's too early to get up," Jared complained when Cora prompted him to get out of bed Thursday morning.

"You've got school today. Did you forget?" She gestured to his clothes piled up on the floor. "And when you get home, I expect you to get this messy room cleaned. You weren't born in a barn, Jared, and I'm getting tired of reminding you to pick up after yourself."

Jared moaned, rolling to the edge of his bed. "Okay, I'll do it later today. Maybe after I get back from Scott's."

Cora frowned. "I don't recall giving you permission to go over there after school."

"Yeah, Mom, you did. Said it last night, remember?"

Truth was, Cora had been so tired and stressed out last night, that she barely remembered fixing supper or going to bed. She was sure she hadn't given Jared permission to go anywhere after school. Ever since her visit with Leah Monday evening, when she had learned that Leah was going to marry Cora's own son, she'd been in a fog, trying to decide what to do. She didn't know how she'd made it through work the past couple of days after learning all that, but somehow she had managed to act in a professional manner. That's exactly what it had been: an act. All she'd been able to think about was Adam and poor Mary. Every time Cora had gone into the waiting room to get the next patient, she half expected one of the Amish men waiting there would be Adam. But if Leah had said anything to him, wouldn't Adam have made an attempt to see her by now?

Yesterday, when Cora got home from work, she'd made a decision. She was going to Leah and Adam's wedding, even though she hadn't received an invitation. Cora knew it wasn't the right thing to do, but as soon as she'd gotten out of bed this morning, she'd called her boss at the clinic and said she was sick. She'd thought about taking Jared to the wedding but didn't want him missing any time from school. Besides, Cora still hadn't told him about Adam. She figured that could wait until she'd spoken to Adam and made things right. It would be a shock for Jared to find out he had a half brother.

"Mom, did you hear what I said?" Jared asked, scattering Cora's thoughts.

She jerked her head. "Uh, yes, son, I heard you."

"So can I go over to Scott's after school?"

"I guess it would be okay. But stay out of trouble. Do you understand?"

He nodded.

"Good. Now get dressed, and pick up some of your clothes before you eat breakfast." Cora hurried from the room. She'd wait until Jared left for school before she drove over to Leah's. She felt sure that was where the wedding would take place.

Leah's stomach tightened as she took a seat across from her groom, inside her brother's oversized shop. She'd seen Adam on Tuesday, and again yesterday, when she'd gone to his house to care for the girls, but not a word had been said about Cora. Perhaps Adam had calmed down now that he'd had a few days to think things over. And maybe, if the Lord answered Leah's prayers, at some point Adam would agree to see Cora. She felt sure that his comment about moving if Cora tried to see him had been spoken out of anger and frustration. Surely he wouldn't give up his home and business and uproot the girls now that they were getting settled and used to living here in Arthur.

And what about me? Leah wondered. *Would Adam expect me to leave my folks and the only home I've ever known and move someplace else so that he could run from his past?* Adam's relationship with his mother—or the lack of it—was eating him up, and Leah felt powerless to do anything about it.

She closed her eyes and offered a brief prayer. *Heavenly Father, please soften Adam's heart and heal the pain that's been there for so many years. Help me to be the helpmate he needs, and, if possible, let healing occur between Adam and his mother.*

Opening her eyes and glancing at her soon-to-be husband, Leah couldn't help but notice the perspiration that had gathered on his forehead. Was he as nervous as she was? Could he be having second thoughts about making her his wife? What would she do if he ran out of Nathan's shop?

Get a hold of yourself, and stop thinking such negative thoughts. Leah licked her dry lips and fought the urge to pick at a hangnail on her thumb. If she had noticed it before she'd left home this morning, she would have trimmed it off with nail clippers. But if she started pulling on it now, she'd draw attention to herself, and that would be embarrassing.

Pulling her gaze from Adam, she glanced at her two witnesses sitting beside her. Elaine seemed focused on the sermon being preached by one of their ministers, but Priscilla kept her focus on Elam, sitting directly across from her.

I wonder if she's wishing they were getting married today. The couple had been courting for quite a while, and Leah was still surprised Elam hadn't asked Priscilla to marry him by now.

Maybe he's waiting till he has enough money saved up, Leah thought. *Or perhaps, for some reason, he's afraid of marriage.*

Leah looked at Ben and noticed that he couldn't take his eyes off Elaine. *Now there's someone who's obviously in love. I wonder if Elaine realizes the way Ben feels about her. If it's this apparent to me, I would think it would be to her, as well.*

She looked at Adam again. If anyone had a reason to fear marriage, it was him. She couldn't imagine how it must have been for Adam's father when Cora walked out on her family. It must have been heart-wrenching, not to mention humiliating. She wondered what other people in Adam's Pennsylvania community must have thought. Would there have been some who believed Adam's dad was to blame—that he may have done something to drive Cora away? Or had most folks blamed Cora, thinking she was a terrible person for what she'd done, especially leaving her two small children? Adam certainly believed that. But unless he could forgive his mother, he would never truly be at peace.

As the service progressed, Adam felt himself beginning to relax. He'd come here feeling exceptionally nervous, fearful that something might happen to ruin the wedding. His eyes kept darting toward the door, hoping a particular person didn't unexpectedly show up, although he was certain that he wouldn't recognize her. It had been three days since Leah had admitted telling his mother who he was. Much to his relief, Cora had not gone to see Leah again or tried to contact him. Maybe she'd given up and decided to leave Arthur. That would be the sensible thing to do, because there was no hope of her having a relationship with him or the girls. All Adam wanted was the chance to begin a new life and, with Leah's help, raise Mary and Amos's girls the best way he could.

When Cora arrived at Leah's home, she knew immediately that the wedding was not taking place there because no buggies were parked in the field and there was no sign of a bench wagon or anything else to indicate that a wedding was being held.

Cora tapped the steering wheel. *Let me think. Where might the wedding be held?*

Unsure of where to go or what to do, Cora turned her car around and headed back down the driveway. The only thing she could think to do was drive around the area and see if she could locate the home where the wedding was being held. Surely it couldn't be that hard to spot. She just had to find the right road.

Turning onto the main road, Cora looked at the sky. "At least my son has a beautiful day for his wedding." It was a cold, crisp November day without a cloud to be seen. The air was sharp and so nippy it felt as though she could almost touch it. A sheet of ice glazed over the top of a pond she passed. Most of the trees were nearly bare, with only a few leaves hanging on the branches.

The other morning, driving to work, Cora had seen a few snow flurries. It reminded her of living in Chicago, where she had become used to the wind and snow. At least Cora didn't have snowy roads to contend with today. She was good at driving in the snow, but everyone else worried her. Over the years, she'd witnessed people making terrible mistakes when they drove on icy and snowy roads. But being a nurse and having to drive herself to work every day, Cora had learned to get over her fear and pay attention to what other vehicles were doing.

Cora glanced at her reflection in the rearview mirror. She had chosen to wear a simple outfit because she would be attending an Amish wedding. Her closet was full of fancy dresses she'd brought with her from Chicago, but none of them would have been appropriate. She had attended many hospital functions, weddings, and parties with her now ex-husband, but those dresses were too flashy to wear to a simple gathering such as this. Cora certainly didn't want to bring attention to herself, so she had chosen a dark blue skirt with matching jacket, and a light blue blouse. Since Amish women wore no jewelry, she avoided wearing earrings or a necklace.

Cora took a deep breath and concentrated on the matter at hand, slowing down at each farm she came to, hoping to see a crowd of horses and buggies. So far she'd had no luck. To make matters worse, a few minutes ago, her vehicle had started making sputtering noises.

Oh, please, not now, Cora silently prayed. *I don't need this on top of everything else.* She checked the gauge, but that was okay. She still had a half tank of gas. No other lights on the dash were lit up, and the steering seemed to be okay. Inspection was due sometime soon, but Cora hadn't had a chance to seek out a garage where she could take her vehicle. That was the first thing she planned to do when she went back to work the next day. Perhaps her coworkers could let her know of a reputable place to get her car inspected.

A few more miles down the road, Cora's car sounded normal again.

Sure wish I'd thought to ask Leah where the wedding was going to be. But then, she might not have told me.

Cora clutched the steering wheel tightly and berated herself. "What am I doing?" She was slowly beginning to lose her nerve. "What will I say to Adam if I come face-to-face with him?"

She'd planned out what she would say, but now she was so nervous she couldn't remember the words. She didn't want to talk herself out of it, but her nerves were on edge. What if she located the place where the wedding was being held and found out that she wasn't welcome? Cora didn't think she could handle the rejection.

After driving another mile up the road, she spotted a line of buggies parked in a field. *This must be the place.* Biting her lip, she slowed to let another vehicle pass before pulling in.

She turned up the driveway and parked her car near the edge so that if anyone needed to get out she wouldn't be in the way. Besides, she didn't want to alarm any of the horses, even though most of them were probably used to vehicles. Cora had to admit, she wanted to park in a space where she could get out easily, in case she had to leave quickly.

Opening the car door, Cora froze when the car started drifting forward. She realized then that she'd forgotten to put the gear in Park. After doing so, she sat for a few minutes, taking deep breaths. "Pull yourself together," she whispered. "You came here to see Adam, so you can't chicken out now."

Gathering her courage, Cora grabbed the door handle and stepped out of the car. Despite the butterflies in the pit of her stomach, there was no stopping her now.

CHAPTER 40

Cora heard singing coming from inside the oversized shop on the right side of the property, so she headed in that direction. When she got to the door, she stopped, running her damp hands down the side of her skirt. Earlier she had been concerned that she hadn't dressed warmly enough, given the cool weather. But now, Cora's nerves were keeping her plenty warm enough.

Looking back at her car to make sure it was still parked where she'd left it, Cora wiped her hands one more time then grasped the shop door handle. Taking a deep breath, she stepped inside and slipped quietly onto one of the backless wooden benches on the women's side of the room, near the rear. She couldn't see the bride and groom because other heads blocked her view. Cora sat silently, willing her heart to quit beating so wildly and uncrossing her legs to keep her feet from bobbing.

Leaning slightly forward, she looked past the women in front of her and saw several children. Some sat with their mothers, grandmothers, or some other person, and a few sat with their fathers. Cora wondered which of these children might be Adam's nieces. Then she spotted little Carrie, whom she'd met at the clinic the day Leah had brought her in. The child looked so cute, wearing an olive-green dress with a white apron. Her small hands were folded as she looked straight ahead. On either side of Carrie sat two other young girls. Beside them was an older woman, who Cora recognized as Leah's mother. She'd only seen her briefly the last time she'd gone to Leah's for a foot treatment, but she was sure it was her.

I wish I were the one sitting on the bench with those girls, Cora thought. *I gave up the privilege of knowing my children when they were young, but, oh, I would cherish each moment if I could spend that lost time with my grandchildren now.*

Cora's attention was drawn to the front of the room when one of the men, whom she assumed was a minister, stood and gave a message on the topic of marriage, speaking in German. The language came back to her as if she'd never stopped using it, and Cora was able to understand every word he said.

The focus of the message was on the serious step of marriage, for in the Amish church, the people were taught that divorce was not an option. The sermon and Bible passages emphasized the relationship between husband and wife, as God intended.

Cora had heard something similar the day she'd married Andrew but hadn't really taken it to heart. Today, however, the man's words penetrated her soul. Even though she'd spoken her vows before God and man and promised to be true only unto her husband, Cora had broken that vow the day she'd left Andrew and filed for divorce. Then by some twist of fate, Evan had done the same thing to her. If only she could go back in time and reverse her decision. *What goes around, comes around.* And what she had done so many years ago to her family had certainly come back around to her. *I didn't leave my husband for another man, though*, Cora justified, comparing what she'd done to Evan's reason for divorcing her. Wanting to be a nurse was a burning desire she'd had years ago, but had it been worth it in the end? Cora knew she had done wrong by leaving Andrew and had cheated herself out of the joy of knowing their children and being the kind of mother to Mary and Adam that they deserved. She had also robbed herself of the privilege of knowing her granddaughters. But maybe it wasn't too late for that.

As the minister continued, Cora's face burned with shame. Tears dripped onto her blouse. It felt like he was directing his words at her; yet he was speaking to the bride and groom. *Father, forgive me*, she silently prayed. *I was a selfish woman who knew better but wanted my own way. I know it's a lot to ask, Lord, but I'd like the chance to make amends.*

When the sermon ended, the wedding couple was called to stand before the bishop. Cora craned her head to get a look, and her heart nearly stopped beating when she caught sight of Leah standing beside a young Amish man with blond hair. It was the same man she'd spoken to at the hardware store the other day. Cora knew now why he'd looked so familiar. He resembled his father.

Swallowing against the lump in her throat, Cora couldn't take her eyes off the couple as they said their vows. Her son wasn't the little boy she remembered from long ago. Adam had been such a cute kid, and now he'd grown to be a handsome young man who had taken on the responsibility of raising Mary's daughters. No wonder Leah had fallen in love with him.

Cora continued watching as Leah glanced shyly at Adam. It took Cora back to the day she and Andrew had shared their wedding vows and looked bashfully at each other.

Adam and Leah were asked by the minister if they would remain together until death and if they would be loyal and care for each other during adversity, affliction, sickness, and weakness. They both answered affirmatively, and then the minister took their hands in his, and after wishing them the blessing and mercy of God, he said, "Go forth in the Lord's name. You are now man and wife."

Tears clouding her vision, Cora sat very still as the couple returned to their seats. Then she stood and quietly left the building, hoping neither Leah nor Adam had seen her. She had come here, planning to speak with her son and reveal who she was, but now she realized that this was not the time to make an appearance. She didn't want to spoil Leah and Adam's wedding day, so she would wait for a better time to speak with Adam.

When Leah took a seat after saying her vows, she glanced over at Adam's nieces and smiled. Those precious little girls would be in her care full-time from now on, and she looked forward to that. Unless things changed between her and Adam, she would probably never have any children of her own. That was one more reason for Leah to find satisfaction in being able to nurture and care for Carrie, Linda, and Amy. If the look of happiness on the girls' faces was any indication of how they felt, then they were equally glad that she'd become Adam's wife.

Adam's wife, Leah mused. It was hard to believe, especially given the fact that at one time she hadn't cared for Adam that much. Things were different now. Since Adam had become the caregiver of his nieces, Leah had seen him in a different light. He didn't annoy her like he had before, although he could still be pretty stubborn. If it weren't for the bitterness he carried toward his mother, Leah could give Adam her whole heart.

Turning her attention to the final sermon, Leah listened as the minister praised the institution of marriage and quoted more scriptures. She thought about the vows she'd just spoken and wondered what the rest of her life would be like. Would Adam ever give his heart to her in love? Was there any chance that he would agree to speak with Cora? So many questions and doubts floated through Leah's mind. The best response was to simply take one day at a time and trust God to work things out for everyone.

Adam's throat felt dry as he alternated between listening to their bishop speak about marriage and looking at Leah's rosy cheeks. She'd looked at him so sincerely when she'd answered the bishop's question only moments ago: "Can you confess, sister, that you accept our brother as your husband, and that you will not leave him until death separates you?"

"Yes," Leah had said with a decisive nod.

Why didn't my mother stay true to those vows when she married my daed? Adam wondered. *Did Dad, Mary, and I mean so little to her that she could forget about the promise she'd made before God and the church?*

That old familiar bitterness welled in Adam's soul. It was wrong to harbor such feelings of anger and resentment toward his mother, but he couldn't seem to help himself.

I won't let it consume me, Adam told himself. *My concentration needs to be on raising my nieces and trying to be a good husband to Leah, even though we won't be married in a physical sense.*

He glanced at Leah once more and relaxed a bit when she smiled at him. Adam was convinced that God had brought them together—if not to be husband and wife in every sense of the word, then to make sure that Mary and Amos's girls received the love and care they truly deserved. Although Mary had never met Leah, Adam was sure she would have approved of the young woman he'd chosen to marry.

That evening when Leah and Adam arrived at his house with the girls, Leah told Adam that she would help the girls get ready for bed.

"That's fine," Adam responded. "While you're doing that, I'll put your suitcase upstairs in the room next to Amy's."

Leah nodded. She'd known she would not be sharing a room with Adam downstairs, but the reminder that she'd be sleeping in the guest room was most troubling.

What have I done? she asked herself as she and the girls went into the house. *Marriage is for life, and I've just committed to a man who does not love me and who will never truly be my husband.*

Resolving to make the best of her situation, Leah followed Carrie and Linda up the stairs and into the room they shared, while Amy went to her room next door. After the younger ones changed into their nightclothes and said their prayers, Leah tucked them into bed. After kissing Carrie and Linda good night, she entered Amy's bedroom.

"How come Uncle Adam said he was gonna put your things in the room next to mine?" Amy asked when Leah took a seat on the end of her bed.

Unsure of how best to respond, Leah smiled and said, "I want to be close to you and your sisters right now."

Amy gave Leah a hug, apparently satisfied with that answer. "I'm glad you'll be living here with us now. I don't miss my mamm so much when you're around."

Tears pooled in Leah's eyes. "I'll never be able to take her place, but I want you to know that I'll be here for you in every way." After kissing Amy's forehead and telling her good night, Leah turned off the gas lamp and slipped quietly from the room. When she entered her own bedroom, where her luggage now sat, she went to the window and looked out. A full moon illuminated the yard, and Leah could see Adam's barn clearly. A light shone through the windows, letting her know that Adam was probably tending the horse. She wondered what he was thinking. Did he have any regrets about marrying her? Was he still upset because she'd told Cora about him? He hadn't said anything more about his mother or what he planned to do, and Leah was afraid to bring up the subject. She hoped Adam wouldn't make good on his threat to move. As far as she was concerned, that would be the worst thing to do.

After opening her suitcase, Leah took out her Bible. Taking a seat on the bed, she looked up Isaiah 30:15. "*In quietness and in confidence shall be your strength*," she read to herself.

Closing her eyes, Leah prayed, *Lord, please help me remember to put my trust in You to work everything out according to Your will.*

CHAPTER 41

Leah scurried around the kitchen, getting breakfast on before Adam and the girls came in. It just didn't seem possible that a whole week had gone by since her and Adam's wedding. Even though Leah had been coming over for the past few months to care for the girls, it felt strange to actually be living in Adam's house, knowing she was his wife.

But I'm his wife in name only, she reminded herself. *Adam doesn't see me as anything more than a housekeeper, cook, and someone to take care of his nieces.*

As Leah stirred a kettle of oatmeal on the stove, her thoughts took her back to their wedding night, when she and Adam came home with the girls. After a whole week had gone by, Adam still hadn't mentioned Cora. Was he ever going to say anything? Should Leah bring up the topic? She was confused and didn't know what to do.

"God is not the author of confusion, but of peace, as in all churches of the saints." Leah silently quoted 1 Corinthians 14:33.

"What's for breakfast?" Amy asked, stepping into the kitchen and scattering Leah's thoughts.

Leah smiled as she turned from the stove. "Since this is such a chilly fall morning, I decided to fix *hawwermehl*."

Amy's nose crinkled. "I don't like oatmeal that much."

"I like it, and so does Carrie," Linda said, holding her little sister's hand as they skipped into the room.

"Amy, would you please set the table?" Leah asked. "I'm making toast, so you can have a piece of that."

"What can I do?" Linda wanted to know.

"Why don't you get out the brown sugar and butter?" Leah suggested. "Oh, and Carrie, you can put some napkins by each of our plates."

While the girls did their jobs, Leah turned the stove down and toasted several slices of bread. By the time they came out of the oven, Adam had come inside from doing his chores in the barn.

"Brr. . ." Adam rubbed his hands briskly over his arms. "It feels more like winter than fall this morning. You can really smell the wood smoke in the air. Guess a lot of folks did what we did and fired up their woodstoves and fireplaces this past week." He glanced at Leah and smiled. "Is breakfast about ready?"

Smiling in return, she nodded.

"Great. I'll get washed up, and then we can eat." Adam headed down the hall toward the bathroom. When he returned, everyone took a seat at the table. "I'll bring more firewood in before I leave for work," he said. "That way you can keep the fireplace going."

"Danki, Adam. The warmth from the fire makes the living room cozy." Leah lowered her eyes, feeling the heat of a blush on her cheeks. She appreciated his thoughtfulness, and the gentle way he'd looked at her just now made her feel kind of giddy.

After their silent prayer, Leah dished everyone a bowl of oatmeal and passed Amy the plate of toast. As they ate, Amy and Linda talked about school and how their teacher would soon be giving out parts for the Christmas program. Leah looked forward to attending along with the parents and other family members of the scholars who went to the one-room schoolhouse. For her, Christmas would be different than it had been in the past, since she was no longer living at home with her parents. Now, she was a parent, of sorts.

"Will you be washing clothes today, Leah?" Adam asked. "I spilled some glue on my trousers yesterday, and they need to be cleaned."

"I'll do my best," Leah responded, "but I can't promise that the glue will come out."

"It's okay if it doesn't. They're an old pair of trousers."

"I'll start washing as soon as I get Linda and Amy off to school," Leah said. "I need to get it done before Priscilla comes for a foot treatment."

Adam's eyebrows squished together. "I've been meaning to talk to you about that, Leah. Now that we're married, I'd prefer that you stop practicing reflexology."

Leah stiffened. "But Adam, there are people in this community who count on me to help them with various ailments."

"If they're sick, they can see a doctor." Adam reached for his cup of coffee and took a drink.

"Some folks who see me aren't sick; they may have back problems or—"

"That's what chiropractors are for," he interrupted.

"But, Adam—"

He gestured to the girls. "I rather not discuss this right now. Since you've already scheduled Priscilla to come over, you can go ahead and work on her feet, but you'll need to let her know that this will be the last time you will see her for that." As if the matter were settled, Adam got up from the table and put his dishes in the sink. After he'd said good-bye to the girls and Leah, he grabbed his hat, jacket, and lunch pail, and headed out the door.

It's not fair of Adam to ask me to quit doing reflexology. Leah teared up. *It's my gift.*

As Cora drove to work that morning, she spotted a group of Amish children walking along a path on the side of the road. No doubt they were headed to school. She recognized two of the young girls, as she'd seen them sitting with Carrie at Leah and Adam's wedding. One of the girls looked so much like Mary when she was a little girl that Cora was tempted to stop and talk to them. But she didn't want to frighten the girls. Once more, she thought about how she had cheated herself out of knowing these children. Was it too late for that? If the girls knew she was their grandmother, would they welcome her into their lives?

Cora had to find out, and the only way she could do that was to speak with Adam. She didn't know where Adam lived, but she would go by his hardware store before the week was out. She just hoped and prayed he would be receptive to what she had to say.

That afternoon, Leah scurried around finishing up the housework. She hadn't done the laundry yet, because she'd gone over to her folks' house to get her massage lotion for Priscilla's foot treatment. The old recliner she had always used was still in Mom and Dad's basement, so she would have Priscilla sit on one of the chairs in Adam's living room. Oh, how she dreaded telling her friend that she could no longer practice reflexology. If Leah had known Adam was going to take that away from her, she'd have thought twice about marrying him.

Before Leah and Carrie had gone to her folks', she'd taken Adam's pants to the laundry area and rubbed some spot remover on the area he'd told her about. Now the house was all clean, including the floors, and she had just gotten Carrie up from her afternoon nap. "Do you want to go for a walk with me out to the phone shack, Carrie? I need to check for messages."

Carrie eagerly agreed and got her coat, which hung on a low-hanging hook in the utility room. Hand in hand, they walked to the phone shack, with Coal following close behind. The Lab was so good with the girls, and he'd taken a liking to Leah, as well. She missed seeing Sparky every day, but he was better off staying at home with Mom. No doubt Sparky and Coal would have vied for her attention, and two dogs were just too many for Leah to deal with right now.

"Now just stand here and wait until I check for messages." Leah smiled when Carrie reached for Coal and hung on to the thick fur on the back of his neck, while the dog sat close to her feet.

There was only one message, and it was from Priscilla. Her plans had changed. She wasn't going to be able to make it for a foot treatment after all.

Going back into the house, Leah decided to start the laundry. Hopefully the spot remover had worked and the glue would come out once Adam's pants were washed. Carrie seemed content to sit by the living-room window and watch the birds at the feeder outside.

"Carrie, I'll be right back as soon as I wash your uncle's clothes. Do you want to come with me to the laundry room while I do that, or would you like to stay here and keep watching the birds?"

"I wanna watch the birdies eat," Carrie responded.

Leah reminded Carrie that she wouldn't be long and to come to her if she got tired of watching the birds. There were some children's puzzles Carrie could play with that were kept on a shelf in the laundry area, but Adam's youngest niece seemed quite content to sit quietly looking out the window.

Leah was happy when she saw no evidence of the glue in Adam's trousers after she'd washed them with a few other things. "He should be pleased with that," she murmured, putting the clothes in the basket to take outside to hang on the line.

Setting the laundry basket by the back door, Leah went to check on Carrie, but the little girl was no longer at the window. "Carrie, where are you?" Leah called, going from room to room. "Now where could that child have gotten in so little time?"

Leah looked toward the hook where she'd hung Carrie's coat when they'd come inside earlier. When she saw that it, too, was missing, Leah grabbed her own coat and immediately went outside.

Leah stood on the porch, yelling Carrie's name. Silence. She realized that Coal, who always greeted her when she went outside, hadn't appeared, either. Leah hurried to the barn and checked there, but Carrie was nowhere to be found. Leah continued searching, walking all around the outside of the house. Her heart beat wildly as she raced toward the pond, but luckily she saw no evidence of Carrie or the dog. She'd hoped at first that the girl might be playing hide-and-seek, but now Leah was afraid. "What am I going to do?" She nearly choked on the words.

Just then, she spotted Amy and Linda walking with a few other children, coming home from school. When the girls entered the yard, Leah told them that their little sister was missing.

"Oh, no!" Linda gasped. "What if we never find her?"

"I'll bet she saw something she liked and wandered off someplace," Amy put in.

"Well, we need to find Carrie before your uncle gets home from work," Leah said. "Will you two help me look for her?"

Both girls nodded soberly.

While the three of them searched for Carrie, Leah tried to remain calm. Where was Carrie? Why did she leave the house? How would she explain to Adam what had happened, and what would he think? They'd only been married a week and already something had gone wrong. Leah told the girls to go back in the house while she went to the phone shack to call the sheriff. It was the last thing she wanted to do, but, at this point, she saw no other choice, especially since it would be getting dark in a few hours. After giving a description of Carrie to someone at the sheriff's office, Leah mentioned that there might be a black Lab with her. She was beside herself, but she'd done all she could.

When Leah entered the house, Amy and Linda were sitting in the livingroom crying. Gathering them into her arms, Leah tried to offer the girls hope that their little sister would soon be found. She had to hold things together until they heard something from the sheriff.

Leah looked at the clock above the fireplace and couldn't believe it had been an hour already since she'd first realized Carrie was missing. In that amount of time the child could have gone almost anywhere. *Please, Lord, let her be okay.*

Suddenly, all three of them heard a slight barking sound from outside. Trying to get through the door at the same time, Leah, Amy, and Linda rushed outside. Leah was so relieved when she saw Coal walking next to Carrie, coming toward them from the edge of the backyard. Carrie clutched the Lab's thick fur on the back of his neck. The dog, Leah realized, was Carrie's protector, walking slowly beside the child so her two little legs could keep up with his four. Carrie was smiling, big as you please, while Coal's tail wagged rapidly back and forth.

Leah couldn't get to the child quickly enough. Running down the porch steps, she scooped Carrie into her arms, holding on for dear life.

"You're squeezing so tight." Carrie giggled, while Leah eased up but continued to hug her. Coal was barking loudly now, his tail going in circles.

Linda and Amy bent down and hugged the dog. "Good boy, Coal. Good dog," they said in unison.

After Leah put Carrie down, Linda and Amy hugged their little sister.

"Where have you been, Carrie?" Leah asked. "We were so worried."

"I saw Chippy and went after him, but he ran away."

"I'm glad you saw the chipmunk, but you should not have left the yard," Leah scolded.

Carrie's chin trembled. "Sorry."

Leah gave one of Carrie's braids a gentle tug. "Please, don't ever do that again."

"I won't," Carrie promised. "I'll stay in the yard."

After Leah sent the children inside, she went to the phone shack and called the sheriff's office again, letting them know that Carrie had been found. When she returned to the house, she put another log in the fireplace to warm the house up a little more for Carrie. In the meantime, Linda took some fresh water out on the porch for Coal. When they were all back together in the house, Carrie continued to tell them her story. While she'd been watching out the window, she'd seen Chippy in the backyard under the bird feeder.

"We thought he died," Linda spoke up. "I'm so glad he's okay."

Carrie's lower lip jutted out. "When I went outside, Chippy ran, so I followed him."

"But where did you go?" Leah asked. "We looked everywhere for you."

"I went far away—in a field, where Chippy ran." Carrie paused, tears pooling in her eyes. "Then I didn't know how to get home."

"Didn't you hear us calling for you?" Leah asked calmly, so as not to further upset the little girl.

"Uh-uh. I'm sorry." Carrie hid her face with her arm.

"Come here, sweetie." Leah lifted Carrie onto her lap.

"How did you get home?" Amy questioned.

"Coal kept tuggin' on my coat, so I gave up looking for Chippy." Carrie looked up at Leah and sniffed. "Are ya mad at me?"

"Of course not." Reaching for the child's small hands, Leah squeezed them gently. "We're just glad you're home, safe and sound."

Leah was so happy she was about to burst. As a reward for bringing Carrie home, Leah had thought about letting Coal come inside. That way he, too, could enjoy the warmth of the house. She decided to wait until Adam got home, however, since Adam had made it clear that he didn't want the dog inside. Leah hoped that after he heard the details of Carrie's safe return, Adam would change his mind and let Coal come in.

When Adam got home, Leah explained what had happened with Carrie. His heart hammered in his chest, thinking about what could have happened, but he'd quickly calmed down, seeing that Carrie was okay. Leah had apologized for not watching Carrie closer, but Adam knew she couldn't be with the child every moment of the day.

Like he normally did each evening after supper, Adam had gotten a bowl ready and fixed Coal's food, but this time he'd opened the door and called the dog inside. As Coal came running in, Adam stole a glance at Leah and the girls and grinned back at them as Coal hungrily slurped his chow.

Adam turned off all but one of the gas lamps and stood by the wall where the glow of light reflected. Even Coal, who'd been lying near Leah's feet, looked up and watched.

"Can any of you guess what this is?" Adam asked, making a shadow figure on the wall.

"It looks like a dog!" Linda shrieked with delight, while Carrie clapped her hands. Even Amy wore a grin.

Next, Adam made a bird and flapped his hands, making the shadow look as if it were flying. After that, he made a rabbit and several other animals. Linda was so intrigued that she jumped up and joined Adam, asking if he would teach her how to do it.

"Okay, now you put your hands like this." He positioned her hands and showed her how to make an easy hand shadow. "This one you can do with one hand, raising your index finger a little."

"It looks like a dog," Linda squealed.

"Now make him bark by moving your thumb up and down a little." Adam watched as Linda succeeded in making the motion.

Carrie came forward, and Linda showed her how it was done, while Adam stood off to one side. He glanced at Leah, who smiled as she, too, sat watching the girls. Being here with his nieces and Leah made Adam feel like he was complete, like he had a family. How could he have ever been content to keep to himself for all those years?

Only one thing was missing, and that involved Leah. Did he dare express the way he felt about her? He'd be taking a risk if she didn't share his feelings of love. Adam knew from the way Leah responded to the things he said that she respected him as the head of the house. But he wanted more.

As Adam sat down on the couch next to Leah, he made a decision. When the time was right and he felt a little more confident, he would open his heart to Leah. But he couldn't do that until Leah showed some sign that she loved him, too.

"That's really good, girls," Adam said, focusing once more on Carrie and Linda. "The hand shadow you made looks just like a bird. Now see if you can make him fly."

Unexpectedly, a vague memory worked its way into Adam's consciousness. He remembered someone else making shadow figures on the wall when he was a child. Until now, he'd kept this memory buried all these years. *My mother taught Mary and me how to do this.*

"Are you okay, Adam?" Leah asked. "You've become very quiet."

"I'm fine. Just watching the girls." Adam broke out in a sweat. There was no way he was going to let this one little memory make him forget what his mother had done to him and Mary, not to mention Dad. *We suffered all those years without a mom, and I won't let one good memory erase all of that.*

CHAPTER 42

When Jonah entered his buggy shop on Friday morning, he found his father hard at work. "Am I late?" Jonah asked. "Thought I was getting here right on time."

"You are." Dad grinned. "I woke up early this morning and decided to come on into the shop and get started. We've still got two buggies we need to complete before Christmas, you know."

Jonah nodded. "And I'm ever so thankful to have you working with me, Dad."

"How are Sara and the boppli doing?" Dad asked, reaching for one of his tools.

"The baby is doing well, but I'm worried about Sara." Jonah moved across the room to his desk.

Dad's forehead creased. "What's wrong? Has she been doing too much?"

"Not really," Jonah replied with a shake of his head. "Between Mom and Sara's mamm, now that she's arrived, they're taking over the household chores and cooking." He grimaced. "I think Sara's MS is flaring up. She's had a few dizzy spells, and her legs have been kind of weak. She's been using a cane to get around the house, and I can't help but worry."

Dad set his work aside and joined Jonah at his desk. "Try not to worry, son. Remember what God's Word says in Philippians 4:6: 'Be careful for nothing; but in every thing by prayer and supplication with thanksgiving let your requests be made known unto God.'"

Jonah clasped Dad's shoulder and squeezed it. "That's good advice. Danki for the reminder."

❧

Dianna parked her bicycle and joined Leah by the clothesline, where she was removing her clean laundry.

"It's good to see you. What brings you by here today?" Leah asked.

Dianna smiled and gave Leah a hug. "Can't a mother drop by to see her daughter without there being a reason?"

"Of course." Leah placed one of the little girls' dresses in the basket. "I just thought maybe you came by for a special reason."

"I did. Came to see you." Dianna playfully tweaked the end of Leah's nose, like she'd done many times when Leah was a child. "So, how are you doing?"

Leah dropped her gaze to the ground. "Just trying to get these clothes off the line. I left them hanging outside all night."

"I can see that. But I didn't ask what you were doing; I asked how are you doing?"

"Okay, I guess."

"Just okay? You're a new bride, for goodness' sake. You ought to be smiling from ear to ear."

When Leah made no comment, Dianna felt concerned. "Is something wrong, Leah? You look unhappy this morning."

"I am unhappy, Mom." Leah glanced at Carrie playing with Coal on the porch, and lowered her voice. "When I told Adam yesterday morning that Priscilla would be coming by for a foot treatment, he said he didn't want me doing that anymore."

"Really? Why not?" Dianna could hardly believe Adam would object.

"He didn't explain. Just said he didn't want me doing it anymore, and then he left for work."

"Don't you think you ought to find out the reason for his request?"

"Jah, but I don't want to do it in front of the kinner. They don't need to hear Adam and me involved in a disagreement—especially now that we're married."

Dianna shook her head. "I should say not." She was tempted to say more on the subject but decided it would be best to let Leah and Adam work out their differences. It might be that after Adam had time to think about it, he would change his mind.

"I'll help you get the clothes off the line," Dianna said, reaching up to remove another dress."

"Danki."

Dianna remained quiet as she and Leah finished the job. When they stepped onto the porch, Carrie announced that she was hungry.

"Guess it is about time for lunch," Leah said. "Would you like to stay and join us, Mom? Thought I'd reheat some chicken noodle soup I made for supper last night. Does that sound good to you?"

"That'd be nice." Dianna smiled. "While you're doing that, I'll fold the clothes and put them away."

"Come on, Coal. You can come inside, too." Leah held the door open until Coal walked through.

Dianna followed Leah and Carrie into the house, and when they went to the kitchen, she took the clothes to the dining room, where she placed them on the table to fold. Once that was done, she carried Adam's trousers down the hall, remembering that when she'd been watching the girls, Linda had mentioned that her uncle's room was downstairs.

Dianna stepped into the bedroom and opened the closet door to hang up the trousers. *Now that's sure strange. Where are all of Leah's dresses?* she wondered, looking around.

Going to the dresser, she opened each of the drawers, but there was nothing in any of them to indicate that Leah shared this room with her husband. *What in the world is going on here? Could Leah have moved her things to one of the rooms upstairs because she was upset with Adam after he'd said she couldn't practice reflexology? Should I say something to Leah about this or just let it go? If Leah and Adam are having marital problems, she may need someone to talk to about this. Maybe I'd better discuss it with Alton first and see what he thinks I should do.*

During lunch, Leah chatted with Mom about the usual things going on with her friends and how some of the stores in Arthur were having preholiday sales.

When Carrie finished eating, she went to the living room to be with Coal, who had bedded down by the fireplace. "Since Carrie's in the other room, now's a good time for me to tell you what happened yesterday."

"What was that?" Mom asked.

Leah explained how Carrie had run off and how frantic she'd been when she couldn't find her. "Even when I realized that Coal was with her, I was still scared." Leah continued to explain the details of how Carrie and the dog came back and how Adam had allowed the dog to come in the house last night.

"I would have done the same thing myself," Mom said. "And I'm pleased to hear that everything worked out okay."

Leah was about to say more, when Carrie yelled for them to come quick. Thinking something must be seriously wrong, Leah jumped up and hurried into the living room. There stood Carrie by the fireplace, giving the dog her own performance of making shadow figures on the wall.

When Cora got off work that afternoon, she headed straight for Adam's store. She'd gone there yesterday, but because she worked later than usual, by the time she'd arrived, the hardware store was closed.

As she drove along, she noticed a horse and buggy pulled off to the side of the road. An Amish man with his back to the road was squatted down by the buggy wheel, as though there might be a problem.

Cora pulled in behind the buggy and got out of the car. "Is there anything I can do to help?" she asked.

When the man turned around, Cora felt as if her heart had stopped beating. She'd seen him at the hardware store the day she'd gone looking for lightbulbs and an extension cord. She had seen him again a week ago, when he'd stood before the bishop with Leah, saying his wedding vows.

"I appreciate you stopping, but I don't think there's much you can do," he said.

He doesn't recognize me. He has no idea I'm his mother. Cora moved closer to Adam. "You don't know who I am, do you?"

He stared at her several seconds. "Oh, now I remember. Aren't you the lady who came into my store a week or so ago, looking for lightbulbs?"

"Yes, Adam, that was me."

He blinked rapidly. "How do you know my name? Don't think I introduced myself when you came into the store."

Barely able to get the words out, Cora murmured, "My name is Cora. I'm your mother."

CHAPTER 43

Adam's throat tightened as he stared at the person claiming to be his mother. She was the same woman who'd come to his store, but he hadn't recognized her then, nor did he now. "You're not my mother," he mumbled, forcing himself to look into her eyes. "A real mother would not have abandoned her own flesh-and-blood children."

Cora reached out her hand but pulled it back when Adam moved aside. "I know what I did was wrong, and I—"

Adam held up his hand. "I don't want to hear your excuses, because that's all they would be, excuses. A real mother loves her children and wants to be with them. A real wife doesn't run off and get a divorce for no reason." Adam's hands shook as he dropped his arms to his sides. "Didn't the vows you took when you married Dad mean anything?"

"I thought they did at the time, but then things changed."

"You mean, *you* changed! One day you were my mother who wiped my nose when I had a cold and created hand shadows on the wall when I was afraid of the dark. The next day you were gone." Adam gulped in a breath of air. "You never returned or kept in touch with me or my sister."

"I know how it must seem, but if you'd just let me explain—"

"I'm not interested in your explanation. Nothing you could say or do would ever make up for all those years that you were not a part of our lives."

Tears welled in Cora's eyes, but Adam felt no pity. Why should he? Had she felt pity for him or Mary when they'd called out for their mother and cried themselves to sleep so many nights? Did she care that she'd not only broken her husband's heart but had also left him to raise their children alone?

"You're not welcome here." Adam motioned to her car. "You left me and my sister by your own choice. Now I'm asking you to leave again, but this time it's my choice."

Cora shook her head determinedly. "I can't do that, Adam. I lost you once. I won't let that happen again."

"You lost me?" His jaw clenched so tightly it was a miracle he didn't break a tooth. "You didn't lose me. You threw me away! If you don't leave Douglas County, I'll have no choice but to take my family and move."

Cora gasped. "Oh no, Adam. Please, don't do that. I have a new job here, and it's given me a new start. I promise I won't bother you or try to force myself on you at all. If the day ever comes that you reconsider and allow me to be a part of your life, then—"

"That will never happen!" Adam turned away abruptly. "Now please go."

As he moved back to his buggy, Adam heard her car door open. When the engine started, he let out his breath in relief. Even if Cora didn't come around or try to see him and the girls, she'd still be in the area, and Adam would no doubt see her from time to time. He wasn't sure he could deal with that painful reminder of the past and be constantly looking over his shoulder for fear of running into her again. It might be better for him and the girls if he did leave Arthur, and it would serve Cora right!

"Alton, I need to speak to you about something," Dianna announced when she arrived home from Leah's that afternoon.

Alton set his newspaper aside. "What is it, Dianna? You look umgerennt."

She took a seat on the couch beside him. "I am upset. I was at Adam and Leah's today, and when I went to put some clothes in their bedroom, I discovered that none of Leah's things were there—only Adam's."

Alton gave his beard a quick tug. "Are you sure about that?"

She nodded.

"Did you talk to Leah about it?"

"No, I wanted to discuss it with you first." Dianna sighed. "Leah said something while I was there that troubled me, too."

"What was that?"

"She said that Adam asked her to stop doing reflexology."

Alton's expression turned grim. "Did she say why?"

"No, but it got me to thinking that if Leah is upset with Adam about this, maybe she moved her things out of their room and is sleeping upstairs in the guest room or with one of the girls."

Alton crossed his arms. "I'm thinking maybe I should have a little talk with our new son-in-law. Find out why he doesn't want Leah doing foot treatments anymore. I'm also going to ask how come they are sleeping in separate rooms."

"Oh, dear." Dianna clutched the folds in her dress. "I hope Adam won't think you're interfering in things that are none of your business."

Alton's knuckles whitened as he clasped his hands tightly together. "Anything that concerns our daughter is very much my business."

Cora was beside herself and barely remembered driving home. Her talk with Adam had gone all wrong, and now because of her, he and his family might move. What would she do then, after just finding him? Adam had made it clear that he wanted nothing to do with her. She didn't even get the chance to tell him about Jared. Maybe he wouldn't have cared to know that he had a half brother. Would it be easier for her to move so that Adam and his family could remain here in Arthur? Cora didn't feel right about him feeling forced to leave. At the same time, if she moved back to Chicago, she might never repair the damage she'd done to her son—if that was even possible.

Cora got out of the car and was fishing for her house key that had somehow disappeared to the bottom of her purse, when Jared flung open the front door and stepped outside.

"Jared, you startled me. I didn't expect you'd be home yet. I thought you'd made plans with Scott after school."

"I did, but Scott had a dental appointment. Said he forgot till his mom reminded him this morning."

"Oh, I see." Cora followed him into the house. *Should I tell him about Adam? Would it help anything if he knew he has a big brother?*

Exhausted, she shuffled into the living room and flopped down on the couch. With all that had happened today, plus the decisions she needed to make, Cora couldn't decide anything right now. If she moved back to Chicago, she'd never resolve things with Adam. If she stayed, it would most likely drive him away. She needed to take a few days to think about things and, yes, even pray.

Leah had started making supper and was getting ready to set the table, when Adam entered the house, red-faced and nostrils flaring.

"Adam, what's wrong?" she asked, feeling concern.

He glanced around the room. "Where are the girls?"

"In the bathroom, washing up."

"That's good. I don't want them to hear this."

"Hear what, Adam?" Leah set the dishes down and moved toward him.

"On my way home from the hardware store, I stopped along the side of the road to check a wobbly wheel." Adam paused and glanced toward the doorway leading to the hall where the bathroom was located. Leah figured he was worried that the girls might come into the kitchen. "While I was stopped, a car pulled up behind my buggy and a woman got out, asking if I needed any help."

Leah waited as Adam paused again. He sank into a chair at the table. "She introduced herself and said she was my mother."

Leah gulped. "Cora?"

"Jah."

"Did anything get resolved between you?" Leah asked hopefully.

His lips curled slightly as he shook his head.

"I'm sorry to hear that. I was hoping once you two had—"

"I asked her to leave Douglas County, but she flatly refused."

"That's understandable, don't you think? I mean, she wants to make things right between you, and I'm sure she'd like to get to know her granddaughters."

Adam slammed his fist on the table. "That will never happen!"

"But don't you think—"

"If Cora won't move, then I'm going to put the store up for sale, and we'll move to another part of the country." The determined set of Adam's jaw and the cold, flinty look in his eyes told Leah that he was serious. Thanksgiving was next week, and her parents, along with her brother Nathan and his family, would be coming for dinner. Then there was Christmas. Surely Adam wouldn't think of uprooting everyone before the holidays. Leah knew it was imperative that either she get a hold of Cora and convince her to move, or figure out some way to get through to Adam. But that seemed impossible.

"I'm going out to the barn to feed the *katze*," Sara told her mother.

Mom's dark eyebrows furrowed. "Can't that wait till Jonah comes up to the house? I'm sure he'd be willing to do it. Or your daed can feed the cats when he comes out of the bathroom."

"Jonah will have enough to do feeding the horses, along with his other chores this evening." Sara slipped into her sweater. "Besides, the fresh air will do me some good. I've been cooped up in this house since we brought the boppli home from the hospital."

Mom turned from the stove, where she'd been stirring a kettle of stew, and nodded. "All right then, but don't be too long. Supper will be ready soon, and when Jonah gets home, we can eat."

Sara smiled and stepped out the back door. The air was a bit nippy this evening, but it felt refreshing. She walked halfway to the barn and paused, breathing in the odor of decaying leaves, mingled with wood smoke from the fire Dad had built in the fireplace before he'd gone to take a shower.

After several minutes, Sara moved on. When she entered the barn, she identified another aroma: horseflesh coupled with the scent of baled straw stacked against a wall. It felt good to be out here with the animals, even if she did feel a bit weak and shaky. But that was to be expected since she'd recently given birth.

Not seeing any of the cats, Sara picked up their metal dish and banged it a couple times with a small shovel. Then she poured some food into the dish and waited. A few seconds later, Fluffy, the mama cat, along with three of her six-week-old babies, darted across the barn and poked their heads into the dish.

That's strange, Sara thought. *Where is Fluffy's other kitten?*

No sooner had Sara thought the words, when she heard a faint, *meow*!

Sara looked up. There sat a little gray-and-white kitten in the loft overhead, looking down at her so pathetically. *Meow! Meow!*

"What's the matter, little guy?" Sara tipped her head back for a better look. "You found your way up there, so why can't you find your way down?"

Meow! Meow! The kitten continued to cry.

"Oh, all right, I'll come up and get you." There was no way Sara would chase a kitten all over the loft. If it wasn't where she could easily reach it, then it would have to find its own way down.

Grasping the sides of the ladder, Sara made her way slowly up, while the kitten sat patiently waiting for her. "Now don't you move. I'm almost there."

She was nearly at the top, when her right leg gave out and she missed the next rung. It threw her off balance, and letting go with one hand, she tried to regain her balance. Just then, the kitten screeched, leaped onto Sara's right shoulder, and dug its needlelike claws into her skin.

The room started to spin, and as an inky blackness moved in, Sara lost her grip on the ladder. Her last thought as she tumbled toward the floor was, *Dear Lord, take care of my family.*

CHAPTER 44

Jonah whistled as he made his way from the buggy shop to the house. It had been a long day, and he was anxious to see how Sara and the baby were doing. He looked forward to spending some time with Mark, too, and enjoying a pleasant evening visiting with his in-laws during supper. It was a comfort having Sara's folks there to look after things while Jonah was working; although he knew his own parents would have continued that task if Rueben and Martha hadn't come to see their new granddaughter.

Jonah looked forward to being with both sets of parents on Thanksgiving. His twin sister, Jean, and her family would be there as well. Jonah had always longed for a wife and children, and now that he had them, his life seemed complete. He loved Sara and their children with all his heart and would do anything for them.

When Jonah entered the house, he found Sara's mother standing at the sink, washing a head of lettuce. "Guder *owed*, Jonah." She turned and smiled at him.

"Good evening," he responded. "How's my fraa doing? Is she resting like the doctor told her to do?"

Martha motioned to the kitchen window. "Said she wanted some fresh air and insisted on going out to the barn to feed the katze."

"How long ago was that?"

"Now that I think about it, it's been quite a while." Martha glanced at the clock on the wall near the stove. "She really should have been back by now unless she found something else to do out there in the barn."

Jonah frowned. "Sara shouldn't be doing anything in the barn. I'll go out and see what she's up to." He turned and headed back outside.

When Jonah entered the barn, it was dark, so he called Sara's name.

No response.

Could she have left the barn and gone into the house without Martha seeing her?

Jonah lit one of their gas lamps. Holding it up so he could see better, he moved across the barn. The mama cat was sitting on a bale of straw, and her kittens were grabbing at her tail. Below them sat the cat dish, but it was empty. Looking back at the cats, Jonah noticed that one of Fluffy's kittens was missing. He walked over to the mama cat and stroked her head. "Where's your other little one?" He smiled as the cat leaned in, purring, while rubbing her whiskers on the back of his hand.

When Jonah went farther into the barn, he heard a faint *meow*. "Where are you, kitty? Here, kitty kitty."

As he looked around, he froze. Sara's twisted body lay on the floor beneath the ladder leading to the loft. Wedged under her arm was the missing kitten. "Sara!" Jonah dropped to his knees in front of his wife, setting the lamp on the floor. "Sara! Sara, what happened? Can you hear me?"

When Jonah picked up Sara's arm to hold her hand, the kitten took advantage and ran out. Her hand was like ice. He felt for a pulse, but his hands shook so badly he couldn't find it. She was so still. He detected no movement or response from her whatsoever. She looked like a sleeping angel.

Jonah checked for any sign of breathing. Then he put his ear against her chest and held his breath, praying to hear the beating rhythm. Silence. He realized then that sweet Sara, his beloved wife, was gone.

Adam was getting ready to check on the horses when he heard a noise. Turning, he came face-to-face with Leah's dad. "Alton! You startled me. Have you been here long?"

Alton shook his head. "Just got here. I was heading to the house till I saw light coming from the barn."

"Jah, we just finished eating supper, and I'm checking on the horses." Adam didn't like the furrow of Alton's brows. "Is something troubling you? Sure hope you didn't come with bad news."

Alton moved closer. "I came to ask you a question, and I'd appreciate it if you were up front with me."

"Sure, Alton." Adam nodded. "What did you want to know?"

"It's about you and Leah." Alton cleared his throat. "Are you two having marital problems? Is that why her things are not in your room?"

Adam winced. "Did she tell you that?"

"No, her mamm did."

Adam was on the verge of asking how Dianna would know anything about his and Leah's sleeping arrangements, when Alton spoke again.

"My wife was here earlier, helping Leah with the laundry. When she took some things into your room, she was surprised not to see any of Leah's clothes there."

Adam shifted his weight and leaned on the stall door, feeling the need for support. "Well, you see—"

"Dianna also said that you asked Leah to stop doing reflexology. Is that true?"

Adam nodded slowly.

"Is that the reason she moved her things out of your room?"

"Well, no, but—"

"Leah's ability to help people through the use of reflexology is her gift. How could you take that from her, Adam?"

Adam pulled nervously on his shirt collar, feeling like he'd been backed into a corner. Should he tell Alton the truth? Well, what did he have to lose? Sooner or later, Leah's folks, and maybe others, would figure out that his and Leah's marriage wasn't based on love, but on a very special need.

"Okay, there's something you need to know," Adam began cautiously. "Leah and I got married so she could give my nieces full-time care."

Alton's eyebrows shot up. "I knew Leah was fond of the girls, but I didn't think she'd marry you just to be their substitute mother."

"She's more than that," Adam interjected. "She's also my friend."

"Humph!" Alton screwed up his face. "If she were your friend, you wouldn't have asked her to give up something she feels is so important."

Adam felt like a heel, but in order to explain his reasons for asking Leah to stop foot treatments, he'd have to tell Alton about his past.

I may as well tell him, 'cause if I don't, Leah probably will. Maybe she already has. I just won't mention that Cora is living here in Arthur.

Adam took a step closer to Alton. "I think you should know the reason I asked Leah to give up reflexology."

"I'm all ears."

Adam quickly told the story about his mother leaving when he was a boy and how she used to do reflexology, even though his dad disapproved. He heard them arguing about it and had always wondered why she wouldn't give it up when Dad had asked her to. When she finally did give it up, it was to become a nurse—something she couldn't do and remain Amish. She obviously cared more about helping other people than taking care of her own family.

Alton stood silently for several minutes, as though trying to let everything Adam had said sink in. Slowly, he reached out his hand and touched Adam's shoulder, giving it a squeeze. "Sounds like you went through a lot as a child, and I'm real sorry about that. But the past is in the past, and just because your mamm practiced foot doctoring and left to become a nurse doesn't mean Leah would do that, too. She's a good woman, devoted to God, your nieces, and I believe to you. Don't you think you oughtta give her the chance to prove that, Adam?"

Adam swallowed hard, trying to dislodge the lump in his throat. "Maybe you're right. I'll tell Leah that I've changed my mind. As long as it doesn't take time away from the girls, she's free to see people here in our home for reflexology treatments."

Alton gave Adam's shoulder another squeeze. "That's good to hear. Jah, real good."

Adam was tempted to tell Leah's dad about the sudden appearance of his mother, and how he was thinking of moving, but then he thought better of it. He needed to do something he should have done sooner. He needed to commit everything to prayer.

Cora turned off the kitchen light and was about to head for the living room to watch TV and spend a little time with Jared, when her cell phone rang. She paused. Seeing that it was her ex-husband, she answered the call. "Hello, Evan."

"Hey, Cora. How's it going?"

How do you think it's going? she silently screamed. *I'm here trying to raise our rebellious son by myself, and I've just met my other son, whom you know nothing about, but unfortunately, he would barely speak to me.* "Fine, Evan. Everything's just fine and dandy," she said dryly.

"Okay, good. Well, the reason I'm calling is I thought I'd drive down to Arthur on Tuesday and pick up Jared so he can spend Thanksgiving with me and Emily."

Oh, great. Now you want to spend time with our son. Cora was tempted to say that she'd made plans for her and Jared's Thanksgiving, but the truth was, she had no real plans. Besides, it might do Jared some good to spend a little time with his dad. After all, they hadn't seen each other since Cora and Jared left the city.

"Sure, Evan, that would be fine. I'll let Jared know right away. I'm sure he'll be glad."

"Okay, great. I'll be there late Tuesday afternoon to pick him up, and I'll bring him back on Sunday."

"That sounds fine."

When Cora hung up, she headed to the living room to give Jared the news. She knew he'd be glad, and she was happy for him, too, but oh, how she dreaded spending Thanksgiving alone.

CHAPTER 45

Saturday morning, Adam awoke at the crack of dawn. He'd spent several hours last night praying and mulling over the things Leah's father had said to him. He'd come to the conclusion that asking Leah to give up reflexology just because his mother used to practice it probably wasn't fair. Perhaps Alton had been right when he'd said Leah had a gift for helping others. He remembered how Amy had said Leah's foot treatment had relieved her headache, so maybe foot doctoring wasn't hocus-pocus. Maybe he'd just associated it with that because of negative things his dad had said.

Could my mother have had that gift as well? Adam threw the covers aside and crawled out of bed. He wouldn't think about his mother right now. Even if she'd had the gift, she quit doing it and ran off to become part of the English world. No God-fearing Christian woman would have done something like that. Not if they had been in their right mind.

Adam shook his head and muttered, "It would be a lot easier to forget about the past if she hadn't shown up." He still had to make a decision about whether to sell out and move to another state. If Cora would just leave, he wouldn't even consider moving. But how could he get her to do that?

I need to clear my head. Maybe I'll take a walk before breakfast and have another talk with God.

After getting dressed, Adam left the house, being careful to close the door quietly so he didn't disturb Leah or the girls while they slept upstairs. He'd just reached the end of his driveway, when Jonah's father, Raymond, pulled in with his horse and buggy.

"Guder mariye," Adam said, stepping up to the buggy. "You're sure out and about early this morning."

Raymond's grim expression gave Adam cause for alarm. "Is something wrong?"

The older man nodded. "I came with bad news."

"What's wrong?"

"Sara passed away last night. Since she and your wife were friends, I thought she'd want to know."

Adam drew in a sharp breath. "What happened?"

"Jonah found her in the barn, lying on the floor beneath the ladder leading to the loft. He thinks she may have climbed up to get one of their kittens and fallen." Raymond's voice faltered, and his eyes glassed over. "It appeared that her neck was broken."

Stunned by this news, Adam touched his pounding chest. "That's baremlich! I'm so sorry for your family's loss. Please let us know when the funeral arrangements have been made and also if there's anything we can do to help out."

Raymond nodded. "Guess I'd better move on. I still have others in the community that I need to notify this morning."

Adam turned and shuffled back to the house. He dreaded telling Leah this news.

Leah yawned as she entered the kitchen to start breakfast. She hadn't slept well last night, tossing and turning as she thought about the situation with Adam. Seeing his tender way with the girls had made her fall in love with him, but Adam's bitterness toward his own mother troubled Leah. It was a wedge that would always stand between them unless Adam's heart softened and he became willing to forgive Cora for what she'd done.

I need to keep praying about the situation, she told herself as she opened the refrigerator and removed a carton of eggs. There was no time to dwell on this now; the girls and Adam would be up soon and they'd expect to have breakfast ready.

Leah took out a bowl and cracked open several eggs. She'd just begun mixing them, when the back door opened and Adam entered the room.

"Ach, you startled me, Adam." Leah gestured to the bowl. "I was just getting breakfast started and figured you were still in bed."

"I went outside to clear my head, but then. . ." Adam paused and moved closer to Leah. "Raymond Miller stopped by to deliver some very distressing news."

"What is it, Adam? You look umgerennt."

"I am upset, and you will be, too, when you hear what I have to say."

Leah held her elbows tightly against her sides. "Adam, what is it? Tell me what's wrong."

"It's Sara Miller. She. . .she's dead."

Leah clasped her hands over her mouth to cover a gasp. "Oh, no! Oh, no! That just can't be. What happened, Adam?"

She stood in stunned silence as Adam told her everything that Raymond had said. Her legs felt so weak she could barely stand. Had it not been for the fact that Adam had taken hold of her arm, she might have collapsed.

As the reality of the situation sank in, Leah began to sob. Sara had visited her regularly for foot treatments, and they'd gotten to know each other quite well. In addition to Elaine and Priscilla, Sara was Leah's good friend. She had confided in Leah many times during her treatments, and Leah's heart had gone out to Sara when she'd learned that she had MS. Then when Sara married Jonah and had his baby, Leah had shared in their joy. Poor Jonah was alone now with the responsibility of raising Mark and baby Martha on his own. It wasn't fair. Life wasn't fair. Where was God in all this?

Adam pulled Leah into his arms, gently patting her back. "It's all right, Leah. Let the tears flow and grieve all you want."

Despite her pain, Leah found comfort in Adam's embrace. It was the first time they had been this close, emotionally or physically.

When Leah's sobs subsided, Adam leaned down and gently kissed her forehead. "This may not be the best time to say this, but there's something I need to get off my chest."

She tipped her head back and looked up at his face. "What is it?"

"Your daed came by last night while I was in the barn."

"Really? I didn't know Dad was here." Leah paused to use her apron to wipe at the tears wetting her cheeks. "Go on, Adam. Tell me the rest."

"You were probably preoccupied doing something with the girls and didn't hear his horse and buggy come in."

"What did Dad want?"

"He wanted to talk to me about something."

Leah waited for Adam to continue, finding comfort in his embrace.

"He thinks we're having marital problems."

Leah blinked. "What made him think that?"

"Apparently your mamm was in my room putting some laundry away, and when she saw that none of your things were there, she figured out that you don't sleep there. So she just assumed—"

Leah groaned. "Oh no."

"Your daed also said that your mamm had told him that I'd asked you to stop doing reflexology."

Leah pulled away from Adam and sank into a chair at the table. Not only did she need to deal with her grief over Sara's death, but now she also faced having to explain her relationship with Adam to her folks.

Adam pulled out the chair beside her and sat down. "I admitted to your daed that the reason we got married was so you could live here full-time and help me care for my nieces." He paused. "I could tell that Alton was none too happy about that. He accused me of marrying you just so you could be a substitute mother for the girls."

"Didn't you?"

"Well, yes, but that wasn't the only reason." Adam's cheeks colored. "The truth is, Leah, I care about you, and you've become a good friend."

Just a friend? Is that all I am to you, Adam?

"That's not the only thing I told your daed, Leah." Adam rushed on. "I told him about the situation with my mother—how she used to practice reflexology and then ran out on me, Mary, and our daed."

"Does he know that your mother is here in Arthur and that she wants to make amends with you?" Leah questioned.

Adam shook his head. "I figured, at that point, enough had been said."

"Sooner or later, it's bound to come out, Adam."

"Not from me, it won't. And I hope you won't say anything, either."

"I won't say anything without your approval, but we can't know about Cora. She could tell someone she works with or anyone else she may know."

"I'll deal with that when the time comes. Right now, we have issues of our own to deal with." Adam touched Leah's flushed cheeks, lightly brushing away her tears. "I thought hard and prayed about things last night, Leah, and I've decided that it was wrong of me to ask you to give up reflexology. Since my mother practiced it when I was a boy, I saw it as something evil, like her."

Leah shook her head. "No, Adam, I don't think Cora is evil. What she did was wrong, but I believe she's truly sorry and regrets her decision to leave like that. I think she deserves another chance."

Adam lowered his gaze. "You might be right, but I don't think I'm ready for that. I do want you to know, however, that if you'd like to continue doing foot treatments, you have my blessing. I may even ask you to work on my feet once in a while."

"Really, Adam? You don't mind if I do reflexology here in this house?"

He shook his head. "As long as it doesn't interfere with the care of the girls, you can foot doctor whenever you like."

Leah smiled, despite her tears. "Danki, Adam. Danki for that."

CHAPTER 46

Cora stared out the living-room window at the falling rain. It was such a dismal day, which only added to her depression over having to spend Thanksgiving alone. She'd thought about going out to dinner at one of the restaurants that were open on the holiday, but the idea of eating by herself held no appeal. So she'd stayed home and fixed a small turkey, just so she would have the leftovers for making sandwiches and soup.

Cora moved away from the window and took a seat in the rocking chair to be closer to the warmth of the fireplace. *I wonder what Adam and his family are doing today?* She squeezed her eyes tightly shut, willing herself not to cry. She'd done enough of that already, and where had it gotten her? Tears wouldn't change the fact that she'd been dumped by Evan, nor would they bring Adam back into her life. Crying and feeling sorry for herself wouldn't give her a good relationship with Jared, either. He'd been angry with her ever since the divorce and hated living here in Arthur.

Maybe it would be best for everyone if Jared and I did move back to Chicago. Since my house hasn't sold, we could take it off the market and move into it. And I don't think it would be that difficult to find a nursing job. It just won't be at the hospital where I'd have to see Evan and Emily.

A horn tooted from outside, and Cora's eyes snapped open. Obviously a car had pulled into the yard. Moments later, the front door opened and Jared stepped in.

"Jared! What are you doing here?" Cora asked in surprise. "I didn't expect you to come back until Sunday."

Jared frowned and tossed his coat on a chair. "As soon as we finished eating dinner today, I asked Dad to bring me home."

Cora's eyebrows rose. "How come?" *Did Jared just call this place home?*

"Dad didn't really want me there, Mom." Jared grunted as he flopped onto the couch. "The first night I was at their house, he and Emily went to a party and left me home alone. Then on Wednesday, they both went about their business as though I wasn't even there." He folded his arms. "Guess they thought I could entertain myself by watching TV or playing some computer games."

Cora frowned. "I thought he wanted to spend some quality time with you. That's what he said when he called." She glanced at the door. "What'd he do—just pull into the driveway and drop you off?"

Jared gave a nod. "He's bent out of shape because I asked him to bring me home. Guess he didn't like being pulled away from his fancy friends."

"What friends?"

Jared shrugged. "Beats me. I can't remember any of their names, but I think they were all doctors from the hospital. A few of them brought their wives and kids along."

"Did Emily host the meal?"

"Nope. The dinner was held at one of the other people's homes, but Dad pretty much ignored me the whole time. Made me feel like a stranger—even to him. To tell you the truth, Dad seems like someone I don't know anymore."

"I'm sorry, Jared." Cora got up and sat on the couch beside him. "I was hoping you would have a good time."

"Yeah, me, too."

"Do you still want to move back to Chicago?" she asked.

He shook his head. "No way! Being around Dad, Emily, and their snooty friends made me anxious to get back here to be with you."

Cora's heart melted, and she gave Jared a hug. "I'm glad you're back, because I missed you. It wasn't Thanksgiving without you."

"Same here."

"If you're hungry, I have some leftover turkey. Would you like some of that?"

Jared shook his head. "Not now, Mom. Maybe later, though."

"Okay." Cora smiled. Today had turned out better than she'd imagined, at least where she and Jared were concerned. She didn't know when or if she would ever mend fences with Adam, but at least she had Jared, and for that she was thankful.

The day after Thanksgiving as Elaine stood beside Ben, along with several others who had come to the cemetery to say their final goodbyes to Sara, her heart went out to Jonah. He stood beside Sara's parents, holding little Mark, while his mother-in-law held the baby. On the other side of Jonah were his parents and his sister and her family. Obviously they were all in pain. Sara and Jean had been good friends, so Sara's death had been a huge blow to everyone in the family.

Jonah's drooping shoulders and dull-looking eyes let Elaine know that in addition to his grief, he hadn't had much sleep. Losing a loved one was difficult in any situation, and an unexpected tragedy such as this had to be devastating. Elaine wished there was something she could do to ease his burden. It would be difficult for him to go on without Sara. But Jonah was strong, and Elaine felt sure he would make it through with the help of his folks and Sara's. Others within their Amish community would be there for Jonah and his children, too.

As Jonah stood on shaky legs, staring at Sara's simple wooden coffin being lowered into the ground, he struggled to keep his emotions under control. For little Mark's sake, he did not want to break down.

It still didn't seem possible that such a tragedy had happened. Things had been going along so well, and he and Sara had been so excited about the safe arrival of their new baby girl. It grieved him to know that their precious daughter would never get to know her mother—at least not on this earth. He loved Sara and wondered how he could make it without her. For the sake of his children, though, he had to find the courage and strength to go on.

He remembered the words to Isaiah 30:15, a verse of scripture their bishop had quoted during Sara's funeral service: *"In quietness and in confidence shall be your strength."*

Jonah would need to memorize that verse and quote it many times in the days ahead, for he had never been more fully aware that he could do nothing in his own strength. He needed every bit of help he could get—from his family and friends, but most of all from God.

Leah's heart was saddened as she stood beside Adam and recited the Lord's Prayer along with the others in attendance. She was confident that Sara was in a better place, but she would be sorely missed by her family and friends—especially Jonah. Mark was still young, and even though he would miss his mother, in time his memory of her would fade. And the precious baby girl would have no memory of Sara at all. *What will Jonah do now?* Leah wondered. *Will he eventually remarry or simply rely on his family to help him raise Martha and Mark?*

Leah knew how important the children were to Jonah. She'd been convinced that he'd married Sara mostly to be a father to Mark. That wasn't to say that he didn't love Sara. No, it had been quite evident from Jonah's tender, caring ways that he was committed to Sara and their marriage and would have done most anything for her.

She glanced over at her brother, Nathan, and his wife, Jean, who stood near Jonah and his parents. *Poor Jean, seeing her brother go through something like this. It seems so unfair to all of them.*

"Leah, are you ready to go?" Adam asked, placing his hand on her arm while leaning close to her.

She blinked a couple of times and slowly nodded. She'd been so immersed in her thoughts that she hadn't even realized the service was over.

Leah followed Adam over to offer their condolences to Jonah once more. "If there's anything you need, please let us know," Leah said, swallowing against the sob rising in her throat.

"Jah," Adam agreed. "We'll do whatever we can to help."

"Danki for your kindness." Jonah tousled Mark's hair. "It's going to be tough, but with the support of family, friends, and most of all God, we'll make it through."

Several others came up then, so Leah moved aside and followed Adam to their horse and buggy at the hitching rack just outside the fence surrounding the cemetery. They'd left the girls with Leah's mother today, thinking the funeral might be a harsh reminder of their own parents' death.

Adam helped Leah into the buggy, untied his horse, and took his place in the driver's seat. Turning to Leah, he said, "There's something I think you should know."

"What's that?"

"I've been thinking about our marriage and how it's only a marriage of convenience." He clasped her hand. "What I'm trying to say is that I've been dead inside, but you've brought me back to life. I'm in love with you, Leah, and I'd like us to be married in every sense of the word."

"I love you, too, Adam, and I love Carrie, Linda, and Amy. I've come to realize that you and the girls are God's gift to me. But we need to work out some things."

"You mean about my mother?"

Leah nodded, while squeezing his hand. "We are Christians, Adam, and God's Word says we need to forgive others."

"I know, and I've been praying about that. I'm not ready yet to establish a relationship with Cora, but God's helping me to be able to forgive her." Gently, he caressed Leah's face. "You don't have to worry about me selling out and moving, either, because we'll be staying put."

Tears welled in Leah's eyes, clouding her vision. "I'm so glad."

"I've been meaning to ask you something. That night when you told me about Cora, it seemed that you were going to say something else, but I cut you off. Was it important, Leah?"

"Jah, I think it was, but I didn't say anything because it seemed as if you'd made up your mind, and I was waiting for just the right time."

"What is it, Leah? I'm willing to listen."

"Cora told me that awhile after she'd left you, Mary, and your daed, she'd come back to see you, but you'd moved, and no one would tell her where you had gone."

"She really came back?"

Leah nodded. "That's what she said."

"Do you think she planned to stay, or was it just for a visit?"

"I'm not sure. That's something you'd have to ask her yourself."

"Maybe someday, I will." Adam leaned closer and gently kissed Leah's lips.

His words gave Leah hope. Maybe after a little more time, Adam would be willing to talk to his mother and would learn that he had a half brother. Perhaps someday soon, he'd allow Cora and Jared to be a part of their family. Now that would be the best gift of all.

LEAH'S CHOCOLATE-CHIP CHEESE BALL

Ingredients:
1 (8 ounce) package cream cheese, softened
½ cup butter, softened
¼ teaspoon vanilla
¾ cup powdered sugar
2 tablespoons brown sugar
1 (10½ ounce) package mini chocolate chips
¾ cup nuts, finely chopped

In mixing bowl, beat cream cheese, butter, and vanilla until fluffy. Gradually add powdered sugar and brown sugar until combined. Stir in mini chocolate chips. Cover and refrigerate for 30 minutes. Place on large piece of plastic wrap and shape into a ball. Refrigerate at least 1 hour before serving. Roll ball in nuts. Serve with graham crackers or any other cracker you like.

LEAH'S HUMMINGBIRD CAKE

INGREDIENTS:

1 package yellow cake mix
⅓ cup vegetable oil
1 (8 ounce) can crushed pineapple, well drained with juice reserved
3 eggs
1 teaspoon cinnamon
1 ripe banana, cut up
¾ cup walnuts, chopped and divided
1 (12 ounce) jar maraschino cherries, well drained, chopped, and divided

GLAZE:

4 ounces cream cheese, softened
¼ cup powdered sugar
2 to 3 tablespoons milk

Preheat oven to 350 degrees. Coat 10-inch Bundt pan with cooking spray. In large bowl, combine cake mix, oil, pineapple, eggs, and cinnamon. Add enough water to reserved pineapple juice to make ½ cup. Add to bowl and beat thoroughly until mixture is combined. Stir in banana, ½ cup walnuts, and ¼ cup cherries. Mix well. Sprinkle remaining nuts and cherries in prepared pan then pour in batter. Bake 40 to 45 minutes, or until toothpick inserted in center comes out clean. Let cool 15 minutes then invert onto serving platter and cool completely. In medium bowl, combine cream cheese, powdered sugar, and milk. Beat until smooth. Drizzle glaze over cooled cake.

DISCUSSION QUESTIONS

1. Leah felt that her ability to help people with reflexology was a gift from God. But some people, like Adam, didn't see it that way. Have you ever had an ability that you felt was God's gift but others did not? How did you deal with their negative comments?

2. Since Adam's mother had abandoned him when he was a child, he was afraid of establishing a relationship with any other woman because she might reject him. Have you or someone you know ever been in a similar situation? How did you deal with those feelings?

3. What can we do to help someone whose parents have abandoned them? What are some verses of scripture that might help someone like Adam cope with their past?

4. Cora made several unwise decisions during her adult life, including her decision to leave the faith of her people. How did walking away from the faith that she'd been taught during her childhood change the course of her life?

5. Should Cora have included her son Jared in the decision to leave their home in Chicago and move to Arthur where they had no friends or family? Do you think Jared may have been more receptive to change if he'd been included in the plans?

6. After Cora's divorce, her son became rebellious. How can a single parent deal with a defiant teen?

7. Jonah suffered yet another loss when an unexpected accident shattered his world. What are some things we can do to help someone get through a tragic loss?

8. Despite his decision to remain single, Adam felt the need for a wife. His marriage was one of convenience, rather than love, since he needed someone to help him raise his nieces. Was that the best course of action for Adam, or should he have looked for a full-time babysitter?

9. Leah agreed to marry Adam even though he didn't love her. Leah's love for Adam's nieces was a driving factor. Is there ever a time when a couple should marry without love? What obstacles would they have to overcome in order to make the marriage work?

10. Leah's friend Priscilla became tired of waiting for her boyfriend to propose and was thinking about breaking up with him, but she didn't tell him why. Do you think Priscilla should have been up front with Elam, or should she have been more patient and waited awhile longer to see if he would bring up the subject of marriage? How long do you feel a couple should date before marriage?

11. Was it fair for Leah's friend Elaine to allow Ben to court her when she still had feelings for Jonah?

12. When Leah knew she had feelings for Adam, she kept them to herself. Should she have opened up and admitted how she felt instead of fearing rejection?

13. Forgiveness, acceptance, and tolerance of others are some of the themes in this book. What verses of scripture were mentioned in the story? Can you think of some other helpful Bible verses that deal with these topics?

14. What life lessons did you learn from reading this book? Were there any particular verses of scripture that spoke to your heart?

15. Did you learn anything new about the Amish by reading this story? What are your thoughts about their way of life?

The RESTORATION

To Dianna Yoder, a special friend.

[Jesus said,] "For if ye forgive men their trespasses,
your heavenly Father will also forgive you."
MATTHEW 6:14

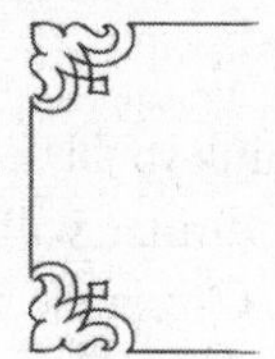

CHAPTER 1

Arthur, Illinois

Priscilla Herschberger shivered as she hurried across the yard, anxious to get out of the cold. It was only the first week of December, but with fresh-fallen snow and blustery winds, it felt like the middle of winter. Despite her chattering teeth and tingling hands and feet, this weather stirred Priscilla's feelings like it had when she was a child, filling her with hope that they might have snow for Christmas.

Entering the small store where she and her mother sold jams, jellies, and several other types of home-canned goods, she quickly shut the door. Business was slow this time of year, so they opened the store only a few days a week. Priscilla had come to get several jars of strawberry jam to serve at a dinner for tourists hosted by her friend Elaine Schrock. Elaine's helper, Karen Yoder, couldn't be there this evening, so Priscilla had volunteered to take her place. She looked forward to going—not only to help but also to spend time with Elaine.

"Sure hope everything goes okay," Priscilla murmured. She'd never helped with one of Elaine's dinners before, but she had plenty of experience in the kitchen, helping her mother. *It should be fun*, she told herself, placing the jars inside a cardboard box. From what Elaine had told Priscilla, these dinners often provided unexpected chuckles. Once when Elaine's grandmother was alive, her parakeet, Millie, had gotten out of its cage and created quite a stir among their dinner guests. Another time, a man had made everyone laugh by his constant burping. He'd later explained that, in his country, burping was a custom that showed appreciation for a good meal.

Priscilla always enjoyed listening to Elaine's stories, but she hoped nothing she said or did tonight would cause anyone to laugh.

Leaving the store, she put the box in her buggy and headed back to the house to tell her mother good-bye. She found Mom in the sewing room, cutting a pattern for a new dress. "I got the jam, and I'm leaving for Elaine's now."

Mom looked up and smiled. "What time do you think you'll be home?"

Priscilla shrugged. "I'm not sure how long the dinner will last. It starts at six o'clock, so it may be over by eight or so. Of course, I'll stay awhile after that to help Elaine clean up and do the dishes."

"Please be careful. The roads could be icy tonight." Mom's depth of concern was revealed in her ebony-colored eyes.

"I'll take it easy. Tinker is a good horse. I've never had a problem with her in the snow."

"There's always a first time." Mom's face tightened. "Just because a *gaul* is easygoing, doesn't mean it won't spook. Remember to keep a tight rein. Some people don't take the road conditions seriously enough."

"Try not to worry, Mom. I'll be okay." Priscilla knew her mother was concerned, but sometimes she tended to be overprotective. Maybe it was because Priscilla was the youngest of five children and the only girl. *Once I'm married and living in a place of my own, Mom won't worry about me so much. Of course, that won't happen if Elam never asks me to marry him.*

"*Danki* for coming to help on such short notice," Elaine said when Priscilla entered her house that evening and set the cardboard box on the table.

Priscilla hugged her friend. "It's not a problem. I'm glad you asked." Before Elaine hired Karen, Priscilla and their friend Leah had offered to help Elaine many times, but Elaine had always said she could manage by herself.

"How are the roads?" Elaine questioned.

"Not too bad. Right now they're just wet, but they could get worse when the temperature drops." Priscilla motioned to the jars of jam. "Where would you like me to put these?"

"You can put them in glass bowls and place two on each of the tables I've set up in the other room." Elaine smiled. "I appreciate all this jam and will gladly pay for it."

Priscilla shook her head. "There's no need."

"You won't let me pay you for helping tonight, so I insist on paying for the jam."

Priscilla knew she wouldn't get anywhere arguing with her friend, so she nodded and took the jam and dishes into the generously sized room next to the kitchen. Elaine's grandfather had added it on to the house when his wife started serving dinners for tourists many years ago. It could accommodate as many as one hundred people and had been used to hold church services when needed, in addition to groups of people who came for the meals. Elaine had continued offering the dinners after her grandparents died. It gave her something meaningful to do and had become a favorite event for tourists, as well as some of the locals.

Priscilla looked around as she set the bowls of jam on the three tables. Elaine had covered each table with a bright red cloth and draped white lace over the top. Beside each plate was a green cloth napkin, and chubby red pillar candles with a bit of greenery at the base served as centerpieces. Between the tantalizing aromas coming from the kitchen, the scent of pine from the greenery, and the overall festive appearance, the room was ready to welcome their guests. Just being in it made Priscilla look forward to Christmas.

She wondered if the holiday would be special for her and Elam. Last year she'd hoped for that, too. Unfortunately, nothing had changed—they were still courting, but Elam had not proposed. It did no good to analyze his reasons, so she reminded herself to focus on other things.

Priscilla returned to the kitchen, where Elaine was slicing freshly baked bread. "That room sure looks festive," Priscilla commented. "I had to look closely at the candles before I realized they were battery operated."

Elaine filled a basket with bread and began slicing another loaf. "Besides being safer, battery-powered candles last for hours, with no dripping wax to worry about."

"That's true. Now, what would you like me to do?" Priscilla questioned.

"The salads are made and the chicken's in the oven. Why don't we have a cup of tea and visit until it's time to start the potatoes?"

"Are you sure? I came here to work, you know."

Elaine chuckled. "Don't worry, you'll have plenty to do as soon as our fifty guests arrive."

Priscilla's mouth opened wide. "Fifty? I didn't realize there would be so many people to serve."

"Guess I forgot to mention it, but don't worry, we'll manage okay." Elaine poured tea, and they took seats at the table. "The people coming here tonight are family members who wanted to do something different to celebrate Christmas."

"This is only the first week of December. Why would they celebrate Christmas so early?" Priscilla scooted her chair closer to the table.

"Some people who'll be coming live in the area, but others are from out of town. They're having a get-together now because it's the only time they could all manage to gather." Elaine pushed a strand of shiny blond hair back under her white head covering.

Priscilla took a sip of the warm tea, enjoying the familiar pumpkin-spice flavor. "Speaking of Christmas, if you haven't made plans, I'd like you to come over to our place that day."

"I appreciate the invitation," Elaine replied, "I'll be joining Ben's family for Christmas Eve dinner, but I have no plans for Chrismtas Day."

"You two have been seeing each other awhile now. Has there been any talk of marriage?"

Elaine nodded. "Ben proposed several weeks ago."

"Really? How come you're just now telling me?"

"Since I haven't given him an answer yet, I figured there was no point mentioning it." Elaine blew on her tea. "Ben's a wonderful man, and I care for him, but I'm not sure what I feel is deep enough for a marriage commitment."

"That makes sense." Priscilla knew Elaine had once been in love with Jonah Miller, but in all the time Ben had been courting her, Priscilla had never seen Elaine look at him the way she used to look at Jonah. It was unfortunate that Jonah's wife, Sara, had died. Recently, Priscilla had wondered if Jonah and Elaine might get together again someday. Of course, she'd never voice her thoughts to Elaine. It hadn't even been a month since Sara fell from a ladder in their barn. It was too soon for Jonah to take another wife, although he might eventually feel the need for someone other than his folks to help care for his baby girl and stepson.

Elaine bumped Priscilla's arm. "You're awfully quiet all of a sudden. What are you thinking about?"

"Love and marriage."

"Has Elam finally proposed?"

Priscilla sighed, looking down at the table. "No, and maybe he never will. I'd probably be smart to break things off with him."

"As I recall, you were thinking about breaking up once before." Elaine placed her hand on Priscilla's arm, giving it a motherly pat. "You love him very much, don't you?"

"Jah." Priscilla lifted her head. "But if he doesn't want to marry me, I may as well accept it and move on with my life."

"I'm sure Elam loves you, Priscilla. You just need to be patient. He's probably waiting for the right time to propose."

"Maybe so." After a brief pause, she said, "I haven't talked to Leah for a while. Do you know how things are going with her and Adam?"

"I dropped by their place yesterday, to give the girls some cookies. Leah said things are going well. Unfortunately, though, Adam still hasn't resolved things with his mother."

"It's a sad situation any way you look at it. I was glad when Leah finally explained how Adam's mother had abandoned him and his sister when they were children. It's ironic that Cora used to practice reflexology." Priscilla directed her gaze across the room to look at the clock. "Guess it was the reason Adam was so set against Leah working on people's feet. Most likely, it reminded him of his mother."

"That's understandable, at least from a child's point of view. But as an adult, Adam should have been able to see past all that and realize Leah is nothing like his mother." Elaine paused to drink some tea. "It seems a shame that Adam's mother is now living here in Arthur, and yet Adam won't have anything to do with her."

"I hope everything works out for them. Life's too short to hold grudges that can separate people from their families." Elaine pushed away from the table. "Guess I'll get the potatoes out now and start peeling."

When the lively group of people arrived, most dressed in fancy Christmas attire, Priscilla scurried about, making sure everyone found a seat. Some brought gifts for family members, which they placed on a smaller table, to be opened after the meal.

Priscilla noticed Evie, a boisterous woman with dyed blond hair. Her bright red dress had slits in the sides of the skirt, and the bodice was low cut. When Evie laughed, her whole body shook, making the shiny gold bells in her hair clink together and jingle.

Pricilla had begun to pour water for everyone, when Evie flipped her head around and bumped Priscilla's arm. Water splashed out, some landing in the woman's lap.

Priscilla gasped. "I am so sorry." She handed Evie several napkins.

Blotting her skirt, Evie chuckled. "Don't worry, dear. It's only water. It won't leave a stain."

Relieved, Priscilla hoped the rest of the evening would go by without any other mishaps.

During the meal, everyone visited, and several people told jokes or humorous stories. After Elaine brought out three kinds of pie, they all settled down, and for a while everything got quiet.

"This apple pie is delicious, darlin'," a dark-haired man wearing a battery-operated lighted Christmas tie spoke up. "Would ya mind sharin' the recipe with my wife?"

Elaine's cheeks flushed. "I'm glad you like it. The pie has no refined sugar in it, so it can be enjoyed by those whose diets are restricted. I'll be happy to give you a copy of the recipe before you go home."

"That'd be wonderful." The bells in Evie's hair tinkled as she bobbed her head. "You should put together a cookbook and sell it to those who come here for your delicious dinners. I know I would enjoy having a few of your recipes."

Elaine's eyes sparkled. "I've thought of doing that but haven't taken the time."

"If you decide to do a cookbook, I'd be happy to help you with it," Priscilla volunteered.

"It's nice of you to offer. I may just take you up on that, because it'll be a lot of work to do on my own."

"Well, just let me know whenever you're ready to begin."

Elaine and Priscilla headed back to the kitchen to get more coffee for the guests.

"Everyone seems to be having a good time," Priscilla commented.

"They're in the Christmas spirit, and it gets me excited, too." Elaine gave Priscilla's shoulder a tender squeeze. "I appreciate you helping me tonight."

"I'm glad I could do it. It's been fun, even if I did spill water in Evie's lap."

Elaine snickered. "She took it quite well." She moved toward the stove but paused before picking up the coffeepot. "Umm. . . I have a favor to ask, Priscilla."

"What's that?"

"Karen won't be coming back to work for me."

"How come?"

"She and her family are moving to Indiana next week. Since I have two more dinners scheduled between now and Christmas, I'm kind of in a bind. Would you be able to help until I find someone to take Karen's place? I'll pay you what I paid her, of course."

Priscilla smiled. "I'd be happy to help, and you don't have to worry about finding anyone else. Mom and I won't have much to do in the store until spring, when we'll make more jams and jellies to sell. I just have one question. Are all your dinners like this one?"

Elaine shook her head. "Every group of people is different, but they're all quite entertaining."

Priscilla grinned. "I'm sure it'll be an experience."

After the people went home, Priscilla cleared the dishes and began washing them. Elaine came in and said, "As the last guests were leaving, I noticed it was snowing pretty hard. I think you ought to spend the night. If the weather improves, you can go home in the morning."

Priscilla shook her head. "I should be fine if I leave as soon as we finish washing the dishes. If I don't show up, my folks will worry. Even if I call and leave a message, they probably won't check their voice mail till tomorrow morning."

"I suppose you're right. You'd better go now then, before the snow gets any worse."

"What about the dishes? I don't want to leave you stuck with those."

"I don't mind." Elaine gave Priscilla a hug. "You go on now and be safe."

"Okay, if you insist." Priscilla put on her outer garments and headed for the door. "I'll call you tomorrow morning," she called over her shoulder.

A short time later, Priscilla headed down the road with her horse and buggy. She'd only gone a short ways when she caught sight of a motorcycle going in the opposite direction. Wondering why anyone would be riding a cycle on a night like this, Priscilla gripped her horse's reins a little tighter. Suddenly, a flash of brown ran in front of the motorcycle. When the driver swerved to avoid hitting it, he slid off the road and slammed into a stop sign. The bike flipped over, sending the driver into the snowy ditch.

"Whoa, Tinker! Whoa!" Priscilla directed her horse to the side of the road. She had to see if the rider was hurt.

CHAPTER 2

Priscilla's hands shook as she guided her horse and buggy to the side of the road. She hopped out and tied Tinker to a nearby tree. She grabbed a flashlight and rushed over to the victim. Shining the light on his face, she gasped. It was David Morgan, a young English man she'd known since they were teenagers. David lived in Chicago and had been coming to Arthur off and on over the years to visit his grandparents. Even though Priscilla hadn't seen him for some time, she recognized his sandy blond hair and vivid blue eyes.

"David, are you hurt?" Panting, she dropped to her knees in the snow beside him, relieved to see he was conscious.

He blinked several times. "Priscilla Herschberger, is. . .is it you?"

"Yes, it's me." Priscilla nodded. "Are you hurt?" she repeated, lowering the flashlight and placing her hand gently on his arm.

"My leg. . . I think it might be broken. My head and ribs hurt, too. It–it's hard to breathe."

"Oh, David, I'm so sorry. I need to get you some help."

"My cell phone's in my jacket pocket. You'd better call 911."

Priscilla's fingers trembled as she reached into David's pocket and retrieved his phone. She hoped help would come soon, because it wasn't good for him to lie out here in the cold. She wasn't strong enough to move him, which might do more harm than good anyway.

After she made the call, Priscilla took a blanket from her buggy to cover David, who was shivering badly. She thought about placing something under his head, but worried he might have a neck injury, so decided against it. Using a clean towel she kept in a plastic bag under her buggy seat, she wiped the snow off his face.

"I'll stay right here beside you till help comes," Priscilla knew she needed to keep him talking so he would remain awake. If David had a concussion, he shouldn't fall asleep.

"I didn't know you were in the area," she said as the falling snowflakes melted on his face.

David's teeth chattered, and he tried to sit up.

"You'd better lie still," she cautioned, placing her hand on his shoulder. "Your injuries could be serious."

"Priscilla, you're my angel of mercy." He closed his eyes.

"Don't fall asleep. Talk to me, David. Tell me why you've come back to Arthur after being gone two years." Gently, Priscilla continued drying the melted snow from his face with the towel.

"Came back to see if..." His voice trailed off as he sucked in a shallow breath. "It hurts, Priscilla. It hurts to breathe."

"I know it's hard, but try to relax and keep talking to me. Help will be here soon."

Priscilla didn't know how many minutes had passed, but it seemed like forever before the EMTs arrived. "What hospital will you take him to?" she asked one of the paramedics.

"We'll go to Sarah Bush in Matton. Depending on how severe his injuries are, he may be transferred to either Carle in Urbana or DMH in Decatur."

Priscilla moved close to the stretcher where David lay. "I'll let your grandparents know what happened. I'm sure they'll go to the hospital right away."

"W–will you come, too, Priscilla? I'd f–feel better if you were there."

She nodded and squeezed his hand. "I'll be with them, David; you can count on it."

❧

When Priscilla pulled her horse and buggy into the yard of David's grandparents, she was relieved to see lights in the window. Thank goodness someone was still up.

Although she didn't know Walt and Letty Morgan well, she had met them several times when their grandson visited, and she and Elam had gone there to see him. David spent most of the time, though, at either Priscilla's or Elam's. Priscilla had never understood why David enjoyed hanging out with her and Elam, but he'd always seemed to enjoy their time together and had even teased about becoming

Amish someday. Of course, Priscilla knew he was only kidding. After all, why would David, who'd grown up with modern things, want to give up his dream of becoming a veterinarian? He'd attended college for the last two-and-a-half years and had only been back to Arthur once since then. Priscilla and Elam first met David when some of the young people in their area got together to play volleyball. Priscilla had always gotten along well with David, and if he were Amish, she may have been interested in him as more than a friend. Of course, she'd never told anyone. It was silly, Priscilla knew, but when things weren't going well between her and Elam, the notion of being with David sometimes popped into her head.

Shaking her thoughts aside, Priscilla secured Tinker to a fence post and hurried to the house. As she reached out to knock on the door, it opened, and Letty greeted her. "Well, for goodness' sake, I thought I heard a horse and buggy pull in. Walt said I was hearing things, but my hearing's just fine. I know the sound of a horse's whinny." Letty peered at Priscilla over the top of her plastic-framed glasses. "You're Davey's friend Priscilla, aren't you?"

Priscilla nodded. "I came here to tell you—"

"Davey's on his way here right now. He called yesterday and said he should arrive sometime this evening." Letty's brows furrowed. "Walt and I expected him hours ago."

Rubbing her arms briskly beneath her woolen shawl, Priscilla said, "I'm sorry to tell you this, but David's been in an accident."

Letty gasped. "How did it happen? Has Davey been hurt?"

"What I believe was a deer ran in front of his motorcycle. David lost control and slid off the road. He complained of his head and ribs hurting and said he thought his leg was broken," Priscilla explained. "I called 911, and he's been taken to Sarah Bush Hospital."

"Oh my!" Letty motioned for Priscilla to step inside. "Walt, our Davey's been in an accident!" she called. "We need to go to the hospital right away!"

A few seconds later, Letty's husband appeared, wearing a pair of gray sweatpants and a matching T-shirt. "I'll change my clothes and get the car out of the garage."

"Would it be all right if I go with you?" Priscilla questioned. "David asked if I'd come, and I'd like to know how he's doing."

Letty gave Priscilla's arm a gentle pat. "Of course you can come. Walt can put your horse in our barn."

"Thank you." Priscilla hesitated. "May I use your phone? I'll need to leave my folks a message so they know where I am and don't worry."

"Not a problem." Letty pointed to the kitchen. "The phone's in there."

"I wonder why Priscilla isn't home yet." Iva glanced at the grandfather clock her husband had given her as a wedding present thirty-four years ago. "It's ten thirty. I would think she would have been here by now."

Daniel set his book aside and clasped Iva's hand. "Try not to worry. With the way the weather is tonight, Priscilla may have decided to spend the night at Elaine's."

"That makes sense. I'd better go out to the phone shack and see if she left us a message. If she decided to stay over, I'm sure she would have called."

Daniel stood. "I'll do it. There's no need for you to go out in the cold."

"Danki, Daniel." Iva smiled as he put on his jacket and went out the door. Her husband had always been considerate of her needs, and she appreciated his thoughtfulness. She hoped Priscilla would find a man like her father. Elam Gingerich seemed nice enough, but Iva wasn't sure how committed he was to her daughter. He'd hung out with Priscilla since they were teenagers and had been courting her for well over a year with no mention of marriage.

Iva thought about her married sons, Alan, Edward, James, and Thomas, with just two years between them. They'd all fallen in love with lovely young women and proposed marriage after the first year of courting. *Guess I shouldn't worry about Priscilla and Elam's relationship*, Iva told herself. *Priscilla hasn't said much about it to me, so perhaps she's content with the way things are right now. One of these days Elam might surprise us all and pop the question.*

Iva clasped her hands behind her neck and rubbed the knotted muscles. Her neck had been hurting most of the day. If it didn't let up soon, she would make an appointment with Priscilla's friend, Leah, for a reflexology treatment. The last time Iva's back acted up, Leah had been able to relieve the pain. Hopefully, she'd be able to work out the kinks in Iva's neck as well. With Christmas a few weeks away and so much baking and cleaning to do yet, Iva would be in better shape if she were free of pain.

When Daniel returned to the house, his expression was grim.

"What's wrong?" Iva asked, seeing the look of distress on her husband's bearded face. "You look *umgerennt*."

"I'm not upset as much as concerned." He removed his jacket and took a seat in the recliner across from Iva. "Our daughter left a message, but it wasn't about spending the night with Elaine."

Iva tipped her head. "What was it then?"

"Priscilla is at the hospital with David Morgan's grandparents. Apparently he was injured when he fell off his motorcycle. Priscilla witnessed the accident on her way home from Elaine's."

Iva's hands went straight to her mouth. "*Ach*, my! Is David badly hurt?"

"Priscilla didn't say. Just said she was heading to the hospital with Walt and Letty and would fill us in on the details when she gets home."

Mattoon, Illinois

At the hospital, Priscilla paced nervously as she waited for a report on David's condition.

His parents will probably come as soon as they hear the news. Priscilla thought about David's father, a veterinarian. He and his wife lived in Chicago. From what David had said, his dad expected him to follow in his footsteps. It was the reason David had gone to college and would eventually attend a veterinary school.

I'll bet his grandparents have missed him, Priscilla thought, glancing at Walt and Letty sitting across from her with anxious expressions. Walt had called David's folks to notify them of the accident and then returned to the waiting room to sit beside his wife.

"Had to leave them a message," Walt grumbled. "As usual, our son, Robert, didn't answer his phone."

Priscilla figured David might be on Christmas break and had come to Arthur to spend the holiday with his grandparents. Perhaps his parents would be joining them. Since David was an only child, surely they wouldn't spend the holiday alone.

The ride to the hospital had been slow. With the icy roads, Priscilla was thankful David's grandfather had driven cautiously. His grandparents were probably more concerned for David's welfare than even she was. Broken bones could heal. What worried Priscilla the most was his head injury. If he'd been wearing a helmet, he would have been better protected. She hoped none of his injuries were serious.

"Sure wish we'd hear something." Letty fidgeted in her chair. "I can't stand sitting here doing nothing, not knowing how Davey is doing."

"I don't like waiting, either." Walt patted her hand. "There's not much we can do except try to be patient and pray for David."

"I've been praying for him, too," Priscilla said.

Letty offered her a weak smile. "It was nice of you to come along, and we appreciate the added prayers."

A nurse entered the waiting room and walked over to Letty and Walt. "The doctor's with your grandson now. He's been asking for you."

David's grandparents rose from their chairs. "One of us will come back and tell you how David is doing as soon as we've talked to the doctor," Letty said to Priscilla.

She nodded slowly and closed her eyes in prayer as Letty and Walt left the room.

CHAPTER 3

Gram. . . Gramps. . . I'm sure glad you're here." David was relieved to see his grandparents beside his bed. "Where's Priscilla? Didn't she come with you?"

"She's in the waiting room," Gram said. "The doctor explained what your injuries are, and we wanted to see you first, before Priscilla comes in."

"So let me have it. Am I gonna be okay?"

"Of course you are." Gramps moved closer to David's bed. "Your left leg is broken, along with a couple of ribs."

"You also have a mild concussion." Gram took David's hand. "We're thankful you weren't hurt any worse. When you called to let us know you were coming, we thought you'd be driving your car. Riding a motorcycle in this kind of weather is dangerous, Davey."

"Yeah, I know. It's a good thing Priscilla came along when she did." David glanced toward the door. "Will you ask her to come in?"

"In a minute." Gramps's forehead creased as he took a seat in the chair beside David's bed. "I need to talk to you about something."

Here it comes. I bet they've already called my folks and told 'em I've been in an accident.

Gramps leaned closer to David. "I called your dad to let him and your mom know you'd been injured, but got no answer so I had to leave a message." He glanced at Gram, seated on the other side of David's bed. "I'm sure as soon as your folks get the message they'll come."

David grimaced. "Can we talk about this later? I'm tired, and I'd like to talk to Priscilla before I conk out."

"Certainly. I'll go get her." Gram rose from her chair. "Are you coming, Walt?" She leaned over and kissed David's forehead before heading for the door.

"Yeah, sure. We'll talk to you later, David." Gramps got up and followed her out of the room.

Struggling to keep his eyes open, David kept his focus on the door, waiting for Priscilla to show up. She was the one person who would understand his reason for leaving Chicago. She'd always been supportive of his decisions. He remembered how after he'd decided to go to college, Priscilla had encouraged him, saying she thought he was smart and would do well academically. If she'd approved of him going, surely she would support his decision to drop out. *Or will she think I'm a failure?*

Yawning, David glanced around the room in an effort to stay awake. *How far down the hall am I?* he wondered. The room was spotless and actually smelled clean. Looking through the slats of the open window blinds, he saw in the glow of lights that it was still snowing. Hopefully, by the time his grandparents and Priscilla left, the weather would improve.

Reliving the accident and how fast it had happened, David was glad it hadn't been any worse. Although he wished it hadn't happened at all.

While he waited for Priscilla, David picked up the TV remote and surfed through the channels. He stopped when he caught the tail end of a local news channel, reporting on his motorcycle accident.

When the door opened and Priscilla stepped in, David smiled, despite the throbbing in his head, ribs, and leg. Dark hair, ebony eyes, and a slightly turned-up nose—she was as beautiful as he remembered. Quickly, he turned off the TV.

"How are you feeling?" Priscilla crossed over to his bed.

"Much better since you're here."

Priscilla's cheeks flushed, making her dimples more pronounced. "I've been worried about you. Your grandmother explained the extent of your injuries. While I'm sure you're in pain, I'm just glad they aren't worse."

"Same here. What about my cycle? Did it get banged up pretty bad?" He made no mention of the news report he'd seen briefly.

She shrugged. "I don't know, David. When the sheriff showed up at the scene of the accident, he said he would make sure your bike was picked up."

"Guess I'll ask Gramps to check on things for me in the morning, 'cause it doesn't look like I'll be getting out of the hospital till the doctor gives the okay." David gestured to the chair on the right side of his bed.

"Why don't you take a seat?"

"You know, David, you've been through a lot tonight, and I'm sure you're tired, so I'd better not stay too long."

"They gave me something for the pain, and I can't promise I won't fall asleep, but you're welcome to stay as long as you like."

Priscilla pulled the chair closer to his bed and sat down. "Before the EMTs showed up, you were about to tell me what brought you back to Arthur. Is it to spend Christmas with your grandparents?"

"Partly, but the main the reason I came is to see if I'd fit in."

She tilted her head in his direction. "I don't understand."

"Fit in. . . Amish way of. . ." David's tongue felt thick, as his eyelids grew heavy. The last thing he remembered before succumbing to sleep was the curious expression on Priscilla's face.

Arthur

Elam Gingerich stepped onto the Hershbergers' porch and knocked on the door. He was anxious to invite Priscilla out to supper.

"*Guder mariye*," Iva said when she opened the door.

"Mornin'." Elam smiled. "Is Priscilla at home?"

"Jah, but she's still in bed."

"Really? I figured she'd be up by now."

"Normally she would, but she was at the hospital last night and didn't get home till the wee hours."

Elam felt immediate concern. "Why was Priscilla at the hospital?"

"She went there to see David Morgan."

"I didn't know he was in town. What was he doin' at the hospital?"

"David was in an accident. Priscilla witnessed it when a deer darted in front of David's motorcycle."

Elam pursed his lips. "Sorry to hear about it. Is he gonna be okay?"

"His injuries are not life threatening, but he did break his leg and a couple of ribs. He also has a mild concussion." Iva frowned, rubbing her forehead. "I broke my wrist when I was a girl, and it was quite painful. I can't imagine how much pain David must be in."

Elam nodded. "I haven't seen him in a long time."

"From what Priscilla said, David was on the way to his grandparents' when the accident occurred."

"It's a shame. I'll stop by their place soon to see how he's doing."

Iva opened the door wider. "You're welcome to come in if you like. I'm sure Priscilla will be up soon. Maybe you'd like to have a cup of coffee while you're waiting for her."

He shook his head. "I'd better not. My *daed*'s store opens in an hour, and he expects me to work there today. Would ya tell Priscilla I dropped by? Oh, and unless I hear differently, I'll come by around six to take her out to supper this evening."

"I'll give her the message." Iva smiled. "It was nice seeing you, Elam. Tell your *mamm* I said hello."

"I will." Elam stepped down off the porch and sprinted to his buggy, leaving more boot prints in the freshly fallen snow. It had been two years since he'd last seen David. *I wonder why he waited so long to pay his grandparents a visit.*

"Guder mariye," Mom said when Priscilla entered the kitchen, rubbing her eyes.

"Good morning." Priscilla glanced at the clock on the wall and grimaced when she saw it was almost ten o'clock. "I didn't realize it was so late. Why didn't you wake me, Mom?"

"I figured after being out so late last night you'd be exhausted and need to catch up on your sleep." Mom handed Priscilla a cup of coffee and motioned to the table. "Have a seat; I'll fix you some scrambled eggs."

Priscilla moved to the window, squinting as the sun glared off the new snow. "It's so bright out there. Looks as if we got a couple more inches overnight."

"The snow is sure pretty." Mom turned on the gas burner to heat up the frying pan. "I must say, though, I was relieved when you finally got home last night."

"David's grandpa is a good driver and took his time on the road. I was careful with my horse and buggy when I brought it home, too." Priscilla took a seat at the table. "Don't trouble yourself, Mom. I'm not really *hungerich* this morning."

"You may not be hungry, but you need to eat." Mom went to the refrigerator and took out a carton of eggs. "I've never understood why you and your daed think you can start your day with only a cup of *kaffi*."

Priscilla smiled. She did take after Dad in some ways. But Mom was right; she would have more energy if she ate a good breakfast.

"Elam was here awhile ago," Mom said, cracking two eggs at the same time into a bowl.

"What'd he want?"

"He came by to see you. Wanted to know if you'd be free to go out to supper with him this evening."

"Did you tell him about David?"

Mom nodded as she added a little milk to the bowl of eggs then mixed them with a wire whisk. "He seemed surprised to hear David was back in Arthur."

Priscilla blew on her coffee and took a sip. "I'll give Elam a call and let him know I can't go to supper this evening."

Mom tipped her head. "Why? Do you have other plans?"

"I need to check on David. I'm pretty sure Letty and Walt will be bringing him home sometime today."

"Can't you and Elam stop by there before or after you go out this evening?"

"I guess we could. David and Elam are friends, too, so he's probably anxious to see how David is doing. When I finish eating breakfast, I'll go out to the phone shack and give Elam a call."

CHAPTER 4

"It's turned into a beautiful Saturday evening," Priscilla commented as she and Elam headed down the road in his buggy toward Yoder's Kitchen.

Elam nodded. "With all the snow we got last night, I wasn't sure how the roads would be. With the sun's help and the roads being cleared, they're pretty much dry now, making travel a lot safer."

"For a Saturday evening, the traffic is light," Priscilla noted.

"Jah. Guess most people decided to stay home tonight."

As they pulled into the area where buggies were parked, Priscilla noticed the sun was getting ready to set. She wished they could stay outside and watch the show of colors, but Elam had said awhile ago that he was anxious to eat, so they headed inside as soon as he secured his horse.

"Have you heard how David's doing?" Elam asked after he and Priscilla were seated inside the restaurant.

"I talked to his grandma this morning, and she said they'd be bringing him home today."

"He must be doing pretty well if they're letting him go home so soon." Elam's forehead wrinkled. "Guess he's not really going home, though, since he lives in Chicago."

Priscilla's attention turned toward the window, taking in the beautiful sunset. The mix of reds, golds, and pinks was breathtaking.

Elam bumped her arm. "Did ya hear what I said about David?"

Priscilla's face heated. "Sorry. I was watching the sunset. What did you say?"

"Said I guess he's not really going home, since he lives in Chicago."

"His grandparents' place is home for David right now." Priscilla studied the menu. She didn't know why, though. Whenever she ate supper at Yoder's she usually ended up having the dinner buffet, where she enjoyed moist and tasty roasted chicken and plenty of delicious homemade noodles. To accompany her meal, Priscilla ordered a glass of iced tea, while Elam asked their waitress for chocolate milk.

"I know David's been away at college, but you'd think he would have visited his grandparents in all that time." Elam's brows furrowed. "Not very considerate, if you ask me."

"I'm sure Letty and Walt have gone to Chicago to see David and his parents."

"Maybe so. Should we pray before we go to the buffet?" Elam suggested.

"Jah."

They bowed for silent prayer. When they were done, Priscilla and Elam joined several others in line for the buffet. "I see Elaine and Ben ahead of us." Priscilla gestured in their direction. "Would you mind if I asked them to join us at our table?"

Elam hesitated but finally nodded. "If that's what you want to do."

Priscilla stepped out of line and tapped Elaine's shoulder.

Elaine whirled around. "You startled me!"

"Sorry. I wanted to get your attention before you sat down."

Elaine smiled. "Are you here with your family?"

"No, I came with Elam. I was wondering if you two would like to join us."

Elaine looked at Ben. "Is it all right with you?"

Ben's broad shoulders lifted in a brief shrug. "Sure, why not?"

"Our table is right over there." Priscilla motioned to it.

"Okay. Ben and I will join you after we get our food and have told our waitress where we're going."

"Did Priscilla tell you she helped Elaine with her dinner last night?" Ben asked, taking a seat across from Elam.

"Nope." Elam looked over at Priscilla. "How come you never mentioned it?"

"I haven't had a chance." Priscilla cut the meat off her drumstick. "Besides, we've been talking about other things so far tonight."

"True—like David's accident." Elam waited for Priscilla's response but then realized she must not have heard him. Her peculiar expression was hard to read, but ever since they'd arrived at Yoder's, Priscilla's attention seemed to be somewhere else. Like now, as she stared out the window again. *What's she thinking about?*

Elam glanced out the window, to be sure he wasn't missing something. *The sun's already set, so it couldn't be the sky.*

"Who's David?" Ben asked, breaking into Elam's thoughts.

"David Morgan. He's English and used to visit here a lot when we were teenagers," Priscilla explained. "Until last night when I witnessed David's motorcycle accident, neither Elam nor I had seen David for two years."

Elam noticed how Priscilla perked up when David's name was mentioned.

"I remember David." Elaine massaged her forehead. "Was he injured in the accident?"

Priscilla explained what had happened. Since Elam had already heard the story and didn't want his food to get cold, he started eating. When Priscilla finished telling about the accident, Elam jumped into the conversation. "Maybe we oughta stop by the Morgans' place when we're done eating and see how David's doing."

Priscilla's eyes brightened. "Good idea."

As their meal progressed, Elam became irritated. So far, Priscilla had spent more time talking to Elaine than him. He'd hoped to have Priscilla all to himself tonight and had been trying to get in a word with her, but to no avail. Even though he liked the food here, Elam wished they'd gone someplace else to eat supper.

Maybe I shouldn't have suggested we stop and see David on the way home, either. Elam crumpled his napkin. *It'll be one more opportunity for her to visit with someone other than me. Guess it's too late to worry about that now. Said I'd go, so I'll have to follow through. And it will be kind of nice to see David again.*

"Are you all right?"

Elam turned to look at Priscilla. "Huh? I'm sorry. Were you talking to me?"

"No, I was asking Elaine."

"I have a *koppweh.*" Elaine rubbed her forehead again. "I've had it most of the day, but it's suddenly gotten worse."

Ben looked at her with concern. “Should I take you home?”

“I apologize. I don’t want to ruin anyone’s evening, but that might be a good idea.”

“I have a better idea,” Priscilla interjected. “Why don’t you go over to Leah’s and see if she can give you a foot treatment? Reflexology has always helped whenever I have a headache.”

Elaine’s forehead wrinkled. “I hate to bother her at this time of night. She’s probably fixing supper for her family.”

“Maybe they’re done eating by now,” Ben put in. “We ought to drop by and see if she’s free to give you a treatment.”

“It’s worth a try.” Elaine pushed her chair aside and stood. “Danki for inviting us to join you.” She offered Priscilla a weak smile. “Sorry I wasn’t better company.”

Priscilla reached out and clasped her friend’s hand. “It’s okay. I hope you feel better soon.”

While Elam wasn’t glad Elaine had a headache, he was pleased he would finally have Priscilla to himself—at least until they got to the Morgans’ house.

❧

“Are you comfortable, Davey? Do you need another pillow under your leg?”

David shook his head. “I’m fine, Gram. You don’t need to fuss over me.”

Gram squinted at David over the top of her glasses. “If a grandma can’t fuss over her grandson, then she ought to quit being a grandma.”

Gramps chuckled as he seated himself in the recliner across from where David lay on the couch. “You may as well give in, Davey, and just let your grandma fuss to her heart’s content.”

David held up his hands. “Okay, but I really don’t need two pillows.”

Gram placed the second pillow at the end of the couch. “All right, but it’s here in case you change your mind.” She took a seat in her rocking chair across from him. “By the way, as soon as we knew you were being released from the hospital, we called your folks again, to let them know we’d be bringing you here. Said not to worry, that we’ll take good care of you.”

David grimaced as he tried to find a comfortable position for his sore ribs. "I hope you told 'em I'm gonna be okay and there's no need for them to come here."

"Actually, we haven't heard anything from them yet." Gramps frowned. "When I called, I got your dad's voice mail, but he never returned my call."

Gram smiled. "I'm sure we'll hear something from them soon."

A knock sounded on the door, and Gramps went to answer it. When he returned, Priscilla and Elam were with him. David's mood brightened.

"How are you doing?" Priscilla rushed to the couch.

"I've been better, but I could be worse." David managed a smile. "It's good seeing you, Elam. Did Priscilla tell you about my accident?"

Elam nodded and moved to stand beside Priscilla. "Priscilla and I went to Yoder's Kitchen for supper this evening, and we decided to come by here to see how you were doing."

"I'm glad you did."

"Let me take your coats. And please, have a seat." Gram gestured to the love seat near the couch.

After Elam and Priscilla were settled, Grandma went to the kitchen to get everyone something to drink. When she returned with coffee and doughnuts, David sat up so he could eat and drink without spilling.

"Are you in much pain?" Priscilla questioned.

"I'll admit it hurts, but the doctor gave me something to help with the discomfort." David blew on his coffee before taking a sip. "Truthfully, though, I'd rather deal with the pain instead of taking medicine. It makes me too drowsy."

"Rest is what you need right now," Gram interjected.

"She's right. A person's body heals better during sleep," Elam added. "If it were me, I'd be takin' the pain pills."

"I guess so, but I don't like the idea of sleeping all the time; especially since I just got here." David ran his fingers through his thick hair. "While I'm staying here, I'd like to help Gramps with chores especially if something needs to be fixed."

"I appreciate it, Davey, but there's no need to worry about those issues right now."

"Your healing is what's important." Gram looked tenderly at David.

Her smile intensified, causing the laugh lines around her eyes to deepen.

"Your grandmother's right. You were fortunate your stay in the hospital was only overnight. You'll be up and around before you know it."

Priscilla's reassuring words gave David comfort. Deep down, he was glad to be here, surrounded by all this love and attention. He felt fortunate, but at the same time, he was more than ready to change the subject.

"Enough about me," he said. "What's been going on around the area since I've been away?"

While Elam and Priscilla filled him in, another knock on the door sent Gramps to see who it was.

Elam grabbed a doughnut and dunked it in his cup of coffee. "What brings you back to Arthur, David? Was it just to visit your grandparents?"

"I wasn't happy with the way things were going for me in Chicago," David answered honestly. "I left a week before Christmas break and decided to come live with Gram and Gramps for a while—till I figure out exactly what it is I want to do."

"And what would that be, son?"

David blinked when his folks stepped into the room. "Mom! Dad! What are you doing here?"

Dad's bushy eyebrows rose high on his forehead. "What are we doing here? More to the point, what are *you* doing here, David? And what did you mean when you said you left school early and were going to live with my folks for a while? I thought you were coming home for Christmas break."

CHAPTER 5

Well, David, I'm waiting for an answer." David's father tapped his foot impatiently, looking sternly at his son.

Mrs. Morgan stepped forward and placed a hand on her husband's arm. "Stop badgering our son, Robert. We came all this way to see how David is, not ply him with questions about what he's doing here."

"I know why we came, Suzanne, and I don't need you to remind me."

She glared at him.

Priscilla cringed, seeing David's hurt expression and knowing how embarrassed he must be. Having his parents argue like this—especially in front of her and Elam, whom they barely knew—had to be uncomfortable. She'd also found it odd how David's father had jumped on him right away, without giving him any kind of greeting.

"By the way, it's nice to see you, too." David's tone was sarcastic. "But okay, you want to hear the truth, then here it is." David looked directly at his father. "I'm not going back to college after Christmas. I'm gonna stay here with Gram and Gramps until I figure out what I want to do with the rest of my life."

David's father's grim expression made it clear he wasn't happy to hear this news. Knowing David, he wouldn't back down.

"What do you want to do with your life?" Robert stretched out his hands. "I thought you had your heart set on becoming a veterinarian."

"No, you had your heart set on me following in your footsteps. I'm not sure now I have the same dream." David wiped his brow and threw the afghan off his lap.

The room grew quiet when Suzanne pointed at David's cast and gasped. "Oh, son, how bad is your leg?"

"I broke it—in two places," David said dryly.

David's grandpa jumped in and explained that they'd tried calling several times after they found out the extent of David's injuries. "All I got was your voice mail, but apparently you didn't listen to any of my messages."

Mr. Morgan scratched his head. "I did but not till this afternoon, when I turned my phone on." He gestured to his wife. "Suzanne suggested I turn it off last night when we attended a musical, and I forgot to turn it back on."

David then told them about his accident and how lucky he'd been to have Priscilla close at hand.

"I'm so sorry." Suzanne sat on the couch beside David and gave him a hug.

"Not too tight, Mom." David sucked in his breath. "A couple of my ribs are broken, and they're pretty sore, too."

"You should have known better than to take a trip on your motorcycle this time of the year. The weather and travel conditions can turn on a dime," David's dad scolded.

"Robert, we should just be grateful our son wasn't hurt any worse." Suzanne looked at Priscilla and smiled. "Thank you for staying with David until the paramedics arrived."

"It was a good thing you were there." Robert nodded in Priscilla's direction. "But none of this would have happened if David had come home instead of here."

Priscilla was about to change the subject, when David's grandma said, "Why don't we all relax and let our thoughts settle a spell?" Priscilla could tell Letty was trying to smooth things over. "We can talk more about this in the morning. Right now, I need to go upstairs and fix up the guest room. Oh, and Suzanne, when was the last time you and Robert had anything to eat?"

"Don't worry about us, Letty. We stopped on our way here to get something to eat. And please, let me help you get our room ready." Suzanne squeezed David's arm before rising to her feet and following her mother-in-law from the room.

Elam bumped Priscilla's arm. "We really should go now, don't you agree?" It was the first thing he'd said since David's parents arrived.

Priscilla gave a quick nod. "Take it easy, David." She offered him what she hoped was a reassuring smile. "We'll come back in a few days to see how you're doing."

"I'll look forward to seeing you again."

Priscilla gathered up her coat and outer bonnet then followed Elam out the door. She couldn't imagine what it must be like for David to go against his parents' wishes and give up his schooling. In all her twenty-six years Priscilla had never made any major decision that would upset her parents.

"Danki for seeing me on such short notice," Elaine said, taking a seat in Leah's recliner. "I woke up with a koppweh this morning, and the aspirin I took hasn't helped at all. In fact, as the day has worn on, it's gotten worse."

"This must be the day for headaches," Leah rubbed massage lotion on Elaine's feet. "Iva Herschberger was here awhile ago, complaining of a koppweh. I believe hers stemmed mostly from her neck. She's prone to neck problems, but a reflexology treatment always seems to help."

Elaine smiled. "What you're doing is a good thing, Leah. God has given you the gift to help others through reflexology."

"Adam didn't always think so." Leah picked up Elaine's right foot and probed for sore spots.

"But he's come around and seems to be fine with your foot doctoring now."

"Jah. He's even asked me to do his feet a few times."

"That's good. I'm glad things are working out between you and Adam now." Elaine winced. "Ouch. You found a sensitive spot."

Leah held steady pressure on it. "Let me know when it gets better."

"It's easing up now," Elaine said after several seconds passed.

"Let me know if I find more sore spots."

Elaine gave a nod. "It's awfully quiet in here. Are the girls in bed already?"

"I doubt it." Leah continued to probe the bottom of Elaine's foot, and even between her toes. "Carrie, Linda, and Amy are at my folks' house this evening. Mom invited them to help her bake *kichlin* today, and they stayed for supper. Right before you got here, Adam left to get them."

"Sounds nice," Elaine said. "Speaking of Iva Herschberger, we ran into Priscilla and Elam at Yoder's Kitchen this evening, and ended up joining them."

"Iva did mention Priscilla and Elam were going out to supper this evening. How are they both doing?"

"They seemed to be okay, but did you hear about the accident Priscilla witnessed?"

"What accident?" Leah's eyebrows drew together.

Elaine tried to explain all of what Priscilla had told them earlier at Yoder's, including the extent of David's injuries. "To tell you the truth, my head was hurting so bad, I'm not sure I heard everything exactly right. It might be best if you let Priscilla tell you the details of David's accident, since she witnessed the whole thing."

"I'll have to ask her about it, and I'm glad her friend doesn't have life-threatening injuries." Leah paused. "By the way, where is Ben? You said he drove you here, right?"

"He went out to the barn to see if Adam was there. My guess, though, is that Ben's either petting your black Lab or visiting the horse." Elaine tried to relax as Leah continued the treatment. "I'm surprised Ben doesn't have a dog of his own."

"Pets can be a handful sometimes. Coal has become a special member of our family—especially to Adam and the girls." Leah smiled. "Let's hope those *kinner* bring back some kichlin with them, because I'm in the mood for cookies and milk."

"Are they being saved for Christmas or to be eaten now?"

"A little of both." Leah chuckled. "They'll probably come home with their tummies full and won't be able to sleep."

"It's good they can spend time with your parents. Since their paternal grandparents don't live close, your mamm and daed sort of fill the roll."

"Jah, and they love it. Of course, the girls do, too."

"They seem to have adjusted pretty well since you and Adam got married." Elaine winced again. "You found another sore spot."

"Let me know when it's gone." Leah kept a steady pressure on the area. "And you're right about the girls. They're doing much better dealing with their parents' death; although Amy still gets moody sometimes."

"Guess it's to be expected." Elaine sighed. "Losing a loved one is never easy—especially when a parent leaves children behind."

"Are you thinking about Jonah's kinner right now?"

"Jah. Of course they're much younger than Adam's nieces, so it makes a difference. It'll still be difficult for them, growing up without a mother."

"Maybe at some point Jonah will remarry."

Elaine leaned her head back and closed her eyes. Leah didn't voice her thoughts, but she wondered if someday Jonah and Elaine might get together again. They'd loved each other once. Maybe God would bring them together again.

Jonah Miller had put his children to bed and was about to relax and read the newspaper, when he remembered he hadn't done the supper dishes. He could leave them until morning, when his mother came over to watch the children while he was at work, but that wouldn't be fair to Mom. She'd done so much for him since Sara's death. There weren't enough words to express his gratitude to her or Dad. Tonight, Jonah would wash and dry the dishes, giving Mom one less thing to worry about.

Jonah ambled into the kitchen and turned on the gas lamp overhead. As he filled the sink with warm, soapy water, he thought about all the times Sara had stood here, washing the dishes. In the brief year they'd been married, Sara had been a good wife, and he missed her so much. Despite dealing with her symptoms of multiple sclerosis, she'd been a hard worker and had never failed to care for Mark and their baby girl. Sara had always been loving and kind and had looked to the needs of others before her own. Her sweet, gentle spirit had drawn Jonah to her, and he had looked forward to spending many years with his beloved wife. But fate, or the hand of God, whatever a person wanted to call it, had snatched Sara from Jonah. He was now faced with raising their children alone. Even though his mother would be there to help, it wasn't the same as having Sara's presence in this home.

Sloshing the dishcloth over a plate, Jonah groaned. He had been in love with three women, and God had seen fit to take all of them in different ways. First, he'd lost Meredith when her husband, Luke, returned after she'd been told he was dead. Then he'd found love again with Elaine, but she had shattered his world by saying she didn't love him after her grandmother was diagnosed with dementia. Now Sara was gone—senselessly killed in an accident. It should never have happened. If only she'd stayed in the house and rested, like she'd been told to do after having the baby. But no, she'd been determined to go out to the barn to feed the cats. That's when she'd apparently seen the kitten and tried to help it down from the loft.

Did she get dizzy and lose her footing on the ladder? Jonah asked himself for the umpteenth time. Unless someone had been with Sara in the barn that day, Jonah would never know exactly how it happened.

For some reason, his parents' dog, Herbie, jumped into his thoughts. Even though Jonah had considered getting a border collie of his own, he was glad he and Sara had never gotten a dog. Knowing how much Sara loved animals, it would have been one more responsibility she'd have taken on. Right now, it was all Jonah could do to look at the gray-and-white kitten Sara had been clutching when she fell off the ladder. It had never been clear exactly what had happened, but Jonah was quite sure if it hadn't been for the cat, his wife would still be alive.

Jonah gripped the soapy dishcloth and made a decision. He would give that little kitten away. It was too hard having it around the place as a reminder of his and the children's great loss.

Jonah hadn't admitted it to anyone, but Sara's death had really shaken his faith. His only source of comfort was his stepson, Mark, as well as his baby girl, Martha Jean, named after Jonah's twin sister.

Jonah remembered how Sara's parents, who lived in Indiana, had offered to take the children and raise them. Of course, he'd flatly refused. When he married Sara, Mark had become his son, too. It was because of his children that Jonah was able to face the future. Mark and Martha Jean were his only reason for living, and no one but him would raise them, although he did rely on his folks for help.

Jonah was sure he would never marry again. He couldn't take the chance of losing another wife. He seemed destined to lose when it came to love and marriage.

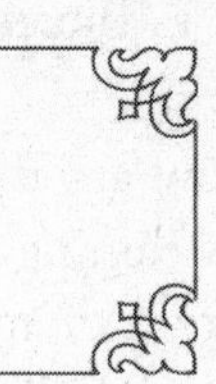

CHAPTER 6

"I'm glad you could both come over for lunch today," Leah said when Priscilla and Elaine entered her kitchen on Monday, shortly before noon. "It's been awhile since we got together like this."

Priscilla smiled. "We need to do it more often."

"How are you feeling, Elaine?" Leah asked. "I didn't get the chance to talk to you at church yesterday."

"Thanks to the foot treatment you gave me Saturday night, I made it through the rest of the weekend without a twinge of pain in my head or neck." Elaine gave Leah a hug. "Is there anything we can do to help with lunch?"

Leah shook her head. "Everything's ready. Just take your seats at the table."

It felt strange not to do anything to help, but after Elaine took a chair, Priscilla did the same. She noticed Leah's peaceful expression. She was obviously happy in her new role as Adam's wife. Even though their marriage had been one of convenience, the couple had fallen in love.

"Have you been busy with reflexology patients?" Elaine asked.

Leah nodded. "My mamm's agreed to keep the girls at her house on Saturdays so I can see as many people as I need to on those days. In fact, Cora Finley made an appointment to see me this coming Saturday."

Priscilla's eyebrows rose. "Does Adam know about her coming for a treatment?"

"Jah." Leah sighed. "Even though he's not ready to accept Cora into his life, he gave me permission to see her as long as the children aren't here."

"Do they know about Cora?" Elaine questioned.

"Adam hasn't told them yet. I hope he will soon, though. They have the right to know."

Priscilla bobbed her head. "I agree."

"How are things going with the girls?" Elaine asked when Leah placed steaming bowls of vegetable soup on the table and took a seat across from them.

"Pretty well." Leah clasped her hands beneath her chin. "Amy can be a challenge sometimes, but even she seems to be coming around."

"Are she and Linda doing well in school?" Priscilla questioned.

"They are. And it's nice having Carrie still here with me. She'll be starting school before you know it."

"They sure grow fast," Priscilla added, thinking about the children she hoped to have someday.

"Why don't we pray? Then we can visit some more." Leah bowed her head. Elaine and Priscilla did the same.

In addition to thanking God for the food and her friends, Priscilla prayed that David's injuries would heal without complications and things would improve between him and his parents. *Maybe I'll stop by and see him on the way home*, she decided. *I want to find out how things are going.*

"How are you feeling, Davey?" Gram asked. "Is there anything you'd like me to get you?"

Hobbling on his crutches to the couch, David shook his head. "I'm fine, Gram. Just need to lie down awhile." Truth was, David's pain medicine hadn't kicked in, so his ribs, leg, and head hurt. He wasn't about to admit his discomfort to Gram. She'd only fuss over him all the more. He didn't mind, really, but he just wasn't used to having someone hovering over him.

If the pain wasn't bad enough, now David had something else to deal with—the itching on his leg underneath the cast. The doctor had warned him this would happen and said it was important not to try using any object to scratch the skin. If the itching got unbearable, the doctor suggested David could use a hair blower, set on cool, aiming it under the cast. If the itching didn't get worse, he could ignore the crawling sensation, but if that didn't work, the doctor would give David a prescription for an antihistamine. David didn't want to resort to more pills. He was determined to find a way to cope with the annoyance.

David's parents had gone home before lunch, and he was glad. Dad needed to get back to his clinic, and Mom had convinced him nothing could be done about David's decision to drop out of school until Christmas break was over and David's injuries had healed. She'd even told David she thought being here with his grandparents would be good for him—a chance to clear his head and think things through.

Mom's hoping I'll change my mind and go back to Chicago, David thought, repositioning the pillow under his leg. Keeping it elevated helped ease the pain. Now if his ribs would quit hurting every time he took a breath. . .

David closed his eyes and was about to drift off, when a knock sounded on the front door.

"I'll get it," Gram called. "Just stay where you are."

A few minutes later, she entered the living room with Priscilla at her side. "Look who's come to visit." After Gram took Priscilla's jacket and outer bonnet, Priscilla sat in a chair near the couch.

"How are you doing, David?" Priscilla asked after Gram left the room.

"Still hurting, but I'll live."

"Are you taking something for the pain?" The depth of Priscilla's concern showed in her eyes.

"I'm taking half a dose, but it only takes the edge off. If I take the full amount, it makes me sleepy."

Her nose wrinkled slightly. "Wouldn't you rather be sleepy and have no pain then suffer through it to stay awake?"

"Nope." David pulled himself to a sitting position. "It would be a shame if I was sleeping right now and couldn't visit with you."

Priscilla's cheeks flushed, and she looked away for a moment. "I didn't see your folks' car parked in the driveway."

"Mom and Dad left this morning."

"I hope you got things resolved with them. I can't imagine being at odds with my parents."

"Nothing's been resolved as far as they're concerned, but on my end it sure has."

"What do you mean?"

David shifted slightly and grimaced when pain shot through his ribs. "I'm not going back to college, no matter what my dad says. As soon as my leg and ribs heal, I'll look for a job in the area." He winked at Priscilla. "I may even decide to join the Amish faith."

Priscilla blinked. "Are you serious or just teasing?"

"I would never tease about something as serious as joining the Amish faith."

"Why would you want to give up your English customs and take on the Plain life?"

"I'm not saying I do. I'm just thinking about it right now." David winked at Priscilla again.

How was she to know if he was teasing or not?

When Cora Finley left the clinic in Arthur where she'd been working as a nurse, she decided to take a different route home. It would be good to see some other scenery for a change, and traveling the back roads could be done at a slower pace.

Living in Arthur seemed peaceful compared to the hectic lifestyle she'd had in Chicago during the years she'd been married to Evan. This rural community had been good for her fifteen-year-old son Jared, too. When they'd first come to Arthur, Jared had been defiant, wanting to live near his dad, but in the last few weeks that had all changed.

"A dad who doesn't care about anyone but himself," Cora muttered. Jared was beginning to see his dad clearly, too.

The end of Cora's marriage to Evan had been life changing and not of her own doing. The challenges it caused hadn't been easy, either. Thanksgiving had begun a turning point for her son, and for the time being, at least, he seemed to understand Cora's motives for moving to Arthur.

As difficult as the divorce had been, Cora's biggest struggle had come about when she'd learned that her son Adam, from a previous marriage, lived in this area. He wanted nothing to do with her. Who could blame him, though? Cora had abandoned Adam and his sister, Mary, when she'd left the Amish faith and divorced their father more than twenty years ago.

Cora wanted to make amends and establish a relationship with her eldest son, but unless Adam changed his mind, it might never happen.

Refocusing her thoughts, Cora looked at the fields on both sides of the nearly deserted road, untouched, as if the snow had just fallen. Back in Chicago, she'd often felt as if she had no place to unwind. Here in Arthur, though, the landscape alone could make her tension melt away.

Approaching an Amish schoolhouse, Cora's thoughts switched gears. Could this be the school Adam's two oldest nieces attended? Cora had met the youngest girl, Carrie, when Leah brought her to the clinic once. But she'd only seen Carrie's sisters from a distance after she'd shown up at Adam and Leah's wedding without an invitation. How she longed to be a part of the girls' lives and fulfill her role as their grandmother. Since Cora still saw Leah occasionally for reflexology treatments, she'd been tempted to ask if Leah could arrange a meeting between her and the girls, but she was afraid to broach the subject. Leah was Adam's wife, and it might cause dissension if he found out Leah had played go-between. Cora didn't want to be the cause of any trouble between them.

She clutched the steering wheel, swerving slightly to avoid a patch of ice. *Maybe I should stop by Adam's hardware store and see if I can reason with him. Oh, Lord, please show me what to do.*

As Cora continued down the road, she caught sight of a group of Amish children trudging through the snow along the shoulder of the road. As she drew closer, Cora's breath caught in her throat when she got a look at one of the girls. Even though the child was bundled up, Cora recognized her from the wedding. *She's my granddaughter. I bet the girl walking closest to the road is her older sister.*

Cora fought the urge to stop and talk to them. But what would she say? She certainly couldn't announce she was their grandmother who used to be Amish. Cora wondered if Adam or Mary had even told the girls about her. Surely they must have asked questions about their maternal grandmother: who she was, where she lived, and why they'd never met her. *Oh, Mary, if only you were still alive and I could apologize for walking away from you and your brother. I should have been content to be an Amish wife and mother who practiced reflexology, instead of giving up my family so I could become a nurse.* Tears sprang to Cora's eyes. *I was immature and selfish. What I did can never be undone.*

Waving at the girls, Cora moved on. She needed to get to the house and see if Jared was home from school yet. When Jared was born, at least she'd been offered a chance to be a better mother. Cora had learned a hard lesson, and from the beginning she'd vowed not to mess up his life.

An image of Jared came to mind—tall and lanky with jet-black hair like his father's and deep blue eyes like Cora's.

Cora bit her lip and winced when she tasted blood. She still hadn't told Jared about his half brother or admitted she used to be Amish. She'd have to find a way to tell her son soon, before he found out from someone else. She was sure Leah, and maybe Adam, had already told a few others about her.

CHAPTER 7

"How's it going?" Adam Beachy asked when he entered his store Saturday morning and found Ben Otto behind the counter. Normally, Adam liked to get there before his employees, but this morning he'd dropped the girls off at Leah's parents', and due to traffic moving slow because of fresh-fallen snow, he was running later than usual.

"No customers so far. But then it's only been fifteen minutes since I put the OPEN sign in the window." Ben smiled. "Scott got here soon after I did. I got him started stocking the shelves in the birdseed aisle. If today ends up like yesterday, I'm sure there'll be plenty of people coming in to buy seed, bags of ice melt, and pellets. Hope it was okay I got Scott started with the birdseed."

Nodding his approval, Adam removed his stocking cap and jacket. "It's chilly out there. If we keep getting snow like this, we'll have a white Christmas for sure."

Ben glanced out the front window. "Seems to be comin' down harder now than when I left home. This weather might keep some folks from going out today."

"Guess we'll have to wait and see how it goes." Adam turned in the direction of his office. "I'm going to get some paperwork done. Give a holler if things get busy and you need my help waiting on customers."

"I will. With Henry off this week because of his wife's shoulder surgery, things have gotten kind of crazy around here."

"That's why you shouldn't hesitate to give me a shout."

When Adam reached his office, he hung up his jacket and cap then took a seat at the desk. Opening the Thermos of hot coffee Leah had made for him this morning, he poured a cup. Somehow while preparing breakfast, she had squeezed in time to make brownies, one of his favorite desserts. Even before he'd entered the kitchen, Adam had smelled them baking.

He picked up his lunch pail and peeked inside. In addition to the egg-salad sandwich Leah had made, the apple and brownies looked appetizing, too.

"Should have never looked at my lunch," Adam mumbled. He'd only arrived a few minutes ago, but the chocolate delights were tempting.

Then Adam noticed a small slip of paper wedged between the sandwich and brownies. Pulling it out, he read: *"I hope you have a nice day."* The simple message made him smile.

Leah's a thoughtful wife, he mused. *Always thinking of others and so good with the girls. I made the right choice in asking her to marry me, even if at first we weren't in love with each other.*

As Adam drank his coffee he reflected on how things had changed between him and Leah. It hadn't taken long before he'd come to love and respect her. Adam looked forward to the future and hoped someday they might have children of their own.

Of course, when they did, he'd make sure it didn't change his relationship with his nieces. Carrie, Linda, and Amy had become orphans when Adam's sister, Mary, and her husband, Abe, were killed because of a tragic accident. Adam had taken the girls into his home to raise as his own. He still remembered the look on Mary's face as she lay dying in the hospital. With her last breath, she'd pleaded with Adam to look after her daughters. At the time, he'd been a bachelor, but he couldn't say no to her request.

Having the girls to look after had been a blessing to Adam in many ways. It had taken him out of his comfort zone, and upset his normal routine, but he'd learned to put his nieces' needs ahead of his own. Walking into an empty, quiet house was something he didn't miss. Having the children in his home had helped Adam deal with losing his sister and had also given him something besides his grief to think about. At first, he hadn't known what to say or do to help the girls deal with the loss of their parents, but Leah had made up for what he couldn't do. Neither of them could take the place of the girls' parents, but they had formed a bond with them. He was sure his nieces were aware of how much they were loved.

"Can I talk to you a minute?" Scott Ramsey asked, stepping into Adam's office and interrupting his musings.

"Of course. What's on your mind?"

Scott shifted his weight, leaning on Adam's desk. The freckles normally present on the teenager's nose had nearly faded with the cold of winter setting in. "Well, my friend Jared needs money to buy his mom a Christmas present. So I was wonderin' if you might have something he could do to help out around here."

Adam rubbed his hand across the growth of his new beard. "To tell you the truth, Scott, I don't have enough work right now for you and your friend. I know you need your part-time job, and I can't hire you both to work in the store."

"You're right, I do need the job, but I was hopin' there might be something Jared could do. Business might pick up around here, since it's only two weeks till Christmas."

Adam's heart had softened since Leah and the girls had come to live with him. Scott was a good kid, and he hated to disappoint him. "Guess I could let Jared do some cleaning for the next two weeks, but I can't promise anything after that."

Scott smiled widely. "Thanks, Adam!"

"A word of caution for you, though. You and your friend will need to work individually. There's to be no fooling around."

Scott shook his head. "No need to worry. We'll both work hard and do whatever we're told."

Adam smiled. "Tell your friend to drop by the store so we can talk. Oh, and he'll need a written note from one of his parents so I know it's okay for him to work for me. Better yet, they can come to the store so I can talk with them personally."

Scott frowned. "If his mom comes in, it won't be a surprise he's working for you so he can buy her a Christmas present."

"I won't tell her about the present, and Jared doesn't have to, either," Adam replied. "But if he's worried about it, he can ask his dad to talk with me. I need to be sure one or both of his parents approves before he does any work for me."

"It won't be his dad." Scott shook his head. "Jared's folks are divorced. He lives with his mom."

Adam grunted. "I know it can be tough. Divorce is hard on a family."

"Yeah. Guess I should consider myself lucky my folks are still together. When my dad was out of work, he and Mom argued a lot." Scott frowned. "A couple of times I thought they might split up, but they hung in there, and now that Dad's workin' again, things are better all the way around."

Adam wished his parents had been able to work things out, rather than Mom running off and getting a divorce. It had been hard on him and Mary, growing up without a mother. What his mom did was hard on his dad, as well. In fact, it had changed his father's whole life, shattering all his dreams.

"Jared's waiting outside," Scott said, breaking into Adam's thoughts. "I'll go tell him what you said. Then I'll get right back to work."

Adam nodded. "As soon as he gets his mother's permission, Jared can get started."

Scott grinned. "Thanks again, Adam. You're a nice man."

Some folks might say otherwise, Adam thought as Scott left his office. *My own mother probably thinks I'm not so nice. But then, she's never walked in my shoes—not even a few steps.*

"How did you talk Adam into letting me come to your house for a foot treatment?" Cora asked, seating herself in Leah's recliner.

"He said as long as he and the girls weren't home, he was okay with it," Leah replied, honestly.

"So he still hasn't forgiven me." Cora sighed as she slipped off her shoes and stockings. "Maybe he never will."

"I'm sure he's forgiven you, but forgiving and forgetting are two different things." Leah poured massage lotion into her hands and rubbed it into the sole of Cora's left foot. "I've been hoping and praying Adam would at least let you see the girls, but he's not ready to allow it yet."

"Will he ever be?"

Leah shrugged. "I don't know, but it's best we don't push the idea right now or it might drive him further away."

"Has Adam even told the girls about me?"

Leah shook her head. "He asked me not to say anything to them, either. Does it hurt here?" She probed Cora's foot, hoping to change the subject. Cora and Adam's relationship was complicated, and she didn't like being caught in the middle of it.

"Yes, there's a sore spot there, but it doesn't hurt nearly as much as knowing my own granddaughters might never know me."

"It must be painful for you, but Adam's endured a lot of pain, too."

Cora looked down. "If I could erase the past, I surely would. I'd go back and redo everything. How could I have been so selfishly stupid?"

Leah said nothing, just continued to massage the sore spot on Cora's foot.

"I haven't told Jared about Adam, either. He knows nothing about my past," Cora gripped the armrests. "To Jared, I've been English all my life, and the only man I've ever been married to is his dad."

Leah stopped pressure-pointing and looked at Cora. "Is it wise to withhold the information from Jared? What if he hears from someone else about you once being Amish and having two children by a previous marriage?"

Cora winced. "I know I need to tell Jared about Adam and Mary and about me being Amish, but I'm so afraid of how he will take it—especially now when things are going better between us." Cora leaned slightly forward. "If Adam would let me back in his life, it might make things easier. At least I'd feel like I had his support."

"It could happen someday, but you can't depend on it." Leah started rubbing Cora's foot again.

"Does Adam know about Jared? Have you told him he has a half brother?"

"No. It's not my place to mention something so personal."

Cora pursed her lips. "You're right, but I think Adam needs to know about Jared."

"Then you should tell him."

Cora grimaced. "I can't simply waltz into his store and announce such a thing." Tears pooled in her blue eyes. "I'm such a coward. My mother's heart hurts more than you can ever imagine—if you can call me a mother, that is."

Leah patted Cora's hand, wishing she could bring this all to a head. If Adam and his mother would resolve their differences, the girls could have a relationship with their grandma. "None of us can change the past, but you're on the right path, Cora. And you're not a coward. Just pray about it. Pray God makes a way for you to tell Adam about Jared and Jared about Adam."

Cora sniffed. "Danki, Leah. You're such a good friend. I'm glad my son married you."

"Oh no, Elam's here," Priscilla groaned as she looked out the kitchen window and spotted Elam's horse and buggy coming up the driveway.

Mom joined her at the window. "I can't believe you're not happy to see Elam."

"I am happy to see him, just not this way."

Mom tipped her head. "What do you mean, 'not this way'?"

Priscilla looked down at her soiled apron. "Look at me, Mom. We've been cleaning all morning. I look a mess."

"I'm sure Elam won't care how you look. He's in love with you."

Priscilla's forehead wrinkled. "I'm not so sure. If he really loves me, wouldn't he have proposed marriage by now?"

Mom slipped her arm around Priscilla's waist. "Maybe he's waiting until the time is right."

"Right for what, Mom?" Tears sprang to Priscilla's eyes. "Most couples who've been courting as long as me and Elam would at least be talking of marriage by now."

"I know Elam must love you, Priscilla. He wouldn't keep coming around if he didn't. Your daed and I have seen the way he looks at you, too."

Using one corner of her apron, Priscilla dried her eyes. "Then you must see something I don't see, because I'm not sure how Elam feels about me anymore. All this time we've been doing things together, I've never gotten a hint of him wanting to take me as his wife."

"How do you feel about him?"

"Mom, don't be silly. I would have broken up with Elam by now if I didn't care deeply for him."

"Caring for Elam and being in love are two different things."

Priscilla faced her mother. "I love Elam, and if he asked me to marry him tomorrow, I'd say yes, for sure."

Mom placed her hands against Priscilla's hot cheeks. "Then bide your time and try to be patient. Good things come to those who wait."

Priscilla didn't argue. She appreciated Mom's advice. But as each month went by, the waiting became harder. She couldn't wait indefinitely, or she'd end up an old maid.

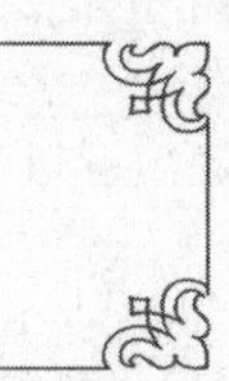

CHAPTER 8

"Hey, Mom, I need to ask ya something," Jared hollered when he entered the kitchen Monday morning.

Cora placed two bowls of steaming oatmeal on the table. "You can ask your question while you eat, because if you don't hurry you'll be late for the bus."

Jared glanced at the clock above the refrigerator before sitting. "There's still plenty of time."

Cora took a seat across from him. "Now what did you want to ask me?"

He spooned some brown sugar on his oatmeal and poured milk over the top. "Is it okay if I go over to Scott's after school? We need to work on a science project. It'll probably take this week and next."

Cora took a sip of coffee. "Christmas break is next week, Jared. Wouldn't you have to turn your assignment in by this Friday?"

Jared gulped down some milk and wiped his mouth with the back of hand. "Actually, it's not due till we go back to school after our winter break, but we wanna get it done before Christmas so we can relax and enjoy our time off from school."

Cora handed Jared a napkin. "Use this to wipe your face, please. I've taught you better than that." Would her son's table manners ever improve? "It's good you're planning ahead. It shows you're being responsible, rather than waiting until the last minute."

"So you're okay with me going there after school?" Jared asked around a mouthful of oatmeal.

"Please don't talk when there's food in your mouth," she admonished.

"Sorry," he mumbled after he'd finished chewing. "So is it okay if I go over to Scott's?"

Cora nodded. "Just don't stay too late. You need to be home in time for supper, and don't forget your chores." Cora had insisted on one thing when she'd rented this house: Jared had to pick up after himself. A place this small could become overrun with clutter if things didn't get put away.

"No problem, Mom. I'll be home in plenty of time."

Cora smiled. It was nice to see her son in such a good mood.

Adam pulled out his pocket watch and whistled. Where had the day gone? In two-and-a-half hours it would be time to close the store. He looked forward to locking up, knowing Leah would have supper ready and he could find out about her day. He was anxious to see the girls and talk about their day at school, as well. Going home after work was so different now that he had a family. Adam wouldn't trade it for anything. No matter how tired he was after a busy day at the store, seeing his family brought a smile to his lips. *I'm blessed*, he thought, moving toward the front of the store to see if Ben needed help with customers.

Approaching the counter, Adam saw Scott enter the store with his friend. Adam had met Jared a few times when he'd come by to visit Scott. The first few times, the boy had carried an attitude, but the last time Jared had stopped by to see Scott, he seemed more settled.

"You here to work?" Adam asked Scott.

The teen nodded. "So is Jared. He brought a note from his mother."

Jared handed a piece of paper to Adam. "My mom said it was okay for me to work here, and I appreciate the job."

Adam read the note:

Dear Mr. Beachy:

My son, Jared, has my permission to work at your store after school and on Saturdays. Thank you for giving him this opportunity.

Sincerely,
Mrs. Finley

Adam lowered the paper. "Since your mom approves, I'm okay with it, but you'll have to work hard. And there's to be no fooling around or visiting with Scott during work hours."

"No problem, sir. I'll do everything I'm told."

"Great. Now if you boys will follow me to the back room, I'll get you started stocking some shelves."

"Yes, sir," Scott and Jared said in unison.

Adam smiled at their enthusiasm, but something else caught his attention, although he couldn't put his finger on it. Something about Jared reminded him of himself back when he was around the same age.

"Since the laundry has been brought in, would you mind if I go out for a while?" Priscilla asked her mother. "Dad said he was planning to work late today, so I'm guessing we won't eat till sometime after seven."

Mom nodded. "True, but would you mind telling me where you're going?"

"To the Morgans' place. I want to see how David's doing."

"I don't think it's a good idea for you to be going over there so much." Mom clicked her tongue. "Some folks might get the wrong idea."

"What do you mean?" Priscilla's eyebrows rose. "The wrong idea about what?"

Mom folded the last towel and placed it on top of the stack. "You and David. Some people might wonder if you're interested in him."

Priscilla's defenses rose. "I am interested in David, but not seriously. You know David and I have been friends for several years. He's Elam's friend, too."

Mom placed her hand on Priscilla's shoulder. "I understand, but—"

"There's nothing for you to worry about, and I don't care what others may think."

"Just be careful you don't give David any ideas by going over there too often," Mom cautioned. "It wouldn't be good if he became romantically interested in you. He might try to persuade you to go English."

"It will never happen, Mom. David and I are just friends." Priscilla gave Mom a reassuring hug, grabbed her outer bonnet and jacket, then hurried out the door.

I can't believe Mom is worried about me and David, Priscilla thought as she made her way to the barn to get her horse. She stomped inside, scattering the barn cats in every direction. *I'm sure David doesn't see me as anything more than a friend.*

"It's nice to see you." David's grandma greeted Priscilla at the door. "I know Davey will be glad, too. He's been down in the dumps all day."

"Is he still in a lot of pain?" Wet with snow, Priscilla stopped to wipe her feet on the throw rug inside the door.

"Not as much as before. It's hard for him to be laid up. Davey's like anybody else—it's difficult not to be able to do things."

Letty led the way to the living room, where David sat in Walt's recliner. His eyes lit up when he saw Priscilla. "I was just thinking about you."

Priscilla smiled. "I've been anxious to see how you're doing."

David gestured to his cast. "I'm not running any marathons."

"You won't be for a while, either." Letty tapped David's shoulder. "You'll have to learn some patience till that leg of yours heals."

"Your grandma's right," Walt said, entering the room with a cup of coffee.

Letty moved closer to Priscilla. "I'll hang your jacket and outer bonnet in the hall closet till you're ready to go."

"I have a better idea," David spoke up. "Priscilla, why don't you leave your coat and bonnet on and take me for a ride in your buggy? I need to get out for some fresh air." He grinned at her. "Even though it's not snowing today, there's still plenty of white stuff on the ground. I'd enjoy getting out and seeing the beauty of it."

"You're not up to riding in a buggy, Davey." Letty shook her head. "Travel would be a lot rougher than riding in a car. You'll get jostled around."

"I'll be fine, Gram. Now would you mind gettin' my jacket?"

"I'll get it." Walt set his cup on the coffee table and left the room. When he returned, he had David's coat and a knitted cap, like the ones many of the Amish men wore in the area during the winter months.

Using his crutches to pull himself up, David stood. With his grandpa's help, he slipped on his jacket. "I really don't need the cap, since I'll be inside Priscilla's buggy. You do have a heater in there, right, Priscilla?"

She nodded. "It's in the dash, but if the wind picks up, it could still be a little chilly. I'd wear the knitted cap if I were you, David."

"Okay." David put the cap on his head and hobbled out the door.

Priscilla turned to face Walt and Letty. "We won't be gone long. I'll make sure my horse goes slowly so David won't get jostled too much."

Letty smiled. "Enjoy the ride, you two. I'll have hot chocolate waiting when you get back."

As they headed down the road a short time later, David reached over and touched Priscilla's arm. "There's something I've been wanting to ask."

"Oh?"

"How come you never answered any of my letters?"

Her brows drew together. "What letters?"

"The letters I wrote you when I first went to college."

"I never got your letters, David. The night of your motorcycle accident was the first I'd seen or heard from you in two years." Priscilla noticed David's deep frown. "Maybe you sent them to the wrong address, or perhaps the letters got lost in the mail. Unfortunately, it happens sometimes."

David grunted. "I know where you live, Priscilla, so I didn't use the wrong address. And it's not likely half-a-dozen letters would get lost. Maybe one of them, but not all."

Priscilla pursed her lips, clutching the horse's reins a little tighter. "Very strange." *Could Mom or Dad have intercepted David's letters? If so, why? When I go home I'm going to ask.*

CHAPTER 9

"Riding in your buggy is great!" David looked over at Priscilla and smiled. "I haven't felt this relaxed in days."

She returned his smile. "I'm trying to take it slow and easy so you don't get bumped around."

"I like going slow like this. Gives me a chance to really see the snowy landscape—not to mention the ride will last longer."

"It is beautiful." Priscilla held the reins firmly and kept her horse going at a steady pace.

"I may want to try driving a horse and buggy sometime."

"Really?"

He gave a nod. "It might be fun."

"It is, but it can also be hard and sometimes stressful when the horse doesn't want to cooperate."

"I'd still like to give it a try. Will you teach me, Priscilla?"

"Sure, if you want."

"Oh, and before you head home today, would you sign my cast?"

Priscilla felt David's eyes on her and immediately brought a hand to her warm cheek. Clearing her throat, she asked, "What for?"

"Usually when someone breaks a bone, it's fun to have friends or family sign their cast."

"Did your grandparents sign yours?"

"Not yet. You can be the first. Have you ever signed anyone's cast?"

She shook her head. "But I'm willing."

"You can do it when we get back to my grandparents' house." David's eyes shone as he grinned at her. "On another note, what are you doing for Christmas?"

"We'll get together with my brothers and their families on Christmas Eve, as well as Christmas Day," Priscilla replied, her composure now back to normal.

"You're lucky to have a big family." David dropped his gaze. "Since

I'm an only child, Christmas has always been kind of boring for me."

"Even when you've come to visit your grandparents?"

Looking up, he shook his head. "The Christmases we've spent here have always been great—the best, in fact."

"Will your parents be with you and your grandparents for Christmas this year?" Priscilla questioned.

"Probably, but I'm not looking forward to it."

"How come?"

"You heard the way my dad carried on when he and Mom showed up the day after my accident. If they come for Christmas, Dad will probably bring up the topic of me dropping out of college." David pulled his knitted cap down over his ears. "Let's not talk about this anymore. I want to relax and enjoy the ride."

Amy and Linda bounded into the kitchen at the moment Leah took a loaf of bread from the oven. Carrie, who'd been sitting at the table, pointed to the picture she'd been coloring. "See what I did while Leah was makin' bread?"

"That's nice." Linda peered over Carrie's shoulder.

"You stayed in the lines real good," Amy interjected.

Carrie grinned. "Danki."

"How was your day, girls?" Leah closed the oven door and wiped her hands on her apron. Then she gave Linda and Amy a hug.

"It was good for a Monday," Amy said. "It went pretty fast, too."

Linda nodded. "We practiced for the Christmas program."

Leah gave the girls a glass of milk. "I remember when I was young and took part in Christmas programs. Did you know I went to the same school you attend?"

"Wow! It must have been a long time ago." Linda looked up at Leah innocently.

Leah laughed, understanding how adults seemed much older through a child's eyes. She tweaked the end of Linda's nose. "I'm not old yet."

The girls all giggled.

"Did you see the sweet cake?" Carrie asked her sisters.

Leah's mouth twisted. She hoped Carrie wasn't talking about the chocolate cake she'd mentioned to her earlier. She'd planned to surprise Linda and bake it for her birthday this coming Friday. This would be the first birthday for one of Adam's nieces that they'd celebrated since the death of the girls' parents, and Leah wanted it to be special.

"Sweet cake?" Amy looked at the counter where the bread was cooling. "I see the *brot* Leah took out of the oven, but there's no cake."

Leah chuckled. "What I beleive Carrie meant was, did you see the suet cake?"

"What's a suet cake?" Linda asked.

"It's a small square-shaped block of seed held together by a mixture of beef fat," Leah explained. "Your uncle Adam sells them in his hardware store, and the birds love it."

Carrie's eyes brightened. "It's in a *kewwich*."

"You're right." Leah nodded. "You put the suet in a little cage designed to hold each cake. The cage makes it easy for the birds to grip the sides of the cage so they can peck at the suet."

"Where do you hang it?" Amy questioned.

"In a tree or suspended on a hook in a spot where the birds will easily find it. It'll be fun to watch the birds visit our yard this winter. In fact, I hung a suet cake in the small tree close to our living-room window."

No sooner had Leah said the words than all three girls raced into the living room. Smiling, Leah joined them at the window, where they could see a blue jay eating from the feeder. Seeing the look of joy on the girls' faces filled her with peace. She felt privileged to help Adam raise his nieces.

Iva was standing at the sink, peeling potatoes when Priscilla entered the kitchen at five o'clock.

"How'd your visit with David go?" she asked, turning to face Priscilla.

"It went well. I took him for a buggy ride." Priscilla removed her wrap and hung it up. "Letty had hot chocolate and brownies for us when we got back. After we finished eating, I signed David's cast."

Iva's eyebrows lifted, but she made no comment. She hoped Priscilla wouldn't make a habit of spending time with David. His modern English ways might rub off on her.

Priscilla moved closer to the sink. "I need to ask you a question, Mom."

"Ask away." Iva turned back to the potatoes.

"David said he sent me some letters during his first year of college, but I didn't get any of them. Would you know anything about that?"

The peeler slipped from Iva's fingers, and she drew in a sharp breath. She fixed her gaze out the window, barely aware of how the sunset made the snow look pink. Should she admit she'd intercepted the letters or pretend she knew nothing about them? Back then, Iva had rationalized that she was only trying to protect her daughter.

What I did was bad enough. I can't lie to my own daughter about this now. It would go against what I believe—especially when Daniel and I have taught our children to be honest and upright, as the Bible says.

Swallowing past the constriction in her throat, she turned and looked at Priscilla. "I–I'm ashamed to admit this, but the truth is, I threw away David's letters."

Priscilla gasped. "Why would you do something like that, Mom?"

"I saw the way David hung around you whenever he came to visit his grandparents. I was afraid he might talk you into becoming part of his English world."

"David has never tried to influence me to do anything, Mom. Even if he had, you ought to know I would never go English." Priscilla's shoulders tightened. "I'm disappointed you would keep David's letters from me. Not to mention all this time David has wondered why I never wrote back."

"I'm sorry, Priscilla." She placed her hand against her breastbone, and when she spoke, her voice cracked. "What I did was wrong. I hope you'll accept my apology."

"I forgive you, Mom, but from now on, if you're worried about something involving my life, I'd appreciate it if you would please come talk to me about it."

Iva hugged her daughter. "I will, and again, I'm truly sorry."

David lounged on the couch, barely watching the TV, while Gramps read the paper and Gram knitted a sweater. His favorite show was on, but he had no interest in it. He glanced at his cast, studying the words Priscilla had written with a marking pen. *Keep the faith.*

David realized those three simple words could have more than one meaning. Did Priscilla mean he should have faith to believe he would heal quickly? Or perhaps she'd meant something else.

Riding in Priscilla's buggy and enjoying Gram's hot chocolate and brownies afterward had lifted David's spirits. He liked being with Priscilla and looked forward to seeing her again.

As David's eyelids grew heavy, he let his imagination run wild. *What would it be like if I became Amish and married Priscilla?*

"Did you and Scott get a lot done on your school project today?" Cora asked while she and Jared ate supper.

"Uh. . .yeah. . .but we still have a lot to get done."

"I always enjoyed science when I was in school, so I'm anxious to hear all the details."

Jared grabbed his glass of water and took a drink. "There's not much to tell. I'll fill you in when the project's done. We're just in the starting stages."

"I understand."

They ate in silence for a while, until the telephone rang.

"I'll get it!" Jared dropped his fork and raced into the other room. He returned with a big grin.

"Who called, Jared?" Cora asked. "Was it your father?"

"Nope. It was my friend Chad."

"Chad from Chicago?" Cora hoped not, because when Jared used to hang around Chad, he'd usually gotten into trouble.

"Yeah, Mom, it was Chad from Chicago." Jared flopped into his chair.

"What did he want? How'd he get our number?"

"I gave him the number. He wanted to know if he could come here for a few days during Christmas break."

Cora frowned. "I hope you told him no."

"I didn't say he could, but I didn't say no, either."

"What did you say?"

"Said I'd ask you if it was okay."

"Well, I'm glad you respected me, Jared, but unfortunately, it's not okay. Your so-called friend is nothing but trouble, and I don't want him staying here, so you'd better call him right back and tell him not to come." Cora pursed her lips. "I can't imagine Chad's parents allowing him to drive all those miles—especially with the cold, snowy weather we've been having."

"Chad's folks are goin' on a cruise the day after Christmas, so they won't care what he does."

"Well, they should care. He's only seventeen. No wonder Chad gets into trouble, the way his parents let him do whatever he wants. They must not believe in parental supervision."

"Chad turned eighteen a few weeks ago, Mom. He graduated from high school in June."

"What's he done since then, Jared? Does he have a job? Is he attending college somewhere?"

Jared turned his hands palms up. "Beats me. He never said. I didn't ask."

"Figures. He'll probably sponge off his parents for as long as he can." Cora sighed. "I want you to call Chad back as soon as we're done eating and tell him not to come."

"Okay, Mom, whatever you say." Jared grabbed his hamburger and took a big bite.

Cora felt relieved. At least Jared hadn't argued about her decision. Their house was barely big enough for the two of them. The last thing she needed was Chad coming around and undoing all the good that had developed between her and Jared this past month.

CHAPTER 10

Adam went to the office to get his jacket and hat. He was anxious to get home early because they were celebrating Linda's eighth birthday. Since Scott and Jared had already arrived, he was leaving Ben in charge of overseeing the boys and closing up for the day.

Adam opened his filing cabinet drawer and retrieved the gift bag with the book he and Leah would give Linda for her birthday. He was glad the store had this particular book about birds specific to the state of Illinois—especially since Leah had recently hung out a suet feeder. They both felt Linda would enjoy learning from it.

"See you in the morning," Adam called as he waved good-bye to Ben and headed out the door. Already, he imagined how good the house would smell once he got there. Leah probably had the cake made, and the meat loaf was likely in the oven. Adam's favorite dessert was brownies, but chocolate cake with peanut butter icing was high on his list of favorites, too.

"Come on, Flash. Let's get moving." Adam clucked to his horse. Leah's parents were no doubt there already. This was one evening when he wouldn't mind if Flash felt frisky.

Everything was going according to plan when the girls got home from school Friday afternoon. Even though this was Linda's first birthday without her parents, she seemed to be handling it well. Amy and Carrie were excited about their sister's birthday, too.

Leah had baked Linda's birthday cake earlier in the day, while Carrie was napping. Adam was the only one aware of the three-layer chocolate cake with peanut butter icing. Even the corn on the cob, hidden in the lid-covered pot on the stove, would be a surprise for the girls.

Leah glanced at the clock, noting Adam should be home shortly.

"Danki for bringing the corn," she told Mom, who stood at the counter, mashing potatoes.

Mom smiled. "You're welcome. We had an abundance of corn in our garden this past summer, so I was able to freeze and can quite a bit."

Leah peeked out the window. "I see Dad's still chopping wood, and Coal's there to keep him company."

"Jah, he likes to keep busy. Bringing in more wood for you is his way of helping out."

"It's appreciated." Walking back to the stove, Leah double-checked all the food. "Everything should be ready as soon as my husband arrives." She smiled inwardly, remembering the days when she'd had no interest in Adam. For a time, he'd actually gotten on her nerves. But that was before Amy, Linda, and Carrie came to live with him. After the girls had been in his charge for a while, a change had come over Adam. Leah loved him more than she'd ever thought possible.

"Those girls are sure focused on the window in there." Mom gestured to the other room.

"They love watching the birds eat from the suet cake." Leah opened the oven door to check on the meat loaf one more time.

Just then, Adam and Dad walked into the house. Before they could say anything, Linda started crying. "What's going on?" Adam asked.

Leah shrugged. "I don't know."

All three girls dashed into the kitchen. Still crying, Linda raced out the back door.

"What happened?" Leah looked at Amy.

"A bird flew into the window." Carrie sniffed.

Amy's sober expression let Leah know she, too, was on the verge of tears.

Leah turned down the stove and oven and followed Adam and her folks out the door. She found Linda on the porch, tears streaming down her face. "Is. . .is it dead?" She gulped on a sob, lifting her cupped hands out to reveal the still form of a black-and-white bird.

Time hung suspended as everyone stared at the bird. Adam pointed to Linda's feathered friend. "Look, its eyes are blinking."

"Its little head is moving now, too." Amy moved in closer to Linda.

Linda's eyes widened when the bird hopped to her finger, clutching with its tiny feet. It sat, looking around, as though quite comfortable at being the center of attention.

Leah's voice lowered so she wouldn't startle the bird. "I believe, looking at the markings and color, it's a male downy woodpecker."

"You're right," Adam agreed. "You can tell by the little red area on top of its head. The females are black and white."

Before anyone spoke again, the little bird flew off and landed in the nearest tree. Everyone clapped, watching it fluff its feathers. Leah was thankful the woodpecker's adventures hadn't spoiled Linda's birthday.

"Maybe you should hang the suet feeder a little farther from the house," Leah's mother suggested.

Leah nodded. "Good idea. We can hang it from the tree over there, where we can still see from the window."

"I'll bet the bird saw its reflection in the window and thought it was another bird," Leah's father interjected.

"You might be right, Dad," Leah agreed.

Adam moved toward the door. "I don't know about the rest of you, but I'm ready to eat and help someone celebrate her birthday." He winked at Linda.

"Me, too!" Giggling, she clapped her hands.

"Okay, girls, after you've washed your hands, you may take your seats." While the girls went to wash up, Leah took the meat loaf from the oven, and Mom put the mashed potatoes and broccoli in serving bowls. Adam set the corn on a plate, and Dad took each item to the table.

Soon Linda and her sisters joined them at the table. The look on Linda's face was priceless as she pointed to the steaming corn on the cob. "Yum! Everything looks *appeditlich*!"

"It's time to give thanks for this delicious food." Adam bowed his head, and everyone else did the same.

"This is the last dinner I'll be hosting this month." Elaine removed a pumpkin pie from the oven and smiled at Priscilla. "I could never have done all these dinners so close to Christmas without your help."

Priscilla took the second pie from the oven. "I'd have been happy to do it even if you weren't paying me. It's given us a chance to visit more than usual, and I've certainly met a lot of new, fascinating people."

Elaine laughed. "Some of them have been rather unusual—like the man with the musical tie who came to the dinner last night."

Priscilla snickered. "Don't forget the woman with little silver bells. Every time she moved, they jingled."

"Thursday night's dinner guests were quite the musical group. It'll be interesting to see what tonight's group brings." Elaine got down the teapot. "Let's take a break before we start setting the tables."

"Sounds good." Priscilla got the cups, while Elaine brewed the tea; then they both took a seat at the kitchen table.

"Other than helping me here, how's your week gone?" Elaine questioned. "We were so busy with the dinner last night, I didn't get a chance to ask."

"I helped my mamm do some cleaning, and I visited David." Priscilla blew on her tea before taking a tentative sip.

"How's David doing?"

"A little better; although he's still having some pain." Priscilla smiled. "David was getting tired of being cooped up, so I took him for a buggy ride."

"Was Elam there, too?"

"No, just me and David."

Elaine quirked an eyebrow. "I don't like to be so direct, but is it good for you to spend so much time with David? Won't Elam be *vergunne*?"

Priscilla shook her head. "There's nothing for him to be envious about. David and I are just good friends. David is Elam's friend, too." Why was Elaine giving her a hard time about this? Had she talked to Mom?

"True, but some folks, and maybe Elam, might get the wrong idea if you spend too much time with David."

"Now you sound like my mamm. She's worried for the same reason." Priscilla frowned. "I just learned that David wrote to me several times during his first year of college, but Mom intercepted his letters."

"What?"

"She threw the letters away and never told me about them. The other day, the truth came out."

"Why would she do something like that?"

"Said she was worried David might influence me to leave the

Amish faith." Priscilla clenched her fingers tightly, causing some tea to spill out of the cup.

"Be careful you don't burn yourself." Elaine grabbed a napkin and wiped up the spill.

"I'm okay. Talking about those letters I never got to read upsets me."

"I'm sure it does."

"Mom apologized, of course, but it hurt to know she would do such a thing."

Elaine drank more tea, and sat several seconds before responding. "What your mamm did was wrong, but I suppose she was only trying to protect you."

"I didn't need it then, and I don't need it now. David has never tried to influence me to go English."

"You wouldn't consider leaving, would you?"

Priscilla shook her head. "I have no desire to give up my Plain life."

"Whew! Good to hear. I can't imagine going English, either. Our Amish values and the support we get from one another are important to me."

"Speaking of support, my daed mentioned this morning he'd seen Jonah Miller yesterday."

"Oh?"

"He said Jonah's not doing well."

"Physically or emotionally?"

"Emotionally. Losing Sara has been hard on him. Not only does he have the responsibility of raising his stepson and daughter, but he has his buggy shop to run as well. Poor little Mark has lost both of his birth parents. Fortunately, he's truly taken to Jonah, and in every respect has become his son."

"Losing a loved one is never easy, even for someone so young. At least Jonah's folks live nearby and are available to help out and offer their support." Elaine took her cup to the sink.

"Do you still have feelings for Jonah?" Priscilla dared to ask.

"Ben's asked me to marry him," Elaine stood at the sink, staring out the window.

"But you haven't given Ben your answer, right?"

"No, I haven't."

"If you still care for Jonah, maybe you two will end up together."

"Jonah loved Sara, and it's too soon for him to even consider getting married again. Besides, what Jonah and I once had is in the past. There's no point talking about this." Elaine moved toward the room where they'd be hosting their meal. "Let's go in now and get the tables set. There's still much to be done before the dinner guests arrive."

Priscilla pushed away from the table. From the way her friend had quickly changed the subject, she had a hunch Elaine still had feelings for Jonah. *I hope she doesn't end up marrying Ben. I've never told Elaine this, but they're not suited to each other.*

"I'm surprised you're eating supper with us tonight." Elam's mother passed him the basket of rolls and some butter. "Don't you and Priscilla usually have something planned on Friday evenings?"

"She's helping Elaine host another dinner," Elam mumbled.

Mom's eyebrows rose. "Again? Didn't Priscilla help Elaine with a dinner last night?"

Elam nodded, spooning some mashed potatoes onto his plate. "I have a feeling Priscilla's been avoiding me lately."

"Why would she do that?" Dad asked. He took a piece of chicken and handed the platter to Elam.

Elam shrugged. "She didn't even tell me she was doing the dinners till the night we went to Yoder's Kitchen. Then it was only brought up because Elaine, who was there with Ben Otto, mentioned it."

"I'm sure Priscilla wasn't keeping it from you on purpose, son." Mom took a piece of chicken. "She probably got busy and forgot to mention it. Besides, Elaine's helper left town suddenly, so Priscilla had to fill in rather quickly."

Dad nudged Elam's arm. "If you'd marry the girl, you wouldn't have to worry about her not telling you things. You and Priscilla have been courting awhile now. Maybe she feels you're not interested since you haven't asked her to marry you."

Elam grunted. "I'm not ready for marriage yet, Dad. Even if we were married, there's no guarantee Priscilla would tell me everything."

Dad chuckled, looking at Mom. "Some women like to keep their men guessing. Right, Virginia?"

Mom rolled her eyes. "Now, Marcus, you know I'd never do that. Let's talk about something else while we eat supper, okay?"

Elam and Dad both nodded.

As Elam's parents discussed the weather, Elam tuned them out. The only thought on his mind was Priscilla. How he wished he felt free to ask her to marry him now.

CHAPTER 11

Monday morning, Cora headed toward the Amish schoolhouse on her way to the clinic. She'd gone to and from work this way since she'd first spotted her granddaughters walking on the shoulder of the road.

So many thoughts went through her head as she drove along the winding country road. *Too bad Jared didn't grow up around here instead of the big city. Maybe he would have a different attitude about things.*

Lately it seemed he'd been trying, but a friend's influence could change it all. In the Arthur area, life seemed so much simpler, although not immune from normal life experiences. The tragic accident that took her granddaughters' parents was a prime example.

Tears welled in Cora's eyes, thinking of those poor little girls. *They're so young to have gone through such a tragedy.* Wiping a tear that had fallen to her cheek, she felt consoled knowing the girls had Adam and Leah now and were being brought up in a good home. Being as young as they were had its good points, though. Children were more resilient than adults and, in some cases, accepted things quicker. Other situations could mess up a person's life forever. Cora would never know how her deceased daughter, Mary, felt about her, but unfortunately, Adam had made his feelings quite clear.

"I wish I could talk to my granddaughters," she murmured. "I wouldn't have to tell them who I am. Just say a few words."

Cora clenched the steering wheel until her fingers ached. *But would talking to them be enough?* She really wanted to be part of their lives—to spend time with them and get to know them.

Some days, Cora thought she deserved a second chance. Other times, she berated herself for running out on Adam and Mary and figured she was getting what she deserved for being a terrible mother. She'd asked God's forgiveness; now if she could only forgive herself. If she had the chance to be the girls' grandmother in every sense of the word, maybe it would help make up for the past. Cora was well aware that the only chance she had of making up for her past would be if she could work her way back into Adam's life. She would not force herself on Adam, though; doing such a thing would only push him further away.

Cora had started attending a local church and had tried getting Jared involved with the youth group so he would have some new friends, but so far he hadn't shown much interest.

Worshipping helped to strengthen her faith, but she hadn't made any new friends there.

As she rounded the next bend, Cora noticed a lone tree in the middle of a field. From its size, she figured the tree must have been there for years, but she'd never noticed it before. Barren of leaves and silhouetted against the sky, it stood in stark contrast against the snow-covered landscape.

Cora sighed. *I feel like that tree: all alone with no one surrounding me.*

Up ahead, Cora spotted a group of children on their way to school. It didn't take long to realize two of them were Adam's nieces, especially since one looked so much like her daughter, Mary, when she was around the same age.

Heart thumping in her chest, Cora pulled her car to the side of the road and got out. "Good morning. Can any of you tell me where I might be able to buy some fresh eggs?" To hide her swirling emotions, Cora took slow deep breaths. Her nerves were at the breaking point from being this close to Mary's girls.

"Don't know of anyone sellin' eggs on this road," the younger girl said. "But on the next road over, there's a place where you can buy 'em."

"Good to know. I'll check on it soon." Cora smiled. "You must be heading to school."

The girls nodded. "We can't be late, neither, 'cause tonight's our Christmas program and we've gotta practice," the younger one said.

The older girl spoke up. "Come on, Linda, we don't have time to talk or we're gonna be late. Besides, you know what Uncle Adam's told us about talking to strangers."

I'm not a stranger. Cora rubbed her arms where the cold seeped in under her coat. *I'm your grandmother.* Oh, how Cora wished she could utter those words. But she didn't want to alarm the children. "I'll let you go. Danki for telling me where I might find some fresh eggs."

The girls looked at her strangely then hurried along. Were they wondering why she'd said the Pennsylvania Dutch word for *thank you*?

I've made a decision. I am going to that Christmas program. Cora returned to her car. *I'll sit at the back of the room so I won't be noticed.*

"Are you two excited?" Leah asked, helping the girls into Adam's buggy that evening.

"I'm *naerfich*." Linda climbed into the backseat next to Carrie.

"There's no reason to be nervous." Leah stepped aside so Amy could get in. "I'm sure you and your sister will do fine."

"Leah's right," Adam chimed in as he settled in the driver's seat. "And I'll tell ya a little secret. She and I have been looking forward to this all week."

Leah smiled at Adam's sincerity as he talked to Linda and Amy. He had come a long way in his relationship with his nieces.

As they approached the end of their driveway, preparing to enter the road, Adam reached across the seat and clasped Leah's hand. "Tonight's gonna be a good night."

Leah squeezed his fingers gently and smiled. "Jah."

Carrie, Linda, and Amy chatted as they traveled while Leah sat quietly, listening to the *clip-clop* of the horse's hooves, and watching the gentle snowflakes starting to fall. It was pretty to see how the little flecks of white clung to the horse's mane and tail.

In no time, they pulled into the school yard where many other buggies were already parked. The program they'd soon be watching brought Leah fond memories of when she was a girl. One year in particular, she, Priscilla, and Elaine had taken part in a play depicting the birth of Jesus. Leah and Elaine had been angels, while Priscilla played the role of Mary.

"You and the girls can go inside while I tie my horse to the hitching rail." Adam touched Leah's arm, pulling Leah out of her musings.

"Okay." She got out of the buggy and helped the girls down. Then they all tromped through the snow to the schoolhouse.

Cora paused at the door of the schoolhouse, hoping she could sneak in the back, unnoticed. She'd seen other cars parked outside, which meant she wasn't the only Englisher who'd come tonight. Since Jared was doing homework at Scott's this evening, it gave Cora the chance to attend the program without him knowing where she was. He'd probably wonder why his mother wanted to attend an Amish school program, and she wasn't ready to explain. How would Jared respond if he knew she had grandchildren? All his life she'd let Jared assume he was an only child.

Pulling her head scarf a little closer to her face, Cora seated herself on a wooden bench along the back wall of the schoolhouse. Coming here reminded her of the day she'd slipped into Leah and Adam's wedding without them knowing. She'd left early that day, not wanting to be noticed, and would leave tonight as soon as she saw her granddaughters perform.

Cora glanced around the room, looking for Adam and Leah. All she saw were the backs of people's heads, so she couldn't be certain where they were seated. *I hope no one recognizes me. If Adam knew I was here, he'd be upset. It's asking a lot, but I wish he'd give me a second chance.*

Cora sat in rapt attention as the program began. Several scholars sang and gave their recitations, some shyly, some wiggling and giggling. A lump formed in her throat when the two young girls she was certain were her granddaughters said their parts. *If only I felt free to tell them who I am*, she thought once more. *How much longer can I go without talking to Adam again?*

"I thought you were going to the school Christmas program tonight," Mom said when she came into the kitchen where Priscilla sat at the table, making Christmas cards.

"I was planning to go, but I've been busy helping Elaine with her dinners and haven't had time to make cards, let alone do any Christmas baking or buy gifts." Priscilla frowned. "I'm not even sure what to get for Elam or David."

Mom pursed her lips. "Why would you buy David a Christmas

present? He hasn't been courting you."

"I realize that, Mom, but David's a good friend, and he's laid up with a broken leg. I thought it would be nice to get him something." Her defenses rising, she plunked the rubber stamp she'd been using into the ink pad a little too hard. "I'll bet Elam plans to buy David a gift, too."

"Does Elam know you're planning to give David a gift?"

"I haven't told him, but I'm sure he'd have no objections."

Mom folded her arms across her chest. "I hope you won't take this the wrong way, daughter, but you're making a *fehler*."

"It's not a mistake." Priscilla realized where this was going and was ready to nip it in the bud if Mom went too far with giving her opinion about David. She'd already expressed her disapproval, but Priscilla thought her mother was wrong. Time and again, Priscilla had reiterated there was nothing but friendship between her and David. She was sure Elam was aware of it, too.

Mom took a seat at the table. "If you keep showing David so much attention, Elam is bound to be jealous."

Priscilla shook her head determinedly. "I think you're wrong, and I'm sorry you disapprove of David. I can assure you, though, my friendship with him is not going to come between me and Elam."

"I hope you're right." Mom turned and ambled out of the kitchen.

Looking at her ink-stained fingers, Priscilla huffed. *If Mom got to know David better, she'd see how nice he is. I wish she wasn't so controlling.*

"That was a nice Christmas program," Leah said as they headed home. "Amy and Linda, you did a good job."

Adam nodded. "I agree. And you didn't seem naerfich at all."

"I was at first," Amy admitted. "But when I looked out and saw you and Leah smiling at us, I didn't feel nervous anymore."

"Me, neither," Linda agreed. "It was kinda fun. That nice lady sittin' in the back of the room smiled at us, too."

"What lady?" Adam questioned.

"I don't know her name. She left as soon as me and Amy were done."

Leah glanced over her shoulder. "Was it Elaine, Priscilla, or one of our other Amish friends?" She'd invited several of their close friends to attend but hadn't seen Priscilla or Elaine among those in attendance.

Linda shook her head. "It was that English lady who stopped and talked to us on our way to school this morning. She wanted some *oier*."

Leah's forehead creased. "Why would anyone think you had eggs?"

"She didn't think that," Amy explained. "The woman asked if anyone sold fresh eggs in the area."

"Are you sure she was the same person you saw at the program tonight?" Adam questioned.

Linda shrugged. "I think so." She turned to Carrie. "Next year when you go to school, you'll have a part in the program, too."

Grinning widely, Carrie bobbed her head. "It'll be fun."

Turning to face the front of the buggy, Leah reflected on what Linda had said. *I wonder who the English woman was. How come she left early? I wish I'd thought to turn and look in the back. I may have recognized her.*

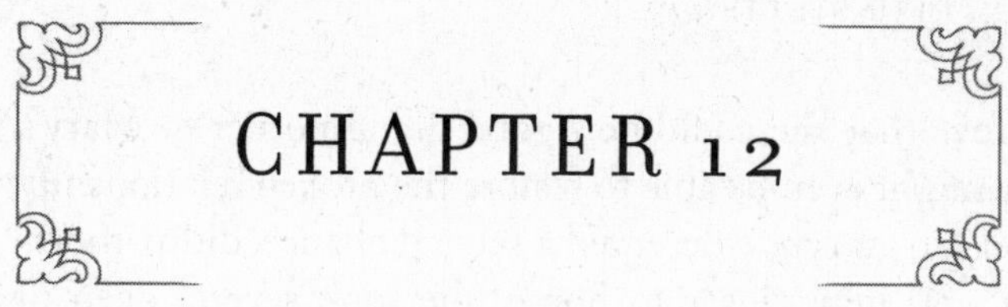

CHAPTER 12

As Cora drove home, with Christmas music playing on her car radio, she thought about the program she'd just attended. It had been difficult to sit at the back of the room, watching the Amish children say their parts, unable to acknowledge her granddaughters in public. Leaving before the program was over had been just as hard. Cora imagined what it had been like after the play, when parents, relatives, and friends greeted the children. *If only I could have been a part of tonight, giving hugs to my granddaughters and telling them how well they'd both done. When I see Leah again, I may ask her to speak to Adam on my behalf.*

Since Christmas was a few days away, Cora would wait until the holiday was over.

Maybe I should send anonymous gifts to the girls. Cora's shoulders tensed. *Guess that's not a good idea. Adam would probably figure out who had sent them and pull away even further.*

Cora felt sure this was part of her punishment. She felt cheated not being able to share in tonight's activities. She wondered how it had been for Adam or Mary when they'd taken part in school Christmas programs. How terrible it must have been for them to look out into the audience and not see their mother.

Cora realized this Christmas would be bittersweet. The sweet part would be spending time with Jared—especially since they'd been getting along better. The bitter part was being unable to repair her relationship with Adam. She also longed for a connection with her granddaughters, instead of seeing the girls from a distance or speaking to them as a stranger. *If I'd known who little Carrie was the day Leah brought her to the clinic after she'd been stung by bees, I would have given her a hug.*

The more time that passed without speaking with Adam, the more frustrated Cora became. The damage she'd done by leaving Adam and Mary could not be repaired. But if he would give her a chance, she would prove that she could be a good grandmother to Mary's girls. In time, she might even be able to restore the broken relationship with her son. After all, everyone deserved a second chance, didn't they?

As Cora drew closer to home, she took several deep breaths to calm her nerves. It wouldn't be good if she walked in the door, tense and moody. When Jared returned from Scott's, it wouldn't be good if she was tense and moody. He might ask questions she wasn't ready to answer.

When Cora pulled into her driveway, she was surprised to see a parked car blocking her access to the garage. At first she thought it might be Scott's dad dropping Jared off. But she'd seen his vehicle before, and this car definitely was not his.

Turning off the ignition, Cora stepped out of her car. Being careful not to slip on the icy sidewalk, she made her way to the house.

When she entered her living room, she was taken by surprise. Jared sat on the couch watching some crazy TV show. His friend from Chicago sat beside him.

"What's going on?" Cora stood between the boys and the television. She grabbed the remote from the coffee table and hit the mute button.

"Oh, hi, Mom. Where have you been?" Jared looked up at her and smiled. Did he really expect a smile in response?

"Yes, I am, and never mind the meeting. I thought you were studying with Scott this evening." She motioned to Chad. "What are *you* doing here, young man?"

"He came to see me," Jared responded before Chad could open his mouth.

Cora tapped her foot. "I thought I had made it clear. . ."

"My mom and stepdad kicked me out." Chad frowned. "Can you believe they'd do somethin' like that right before Christmas?"

"I thought your parents were on a cruise." Either Jared had lied to Cora, or Chad lied to him. Either way, Cora was going to find out the truth.

Chad reached for the can of soda pop on the coffee table and took a drink. "They were gonna go, but then somethin' came up and they had to cancel at the last minute."

Cora didn't know whether Chad was telling the truth or not, but she did know this young man had been deceitful when he'd hung around Jared in Chicago. "Would you mind telling me why they kicked you out?"

Chad shrugged his shoulders. "Beats me. Shawn's never liked me much. And Mom, well, she goes along with whatever he says."

Jared left his seat and stood beside Cora. "Look, Mom, Chad came all the way here, and he has no place else to go. Is it okay if he spends the night?"

Cora clenched her teeth. She couldn't very well send the kid out into the cold, but having him stay here was not a good choice, either.

"Please, Mom." Jared tugged on her arm. "I know we don't have a spare bedroom, but Chad can sleep on the couch, or on the floor in my room."

Unable to keep from sighing, Cora said, "Okay, but it's only for tonight. Understand?"

Jared nodded.

"Thanks, Mrs. Finley." Grinning, Chad ran his fingers through the ends of his shaggy blond hair. "I sure appreciate it."

"The couch will be more comfortable than sleeping on the floor. I'll get you a blanket after I have some tea." Handing the remote to her son, Cora reminded him to keep the volume lowered.

I must be out of my mind, Cora thought as she made her way to the kitchen to brew some tea. In the morning, she would fix Chad some breakfast and insist he go home. Surely his parents would take him back.

"Danki for making *penuche* this morning," Amy said as Leah and the girls sat at the breakfast table the next morning. Since he needed to open the store a bit early this morning, Adam had already left.

"You're welcome." Leah smiled. "I know how much you girls like pancakes."

"I like french toast, too," Linda said around a mouthful of food.

"Please don't talk with your mouth full," Leah reminded. "It's not polite."

Linda finished the pancake and grabbed her glass of milk. "Sorry 'bout that."

Leah noticed a blotch of syrup on Carrie's chin, so she reached over and wiped it with a napkin.

"I've been wondering about something." Leah leaned closer to Linda. "The woman you mentioned who asked you about eggs, what did she look like?"

Linda shrugged, but Amy answered Leah's question. "She had red hair."

"Was she young or an older woman?"

"Older, I guess." Amy paused to take another pancake. "Course she wasn't old like our bishop's wife. Margaret has lots of wrinkles."

"Wrinkles can be a sign of several things, Amy. They can be an indication of many years of life. Unfortunately, wrinkles can also be due to stress, or even pain someone is dealing with," Leah explained.

"Sorry. Guess I shouldn't have said that." Amy lowered her head.

"We learn from many lessons in life, so I'm glad you understand." Leah patted the child's arm. "Do you remember the color of the lady's car?"

"It was gray," Linda spoke up.

Leah dropped her fork. *Could it have been Cora who talked to the girls? Was she at the schoolhouse last night, watching from the back? I'd better not say anything to Adam about this. At least not until I know if it was Cora.*

Cora entered the living room and groaned. Chad lay sprawled on the couch in a pair of sweat pants, but no shirt. With his bare arms and shoulders exposed, she couldn't help noticing several tattoos. *What was that boy thinking, and where were his parents when he marked up his body that way?*

Since she was a nurse, Cora had seen a good many people with tattoos that they had chosen to get. But seeing Chad's and knowing he was barely eighteen made her wonder how long ago he'd done it and whether he'd had his parents' permission.

Moving into the kitchen, Cora was surprised to see Jared at the table, eating a bowl of cereal. "You workin' today, Mom?" he asked, barely glancing at her.

"Yes, of course I am, and when I get home this afternoon, I expect your friend to be gone. Is that understood?"

Jared's posture slumped. "So you're just gonna throw Chad out on the street, the way his folks did?"

"I am not throwing him on the street. He doesn't belong here, Jared. I went against my better judgment letting him even spend the night."

"If Chad leaves here, he'll have no place to go and will spend Christmas alone."

"Chad doesn't have to be alone. He can go home and make things right with his mother and stepfather." Cora moved across the room to get some coffee started. "If I'd known you were going to give me a hard time about this, I would have insisted Chad leave last night."

Jared's chair scraped the floor as he pushed away from the table. "I promise, when you get home from work today, Chad won't be here."

"That's good." The last thing Cora needed was one more problem. All she wanted was for her and Jared to enjoy a nice, quiet Christmas without any issues or complications.

Mattoon

"I'm glad you were free to go shopping with me this morning." Priscilla smiled as she and Elaine made their way down the aisle at Wal-Mart. "In addition to picking up a few things I need myself, I want to get a Christmas present for David."

Elaine tipped her head. "Really? I thought you'd be buying something for Elam."

"I am. I'll be going to the Country Shoe Shop to buy a new dress hat for Elam." Priscilla wrinkled her nose. "The one he's been wearing for church has seen better days."

"A hat sounds like a nice gift. I'm sure he will appreciate getting a new one."

"I hope so." Priscilla gestured to the books. "This is what I'm looking for. David enjoys reading stories set in the Old West, so I'll buy him a paperback novel, but it needs to be from the inspirational section."

Priscilla looked at several books and finally settled on a historical novel, written by a Christian author. "What are you giving Ben for Christmas?"

Elaine rubbed the bridge of her nose. "I've been so busy with all the dinners we've hosted lately, I haven't had time to do any shopping until today."

"Do you know what he would like?"

"I'm not sure. Maybe I'll ask one of Ben's sisters."

Priscilla looked to her left and spotted Jonah's mother, Sarah Miller, heading their way.

"I see I'm not the only one out shopping on this chilly morning." Sarah smiled. "Are you two looking for Christmas presents or just shopping for general items?"

"A little of both." Priscilla gestured to Sarah's shopping cart, full of grocery items. "Are you buying for Christmas dinner?"

"Jah." Sarah pushed a strand of silver-gray hair back under her head covering. "We're keeping Christmas fairly simple this year, what with Jonah losing Sara and all. But it's still important to share a nice meal and do something special for the kinner."

"Speaking of Jonah's children, where are Mark and the baby today?"

"They're with the parents of Sara's first husband this morning. It would have been too difficult for me to get any shopping done with the two little ones. Besides, Mark's grandparents have a right to spend time with him, and it's good for them to get to know Mark's half sister, too."

"How is Jonah doing?" Elaine asked, joining the conversation.

Sarah sighed. "He's still struggling with his wife's death, but taking one day at a time. Raymond and I are doing our best to help him get through it. Fortunately, the baby is too little to know what's happened to her mamm, but for Mark's sake, we need to put on a happy face and make Christmas special. He still cries for his mother and clings to Jonah when he comes home from work at night." Tears welled in her eyes. "Jonah has been working twice as hard since Sara died, so he doesn't spend as much time with the children as he should."

"Maybe he needs to stay busy in order to keep going." Elaine rubbed her arms, as if she were cold. "That's how I got through the loss of my grandmother."

"I suppose you're right. I'm thankful Raymond and I left our home in Pennsylvania and moved here when we did. Not only has it given

Jonah and his daed the chance to work together again, but we're clearly needed to help raise Jonah's kinner." Sarah turned her shopping cart around. "Guess I'd better get checked out. I've kept my driver waiting long enough."

When Jonah's mother moved on, Priscilla noticed Elaine's pained expression. She felt certain her friend had never stopped loving Jonah. No doubt Elaine wanted to reach out to Jonah but didn't think it would be appropriate so she was holding back.

Priscilla wondered how things would be right now if Jonah had married Elaine and not Sara. Certain events that happened to people could cause them to take a different course than they'd originally planned. It was hard to know sometimes which way to go. David was a prime example, for the course of his life had changed the day he'd given up the idea of becoming a vet and dropped out of school. Priscilla wondered whether he would stay in Arthur or return to Chicago and resume his schooling to study for some other profession. If he stayed here, what would he do for a living?

CHAPTER 13

Arthur

Where's Priscilla?" Daniel asked as he entered the kitchen where Iva was busily putting ginger cookies into a container. "With everything to be done before our family arrives for Christmas Eve, I thought she'd be here helping you."

"She left a few hours ago. Said she had Christmas gifts she wanted to give to a few of her friends." Iva handed her husband a cookie. "I'm guessing David might be one of those friends. She's been seeing a lot of him lately, and I'm *bekimmere.*"

"Why are you concerned?" Daniel bit into the cookie. "Yum! Nice and chewy, just the way I like 'em."

"I'm worried David might be interested in our daughter and persuade her to leave the Amish faith."

Daniel shook his head. "That's not likely. We need to put our daughter's situation in the Lord's hands and not meddle in her life. She's an adult and has a good head on her shoulders."

"You're right, Daniel."

"Have you been praying for Priscilla?"

Iva's hands went straight to her hips. "Of course I've been praying, but David could win Priscilla over if Elam doesn't ask her to marry him soon."

"Just give him some time."

"How much time does he need? If Elam really cares about our daughter, then he ought to be committed enough to marry her, don't you think?"

Daniel reached into the container and took another cookie. "Not every man is as eager to propose as quickly as I did." He leaned closer and kissed her cheek. "I could tell you were a good woman when we first met, and I wasn't about to let ya go."

Iva snickered and snapped the lid on the container before he could snatch another cookie. Sobering, she said, "Priscilla was umgerennt when I told her I'd intercepted those letters David sent her when he went off to college."

Daniel's brows lifted. "You did what?"

"Even back then, I thought they were getting too close, so when I found his first letter in our mailbox, I threw it away." Iva's eyes watered. "I knew it was wrong, but when more letters came, I intercepted them as well."

Daniel frowned. "When did you admit this to Priscilla?"

"The other day. As I said, she was very upset."

"And with good reason."

"After David told Priscilla he'd written to her several times and wondered why she never responded, she asked if I knew anything about the letters." Iva pursed her lips, heat spreading across her face. "What I did back then was bad enough. I couldn't look my daughter in the face and lie about it now. I wish I could change the past."

"Did you apologize to Priscilla?"

"Of course."

"What's done is done." He took a glass from the cupboard and filled it with water. "There's no going back, and hopefully you learned from the mistake."

"I certainly did."

"Now, getting back to the situation with Priscilla and Elam. If you like, I could have a talk with him—find out what his intentions are."

Iva smiled. "Good idea. Maybe all Elam needs is a little nudge."

"What's this?" David asked when Priscilla handed him a gift.

"It's a Christmas present."

He grimaced.

"What's wrong? Don't you like gifts?"

"It's not that." David propped his foot on the coffee table and leaned into the sofa cushions. "I'm sorry, Priscilla, but I have nothing to give you. Gramps's back went out two days ago when he hauled in the Christmas tree, and Gram has been too busy taking care of him to drive me into town."

Taking a seat beside him, Priscilla shook her head. "It's okay. I didn't expect a gift in return. Besides, what I got isn't anything big, but I hope you'll like it."

David was about to open the gift when his grandmother entered the room.

"Hello, Mrs. Morgan." Priscilla stood. "I'm sorry to hear about your husband's back. I know it means extra work for you right now, so if there's anything I can do to help out, let me know."

"Honey, you didn't have to get up on my account." Letty smiled. "It's nice of you to offer to help, but Walt's doing some better today, and I have things pretty much under control. We're going to have a nice, quiet Christmas."

"Which is fine by me," David put in. "I like being here where it's quiet and peaceful."

Letty's eyes shone as she looked lovingly at her grandson. "We like having you, Davey. And Priscilla, please call me Letty."

After Letty left the room to check on Walt and the cookies she had baking, David opened his gift. "Hey, thanks! How'd you know I like western novels?"

"You mentioned it once."

David held the book up. "This will help keep me from being bored while my leg's healing and I'm waiting to get back on both feet."

"What are your plans once your cast comes off?" Priscilla asked.

"I'll probably have to do some physical therapy."

"I meant after that. Will you return to Chicago and get more schooling?"

He shook his head. "My mind's made up about not becoming a vet."

"I thought you might go back to school to study something else."

"Nope. I'm staying right here. Maybe I'll follow in my grandpa's footsteps and learn the carpentry trade. I've always been pretty good with my hands. Bet he'd be happy to teach me the trade, too." David rubbed the back of his neck. "Unless there's no room in this area for another Amish carpenter."

Her brows drew together. "What do you mean?"

"Like I told you before, I'm considering becoming Amish."

"You're such a tease." Playfully, she swatted his arm.

"I'm not teasing, Priscilla. I might be happier living the simple life."

"Our life is not simple, David. We face as many complications and trials as the rest of the world."

"I realize that, but I admire your lifestyle and values." He touched her shoulder. "I'd really like to know more about them."

"I'd be happy to answer any questions, but if you're seriously interested in joining the Amish church, you'll need to meet with our ministers and discuss what needs to be done."

"Sure, I'm willing to do that."

Priscilla could hardly believe David was considering such a thing. He'd probably feel differently once he found out what changes he'd have to make.

When Elam pulled his rig into the Morgans' yard, he spotted Priscilla's horse and buggy parked by the garage. Apparently she was here to see David, same as him.

Elam looked forward to having Christmas dinner with Priscilla and her family. Besides enjoying all the good food, he would get to visit with Priscilla. When he had enough money saved up, he was going to ask her to marry him.

Elam knocked on the front door, expecting one of David's grandparents to answer. Instead, Priscilla greeted him.

"Hey, Elam, I didn't expect to see you until tomorrow." She smiled up at him.

"Came by to see how David's doing and wish him a merry Christmas."

"That's why I came, too." Priscilla led the way to the living room, where David sat on the couch.

"Good to see you." David grinned and held up a book. "Look what Priscilla gave me for Christmas."

"Looks like you'll have some reading to do." Elam wished he'd brought David a gift. He was surprised Priscilla had. Seeing the way David smiled at Priscilla made him feel a bit jealous. Could David have more of an interest in her than friendship?

"Take a seat so we can all visit." David motioned to the recliner across from him.

Elam lowered himself into the chair, wondering why Priscilla had taken a seat on the couch beside David. He glanced at the only other chair in the room and realized a little black terrier occupied it. *Guess she didn't want to disturb the* hund.

Priscilla looked at David. "Why don't you tell Elam what you told me awhile ago?"

"You mean about joining the Amish church?"

"Who's joining the church?" Elam asked.

David pointed to himself. "Me. Well, not right away of course, but eventually."

"Really? A change like that isn't simple, David. Fact is, there aren't many who can make it." Elam looked at Priscilla. "Was this your idea?" It would be just like impulsive Priscilla to suggest such a thing.

She shook her head. "No, of course not."

Elam's gaze went to David again. "If you're born into the Amish life, it becomes a part of you, but to be raised in the English world and then give up those modern conveniences is a challenge. One I'm sure you're not up to."

David sat up straight. "Why not? I'm not a wimp, you know."

"Never said you were. You just don't realize what the changes would involve."

David shrugged. "I won't know till I try."

Hearing this caused Elam to worry. What if David joined their church and decided to go after Priscilla?

Don't be ridiculous, he told himself. *Neither of those things is likely to happen.*

CHAPTER 14

"Sure was a nice evening." Ben reached across his buggy seat and took Elaine's hand. "I'm glad you could spend Christmas Eve with me and my folks."

Elaine smiled. "It was fun. I enjoyed getting to know your sisters and their families, too."

"I'm glad we could all be together." Ben paused, taking a slow, deep breath. Giving her fingers a gentle squeeze, he said, "I was wondering if you've thought any more about my marriage proposal."

Elaine swallowed hard. Truth was, she had thought about it but wasn't ready to give him an answer. Being with Ben was like wearing a comfortable pair of slippers. But when she looked at him or he touched her, she didn't feel any sparks or tingles of anticipation. Ben was more like a big brother. If she married him, he would be a good provider, kind, and nurturing, but was it enough? In order to say yes, shouldn't she feel something more—something like she felt when she was being courted by Jonah? If she and Jonah might get back together, she wouldn't consider marrying Ben. But Jonah might never feel ready to marry again. Besides, the love he'd felt for her had ended when he married Sara.

"Your silence makes me wonder if you don't want to marry me."

Elaine jerked her head. "It–it's not that. I just need a little more time. Marriage is an important decision—not to be taken lightly."

"You're right, and if you're not ready to make that commitment, I understand." Ben let go of her hand. "Would you rather I stopped seeing you, Elaine?"

"No, Ben. I enjoy your company."

"But you don't love me. Is that it?"

"I. . .I care for you, Ben. But I'm not sure what I feel is love." Elaine held her elbows tightly against her sides, unable to look directly at him.

"Maybe after we've courted longer, your feelings will change."

Ben's tone sounded hopeful, and maybe he was right. "Jah," she murmured. "Sometimes love needs a chance to grow."

"You're right. When you make a decision, please let me know."

"I will."

Elaine remained quiet the rest of the way home. She felt bad stringing Ben along, but if she didn't keep seeing him, she might never know if he was the one. If she said yes to his proposal now, one or both of them might regret it later on. One thing was certain: she didn't want to hurt Ben. *Lord, I need Your guidance. Please show me what to do.*

Leah smiled, watching Adam with Linda and Amy on either side of him and Carrie curled up on his lap. They'd had a wonderful Christmas Eve, just the five of them. After a delicious dinner of baked chicken, mashed potatoes, green beans, homemade rolls, and a platter of fresh vegetables, everyone had helped with the cleanup. Then they'd all bundled up and taken a walk toward the fields behind the property. While they sang Christmas carols, Coal bounded ahead, with snow flying off his feet. At times the dog would stop to bury his nose in the snow, most likely because of a scent he'd picked up. As far as the eye could see, the radiance of light had illuminated every object. Leah still remembered the smell of wood smoke permeating the air.

Returning to the house, where it was warm and toasty, Leah had fixed hot chocolate and popcorn; then they'd gathered in the living room to listen to Adam read the Christmas story. Even Coal joined them, lying near the fireplace with his nose between his paws.

Like most children on Christmas Eve, the girls had been wound up but were getting sleepy now, and they would soon need to be tucked into bed. Tomorrow they'd visit Leah's folks for the day and enjoy Christmas dinner. Leah's brother, Nathan, and his family would be there, too. The girls got along well with Leah's parents and had recently started calling them "Grandma" and "Grandpa."

As much as Leah looked forward to being with everyone, she couldn't imagine feeling any more joy than she did now. Adam looked relaxed with his nieces clustered around him, and Leah was content just watching the scene. The only thing that would make it any better would be if Cora could have been here to spend Christmas with her son and granddaughters.

Leah had a hard time understanding how Cora could have left her Amish family so many years ago. But from talking with Cora, it wasn't hard to figure out how much the poor woman regretted it. How long must a person pay for mistakes they'd made years ago? Leah could only imagine how much it hurt Cora to have her son reject her like this. But Adam and his sister had been rejected, too—not to mention Adam's father. No matter how one looked at the situation, it was horrible. The selfish mistake Cora had made back then was coming back at her, full circle.

Leah wouldn't push Adam to forgive his mother, however. If he and his mother were going to establish a relationship again, it had to be his decision.

Hope welled in Cora's soul as she stared at the twinkling lights on their artificial tree. In addition to Jared's friend Chad returning home to his family, she'd gotten a call from her Realtor yesterday morning, saying an offer had come in on her house in Chicago. The offer was fair, so she'd accepted it without reservation. Once the deal closed and Cora received the money, she'd look for a house to buy in this area—something bigger and more updated than their tiny rental. Maybe by next Christmas she'd be able to get a real tree; perhaps a potted one that could be planted in the yard in the spring.

"Are we gonna open our Christmas presents now, Mom, or did ya plan to stare at the tree the rest of evening?"

Jared's question drove Cora out of her musings, and she turned to face him. "Sorry. I was lost in the moment."

"Yeah, I could tell."

"We can open gifts now, but wouldn't you rather wait until tomorrow morning?"

He shook his head. "We've always opened gifts on Christmas Eve."

"True, but it might be nice to do something different this year. We could start a new tradition." Cora's mind flitted back to the last Christmas Eve she and Jared had spent in Chicago, when she was still married to Jared's father. The three of them had sat around their stately tree, drinking hot cider, eating open-faced sandwiches, and opening the mounds of presents under the tree. Evan had spared no expense when it came to buying gifts. Cora thought his gifts were too lavish and they were spoiling Jared, but she never said a word. Evan was king of his domain, and since he made the bulk of the money, Cora seldom questioned his financial decisions. Now, even though Evan paid child support, money was tight, and Cora had been forced to learn the art of penny-pinching.

"You're phasin' out on me again." Jared nudged Cora's arm. "I like our old traditions. Let's open our gifts now."

"Okay." Cora picked up a gift and handed it to him.

Jared's nose wrinkled when he opened the box and pulled out a pairs of jeans and two shirts. "Aw, Mom, you know how I hate gettin' clothes for Christmas."

"With the way you've been growing, you really need them." Cora placed another gift in Jared's lap. "See what you think of this."

Jared tore the paper aside and let out a whoop when he opened the smaller box. "My own cell phone! Thanks, Mom!" He leaped out of his chair and gave Cora a hug. "Now here's a gift from me." Jared grabbed a gift bag from under the tree and handed it to her.

Cora figured he'd made something or picked it out at the Dollar General. Instead, she discovered a birdhouse made to look like an Amish buggy.

"Since we live in Amish country and you enjoy watchin' the birds so much, I thought you might like this." Jared grinned.

"It's a wonderful gift, but where did you get the money to buy it?" Something this precise was obviously not made by Jared. Besides, he didn't have the tools necessary to build anything like this.

"I've been workin' at Beachy's Hardware Store the last two weeks so I could earn some money." Jared slumped in his chair. "Sorry for lyin' to you about workin' on a project with Scott. I wanted your gift to be a surprise."

Cora's heartbeat picked up speed. "You—you've been working at Adam Beachy's?"

He bobbed his head. "That's where I bought the birdhouse."

Cora gulped. Did Adam know who Jared was? "I appreciate you

wanting to get me a nice gift, Jared, but what you did was wrong. And I can't imagine Mr. Beachy hiring you without my permission. You're still a minor."

Jared hung his head. "I asked a friend at school to write a note for me. She signed your name."

Cora's mouth dropped open. "I can't believe you would do such a thing, Jared. Didn't you know what you were doing was wrong?"

"Calm down, Mom. Your face is red. I know what I did was wrong, but I thought you'd appreciate that I bought the gift with my own money. Money I worked hard for, by the way."

"I am proud of you in that respect, but I can't condone your deceit." Cora's hands shook as she set the birdhouse on the coffee table. "Did Mr. Beachy say anything about me?"

"Yeah. When I went there with Scott to ask for a job, he said I'd have to get one of my parents' permission."

"How did this so-called friend of yours sign my name?"

"Mrs. Finley."

"Is that all? She didn't include my first name?"

Jared shook his head. "Why does that matter?"

"It—it doesn't, I guess." Cora's mind filled with scattered thoughts. If the note Jared gave Adam was only signed "Mrs. Finley," then Adam wouldn't have realized Cora was Jared's mother. The day she'd spoken to Adam on the road and revealed that she was his mother, Cora hadn't mentioned her last name was Finley now.

Massaging her pulsating temples, Cora made a decision. After work on Monday, she would stop by Adam's store and tell him about Jared. If she didn't reveal the truth, it was bound to come out sooner or later. Now she needed to figure out how and when to tell Jared.

CHAPTER 15

"I wish your folks could have joined us today." David's grandma placed a pitcher of grape juice on the table and took a seat beside him. "It doesn't seem right them spending Christmas in Chicago with their friends instead of here with family."

"It's probably for the best." David's face tightened. "If Dad and Mom were here right now, Dad would hound me to go back to school, and everyone's Christmas would be ruined."

Gramps nodded. "Although it would have been nice to have our son and his wife here today, I think you're right. We don't need a repeat of what happened when they came here after your accident."

If Mom and Dad were to find out I'm thinking of joining the Amish church, they'd really be upset. David bowed his head. *Please, God, give me the courage to tell Gram and Gramps. I pray they'll support my decision.*

When David opened his eyes, he noticed his grandparents' inquisitive expressions. "What's wrong? Why are you both looking at me like that?"

"Were you praying, Davey?" Gram asked.

"Yes."

"But we usually pray out loud before our meals."

"I was praying the Amish way. Besides, we already prayed out loud." David poured some juice into his glass and took a drink. "This is good stuff, Gram. Is it some you made from the grapes in your yard?" He liked having grape juice with dinner. It was a nice change from water or milk.

She nodded slowly. "What made you decide to pray the Amish way?"

He took another drink and swallowed it down. "I'm practicing."

Gramps's brows furrowed. "Practicing for what?"

"For the day I become Amish."

"What?" his grandparents questioned.

Before he could lose his nerve, David explained his decision.

"When did you come up with such a crazy notion?" Gram's voice rose as she leaned closer to David.

"I've been mulling it over quite awhile, actually."

"But why?" Gramps asked.

"I'm sick of the English rat race. I'm ready to live a simpler life."

"Your grandfather and I live a fairly simple life, and we didn't have to go Amish to do it." Gram clenched her fists, something she did when she wanted to make sure she got her point across.

"I know, but it's not the same. You still have modern conveniences in your home, and you both drive a car. The Amish—"

"We know how the Amish live," Gramps interrupted. "We've lived among them a good many years."

Gram placed her hand on David's arm. "There are so many changes you'd have to make—not just giving up modern conveniences, but learning to drive a horse and buggy."

"Don't forget learning a new language," Gramps chimed in.

"I realize it won't be easy, but the only way I'll know if the Amish way of life is right for me is if I try to make a go of it."

"Is this about your friend?" Gram peered at David over the top of her glasses.

David jerked his head. "What friend?"

"Priscilla." Gram's eyes narrowed. "Are you hoping if you go Amish she'll date you?"

David shifted in his seat. This conversation was not going well. He'd hoped his grandparents would support his decision. Now Gram was basically accusing him of trying to take Priscilla from Elam. *Is that what I'm hoping for?* David asked himself. *If I did become Amish, would Priscilla see me as more than a friend?*

"I'm glad we waited till today to open our gifts." Priscilla smiled as she and Elam took seats on the couch in his parents' living room. Since Priscilla had spent Christmas Eve with her family, her folks said they didn't mind if she went to Elam's to be with his family today. "It's more fun when we can do it together," she added.

Elam glanced toward the kitchen, where his mother and sisters had gone to get things started in the kitchen. Priscilla had offered to help, of course, but they'd said she could join them after she and Elam had opened their gifts to each other. Priscilla figured they wanted to give her and Elam some time alone. And since the men and Elam's younger brothers were in the barn, looking at the new horse his dad had recently acquired, Priscilla and Elam were truly alone.

"Do you want to go first, or should I?" Elam asked.

"It doesn't matter to me." Priscilla shrugged; although she was anxious to see what Elam thought of the new hat she'd bought him.

"Okay, I'll go first." Elam handed Priscilla a small box wrapped in tissue paper. Inside, she discovered six crisp white hankies, each with the letter *P* embroidered in the corner.

Priscilla forced a smile and said, "Danki." After all the time she and Elam had been courting, she'd expected something a little more than this. She wished he had given her something to put in her hope chest. It would give an indication that he planned to marry her someday.

As though sensing her displeasure, Elam took Priscilla's hand, giving her fingers a gentle squeeze. "I wanted to get you something more expensive, but I'm a little short on cash right now."

Struggling to keep her composure, Priscilla managed a nod. She realized Elam's only job during the winter months was working in his parents' store. But couldn't he have saved some money to buy her a nicer gift? Since the hankies held no promise of a marriage proposal, Priscilla wondered once again if Elam had any plans of marrying her.

Blinking back tears of frustration, Priscilla cleared her throat and handed Elam his Christmas present. "I hope you like what I got." She held her breath, waiting for him to open it.

Elam's cheeks colored when he removed the black hat from the box. "Wow, Priscilla, I really feel cheap. A *hut* like this is expensive."

"It doesn't matter. I've earned some extra money helping Elaine host dinners. Besides, your old dress hat is showing some wear. I thought it was time you had a new one."

"I sure appreciate it, but it really wasn't necessary. My old one was gettin' me by just fine." He plunked the hat on his head. "How's it look?"

She smiled. "Good. Real good, in fact."

Elam leaned close and gave her a quick kiss. Priscilla was glad no one else was in the room. "Know what I might do?"

"What?"

"I'm gonna look for another part-time job. That way I'll have more money comin' in, which will mean I can buy you a better gift next year."

Priscilla wondered how things would be between her and Elam by next Christmas. Was there a chance they could be married by then, or would things still be as they were now?

Feeling the need to be alone for a while, Jonah excused himself from the family gathering at his parents' house and went for a walk. It was a crisp afternoon, with a clear blue sky, which meant no threat of more snow, at least not for today. Toward the east, the moon, although faint, could be seen in the cloudless sky.

Jonah had been doing his best to put on a happy face and engage in conversation all morning, but as the day wore on it became more difficult. Watching his twin sister and her husband with their children was the hardest part. They were a complete family; not one parent trying to raise two children on his own.

Of course, I'm not really raising them alone, Jonah reasoned as he trudged through the snow along the edge of the road. Jonah's mother had been a big help watching Mark and the baby while Jonah was at work. Most evenings, she stayed to fix supper and help put the children to bed. But that wasn't the same as having a wife to come home to every night.

He paused and drew in a deep breath. *Oh, Sara, if only you hadn't climbed up after that stupid* katz.

Jonah was glad he'd found a new home for the cat, but once again, bitterness welled in his soul as he thought about the injustice of it all. Things could be going along fine one minute, and the next minute a person's world might be turned upside down.

He wished he'd spent more time with Sara and the children when she was alive. It wasn't that he'd ignored them; he'd just worked too many hours in the buggy shop, when he should have been with his family.

Regrets. Regrets. So many regrets. But they wouldn't change a thing.

Shivering from the cold seeping in around the neckline of his jacket, Jonah turned in the opposite direction. *I may as well quit feeling sorry for myself and head back to the house where it's warm.*

Heading down the road toward the Hershbergers' house, where she'd been invited for Christmas dinner, Elaine spotted an Amish man walking along the shoulder of the road. When he slowed his steps and turned as her buggy approached, she realized it was Jonah.

Elaine guided her horse to the side of the road and opened her buggy door. "Are you all right?" She noticed Jonah's slumped posture as he stared at her with a dazed expression. Poor Jonah had been through so much; she wished she could offer him comfort. The joy of becoming a father to a healthy baby girl had been overshadowed by the tragic loss of his wife just a month ago. How could a person cope with such unfairness?

Jonah blinked, as though seeing Elaine for the first time. "I–I'm fine. Just out for a walk. Now I'm heading back to my folks' place."

"You look cold. Would you like a ride?"

Jonah hesitated but finally nodded.

Elaine held the reins tightly until he got into the passenger's side, then she directed her horse onto the road.

"Where are you headed?" Jonah asked, glancing quickly at Elaine before staring straight ahead with rigid posture.

"I've been invited to have Christmas dinner at the Hershbergers'."

"I'm surprised you're not spending the day with Ben. I assume you're still seeing him?"

"Jah. I was at his folks' house for Christmas Eve."

Jonah made no comment.

"How are you doing, Jonah? You've been in my prayers."

"I'm gettin' by," he muttered, "but you can save your prayers. If prayer changed anything, Sara would still be with me." His mouth twisted at the corners. "I prayed for Sara's safety every day of our marriage, and look where it got me—she's dead."

"It's painful to lose someone you love. But God will give you the grace to get through it."

"It's gonna take more than grace to get me through the loss of my *fraa*."

Elaine winced at Jonah's bitter tone. He truly was hurting. *Please, Lord, give me the words to offer him comfort.*

"Remember, Jonah, Psalm 147:3 says God 'healeth the broken in heart, and bindeth up their wounds.'"

A muscle on the side of his neck quivered. "I doubt my wounds will ever heal." He released a shuddering sigh. "One thing's for sure: I will never get married again."

CHAPTER 16

Monday morning, as Cora finished her breakfast before leaving for work, she thought about her decision to tell Adam about his half brother. Jared wouldn't be working at the store anymore because the Christmas rush was over, so did she really need to tell Adam? But no matter when her sons learned that they were half brothers, it wouldn't be easy. Still, wouldn't it be better if she told them now, before they found out on their own? Although Leah had never met Jared, she knew about him and might end up telling Adam, even though Cora had asked her not to say anything.

Pulling in her bottom lip, Cora took a last sip of her coffee and thought things through. *Should I say anything or keep quiet awhile longer?*

"Hey, Mom, what's for breakfast?"

Cora's head jerked at the sound of Jared's voice. "I thought you'd sleep in, since you have no school this week."

Jared stretched his arms over his head and yawned. "I was gonna go to Beachy's Hardware Store and see if he could use my help this week, but then I remembered he said things usually slow down after Christmas. Besides, I wasn't sure you'd want me workin' there anymore."

Cora's spine stiffened. "You're right, Jared. I don't want you working there, or anywhere else without my permission."

"No problem, Mom. Scott will be workin' at the hardware store this week, though, so I may drop over there later and see how he's doing."

Cora shook her head. "I'd prefer you stay home today."

"How come?"

"I'm expecting a package, and someone needs to be here to sign for it." It wasn't a lie exactly. Cora was expecting some vitamins she'd ordered online but wasn't sure if it would be necessary to sign for the package. She couldn't have Jared going into Adam's store today, however—not before she'd talked to Adam. Once that was done, she would tell Jared about Adam.

Cora got up to start putting her lunch together. *What a mess I've created. It all started the day I walked away from my Amish husband and children. How did I ever think my selfishness would not come back to bite me?*

Cora opened the refrigerator door and withdrew a container of leftover turkey. When she set it on the counter and opened the lid, she was surprised to discover only two pieces left.

She turned to face Jared. "What happened to all the turkey? There was more than this left after dinner last night."

"Umm. . . well, I may have eaten it."

Cora frowned. "What do you mean, 'may have'? Either you did or you didn't."

Jared looked away. "Okay, I ate it."

Normally, Cora was able to tell when her son was lying, but now she wasn't so sure. If Jared hadn't eaten the turkey, then who had? Unless Cora had begun to sleepwalk and gotten up in the middle of the night for a snack, she wasn't responsible for the missing slices.

Cora shrugged. "That's fine. I'll use these last two pieces of turkey to make my sandwich."

"You're gonna make a sandwich?"

"That's what I said."

"That might be a little hard to do, 'cause there ain't no bread."

Cora clenched her teeth. "The word is *isn't*, and why is there no bread? I saw some in the bread box yesterday."

Jared moved toward the pantry and took out a box of cold cereal. "Guess I must have eaten all the bread, too."

She put one hand on her hip. "So you ate most of the turkey and all of the bread?"

"Yeah."

"When did you do this, Jared—at midnight? In case you've forgotten, yesterday was Sunday, and we were together all day."

"Not all day, Mom. You took a nap in the afternoon."

"True, but. . . Never mind. I'll stop at the convenience store on my way to work and pick up something for lunch." She put the turkey back in the refrigerator. "I'll go by the grocery store on my way home and get some lunch meat, cheese, and a loaf of bread. You can eat what's left of the turkey for your lunch today."

"Sure, Mom, whatever you say."

Cora wished she didn't have to go to work and leave Jared home by himself, but he wasn't a little kid anymore and could manage on his own.

Elaine stood at the kitchen sink, staring out the window at the dismal day. The gray sky and dark clouds were in stark contrast to the beautiful weather they'd had over the weekend.

She thought about Christmas Day, when she'd seen Jonah walking along the side of the road. Her heart ached, thinking about the sadness she'd seen on his face. What really concerned her was the bitterness he obviously felt over losing Sara. To say he would never marry again meant Jonah must have loved Sara very much.

Elaine gripped the edge of the sink. *More than he loved me, no doubt. What a fool I was to send Jonah away and let him believe I didn't love him. If I had married him, Sara may have found someone else, and she might still be alive.*

Elaine needed to stop thinking like this and concentrate on something else, but first she needed to pray for Jonah.

Taking a seat at the table, she bowed her head. *Heavenly Father, please be with Jonah. Let him feel Your presence, and send someone to help him work through his grief. Please be with Jonah's precious children, and give him the courage and wisdom to raise them in a godly manner. Amen.*

Elaine finished her prayer just as a knock sounded on the back door. When she opened it, Priscilla stood on the porch, holding a cardboard box.

"Guder mariye." Priscilla smiled. "I came ready to work, and I even brought lunch."

"Good morning." Elaine opened the door wider. "What'd you bring?"

"I made Friendship Salad, and Mom gave me a loaf of homemade wheat bread."

"Both sound delicious." Elaine led the way to the kitchen. "You can put the box on the table. I'll take the salad and bread out while you remove your shawl and outer bonnet."

"Are you as anxious as I am to start working on that cookbook we talked about putting together?" Priscilla asked after she'd removed her wraps.

"Sure am." Elaine put the salad in the refrigerator and placed the bread on the counter. "I have so many tasty recipes Grandma used to make. She served many of them to her dinner guests. It'll be nice to get them compiled and put into a cookbook I can offer to those who come for future dinners."

"Speaking of dinners, when is your next one scheduled?" Priscilla took a seat at the table.

"This Friday evening."

Priscilla's eyebrows rose. "On New Year's Eve?"

Elaine nodded. "That won't be a problem for you, will it?"

"I guess not, although Elam mentioned the two of us getting together."

"The dinner shouldn't last too long—probably not much past eight o'clock. Could you get together with Elam after that?"

"I suppose, but by the time I help you clean up, it could be nine or after, and I'll be tired, so. . ."

"That's okay. If you and Elam make plans for later, I'll take care of the cleanup myself."

Priscilla shook her head vigorously. "I won't even consider that. I'll see if Elam would be willing to wait till New Year's Day to get together."

Elaine could see by the determined set of her friend's jaw she'd made up her mind. "Okay. Now since that's all settled, should we start looking through some of Grandma's recipes?"

Priscilla nodded. "After we work on it awhile, we can enjoy the Friendship Salad."

"How are things going up here?" Adam joined Ben behind the front counter.

"Good. We've had enough customers to keep me busy but not so many I needed to call on you for help." Ben smiled. "You were busy in your office, and I didn't want to ask unless it was necessary."

"I did get a lot done, so thanks for taking care of the customers."

Adam glanced at the clock near the front door. "Has Scott showed up yet?"

Ben shook his head. "No, he hasn't. I figured since he was on break from school this week he'd come in this morning. But here it is past noon, and he hasn't come in."

Adam's forehead wrinkled. "That's strange. I thought when Scott and his friend Jared, were working here last week Scott said he'd be in early today."

"Maybe he got sick over the weekend."

"If that were the case, his mother would have called to tell me he wouldn't be coming in." Adam pulled out his handkerchief, hoping to ward off a sneeze he felt coming. He'd just put the hanky away when the front door opened and Cora walked in. Adam froze. *I wonder what she's doing here.*

"I'm sorry to bother you, Adam." She stepped up to the counter. "I'm on my lunch break. Could I speak to you alone?"

Adam was on the verge of telling her no, but feeling Ben's eyes on him, he mumbled, "Sure. Let's go to my office."

Leading the way to the back of the store, Adam remained quiet until he and Cora were in the room. "I'm kind of busy right now, so I hope this isn't going to take long."

She shook her head.

Adam gestured to the chair on the other side of his desk. "You can sit there, if you like."

"No, that's all right. I'll stand." With her gaze fixed on him, Cora drew in a quick breath. "I understand you hired my son to work for you before Christmas."

Adam scratched the side of his head. "Huh?"

"Jared. You hired Jared to work for you."

Adam's eyes widened. "You're Jared's mother?"

She nodded slowly. "He's your brother, Adam. Well, half brother, anyway."

Adam tried to digest what she'd said. Then as Cora's words sank in, he sank into his chair. "How long were you planning to keep me in the dark about this?"

"I—I wanted to tell you a few months ago, but you didn't want to hear anything I had to say."

"Why are you telling me now?" The words stuck in Adam's throat as he fought for control. *No wonder Jared reminded me of someone. It was probably myself.*

"When Jared admitted he'd been working at your store, without my permission, I was afraid you might have said something about me to him."

Adam shook his head. "I didn't know he was your son, so why would I say anything about you?"

"I don't know. I just thought. . . And by the way, that note he gave you was written by one of his friends, not me." Cora reached into her purse for a tissue to blot the tears dribbling onto her cheeks. "Has Leah ever said anything to you about Jared?"

Adam stiffened. "Are you saying my wife knows I have a half brother?"

"Well, she's aware I have a son by the man I married after I divorced your father. But she's never met Jared."

Adam put his arms on his desk, clenching his fingers. "I can't believe Leah didn't tell me."

"I asked her not to."

"Is that so? What gives you the right to expect my wife to keep secrets from me?" Adam's face heated to such a degree, he felt as if he'd acquired a sunburn.

"I'm sorry, Adam. I should have told you about Jared sooner."

What you should have done was remained Amish and raised your son and daughter, like any good mother would do. Adam swallowed against the bile rising in his throat. Just when he'd thought he'd gotten past the bitterness he felt toward his mother, she hit him with this.

"Does Jared know about me?" Adam asked.

"Not yet. I'd planned to tell him, but I didn't want to until I'd told you."

"Tell me what, Mom?"

Cora whirled around, and Adam leaped out of his chair. Jared stood inside the door of his office beside Scott. *Okay, Cora,* Adam thought. *Let's see how you're going to deal with this.*

CHAPTER 17

Cora's heart pounded as she stood face-to-face with Jared. "We should go, son. We can talk about this when we get home."

"Talk about what, Mom? What were you and Adam talking about when I walked in?"

"What are you doing here anyway?" Cora quickly changed the subject.

"Came to see Scott. Wanted to ask him something." He turned and motioned to his friend, standing inside the doorway.

"You're late for work, Scott, but since you're here now, I think you'd better get busy," Adam spoke up.

Scott glanced at Jared questioningly then left the room.

"Let's all have seats, and we can talk about this." Adam pulled two more chairs up to his desk, then closed the door.

Feeling like a mouse caught in a trap, Cora sat. Glancing toward the office door, she rubbed her brow, wanting nothing more than to bolt. This was not the way she'd planned to tell her son that Adam was his older brother.

Cora waited until Adam and Jared took seats, then she drew in a quick breath and began. "In all these years, Jared, I've never talked to you about my childhood." She closed her eyes to say a quick prayer. *Give me strength and the right words.* "The truth is, I grew up in an Amish home."

"Say what?" Jared blinked a couple of times, and his eyes widened.

"I used to be Amish before I met your dad. I was married to an Amish man. His name was Andrew Beachy. We lived in Pennsylvania." As the words poured out, Cora paused to collect her thoughts. "Andrew and I had two children—Adam and Mary."

"So are you sayin' that Adam and me are brothers?" Jared leaned forward.

"We're half brothers," Adam interjected.

Jared glared at him. "You knew about this but never said a word? Is that why ya let me work for you, 'cause we're related?"

Adam shook his head vigorously. "I only found out Cora's your mother a few minutes before you got here. I was as surprised by this as you are."

Jared looked back at Cora. "Well, keep talkin', Mom. I wanna hear all the details."

Cora gripped her hands as she continued to tell Jared how she'd left the Amish faith to pursue a career in nursing.

"Did your Amish husband leave, too?" Jared questioned.

Cora shook her head.

"So you took your kids and left him?"

Cora swallowed hard. Her throat felt so tight she could barely speak. "No, I—I left our children with Andrew."

Jared's face reddened as he leaped out of his chair. "You walked out on your husband and just left your kids?" He pointed a trembling finger at her. "And you think Dad was terrible for cheatin' on you and runnin' out on your marriage!"

"I—I didn't cheat on Andrew." Cora's voice trembled. "I was young and had dreams of becoming a nurse. Please understand, Jared. I begged Andrew to go with me, but he refused." She halted for a breath, to compose herself. She wanted to remain silent, to let all this sink in, not only for Jared, but for Adam as well. But the need to tell her side of things made Cora continue. "I wanted to take the children, but he said if I tried, he would move and I'd never find them."

"Apparently you did." Jared motioned to Adam.

"It was a surprise to me when I found out Adam lived here in Arthur. I'd tried to find him and his sister before, but never could because my first husband took them and left Pennsylvania to begin a new life somewhere else." Cora sighed. No one there would tell me where they'd moved. Because I'd left my husband and filed for divorce, I was shunned."

"So I have a half sister, too?" Jared blinked rapidly.

"Yes, her name is Mary. She and her husband were killed in an accident. Adam and his wife are raising Mary's three girls." Cora would have said more about how Mary died, after what she'd learned from Leah, but thought Adam should do that, perhaps another time, when he and Jared could talk more and get to know each other better.

"Cousins." Jared sank to his chair again, shaking his head in disbelief.

"No, Amy, Linda, and Carrie are my nieces," Adam corrected. "It makes them your half nieces."

Jared groaned. "Wow, this story keeps getting better and better." He glared at Cora. "Besides the fact that you were a lousy mother for runnin' out on your kids, you had no right to keep all this from me."

"I know, Jared, and I was planning to tell you. I couldn't seem to work up the nerve. I didn't think you would understand." Cora pinched the bridge of her nose, trying to squelch the tears dribbling onto her cheeks.

Jared reached his hand out to Adam. "It's nice to meet ya, big brother. Maybe I'll come by the store sometime and you can tell me what it was like bein' raised with no mother. Seems a whole lot better than bein' raised by a mother like mine, though." Jared jumped up and raced out of the room, flinging the door open so hard it banged against the wall.

Cora looked at Adam, unable to read his expression. "I need to go after him, but I'd like to talk with you more some other time."

Adam shook his head. "I have nothing more to say to you, Cora. You messed up my life. Now you'd better see if you can patch things up with your other son, or you won't have a relationship with him, either."

Tears coursed down Cora's cheeks as she fled Adam's office. Not only had she estranged herself from Adam, now Jared was upset with her, as well. She wished she didn't have to go back to work this afternoon. *Lord, help me. I can't lose Jared, too.*

When Cora left the store, hoping to catch up with Jared, she spotted him getting into a car. It looked like the same vehicle Chad had been driving the night he'd shown up at their house. *But that can't be—Chad went back to Chicago before Christmas.*

When Priscilla left Elaine's that afternoon, she decided to stop by the Morgans' to see how David was doing. It had been a few days since he'd told her he wanted to go Amish, so she figured he could have changed his mind by now. Completely changing his lifestyle would not be easy. As Priscilla approached Walt and Letty's place, Cleo, their little black terrier, raced down the driveway, barking and nipping at Tinker's hooves. During other visits, the dog had been calm. After greeting her with a few sniffs, the little mutt would return to her doggie bed in the corner of the living room. Maybe this afternoon they'd let her out for some exercise.

As the terrier made circles around the buggy, her barking became more intense. Priscilla's horse started kicking and thrashing about, which made the dog act crazier.

"Calm down, Tinker." Priscilla opened her door, and shouted at the dog to stop, but Cleo kept barking and carrying on.

Closing the buggy door, Priscilla gripped the reins and hollered at her horse to stop.

Somehow Priscilla managed to get the gelding and buggy turned up the driveway, but the dog kept nipping, while Tinker continued to kick. When Priscilla thought it couldn't get any worse, Tinker kicked the terrier, sending the poor pooch flying into the Morgans' yard. At the same moment, the shaft connecting the horse to her buggy snapped. Priscilla screamed as the horse broke free and her buggy tipped on its side.

Inching her way along the seat to the passenger's side, Priscilla managed to get the door open and climb out. Her feet had barely touched the ground when David's grandpa came out of the house. "Are you hurt?" he called, making his way down the driveway as quickly as possible. Fortunately, the snow had been cleared, but it was still slippery in places.

"I think I'm okay." Priscilla touched her sore elbow. "I may have a few bruises, though."

"What happened?" Walt asked. "I heard Cleo barking, and when I looked out the window I saw the buggy flipped over and your horse running up the driveway.

Priscilla explained what had happened. "I fear Cleo might be dead." With the dog quiet, Tinker stood, shaking his mane and pawing a hoof on the ground.

Holding her arm, Priscilla watched as Walt calmly talked to the horse, grabbed the reins, and tied him to a post near the garage. Then he and Priscilla went to check on the dog. They found her in a clump of weeds, unmoving.

Walt bent down to examine Cleo. His somber expression told Priscilla it wasn't good news.

"I'm afraid she's dead." Walt rose to his feet. "I'll bury her body out back after we get your buggy taken care of."

"I'm so sorry," Priscilla sobbed. "I tried to get her and my horse calmed down, but neither of them would listen."

"It wasn't your fault. I don't normally let Cleo outside by herself, but I got sidetracked and wasn't paying attention." Walt touched Priscilla's shoulder. "You'd better come inside with me so Letty can tend to your injuries while I call for help. A friend of mine has a flatbed truck we can put the buggy on. I'll ask him to haul it over to Miller's Buggy Shop for repairs."

Tearfully, Priscilla followed Walt into the house. She was greeted by David, who stood near the door on his crutches.

"I saw what happened out the window, Priscilla."

"Are you okay?" Letty asked, wide eyed as she joined them.

"I think so, but I'm sorry to say, Cleo is dead, and I feel responsible."

"It's not your fault," Letty said tearfully. "But I'm sure going to miss that spunky little terrier."

"Come take a seat on the couch." David nodded toward the living room.

Once they were seated, and Letty had made sure Priscilla had no serious injuries, she left the room to get something for Priscilla to drink and some ice for the bruise on her arm. Letty never said a word, but it broke Priscilla's heart to see tears in her eyes. She was obviously upset over the loss of her dog but was nice enough not to let on.

Emotionally drained, Priscilla broke down and sobbed. "I came over to see how you were doing and never expected something like this to happen."

"No one ever expects an accident to occur. It's why they shake us up so badly." David put his arm around Priscilla. "I'm glad you weren't seriously hurt."

"Me, too." Within the circle of David's arm, Priscilla felt safe and cared for. As he gently moved her head toward the crook of his shoulder, his fingers caressed the side of her face. Priscilla's stomach fluttered. *It must be nerves.*

CHAPTER 18

Somehow Cora made it through the rest of her shift, but when she got home, Jared wasn't there. Was he so upset that he'd decided not to come home?

Cora sank into a chair at the kitchen table. *Who picked Jared up at Adam's store? Whoever it was, Jared's probably with him right now, complaining about what a terrible mother he has.*

Cora tapped her fingers on the table. It worried her to think of Jared riding around with one of his friends, going who knew where? If Jared told Scott or any of his friends what he'd learned today, the news would be all over the county that Cora was an unfit mother who used to be Amish and ran out on her kids. Worse yet, if this information got back to Evan, he might use it against her to try and get custody of Jared. She couldn't worry about herself right now. Except for her sons, it didn't really matter what others thought of her. Cora just needed to know Jared was okay and would be home soon.

"What am I going to do?" Cora cried. "I've messed up so many lives. There's no way to wipe the slate clean with Adam, and now Jared. How can I make them both understand how sorry I am for all my mistakes?"

Cora dropped her head to the table and wept. *I'm sorry, Lord. I don't deserve a second chance with Adam or Jared, but if I should get one, I promise I'll do my best to make up for what I've done.*

Cora looked up when she heard the back door open then slam shut. A few seconds later, Jared stomped into the kitchen. She wiped her eyes. Jared stood on the other side of the table, staring at her.

"Where have you been?" she asked, tearfully.

"What do you care?"

"Come on, Jared. Let's try to be civil. I am still your mother, and you don't need to be rude. Now, I'll ask you again: Where have you been?"

He shrugged. "Nowhere in particular; just riding around, thinkin' about all the things you've kept from me."

"Whose car were you in?"

"I was with a friend."

"It wasn't Chad, was it, Jared?"

He shook his head then moved over to the refrigerator. "What's here to eat? Did ya stop by the store to get lunch meat and bread?"

Cora rubbed the bridge of her nose. She'd been so worried about Jared that she'd forgotten to go to the store. "I didn't pick up any groceries. We can go out for pizza if you like."

"No, that's okay. I just wanna go to my room and be left alone."

"Okay, I'll run to the store and be back in a little while. Is there anything you'd like me to get?"

"Nope."

Cora was tempted to engage Jared in more conversation but thought better of it. He obviously needed some time to think about the things she'd told him. Truthfully, she needed to be alone this evening with her thoughts, too.

"Priscilla, you're limping. What's wrong?" Mom's concern was obvious as she looked up when Priscilla entered the house.

"I had an accident with my horse and buggy today. David's grandpa drove me home and he had my buggy picked up and taken over to Jonah Miller's shop."

Mom's mouth opened wide. "What happened? How bad are you hurt?"

"I'm okay—just a few bumps and bruises."

"I'm glad you're not hurt bad, but how did the accident occur?"

"Let's take a seat in the living room, and I'll tell you about it."

As Priscilla explained what had happened, her mother kept interrupting with more questions. By the time Priscilla finished talking, she was exhausted and feeling a little perturbed. *Why couldn't Mom have just let me explain what happened without asking so many unnecessary questions?*

Then Dad came into the house, and Priscilla had to tell the whole story again.

"I'll go over to Jonah's buggy shop in the morning to find out how much damage was done to your buggy and what it's going to cost. I'll also stop by the Morgans' and get your horse." Dad shook his head. "It's a shame about the Morgans' dog. I'm sure David's grandparents are upset."

"Walt and Letty said they knew it wasn't my fault. When Walt gave me a ride home, he said their dog had a bad habit of chasing cars, horses, and anything that moves. He also said he had gotten sidetracked today and didn't realize Cleo was outside by herself." Priscilla rubbed her head, wishing she could forget the horrible incident.

"We should get them another *hund*," Mom said.

Dad bobbed his head. "I'll take care of that in the morning, too." He looked over at Priscilla. "By the way, Elam came by earlier, wanting to talk to you about New Year's Eve."

Priscilla rubbed a throbbing spot on her elbow. "I have to help Elaine host a dinner that night. I'll let Elam know we can get together on New Year's Day."

"He will be disappointed," Mom interjected.

"I'm disappointed, too, but I won't leave Elaine in the lurch. She can't host such a big dinner by herself."

"You're right," Mom agreed. "Now, let me take a look at your elbow and knee. You may need some arnica to help with the pain and swelling."

Priscilla appreciated her mother's concern. Someday when she became a mother, she would do the same for her sons or daughters. Of course, she'd have to get married first.

Elam whistled as he made his way to the phone shack, pushing snow aside with a shovel. No one had checked for messages over Christmas, so the path hadn't been cleaned.

Inside the small building, Elam found a message from Priscilla. He frowned when he heard she'd made plans to help Elaine on New Year's Eve and couldn't spend the evening with him.

"I don't get much time with her anymore," Elam mumbled. Priscilla had said they could see each other on New Year's Day, but Elam knew whether he went to her house or she came to his, several family members would be around. Of course, that's how it was most of the time. The only opportunity he and Priscilla had to be alone was when they went on a buggy ride, which they hadn't done in a while.

Maybe we can do that on New Year's Day, Elam thought as he left the phone shack and headed back to the house. *Because if I find another job, we'll have even less time together.*

As Leah set a few things out for supper, Adam stepped into the kitchen.

She smiled and gave him a hug. "You're home early today. The girls are upstairs playing, and I don't have supper ready yet, so I hope you're not too hungry."

"No, I'm not. In fact, the last thing on my mind right now is food."

"What's wrong? You look umgerennt."

"I'm very upset. Cora came to the store today and gave me some shocking news."

Leah tipped her head. "What'd she say?"

"Let's sit down, and I'll tell you about it." Adam took a seat, and after Leah poured him a cup of coffee, she joined him.

Leah listened intently as Adam told her what had transpired.

"According to Cora," he added, "you knew about Jared."

"I knew she had a son, but I've never met him."

"How come you didn't say anything to me about this?"

"You told me not to talk about her." She hesitated. "Also, Cora asked me not to say anything about Jared. She wanted to be the one to tell you about him."

Adam took a drink, and as he set his cup down, some coffee sloshed onto the table. "If I knew something that important about one of your siblings, I would have told you. I feel like you betrayed me, Leah."

"You're home already?" Linda squealed as the three girls bounded into the kitchen. "We were upstairs drawing pictures. Wanna see?"

Three pairs of eyes looked intently at Adam. "Not right now, girls. Leah and I are talking."

The children must have sensed Adam was not in a good mood, for they hurried out of the kitchen.

"I shouldn't have been so abrupt with them." Adam rested his forehead in his hands. "I'll apologize. I just wish you had told me Jared was Cora's son, Leah."

She left her seat. Placing her hands on his shoulders, she gently massaged him. "I wanted to tell you, Adam, and I almost did several times. But it wouldn't have been right to go back on my word to Cora."

"So Cora's more important than me? Is that how it is?" Adam's shoulder muscles tightened.

Leah winced, hearing the hurt in his voice. She didn't like being the cause of it. "Of course not, Adam. You're my husband, and I love you."

"Then you should have told me about Jared, regardless of what Cora may have asked."

"What more can I say, Adam, except I'm sorry?"

Adam pushed his chair away from the table. "I need to be alone right now."

"What about supper? I'll have it ready soon."

"You can fix something for you and the girls, but I'm not hungry. Right now, I need to apologize to the girls." Adam got up and quickly left the room.

Leah rubbed her forehead as she listened to Adam's footsteps heading up the stairs. *Oh, dear, what have I done? Just when things were going along so well between me and Adam. Now I may have ruined everything.*

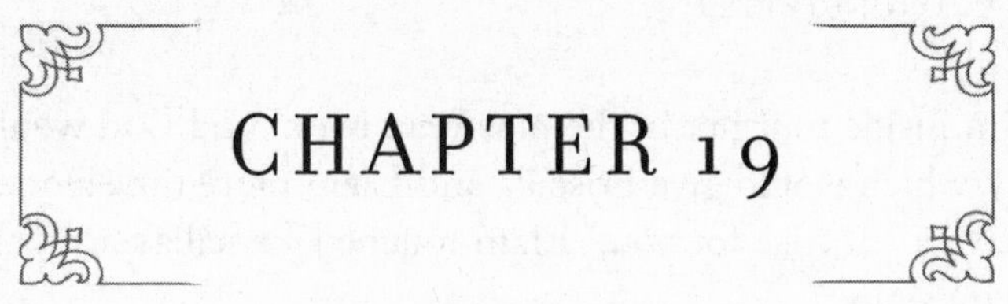

CHAPTER 19

Cora sat quietly in front of the TV, struggling not to give in to self-pity. It was New Year's Eve, and she was alone. Of course, it was her own fault, because she'd let Jared go over to Scott's. Things had been strained between her and Jared since he'd found out about Adam. Cora hoped as time went by he would forgive her for not telling him sooner about her past. She needed to give Jared more time to let everything sink in.

"One more mistake to add to all the others I've made," she murmured. "Am I ever going to be capable of making good decisions?"

Cora reached for her glass of eggnog and took a sip, letting its sweetness roll around on her tongue. At least she had one thing to look forward to—getting the money from the sale of her house. But what good would it do if her relationships with her sons remained as they were now?

Forcing her negative thoughts aside, Cora picked up the remote to change the TV channel, hoping for a weather report. What she found instead was a news bulletin telling about a car accident that had just occurred, involving two teenage boys. One boy had been pronounced dead at the scene of the accident. The other was en route to the hospital. No other details were given, nor did the announcer give the boys' names.

Those kids shouldn't be out on New Year's Eve, Cora thought.

Seated on the passenger side of Elam's buggy, Priscilla glanced over at him and smiled. Instead of giving up their New Year's Eve plans entirely, Elam had agreed to pick Priscilla up this afternoon and drop her off at Elaine's to help with the dinner. He'd return for her later this evening, after everyone had gone and Priscilla had helped Elaine clean up. Priscilla looked forward to the ride home with Elam and planned to invite him inside to usher in the new year. Mom and Dad would go to bed early, which would give Priscilla and Elam more time alone.

"I have a surprise for you." Elam touched Priscilla's arm, breaking into her musings.

"What is it?"

He gave her a teasing glance. "You'll have to wait till later, when I pick you up."

Priscilla relaxed against the seat, tapping her foot to the rhythmic beat of the horse's hooves. Goose bumps erupted on her arms as a chill coursed through her body. Was it the cold night air or anticipation of Elam's surprise? *I wonder if Elam's planning to propose to me. Wouldn't that be a great way to start off the new year?*

"This is the last dinner I have scheduled until Valentine's Day," Elaine told Priscilla as they worked together getting the tables set before the guests arrived.

"Is there a chance one of the tour groups in the area might call to schedule something before then?" Priscilla placed the last of the glasses on the table.

Elaine shrugged. "I suppose it's possible, but most tourists don't visit until spring."

"What will you do to make money between now and then?"

"I'll be okay; I have enough money saved up." Elaine smiled. "And I'll use the time to work on my cookbook."

"Don't forget I'm available to help, and Leah said she'd be willing to work on the cookbook, too."

"She did offer, but between her reflexology treatments and taking care of the girls, I doubt she'd have much free time right now." Elaine moved toward the kitchen. "Guess we'd better check on the food. I don't want anything to burn."

Priscilla followed Elaine into the adjoining room. "Is there anything else you'd like me to put on the tables right now?"

"Not till closer to when the people arrive. Then we can set out the salad dressings and some of your homemade jelly."

"Okay. What would you like me to do now then?"

Elaine lifted the lid on the potatoes and poked them with a fork. "As soon as these are done, you can mash them. Then we'll keep them warm on the stove. In the meantime, why don't you sit and relax? I'll join you as soon as I'm sure all the food's okay."

"Should I pour us some coffee?"

"That'd be nice. We'll probably need the caffeine in order to keep up with everything tonight." Elaine chuckled.

Priscilla got out two mugs and filled them with coffee. She placed them on the kitchen table, along with cream and sugar, then took a seat. "Elam will be coming by to pick me up later this evening, and we'll usher in the new year at my place."

"I thought you were getting together with him tomorrow."

"We are, but Elam wanted to see me tonight, too. He said he has a surprise for me."

Elaine joined her and blew on her coffee before taking a sip. "Do you know what it could be?"

"I'm hoping it's a marriage proposal." Priscilla's fingers curved around the bottom of her cup, enjoying the warmth.

"For your sake, I hope so, too. You've wanted that for some time." Elaine sighed. "Speaking of marriage, I've been considering Ben's proposal."

"What have you decided?"

"I'm not getting any younger, and I would like to have children."

"I sense some hesitation. Do you still have feelings for Jonah? Is that why you haven't responded to Ben's proposal?"

Elaine dropped her gaze. "Jah. I often wonder how things would be for me now, if I hadn't pushed Jonah away when Grandma became ill." She sighed deeply. "Sara might still be alive today and married to someone else."

Priscilla left her seat and slipped her arm around Elaine's waist. "You shouldn't think of the what-ifs. It will drive you crazy. You need to think of your own happiness. Don't settle for someone you really don't love."

"But if I don't marry Ben, I may not find someone else or have any kinner. Having a family is important to me."

"I understand, because I want children, too. But how can you be sure there's no hope of you and Jonah forming a relationship again?"

Elaine shrugged her shoulders. "He's shown no interest in me and probably won't. Jonah still loves Sara. When I saw him out walking on Christmas Day, he said he will never get married again."

"God has things under control, so wait for His answer. Whether things should ever work out for you and Jonah or not, my advice is don't marry Ben unless you are sure you love him."

"I won't." Elaine moved over to the stove. "I hear some vehicles pulling in, so we'd better get going."

"How come you're sitting in the dark?"

Jonah jumped at sound of his mother's voice. He'd been sitting in the kitchen by himself since Mom went upstairs to put his children to bed.

"Sorry if I startled you." Mom turned on the gas lamp overhead.

Jonah blinked against the invading light. "It's okay. I was just sitting here thinking."

Mom took a seat across from him. "About what?"

"About my life. . .the kinner. . ." Jonah pulled his fingers through the ends of his thick, curly hair. "I don't think I can do this, Mom."

"Do what?"

"Raise them without a mother."

"Do you want to get married again?"

Jonah shook his head. "I've given up on love and marriage, but Mark and the baby need a stable environment, which I can't give them."

"Their environment is not unstable, Jonah. The kinner have you, me, and your daed. They also have Sara's parents—although it's too bad they don't live closer."

Jonah moved over to the stove. The coffeepot was still warm, so he poured himself a cup. "I can't give Martha Jean and Mark what they need. Would you mind if they moved in with you and Dad? That would save you from having to come over here every day. I'd come visit them, of course," he quickly added.

"I don't mind coming over, but I think it would be wrong to uproot the children. You are their father, and they need to be here in a familiar environment. They also need to spend as much time with you as possible." Mom got up and stood beside him. "In a few hours, we'll be starting a new year. Each new year brings something to look forward to. Rather than feeling sorry for yourself and underestimating your abilities, you ought to focus on your precious children and trying to be the best daed you can be."

"I want to be, Mom. I'm just not sure I can."

"If you put your faith and trust in God, you can look to the future with hope and purpose. Remember Philippians 4:13: 'I can do all things through Christ which strengtheneth me.'" She placed her hand on his shoulder. "You can't do it on your own strength, son, but you can do it with the Lord's help. He has given you two precious children to raise. He will help you be the kind of father they need."

"I'll do my best to be there for my kinner, but I'm not sure I can trust God for anything. He's let me down three times now. I can't take any more."

Mom gave Jonah's arm a tender squeeze. "God did not let you down, son. He is always with you. Just reach your hand out to Him, and He will see you through any troubles you may have to face. It's not been that long since Sara's passing. You need to give yourself time to grieve."

"I know." Jonah could barely get the words out.

"Cherish your memories of Sara and keep her alive in your heart. She wouldn't want you to give up on life now that she's gone."

Jonah's throat burned as he struggled to hold back tears. In the last month and a half since Sara's death, he'd done enough crying and complaining. Regardless of whether he could trust God again, he would do his best to be strong for his children.

CHAPTER 20

"How'd things go tonight?" Elam asked as he and Priscilla headed toward her home later that evening.

"Quite well. They were a group of farmers' wives, and everyone seemed to have a good time. Elaine got many compliments on her cooking, too," Priscilla responded. "We only had one person who seemed to have started New Year's a little early. She was a real character."

"Did something happen?" Elam questioned.

"Nothing big, just funny." Priscilla chuckled. "She was a cute little lady, maybe in her eighties, named Agnes."

"Sounds pretty normal so far."

"Not really. Her hair was dyed red on one side and green on the other. Plus, she wore a purple headband around her forehead with blinking lights, spelling out, 'Happy New Year.' Kind of unusual, wouldn't you say?"

Elam snickered. "Different, anyway."

"I'll say. Each time she heard someone in the group say the word *celebrate*, Agnes stood up and yelled, 'Happy New Year!' One of the other ladies whispered to me that Agnes liked to keep things lively." Priscilla smiled. "I could tell the other women were fond of Agnes, and they all went along with her antics. I think some of them said *celebrate* just so Agnes would respond."

"She sounds like a character, all right."

While Priscilla enjoyed talking about her evening, she wished Elam would reveal his surprise. If he didn't tell her soon, she would ask.

A few snowflakes began to fall. "I hope the snow doesn't amount to much," Priscilla commented.

He glanced over at her. "You don't like the snow?"

"It's beautiful, especially around Christmas, but it can also be dangerous when the roads get nasty."

"Good point."

They rode in silence awhile. Then Elam reached across the seat and took Priscilla's hand. "Would you like to hear my surprise now?"

"Jah." Priscilla's heart pounded, and she held her breath. If Elam asked her to marry him, she was prepared to say yes. Unlike Elaine, who wasn't sure whether she loved Ben enough to become his wife, Priscilla had been sure for some time she and Elam were meant to be together. Priscilla knew she shouldn't be thinking this way, but Christmas had come and gone without a proposal from Elam. Now it was New Year's Eve. What better time for new beginnings?

"I found another part-time job today," he said.

"What was that?" Elam's comment had barely registered because she was so caught up in her thoughts.

"I found a second job. Whenever I'm not at my folks' bulk food store, I'll be working for the English cabinetmaker on the other side of town. He said he'd have some evening work for me, and some Saturdays, too."

"That was your surprise?" Priscilla couldn't hide her disappointment.

"Jah. I'll be making more money now."

Money for what? Priscilla wondered, but she didn't voice the question. She felt like crying. She'd gotten her hopes up, expecting a marriage proposal, and all Elam was thinking about was making more money.

"If having a second job is what you want, then I guess we won't be seeing each other much anymore." Priscilla looked straight ahead so Elam wouldn't see her displeasure. Her dreams felt like snowflakes falling, melting away, disappearing. With him about to become busier, they may as well not be courting at all.

"I won't be working every evening, and of course, not on Sundays." Elam squeezed Priscilla's fingers, as if to reassure her. But she felt no reassurance. The only thing she felt was frustration. It seemed that David was more eager to spend time with her than Elam was these days.

"Say, I have an idea. Why don't we stop by the Morgans' and see David?" she suggested.

"Now?"

"Jah. David's grandparents have most likely gone to bed by now, and David might be sitting by himself with no one to ring in the new year."

"Or maybe he's in bed, too. Even if he's not, this is supposed to be our night, Priscilla. We can see David some other time."

"I realize it's our night, but if David's by himself, he'd probably appreciate some company."

"Okay, if that's what you want, but let's not stay too long."

At least Priscilla isn't going by herself to see David, Elam thought. *David's my friend, too, but he's been seeing too much of Priscilla. I wish he'd go back to Chicago.*

When they arrived at the Morgans' house, Elam saw light in a few of the downstairs windows. Someone must be up. He stepped down from the buggy and secured his horse to a fence post. By the time he went around to help Priscilla down, she was already out of the buggy and walking toward the house.

Elam was surprised when they knocked on the door and David's grandma answered. Smiling, she invited them in. "Walt and I are about ready to head for bed, but Davey's awake. I'm sure he'll be glad to see you." Letty yawned, before gesturing to the living room. "Please, go on in and stay for as long as you like. I'm pleased Davey won't have to ring in the new year by himself."

When Priscilla and Elam entered the living room, David, who'd been reclining on the couch, grabbed the remote and turned off the television. Elam was tempted to tell him if he wanted to become Amish he should start by giving up TV.

"Thanks for stopping by." Smiling, David sat up. "Gram and Gramps were trying to stay awake so I wouldn't be alone at the stroke of midnight, but I insisted they go to bed. Now that you two are here, I'll have someone to greet the new year with."

"We weren't planning to—"

"We'd be happy to stay until midnight." Priscilla cut Elam off before he could finish his sentence.

Elam groaned inwardly. It wasn't that he disliked David. He simply wanted to be alone with Priscilla. After he and Priscilla removed their jackets and took seats, David asked if Elam would like to sign his cast.

Elam shrugged. "Sure, why not?"

David pointed to the marking pen lying on the coffee table, and stretched out his leg. "Priscilla already signed it."

"Oh? When was that?"

"One day when she took me for a ride in her buggy."

Elam clenched his teeth. *I wonder why Priscilla didn't mention that to me.*

"By the way, Priscilla, I have a late Christmas gift for you." David grinned at her. "Gramps drove me into town yesterday so I could pick something out. I hope you like what I got."

Priscilla shook her head. "You didn't have to get me anything, David."

"Hey, I wanted to." David motioned to a box on the coffee table, wrapped in tissue paper. "Go ahead and open it."

Elam watched with irritation as she opened the box and removed a cut-glass dish full of candy.

Priscilla smiled. "Thanks, David. How thoughtful of you."

David grinned. "Those chocolates have maple centers. They're really good. I sampled a few at the store."

"Those are my favorite kind."

"That's what I thought. I remembered you mentioning it once."

Elam thought about the gift he'd given Priscilla for Christmas. Compared to David's present, the hankies seemed cheap and impersonal. *Someday after I save up more money*, he thought, *I'll be able to give Priscilla everything she wants.*

"I had a feeling they wouldn't be able to stay awake until midnight," Leah said when she and Adam returned to the living room after tucking the girls in bed.

Adam chuckled. "Carrie was the first to conk out, but Linda and Amy weren't far behind." He took Leah's hand and led her to the couch. "Guess it's just the two of us to see the new year in. Unless you're too tired and want to go to bed now."

"No, I'm fine." Leah scooched in beside him, enjoying the quiet and a chance to be alone with the man she loved. She looked forward to the new year and seeing what the future held for her, Adam, and their ready-made family. Sadly, one thing was missing in their life right now—a resolution to the situation between Adam and his mother.

"I hope you won't get upset by what I have to say," Leah said, "but I've been wondering when you plan to tell the girls about Cora."

Adam jerked his head. "I don't see why they'd need to be told."

Leah paused, trying to collect her thoughts. "They're being cheated out of knowing their grandmother, Adam."

"Humph! If she'd wanted to know her grandchildren, she shouldn't have abandoned me and Mary when we needed her."

Leah turned to face him. "Won't you ever let it go? What are you accomplishing by rehashing the past?"

"Nothing, I guess, but I won't allow Cora to mess up Carrie, Linda, and Amy's lives the way she did mine and Mary's."

"From what I can tell, Cora's not the same person she was back then. I doubt she'd do anything to mess up their lives. If anything, she could give them something they're lacking: having a grandmother living close by."

Adam slowly shook his head. "I don't know, Leah. I'm not comfortable with Cora coming in contact with the girls. And how would I explain to them who she is?"

Leah reached for his hand. "Pray about it, Adam. I'll be praying, too. And don't forget, you have a younger brother who needs you, especially since his dad doesn't live close by."

"I will pray about it, Leah." He gestured to the crackling logs in the fireplace. "Right now, let's just sit together quietly and enjoy the warmth of the fire."

Leah leaned her head against his shoulder and closed her eyes. When they woke up tomorrow morning, they would start a brand-new year. Perhaps, Lord willing, things would be different for all of them soon.

When the clock struck midnight, Leah bowed her head in silent prayer. She decided to make Matthew 6:33–34 her verses for the new year: "But seek ye first the kingdom of God, and his righteousness; and all these things shall be added unto you. Take therefore no thought for the morrow: for the morrow shall take thought for the things of itself."

Cora had been sleeping awhile, when a knock sounded on the door. Rising from her chair in a somewhat dopey state, she peeked out the window and was surprised to see the sheriff's car in her driveway.

Cautiously, she opened the door.

"Mrs. Finley?"

Cora nodded. "What can I do for you, Sheriff?"

"I'm sorry to tell you this, but there's been an accident involving two cars. Your son Jared was riding in one of them."

Stunned, Cora remembered the news bulletin she'd seen on TV. "Pl–please tell me my son is not dead."

The sheriff shook his head. "His injuries are serious, but the driver of the car he was riding in didn't make it."

Muffling a sob, Cora leaned against the door for support. *Dear God, please don't take my son.*

CHAPTER 21

Priscilla rolled over to look at the clock beside her bed. It was already 7:30 a.m.—well past the time she normally got up. Elam hadn't gone home until well after midnight last night, and even though she'd gone to bed as soon as he'd left, she hadn't fallen asleep right away. So many thoughts went through her mind as she pondered where her life was going. All these years she had assumed her future was pretty much set, but lately she wasn't so sure.

Taking in a deep breath, all the smells drifting up the stairs told Priscilla that Mom had already started breakfast. Rubbing her pounding temples, she groaned and pulled the covers over her head. If she got up now, she'd never make it through the day without dozing off. She might even get sick because of her headache.

Priscilla wanted nothing more than to lie here, enveloped under the darkness of the covers, where most of the morning sounds were muffled. Regrettably, it wasn't an option. Mom always counted on Priscilla helping with the breakfast, so she forced herself out of bed. After putting on her robe and slippers, she made her way down the stairs, where she found Mom in the kitchen, mixing pancake batter.

"I'm surprised you're up so early, since you had a late night." Mom turned from the stove and frowned. "Ach, Priscilla, you look *baremlich*. Did you look in the *schpiggel* at those dark circles under your eyes?"

Priscilla massaged her forehead. "I feel terrible—like I haven't slept at all. And no, I did not look in the mirror. I came downstairs to let you know I have a koppweh."

"Then you'd better go back to bed." Mom gestured to the door from which Priscilla had entered. "If you sleep a few more hours you may feel better before your brothers and their families arrive. Elam's still planning to come, too, isn't he?"

Priscilla nodded, wincing at the beam of light shining through the kitchen window. At least it wasn't snowing this morning. "Danki for understanding, Mom. A little more sleep is what I need right now." She started out of the room but turned back around. "Please wake me before they get here. I'll need to take a shower and make myself look presentable."

"I'll make sure you're up."

"By the way, what smells so good?" Even though Priscilla knew she couldn't eat anything, whatever her mother had made smelled delicious.

"A scrambled egg and green pepper quiche. But don't worry, once it cools, I'll wrap a piece and you can have it later."

"Danki, Mom." As Priscilla headed back to her room, she thought about how strangely Elam had acted when they'd stopped to see David last night. *It almost seemed as if he was jealous of David's attentions toward me. But why?* she wondered. *David and I are just friends.*

Leah smiled as she stood at the kitchen window, watching Adam shuffle toward the phone shack, where he'd gone to check for messages. Last night it had snowed a bit, and the path was most likely slippery, since the sun wasn't high enough yet to melt it.

It was still early, and the girls weren't awake yet, so Leah hesitated to start breakfast. When Adam came back to the house, she would fry eggs and bacon. In the meantime, she may as well get some coffee started. One thing Leah had learned about Adam was that he liked to have a cup of coffee every morning to start his day.

Humming, she filled the coffeepot with water and set it on the stove. While she waited for it to perk, she took out a carton of eggs and a slab of bacon. Then she sat at the table with her Bible, to read a few verses.

She turned to Isaiah 26:3–4: *"Thou wilt keep him in perfect peace, whose mind is stayed on thee: because he trusteth in thee. Trust ye in the LORD for ever: for in the LORD JEHOVAH is everlasting strength."*

Those verses are a reminder of the importance of putting my trust in God, she thought. *I need to remember His teachings, and trust Him to work things out between Adam and his mother.*

Leah closed her Bible as Adam entered the room, blinking rapidly, elbows pressed tightly against his sides.

"What's wrong, Adam?"

"Cora left a message on our answering machine. Jared was involved in an accident last night." Adam swiped the palm of his hand across his forehead. "He's in the hospital, in serious condition."

Leah gasped. "Oh, no!"

"I'm going to the hospital, Leah. I called my driver. He will pick me up in twenty minutes."

"I'll go with you. We can drop the girls off at my folks'."

"What if Jared doesn't make it?" Adam asked. "What if I never get the chance to really know my little *bruder*?"

Leah wished she had an answer for Adam. All she could do was give him a hug, hoping to offer reassurance. Then she remembered the scripture she'd just read. "Trust God, Adam. The Lord Jehovah is our everlasting strength."

Cora's eyes felt as gritty as sandpaper. She'd been at the hospital all night, waiting for news on Jared's condition. When she'd first arrived, she'd been told he had a ruptured spleen and some other internal injuries, as well as several broken bones. As soon as she signed the papers, he'd been taken into surgery. Two hours ago, when Jared was in the recovery room, he'd gone into cardiac arrest. They were trying to stabilize him and insisted Cora take a seat in the waiting room. All she could do was wait and pray. The waiting was difficult, but Cora hoped her prayers would be answered. She couldn't imagine what her life would be like without Jared.

Cora had called Adam and left a message early this morning, and last night she'd tried to get in touch with Evan. He hadn't answered the phone, nor responded to the message she'd left. *I'll bet he was out partying with his new wife*, Cora thought bitterly. *If Evan's suffering from a hangover this morning, it could be hours before he checks his messages.*

Normally, Evan didn't have a problem with alcohol, but Cora had seen him drink too much on a few occasions—like when they'd been celebrating some event. *Call me, Evan. Call me.*

Cora ground her teeth together. *Evan should be here right now, waiting with me to find out whether our son is going to live or die.*

Her focus switched to Adam, wondering what his response would be when he got the news his brother had been seriously injured and might not live.

Tears welled in Cora's eyes, dribbling down her cheeks. *It's my fault this happened to Jared. I never should have said he could spend New Year's Eve with Scott.* Of course he hadn't gone to Scott's. Jared had been riding in Chad's car, and now Chad was dead.

New Year's Day was supposed to be a time for new beginnings and hope for the year ahead. She grimaced, turning in her chair in an attempt to find a comfortable position.

I don't think I can go on if Jared doesn't make it. Cora struggled to hold herself together, even though she thought she might lose control at any moment. If she let the what-ifs take over, she would be devastated. *I have to think positive. Jared's going to make it. Lord, please save my boy. I know I don't deserve anything, but please spare him so I can have the chance to bring him up right and teach him to love You.*

Cora's thoughts turned to Chad. Deep down she'd always felt sorry for him but had focused more on her concern for Jared hanging around someone of his poor character. She'd seen it happen so many times with other parents during the years they'd lived in Chicago. Children who were brought up in a secure, happy home would get in with the wrong crowd and cause their parents to worry.

Thinking back on it now, apparently Chad had never gone home like Jared said. Cora had no idea where the boy had been all this time. Maybe all the missing food had been going to Chad. The food didn't matter now. She only wanted Jared to wake up.

I wonder how Chad's parents are handling the news of their son's death. Cora had been informed they'd been notified, but she hadn't seen them at the hospital yet. *Please, God, comfort Chad's parents, and don't let me lose Jared, too.*

Cora picked up her cell phone and was about to call Evan again, when Adam and Leah entered the room.

Leah moved swiftly across the room and gave Cora a comforting hug, while Adam stood off to one side with a strained expression.

"I am so sorry." Gently, Leah patted Cora's back. "Is Jared going to be okay?"

Cora sniffed deeply. "I don't know. His heart stopped beating in the recovery room, but they managed to revive him. Now it's just wait and see."

"We can pray," Adam spoke up. He looked at Cora with earnest eyes, as if reminding her of all she'd been taught.

"I have been praying. I just don't know if it's enough."

"We need to pray and trust." Leah spoke softly, leading Cora back to her seat.

"Where's my son, and who are these people?"

Cora jumped at the sound of Evan's deep voice as he bounded into the waiting room. Thank goodness he had come, but should she take the time to explain about Adam being her son and Leah his wife? It wasn't important right now.

"I'm glad you got my message." Cora moved closer to Evan, moistening her parched lips with the tip of her tongue. "Jared's seriously injured, and he. . ." She nearly choked on the words. "He might not make it."

Evan looked around the room, as though searching for someone. "I want to see him now."

Cora nodded. "Me, too, but we can't go in until they say it's okay."

Evan sank into a chair with a moan. "I never should have let you and Jared leave Chicago. If our son dies, I'll never forgive you, Cora." He clasped his hands behind his neck and stared at the ceiling. Cora could see his Adam's apple moving up and down as he swallowed.

Cora spread her fingers out and pressed them against her breastbone. She had been prepared for Evan to blame her for what had happened tonight, but was Evan saying what she thought he was saying? Did he wish he'd never filed for divorce and married Emily? Did he regret the three of them no longer being a family?

Except for the occasional calls over the PA system, all was quiet. It was nerve-racking to hear the muffled sounds of nurses walking past the waiting room. Only their shoes could be heard going down the spotless hallways, and each time the squeakiness drew near, Cora held her breath, wondering if someone was coming to give her bad news.

CHAPTER 22

The next several hours seemed like days to Cora, as she sat with Adam, Leah, and Evan, waiting for news on Jared's condition. Several times she saw Adam and Leah with their eyes closed and heads bowed, but Evan either paced or sat impatiently tapping his foot. Cora had introduced Adam and Leah to Evan, but just as Amish friends. Now was not the time to tell Evan the truth about her previous life. It would upset him and probably make matters worse. Thankfully, neither Leah nor Adam made any reference to Cora being Adam's mother. Right now, everyone's focus was on Jared, hoping he pulled through.

Cora shifted in her seat. She'd been trying to do as Leah had suggested and trust God, but the longer they waited for news on Jared's condition, the more apprehensive she became.

"Why don't Adam and I get us all some coffee?" Leah rose from her chair.

"Good idea." Adam stood, too. "Four coffees coming right up. Is black okay, or do we need some cream and sugar?"

"Black is fine for me," Cora replied.

Evan gave a nod. "Same here."

After Leah and Adam left the room, Evan turned to Cora. "Would you tell me exactly why our son was with Chad, driving around in bad weather?"

"Jared lied to me, Evan. He was supposed to spend the night with his friend Scott. I had no idea Chad was still in Arthur. When he first showed up here and said his folks had kicked him out, I made it clear he needed to go back to Chicago and try to work things out. I thought he'd gone back, but I was wrong. Apparently he'd found someplace else to stay, but we won't know any details until Jared wakes up."

Cora sighed. "But really, Evan, why does it matter now why Jared was with Chad? Think what Chad's parents are going through, hearing their son was killed." She gulped. "I just want our son to be all right."

"So do I, but something else is puzzling me."

"What's that?"

"You introduced those Amish people as your friends, but why would they be here at the hospital with you? I mean, it's not like they're family or anything."

"Actually, they are. Adam's my son, and Leah's my daughter-in-law." Cora covered her mouth. She couldn't believe she'd blurted the truth out, especially after deciding this was not the time or place.

Evan blinked rapidly. "Have you lost your mind, Cora? Or are you so upset over Jared's condition you've become delusional?"

"I am not delusional." Cora's spine stiffened, but at the moment she felt quite brave. "I never told you this before, Evan, but I used to be Amish."

Evan sat with a stony face, then he snorted. "Of course you were. You drove to nursing school in a horse and buggy, wearing a dark-colored dress and a white cap."

"Very funny, Evan."

He crossed his arms. "Seriously, you don't expect me to believe you used to be Amish."

"You can believe whatever you want, but it's the truth." It felt good to get this all out, instead of keeping it bottled up like she'd done since she met Evan. "My parents were Amish, and when I grew up, I married an Amish man."

"No, you didn't; you married me."

"That was later. Ours was my second marriage."

Evan leaped to his feet. "What? You are kidding, right?"

"No, Evan, I'm not kidding. I married an Amish man, and we had two children—Adam and Mary. We'd been divorced for some time before I met you."

"Adam is really your son?"

"Yes, but I lost touch with him and his sister after I left."

Evan took a seat in the chair beside her. "What do you mean, 'left'?"

Cora's heart pounded as she struggled to keep her composure. "I wanted a career in nursing, but I couldn't talk my husband into leaving the Amish faith, so I left."

Evan's eyes widened. "Without him?"

She nodded slowly, swallowing around the lump in her throat. "Yes."

"What about the children? Did you take them when you left?"

Cora slowly shook her head, feeling the shame of what she'd done. "Andrew wouldn't allow them to go with me, and when I went back to see them, they were gone."

"What do you mean?"

"My children's father had sold our home and moved somewhere else." Cora sniffed as tears filled her eyes. "I was shunned by those in my Amish community, and no one in the area would tell me where Andrew and the children had gone."

Deep wrinkles formed across Evan's forehead. "And you think I'm a bad person. At least I don't have a sordid past I never told you about. I didn't abandon my children to seek a career, either."

Anger bubbled in Cora's soul. "You may not have left to seek a career, but you abandoned Jared when he needed you the most." She pointed a shaky finger at him. "You divorced me for a woman you thought was better." Cora narrowed her eyes and looked around. "If Emily is so wonderful, then why isn't she here with you right now? I've been meaning to ask about her since you first arrived."

Evan held up his hand. "Leave Emily out of this, shall we? She didn't get much sleep last night and wasn't feeling well after our New Year's Eve party. Besides, Jared's my son, not hers."

"She should have come to support you. I would have if the tables were turned." Cora picked up a magazine and slapped it against the table in front of her. "We shouldn't be having this conversation right now. Our thoughts should be on Jared."

"You're right, and mine are." Evan grunted. "But since we can't do anything for our son at the moment, we may as well finish this conversation."

"What more is there to say?"

"You can start by telling me how you happened to find your long-lost Amish son. Did you move here to Arthur on purpose, so you could reestablish a relationship with him and his sister?"

She knew it was time to admit everything, even if it meant telling Evan about every bad decision she'd made. "I had no idea Adam lived here. I came to Arthur because of an opening for a nurse at the clinic." She paused and drew in a breath. "And I have not connected with my daughter at all, because Mary is dead. I found out about my daughter after we moved here. She and her husband were killed in an accident. Now Adam and Leah are raising their three girls."

Evan's eyebrows shot up. "So you're a grandmother, too?"

Cora nodded briefly, then she reached into her purse for a tissue to dry her tears. "I haven't established a relationship with them, because Adam won't let me. In fact, I don't have a connection with him, either. He hasn't forgiven me for leaving when he was a boy."

Evan scowled at her. "Can you blame him? Do you think any man would want a relationship with a woman who cared more about chasing after a career than being his mother?"

Cora winced. Evan's sharp words pierced her like a sword. "You're right. I am a terrible person, and I probably don't deserve a second chance with my son. But you can't deny I've been a good mother to Jared. And right now, he's my only concern."

A picture on the wall caught Cora's attention. A beautiful wooden frame bordered the serene painting of a cottage surrounded by trees. In the background were deer feeding in a meadow. Cora wished she could transport herself into the scene, where everything looked so peaceful—a place where no problems existed.

"Let's take a seat here in the cafeteria and drink our coffee," Leah suggested. "When we're done we can take some back to Cora and Evan."

Adam's eyebrows squeezed together. "Why don't you want to go back now?"

"I thought it would be good if we had some time to talk. Maybe Cora and Evan need time alone, too."

"That's fine, but I don't want to be gone long. The doctor might give us some news on Jared's condition soon, and I want to be there to hear it."

"I understand, and we don't have to sit here at all if you'd rather not."

Adam shook his head. "No, it's okay." He seated himself at an empty table, and Leah took the chair beside him.

"Cora will be devastated if she loses Jared," Leah said.

"I will be, too." Adam rubbed his forehead. "I haven't even had the chance to really get to know my half brother."

"Once he gets better maybe we can have Cora and Jared over to our house so they can get acquainted with the girls."

Adam grimaced. "I'm not sure I want my nieces to know their grandmother."

Leah leaned closer. "Adam, you need to forgive your mother for what she did in the past."

"I know, and I've tried. I just don't think I can let her back into my life."

"Ephesians 4:32 says, 'Be ye kind to one another, tenderhearted, forgiving one another, even as God for Christ's sake hath forgiven you.'" She touched his arm. "Restored relationships aren't easy, but by the grace of God they're possible. Cora has expressed sorrow over what she did when you were a boy, and she's asked your forgiveness."

Adam dropped his gaze to the table. "I thought I had forgiven her, but it's hard to forget what she did."

"I'm not suggesting you forget it, Adam," Leah said softly. "But you don't have to carry a grudge." She waited a few seconds then spoke again. "Your mother's repentance and your forgiveness can be the glue that repairs your broken relationship."

Adam gave a slight nod.

"Cora needs you right now. If you really think about it, you need her, too. I believe the young man fighting for his life right now needs a big brother."

"I've been praying fervently that God will spare Jared's life."

"Cora has no one but us to help her through this, Adam. Her ex-husband doesn't seem to be offering much support. I saw his attitude the minute he stomped into the waiting room. He's only worried about himself and doesn't care what Cora's going through."

"You're right." Adam looked at Leah, tears shimmering in his eyes. "With God's help, I'll let my mother back into my life. Now I need to figure out the best way to tell the girls about her."

Elam's footsteps quickened as he made his way across the yard to the Hershbergers' house, where he'd been invited to share their noon meal. Several other buggies were parked near the barn, meaning the rest of Priscilla's family were here, too.

When he knocked on the door, Priscilla's mother answered.

"I'm sorry to tell you this," Iva said, "but Priscilla has a headache and is resting in bed. She thought she'd feel better by now, but the pain has gotten worse. I don't think she'll be down at all today, but you're welcome to stay and have dinner with the rest of our family."

"Danki for inviting me, but it wouldn't be the same without Priscilla. Guess I'll go on home and eat dinner with my folks." Elam couldn't hide his disappointment. He'd been looking forward to being with Priscilla today. "I hope she feels better soon. Please tell Priscilla I look forward to seeing her in church tomorrow morning."

Iva nodded. "I'll let her know."

With shoulders slumped, Elam made his way back to his horse and buggy. This new year hadn't started out anything like he'd hoped. *Things will be better once I have some money saved up*, he told himself. *A few months working at my second job and I should be ready to ask Priscilla to marry me.*

When Adam and Leah returned to the waiting room with coffee, Evan sneered at Adam. "It's about time. What took you so long?"

"There's no reason for you to talk to Adam like that," Cora snapped. "Just be glad he brought us some coffee."

"Thanks," Evan mumbled, taking the offered cup.

"Sorry for the delay." Leah gestured to Adam. "We sat for a while so we could talk. We thought maybe you and Cora needed some time alone to visit, too."

"It's okay. We haven't heard any news yet." Cora forced a smile she didn't really feel. How could she smile about anything right now?

Evan drank his coffee and started pacing again. "I'm a doctor, for crying out loud. They shouldn't keep me in the dark about my son's condition."

"Waiting is the worst part," Leah agreed, "but hopefully you'll hear something soon."

Unable to drink her coffee, Cora placed the cup on the table and lowered her head into her outstretched hands. She was surprised when Adam took a seat beside her and laid his hand on her shoulder. "With

God's help, we'll get through this—together."

Her head jerked up. "Really, Adam?"

He gave an affirmative nod. "Let's leave the past in the past and move on from here."

Tears sprang to Cora's eyes and ran down her cheeks. The urge to reach out and grasp Adam's hands was overpowering, but she held back, fearful of scaring him away. "Oh, Adam, thank you." She gulped on a sob. "I can't change the past, or make up for what I did, but I promise from this day forward to be the kind of person God wants me to be."

Evan looked at Cora and grunted. "Since when did you start talking about God?"

"Since I realized all the things I'd been taught when I was a girl were important; I just wasn't listening or putting them into practice. I was selfish and self-centered when I should have put God first and looked to others' needs instead of my own."

A middle-aged doctor entered the room and walked over to Cora. "Your son's stable now, and things are looking positive. He's sleeping, but you and your husband are welcome to see him now."

Cora didn't bother to tell the doctor that Evan was no longer her husband. All she could think about was how grateful she felt that Jared's condition was stable and Adam had just agreed to begin again. *Thank You, Lord, for answers to prayer.*

CHAPTER 23

Cora had just come from the waiting room, where she'd gone to take another look at the picture on the wall. For some reason, after noticing the painting that first night, something about the tranquil scene drew her each time she went to the hospital. Whenever she stopped to gaze at it, Cora noticed things she hadn't seen before—wildflowers of different hues where deer grazed, flower boxes on all the windows, and a glider swing on the front porch. Even a family of bluebirds splashing in a birdbath adorned this colorful painting. Cora almost lost herself in the beauty of the picture, but the cottage, nestled among a canopy of trees, tugged at her heart the most. *If only I could find a place like that for me and Jared. But that type of home probably doesn't exist in this area. If it did, surely I would have seen it.*

It had been two weeks since Jared's accident. Even though his injuries were healing, he hadn't responded well to any of Cora's visits. In addition to being angry with her for not telling him about her past, Jared blamed Cora for the accident that had taken his friend's life. He told her that if she'd let Chad stay with them, he'd still be alive. Cora had countered that Chad could have gotten in an accident no matter where he was staying. She'd also reminded Jared he had been dishonest with her about spending the night at Scott's, when all along, he planned to be with Chad.

As Cora headed down the hospital corridor toward Jared's room, she lifted a silent prayer. *Please, God, soften my son's heart toward me, and let this be a good visit. I don't know if Chad would be alive or not if he and Jared hadn't been out joyriding, but I wish I hadn't said yes to my son's request to spend the night with a friend. I should have insisted he stay home with me on New Year's Eve.*

Cora had a knack for blaming herself for things, and now was no exception. She'd messed up so many times in the past, it was hard to know sometimes when something was actually her fault.

Her thoughts turned to Evan. He'd hung around long enough to make sure Jared was okay, but he'd hightailed it back to Chicago to resume his life. In all fairness, Cora reminded herself that Evan had a medical practice and patients to tend to. But she couldn't help thinking Evan was most likely anxious to get back to his new wife. Why wasn't Jared mad at his father? Evan was certainly no saint.

Cora was glad she'd finally told Evan about her past Amish life. That day, Cora's emotions had teetered between fear and bravery. It was getting easier to take Evan's reactions, since they were no longer married, although she still missed what they'd once had. Right now, though, she had more important things to think about.

The one bright spot in Cora's life was that she and Adam had finally made peace. Due to her job and numerous trips to the hospital to see Jared, Cora hadn't had the chance to visit her granddaughters yet, but she would do that as soon as she got the go-ahead from Adam. He wanted to talk to the girls first and prepare them for her meeting. Cora hoped they would welcome her into their lives.

I can't think about that situation now, either. I need to concentrate on Jared.

Drawing in a deep breath to steady her nerves, Cora entered Jared's room. She was surprised to see Adam sitting beside Jared's bed, carrying on a conversation.

When the door closed behind Cora, Adam looked her way and smiled. "I'm glad you're here. I have to get to the store and I didn't want to leave Jared alone."

"Why? Is there a problem?" Cora held her arms tightly against her sides.

Adam shook his head. "Jared's doing okay physically, but he seems kind of down today."

I doubt I'll be able to cheer him up, Cora thought, but she didn't speak the words. Instead, she moved to stand at the foot of Jared's bed. "How are you feeling, son? Is there anything I can do for you?"

With his gaze fixed on the ceiling, Jared grunted. "It's a little late for that."

Cora winced. Apparently this was going to be a repeat of her last visit, with Jared making snide remarks or giving her the cold shoulder.

"Don't you think this has gone on long enough?" Adam touched

Jared's arm. "Your mom has taken good care of you. I can tell she loves you very much."

Jared made no reply.

"If you remain angry at your mother, it won't change a thing. It'll only fester like an unremoved splinter, causing you nothing but pain. Believe me, I know what I'm talking about."

Jared remained silent.

"It's all right, Adam," Cora said. "If you need to get to work, you'd better go."

He shook his head. "I'm not leaving till Jared listens to me."

"I can hear ya just fine." Jared turned his head toward Adam. "I don't need no lectures today."

"Admit it, Jared, you do." Adam scooted his chair closer to the bed. "Look, if I could forgive your mother for what she did when I was a boy, then don't you think you should be able to forgive her as well?"

Jared blinked a couple of times but gave no verbal response.

Cora stood motionless, trying to keep her emotions in check. *Please, Lord, please let Adam get through to his brother.*

"Jared, do you believe in God?" Adam prompted.

"Yeah, I guess so."

"The Bible is God's Word, and in Matthew 6:14 it says that Jesus said, 'If ye forgive men their trespasses, your heavenly Father will also forgive you.'" Adam paused, glanced at Cora, then back at Jared. "It took a long time for that verse to penetrate my heart. When it did, I was able to forgive. Then I felt a heavy burden being lifted from my shoulders. We've all made mistakes we wish we hadn't, and it's not our place to judge others. What I'm trying to say is, God spared your life, and you've been given a second chance. Don't ruin it by cutting your mother—our mother—out of your life."

Tears welled in Cora's eyes, and she nearly choked on the sob rising in her throat. Hearing Adam refer to her as his mother was healing balm to her soul.

"It's going to take time, Jared," Adam continued, "but with God's help, we can all learn to love each other and get along. We need to put the past behind us and look to the future. Do you agree?"

Jared nodded as tears slipped from his eyes and splashed onto his cheeks. "I'm glad I have a brother." He looked at Cora then and gave her a weak smile. "I forgive you, Mom. Will you forgive me?"

The tears let loose, coursing down her cheeks. Cora rushed to the side of Jared's bed. "Of course I forgive you, Jared." As much as she would have liked it to be, everything would not be perfect. No doubt there would be some troublesome days ahead, but from this moment on, she would try to be a good mother to both of her sons.

"Priscilla, have you seen my favorite scrubby? I can't do the dishes without it."

Priscilla brought more of the breakfast dishes to the sink and handed them to her mother. "Sorry, Mom, but I haven't seen it. Would you like me to look in one of the drawers for another scrubby?"

"None of the others are as big as that one." Mom squinted at Priscilla over the top of her glasses. "Did you know most Amish women would walk half a mile to buy a good scrubby like mine?"

Priscilla chuckled. "I'll keep looking, Mom."

She went through every drawer and cupboard, but still the large scrubby wasn't found. "Sorry, Mom, it doesn't seem to be here. Do you think maybe Dad may have taken it?"

"I don't know why he would. He certainly won't be washing dishes out in his shop. Things don't just vanish, though." Mom's brows furrowed. "I surely wish I knew where it was."

Priscilla didn't understand why Mom was making such a fuss over the missing scrubby when a lot worse was happening in the world, even right here in Arthur.

"I'll tell you what," Priscilla said, "I'll get my horse and buggy out and go to the store. I'm sure I can find another big scrubby."

"No, that's okay. It's too cold out to go anywhere today." Mom grabbed a dishcloth and started washing the dishes.

"I really don't mind. I was planning to go see David anyway."

Mom frowned deeply. "Again? Seems like you're always with David."

"I haven't seen him for over a week. The last I stopped by the Morgans' David said he'd be getting his cast off this Monday. I'm anxious to see how it went."

"I really think you're seeing too much of David." Mom turned on the warm water and rinsed a glass. "You're being courted by Elam, and it doesn't look right for you to spend time alone with David."

Priscilla sighed. "David and I aren't usually alone—his grandparents have been there. Besides, Elam's working a lot these days. I doubt he cares what I do in my free time."

"You're wrong about that," Mom argued. "Any man who loves a woman cares about what she does and who she sees socially."

"If Elam loves me so much, then why hasn't he proposed? We've been courting long enough."

Mom pursed her lips. "You need to stop worrying about it. I'm sure Elam will ask in good time."

"We'll see." Priscilla laid the dish towel down and grabbed a tissue to wipe her nose. For some reason, it had started to run all of a sudden. Could she be allergic to the new dishwashing liquid Mom was using?

Priscilla lifted the lid on the garbage can to throw the tissue away but stopped short. Inside was Mom's large scrubby. "Well, for goodness' sake."

"What is it, Priscilla?" Mom asked.

Priscilla pulled out the scrubby, holding it up for Mom to see.

"Ach, my!" Mom's eyes widened. "How on earth did it get in there?"

"Maybe Dad tossed it out, thinking it had seen better days. It has had a lot of wear."

Mom crinkled her nose. "It's too full of germs to use now. Just toss it back into the garbage. The next time I'm out running errands I'll get a new one."

"I'll get one for you today, after I've seen David."

Mom didn't argue, but Priscilla could tell by the firm set of her mother's jaw that she was none too happy about it.

She really has nothing to worry about.

"Sure is nice to have my cast off and be able to move around easily on my own." David took a seat at his grandmother's breakfast table.

She gave a nod. "Your grandpa and I are pleased about that, too. Aren't we, Walt?"

"Yep. Sure are." Gramps smiled at David from across the table.

"Course, I'll be going to physical therapy twice a week until my leg's moving better." David reached for his glass of milk and took a drink. "Oops!" He set it back down. "I forgot to pray." Closing his eyes, he bowed his head and offered a silent prayer. When David opened his eyes, he noticed Gramps staring at him. "What's wrong?" David asked.

"Are you still practicing to be Amish?" Gramps tipped his head, looking at David curiously.

"I'm not practicing. Just doing what will soon be expected of me."

Gramps leaned his elbows on the table, looking right at David. "Want to know what I think?"

"Sure." David drank the rest of his milk.

"I think becoming Amish is just your way of getting under your dad's skin."

David shook his head. "No, it's not."

Gram placed a plate of scrambled eggs on the table, along with some sausage links, before pulling out a chair to join them at the table. "Can we please eat breakfast peacefully and not talk about this right now?"

"Yep, it's fine by me." David forked two sausages onto his plate and passed the platter to Gramps. "What would you like to talk about, Gram?"

"I don't know." She took some eggs and passed the plate to David. "We could talk about the weather, I suppose."

"Humph! The weather we've been having is not much to talk about. There's still too much snow on the ground to suit me," Gramps mumbled.

Gram gave a nod. "Yes, and unless it warms up considerably, the snow will probably stay on the ground for several more weeks."

"I forgot to tell you, Daniel Hershberger came by the other day and asked if we'd like another dog." Gramps smiled at Gram. "Said he was willing to get us one but wanted to ask first."

She shook her head. "He doesn't have to get us a dog. Besides, I'm not sure I want one—at least not yet."

"I've been thinking the same thing but wasn't sure how you felt about it."

David ate silently while his grandparents discussed the situation.

He'd just finished his breakfast when someone knocked on the door.

"I'll get it," he said. "It's easier for me now, since I'm not using crutches."

When David opened the back door, he was pleased to see Priscilla on the porch.

"Hey, look at you." She smiled up at him. "No crutches and you got your cast off."

He grinned. "I feel like a new man."

"I'll bet you do."

"I'm glad you came by." David motioned for her to step inside. "I'm planning to see your bishop today, and I'd like you to go along."

"You're really serious about joining the Amish church?"

"Absolutely! The sooner the better."

CHAPTER 24

Two more weeks went by before Cora brought Jared home. Last evening he'd been released from the hospital, and as soon as she'd gotten him settled, she'd called Adam, as well as Evan. No doubt Adam would either call or come by in the morning, but Cora wasn't sure about Evan. He'd called a few times to check on Jared's progress but hadn't come to see him since New Year's Day. What was going on back there in Chicago? Surely Dr. Evan Finley couldn't be that busy.

Cora was grateful for Evan's good insurance, knowing it would cover most of Jared's hospital bills. She certainly could not have paid them on her own, even with the sale of her house. The money, when she got it, would be used to buy a home here in Arthur. If any was left, it would go into the bank for Jared's future schooling.

This morning, Cora had awakened early and tiptoed into Jared's room to check on him. The sun was up and reflected on the far wall of his room. She was glad he was still asleep, because he needed to rest as much as possible right now. She closed the curtains before leaving his room. Maybe later they'd put on their coats and sit outside for some fresh air. A little sun therapy couldn't hurt.

Cora had taken some time off work, since Jared wasn't strong enough to return to school yet. She certainly wouldn't leave him at home alone. The clinic hired a temporary nurse to take Cora's place but assured Cora that her job would be there when she returned.

After taking a seat at the kitchen table, Cora reflected on her last visit with Adam. He'd gone to the hospital to visit Jared again, and after Jared fell asleep, he and Cora went to the waiting room to talk. Adam had said she was welcome to come by his house to meet her granddaughters whenever she felt ready. However, he suggested they not tell the girls any details about Cora abandoning her husband and children. He felt they were too young to hear it right now. Adam thought it would be best to simply introduce Cora as their grandmother and say she used to be Amish. When the children were older, if they raised any questions, he'd explain whatever details he thought were necessary. Cora looked forward to getting to know her granddaughters. Their first meeting wouldn't happen, though, until Jared was stronger.

When the telephone rang, Cora dashed across the room to answer it before Jared woke up.

"Hello."

"Hey, Cora, it's me."

"I'm glad you called, Evan. Did you get my message saying I'd brought Jared home from the hospital?"

"Yeah, that's great news."

Cora waited as Evan became silent. Was that all he had to say? Wasn't he going to ask how Jared was doing?

"Listen, Cora, there's something we need to discuss. Can I come down there this weekend so we can talk?"

"About what?"

"I'd rather not discuss this over the phone. It's better to do it in person." Once more, Evan paused. "Oh, and I want to see my boy. I'm glad he's well enough to be home."

Shifting the receiver to her other ear, Cora said, "What day were you thinking?"

"How about Sunday? Will that work?"

"I suppose, but if Jared's feeling up to it, we'll go to church in the morning."

"Since when did you start going to church?"

"Since I made things right with God."

"Humph! Interesting."

"What do you mean?"

"Nothing. Forget it, Cora." Evan cleared his throat. "What time on Sunday should I arrive?"

"Would one o'clock work for you?"

"I guess so. See you then. Oh, and tell Jared I'm looking forward to seeing him." Evan hung up before Cora could respond.

I wonder what Evan wants to talk about. She moved back to the kitchen. *He seemed insistent on coming here. I hope he won't start any trouble.*

❧

Leah's stomach gave a lurch as she stood at the stove making scrambled eggs for breakfast. The smell of eggs cooking had never made her nauseous before. *Could I be coming down with the flu? I hope not*, she fretted. *I have too many responsibilities to be sick right now.*

In addition to taking care of Carrie, while Linda and Amy were in school, Leah had scheduled two people for reflexology treatments today. One was her friend Elaine, who'd be coming by this afternoon. And their bishop's wife, Margaret Kauffman, had an appointment at ten o'clock this morning. Leah didn't want to disappoint either woman and hoped by the time they got here she'd feel better.

"Guder mariye." Adam stepped up to Leah. "I see you're making scrambled eggs for breakfast."

She nodded, and another wave of nauseous coursed through her stomach.

"Are you okay?" he asked with a look of concern. "You look kind of pale this morning."

"Just feeling a little queasy is all. I hope I'm not coming down with the flu."

Adam touched her forehead. "You don't seem to be running a fever. Do you feel achy or chilled?"

She shook her head. "Just nauseous."

He tipped her chin so she was looking into his eyes. "Are you *im familye umschtende*, Leah?"

Leah blinked rapidly as his question sank in. "I suppose I could be expecting a *boppli*." Her monthly was often off, so until now, she hadn't given it much thought. *Now wouldn't that be something?*

A wide smile stretched across Adam's face, and he slipped his arms around her waist. "If you are carrying our child, it would be *wunderbaar*, Leah."

"Jah, it surely would." Leah smiled, glancing at the calendar on the wall. She had missed her monthly in December and hadn't had it this month, either. Perhaps the nausea she felt was actually morning sickness. "I'll make an appointment to see the doctor. Then we'll know for sure."

❧

"I'm nervous," David said from the passenger's seat in Priscilla's buggy.

"About what?"

"When I talked to your bishop the first time, he gave me a lot to think about. I hope he believes I truly want to become Amish. Last time, he may have thought it was just a passing fancy." David pulled his fingers through the sides of his hair.

"You didn't seem nervous when we went there."

"That's because I didn't have much time to think about it. Now I've had two full weeks to ponder everything he told me."

Priscilla let go of the reins with one hand and reached over to touch David's arm.

"Are you having second thoughts about joining the Amish church?"

He shook his head. "No second thoughts. I'm just not sure I can do everything expected of me."

"Anything specific?"

"Learning the language, for one thing. Then there's the matter of driving a horse." David sighed. "I know you said you would teach me, but I've never been good with horses. Truthfully, they make me naerfich."

Priscilla smiled. "That's one Pennsylvania Dutch word you've learned well." She sobered. "All kidding aside, if becoming Amish is something you really want to do, then everything will fall into place—including learning to handle a horse and buggy."

His face seemed to relax. "You're a good friend. I appreciate your support, because I'm sure not getting any from my folks these days. When I told them what I was planning to do, Mom started to cry and Dad called me crazy."

"I'm sorry, David. I was hoping they would understand."

"Yeah, me, too." David folded his arms. "Do you have any idea what the bishop might want to talk to me about today?"

"When you spoke to him two weeks ago and expressed your interest in becoming Amish, he didn't go into much detail about everything you'd need to do. So he will probably give you more information during your meeting with him today."

"Yeah. Last time he mostly talked about Amish values and said I should take some time to think more about my decision before deciding if becoming Amish is what I truly want to do." David's lips compressed. "I just hope he won't give me the third degree."

Priscilla snickered. "I doubt that very much."

"Since I've visited this area several times I already know some things about the Amish life. But I guess there are still plenty of things I don't know. Can you enlightened me any?"

"Is there something specific you're curious about?" she questioned.

David gave a slow nod. "Jah—that's how you say yes, am I right?"

She nodded. "What are you curious about, David?"

"I'm curious about you."

Priscilla's face felt like it was on fire. "Wh–why would you be curious about me?"

He touched her arm. "I want to know everything about you."

"We're not here to talk about me," she admonished. "We're heading to see the bishop, to talk about you and your desire to join the Amish church."

"Oh, that's right; I almost forgot." David's eyes twinkled as he grinned at Priscilla. "Seriously, though, I do need to know as much in advance as I can before I speak to your bishop again."

"Okay then, here are a couple of tips." Priscilla held up one finger. "Before deciding to join the Amish church, you need to learn as much as possible about our religion, history, and lifestyle."

"Great! Please fill me in."

"Well, I can't begin to tell you everything in one day, but to begin with, you might be interested in knowing that the Amish communities of today are descendants of Swiss Anabaptists. They came to America in the early 1700s, and the largest Amish community is in Holmes County, Ohio."

"Are there Amish in every state?" David asked.

Priscilla shook her head. "Some states, like Washington and Oregon, had an Amish settlement for a while, but unfortunately, they didn't last long."

"That's a bummer. I wonder how come they didn't make it."

"I'm not sure, but it's not easy for new communities to start out—especially in areas where there aren't other Amish. Even so, it's my understanding that there are Amish living in twenty-eight states and also some in Canada." Priscilla smiled. "There's even a small community in Sarasota, Florida, where some Amish and Mennonites vacation or spend their winters."

David's eyes widened. "Wow! Guess the Amish must enjoy going to the beach as much as I do." He stretched his arms out in front of him then locked his fingers and placed his hands behind his head. "I can see there's a lot for me to learn. Think I'll go online and search for more information about the Amish way of life."

"You could do that all right, but some of it might not be accurate," Priscilla said. "Really, the best way to learn is for you to become part of the Amish community."

"Guess that makes sense. Think I'll do that as soon as I get back to Gram and Gramp's house."

Priscilla didn't say much, but she wondered why David preferred to learn about the Amish through the Internet, when he had the real thing right here in front of him.

As they continued down the road, Priscilla enjoyed her time with David. He was easygoing and fun to be with and seemed to like their ride as much as she did.

It was the end of January, and still quite cold, although today she could feel the sun's warmth. Snow still lay in the shadowy areas, but it had melted in places where the sun hit regularly. Only a few more months of winter remained, but on days like today, Priscilla was anxious for spring.

"What are you thinking about right now?" David asked, breaking into Priscilla's musings.

"Oh, just enjoying the moment. After all the snow we've had, it's nice to see it melting in spots."

"Sort of makes ya hanker for spring, huh?"

She smiled. "I was just thinking the same thing."

David leaned back, putting his hands behind his head again. "Before I forget, I saw Elam the other day."

"Did he drop by your grandparents' house to see how you're doing?"

"No, I saw him at Adam Beachy's hardware store. He was there getting some things his father needed."

"Did he tell you he's working a second job?"

"Jah." David winked at Priscilla. "See, I can say that word pretty good, too."

"Yes, you can." Priscilla never could tell whether David's winks were flirtatious or just his way of showing his humor. Whatever it was, she always felt embarrassed when he winked at her.

"Since Elam's working two jobs, I'll bet you don't get to see him much anymore."

"You're right. I don't."

David looked at her curiously. "Are you okay with it?"

She shrugged. "If Elam's thinks he needs more money, there's not much I can do about it. I do miss seeing him, though."

"Maybe he's saving up enough money to buy you a house."

"I doubt it. Elam hasn't even asked me to marry him yet."

"You think he will?" David prompted.

"I don't know. I'm beginning to think maybe not."

"He's a *dummkopp*. If I had a girlfriend as sweet and pretty as you, I'd have proposed to her by now. If I were Elam, I'd be worried someone might come along and snatch his girlfriend from him."

Priscilla's face heated. She wasn't used to such compliments. Even though she and Elam had been courting quite awhile, he'd never told her she was pretty—at least not so directly.

"Here we are." Priscilla guided her horse and buggy up the lane leading to the Kauffmans' house. "Would you like me to go in with you, or would you rather speak to the bishop alone?"

David took Priscilla's hand, giving her fingers a gentle squeeze. "I'd be more comfortable if you came with me."

"I'd be happy to." Priscilla hoped things would work out for David to become Amish. It would mean he'd stay in Arthur and they could spend more time together. Of course, if she and Elam ever got married, she'd have to stop seeing David by herself. It wouldn't look right for a married woman to hang around an unmarried man—especially one as good-looking as David.

CHAPTER 25

When Adam took a seat on a backless wooden bench inside Jonah Miller's buggy shop Sunday morning, he felt grateful. Not only had he reestablished a relationship with his mother and begun building one with Jared, but they'd learned this week Leah was definitely pregnant. The baby would be born in late August or early September.

They hadn't told anyone yet—not even the girls. Leah wanted to wait until she was a little further along in her pregnancy. Adam had agreed but was bursting at the seams, eager to share their exciting news. Because of the bitterness he'd harbored for so many years toward his mother, Adam had determined never to marry and have children. His life had changed when he'd agreed to raise his nieces and married Leah. Since he was raising three girls, he'd had a little practice at being a father, so having a child of his own should come naturally.

Shifting his thoughts, Adam remembered his mother would be coming by next week to meet the girls. *Sure hope the visit goes well.* He repositioned himself on the unyielding bench. It had taken awhile, but Adam had finally come to realize accusations and blame did nothing to change what had happened. Blaming his mother for everything that had gone wrong in his own life had made Adam bitter and caused him to pull away from others.

At one time, he'd thought shutting himself off from others would keep him from getting hurt again. But that was running from his past and brought Adam no peace. Every day, he thanked God for bringing Leah and the girls into his life. The love he felt for them and his recommitment to God had softened Adam's heart. When Jared's accident happened, Adam had finally let go of the past and truly forgiven his mother.

He smiled as the congregation sang another song from their hymnal, the *Ausbund. I wonder what my mother will say when she learns Leah is expecting a baby—another grandson or granddaughter for her.*

David glanced at Elam, sitting beside him on a wooden bench with no back. Unlike himself, Elam had joined the others in song, but then Elam was familiar with this type of worship and understood everything that was going on. It was frustrating not to be able to read the strange words on the page of the Amish hymnal. And every song they sang seemed to be longer than the one before. David hoped after a time he would feel more a part of things, but right now he felt like a bird with no tree to land in.

As the service progressed and the first message was preached, David's eyelids grew heavy. The preacher spoke in German, which of course, David didn't understand, either. He wished now he'd taken German instead of Spanish in school. But then, how was he to know he was going to need the language of the Amish someday?

To complicate things, the Amish spoke another dialect when they conversed with each other. They referred to it as "German Dutch" or "Pennsylvania Dutch." The higher form of German was only used during their church services, weddings, and funerals.

David hadn't attended a wedding or funeral yet, but Priscilla had tried to explain what they were like. He'd determined they weren't too different from Sunday services, except weddings included a bit more, with the formal vows and messages about marriage. From what Priscilla had said, funerals were different, too, because the casket with the body of the deceased was present. During a funeral service, the message would be geared toward the topic of death, whereas a sermon during a regular preaching service could be based on any passage from the Bible. While David found the Amish way of life quite fascinating, it still seemed a bit foreign to him. There were times, like today, when he wondered if he really should take the necessary classes to join the Amish church. Other days, when he was with Priscilla, David felt confident he could handle almost anything—including a horse and buggy—with ease.

He reached around to rub a tender spot on his back, wondering how much longer until the service ended. It was hard to get comfortable on the rigid bench with no back support. But he did his best to deal with it. In addition to the discomfort in David's back, the leg he had broken started to throb. Even though the break had healed and his cast was off, sitting in the second row gave him little room to stretch out his leg. Hoping no one would notice, David wiggled his ankle around, to get the circulation moving. It helped some, but it wasn't enough. He was anxious for the service to end so he could go outside where he could walk around and stretch his legs.

When another minister stood to deliver a second message, David closed his eyes, succumbing to sleep. He was awakened by a sharp jab to the ribs, and grimaced when he saw Elam glaring at him.

Elam couldn't believe David had dozed off here in church. *If this guy can't even stay awake during one of our preaching services, how's he ever gonna join the Amish church and become one of us?*

Glancing around the room, Elam noticed Ray Mast, a widower in his nineties, was sleeping, too. Ray had been a farmer for as long as Elam remembered. In fact, Ray still helped his sons farm their land, so it was a little more understandable why he might be snoozing. *Sure hope if I reach Ray's ripe old age, I'll be as active as him.*

Elam glanced back at David. *Maybe I should have let him keep sleeping. He might have started snoring and embarrassed himself. I wonder what Priscilla would have thought.*

Elam stole a peek at the women's side of the room and caught Priscilla looking his way. Had she seen what happened with David just now? Did she, too, think David wasn't cut out to be Amish? *I liked him better when he was just our English friend who came to visit his grandparents once in a while. Having him here, hanging around Priscilla so much, is irritating. Sure hope he doesn't have any idea about taking my girlfriend from me. I won't stand for that!*

Elam was eager to spend time after church with Priscilla today. He hoped David wouldn't expect to be included in their afternoon plans.

Cora had finished clearing the table from the meal she and Jared had shared after church, when she heard a car pull in. *It must be Evan.*

Jared had gone to his room to rest, so Cora wiped her hands on a dish towel and went to answer the door. When she opened it, Evan greeted her with a smile—one of those phony-looking ones she'd seen him use whenever he wanted something.

"Come in." She gestured to the living room, her guard already up. "Make yourself comfortable while I fix some coffee."

"Don't bother. I drank plenty on my way here, so I've had more than enough caffeine today."

"Would you like something else to drink?"

"Maybe some water with lots of ice."

"Okay. I'll be right back." Cora went to the kitchen. She hoped Jared would remain in his room, at least until Evan had told her what he'd come here to talk about.

When Cora entered the living room, she found Evan standing with his back to the fireplace, surveying the room. "This place is sure small," he muttered. "A far cry from our home in Chicago."

"It's sufficient for our needs at the present time. Actually, I find it to be rather cozy." She shifted her weight. "And speaking of the home we used to share, I finally have a buyer for it."

"Is that so? Mind telling me how much you'll be getting for it?"

Cora bristled. Why did he need to know that? Part of the divorce agreement was that she would get the house, free and clear. It was none of Evan's business how much it sold for, and she wasn't about to give him those figures. "I'll just say I got enough money to buy another place when I find it and still have some left over to put in Jared's college fund."

Evan took a seat on the couch. "Speaking of our son, I want Jared to come live with me and Emily."

Every muscle in Cora's body tightened. "What brought that request on all of a sudden?"

"You obviously can't control what our son does, or he wouldn't have been off joyriding with a troubled kid like Chad. Those boys should not have even been out on New Year's Eve!"

Cora bit her lip to keep from shouting at him. "For your information, Evan, I did not know Jared would end up riding in Chad's car. I thought he was spending the night with his friend, Scott, who is a nice kid. That's what Jared told me he was doing, and I took his word on it."

"Maybe you should hold a tighter rein on the boy and check things out before you let him go running off with any of his friends." Evan paused, leaning forward with his elbows on his knees. "Emily and I have talked it over. We want Jared to come live with us."

Cora's mouth dropped open, but before she could say a word, Jared burst into the room.

"I won't go back to Chicago, Dad! I belong here with Mom and my brother, Adam. Mom's right, too. I lied when I said I was gonna be with Scott, 'cause I knew she'd never let me go anywhere with Chad."

Cora whirled around, surprised not only because Jared had overhead their conversation but also because he really didn't want to move back to Chicago. There was a day when all Jared talked about was going back so he could be closer to his dad. It did her heart good to hear her son admit he'd lied to her, too. It took a lot for a person to acknowledge when they'd done something wrong and not try to justify their actions. She couldn't feel any prouder of her son.

"Your brother?" Evan scoffed, pointing a finger at Jared. "You mean you'd rather hang around an Amish man who's twice your age and whom you barely know, than live with your father?"

Jared nodded. "At least Adam came to visit regularly when I was in the hospital. How come you only came to see me once, Dad?"

Before Evan could respond, Jared continued with his tirade. "You think I've forgotten all about Thanksgiving, when you had no time for me? No, instead of spendin' time with your son, you wanted to be with your friends and couldn't have cared less if I was there or not." He paused long enough to take a deep breath. "I couldn't stay in Chicago another day. That's why I asked you to bring me back to Arthur earlier than planned."

Evan's face colored. "I've been busy with my practice, or I'd have been back to see you sooner. And whether you know it or not, I did call the hospital several times to find out how you were doing." His eyes narrowed. "As far as Thanksgiving goes, you acted in a selfish and immature manner that day. I only took you home because you insisted, and I didn't want you to make a scene in front of my friends."

Cora was tempted to say how a visit from Jared's dad during his hospital stay would have meant a lot more than a phone call he knew nothing about, but she held her tongue. There was no point putting

Evan on the defensive even more. Besides, Jared was starting to figure things out for himself.

Jared moved closer to Cora but kept his focus on Evan. "If you make me move back to Chicago, I'll run away like Chad did. He was so desperate to get away from his stepdad that he chose to sleep in one of our neighbor's barns after Mom said he couldn't stay here."

Cora gulped. So that's where the boy had been hiding out between Christmas and New Year's. She couldn't help wondering whether he might be alive today if she'd allowed Chad to stay with them. *I can't carry the blame for this*, she told herself. *Jared's friend should have gone home, like I told him to.*

"I'd never be happy livin' with you and Emily, Dad," Jared continued. "I'd come right back here to be with Mom. She needs me, Dad, and I need her."

Evan grabbed his glass of water and took a drink. "Okay, okay, Jared. I won't force you to leave here, but I want you to think more about my offer. If you change your mind, give me a call, and I'll come get you. And don't forget, you're welcome to visit any time you want."

"Yeah, all right, Dad." Jared flopped into a chair and put his feet on the footstool.

Cora breathed a sigh of relief. She had no objections to Jared visiting his father, but she didn't know what she would have done if Jared had wanted to move back to Chicago. It seemed in only a matter of weeks her son had grown up. If anything good had come from his accident, it was the relationship she'd established with both of her sons. She looked forward to meeting her granddaughters next week, too, and if all went well, she would schedule a meeting between Jared and the girls.

CHAPTER 26

Before noon on Friday, Priscilla went by horse and buggy to pick up Elaine. They'd been invited to have lunch at Leah's house. It had been awhile since the three of them had gotten together, so Priscilla looked forward to the occasion.

"Seems we may see more snow before the day is out," Elaine commented after she climbed into Priscilla's buggy.

Priscilla nodded. "I was getting used to seeing the bare ground in spots where the snow had been melting. It's nice seeing some grass after all this time, even though it's brown."

Elaine sighed. "Hopefully the snow will hold off till we get back home later this afternoon."

"I hope so, too. It's a little scary being out with the horse and buggy when the snow's coming down." Priscilla frowned. "Makes it hard to see out the front window, and my hand-operated windshield wiper can't keep up with it."

"When the roads are bad, I don't like being out with the horse and buggy, either." Elaine looked over at Priscilla and smiled. "Is there anything new going on with you lately?"

"Not really—just keeping busy tutoring David so he can learn our language, and of course helping Mom around the house. David wants me to teach him how to drive the horse and buggy, but it would be safer to wait till the roads are clear of snow before I take him out."

"I'm surprised he didn't ask Elam to teach him. They're good friends, too, aren't they?"

"Jah, but maybe he feels more comfortable with me. Elam can be impatient sometimes. Plus, he's working two jobs now, so he wouldn't have time."

Elaine pulled her woolen shawl up around her neck. "So David still wants to become Amish?"

"That's right. He seems quite determined, in fact." Priscilla held the reins steady, giving her horse the freedom to move at his own pace, but in readiness to take control should he decide to go fast. "Of course, Elam doesn't believe David will make it." She sighed in exasperation. "Some of the things Elam has said sound as if he's hoping David will fail."

"Why would he hope that?"

Priscilla shrugged.

"Could Elam be jealous?"

"What does he have to be jealous about?"

Elaine gave Priscilla's arm a light tap. "David's attention toward you. It doesn't take a genius to see he's smitten with you."

"Oh, no, he's not—"

"Surely you've noticed the way David looks at you. Ben even mentioned it to me the other day. I'm sure there are others, including Elam, who've seen it, as well."

Priscilla's brows furrowed. "You and Ben have been discussing this?"

"Well, Ben brought it up after our last church service."

"What exactly did he say?"

"He could tell after talking to David awhile, as well as watching his expression whenever you're around, that he's interested in you."

Here we go again, Priscilla thought. "David and I are just good friends." *How many times have I said that recently?* Priscilla concentrated on the road while listening to everything Elaine said.

"While that may be true, it seems as if David might want your friendship to be more."

"David knows Elam is courting me." Priscilla couldn't accept what her friend was saying. She was certain David had no thoughts of horning in on her relationship with Elam.

"Some men become bold if they love a woman."

Priscilla's fingers tightened on the reins. If she were being honest, she'd have to admit she had wondered a few times if David might see her as more than a friend. Truth was, with Elam dragging his feet on a proposal, she'd found herself thinking a lot about David—even wondering if what she felt for him was more than friendship. She'd dismissed the idea, however. It was just a silly notion because she'd been courted so long without even a hint of marriage from Elam.

"Is the dinner you're planning to host on Valentine's Day still going to happen?" Priscilla asked, feeling the need for a change of subject.

Elaine nodded. "Are you still available to help out?"

"Of course. You certainly can't do it alone."

"I thought you might have plans to spend Valentine's Day with Elam." Elaine paused. "Or even David."

"No plans have been made with anyone. Even if Elam had asked, I would have told him I'd be helping you on the fourteenth. If he wants to do something, maybe we can get together the evening after Valentine's Day." Priscilla chose not to comment on what David might be planning for that day. Since he knew she and Elam were courting, surely he wouldn't expect to spend Valentine's Day with her.

"What about you and Ben?" Priscilla glanced at Elaine. "Has he asked you to do anything with him that day?"

Elaine shook her head. "But then I'd already mentioned my plans to host a dinner, and Ben seemed to understand."

"I like Ben. He's so easygoing. Will you give him an answer to his proposal soon?"

Elaine nodded. "By the way, did I mention the dinner on Valentine's Day will be another family group?"

"I don't believe you did."

"The parents of this group have four grown daughters. Each of them got married on Valentine's Day, but in different years. When the mother called to make the reservation, she explained how she and her husband were also married on Valentine's Day. That's why their daughters chose the same date for their weddings. So this is going to be a big anniversary dinner for all of them."

"Sounds nice." Priscilla tried to sound enthusiastic. She was reminded once again how she was the only sibling in her family not married yet. Of course, her four brothers were older than she. Even though they never teased her about it, she was sure they all wondered why Elam hadn't popped the question to their little sister yet.

They rode in silence until Priscilla guided the horse and buggy into Adam and Leah's yard. A short time later, they sat at Leah's table eating chicken noodle soup, with homemade wheat bread and the strawberry jam Priscilla had brought along.

Little Carrie sat beside Leah, chattering away and giggling when some of the jam stuck to her nose.

Priscilla noticed how patient Leah was with the child. And the look of adoration on Carrie's face said it all—she loved Leah beyond measure.

When they finished their meal, Carrie went to the living room to play, while Priscilla and Elaine helped Leah wash and dry the dishes.

"I have some news I want to share," Leah said once the dishes were done.

"Is it good news or bad?" Priscilla asked.

"Adam and I think it's good news." Leah placed her hand on her stomach and smiled. "I'm expecting a boppli."

"Oh my! This is wunderbaar! I'm so happy for you." Elaine hugged Leah and was quickly joined by Priscilla.

"When is the baby due?" Priscilla questioned.

"Late August or early September." Leah glanced toward the door leading to the living room. "The girls don't know yet. Adam and I decided to wait a bit longer to tell them, but it'll probably be soon."

Elaine smiled. "I'm sure they'll be excited about it."

"I hope so." Leah went on to say that Adam's mother was coming over to meet her granddaughters that evening. "I'm hoping it goes well."

"It'll be fine. Don't worry." Elaine gave Leah another hug. "Does Cora know you're expecting a baby?"

Leah shook her head. "Not yet, but my guess is she'll be pleased to have another grandchild."

As Priscilla listened to Leah talk more about the baby and the future of her little family, she struggled with feelings of envy. It was wrong to be envious of her friend, but oh, how she wanted to get married and have a family of her own. At the rate things were going, it was doubtful she'd get married any time soon.

Cora's heart pounded as she drove to Leah and Adam's place. She was finally going to meet her granddaughters, but she had no idea what to say. Would they accept her as their grandmother? Would they be too shy to talk to her? She was, after all, a stranger to them.

Cora's thoughts took her back to the day Leah had brought Carrie into the clinic with bee stings. The child had responded well to Cora then. And when Cora spoke to the two older girls near the schoolhouse several weeks ago, neither of them had seemed standoffish.

"Maybe I'm worried for nothing." Cora rolled down her window and breathed in the fresh air, which helped her relax and think more clearly. *Lord, please give me the right words when I talk to the girls.*

A short time later, Cora pulled her vehicle into Adam's yard. When she stepped out and approached the house, her palms grew sweaty, and her feet felt like lead. Just when she'd thought she was beginning to relax, her nerves had taken over again.

Breathe deeply, she told herself as she knocked on the door. *Breathe deeply and think only positive thoughts.*

Leah answered the door and gave Cora a hug, inviting her into the living room. "Relax. It'll be fine," she whispered, as if reading Cora's mind.

When she entered the room, three beautiful little girls sat on the couch, looking curiously at her. Adam had been sitting in his recliner, but he rose to his feet as soon as he saw her. "We're glad you're here. I've told the girls about you, and they've been waiting for your arrival." He motioned to the children. "Cora, this is Carrie, Linda, and Amy."

Cora moved slowly toward the couch, resisting the urge to grab each of the girls in a hug. She didn't want to frighten them. "It's nice to meet all of you." She tried to wet her lips as her mouth went suddenly dry.

"Would you like something to drink?" Leah offered.

"Yes, please," was all Cora could get out. Her throat felt so tight she could barely swallow, let alone speak.

"I know you," Linda spoke up. "You talked to us near the schoolhouse, asking for eggs."

Cora nodded.

"Carrie, you met Cora once when we went to the clinic because you'd been stung so many times," Leah interjected before heading to the kitchen.

Carrie bobbed her head.

"Ich hot sie net gekennt." Cora was glad she'd found her voice again.

The girls' eyes widened.

"You speak our language?" Amy questioned, apparently quite

surprised that Cora had said in Pennsylvania Dutch, "I did not know her then."

Cora smiled. "I grew up in an Amish home." Cora hoped they wouldn't pursue this topic. How would they understand her reason for leaving? She wasn't proud of what she'd done back then. If the girls had any knowledge of how selfish she'd been, they'd want nothing to do with her.

Cora took a seat on the sofa between Carrie and Linda, sitting quietly as she relished this special feeling. *If only Mary could be here to see me sitting with her daughters.*

When Leah returned a short time later, she gave everyone a bowl of popcorn as well as a glass of apple cider.

While they enjoyed the treat, Cora questioned the girls about school and their favorite things to do. If she kept them busy talking about themselves, maybe they wouldn't ask her too many personal questions.

"If you're really our grandma, how come we never met you before?" Linda tipped her head, innocently looking at Cora.

"She lived in a different state than us," Adam responded. Cora was glad he'd spoken up.

The child seemed to accept his answer and continued to munch on popcorn.

"If you grew up in an Amish home, how come you're not wearin' Amish clothes?" Amy questioned.

Cora drew in a deep breath. This was a question she'd hoped she wouldn't be asked. But then why wouldn't one of the girls ask about the way she was dressed? Most women who spoke the native dialect of the Amish didn't wear burgundy-colored dress slacks and a matching blazer. "Well, I'm not Amish anymore." She hoped her simple answer would be good enough.

Seemingly satisfied, Amy looked at Leah and said, "Is there any more popcorn?"

Leah smiled and patted Amy's head. "Of course. I'll bring another batch out, and you can refill your bowl."

"Me, too." Carrie clapped her hands. "I love popcorn!"

Adam chuckled. "You're not the only one, Carrie. It's always been my favorite snack."

Cora swallowed hard as the memory of her little boy eating a bowl of popcorn flashed into her head. Whenever Adam's bowl emptied, he would snitch some of his sister's popcorn.

"Do you girls have any pets?" Cora asked.

"Just Coal, but he's really Uncle Adam's dog," Linda responded.

"He's everyone's dog," Adam said. "That mutt is a real people-person." He winked at Linda. "I mean people-dog."

Everyone laughed, including Cora. It was nice to see this humorous side of Adam. He seemed relaxed with the girls and would certainly make a good father if he and Leah ever had children of their own.

As the evening progressed, Cora completely relaxed. When she rose to go, she told the girls she would be back soon for another visit. "Next time I come, I'll bring my son Jared with me. He's your uncle, too."

CHAPTER 27

Cora's visit with the girls went well, don't you think?" Leah asked Adam after the children had gone to bed.

Adam nodded. "I was glad they didn't ask a lot of personal questions, like why Cora left the Amish faith. Eventually they might, and it won't be easy to explain."

Leah moved a bit closer to Adam on the couch and clasped his hand. "God will give you the right words if they do ask more questions."

"I hope so. I'm also hoping things go well when Cora—I mean, when my mother—brings Jared to meet the girls."

"It may seem strained at first, but after they get to know one another, everything will be fine."

"Life is full of changes, isn't it?" Gently, Adam stroked her fingers. "Some good, some not so good."

"You're right, and it's how we handle those changes that can make the difference in our attitudes and the example we set for others."

"I hope my mother gets home okay." Adam had been worried since it started snowing.

"I'm sure Cora will be fine. Remember, she lived in Chicago and had plenty of practice with winter weather, pretty much like ours," Leah assured him. "It's nice to know you're concerned about her."

"You're right on both counts." Adam reached over and placed his other hand on Leah's stomach. "How have you been feeling today? Any morning sickness?"

She shook her head. "Not today, thankfully. The herbal tea I've been drinking has actually helped."

"I'm glad." Adam knew it would be difficult for Leah to fulfill all her responsibilities if she kept feeling nauseous. If that turned out to be the case, he would have to hire someone to help out.

They sat in silence, until Leah squeezed his fingers and said, "Do you think we should tell the girls about the boppli soon, before I start showing?"

"Jah, I believe we should."

"Sure is nice to be with you tonight." Elam moved closer to Priscilla and took her hand. He'd been invited to her house for supper, and her parents had gone to bed a short time ago. Elam wondered if Iva and Daniel were tired, or if they had simply wanted to give him and Priscilla some time alone. Whatever the reason, he was glad for this opportunity to be with the woman he loved—especially since, thanks to him working two jobs, they didn't get to see each other as often as he liked.

Priscilla turned her head and smiled at him. It was such a sweet smile it took all Elam's determination not to blurt out a marriage proposal. "I'm enjoying this evening, too."

He stroked her hand with his thumb. "Valentine's Day is coming up soon. Should we eat supper at Yoder's Kitchen that evening? I can never get enough of their good food."

Tiny wrinkles formed across Priscilla's forehead. "I wish I could, Elam, but remember, I'll be helping Elaine host another dinner that night."

"Oh, that's right. Guess you did mention it." Elam was sorely disappointed.

"What about the day after Valentine's? Could we go out then?" Priscilla asked.

"Guess it would be okay." Elam would much rather go out on Valentine's Day, but he understood Priscilla had to keep her promise to help Elaine with the dinner. There might be fewer people going out the night after Valentine's Day, too.

Elam leaned closer and was about to kiss Priscilla, when he heard a car pull into the yard. Priscilla must have heard it, too, for she left her seat and went to the window to look out.

"If I'm not mistaken, that's David's grandfather's car," Priscilla said. "But it's hard to tell, since it's dark outside." She hurried to the front door.

A few minutes later, Priscilla returned to the living room. David was with her.

Oh, great, Elam groaned inwardly. The last thing he needed was David interrupting his evening with Priscilla. It seemed like this fellow had a knack for showing up at the wrong time.

"Look who dropped by with an apple pie." Priscilla's smile stretched across her face.

Wearing an eager expression, David bobbed his head. "Gram made it."

"How nice. Please tell Letty I said thank you." Priscilla took the pie. "I'll take this to the kitchen and cut us each a piece."

David nodded. "Sounds good to me."

When Priscilla left the room, David moved to the couch and took a seat beside Elam. "How's it going with your new job?"

"Fine. Between that and working for my dad, I'm keeping plenty busy." Elam gritted his teeth. Apparently David hadn't stopped by just to drop off the pie. He planned on staying. Elam wished now he'd taken Priscilla out to a restaurant for supper this evening instead of coming here.

"Gramps has been teaching me some things about woodworking. It won't be long before I can look for a job in that trade."

Elam grunted. "Bet that's something you never learned in college."

David chuckled. "You're right."

"So what else can you do?"

"Before starting college, I worked part-time at my dad's veterinary clinic. Haven't had a job since then, though. There was no need to, since my folks paid for my schooling and gave me spending money." David pulled on his chin, like Elam's dad did when he tugged on his full beard. "Oh, and I had a paper route when I was fifteen, but I didn't make much money doing that."

Elam resisted the urge to roll his eyes. He thought David was a spoiled Englisher whose parents gave him everything. Elam didn't see how David could ever fit into the Amish way of life. Especially since he could barely stay awake during church.

"I'll go see if Priscilla needs any help." Elam jumped up and hurried into the kitchen.

"How are we gonna get rid of David?" Elam whispered to Priscilla as she placed pie and coffee for the three of them on a serving tray.

Her mouth puckered. "David's our friend. Why would we want to get rid of him? I can't believe you even suggested it, Elam."

"This is supposed to be our night. I was hoping we could be alone."

"I wanted it, too, but it would be rude if we asked David to leave. We are the only real friends he has in this community."

Elam couldn't argue the point, but he wasn't sure how much he considered David a friend anymore. If David was really his friend, he wouldn't try to move in on his girl. *Of course*, Elam reasoned, *he may just be lonely and finds Priscilla's company fills that void. Could be he doesn't have a romantic interest in her at all.*

"Would you mind carrying this tray to the living room?" Priscilla asked. "While you're doing that, I'll make a batch of popcorn."

"Okay, sounds good." Elam preferred popcorn over apple pie anyway, and Priscilla knew that. If the pie David brought had been cherry or banana cream, it would have been different: those were two of his favorites.

When Elam returned to the living room, he set the tray on the coffee table.

"Where's Priscilla?" David asked.

"She's making popcorn." Elam sat on the couch beside David. He figured when Priscilla came in, she'd sit on the other side of him, and David wouldn't talk to her so much. Maybe after David ate his pie, he'd take the hint that Elam wanted to be alone with Priscilla and decide to go back to his grandparents' house.

"I've been wondering about something." Elam turned to face David.

David reached for a piece of pie and took a bite. "What about?"

"How come you only wear Amish clothes when you go to church and not for every day?" Elam gestured to David's blue jeans and plaid shirt.

"Since I'm not officially Amish yet, I didn't think it would matter that much." David smacked his lips. "This is sure good pie. You'd better eat yours soon or it might disappear."

"You can have my piece if you want." Elam glanced toward the kitchen, sniffing the air as a buttery aroma drifted into the living room. "Priscilla knows I prefer popcorn."

"I like popcorn, too, so maybe I'll have some of that as well."

Elam tapped his foot impatiently, wishing once again David would leave. At the rate things were going, the night would be over and he'd never get to give Priscilla a kiss.

David might be dumb about certain things pertaining to the Amish, but he wasn't stupid when it came to knowing someone didn't want him around. He'd been here less than an hour—long enough to eat two pieces of pie and a bowl of popcorn, but in all that time the only thing Elam said to him were questions that made him look foolish. Just now, Elam looked right at David and said, "How's it going with your language lessons?"

"So-so."

"Do you know what the word *hochmut* means?"

David had to admit he wasn't familiar with the word. Learning a new language was proving to be a challenge. "Sorry, but I don't."

"Hochmut means pride."

"Oh, I see."

"So how would you respond if someone who wasn't Amish said or did something to humiliate you?" Elam asked.

Like you're doing to me now? David squirmed on his end of the couch. *Is Elam trying to make me look foolish in front of Priscilla? If so, he's doing a good job.*

"Guess the first thing I'd do is ask them to stop," David said.

"What if they didn't?" Elam leaned closer to David. "What if they hit or pushed you? What would you do then?"

"I'd hit 'em right back."

Priscilla gasped. "Oh, David, that would be wrong. As I've told you before, we Amish are pacifists."

David's face heated. "Are you saying I should just stand there and let someone do me bodily harm?"

"It might be the best thing," Elam interjected. "The Bible says if someone hits us, we are to turn the other cheek."

This bit of knowledge didn't sit well with David. If he had to sit idly while someone gave him a punch, he wasn't sure he could ignore it and not retaliate. Maybe he needed to rethink his desire to join the Amish church. But if he didn't see it through, he'd be admitting defeat, and he'd never been a quitter—except for college, that is.

Looking at Elam, David forced a smile. "Guess I need to read my Bible a little more so I can learn how to react to any situation." He stood and stretched his arms over his head. "Think I'm gonna head back to Gram and Gramps' place now. It was starting to snow earlier, so before the roads get too bad, I'd better get going." David grabbed his jacket and headed for the door. "You two enjoy the rest of your evening."

"What about your grandma's pie?" Priscilla called.

"Keep the rest of it. The pan is disposable. You can share the pie with your folks."

"Thanks for dropping by with the pie. I'm sure my mom and dad will enjoy it, too. Oh, and I'll be over with the buggy tomorrow to start your driving lessons." Turning to Elam then, Priscilla said, "Unless you'd rather teach David to drive a buggy. He needs to learn soon so he can start using one instead of his grandparents' car."

Elam shook his head. "No, that's okay. You said you'd do it, so go right ahead. I don't have much free time anyway."

"I'll see you both later, then." David opened the door and stepped outside. Lifting his face toward the sky, he felt wet snowflakes moisten his skin. As he stood with his hands in his pockets, battling mixed emotions, the coldness seeped through his sneakers. *Guess I shoulda worn boots tonight.*

Before heading to the car, David glanced back at the house. Priscilla was a special friend. He couldn't help wishing she was his girlfriend instead of Elam's.

David's shoulders slumped. *My visit didn't go well this evening—at least not with Elam. Think he senses my interest in Priscilla, and it's why he made those catty remarks.*

As David tromped through the snow to his car, he made a new decision. Elam might be his friend, but he was not going to let him belittle him again—especially in front of Priscilla. The next time he went to see her, he'd make sure Elam wasn't there.

CHAPTER 28

"Are you nervous about meeting your nieces?" Cora asked as she and Jared approached Adam and Leah's house.

He shrugged. "Maybe a little. I really don't know what to say to kids younger than me, 'cause I've never been around many before. And since they're girls, we don't have a whole lot in common."

"I realize it, Jared, but you do have one thing in common."

"What?"

"You're their uncle Adam's younger brother."

"Yeah, but we both have different dads. How am I supposed to explain to the girls if they ask?"

"You don't need to worry about it right now. None of them questioned me about my husbands, so I doubt they'll ask you, either."

"But what if they do?"

"If they ask, then either Adam or I will try to explain." Cora could tell how apprehensive Jared was by the way he was fidgeting. She couldn't really blame him, though. She had felt the same way when she met her granddaughters for the first time. It pleased Cora that Jared wanted to come along this evening. She felt proud of him for so many reasons. He had grown up quite a bit since his accident. Even though Jared's injuries were something Cora wouldn't wish on anyone, she wondered if things such as his accident happened for a reason. She remembered reading in Romans 8:28: "And we know that all things work together for good to them that love God, to them who are the called according to his purpose." Right now, Cora felt very blessed.

Jared's recovery was going well. He was off the pain medication he'd taken at first, and he didn't spend so much time sleeping. Cora was glad he spent more time with her, no longer hiding out in his room the way he'd done when they first moved to Arthur. Seeing Jared go through all he'd faced after the accident had been hard, and she was grateful for the time off they'd given her at work. Even if the clinic hadn't held her position, she would have quit in order to be with Jared during his ordeal.

Cora let go of the steering wheel with one hand and reached over to give Jared's arm a reassuring squeeze. "Try not to worry about anything. Just relax and enjoy the evening."

"Yeah, okay."

She glanced briefly at the paper sack on the floor by his feet. Since tomorrow was Valentine's Day, she'd bought something for each of the girls. Cora didn't want to give them candy, so in addition to cards, she had purchased coloring books, crayons, and stickers. Hopefully they would like her gifts.

"Your grandmother is here," Leah announced, peeking out the living-room window after hearing a car pull in. She smiled at Carrie, Linda, and Amy sitting on the couch with expectant expressions. "Are you ready to meet your uncle Jared?"

All three girls nodded, but no one said a word. Normally when someone was coming to visit, the girls were little chatterboxes. Leah sensed their nervousness, but they'd done well meeting Cora last week, and she felt sure things would go fine this evening.

Adam rose from his recliner. "I'll get the door."

When Adam returned with Cora and Jared, Leah took their coats, and introductions were quickly made. After Jared took a seat in a chair near Adam's, Cora seated herself on the couch and gave the girls their gifts. Leah noticed that Jared appeared to be as jittery as the girls.

"These are for you." Cora smiled. "A little something for Valentine's Day."

The girls eagerly opened the gifts. "Danki," they said in unison.

"*Du bischt willkumm*," Cora responded.

Jared's eyebrows shot up. "What'd you just say to them, Mom?"

"They said 'thank you,' and I said, 'You are welcome.'"

"Is that German?" he questioned.

"It's German Dutch, or some people call it Pennsylvania Dutch," Adam interjected. "It's what we Amish speak on a daily basis. We also learn German, because it's the language spoken during our church services."

"Interesting." Jared looked at his mother. "I'd like to learn Pennsylvania Dutch. Can you teach me, Mom?"

Cora smiled. "I'd be happy to, son."

Leah was pleased with how well things were going. Jared seemed more relaxed now, and so did Carrie, Linda, and Amy. They were all smiles, looking at their coloring books and removing some of the stickers to put on the pages. With everyone sitting here, visiting in a relaxed manner, it seemed as if they were finally a real family. It was especially touching when Carrie climbed up beside Jared and gave him a hug.

"I'll go to the kitchen and get some refreshments." Leah smiled at her husband. "Would you mind helping me, Adam?"

"I'd be happy to." Adam followed Leah into the next room.

"How would you feel about telling Cora, Jared, and the girls we're expecting a boppli?" Leah asked, taking a chocolate-chip cheeseball from the refrigerator.

"You mean tell them now, when we are all together?"

"Jah. Now's a good time to do it, especially since Jared is here. It might help him feel included and an important part of our family."

Adam hesitated a minute but finally nodded. "Cora and Jared are part of the family now, so they have the right to know."

She smiled, reaching up to tweak the end of his nose. "That's what I think, too." Leah couldn't be happier, with Adam and his mother back in each other's lives. She had prayed for it many times and felt thankful those prayers had been answered.

When Leah and Adam returned to the living room with the refreshments, she suggested they all take a seat at the dining-room table.

Once everyone began eating their treat, Adam said he had an important announcement to make.

"What is it?" Amy asked, spreading a graham cracker with some of the chocolate-chip cheeseball.

Adam smiled at Leah, and her cheeks warmed. "My fraa is expecting a boppli."

Cora leaped to her feet and gave Leah a hug. "That's wunderbaar news!"

Jared sat, looking perplexed, as the three girls stared at Leah's stomach.

"Wait a minute." Jared held up his hand. "What are you guys talking about? I didn't understand some of the words you just said."

"Sorry, Jared." Adam moved around the table and placed his hands on Jared's shoulders. "What I first said is my wife is expecting a baby. Then your mother—our mother—said it was wonderful news."

Jared's face broke into a wide smile. "Does this mean I'm gonna be an uncle again?"

"Yes, it does." Cora placed her hand on Leah's arm. "I'm going to be blessed with another grandchild."

After Elaine finished doing the supper dishes, she decided to make a list of things she and Priscilla would need to do tomorrow afternoon, in readiness for the dinner they'd be hosting. How thankful she was for her friend's help. She couldn't imagine trying to do these meals alone, especially one as important as a Valentine's Day dinner.

Opening a drawer in the rolltop desk, Elaine took out a notebook, but she spotted something else. It was an old Valentine Jonah had given her when they were courting. Her hand trembled slightly as she picked up the card. The front of it read: "Happy Valentine's Day to Someone Special." Elaine had memorized the inside, from reading it so many times, especially right after Jonah had given it to her. Still, she opened the card and read the note aloud. "To the love of my life. I thank God for bringing us together. I'll love you always. Jonah."

A sob caught in Elaine's throat. How things had changed since then. She'd kept the Valentine, even though the possibility of her and Jonah being together was slim. It was hard to come to terms with the reality of it, but Elaine had accepted facts the best she could. Despite Jonah being a widower, the chance of them having a future together was unlikely. Jonah had made it perfectly clear when he'd said he would never marry again.

Hearing the whinny of a horse, Elaine put the Valentine down and dried her eyes. She didn't want whoever had come to ask questions about why she'd been crying.

Going to the door, she was pleased to see Ben getting out of his buggy. She hadn't known he was coming by and didn't think she'd see him until their next church service.

"I hope I haven't interrupted anything," Ben said, stepping onto the porch.

"No, not at all. I was just getting ready to make a list of things I need to do before tomorrow night's dinner."

"I remember you said you'd be doing the dinner, so I came by now to bring you this." Ben handed Elaine a package. "Happy Valentine's Day. I bought you a box of chocolates and a card."

"Danki, Ben. How thoughtful of you." Elaine opened the door wider. "Would you like to come in for coffee and pie? I did some baking today for tomorrow's dinner and I made two extra chocolate–peanut butter pies."

Ben smacked his lips. "Now when did I ever turn down a dessert?"

When they entered the kitchen, Ben hung his coat over the back of a chair, and Elaine set the pie and coffee on the table. As they ate, they talked about the weather, which seemed much colder.

"Makes me wonder if there's more snow on the horizon," Ben commented. "All these little snows we've been getting lately could be leading up to something big."

"I hope not." Elaine frowned. "It's only the second week of February, but I'm more than ready for spring. I was getting used to the snow melting awhile back."

"Me, too," Ben agreed. "It'll be nice when we can spend more time outdoors. After a while, being cooped up can get to a person. Know what I mean?"

"I certainly do." Elaine motioned to the coffeepot. "How about more coffee?"

"No, I'm good. I'm wondering, though, if you're ever going to open the card I brought you."

"Oh, of course." Elaine giggled self-consciously. As she tore open the pink envelope and started reading the card, she tried to hide her disappointment by forcing a smile. It was a cute card but not romantic like Jonah's card had been.

"The card is nice, Ben, and so is the box of candy. Danki for thinking of me."

"You're welcome."

Elaine hesitated, realizing she hadn't gotten Ben a card. *He must think I don't care about him.*

"This pie is sure good, Elaine." Ben smacked his lips.

"I'm glad you like it. Oh, and please forgive me for not getting you a Valentine's card. With my work here, I haven't gone out of the house all week."

"No problem. This pie is better than a card anyway. Being here with you makes it even more special."

Elaine's face heated, and as she finished the last of her pie, she noticed Ben looking over his shoulder. *What is he looking at?* she wondered.

"Did you get a Valentine's card from someone else?" Ben looked toward the rolltop desk.

It was then that Elaine realized he had seen Jonah's old card. She jumped out of her chair and picked up the card, fumbling for something to say. The look on Ben's face told Elaine that he had a clear view of the front of the card.

He leaned forward, squinting, as though for a better look. "Looks like one of those romantic cards."

Elaine noticed the tightening under Ben's eyes and knew she had better explain. "Before you arrived, I was getting ready to write some things down for tomorrow's dinner. When I opened the desk drawer to get out a tablet, I noticed the card—a card I had forgotten I still had."

"Oh, I see." Ben tilted his head to one side.

While several seconds passed between them, Elaine became unnerved. It was uncomfortable, watching Ben run his fingers through his hair as he stared at her. What else could she say? He was obviously a bit distressed.

"Mind if I ask who gave you the Valentine?"

"Jonah Miller, but it was before he married Sara."

"I noticed when I first got here, it looked as if you'd been crying. In fact, your eyes are still puffy." Ben leaned even closer and pointed to the card still in Elaine's hand. "Was it because of that?"

"Sort of." Elaine quickly put the card back inside the drawer. "It made me think of everything Jonah has gone through. Losing his wife hasn't been easy for Jonah—especially with two small children to care for. Furthermore, he had to get through the holidays, and so close to when Sara's accident happened." Elaine could tell Ben had some doubts. "You know me," she quickly added, hoping to make light of the situation. "I get emotional about things."

"Guess it makes sense." Ben got up and took his cup and plate to the sink. When he turned around and sat back down, she joined him at the table. They continued to visit, but the conversation was strained. When Ben said he'd better go so Elaine could do whatever she needed to do in preparation for her dinner, she felt relieved.

Elaine walked him to the door. "Danki for coming, and also for the candy and card."

"You're welcome." Ben leaned down and gave Elaine a kiss. "See you soon."

After Elaine returned to the kitchen, she paused, touching her lips. She couldn't help comparing the way she'd felt when Ben kissed her to how she used to feel when Jonah kissed her. *Why didn't I put Jonah's card away after I first looked at it? Did Ben's kisses always feel this way?* It was terrible, but Elaine couldn't remember any of Ben's kisses and how they made her feel afterward, yet she could still recall the fluttering of her heart whenever Jonah had kissed her in the past. She hated to compare things between Ben and Jonah, but not only were their kisses different, the Valentine's cards they'd given her had been nothing alike.

I need to stop thinking about Jonah, Elaine admonished herself. *I have no future with him.*

Jonah groaned as he entered the living room and flopped onto the couch. Things had been unusually busy in his buggy shop, and he'd had an equally busy evening, taking care of his children. Mom stayed with Mark and baby Martha during the day, but after she fixed supper for them, Jonah had insisted she go home and spend the evening with Dad. Jonah's folks had been supportive since Sara died, but Jonah didn't want to take advantage of them. They had a life, too, and it was Jonah's responsibility to take care of his children.

Martha and Mark were both asleep now, so it was Jonah's time to relax and unwind. Glancing at the calendar on the wall nearby, he realized tomorrow was Valentine's Day. His thoughts took him immediately to Sara and how happy she'd been when he'd given her a Valentine's card the previous year. Of course, she'd always been appreciative of everything he'd done, even something as small as a card.

Jonah wasn't the only one hurting, though. He thought about Mark, and how Sara's death had affected the dear little boy. Mark was only three—not old enough to understand the meaning of death. What the poor kid did realize was his mama wasn't around anymore. Mark's young mind couldn't comprehend why she had suddenly disappeared, and Jonah probably hadn't done a good job trying to explain it to him.

Right after Sara died, every morning when Mark would wake up, he'd cry for his mother. During the day, one or both of the little guy's grandparents played with Mark and kept him busy while Jonah was at work. In the evenings, when Jonah took over the children's care and put Mark to bed, he cried himself to sleep, asking for his mama. It tore at Jonah's heartstrings, but he hoped in time things would get better.

Thankfully, Mark's need for Sara was lessening, but tonight the little guy had another episode, sobbing for his mother. By the time he finally rocked his stepson to sleep, Jonah was exhausted.

Unbidden tears sprang to Jonah's eyes, and he blinked to keep them from falling onto his cheeks. Seeing the Bible on the coffee table, he opened it and read several passages. One in particular grabbed his attention: "We are troubled on every side, yet not distressed; we are perplexed, but not in despair," 2 Corinthians 4:8.

Closing the Bible, Jonah silently prayed, *Help me, Lord. Help me not to give in to despair. For my children's sake, please give me the strength to be a good daed.*

CHAPTER 29

"How were the roads on your way over here?" Elaine asked as she and Priscilla prepared for the Valentine's Day dinner they'd be hosting.

"Not too bad with my horse and buggy, but I noticed a few cars sliding on the road a bit. It's begun snowing again, too."

"Let's hope the weather doesn't get any worse, or our guests may end up canceling." Elaine gestured to the food cooking on the stove. "I don't know what I'd do with all this if the people don't show up."

"Maybe it's just a few flurries and won't amount to much." Priscilla tried to make her tone sound hopeful. Truth was, she had some concerns about the weather.

"I hope you're right. Sometimes, though, the lighter snows can be as treacherous as the deeper ones."

"Let's try not to worry about it." Priscilla gave Elaine's arm a gentle pat. "I'm sure everything will be fine."

Elaine smiled. "I appreciate your positive attitude."

"Not always, but I try to be. As my grandma Herschberger used to say: 'It's always best to look on the bright side of things.' Besides, there's no use worrying about something if it hasn't happened yet."

Elaine nodded. "Good advice."

Priscilla gestured to the card on the desk. "Looks like you received a Valentine's Day card. Bet I know who gave it to you."

"Ben dropped it by last night, along with a box of chocolates."

Priscilla smacked her lips. "Yum. Where are you hiding the candy?"

Elaine snickered. "I put it in the pantry so I wouldn't be tempted to eat all of it at once. Would you like a piece?"

"Maybe later. It'll be a nice treat to indulge in after our guests have gone home."

"You're right. Did Elam give you anything for Valentine's Day?" Elaine asked.

"Not yet. Elam is working at his folks' bulk food store today, but we do have plans to go out to dinner tomorrow evening, so maybe he'll give me something then."

"I wouldn't be surprised." Elaine moved closer to Priscilla. "I don't suppose he's said anything about marrying you yet."

"No, and I'm wondering if he ever will." Priscilla wished her friend hadn't brought the topic up. It was hard to keep a positive attitude whenever she thought about how long Elam had been courting her without a marriage proposal. What made it worse was when others asked about it. Now was definitely the time for a change of subject.

"How many people did you say will be here tonight?" Priscilla asked.

"Five couples. And since they are all celebrating their wedding anniversary, it's a very special occasion."

Another discussion about marriage. How am I ever going to stop thinking about Elam and the proposal I long for?

"Say, I've been wondering something," Iva said as she and her husband sat in the kitchen, eating an early supper of roast beef with potatoes and carrots. It was one of Daniel's favorite meals, and Iva enjoyed preparing it for him.

Before he took a bite, he set his fork down and gave Iva his full attention. "What have you been wondering about?"

"Some time ago you mentioned you might speak to Elam and ask what his intentions are toward our *dochder*. Just wondered if you did, and if so, what his response to it was."

Daniel shook his head. "After thinking it through a bit more, I decided not to say anything."

"Oh? Why not?"

"Thought Elam might not take kindly to me butting into his personal business."

"But if his business involves our daughter, then it's our business, too." Iva wondered if she ought to speak with Elam's mother about this.

"I don't want it to seem as if we are desperate to get our daughter married off. And we sure can't force Elam into something he's obviously not ready for yet."

Iva tapped her foot impatiently. "I see your point, but I really wish there was something we could do to speed things along. Makes me wonder if Elam is afraid of marriage."

"The best thing for us to do is to pray for Elam—that he will follow the Lord's leading. If they are meant to be married, it will happen in His time." Daniel shrugged. "Or maybe someone more suited to Priscilla will come along." He picked up his fork and started eating again.

Iva's forehead creased. She hoped the "someone" wasn't David. She'd seen the way he looked at Priscilla, and she couldn't help but worry, especially now that he planned to join the Amish faith, which meant he would most likely stay in the area. *Maybe I will speak to Elam's mamm. Virginia might have some influence on her son.*

By the time Elaine and Priscilla's guests arrived, the snow had gotten worse.

"The roads are treacherous," one woman said as they all took seats at the table. "But from the delicious aroma of the food you've cooked, it was worth coming out on a snowy night to celebrate all our anniversaries."

Everyone nodded affirmatively, and Priscilla and Elaine set out the food.

The dinner guests consisted of an older couple, Tracey and Steve Munroe, and their four daughters with their husbands. The Munroes had gotten married fifty years ago, and Priscilla suspected from their tender expressions as they looked at each other that they were still very much in love.

As Priscilla stood beside Elaine, making sure the celebration ran smoothly, she enjoyed listening to the older couple share memories of the years they'd been together. As they did so, their daughters listened attentively, while casting loving glances toward their husbands.

Priscilla thought it was sweet when some of the couples held hands. They were all obviously in love.

Mrs. Monroe had tears in her eyes as she smiled at Priscilla and

Elaine. "Early in our marriage, times were tough, but if I had to do it all over again, I wouldn't change a thing. God has given us a loving, caring family, and we certainly feel blessed."

Mr. Monroe nodded in agreement.

Priscilla turned her back, using her apron to dab at the tears threatening to fall. When she turned back around, she noticed some of the others using their napkins to wipe their eyes, too.

Mr. Munroe stood, clearing his throat, and added some humor, as well. It was funny, hearing him recount how things had been growing up in a house with all brothers. "Now I know how my mother felt about being the only woman in a houseful of men." But as he continued to speak, his eyes glistened with tears. "No man could be any happier than I, sharing a life with my special girls."

Everyone clapped and wished one another many more years of happiness.

As the family ate heartily, laughing and talking, each had a story to tell about how they'd met. Priscilla enjoyed listening, although it made her long all the more for a marriage proposal. It seemed each of the Monroes' daughters had chosen February fourteenth for her wedding day, with the hope of having the same special relationship her parents had. The youngest daughter was the last to share her story, and afterward, her husband stood up. Hugs and congratulations went around the room when he announced they were expecting their first child.

Priscilla sighed. Having a baby was another dream she hoped would come true someday.

They had just set the pies out for dessert, when someone knocked on the back door. Elaine went to answer it, while Priscilla poured coffee and tea.

When Elaine returned to the dining room, Priscilla was surprised to see David with her.

He grinned at Priscilla and handed her a gift bag. "I remembered you would be here helping Elaine tonight. So I came by to give you this. Happy Valentine's Day, Priscilla."

Her breath caught in her throat. She hadn't really expected a card from him, much less a gift.

Suddenly, the room became quiet; all eyes seemed to be on her and David. "That was very thoughtful of you, David," Priscilla whispered. Thinking it would be best not to open David's present in front of their dinner guests, Priscilla suggested she and David go to the kitchen.

"Would you please excuse us?" Priscilla glanced at each of the guests. Grins and nods were given her as the room became alive with conversation again.

"Go right ahead." Elaine stepped aside as David followed Priscilla out of the room.

"The roads are sure nasty tonight." David leaned on the kitchen counter as Priscilla set the gift bag on the table.

"Our dinner guests said the same thing. I'm surprised they didn't cancel." Her brows puckered. "For that matter, how come you ventured out in this weather?"

David grinned at her as he shook his head. "Aw, I'd never let a little bad weather keep me from bringing you a Valentine's Day gift."

Priscilla felt the heat of a blush. Pulling her gaze away from him, she opened the bag. In addition to a card, she found a package of stationery and a pretty pink pen with her name on it.

"Danki, David. This is very nice."

"Du bischt willkum. Did I say 'you're welcome' right?"

She nodded.

David gestured to the card. "Go ahead, open it."

Priscilla did as he asked, silently reading the card. *For Someone Special. I hope your Valentine's Day is filled with lots of good things, because you're someone very special to me. With Love, David.*

Oh my! Priscilla sucked in her breath. *Could others be right? Does David see me as more than a friend?*

"You're awfully quiet, Priscilla. Don't you like the card?"

"Uh. . ." She felt tongue-tied and wasn't sure how to respond. "It's a nice Valentine, David."

He stepped forward and kissed her cheek. "I'm glad you like it, because it's how I feel about you."

Priscilla sank into the nearest chair, holding the card to her chest.

"I hope I haven't overstepped my bounds." He sat beside her.

"As you know, Elam and I have been courting for some time."

David nodded. "Yes, and I'm not trying to come between you. It's just that—well, I feel complete when I'm with you, Priscilla. In fact, I think I might be falling in love with you." He paused, smiling at her. "I won't pressure you to make a decision, but if you have any feelings other than friendship for me, maybe you should rethink your relationship with Elam."

Priscilla sat quietly, mulling things over. She'd never expected such a bold proclamation. *Why didn't I see this coming? Did I do something to encourage him? David has been pretty attentive since he came to Arthur. What do I really feel for him?*

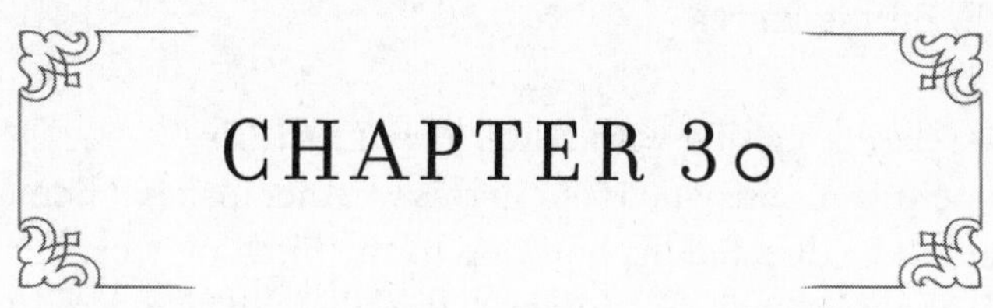

CHAPTER 30

Adam's brows furrowed, and Leah noticed the determined set of his jaw as he clenched the reins. They had taken the girls out for supper this evening to celebrate Valentine's Day, but now she worried whether they would make it home or not. The snow flurries that had begun earlier in the day had become thicker, and the harsh wind caused blizzard-like conditions. Huddled in the back of their buggy, the girls didn't seem to notice the hazardous conditions as they giggled and chattered away like magpies. Maybe it was good the children didn't realize how dangerous the driving conditions were. Leah didn't want them to worry about such things.

Leah remembered how when she was a child she hadn't worried about snow on the roads. She also recalled how much fun it had been to play in the snow.

Please, Lord, Leah prayed, *help us to get home safely.*

"Try not to worry," Adam said, as though sensing her fears. "My horse knows the way home even without me guiding him."

"But this wind, and the snow. . . It's so fierce all of a sudden." Leah lowered her voice so Amy, Linda, and Carrie couldn't hear, as she clung to the edge of her seat. "It's hard not to be concerned when our buggy is rocking to and fro. And what if the cars don't see us in time?"

"We're almost there." Adam spoke in a reassuring tone.

"How do you know? I can barely see the road."

"See how my horse is picking up speed? He always does when we get close to home."

Leah had to admit it was true. Her horse did the same thing.

A short time later, they were turning up the driveway leading to their home. It was dark outside, but Leah could see a ray of light coming from the battery-operated lantern Adam had turned on and placed in one of the barn windows before they left for supper. Coal stood barking from the porch, and his greeting was like music to Leah's ears.

Leah relaxed, sighing with relief. *Thank You, Lord.*

"I hope anyone else who is out in this weather makes it home safely," Adam said as he directed his horse up to the hitching rack.

Leah thought about Elaine and Priscilla and wondered whether the foul weather had kept people from coming to their dinner this evening. If they had come, she hoped everything at Elaine's house was going okay.

"Oh my, we'll never make it home in this weather!" Tracey Monroe, who had set up the dinner with Elaine, stood at the window, shaking her head. "I probably should have canceled this evening as soon as the snow started falling earlier today. I just had no idea it would get this bad. Why, I can't even see where our cars are parked anymore." Her voice was tight with worry. "I was hoping the snow wouldn't amount to much—especially since we were all looking forward to this family celebration."

"It's okay, sweetheart." Tracey's husband, Steve, slipped his arm around her waist. "None of us could have known the weather would get worse. We all wanted to be here as much as you did."

"I'd feel better if you didn't try to drive home tonight," Priscilla said. "It's too dangerous to be out on the roads."

Tracey turned to face her. "What other choice do we have?"

"You can spend the night here," Elaine spoke up. She looked at Priscilla and then David, standing nearby. "That goes for both of you, too."

"That's very generous of you," Tracey said. "But we couldn't put you out. Besides, I'm sure you don't have enough beds to accommodate all ten of us, plus the three of you."

"There are six bedrooms in this house, so each couple can have their own room. Priscilla and I will share my room, and David can sleep there." Elaine gestured to the couch in the living room. "Hopefully by morning, the weather will have improved. There's plenty of food here for breakfast, too."

"Guess we'd better start making some phone calls." Steve pulled out his cell phone, and several others did as well, including David.

"I'll let Gram and Gramps know," he told Priscilla. "Should I call your folks, too?"

"I'd appreciate it." Priscilla clutched the folds in her dress. "I hope one of them thinks to check for messages and, if they do, that they're able to find the phone shack in all of this snow."

Everything was done. The dishes had been washed, dried, and put away. All the bedrooms were clean and ready for the unexpected overnight guests who were here at Elaine's house this evening. All she needed to do yet was get out some blankets for David to use when he slept on the couch.

Everyone settled in the living room for a while, and Priscilla made a big bowl of popcorn to pass around. As they sat visiting, where it was warm and cozy, the snow continued to fall, and the wind whistled eerily as it whipped tree branches against the windowpanes outside.

Steve Munroe had everyone's attention as he recounted a winter from his boyhood. "I was one of nine brothers," he said, grinning. "Much like this blizzard, it took all of us helping my dad to get the cows into the barn before the subzero temperatures set in."

Elaine's eyes grew heavy as she listened to his story. She recalled her grandparents telling her of a time, many years ago, when they'd lived through such a snowstorm.

Suddenly, a loud crash outside broke the silence, causing everyone to jump. It was followed by the sound of glass breaking, as the wind grew louder.

Elaine gasped. "What was that?"

"Don't worry; we'll take a look." David jumped up, and he, as well as the other men, grabbed their coats and headed out the door.

"I hope there's no serious damage," one of the Munroe daughters said.

"I don't feel any cold air coming in, so hopefully no windows were broken," Elaine commented.

Several minutes passed, before David, Mr. Munroe, and his sons-in-law returned.

"One of the tree limbs broke off by the side of your house.

Unfortunately, it busted a basement window," David explained. "Until you can get the window replaced, if you have some wood in the basement, or something else we can cover the window with, it should help keep the cold air out."

Elaine tapped her chin. "I believe there might be some plywood in the basement by my grandpa's workbench. Could you use that?"

Steve nodded. "It should work out just fine."

Elaine was glad she wasn't alone here tonight. It was a comfort to be with all these good people during the frightening storm. Now all she had to do when the weather improved was to find someone who could replace the broken window downstairs.

"It's getting late, and I'm worried about Priscilla. With the wind and heavy snow that's falling, she could lose her way coming home." Iva nudged her husband's arm. "Do you think you could make your way to the phone shack to check for messages without getting lost? Maybe Priscilla's decided to spend the night at Elaine's."

Daniel rose from the couch. "I'll take a walking stick and my brightest flashlight to help guide the way. Guess I should have done what my folks did and strung a rope from the house to the phone shack. Dad did that, only it was from our home to the barn so he could find his way easily during a blizzard. The blinding snow can get a person turned around and confused as to where they are, even on their own property."

"Please be careful," Iva called after he had put on his coat and hat.

"I will. Don't worry."

When Daniel went out the door, Iva stood at the window with her nose pressed against the glass. Why, she didn't know, because she couldn't see a thing. Breathing on the window caused the glass to steam up. Even though Iva used her sleeve to wipe the moisture off, the snow came down so fast and heavy, it was impossible to make out what her husband was doing.

Finally, realizing the foolishness of it, Iva began to pace while silently praying. *Heavenly Father, please be with Priscilla right now, wherever she is, and help Daniel find his way to the phone shack.*

Several minutes passed before Iva heard the back door open and shut. She rushed to the utility room, calling, "Did you make it okay?"

"Jah." Daniel bobbed his head, brushing the snow off his shoulders. "It's definitely a blizzard we're having, though. I could hardly get the door of the phone shack open because of the strong wind."

"Were there any messages?"

"Just one, from Priscilla. You were right. She's going to spend the night at Elaine's."

Iva touched her chest. "I'm so relieved to hear that. It would have been foolish to try and come home tonight. I'm glad she called."

"Actually, it was David who made the call." Daniel brushed snow off his jacket and hung it on a wall peg near the door.

"David? Why would he be calling for Priscilla?" Iva didn't like the sound of this at all.

"He said he'd dropped by Elaine's this evening, and he, as well as Priscilla and Elaine's dinner guests would be staying at her house overnight."

Iva tapped her foot, while folding her arms. This piece of news didn't sit well with her, but she was glad to know Priscilla was safe.

"Do you think David is interested in our dochder?" Iva asked as she and Daniel moved back to the living room.

He tipped his head. "I know they're friends. Is that what you mean?"

Iva shook her head vigorously. "I'm afraid it's more. I believe David is interested in Priscilla romantically." She stopped talking when she noticed her husband looking across the room at the fireplace instead of at her. "Daniel, are you listening to me?"

"Jah, I heard what you said."

"Well, what do you have to say about my concerns?"

"I suppose David might see Priscilla as more than a friend."

"What are we going to do about this?" She clutched his arm.

He shrugged. "Don't see what we can do, Iva. If David is falling for our daughter, it's between him and her, don't ya think?"

"No, I don't! David is English, and—"

"He's planning to become Amish."

"Humph! He's only trying to change to the Amish way so he can take Priscilla from Elam."

Daniel grunted. "It's not likely anyone is capable of taking Priscilla from Elam. If she breaks up with him, it'll be by her own choosing."

"But David's a smooth talker," Iva argued. "Priscilla might not even be aware of what he's trying to do."

"Let's leave this in God's hands, like we talked about before. Priscilla will know what is right for her. And who knows, Iva—maybe our daughter is supposed to be with David, not Elam." Daniel reached for her hand. "Let's head for bed now, okay? I'm *mied*."

Iva nodded. She was tired, too, but doubted she'd get much sleep tonight. The sooner she talked to Elam's mother, the better, because there was one way to discourage David, and that was for Elam and Priscilla to get engaged.

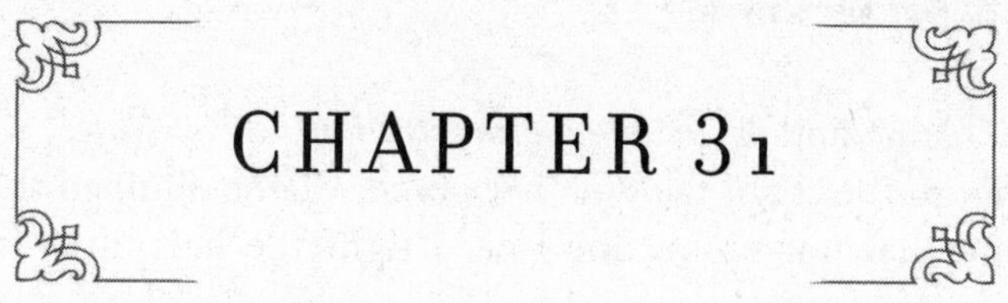

CHAPTER 31

Elaine didn't know where the time had gone, but here it was the middle of April. Snow had been replaced with rain, and they'd gotten plenty of it already. But rain was better than snow, even with all the mud it created. Her horse, Daisy, didn't like the puddles at all, though, and shied whenever they came to one in the road.

"It's okay, Daisy girl. There's nothing to fear." Elaine guided the horse around the puddle. "Let's go now; I'm anxious to get home."

As she continued her journey, Elaine thought about Leah, whom she'd seen at the health food store a short time ago. Leah's pregnancy was beginning to show, and all she could talk about was how she couldn't wait to have the baby. Leah said she'd been feeling well, with no more morning sickness. She still practiced reflexology and had gone to the health food store to buy massage lotion. Little Carrie, as cute as ever, had been with her.

Leah was fortunate to have three little girls to raise. In another four-and-a-half months, she'd have a sweet baby, too.

I wonder if I'll ever have any children, Elaine mused. *If I married Ben, by this time next year, I could be expecting a boppli.*

Dismissing those thoughts, Elaine concentrated on getting home.

When she pulled into the driveway a short time later, Daisy trotted so fast she nearly ran into the hitching rack.Elaine pulled back on the reins. "Whoa, girl. Not so fast!" Elaine's poor horse seemed as anxious to get out of the rain as she was.

Once Daisy stood calmly at the rack, Elaine climbed out of the buggy and unhitched the horse. Stepping around several mud puddles, she led Daisy to the barn, brushed her down and put her in her stall, then fed and watered the animal. After she'd taken care of her horse, Elaine headed to the house, anxious to get out of her wet clothes and fix lunch.

Stepping onto the porch, she fumbled in her purse for the house key but couldn't find it. *Now that's sure strange.*

Going to the small table on her porch, Elaine dumped the entire contents of her purse out. She'd been right the first time. It wasn't there.

Elaine groaned. "Oh no, what am I going to do now, and where is my *schlissel*?"

She stood several seconds, trying to recall. She remembered taking the key out of her purse when she was looking for her wallet at the health food store. *Could I have set it down on the counter and forgotten to put it back in my purse?*

Elaine shivered. Her dress stuck to her skin from the dampness, and the lightweight jacket she wore offered little protection from the rain. She wished she'd had the good sense to bring an umbrella when she'd left home this morning. The only thing Elaine could do was go to the phone shack and call the health food store. If her key was there, she would call her driver so she could pick it up, because she wasn't going to take Daisy back out in the rain.

Stepping off the porch, Elaine moaned as the wind picked up, causing the rain to blow sideways. The driveway was so saturated, it was impossible to dodge all the puddles and mud.

By the time she reached the phone shack, Elaine was thoroughly drenched. Stepping inside, she collapsed into the folding chair and picked up the receiver to make her call. *Oh no! Not something else.* Unfortunately, the phone was dead. Apparently the wind had knocked out the power.

Now what am I going to do? Water dripped from a few strands of hair hanging loosely from her head covering. Elaine wiped at her face; she was saturated straight through to her skin. At this point, her only option was to run to a neighboring Amish home to take shelter.

Jonah had left the drugstore in Arthur twenty minutes ago, after he'd gone to get some ointment to help baby Martha's diaper rash. As he headed back to the house, the rain had gotten worse. It was not a good day to be out walking, but up ahead he spotted an Amish woman, practically sprinting along the shoulder of the road. As he drew closer, he realized it was Elaine.

I wonder what she's doing out here in this weather, with no umbrella.

Jonah pulled his horse, Sassy, to a stop with the buggy alongside Elaine and opened his door. "Where are you headed? Do you need a ride?"

Elaine pushed her black outer bonnet off her face a bit and nodded. "It seems I left my key at the health food store, and I'm locked out of my house. I'd go back to the store to get it, but my horse hates storms. I'm afraid she'll spook if I take her out again." She paused and swiped at the rain running down her face. "If you don't mind dropping me off at my neighbor's place, where I can wait out the storm, I'd appreciate it."

"Get in. I'll take you."

As Elaine climbed into the passenger's side, a thought popped into Jonah's head. "Did you try all your doors and windows? Maybe one of them is unlocked."

Elaine shook her head, sending a spray of water in his direction. "Oops. Sorry about that."

"No problem. A little *wasser* won't hurt me any." Jonah grinned when some drops of rainwater hit him square on the nose.

"I didn't try the doors or windows, because I thought I'd locked them all before I left home," she said. "Guess I wasn't thinking too clearly. Once I realized I didn't have my key, I sort of panicked."

"Why don't we head to your house first? I'll check all the windows for you, and if one is unlocked, you'll have a way inside. When the weather improves, you can go back to the health food store and check for your key. Or better yet, I can take you to the store right now."

"It's out of the way for you. If you don't mind taking the time to try all the windows, why don't we start with that?"

"My daed and Timothy are working in the buggy shop today, which was why I was able to take off to run an errand," Jonah explained. "So I have plenty of time to check your windows."

Elaine smiled. "Danki, Jonah."

"No problem at all."

"How are things with your kinner these days?" Elaine questioned. Before Jonah could reply, she sneezed.

"Bless you." He glanced at Elaine and smiled. "They're doing okay, thanks to my mamm. Don't know how I'd manage without her help, though."

"Martha Jean is sure a sweet baby. When I saw her last Sunday at church I was surprised to see how much she's grown."

"Jah." A lumped formed in Jonah's throat. "It saddens me that Sara won't get to watch our son and daughter grow up."

Elaine reached over and touched Jonah's arm, but when he jerked his head, she quickly pulled her hand aside. "Forgive me for saying this again, but I'm truly sorry for your loss."

All Jonah could manage was a brief nod. He was certain Elaine understood, since she had experienced her own loss when her parents and later her grandparents had died. But that couldn't be as difficult as losing one's mate.

When Jonah turned his horse and buggy up Elaine's driveway, he focused on other things. The rain had let up a little; however, the ground was nothing but mud.

"If you want to wait here in the buggy while I check the windows, at least you'll be out of the weather." Jonah guided his horse to the hitching rack.

"No, it's okay. I'm about as wet as can be, so I'll wait on the front porch."

Jonah climbed down, and so did Elaine. Once he had Sassy secured, he followed Elaine to the porch. Grimacing, he motioned to his boots and her shoes. "Look at all the mud we've picked up."

Her nose wrinkled. "But it couldn't be helped. I'll be glad when summer comes and we won't have nearly so much rain."

"Welp, guess I'd better get busy." Jonah tried each of the lower windows at the front of the house and found them all to be locked. Then he went around back and discovered they were all locked, too.

"Do you have a ladder handy?" he asked after returning to the front porch. "Before I give up, I'd like to check all the upstairs windows."

"There's one in the barn." Elaine gestured in that direction. "But I feel bad making you go through all this trouble."

"It's not a problem. I'm glad to do it."

Jonah sprinted to the barn and returned with a tall extension ladder, which he positioned in front of one upstairs window. "Here I go."

"Please, be careful," Elaine called as she held the ladder for him.

When Jonah reached the window, he was pleased to discover it was slightly ajar. This shouldn't be hard at all.

He lifted it open the rest of the way, and turned around so he could slip in backward. The next thing Jonah knew, he was lying on his back on the floor with his feet in the air. Before he had a chance to roll over, a blob of mud from his boots let loose and landed on his face. "Ugh! I can't believe I did that."

Jonah clambered to his feet, barely taking time to grab a hankie out of his pocket and swipe it across his face. All he cared about was getting the door open so Elaine could come inside where it was warm and dry.

"What happened, Jonah? Are you all right?" Elaine's eyes widened when Jonah opened the back door and stepped out onto the porch.

He saw right away that she was shivering.

"I did a dumb thing," he admitted. Then he quickly explained what had happened and ended it with an apology for not taking off his muddy boots. "I'll clean up the mess I tracked through your house."

"Don't worry, it can be cleaned. You'd better come with me to the kitchen so you can get the mud off your face." Elaine handed Jonah some paper towels. "While you do that, I need to change into some dry clothes. I'll be right back."

Elaine wasn't gone long, and by the time she returned, Jonah's face was clean and he'd set his dirty boots on the porch.

"I feel much better now," she announced. "How about I heat some water and make us a cup of hot tea?"

"Sounds good." Jonah thought how ridiculous he must have looked when he'd come downstairs with mud all over his face, and he almost started to laugh.

Elaine must have been thinking the same thing, for she giggled. Soon, her giggle turned into a full-blown belly laugh. Hearing a person laugh like that was contagious, and soon Jonah joined in. It felt good to have something to laugh about—almost as if he were releasing all the things he'd kept bottled up inside himself. It was the first time since Sara's death he'd found anything amusing, and now that he'd begun laughing he found it hard to stop. Like the Bible said, laughter certainly was good medicine. Jonah realized he needed to look for humor in more things.

By the time Elaine offered Jonah a cup of tea, he was able to get himself under control.

"When I was checking all your windows, I noticed some plywood covering one of the basement windows. I'd considered trying to break through the wood to see if I could get in that way, but it would have been my last resort," Jonah said.

Elaine explained how the Valentine's Day blizzard had caused a tree branch to snap and fall on the window. "Luckily, several people were here when it happened. Priscilla and my dinner guests had to stay the night, due to the roads being impassable. When we heard the crash, the men who were here investigated and put plywood where the broken window had been. I planned to ask someone to replace the wood with glass but never got around to it." She sighed. "I've been so busy I didn't even think about it until now."

Before he could stop the words, Jonah blurted, "Would you like me to replace the window? I'm pretty handy at fixing things—including replacing broken glass."

"I appreciate the offer, but you're busy with your shop, and I'd hate to ask."

"You didn't ask. I offered." Jonah smiled. "Actually, there's a bit of a lull in the buggy shop right now. If anything new comes in, I'm sure Dad and Timothy can take care of it. Anyway, it should only take me part of an afternoon to replace the window for you. I may even have an extra window in my workshop or out in the barn that might fit. Anyway, I'll come by soon to take care of it for you."

"Danki, Jonah, and also for rescuing me today." Unexpectedly, Elaine wet her thumb and wiped a smudge of dirt still smeared on Jonah's face. Immediately she pulled her hand back and averted her gaze. The sweet gesture caused Jonah to think about a time when they'd been courting and she'd done something similar.

Don't start thinking about the past, Jonah reprimanded himself. *What Elaine and I once had is over. She made it quite clear the day she said she didn't love me. Besides, I still love Sara.*

As Cora headed home from work that afternoon, her mind replayed the events of the last two months. Not only had she received the money from the sale of her home in Chicago, but Chad's mother and stepfather's car insurance had covered Jared's medical bills. They'd come by a few weeks ago to visit with Jared, saying they'd waited until they were sure he was ready to talk about the accident. They wanted to know what the boys had been doing right before the crash happened and if Chad had said any last words to Jared.

Cora remembered how Chad's mother, Rita, cried when Jared told her what transpired right before the accident—how Chad had admitted he wasn't a good son and wished he had been a better person. He was afraid his parents weren't proud of him. While nothing could be done to bring Chad back, his mother said she'd found comfort knowing Chad had a friend like Jared who cared about him. It was sad for Chad's parents, as it seemed so many things had been left unsaid between them and their son.

After Rita and her husband went home, Jared told Cora that Chad's fears about his parents were one of the reasons he'd drawn closer to her and set the past behind. Jared didn't want anything to come between him and his mom. Cora was glad Jared had been willing to speak to Chad's folks. It seemed to give him a sense of release.

Her thoughts turned to Jared's father. She felt relief knowing Evan had given up trying to get custody of their son. Apparently he realized Jared didn't want to live with him, and perhaps in some ways, he was actually relieved. Between the responsibilities he faced as a prominent doctor in Chicago, his social commitments, and the need to keep his new wife happy, Evan had little time for anything else.

Thanks to the time Jared now spent with his big brother, he didn't seem to need or miss what he'd once had with his father. Once more, Cora thanked God for the relationship she now had with her firstborn son.

When she rounded the next bend in the road, Cora's breath caught in her throat as a quaint cottage came into view. She'd traveled this way many times and had never noticed this particular home until now. Today, what caught her eye was the For Sale sign posted at the end of the driveway.

What really captured her attention and made this house so special was it resembled the painting of the cottage she'd seen in the hospital waiting room—the same wildflowers of different hues, flower boxes on all the windows, and a glider swing on the front porch. The only thing missing were the deer grazing in the yard.

Cora pulled her car over and wrote down the name of the Realtor. The first thing she planned to do when she got home was call about this home. She sat awhile and looked over the property again. This time, she noticed a birdbath near the backyard with a few birds splashing in the water. Even without looking inside, she felt as if this place already belonged to her and Jared. She couldn't help wondering if seeing this cottage was merely a coincidence or was meant to have happened.

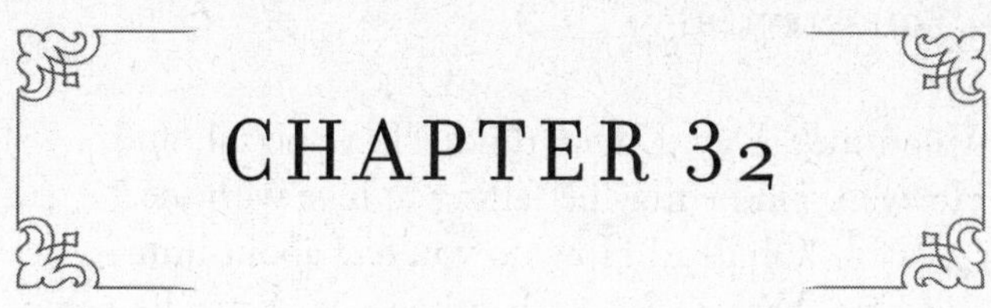

CHAPTER 32

Danki for seeing me at the last minute like this." Priscilla seated herself in Leah's recliner. "I wasn't sure if you'd even be home, much less available to give me a foot treatment."

Leah smiled, taking a seat on the footstool in front of Priscilla. "Since my daed picked up all three of the girls after Linda and Amy got home from school, I'm free until Adam gets off work, closer to suppertime."

"Did they go over to your folks' for a special reason, or was it to give you some time to yourself?"

"A little of both." Leah picked up the bottle of massage lotion and rubbed some on Priscilla's left foot. "Mom said she planned to bake cookies and needed the girls' help, but perhaps it was just an excuse both to give me a break and to spend time with them."

Priscilla smiled. "Those children are fortunate to have so many people in their lives who love and care about them."

Leah nodded. "So tell me why you're here. Is it a *buckelweh*, koppweh, or something else?"

Priscilla sighed. "It's not a backache or headache. I'm having trouble sleeping and can't seem to relax. I was hoping you could help me."

"Is it tender right here?" Leah pressed on a certain spot.

Priscilla's fingers dug into her palms. "It definitely is."

"It signals your adrenals aren't up to par. Are you stressed about something?"

"Jah. I've never felt so stressed."

"Want to talk about it?"

Priscilla nodded. It always seemed to help when she aired out her problems with Elaine or Leah. "I may have two suitors—or at least one who would like to be."

Leah quirked an eyebrow. "David?"

"Uh-huh. I never mentioned this before, but he gave me a romantic card for Valentine's Day. David thinks I'm special, and. . ." Priscilla paused. "He even said he may be falling in love with me."

Leah gasped. "Oh dear! How do you feel about him?"

"I'm not sure. We've seen each other a lot since he came back to Arthur, and sometimes after I've been with him, I fantasize about what it would be like if we were married."

Leah stopped probing Priscilla's foot, and her mouth dropped open. "Are you saying you're in love with David and want to be his wife?"

"I don't know. I'm confused."

"What about Elam? I thought you loved him."

"I do. At least, I think I still do." Priscilla sucked in her breath. "I've never been faced with anything like this before, and I really don't know what to do."

Leah's lips compressed. "I'd say you have some praying to do. Why don't you look up Matthew 6:33–34? God will make things clear if you seek Him and listen for His answers. I'll be praying for you, too, Priscilla."

"Danki, Leah, and believe me, I have already been praying and seeking answers from God, although nothing's come clear to me yet. I'll admit I tend to be spontaneous and don't always think things through. So I need to make sure my feelings for David are real and not just a reaction to the attention he shows me." Priscilla sighed deeply. "If Elam would have proposed to me before David showed up, this wouldn't even be a problem because we'd probably be married by now—or at least planning our wedding."

Leah's forehead wrinkled. "Speaking of Elam, maybe I shouldn't mention this, but I heard something you probably don't know."

"What did you hear?"

"Several weeks ago when I was shopping at the bulk food store, I overheard your mamm talking to Elam's mamm."

"What'd she say?"

"She was asking Virginia if she had any idea why her son hadn't proposed to you yet." Leah started working on Priscilla's foot again. "Virginia said she didn't know, but it might have something to do with his financial situation."

Priscilla's spine stiffened, and she winced when Leah hit another tender spot on the heel of her foot. *Won't Mom ever stop meddling in my life? I need to talk with her about this, and I'm going to do it as soon as I get home.*

❧

When Cora arrived home from work she called the Realtor about the house. He said he'd be more than happy to show it to her and that she was the first to inquire about it. Because of what he'd told her, Cora realized she probably couldn't get it for much less than the asking price, which was fine with her. She could pay cash for it with the money from the sale of her old home. Of course, it all stemmed on whether she liked the inside of the place as much as the outside. She really hoped the cottage was in good condition.

The Realtor set up a time for her and Jared to see it that evening. Cora could hardly wait until he got home from school so she could tell him about it.

Jared had gone over to Scott's after school, but he should be home in time for supper. Since they would be seeing the house at six thirty, Cora thought she'd take Jared out for pizza after the showing. In the meantime, she had some laundry to do, as well as pay a few bills. It was a good thing, too, because Cora was so excited over the prospect of buying the special cottage she needed something to occupy her mind. She sent up a quick prayer. *Please, Lord, let this be the house I've been looking for.*

At five o'clock, Jared showed up, carrying something large, wrapped in brown paper. "What have you got?" Cora asked.

"It's your birthday present, Mom." Jared grinned and handed the item to Cora. "It's a little early, since your birthday's not till Saturday, but I wanted you to have it now. I'm excited to see if you like it or not."

"Are you sure, Jared? I can wait a few more days to open it."

He shook his head. "No, go ahead and open it now."

Cora took a seat on the couch and tore the wrapping aside. "Oh, my!" She stared at the framed picture in disbelief. It was a similar painting—maybe a print—of the cottage she'd seen at the hospital. "Where did you get this, Jared?"

"Got it from Scott's mom, as a thank-you gift for helping out at their yard sale last Saturday. It was something left over that didn't sell."

Jared took a seat beside Cora. "Thought you might like it."

"I love it!" Cora set the picture down and gave Jared a hug. "This is so uncanny I can hardly believe it myself." Cora swallowed the lump in her throat before she continued to explain. "You won't believe this, Jared, but a painting like this one hung in the hospital's waiting room, and I fell in love with it. I even made a mental note of the artist's name and searched for it on the Internet. I found nothing, so I assumed it must have been done by an unknown artist who doesn't have a website showcasing his work."

"Wow, Mom, it's too bad you couldn't find any information, but it's so awesome how this painting was offered to me. Who'd ever guess Scott's mom would have a picture like the one you saw at the hospital?"

"This frame is a little different," Cora commented. "But I actually like this one better." She ran her hands along the oak board framing the outside of the painting. "Where'd Mrs. Ramsey get it? Do you know?"

"Scott mentioned she found it at a thrift store."

Cora stared at the picture, barely able to take it in. "You know something else really weird, Jared?"

"What, Mom?"

"On the way home from work today, I noticed a house a few miles from here. Unbelievably, it looks almost like the one in this picture. The best part is it's for sale."

"Really?"

"Yes, and I made an appointment to look at it this evening."

"Are ya thinkin' of buying it, Mom?"

Cora smiled. "Yes, I am—if we both like it, that is."

As soon as Priscilla entered her house, she went straight to the kitchen, where she found her mother tearing lettuce leaves into a bowl.

Mom turned from her work and smiled. "Oh, Priscilla, you're just in time to help me start supper."

"Mom, I—"

"How'd things go at Leah's? Was she able to give you a foot treatment this afternoon?"

"Jah, but while she was working on my feet, I found something out that has me feeling a bit umgerennt."

"Why are you upset?" Mom started tearing lettuce again.

"Leah mentioned that she'd overheard you talking with Elam's mamm awhile back." Priscilla moved closer to the sink. "Did you tell Virginia you're concerned because Elam hasn't proposed to me?"

Mom's face colored, and she quickly looked away. "I—I did mention it."

"Why would you say such a thing, Mom? Didn't you realize how embarrassing it would be for me?"

Mom turned to look at Priscilla again. "I'm sorry. I was only trying to help."

"Help what?"

"I thought if Virginia knew you've been waiting for Elam to propose—"

"You told her that?" Priscilla smacked the palm of her hand against her forehead.

"Well, not in so many words, but I am sure she understood my meaning."

Priscilla rested her forehead on her outstretched hands. "I can't believe you would do something like that. If this gets back to Elam, he'll think I put you up to asking his mamm." She moaned. "How am I going to explain this to him?"

"You're overreacting, Priscilla. My conversation with Elam's mamm took place several weeks ago. If Virginia had told Elam, which I asked her not to, I'm sure he would have said something to you by now."

"Why would you even take such a chance?" Priscilla took a few deep breaths, finally able to relax a bit. "Please, Mom, don't say anything to anyone else about my situation with Elam. If it's meant for us to get married, he'll ask when he's ready."

Mom's eyes narrowed as she stared at Priscilla strangely. "You don't seem to care so much about this anymore. What's happened, Priscilla? Is it David? Is he the reason you've lost interest in Elam?"

Priscilla cringed. How could she explain her feelings for David—especially when she wasn't sure Mom wouldn't repeat what she said.

Mom touched Priscilla's arm. "Did you hear what I said?"

"Jah."

"Is David the reason you've lost interest in Elam?"

"I haven't lost interest in Elam. He's still special to me."

"And David? What are you feelings toward him?"

Priscilla blew out her breath. "I enjoy being with David, but I'm not sure whether I love him or not."

"Does he love you?"

"I believe so. At least, he said he thinks he's falling in love with me."

Groaning, Mom pushed the bowl of lettuce aside and sank into a chair at the table. "This isn't good, Priscilla. Not good at all. You need to discourage David, and as quickly as possible."

Priscilla blew out a noisy breath. "What have you got against David? He's always been polite when he's come here to visit, and he has shown you and Dad nothing but respect."

"This isn't about being polite, respectful, or even whether he's a nice person or not. It's about him not being the right man for you." Mom gripped the edge of the table until her knuckles turned white. "You're not going to break things off with Elam because of David, I hope."

Priscilla shook her head. "Of course not, but if Elam doesn't show his intentions soon, I may take it as a sign that we're not supposed to be together. Maybe God has other plans for both of us."

"So you'll choose David if Elam doesn't propose?"

"I didn't say that. I'm confused, and talking about this isn't helping." Priscilla pushed away from the table. "I'm going to wash up now, so I can help you with supper." She started for the hall door but turned back around. "Please, Mom, promise you won't say anything to anyone about the things we've just talked about."

Mom gave a slow nod. "As you wish."

When Priscilla headed down the hall toward the bathroom, she made a decision. Having grown up with Elam, she knew him quite well, but she needed to get to know David better. In order to understand how she really felt about David, she'd have to spend a lot more time with him.

CHAPTER 33

"I can't believe how homey this place is." Cora smiled at the Realtor then studied the living room with a sense of awe. The inside of this home was even better than she'd imagined. The living room had a cozy fireplace and two large windows overlooking the expansive front yard.

What a great place for my granddaughters to play. Cora gazed out the window. She could picture a swing hanging from one of the trees and almost hear Carrie giggling as Amy and Linda took turns pushing her on it.

From the outside, the home appeared smaller than it actually was. As the Realtor showed Cora and Jared through the house, she grew more excited, seeing how spacious the rooms were. The open country kitchen, with an area for the table and chairs, as well as the cozy dining room were appealing. The three bedrooms had nice big closets, and hardwood floors ran throughout the home. The master bedroom had its own bathroom, and another bathroom located down the hallway could be used by Jared and guests.

Glancing out the living-room window, Cora's gaze came to rest on the glider swing she'd seen on the front porch as they came in. It appealed to her even more as she envisioned herself watching colorful sunrises early on Saturday mornings. In addition to the glider, many other areas around the property would provide places to enjoy nature. Although Cora was afraid to get her hopes up too high, it was all she could do to keep from shouting, "I'll buy it!" What if Jared didn't share her enthusiasm about this place?

After getting a tour of the entire house, Cora went back to the kitchen. She ran her fingers over the granite countertops, which the Realtor said had recently been installed. This kitchen was almost as big as the one she'd had in Chicago, but it felt homier. The house and yard were almost too good to be true. Cora couldn't see anything she didn't like about it. Nor did she see any need for updates or repairs.

What Cora loved most was at the back of the house, through a doorway in the kitchen. It led to a glass-enclosed patio with a ceiling fan and plenty of room for a few comfortable chairs. This special room overlooked the backyard, where the field by the house could be easily seen, as well as a goldfish pond with a waterfall cascading down some unusually shaped rocks. The outside of the cottage was a pretty, tan-colored mountain stone, and the roof had dark green shingles, matching the window shutters and front door. The yard wasn't real big in the back, but the front yard had a little more grass to mow. Several large trees bordered the back of the property, and to the left of the fish pond stood a tall maple tree that would provide shade for the backyard. *If we move here, I'll have to go to Adam's store and get a birdhouse to hang from the tree. Could this charming property soon belong to me?*

"Know what my favorite part of the house is, Mom?"

Jared's question pulled Cora's thoughts aside. "What would that be, son?"

"I like the finished basement. When Scott, or some of my other friends from school or church come over, we can hang out downstairs."

Cora smiled, pleased to see his enthusiasm. "Shall I make an offer on this house?"

He nodded, grinning widely. "Sure, Mom. Go right ahead."

"I appreciate you coming over to help me clean today." Leah smiled at her mother as they moved about the living room with their dust rags.

"I'm more than happy to do it." Mom gestured to Leah's growing stomach. "You do too much as it is. With a boppli coming, you need to get more rest, which is what you should be doing now instead of helping me."

"I'm fine," Leah insisted. "I get bored if I don't keep busy."

"I understand. You get that trait from me." Mom moved from the fireplace mantel to the window ledges, while Leah dusted the end tables. "Everything is going well, then?"

"For the most part." Leah sighed. "I'm worried about Amy, though."

"What's wrong with her? Is she having problems in school?"

Leah shook her head. "It's nothing like that. Amy's been acting strange ever since my tummy started growing."

"Do you wonder if she's umgerennt you're pregnant?"

Leah shrugged. "I don't know, but it's possible. When we first told the girls, they all seemed happy about it. Now Amy doesn't mention it at all. In addition, she seems quite moody lately."

Mom stopped dusting and moved over to stand beside Leah. "Have you tried talking to her about it?"

"I've tried, and so has Adam, but she just clams up." Leah's brows furrowed. "She's even snapped at her sisters a few times."

"It would be good if you can get her to open up. If Amy feels threatened by the new baby, she will need reassurance."

Leah nodded. "I agree, but I don't think Adam or I will get through to her." I was thinking of asking Cora.

"Danki for offering, but I was thinking of asking Cora. In a short time, she's developed a good rapport with the girls. If Amy will open up to anyone, I'm guessing it will be Cora. I'll check with Adam before I ask her, though."

"You're getting better at this." Priscilla gave David's arm a reassuring pat as he guided her horse and buggy down the road.

"Is gut." He glanced at her quickly and grinned. "I'm not nearly so naerfich now, either."

"I'm glad you think it's good, and that you're not so nervous. Your Pennsylvania Dutch is getting better, too." She smiled, tapping his arm. "And you don't look half bad wearing Amish men's clothing, either."

"Why, danki, Priscilla. I'm doing as well as I am because you're such a good teacher. Oh, and I've been practicing, like you told me to."

Priscilla was pleased David seemed to be trying so hard to become part of the Amish community. If things continued to go well after his classes, he would be baptized and join the church this fall. Sometime between now and then, David would need to move out of his grandparents' house, get a horse and buggy, and find a job in the community. As eager as he seemed to become Amish, Priscilla was surprised he hadn't done those things already. Of course, he'd been learning the woodworking trade from his grandfather, so that should help him find a good job.

"Why don't we stop at the bulk food store and see if Elam's working there today?" David suggested.

Priscilla cringed. If Elam saw her with David again, he might be upset. When she and Elam had eaten a meal out together, which turned out to be several days after the Valentine's Day blizzard, he'd been perturbed when she'd even mentioned David's name. Priscilla had made the mistake of telling Elam that David dropped by Elaine's on the evening of Valentine's Day and ended up spending the night, along with their dinner guests. This information hadn't set well with Elam. Priscilla had been wise enough not to tell him about the card and gift David had given her. She didn't like keeping things from Elam, but if he knew about the gift, it would have caused more tension.

David bumped Priscilla's arm. "Did you hear what I said about stopping at the bulk food store?"

"Jah, I heard, but unless you need something there, I don't see any point in stopping."

"Really? I figured you'd want to see Elam."

Priscilla sucked in her bottom lip. "I'll be seeing him this Friday night. He invited me out for supper."

David's forehead creased. "Oh, I see." She could see that he was clearly disappointed. "Well, I do need to pick up a few things Gram asked me to get."

Priscilla gripped the edge of her seat. *I really hope Elam's not working there today.*

Elam was at the front counter waiting on a customer when he spotted David and Priscilla entering the store. *I can't believe Priscilla's with David again. I wish she hadn't brought him here. Seeing them together is like rubbing salt in my wounds. Don't understand why she wants to spend so much time with that fellow.*

Elam tried to keep his focus on Margaret Kauffman, who was paying for her purchases, but it was hard not to watch David and Priscilla as they made their way down one of the aisles. *Maybe I should quit worrying about money and propose to Priscilla. Then David would know she's mine.*

As soon as he had Margaret's things put in paper sacks and placed her money in the cash register, Elam headed in the direction Priscilla and David had gone. No other customers were in the store at the moment, so it wouldn't matter if he wasn't behind the counter for a few minutes.

"What brings you to the store today?" he asked Priscilla.

She smiled. "We were out with my horse and buggy, so David could practice driving. He needed to stop here to get some things for his grandma."

It now irked Elam that David had turned to Priscilla for driving lessons instead of asking him or one of the other men in their community. David spent more time with Elam's girlfriend than Elam did these days.

"So what is it you need for your grandma?" He looked at David.

"Some Sure-Jell, for one thing."

"It can be found in the next aisle."

"I know what shelf it's on. We were just heading there," Priscilla interjected. Her cheeks colored when David smiled at her.

Is there something going on between them? Elam asked himself. *Maybe David needs a reminder that Priscilla is my girlfriend.*

"Don't forget, Priscilla, I'll be by around five to pick you up for supper on Friday evening." Elam glanced at David then back at Priscilla.

She smiled. "Oh, I haven't forgotten. I'll be ready on time."

"That's great. See you then." Elam walked away, feeling a bit better. At least David saw how things were. If he had any designs on Priscilla, knowing she was still being courted would discourage him.

Elaine had taken some towels off the line when Jonah's horse and buggy pulled in. She waved and greeted him at the hitching rack.

"I came by like I promised to replace your broken window." He stepped down from his buggy.

She smiled. "I appreciate you taking the time to do this for me, Jonah."

"It's not a problem." He went around to secure his horse then took a new piece of glass from the back of his buggy. "This should work fine."

Elaine stepped aside. "I'll get back to taking clothes off the line now, and let you put the new window in place. When you're done, if you have the time, I have some freshly made banana bread we can have with a cup of coffee. Just holler if you need any help."

"Sounds good." Jonah grabbed his tools and the piece of glass then headed off to take care of the task.

While Elaine finished taking the clothes off the line, she thought about the first day she had met Jonah, soon after he'd moved to Arthur from Pennsylvania. She'd been attracted to his good looks right away, but after getting to know him, she realized what a nice man he was. It hadn't taken her long to fall in love with Jonah, either. As they began courting and their relationship grew, she looked forward to the day he would ask her to marry him.

If only I'd felt free to say yes when Jonah did finally ask. Elaine's gaze went to the window he was replacing. *Now I'm faced with another decision concerning Ben.*

Elaine remembered her grandma saying once, "If you love someone, you ought to let them know if not in word, then by your actions."

She clutched a favorite bath towel, heart hammering in her chest. *I still love Jonah and always have, but I can't say anything—especially knowing he's still grieving the loss of Sara. Besides, whatever feelings Jonah once had for me are surely dead.*

Elaine bent down and picked up the basket of laundry. She'd only made it as far as the porch when another horse and buggy pulled in. It was Ben. Setting the laundry basket down, she walked out to meet him.

He stepped down from his buggy. "I came by to see if you wanted to have supper with me, but it looks like you have company."

"Jonah Miller is here replacing a broken window for me." Elaine gestured toward the house.

Ben frowned. "Why didn't you tell me you needed it done? You never mentioned having a broken window."

"It happened on Valentine's evening during the awful blizzard we had," she explained. "I kept putting it off because I've been so busy. Since a piece of plywood had been put over the broken window, I figured it could wait."

Ben glanced toward the house then back at Elaine. "So you asked Jonah to fix it instead of me?"

Elaine shook her head. "I didn't ask him. He offered to do it when he helped me get into the house after I lost my key."

Ben frowned again, a little deeper this time. "You didn't tell me about the key, either."

She turned her hands palms up. "Ben, it wasn't important. Jonah happened by when I was locked out of the house, he found a way in, and I went back to the health food store the next day and got the key I had left there."

"I see." He dropped his gaze to the ground. "Guess our relationship isn't as strong as I thought it was, because to me, something like that is important. Everything that happens to you is important."

Elaine had mixed feelings. On one hand, she felt bad Ben had been hurt by this. On the other hand, she thought he was overreacting. The only thing she wanted to make sure of was not letting him leave here with hard feelings.

"I'm sorry, Ben," she apologized. "I probably should have told you about being locked out, as well as the broken window. It's no excuse, but things have been so hectic around here, with several dinners scheduled, yard work, and keeping up with all the inside chores. I just didn't think to tell you everything that's gone on here."

He stood several seconds without saying a word then finally nodded. "I accept your apology."

She smiled up at him. "Now why did you stop by?"

"To ask if you'd like to have supper with me this evening." Ben folded his arms. "I asked when I first got here, remember?"

A rush of heat traveled up Elaine's neck and quickly spread to her face. "Oh, you're right."

"So how about it? Are you free to go?"

"Not tonight, Ben. I still have laundry to fold and put away, and I can't go anywhere until Jonah's done with the window, either."

"What about Friday night? Would you be free then?"

She nodded. "I have a dinner to host on Saturday but nothing for Friday."

Ben's face seemed to relax. "Good. I'll be by to pick you up around five. Will the time be okay for you?"

"Jah, five o'clock is fine."

"Okay, see you then." Ben glanced at the place Jonah was still working; then he leaned over and kissed Elaine. Had he done it on purpose, hoping Jonah would see? *No, that's ridiculous*, Elaine told herself. *Nothing is going on between me and Jonah, so why would Ben want to make him jealous?*

CHAPTER 34

"It was nice of you to invite us out for supper tonight." Cora smiled at Adam from across the table, where he sat with Jared on one side of him and Linda on the other. Leah was seated on Cora's right and Amy on the left, with Carrie in a booster chair at the end of the table.

Adam smiled. "We wanted to do something special to celebrate your birthday, as well as the purchase of your new home. Sharing a meal at Yoder's Kitchen really benefits all of us, doesn't it, girls?"

Linda and Carrie nodded, but Amy sat, staring at her plate.

"You haven't eaten much. Don't you like your chicken?" Cora asked, leaning closer to Amy.

The child merely shrugged in response.

Cora glanced at Leah, wishing she could ask if everything was all right. Since Leah made no comment about Amy's behavior, Cora thought it best not to say anything, either.

"When do we get to see this new place of yours?" Adam asked. "From what you've told us, it sounds pretty nice."

"Oh, it is," Cora said excitedly. "Our closing date isn't for thirty days, so we can't move in until then. But if you want to see it sooner, I can ask the Realtor to give you a tour of the place."

"No, that's okay. We can wait till moving day. Just be sure to let us know the exact date so we can help you out."

Cora nodded. "Thanks, Adam. I've made arrangements for a professional mover to get our furniture out of storage in Chicago and bring it here. But you could help with the boxes and smaller things."

"It's a really great place, Adam," Jared interjected. "You'll like it—especially the pond out back. It's full of fish."

"Fish for fishing or fish for watching?" Adam questioned.

"Mainly goldfish and some koi. They're sure gonna be neat to watch."

"We were surprised to discover the pond," Cora said. "It's a nice added feature to the outdoor space, and so tranquil."

"I need to use the bathroom." Abruptly, Amy pushed her chair away from the table.

"Would you like me to go with you?" Leah offered.

Amy shook her head. "I'm not a boppli, you know."

"Of course you're not. I just thought—"

Amy hurried away before Leah finished her sentence.

"Amy seems sullen this evening," Cora commented. "Did she have a rough day at school?"

"Nothing happened at school." Leah's voice lowered as she touched her stomach. "But she's been acting strangely ever since I started showing."

"Isn't she looking forward to the baby coming?" Cora whispered.

"I'm guessing she's not."

"Have you asked her about it?"

"I've tried, but she won't talk about it." Leah sighed. "Amy tends to keep her feelings bottled up inside."

"Would you like me to talk to her?" Cora asked.

"I'd appreciate it. In fact, I was going to ask if you might try getting through to her."

"I'll go talk to her right now." Cora left her seat and made her way to the women's restroom. She found Amy at the sink, washing her hands.

"You're kind of quiet tonight." Cora approached the child. "Is everything all right?"

Amy continued washing her hands, offering no reply.

Cora touched the young girl's shoulder. "If you want to talk about it, I'm willing to listen."

Tears filled Amy's eyes, and her chin quivered slightly. "I don't want Leah to have a boppli. She might not care about me, Carrie, and Linda anymore."

"Oh no, Amy. Leah and your uncle love you and your sisters very much. They'll always have time for you." Cora gave Amy a hug. "I admit, the baby will need attention. But just think, with you being the baby's oldest cousin, you'll get to help Leah do lots of things. I'm guessing the little one will look up to you, because you're the oldest."

Amy blinked. "You think so?"

Cora nodded. "I can almost guarantee it. Of course, the baby will love all of you, and your sisters will get to help out some, too."

A tiny smile played on Amy's lips. "Guess it'll kinda be like when Carrie was born and I got to help my mamm with some things."

"That's right." Cora handed Amy a tissue, wishing she had been a part of her granddaughters' lives back then. What she wouldn't give to have experienced the joy of seeing Mary taking care of her daughters.

"Now wipe your eyes, and let's get back to the table before our food gets cold." Cora gave Amy's shoulder a gentle tap. "We wouldn't want to miss having ice cream for dessert now, either."

"Okay." Amy took hold of Cora's hand. "I love you, *Grossmammi*."

A sob caught in Cora's throat, and she swallowed hard, trying to push it down. Hearing the child refer to her as "Grandma" nearly melted her heart. "I love you, too, sweet girl."

"You'd better turn when we get to the next crossroad and take an alternate route to the restaurant," Priscilla suggested as she and Elam headed in the direction of Yoder's Kitchen.

He glanced her way with raised brows. "Why would I do that? This road takes us directly to where we want to go."

"I know, but there's construction up ahead. David and I went through it today when I was giving him driving lessons. If we keep going, we'll probably be stuck waiting there awhile."

Elam shook his head. "I haven't heard anything about construction being done on this road. Besides, it's late, and they should be done working for the day."

"You may not have heard about it, but I know it's there, and you should really turn onto a different road, just in case they're still working on it. It may take us a little longer to get to the restaurant, but it'll be better than having to wait while traffic is redirected." Priscilla squinted, looking out the side window. "Unless you want to sit for a while and wait."

Elam just kept his horse and buggy moving.

"Aren't you going to turn?"

"Nope."

Priscilla frowned as Elam drove right by the roads she'd suggested. What was he trying to prove? Well, he'd see soon that she was right. When they had to stop because of the road construction, she was prepared to tell Elam, "I told you so."

When they approached the section of road under construction and the flaggers came into view, Priscilla did just that. It was wrong to bring it up to him, but Priscilla couldn't seem to help herself.

"Okay, so you were right, and I was wrong. Does that make you happy?" Elam mumbled, bringing his horse to a stop. "I can't believe the road crew is working this late."

Priscilla folded her arms, staring straight ahead. "Of course I'm not happy. I would have been happy if you had taken another route. Now it looks like we're going to be sitting here for a while." Priscilla's stomach protested, almost as loud as she'd spoken.

"We'll get there when we get there." Elam lifted his chin stubbornly.

They sat for nearly twenty minutes, neither saying a word. *If it had been David driving the horse and buggy, I bet he would have listened to me*, Priscilla fumed. *He's not nearly as stubborn as Elam.*

"I'm glad you were free to have supper with me this evening." Ben smiled across the table at Elaine. "We haven't had much quality time together lately."

"I know, and now with spring in full bloom, and summer on the horizon, things will get busier for both of us." Elaine picked up her glass of water, but before she could take a drink, she spotted Jonah at a table across the room with his parents and the children. Mark sat in a high chair beside the table, and baby Martha was in her carrier on the floor near Jonah's feet.

Elaine couldn't resist the urge to say hello, so she excused herself and went over to the Millers' table.

"Guder *owed*." She smiled at the group. "Looks like many in our community are here at Yoder's this evening."

Jonah's mother, Sarah, nodded. "So it would seem. Adam Beachy is here with his family, too. They're sitting toward the back of the room."

Elaine glanced in the direction she pointed. Sure enough, Leah and Adam were here, along with Adam's nieces; his mother, Cora; and her son, Jared. Glancing in another direction, she saw David Morgan and his grandparents, Walt and Letty. There truly were a lot of familiar faces here tonight.

"Your kinner are sure growing." Elaine directed her comment to Jonah, but all he did was offer a brief nod. His coolness caused Elaine disappointment. Earlier in the week when Jonah fixed her window, he'd seem relaxed and friendly. After he'd put the new window in place, they'd sat on the porch eating banana bread, drinking coffee, and visiting. What had happened between now and then to make him appear to be so distant? Could it be because Jonah's folks were with him and he didn't want them to get the wrong idea about him and Elaine? Or perhaps Jonah was preoccupied, having his children to care for this evening. Still, it was a little uncomfortable for Elaine, with him barely acknowledging her.

"It was nice seeing all of you. Enjoy your meal." Elaine tickled Mark under his chin and bent down to stroke the baby's soft cheek.

How blessed Jonah is to have these special children, Elaine thought as she returned to the table where Ben waited. Determined to enjoy her evening, she smiled and said, "Are you ready to order now, Ben?"

He tapped his fingers on the menu. "I've had plenty of time to decide, but you haven't. Mind if I ask why you felt the need to go over to Jonah's table?"

"I wanted to wish them a good evening and say hello to the kinner. They're both adorable, and I feel bad they lost their mother when they're so young." Elaine remembered how hard it had been when she'd lost her parents. She didn't appreciate Ben's perturbed expression, either. How could he be irritated because she'd said hello to the Millers? Then she remembered how he'd acted the other day, when he came by and saw Jonah replacing her window. Elaine wanted to say something about it—reassure Ben he had nothing to be jealous about, but now was not the time or place. Instead, she merely picked up her menu and studied it for the best choice.

"Sure hope some food is left on the buffet," Priscilla muttered as she and Elam entered Yoder's Kitchen.

He grunted. "You worry too much. The restaurant doesn't close for another hour or so. I'm sure they'll keep replenishing the buffet." It irked him to see Priscilla in such a dour mood this evening. Usually when they were together they visited and laughed, but not tonight. Of course, not turning up the road she'd suggested and then having to wait awhile because of road construction hadn't helped any. She was probably as hungry as he was, which could be why she was out of sorts.

The hostess showed them to a table, but instead of looking at her menu, Elam caught Priscilla staring across the room.

"What are ya lookin' at?" he asked. Then he saw David seated at a table with his grandparents.

Can't I ever be alone with my girl without him showing up? I wonder if he knew we were coming and came here on purpose. Elam gripped his menu. *Maybe David won't notice us. Sure hope if he does that he won't come over here.*

Their waitress came and took their order. Priscilla opted for the buffet, and Elam ordered a meal from the menu. They closed their eyes for silent prayer, and then Priscilla left the table to get her food.

Elam watched as she made her way around the buffet, choosing the items she wanted and putting them on her plate. Irritation welled in his soul when he saw David, dressed in Amish clothes, leave his grandparents and make his way to the buffet. When David approached Priscilla and they started talking, Elam's frustration mounted. It took all of his willpower not to walk over and ask David to quit visiting with Priscilla. Of course, if he did, he'd not only look foolish, but Priscilla would probably be even more upset with him than she already was. No, he had to be cautious about what he said or did concerning David. If things kept going well with his two part-time jobs, he'd soon have the money he needed and could ask Priscilla to marry him.

But if he and Priscilla kept having disagreements like they'd had on the way here, he might lose her to David. So rather than make a scene, when David glanced his way, Elam smiled and waved. He was determined to be as pleasant as possible the rest of the evening, wanting it to end on a good note. Elam had been in love with Priscilla for a long time, and he would do whatever he could to make their relationship last. Now if David would just give up his silly notion of becoming Amish and go back to Chicago, everything would be as it should. One thing Elam was sure of: Priscilla would never get serious about David if he remained English.

CHAPTER 35

By the end of May, Cora and Jared were moved and somewhat settled into their new home. It was good to have her own, familiar furniture again. And true to his word, Adam had helped them move boxes. A few other men from his church district came to help, too, including one of Adam's employees, Ben. Several of the women in the area provided meals and helped Cora unload boxes and organize things. She felt blessed to be living in Arthur, and even though she was no longer Amish, she felt like she was a part of the community.

Today was Saturday, and Cora didn't have to work, so she planned to do a little baking. Since it was Memorial Day weekend and the clinic was closed on Monday, she'd have an extra day to get more things unpacked as well.

This morning, when Cora had gotten out of bed earlier than usual, she'd noticed a faint hint of dawn on the horizon. She'd fixed a cup of tea and hurried to the front porch to sit on the glider and watch the sun rise. It had been so relaxing to sip hot tea and watch daylight unfold she vowed never to sleep in again. The rosy dawns were too beautiful to miss.

As Cora looked out the back window, it seemed like spring had suddenly sprung on them in full force. Everything seemed to be blooming, and several people had come into the clinic this week, complaining of allergy symptoms. The pollen count was up, which Cora noticed by all the light green dust on her car. She could probably have written her name across the hood. Fortunately, Cora didn't experience allergy problems, but she felt bad for those who did.

Cora moved away from the kitchen window and took out her baking supplies. *Maybe I'll ask Jared to wash the car sometime today.*

Jared was out back, showing his friend Scott around the yard. No doubt, they'd be making a stop at the pond so Jared could show Scott how the fish carried on when he fed them. Watching the fish certainly had a calming effect for Cora and Jared. He enjoyed having the fish so much and didn't even complain about feeding them or keeping the pond cleaned and full of water.

As Cora passed the window again, to get some more spices from the cupboard, she caught sight of a hummingbird, hovering near the feeder she'd put out earlier this morning. She stopped and watched as the tiny creature landed on the perch and took a drink. It was a male hummingbird, and certain ways he moved his head made the light reflect on the feathers directly under his throat. At times, the feathers looked black; other times they appeared to be red. The little bird was curious, too. Cora giggled when at that moment the hummingbird flew all around Scott's head. Then as quickly as it had appeared, it flew off into the trees.

Cora paused a moment to watch the boys. It was warm enough to have the kitchen window open and let the soft breeze waft in. Jared and Scott had taken a seat in the lawn chairs close to the fish pond. Although she couldn't hear all of their conversation, Cora caught Jared saying something about Chad. It was good to know Jared had a friend like Scott—one he could confide in and express his feelings to. Jared hadn't said much to Cora about Chad or the accident since it happened, but she was glad he was comfortable discussing things with Scott. Cora was certain it hadn't been easy on Jared hearing Chad's last words before he'd died. She would never press him about it, though. If her son wanted to discuss that horrible night with her, he would—in his own good time.

Cora was pleased to see Jared looking so happy. Life felt wonderful right now, and she thanked God every day for it.

Life can be delicate, just like the hummingbird, Cora mused. *How can anyone believe God doesn't exist?* While Cora had never doubted God's existence herself, for a good many years she had lost her faith. Those days were behind her now, for her faith in God had never been stronger.

As Jonah poured nectar into the hummingbird feeder he'd purchased last week at Adam's hardware store, he thought about the cool reception he'd received from Ben, who'd waited on him. Jonah wasn't sure why

Ben had acted so curt. Could it have something to do with Elaine? He'd seen Ben's look of disdain when Elaine came over to their table at Yoder's last month to say hello. It had made Jonah uncomfortable, to the point he could hardly talk to, or even look at, Elaine. Had Ben been irritated because she'd left him sitting alone for a few minutes, or was it something else?

Ben had to be aware that Jonah and Elaine had once been a courting couple. If she hadn't told him, then someone else probably had. *Maybe Ben was bothered because Elaine talked to me. He could even think I'm interested in her, or that I may try to get back what we once had.*

Shaking the notion aside, Jonah's thoughts went to Sara. He remembered how she had taken Mark to watch some hummingbirds get banded at Leah's place last July and said they really enjoyed it. She'd told Jonah she planned to get a feeder for their yard so Mark could watch the little birds zip back and forth. Sara's wish had been granted, only she wasn't here to see the hummers or the expression on her son's precious face when he watched the tiny birds with a look of awe.

Now don't start feeling sorry for yourself again, Jonah reprimanded himself. *I need to get on with the business of living, and focus on the positive things around me.*

He stepped onto the porch, where his mother sat rocking the baby while Mark played nearby with some toys.

"Sure is a beautiful day." Jonah set the empty container of nectar on the porch and took a seat on the wooden bench beside Mom's rocking chair.

She smiled. "It's a good day for sitting and reflecting on the beauty of God's creation."

Jonah nodded. "I haven't seen any hummers yet today, but since the feeder is full now, I'm hoping some will come soon to feed."

"Mark will like that." Mom stroked Martha's rosy cheek. "Can you believe this little *maedel* is already six months old? She's growing like a weed."

"I know. It won't be long and she'll be noticing the hummers, too."

Mom reached over and touched Jonah's arm. "You look content today, son. I'm glad you took the day off to be with the kinner—and me, too. We don't often get to spend quiet time together like this."

Jonah scooched over on the bench so Mark could join him; then he lifted the little guy onto his lap. "Since Dad and Timothy seemed more than willing to work today, I figured I wouldn't have to feel guilty for taking some time off. Since it's Memorial Day weekend, it's nice having these three days."

Mom tousled Mark's head. "And it's well deserved, because this little guy likes to spend time with his daed."

"I like to spend time with him, too." Even though Jonah wasn't Mark's biological father, in every other sense of the word, he was the boy's dad.

"We ought to have a cookout this weekend. Maybe do up some hamburgers and hot dogs over a fire."

"Sounds good to me."

"I'll have to clean the picnic table off today. Even from here, I can see the pollen all over it."

"Oh, look, Mark. Look over there!" Jonah pointed to the hummingbird feeder.

Mark's eyes lit up, and he pointed, too. "*Blummevoggel!*" he exclaimed.

"That's right," Jonah said, smiling at the boy's exuberance. "It's a cute little hummingbird."

"Are you sure you don't want to go with us this evening?" Priscilla's mother asked as she put a batch of brownies into a plastic container. "It's been awhile since we got together with our neighbors for an evening of visiting, games, and refreshments."

"I know, but Elam said he'd be dropping by to take me for a ride. If I'm not here, he'll be disappointed."

"I understand." Mom gave Priscilla a hug. "Enjoy your evening."

Priscilla smiled. "I hope you and Dad enjoy your evening, too."

After Priscilla's parents left, she sat on the front porch and waited for Elam.

Maybe he's not coming, she thought after an hour went by. *Maybe he got busy or just plain forgot.*

A fly buzzed and circled her head. Priscilla slapped at it with irritation. She enjoyed being outdoors, but the pesky bugs could be a nuisance.

More time elapsed, and Priscilla was about to give up and go inside, when she heard the familiar sound of a horse's hooves on the pavement. A few minutes more and she caught sight of a horse and buggy coming up the driveway. Right away she could tell the rig wasn't Elam's.

Priscilla squinted, shielding her eyes against the rays of the setting sun. She was surprised when a few minutes later David stepped out of the buggy. "How do you like it?" he called, waving at her.

Priscilla stepped off the porch and joined him by the hitching rack. "I'm surprised to see you tonight, David. And, where did you get this nice horse and buggy?"

He grinned, like a little boy with a new toy. "They're mine. I took money out of my college fund to buy them." He stroked the horse's mane and gestured to the buggy. "What do you think?"

"They're both very nice. Did you get the buggy from Jonah Miller?"

"As a matter of fact, I did. He had a used one and let me have it for a reasonable price." David's blue eyes seemed brighter than usual this evening. "Wanna take a ride?"

Priscilla hesitated but finally nodded. It was obvious Elam wasn't coming, so why shouldn't she have a little fun with David?

Smiling to himself as he headed down the road with his horse and buggy, Elam felt more anxious than ever to see Priscilla this evening. In addition to getting in more hours at his second job, his dad had given him a raise at the bulk food store.

I can finally ask Priscilla to marry me. Elam snapped the reins to get his horse moving faster. If she said yes, which he was confident she would, by the time they got married he should have enough money set aside. Seeing the way David seemed to be moving in on Elam's territory, he wasn't going to wait any longer. He'd pick Priscilla up, take a leisurely buggy ride, and before he brought her home, he would pop the question.

CHAPTER 36

Elaine hummed softly as she painted a rock resembling a fawn lying on its side. Ben liked deer, so she planned to give him the rock when he came by this evening. Things had been a bit strained between them lately. She hoped by giving Ben a gift, he'd know she cared.

I do care for Ben, but I'm not in love with him. Elaine dipped her brush into the can of white paint to put on the finishing touches. All that was needed to finish the little fawn were the white spots.

Elaine hoped her feelings toward Ben would develop into something more, but the longer they courted, the more doubts she had. Still, he was a good friend, and she didn't want hard feelings between them, regardless of her decision not to marry him.

Elaine stood erect as the thought sank fully in. She could not marry a man she didn't love, and she simply didn't love Ben.

I need to tell him, and the sooner the better. Maybe it would be best not to give Ben the painted rock. She rubbed her forehead. *Oh, dear, what should I do?*

The sound of a horse and buggy pulling onto the driveway invaded Elaine's thoughts.

Peeking out the kitchen, she saw it was Ben. He'd come early.

Elaine set the fawn rock on the counter to dry and quickly put away her painting supplies. Then she hurried to the bathroom to wash her hands. Glancing in the mirror, she was pleased to see no paint had gotten on her face or clothes.

"Guder owed," Ben said when she let him in the back door. "I'm a bit early, but I was anxious to see you tonight."

Even though I must tell him how I feel, I hope he's not going to pressure me to marry him. "Let's go in the kitchen. I have something for you."

Ben followed Elaine into the other room. "Wow, did you paint this?" He pointed to the fawn rock.

She nodded. "Jah, just for you."

"Danki, Elaine." He reached out to touch it, but she stopped him in time.

"It's not quite dry, so you'd better wait awhile to pick it up."

"Oh, okay. I'll get it before I leave." Ben smiled tenderly at her. "How come you made me a gift? It's not my birthday or anything."

"I just wanted to tell you how much I appreciate your friendship."

With his back to the counter, Ben's brows pulled together as he looked at Elaine. "You've said the same thing before, and I'm beginning to think all I'll ever be is just your friend."

Unable to look directly at him, Elaine dropped her gaze to the floor. This was going to be so hard.

He stepped forward and lifted her chin with his thumb. "Your silence is my answer. I'm a good friend, but you don't care about me enough to marry me—right?"

Struggling with her emotions, Elaine nodded slowly.

"Is it because you're in love with Jonah Miller?"

Ben's pointed question brought unwanted tears to Elaine's eyes. She would not hurt Ben by declaring she still loved Jonah. Besides, what good would admitting it do? Jonah didn't love her anymore.

"Ben, this isn't about Jonah." Elaine's voice faltered. "It–it's about me, and my desire to marry for love."

"I get that, but friendship can turn into love. To my way of thinking, a married couple should be each other's best friend."

"I agree, but. . ."

Ben placed a hand on each side of Elaine's face and gently brushed her tears away with his thumbs. "But then, being honest with myself, I have to say, if your friendship with me was going to turn into love, it should have done so by now."

Elaine stood facing him, unable to form a response.

A muscle on the side of Ben's neck quivered. "If you don't love me and can't commit to marriage, then I guess it's over between us."

Elaine swallowed against the sob rising in her throat. When Grandma had gotten ill, she'd sent Jonah away, feeling dejected. Now she was doing it to Ben. Only this time she wasn't pretending, for she'd never truly loved Ben. "Can we still be friends?" she asked hopefully.

Ben reached out and clasped both of her hands. "Of course we can.

Someday, when the time is right, we'll both find the mate God wants us to have. And now, I'm gonna say good night." Turning, Ben hurried out the door but quickly spun around and came back. "Don't worry; things will eventually work out for both of us."

Elaine was startled when Ben gently grasped her shoulders and leaned in toward her face. She closed her eyes and held her breath, but then he surprised her by lightly kissing her forehead before he turned again and walked away.

Feeling completely drained, Elaine sank into a kitchen chair. She sat staring at the table until she heard the *clip-clop* of Ben's horse as he headed out. Then she caught sight of the rock she'd painted for him. He'd left in such a hurry he'd forgotten to take it. Maybe it was for the best. Having the fawn rock might be a painful reminder to Ben that Elaine had rejected his proposal.

Elam arrived at Priscilla's in time to see a horse and buggy coming down her driveway toward the main road. He blinked a couple of times to be sure he wasn't seeing things. Sure enough, David sat in the driver's seat, and Priscilla sat next to him.

Elam pulled his horse up so it was nose-to-nose with the other horse, opened his door, and leaned out. "What's going on, Priscilla? I thought we had a date!"

Priscilla climbed out of the other buggy and came around to Elam's rig. "You said you'd be here over an hour ago, and when you didn't show up, I assumed you weren't coming."

"I had to work late, but you should have known I was coming. I told you I'd be here when we spoke the other day." Elam's eyes narrowed as he stared straight ahead. "That horse and buggy aren't yours, Priscilla. Did David get his own rig?"

She nodded. "David was so excited about getting a horse and buggy he wanted to take me for a ride." Her cheeks flushed a bright pink.

"I was excited to come here tonight and take you for a ride, too, but maybe I'd better turn around and go home, since you'd obviously rather be with him." It might be wrong for him to feel this way, but Elam couldn't help his tone of irritation.

Priscilla shook her head. "I never said I'd rather be with David. You're making too much out of this, Elam."

"Oh, really? I show up a few minutes—okay, an hour—late to pick up my date, and I find her in someone else's buggy." Elam clenched his teeth, causing his jaw to ache. "Any guy who cares for a girl would be upset about that."

"I'm sorry. I really didn't think you were coming." Priscilla gestured to the house. "Why don't we all go inside? I'll make some popcorn, and we can sit and visit awhile. David can take me for a ride some other time."

Elam's spine stiffened. "David? It was me you were supposed to be taking a ride with, Priscilla."

"Well, it was. I just meant. . . Oh, never mind. Do you want to come in for popcorn or not?"

The last thing Elam wanted to do was visit with David this evening. It didn't sit well with him, either, knowing Priscilla wanted to ride in David's buggy. *Are my worst fears coming true?* he wondered. *Am I losing her to David? If so, what am I gonna do?*

Priscilla placed her hand on Elam's arm. "Can't we at least go inside for a little while? I don't want to be rude and tell David he has to go home."

"What about the ride we were supposed to take?" *How am I supposed to ask you to marry me with David around?*

"We could go some other time. Or if David doesn't stay too long, there might still be time for us to take a short ride."

Elam hoped the latter was true. A long, leisurely ride was out of the question now, but anything would be better than nothing. "Jah, okay. Whatever you want to do is fine with me." He figured if he didn't cooperate, he could end up driving Priscilla right into David's arms. Since he was here, he wasn't about to go home and leave David alone with Priscilla. "Okay. Tell David to turn around and head back to the house so I can get up the driveway with my rig," Elam conceded.

Priscilla smiled. "Danki for understanding."

You may think I understand, but I don't. The only thing I understand is that David is wrecking the special night I had planned.

As Priscilla headed back to David's buggy, Elam gripped his horse's reins with such force, the veins on his hands protruded. He hoped before the evening was out, he wouldn't regret his decision to visit with Priscilla and David. If David hung around too long, Elam might not get the opportunity to propose to Priscilla at all.

Priscilla couldn't remember when she'd spent a more miserable evening. So much tension was building between Elam and David she wished she hadn't invited either of them into the house. She would just start a conversation with one of them, when the other would interrupt. At one point, Elam whispered to Priscilla, saying he had something important to tell her and wished they could be alone. Soon after, David told her pretty much the same thing. It felt as if these two young men were in a tug-of-war, and she was the rope.

What's going on here tonight? Priscilla wondered as she got out the popcorn popper. *David and Elam have been carrying on like a couple of schoolboys with a crush on one of the girls. Could they be deliberately trying to aggravate each other? They're both acting pretty immature.*

Shaking the notion aside, Priscilla concentrated on putting the right amount of cooking oil in the bottom of the popper. She turned on the propane stove and was waiting for the pan to heat up, when she felt a sneeze coming on. *Achoo! Achoo! Achoo!* Her nose started to run. It didn't feel like she was coming down with a cold, and Priscilla had never had allergies before, but maybe this year she'd become sensitive to all the spring pollen. Recently, she'd noticed a layer of light green dust clinging to the porch furniture and other things outside.

"When the oil heats up, would one of you mind pouring the popcorn in, while I get a tissue?" Priscilla called to Elam and David, who'd both remained in the living room when she'd excused herself to fix refreshments.

"I'll do it." David smiled as he entered the kitchen.

"If I don't get back before it's done popping, make sure you turn off the burner, okay?"

"No problem." David winked at her. "I've got this under control."

Priscilla smiled. "Danki, David." Handing him the pot holder, she turned and hurried from the room. "Better watch it. The pan will get hot fast."

"No problem," he said with a nod.

When Priscilla entered the bathroom, she realized there were no tissues, so she hollered down the hall to the guys that she was going upstairs for a few minutes.

Priscilla made it to her room just in time to grab the box of tissues she kept by her bed, when another bout of sneezes hit her full force.

Sitting on the side of her bed, Priscilla pulled several tissues out of the box. Over and over she sneezed and blew her nose. "Oh my, why don't these sneezes stop?" At the rate she was going, it wouldn't be long before the box of tissues would be empty. Just when she thought the spell was over, Priscilla started sneezing again. It almost felt like she had pepper up her nose.

"Can this evening get any worse?" She moaned, rubbing her now-itchy eyes. "Oh, I bet I look a mess." She didn't have a mirror to look in at the moment, but Priscilla knew her eyes must be as red as her nose no doubt was. Her eyes felt swollen, too, as they continued to itch and tear. *Maybe I should tell Elam and David to leave. I'm not going to be any fun with my nose running like this.*

Priscilla sat several more minutes, to make sure the allergy attack was over. When she felt comfortable it was, she snatched up the box of tissues and headed back downstairs.

Priscilla's nose twitched, and her eyes began to burn, making her stop in her tracks. *Do I smell smoke? Oh my, I hope David didn't burn the popcorn.*

Hurrying into the kitchen, Priscilla realized it was filling with smoke. There was no sign of Elam or David, though. *That's strange. Where did they go?*

Turning her gaze to the stove, Priscilla gasped when she saw the corn popper engulfed in flames.

"Oh no!" Priscilla grabbed a pot holder. When she reached for the knob to turn off the stove, her sleeve caught fire. In Priscilla's attempt to put it out, the flames ignited her other sleeve. The next thing she knew, heat traveled across her chest. If she didn't get the fire out soon, her whole dress would catch fire.

Panicked, Priscilla screamed and dropped to the floor, rolling one way and then the other. *Please, Lord, help me!*

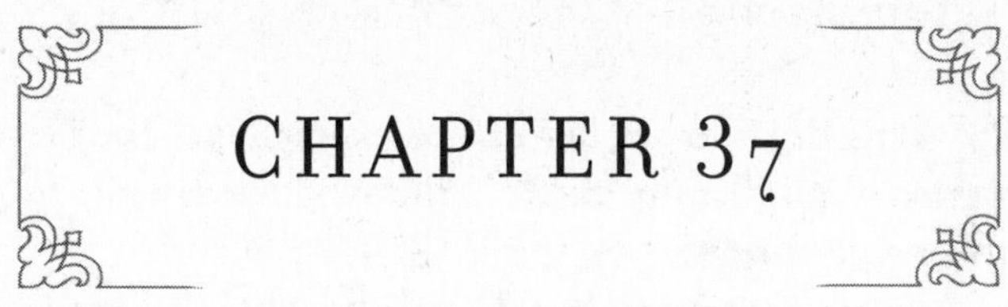

CHAPTER 37

"What's wrong with you, boy?" David stroked his horse's head. A few minutes ago, he had heard the horse carrying on, so he went outside to see what the ruckus was all about. Elam had gone to the use the bathroom, or David would have asked him to finish making the popcorn.

Since David's horse had calmed down, and he didn't see anything other than a cat nearby, all seemed well. As David started back across the yard, he recoiled when he heard bloodcurdling screams coming from inside the house. Something must have happened to Priscilla. He hoped she hadn't fallen down the stairs.

He took the porch steps two at a time, nearly colliding with Elam when he stepped through the door. They raced into the kitchen.

Priscilla was rolling on the floor, with the sleeves and upper part of her dress on fire. David did the first thing that came to mind: he doused her with water.

Meanwhile, Elam, shouting for David to call 911, got the fire put out on the stove.

David's stomach tightened when he saw ugly red blisters had already formed on Priscilla's hands and arms. Thankfully, no sign of blistering showed on her face. Quickly, he took out his cell phone and called for help.

"Do you know where the linens are kept?" David asked Elam, after talking with the emergency operator. "We need a clean, damp sheet to cover her with."

Elam's face was pale as goat's milk as he dashed out of the room. While David waited for him to return, he talked softly to Priscilla. He was glad she was conscious but almost wished she wasn't, so she wouldn't have to suffer such pain. "Don't try to move." He grabbed several dish towels, rolling them up like a pillow to cushion her head. "Just lie still. Help will be here soon."

It tore at his heart to see her pained expression. "The kettle. . .the stove. . . I tried to put the fire out. . . ." She shuddered, while tears trickled down her pale cheeks.

There shouldn't have been a fire, David thought. *I'm sure I turned off the stove.*

Decatur, Illinois

David paced the floor as he waited with Priscilla's parents and Elam for news on Priscilla's condition. He had called his grandparents after the ambulance took Priscilla to the hospital. He'd told them what had happened, without giving all the details, and asked if they'd drive him and Elam to the hospital. Gramps had come right away, of course, and about the time he got there, Priscilla's parents arrived home from their visit with the neighbors. David could still see Iva and Daniel's horrified expressions when Elam told them what had happened to their daughter. After they'd all been dropped off at the hospital, David told Gramps it might be awhile before they heard anything on Priscilla's condition and suggested he go on home.

This is my fault, David berated himself. *In my hurry to get outside and check on my horse, I must have only thought I turned off the stove. If Priscilla's burns are serious and she's scarred for life, I'll never forgive myself.*

"You're gonna wear a hole in the floor if you don't stop pacing."

David halted and looked at Daniel. "I'm worried about Priscilla. From what I saw, her hands and arms were burned badly."

"We're worried, too," Iva spoke up.

"Worry won't change a thing," Daniel interjected. "We need to pray."

Iva glanced at Elam. He hadn't said much since they'd arrived at the hospital. "We know Priscilla was in the kitchen when she got burned, but can you give us more details about how it happened?"

Elam pinched the bridge of his nose. "Priscilla went to the kitchen to make popcorn. Then she said she had to get a tissue for her nose, so she asked David to take over at the stove. Shortly after she went into the bathroom, she hollered that she was going upstairs." He paused and shifted his position in the chair. "Soon after that, I made a trip to the bathroom. When I came out, I heard Priscilla scream. I ran into the kitchen about the same time as him." He glanced briefly at David. "I was shocked to see Priscilla's *frack* on fire, and she was rolling on the floor, trying to put out the flames."

Iva sucked in her breath, covering her mouth with the palm of her hand. "Oh, my poor girl. How on earth did her dress catch on fire?"

"It's my fault," David admitted, unable to bear the burden of what he'd obviously done. Daniel quirked an eyebrow. "How's it your fault?"

David explained how he'd heard his horse acting up and had thought for sure he'd turned off the stove before going outside. "Apparently, I didn't, though, because if I had, the corn popper wouldn't have been ablaze when Priscilla returned to the kitchen." Sweat broke out on his forehead and he reached up to swipe it away. "I feel terrible about what happened."

"You should feel terrible!" Elam's hand shook as he pointed at David. "You shouldn't have gone over to see Priscilla tonight. She's my *aldi*, not yours. I had planned to take her for a buggy ride this evening." His voice raised a notch. "If you hadn't interrupted our date, the accident would never have happened. Instead of her offering to fix us a snack, she'd have been with me in my rig."

David shook his head. "You were over an hour late, and Priscilla never mentioned you were planning to come over."

"Come on, boys, this arguing isn't going to help Priscilla." Daniel held up his hand. "Sounds like you're both acting a bit immature. It was an accident." He looked at David. "Even if you did leave the burner on, it's not your fault Priscilla's dress caught fire."

David felt bad enough, but hearing Elam's angry tone, plus the look of anguish on Priscilla's parents' faces, made it worse. If he hadn't wanted to stick around to hear how badly Priscilla had been burned, David would have called Gramps right then and asked for a ride home.

They sat in silence for a while, until a doctor came in and told Priscilla's folks the extent of her injury. "Your daughter has second-degree burns on her hands, arms, chest, and shoulders," he said in a serious tone. "A burn such as this, covering more than ten percent of a person's body, can be quite serious if not treated properly. We'll keep her here a few days in case infection sets in, and to be sure the burns haven't damaged the deeper layers of Priscilla's skin." He stopped talking for a few seconds, as if to let her parents take in what he'd said. "She will experience a great deal of discomfort, so in addition to treating the burns, we'll give her something for the pain."

"Can we see her now?" Iva's expression was desperate; while Daniel looked like he'd aged ten years.

The doctor nodded. "If you'll follow me, I'll show you to her room."

Daniel and Iva rose from their seats. Clasping each other's hands, they followed the doctor out of the waiting room.

Elam went to the door, watching Priscilla's parents until they turned a corner, then he stood looking down the corridor. It was all he could do not to go with them, but Daniel and Iva needed time alone with their daughter.

Elam's legs felt weak, as if they could no longer hold him, so he quickly took a seat. "I appreciate your grandfather bringing me and Priscilla's parents to the hospital, but you should have gone home with him. There was no need for you to stay." Elam looked at David and frowned. "You oughta go now."

David opened his mouth as if to say something, but then he closed it, turned, and walked out of the room.

As Elam listened to the rhythm of David's shoes as he headed down the hall, he leaned forward, buried his face in his hands, and wept. *Dear God, please let Priscilla be okay. Let her burns heal quickly, and help her not to feel too much pain.*

Elam's tears flowed until he felt none were left. If anything happened to Priscilla, what would he do? She'd been a part of his life for so long. He couldn't imagine even one day without her.

Tonight was supposed to be a special night. It would have started a new beginning for him and Priscilla if she'd said yes to his proposal. She wasn't supposed to be lying in a hospital bed, going through this horrible ordeal. If only he hadn't worried about making extra money before asking her to marry him. Knowing Priscilla, she wouldn't have cared if they had any savings or were just getting by. If he'd proposed sooner, maybe they'd even be married by now.

Rocking back and forth, he felt the seriousness of the situation more acutely. Not knowing how long it would take Priscilla to heal, Elam realized this could delay them from getting married.

Never in a million years had he expected something like this could happen.

CHAPTER 38

Arthur

"I have some bad news," Adam said when he entered the kitchen.

Leah was washing their breakfast dishes and whirled around. "What is it, Adam? Did something happen to someone we know?"

"I'm afraid so." Adam moved quickly across the room and grasped Leah's hands. "I just came from the phone shack, and Daniel Herschberger left a message. An accident occurred at their house last night when he and Iva were away."

Adam's grim expression caused Leah's heart to pound. "Did someone get hurt?"

He nodded. "Priscilla got burned."

Clasping his arm, Leah gasped. "Ach, no! What happened?"

"I don't have all the details, but from what I got out of Daniel's message, something was burning on the stove, and her dress caught fire."

"Oh, Adam, no! How badly was she burned?"

Adam shook his head. "I don't know, Leah. Daniel just said she was in the hospital in Decatur."

"I have to go to the hospital, Adam. Priscilla's one of my best friends. I need to be with her right now."

"I understand. I'll make arrangements with one of our drivers to take us to the hospital. I'm sure your folks will watch the girls."

Leah swiped at the tears on her cheeks. "I wonder if Elaine's been notified. I'm sure she'll want to go with us to see Priscilla."

"Would you like me to call her, or should we drop by on our way to take the girls to your mamm and daed's?"

"We should stop at Elaine's house. I don't know when she'll check her messages, and since we're hiring a driver, she can ride to the hospital with us." Leah glanced at the door leading to the living room, where the girls had gone after breakfast. "It's a good thing this is Sunday and the children don't have school. They can go to church, and even spend the whole day with my parents if necessary."

"They'll be disappointed if we don't take them on a picnic, like we talked about," Adam said.

"I know, but I may want to stay with Priscilla." Leah sighed. "Besides, I'm really not in a picnic mood anymore. All I want to do is see my good friend and let her know I'm there for her. Maybe my folks can do something special with the girls this weekend. I'm sure they'll understand about postponing the picnic."

Adam pulled Leah into his arms for a hug. "Try not to worry. Priscilla is in God's hands. We just need to pray."

"What are you doing, Davey?" Gram asked, looking in through his open bedroom door.

"I'm packing my duffle bag. I'll be leaving soon."

Her forehead wrinkled as she stepped into the room. "Are you going away for a few days?"

"No, I'm not. I'm leaving Arthur for good."

She jerked her head back, as though she'd been slapped. "I don't understand. Why would you leave now, when you're preparing to join the Amish church? Not to mention Priscilla is in the hospital. Don't you want to be here to offer her encouragement as she is being treated for her burns?"

"I'm leaving because of Priscilla's burns."

"I don't understand what you're saying." She took a seat on the edge of his bed. "And I don't understand why you're leaving."

David sank to the bed beside her. "Don't you see, Gram? I'm the cause of Priscilla's burns. If I hadn't left the stove on, the pan wouldn't have been ablaze, and if the fire hadn't started, then Priscilla would never have gotten burned." David groaned, leaning forward, his whole body trembling. "I can't face her, and to make matters worse, Elam is furious with me. He told me to leave the hospital last night and said if I hadn't stopped to show Priscilla my horse and buggy, she would have gone on a ride with him, instead of trying to fix popcorn for the three of us."

Gram put her hand on David's shoulder. "Of course Elam is upset, but you can't carry the weight of this, Davey. It was an accident and could have happened to anyone. I'm sure Priscilla will not blame you for it. Running away won't solve anything, either."

"Yes, it will." David raised his head, struggling not to give in to the tears pricking the backs of his eyes. "I'm in love with Priscilla. I'll admit it: I've been hoping she would choose me over Elam. He obviously knows it, too. I'm sure it's one of the reasons he's so angry with me."

"If you really do care about Priscilla, then you ought to be here to show your love and support as she goes through this ordeal."

"I do, but I can't." David rose from the bed and tossed the rest of his things into the satchel. "This is a lot to ask, but will you and Gramps sell my horse and buggy for me? I'd do it myself, but I want to leave town today. Oh, and you can give my Amish clothes to the thrift store. They're used, but I'm sure someone will buy them."

"Does your grandfather know you're leaving?" Gram asked.

David nodded. "I had a talk with him early this morning before he went outside to mow the lawn."

"What'd he say? Did he try to talk you out of going?"

"At first, but then he said it was my life, and the decision was mine."

"Aren't you even going to say good-bye to Priscilla?"

"No, it's better this way. I'll drop a note in her mailbox, explaining why I left."

Gram stood and gave David a hug. "I don't agree with what you're doing, but we'll be praying for you. Should you change your mind, you're always welcome to come back and live with us."

David swallowed hard, and his vision blurred from more tears. "I love you, Gram, and I'll let you know when I get to Chicago."

Decatur

"I'm scared to go in and see her," Elaine said as she, Leah, and Adam headed down the hospital corridor toward Priscilla's room. "What if her burns are so bad, she's scarred for life?"

"She won't be. Once she gets home from the hospital and her folks can start putting B&W ointment on her burns, she'll heal." Leah tried to sound confident, for her own sake as well as Elaine's.

"The message Daniel left on my answering machine didn't say how badly Priscilla was burned. Did he tell you anything specific?" Elaine questioned.

Leah shook her head, glancing at her husband. "Adam was the one who listened to the message."

"It just said Priscilla's dress caught fire, but no information was given on how severe her burns were," Adam said.

They were almost to Priscilla's room when the door opened and her mother stepped out. The poor woman's eyes were bloodshot, and her lips trembled as she spoke. "Danki for coming. When Priscilla wakes up, she'll be glad to see you."

"If she's sleeping, we'd better not go in there right now." Elaine hugged Iva. "Can we go somewhere to talk?"

"Let's go to the waiting room. Daniel's in the cafeteria getting coffee, but I'm sure he'll find us when he gets back."

"I'll see if I can find Daniel." Adam gave Leah's hand a squeeze before heading down the hall toward the cafeteria.

Leah hugged Priscilla's mother, too. "Oh, Iva, you look exhausted."

"We've been here at the hospital all night."

"Maybe you should try to get a little sleep." Elaine rubbed Iva's arm, obviously trying to comfort her.

"I couldn't sleep, even if I wanted to. If it's okay with you, I'd rather sit and talk. It might help relieve some of my stress."

"Sure, Iva. We'd like to hear the details of how it happened and how badly Priscilla was burned."

Iva led the way down the hall, with Leah and Elaine following. When they entered the waiting room, Leah was relieved to see it was empty, which would make it easier to talk freely.

After they'd all taken seats, Iva gave them the details of what had happened. "As terrible as this is, we are thankful only her shoulders, arms, chest, and hands received second-degree burns. It could be a lot worse if the burns went deeper or the fire had burned other parts of her body." Iva shuddered. "Even so, Priscilla is in a lot of pain, and she had a lot of redness and blistering. She could also have some scarring once it heals. They're keeping her here a few days to watch for infection and dehydration."

"When she comes home will you start using B&W ointment and covering the burns with boiled and cooled burdock leaves?" Leah questioned. With her interest in natural healing, she'd learned the benefits of this home remedy and how it had produced good results in many people who'd been burned.

"Jah," Iva said. "That's exactly what we plan to do. I have a book with instructions, telling how to treat burns of varying degrees, so at least I'll know what to do. There's also an Amish woman in the area who has treated burns like Priscilla's. If I have any questions, I'll seek her advice."

"I've read about it, too." Leah nodded. "The ointment not only helps with pain and healing but infection as well."

"Does the doctor think Priscilla will need skin grafts?" Elaine asked.

"He said maybe, but only if the skin doesn't grow back on its own." Iva's eyes flooded with tears as she looked determinedly at Leah and Elaine. "Please pray the skin grafts will not be necessary and Priscilla will have no permanent scars."

As David sped along the Interstate, he had one thought on his mind—getting as far from Arthur as he could. The roads were dry, but in the distance, dark clouds loomed, so hopefully he'd be in Chicago before any storms hit.

The highway traffic was light, probably because it was Sunday. David took advantage of the open road. It was about a three-hour drive to get to his parents', so he was glad for the 180-mile trip. It would give him time to think and try to sort things out, if that were even possible.

David checked the speedometer. He wasn't going over the speed limit, but for someone who'd had a cycle accident a few months ago David realized he was going faster than he should. His motorcycle had been fixed and was running smoothly, so right now he just didn't care. No one else was in harm's way, since no other vehicles were close to his.

Tears blurred his eyes and dried instantly on his cheek as the air whipped and blew around his helmet. "Oh, Priscilla, what have I done to you?" David's shout was lost in the wind. "Elam was right. I never should have gone to your house last night. If I'd stayed home with Gram and Gramps, none of this would have happened."

All the anticipation of joining the Amish church and possibly developing a permanent relationship with Priscilla was a thing of the past. David knew he had to return to his life in Chicago and leave his dream of living the Amish life with Priscilla behind him. Truth was, that may be all it was—just a fantasy he'd conjured up to show his dad that he could do whatever he wanted, instead of what was expected of him.

David's agony over Priscilla's injury in conjunction with his guilt was worse than anything he'd ever endured. He'd had a sleepless night and felt even worse this morning. Saying good-bye to Gram and Gramps had made it even harder to leave.

How do people cope when they're the cause of someone else's pain? David wondered. Would time heal, as he'd heard Gram say? Maybe it happened to others, but David didn't know if he could ever set things right with himself or Priscilla.

Gripping the handlebars, he steadied his bike as a semitruck came up behind him. When the enormous rig got in the center lane and drove past, the pull was so strong, David had to hold tightly, fearful he might get sucked into the truck's draft. His bike shuddered, just as David was doing, but as the semi got farther up the road, David relaxed. It didn't get rid of the pain in his gut, twisting like an unyielding knife, however. His brain was plagued with one thought after another. Could Priscilla ever forgive him? Would he be able to forgive himself? It would be impossible to look at Priscilla without being reminded of his stupidity and forgetfulness.

"She's better off without me," he muttered. "Wish I'd never left Chicago in the first place. Then none of this would have happened."

Up ahead, David saw high-rise buildings come into view as he approached Chicago. Soon he'd be dealing with the scrutiny of his parents, but that was nothing compared to the remorse eating away at his heart.

CHAPTER 39

Chicago

"I knew you'd never stay in Arthur or become Amish. You're not cut out for a life such as that."

Dad's words cut into David like a two-edged sword. He wished he hadn't felt forced to come back to his parents' house, but he had no place else to go right now. Not until he found a job, at least.

He turned to face his father. "Look, Dad, I don't need you getting on my case right now. I've been on the road for the last several hours, and I'm beat. All I want to do is go up to my room and lie down awhile. I hardly slept last night, and I'm bushed."

Dad's jaw clenched so hard his teeth snapped together. "You just got here, David. You can hide out in your room later on."

Lifting his gaze upward, David shook his head. He was dog-tired from the trip but even more so, from all that had happened with Priscilla. He was in no mood to spar with his father. "Dad, we'll talk later. I need a little shut-eye right now."

"So you're not going to tell us the reason you came back?" Dad moved closer to where David stood near the front door, holding his duffle bag.

"Let the boy alone," Mom spoke up. "Can't you see he's tired? At least he came home to us. You should be happy about that."

"I am, Suzanne, but he owes us an explanation."

David knew his dad wasn't going to let up until he gave them some sort of story, so he looked right at him and said, "I came back because things weren't working out for me in Arthur." It wasn't a lie. Things had definitely not worked out the way David hoped—especially concerning Priscilla.

"So you finally realized the Amish life wasn't for you, huh?" Dad's "I told you so" tone, and his look of anticipation told David that was exactly what his father was hoping to hear.

"Yeah, that's it." David gave a quick nod. "Now if you don't mind, I really need to lie down."

"Would you like something to eat first?" Mom asked, obviously trying to smooth things over.

"No, I'm fine. I stopped for a bite to eat on my way here."

"Okay, we'll see you when you get up." Mom gave David a welcoming hug.

He glanced at his father, to see if he would say anything more, but Dad merely took a seat in his easy chair and buried his nose in the Sunday paper.

As David climbed the stairs to his room, a vision of Priscilla on her kitchen floor flashed into his head. Thinking about her look of panic caused his heart to ache. He'd never forgive himself for what he'd done to her. He hoped the letter he'd left in her folks' mailbox would let her know how truly sorry he was.

Decatur

Priscilla lay in her hospital bed, staring at the ceiling and thinking about everything that had occurred last night. Normally about now, she'd be at church service with her family. If it were not for the pain from the burns she'd received, this would all seem like a dream—a horrible nightmare, really. Other than the tension she sensed between David and Elam, everything had been normal. Now she would be laid up—for how long, she didn't know. It would be at least until her skin had time to heal.

Will I be left with scars? she wondered. *I'm ever so thankful my face didn't get burned.*

Priscilla appreciated Elaine and Leah coming by earlier today. Their friendship and support meant so much, and it was a comfort to know they were praying for her. She clung to the verse Leah had quoted about God never leaving or forsaking her, even when she was enduring so much pain. God would give her the strength she needed to get through this. She was reminded of Psalms 121:1–2, 4: "I will lift up mine eyes unto the hills, from whence cometh my help. My help cometh from the Lord, which made heaven and earth. Behold, he. . .shall neither slumber nor sleep."

She thought about Elam and his sullen expression when he'd dropped by a short time after Elaine and Leah went home. He hadn't said much, except repeating over and over how sorry he was that something so horrible had happened to her. Before he'd left, Elam had kissed Priscilla's forehead and said, "I love you, Priscilla."

Tears welled in Priscilla's eyes as she thought about how long she'd waited to hear him profess his love in that way. "Why now?" she murmured. *Why couldn't he have said those words sooner? What has been holding Elam back all these months we've been courting?*

Priscilla's thoughts went to David, wondering why he hadn't paid her a visit. She was aware that he'd come to the hospital last night, because Mom had mentioned David's grandpa had driven them all here.

Is David afraid to face me? Does he think I blame him for the accident, since he forgot to turn down the stove? He didn't do it on purpose, she reminded herself, but it was hard not to focus on the results of his carelessness.

I should have known better than to try to put out the fire with a dishcloth. I should have thrown baking soda on it. So it's partly my fault, too.

Was it wrong for her to be with David yesterday? Elam was right. She should have known he was coming to take her for a buggy ride and most likely running late. Looking back on it now, it was perfectly reasonable that Elam had been upset. If she had politely told David she had plans with Elam for the evening, none of this would have occurred.

It had been difficult lately, trying to figure Elam and David out. Elam's sudden profession of love confused her even more.

Slowly raising her gauze-covered hands, she stared at them then closed her eyes. *Will I ever be the same again?* All Priscilla wanted right now was to go home where Mom could treat her burns, instead of nurses and doctors hovering around. She wanted to hide out in her house and never let anyone see her ugly red hands and arms.

Walking down the corridor toward Priscilla's voice, Elam heard her crying out in pain. Over and over she screamed, as he moved in her direction. "I'm

coming, Priscilla, hang on!" Elam struggled, concentrating on moving his legs. It felt as if he were stuck in quicksand.

When he finally made it to her room, it seemed to be shrouded in fog. "Why would someone leave the window open?" Elam closed it to keep the cool air out. Then he shut the curtains and turned on the small lamp near Priscilla's bed. "I'm here, Priscilla. It'll be okay." Hoping to reassure her, Elam smoothed the damp hair on her forehead.

"Elam, please take the pain away." Priscilla moaned. "Nothing they've given me has helped."

Elam was beside himself. If the pain medication the doctors were giving her didn't help, what would? He wanted to be strong for Priscilla, and to encourage her every step of the way. Bending over the bed, Elam pulled her into his arms.

Priscilla gasped. "No, Elam, it hurts too much!"

Elam immediately drew back, not wanting to add to her pain. Feeling useless, he thought it might be better to leave, but his heart told him to stay.

"Go away, Elam," Priscilla murmured. "Go away."

Tearfully, Elam turned toward the door but halted when David appeared. Walking past Elam without so much as a word, David went to the side of Priscilla's bed. "I thought I turned the stove off," he murmured. "Will you forgive me, Priscilla?"

Lifting her hands, Priscilla said, "Look what you've done to me. I never want to see you again, David."

Elam sensed David's rejection, for he felt it, too.

David turned to face Elam. "I love her, but I know she'll never be mine." He turned and walked out of the room, disappearing into the darkened corridor.

Elam was on the verge of leaving, too, when Priscilla called out to him: "Elam, don't go! I need you. You're the only one I can trust."

Drenched in sweat and with heart pounding, Elam bolted upright in bed. Shaking from head to toe, it was hard to get air into his lungs. Covering his eyes with his hands and propping his elbows on his knees, he tried to calm himself with the realization it had only been a dream.

The cool evening air blew through his open window as his breathing returned to normal. Elam groaned, using the sheet to wipe perspiration from his forehead. "Will I ever be able to sleep without having nightmares about Priscilla?"

Slowly, he rose from the bed and made his way to the bathroom down the hall. Bending over the sink, he splashed cold water on his face and rubbed some on his neck. Then he took his wet fingers and dampened his hair. He should never have lain down for a nap this afternoon, but visiting with Priscilla earlier today had taken its toll on his nerves. Sleep was the only way he'd been able to escape.

Elam straightened, staring at his image in the mirror. Behind him lightning reflected on the walls, while thunder rolled in the distance as a storm announced its approach. As he took a towel and dried the last droplets of water from his forehead, Elam murmured, "Are things going to get even worse?"

CHAPTER 40

After three days in the hospital, Priscilla came home. It was good to be in familiar surroundings again, but everything had changed. She'd lost her optimistic, spontaneous attitude, and now struggled with depression.

Mom had covered her burns with B&W ointment and placed scalded burdock leaves, now cooled, over the top to hold the salve in place. Once the injury sites had been completely covered with salve and leaves, the area was wrapped with a conforming piece of gauze. The wrapping was firm enough to keep the leaves from sliding, but not too tight to cause pressure or pain.

Following that, Mom wrapped an absorbent pad with a waterproof backing around Priscilla's chest, shoulders, and arms and taped it in place. She would redress the wounds every twelve hours. Even the folds and digits of Priscilla's hands had to be covered with B&W ointment and burdock leaves in order to keep them from growing together.

Priscilla's palms and fingers had to be straightened and flattened while healing. If left un-straightened, they could heal like a claw with a cupped palm, which would disable Priscilla for life.

After dressing Priscilla's hands the same way she had her arms, Mom cut a piece of corrugated cardboard the width of Priscilla's hands and length from her fingertips to her wrist, which she then placed on the back of her hand, over the top of the dressing. The flattened palm and fingers were wrapped against the cardboard with a gauze roll.

Priscilla felt like a scarecrow. She figured she probably looked like one, too. Lying against the pillow, she said, "Well, at least my allergies have quieted down. Guess being in the hospital with the air-conditioning may have helped with that."

"The good rainfall we had on Sunday night washed the pollen off everything, too." Mom got everything ready for the next dressing change.

"Whatever the reason, I'm glad I don't have to blow my nose right now. Don't know what I'll do if that happens."

"We'll worry about it when the time comes, or if you feel a sneeze coming on."

"Let's hope it doesn't." Priscilla groaned. "I sure don't need anyone wiping my nose for me. It's bad enough I'll have to be fed until my arms and hands heal."

"You'll have to swallow your pride and let me or others help you with everything."

Priscilla nodded. "I know, but it won't be easy."

"It's never easy to accept help from others, but there are times when we all need to do it."

"I'll try to cooperate."

Mom smiled. "You'll need to receive plenty of liquids, too, so you won't become dehydrated."

"I know." Priscilla realized someone, probably her mother, would have to hold the glass for her when she drank anything, too. How glad she would be when she could do things for herself again.

"Oh, before I forget, I found this in the mailbox the day after your accident," Mom said. "It's a letter from David. There's no stamp or postmark, so I assume he must have put it there himself."

Priscilla's forehead wrinkled. "Why would he leave a letter instead of coming to see me himself?"

Mom shrugged. "I have no idea. Would you like me to read it to you?"

"Jah, please do. There's sure no way I can hold the letter myself." Priscilla hated sounding so negative. She didn't want to come off as a whiner, but she couldn't seem to help herself right now.

Mom took a seat beside Priscilla's bed and read David's letter:

"Dear Priscilla,

I'm sorry for not coming to see you at the hospital, but I figured I'm probably the last person you want to see. No words can express my sorrow for the agony I've caused you because of my carelessness. If I could take your pain away, I would.

I wish things could have worked differently for us, and I hope you'll find it in your heart to forgive me someday. I'm returning to Chicago today. Things aren't going to work out for me here. I never should have left at all.

Be happy with Elam, and enjoy all that life has to offer. I'll always remember you and the friendship we once had.

Love,

David."

Priscilla lay motionless, letting his words soak in. David felt responsible for her getting burned, but it surprised her that he would leave Arthur. What had happened to his desire to join the Amish faith? Didn't their friendship mean anything to him? Had he determined that he didn't love her after all?

"It's best that he's gone, Priscilla," Mom said. "David wasn't right for you, and he obviously didn't have what it takes to be part of the Amish faith." She patted Priscilla's knee. "Besides, Elam's the one who is meant for you."

"Is he, Mom?" Priscilla's eyes filled with tears. "I'm not sure anyone is right for me anymore." Should she ask her mother to write David a letter, begging him to come back? No, if Mom could destroy the letters David had sent Priscilla before, she might throw out Priscilla's letter to David, as well. *I'll wait and ask Elaine to write the letter. No doubt, she'll come by to see me soon.*

Thinking about Elaine caused Priscilla more discomfort. *I won't be able to help her host any dinners for a long time.*

Elam's hand shook as he knocked on the Hershbergers' door. When he'd called the hospital this morning to see how Priscilla was doing, he'd found out she'd been discharged. Elam knew he had to see her, but the horrible nightmare he'd had last night about Priscilla was still stuck in his brain, and he couldn't stop thinking about it. He hoped she would be glad to see him.

When Priscilla's mother came to the door, Elam jumped. "Oh, Elam, I'm so glad you're here. Priscilla's feeling down right now. Hopefully seeing you will lift her spirits." Iva opened the door wider, and Elam stepped in.

"Is she in a lot of pain?" he asked.

"Not as much as one might expect. The doctor sent some medicine home with Priscilla, but after I put some B&W ointment on her burns, she said the pain lessened."

"I've heard good things about that stuff." Elam glanced into the living room, wondering if Priscilla was there. He saw no sign of her, however.

"Priscilla's resting in the guest room. We moved her things there, since it's downstairs and closer to the bathroom." Iva gestured to the hall. "She's not sleeping, so why don't you go on in? She'll be glad to see you."

"Okay. I won't stay long, though, 'cause I don't want to tire her." Elam headed down the hall with a feeling of dread. When he came to the guest room, the door was ajar, so he poked his head in. "Hey, how are ya doing?"

"As well as can be expected, I guess, considering I look like a scarecrow."

Elam stepped into the room and took a seat beside Priscilla's bed. The sight of her lying there with burdock leaves and gauze dressings covering her burned arms and hands, made his stomach queasy. He could only imagine how her blistered skin must look and feel underneath all of that. "Your mamm said you're not in too much pain right now."

"No, I'm not, but I look baremlich." Her voice trembled. "If my burns don't heal properly and I end up with scars, I'll always look terrible."

Elam shook his head. "No you won't, Priscilla. You'll always be beautiful to me."

Priscilla's cheeks became wet with tears, and Elam reached out and wiped them away.

"I got a letter from David. He's gone back to Chicago."

"He has?" This bit of news almost made Elam's day.

"He feels guilty for not turning off the stove and blames himself for what happened to me."

"I'm glad he's gone." Elam dropped his gaze to the floor. "He didn't belong here, Priscilla."

"How can you say that? It sounds like you're angry with David."

Elam lifted his head. "And you're not?"

"No. Anger toward David won't change what happened to me. It's not his fault my sleeve caught fire when I tried to put out the fire."

Elam rubbed the back of his neck, where a spasm had occurred. "So, you've forgiven him without question?"

"I have to. There's no point holding a grudge. I'm sure David didn't intentionally leave the stove on. It was an accident, plain and simple." She sniffed, while blinking her eyes. "I wish he would come back so I could tell him that."

"It doesn't matter. David's gone, and I'm glad. He was trying to come between us, Priscilla."

"Now you sound like my mamm." Priscilla frowned. "I don't think he was doing that. Maybe he was. . ." Priscilla's voice trailed off. "I'm tired and I'd rather not talk about this right now."

"I understand. Just the trip home from the hospital must've worn you out." Elam pushed back his chair and stood. "I probably should go so you can sleep." He started for the door but turned back. "There's something you should know."

"What's that?"

"The reason I wanted to take you for a buggy ride Saturday night was so I could ask you an important question." Elam paused to see if she would ask him what question. When she didn't, he said, "I was going to ask if you would marry me. But, of course, David being there ruined my plans."

More tears spilled out of Priscilla's eyes.

He came closer. "If you'll have me, I still want to marry you."

"I've waited a long time to hear you say that, but I can't give you my answer right now, Elam. I need time to think about things and focus on getting well."

"I understand." He bent and brushed his lips lightly against hers. "Once you're feeling better, we can talk about this again."

"Okay."

"Get some rest now. I'll come by soon to check on you."

As Elam headed out the door, he felt a little better about things. Priscilla hadn't said no to his proposal, and David was out of the picture. If the Englisher hadn't come back to Arthur in the first place, none of this would have happened. The only good thing that had come from Priscilla getting burned was David had left, even though it was a cruel twist of fate.

CHAPTER 41

Leah had begun giving Cora a reflexology treatment, when Cora said, "You look tired and like something might be bothering you. It's not Amy again, I hope."

"No, she's fine about the boppli now. The problem is with my friend Priscilla." Leah frowned. "She got burned in a kitchen fire a few days ago."

"That's terrible! How badly was she burned?"

"Her arms, hands, chest and shoulders all received second-degree burns."

"I assume she was taken to the hospital?"

Leah nodded. "She was supposed to come home today. Her mother will be taking over her care, using B&W ointment and burdock leaves."

"I know about that particular treatment, and I've heard good things."

"So you're not opposed to it?"

"Not at all. Why would you think I'd be?"

"You're a nurse, and some people who practice traditional medicine don't agree with or understand using more natural methods."

"Since I grew up in an Amish family, I'm well acquainted with holistic medicine. I know it can often bring good results—even where traditional medicines have failed. And sometimes a combination of both healing practices can be helpful." Cora paused to stifle a yawn. "Oh my, excuse me."

Leah giggled when she yawned, too. "I guess it's right what people say about yawning being contagious."

Cora smiled and nodded. "Back to our topic. I was surprised when I learned that the doctors at the clinic where I work often suggest natural methods as an option if the patients prefer to use them rather than conventional ones."

"Yes, in our community it's important to have a doctor who isn't opposed to other methods, and it's the reason we go there when the need arises." Leah poured more lotion on Cora's feet. "I'm glad you have an open mind about this, too."

As Leah worked on Cora's feet, they talked about other things—Leah's pregnancy, the warm spring weather, and Cora's precious granddaughters.

"Maybe you'll have a boy." Cora spoke in a bubbly tone. "I'll bet Adam would enjoy having a son."

"I'm sure he would. However, he's already made it clear he'll be happy with a boy or a girl." Leah grinned. "To tell you the truth, I get the feeling Amy's eager for the boppli to be born so she can fuss over it and pretend she's a little mother."

"Either way, we will all be happy once the baby comes. Even Jared is excited about it."

"How's he doing these days?"

"Quite well. I don't think he's completely gotten over Chad's death, but he spends a lot of time outdoors at our new place. His friend Scott comes over every chance he gets."

"Friends are so important. I can't tell you how many times my good friends Elaine and Priscilla have always been there for me, and I want to be there for them, too."

"How is Priscilla doing?" Elaine asked when Iva let her into the house the following day.

"As well as can be expected—maybe a little better than normal." Iva's lips compressed. "Since we started using the B&W ointment, her pain is less, but she's *verleed*.

"Is she depressed because she can't do much of anything right now?"

"Being immobile is part of it, but she's still worried about the prospect of permanent scarring."

"Many people who have used B&W end up with little or no scarring at all. The stories I've heard about its effectiveness are amazing."

Iva nodded. "I am doing everything the way I was shown by a natural healer in our area, so I'm hoping for a good outcome." She gestured to the living-room entrance. "Priscilla's in there. Why don't you go on in? While you two visit, I'll fix a snack."

As Iva headed to the kitchen, Elaine went to the living room. She found Priscilla stretched out on the couch, her hands, arms, and what she could see of her chest and shoulders had been covered with burdock leaves, wrapped with gauze. She looked miserable.

Elaine took a seat in the chair closest to Priscilla, reaching over to gently stroke her friend's forehead. "How are you feeling? Is there anything I can do for you right now?"

Priscilla shook her head. "Just sit and visit awhile. It might help take my mind off the predicament I'm in."

"I'm sorry you have to go through this. I can't imagine how hard it must be not to be able to use your hands."

Priscilla sighed. "I feel so *nixnutzich* right now."

"You're not worthless at all. Once your hands heal, you'll be able to do things again."

"*If* they heal." Priscilla frowned. "I even have burns between my fingers. That's the reason Mom has them straightened like this." She glanced toward the window. "Look how nice it is outside. I can think of a hundred things I could be doing in the yard if I wasn't in this predicament. But no, I can't do any of it right now."

"Try not to think about all the things you'd like to do. You need to rest and concentrate on healing."

"Now, Elaine, you're starting to talk like my mamm."

"I care about you." Elaine smiled. "After the burns on your fingers begin to heal, you'll have to exercise them. Otherwise, they could become stiff, and you sure don't want that. And don't forget, I'll need your help hosting dinners."

Priscilla stared at her hands. "I won't be doing anything like that for quite a while. I can't even feed myself right now, let alone cook or wash the dishes. You'll need to find someone else to help you with the dinners."

"I already have. Sylvia and Roseann Helmuth came to help me with the dinner I hosted last night, but it took both of them to equal one of you."

"Puh! You're just trying to make me feel better."

Elaine shook her head. "It's true. They were more than willing to help, but neither of them was as fast as you. I had to keep reminding them what to do."

"I'm sure they'll get the hang of it after they've helped with a few more dinners."

"Maybe, but I'll only use their help until you get better."

"Okay, but if you change your mind and decide to keep them working for you, it's fine with me." Priscilla closed her eyes, drawing in a deep breath, then she opened them again. "I need you to do something for me, Elaine."

"Anything. Just tell me what."

"Would you write a letter for me?" Wincing, Priscilla lifted her hands. "I'd do it myself, but as you can see, it will be some time before I can do much of anything with these."

"Of course. Who's the letter going to?"

"David."

Elaine's eyebrows puckered. "Why would you write to David when he lives right here in our town?"

Priscilla shook her head. "Not anymore. He left a note in our mailbox, saying he was going back to Chicago."

"How come?"

"He blames himself for my accident, so he left." Tears formed in Priscilla's eyes and ran down her cheeks.

Elaine wiped Priscilla's face with a tissue. "I'm sorry. I know you think a lot of David."

"Jah. He's a good friend."

"Okay, tell me what to say, and I'll write the letter."

After Priscilla had told Elaine what to say to David, she felt a bit better. She hoped once David read her letter he would return to Arthur. Even if nothing serious came from their relationship, at least they could still be friends. "Why should David give up his plans of becoming Amish because he forgot to turn off the stove?" she murmured. "It's ridiculous!"

"If David comes back, then what?" Elaine asked.

"Hopefully things will go back to the way they were. He'll take classes and continue to learn what he needs to about our ways, and this fall he can join the Amish church."

Elaine tipped her head, looking at Priscilla dubiously. "Mind if I ask you a personal question?"

"Course not. You can ask me anything."

"Are you in love with David?"

"I'm not sure. He's kind and gentle, and he treats me like I'm special."

Elaine's eyebrows squeezed together. "What about Elam? I thought you were in love with him."

"I am. I've loved Elam for a long time."

Elaine shook her head. "You can't love two men at the same time, Priscilla."

"I never thought I could, either, but after spending time with David. . ." Priscilla's voice trailed off. "It doesn't matter anyway. If David doesn't come back, there's no chance of us having a future together."

Priscilla was on the verge of telling Elaine about Elam's marriage proposal but changed her mind. This was something she had to think about and work through on her own. She'd waited a long time for Elam to propose, and now that he finally had, she wasn't ready to give him an answer.

"How's it going, son?" Jonah's dad asked when he entered the buggy shop after running some errands.

"Things got busy after you left. Two people came by with new buggy orders, and three others had buggies needing to be repaired." Jonah motioned toward the back of the shop. "Timothy's started on one of those, while I've been trying to get caught up on some paperwork."

Dad pulled out a chair beside Jonah's desk and sat. "I'll chip in and help as soon as I get the things I bought in town for your mamm unloaded at the house. She needed a few things for the boppli, and I also picked up some groceries she asked me to get."

"I appreciate you taking care of all those things." Jonah smiled. "You and Mom have been a big help since Sara died. Don't know what I'd do without you. Makes me glad you left Pennsylvania and moved here to be my partner."

Dad put his hand on Jonah's shoulder. "We're glad to be here, too—not just to help out in your time of need, but because we enjoy being with you. It's good for us to be working together again, too."

"Jah," Jonah agreed. "When I first moved to Arthur, I thought I could manage on my own, but even with young Timothy's help, I'd get way behind if you weren't working in the buggy shop, too."

"Changing the subject, I assume you've heard about Priscilla Herschberger getting burned?"

Jonah nodded. "I learned about the accident from Adam when he stopped yesterday to get a new wheel for his market buggy. I was sorry to hear such terrible news, but it could have been a lot worse for Priscilla if David and Elam hadn't been there to care for her and call for help."

"You're right about that," Dad agreed. "It's one of many reasons it pays to have good friends."

Jonah pulled his fingers through the back of his hair. "Life is full of ups and downs. One never knows when some tragedy will occur, and of course, we are never ready for it."

"True, but if we put our faith and trust in God, He will see us through."

"That's what I'm trying to do."

"Before I go up to the house, I heard something you should know."

"What?"

"While I was at the grocery store, I overheard our bishop's wife talking to one of the women in our district. She said Ben and Elaine broke up."

"Is she sure it's true?"

"Beats me." Dad shrugged. "But Margaret always seems to be in the know."

Jonah leaned his elbows on the desk. "That's an interesting piece of news, but it doesn't pertain to me." He pushed back his chair and stood. "Think I'll go see if Timothy needs any help."

As Jonah headed toward the back of his shop, he couldn't help wondering what had happened between Elaine and Ben to cause their breakup. From what he'd heard, Ben was pretty serious about Elaine. He'd figured it was just a matter of time before they got married.

Sure wish I knew what happened between them, he thought. *Maybe Elaine did to Ben what she did to me. She may have let the poor fellow believe she loved him and then changed her mind. For Ben's sake, I hope that wasn't the case, because it took me some time to get over the pain of losing Elaine.*

CHAPTER 42

Leah sat on the porch swing beside Carrie, watching the hummingbirds flit to and from the feeders closest to the house. She found their antics not only relaxing but sometimes humorous as they twittered and chirped, vying for their favorite feeder. Some swooped in speedily, took a quick drink, and darted away. Others weren't about to give up their perch and remained for longer periods as they ate their share of the sweet nectar.

Farther over, near the edge of the yard and field, Leah realized the flowers she and the girls had planted toward the back of their property were blooming. Adam had built a raised flower bed, using flat rocks to form the base and a short wall. It was easy to tend, since she didn't have to bend over or get down on her knees.

The baby kicked, and Leah's thoughts switched gears. She placed Carrie's small hand on her stomach. "Can you feel the little kicks, Carrie? It's the boppli in my tummy, and he or she is going to be an active one, because there's sure a lot of movement going on right now."

Carrie's eyes brightened, and she giggled when the next kick came. *"Die* boppli *schpiele gem."*

Leah smiled. "I think you're right, Carrie. The baby likes to play."

Coal had been lying in one corner of the porch, and he lifted his head, looking in their direction. Then he rose and ambled over to Carrie. A few minutes of petting and the dog plodded back to the corner, plopping down again with a grunt.

When Linda and Amy came outside, Leah invited them to feel the baby's kicks.

"When did ya say the boppli will come?" Linda grinned, holding her hand against Leah's stomach.

"The end of August or early September," Leah replied. "Maybe you should practice diapering some of your dolls so you can help me when the baby comes."

Linda wrinkled her nose. "Eww. I don't wanna change *windele*. It's a smelly job."

"I'll change the boppli's diapers," Amy spoke up. "I'll do whatever you need me to do when the baby comes."

Leah gave Amy's arm a gentle pat. "I'm glad you're so willing to help."

"I'll help, too," Linda interjected. "Just no dirty windele."

"No one has to do anything they don't want to for the baby, but I will appreciate whatever help I get." Leah pointed to the buzzing little birds. "Right now, though, let's enjoy watching all these cute hummers."

Linda and Amy sat on the porch steps, staring up at the hummingbird feeders with eager expressions, while Carrie remained on the swing beside Leah.

Linda pointed toward the flower garden "Look! Look over there!"

Leah smiled. "The *blumme* are pretty, jah?"

"Not the flowers. Look between those two rocks."

All heads turned in that direction. Leah didn't see anything at first and was about to ask what Linda had seen, when Carrie squealed, "It's Chippy! He's back!"

"How long has it been since we last saw the little chipmunk?" Amy asked.

"It's been awhile." Leah hugged Carrie. She knew how much the little girl had enjoyed watching the chipmunk when it came into their yard before.

As they sat watching the critter stick its head out then disappear, suddenly another little head appeared.

"Hey, Chippy has a friend!" Amy's eyes twinkled.

"It looks like the little chipmunks have found a good home, too," Leah added. Chippy must have liked the rock wall Adam had built for the flower garden.

Time flew by as Leah and the girls watched the two critters venture from the rocks into the yard. They went back and forth several times, as though they had some sort of plan.

"Can we get some peanuts for Chippy and his new friend?" Carrie tugged on Leah's sleeve.

Leah nodded. "Good idea. There's a bag in the pantry. Let's give him those."

"I'll get it!" Linda jumped up and raced into the house. When she returned with the peanuts, the three girls walked hand in hand to the flower bed. Leah watched from the porch as they dropped some of the nuts on the ground and on the row of rocks. Then they backed up and waited. Shortly, both chipmunks came out. It was cute to see Amy standing behind her younger sisters, with her arms stretched around their shoulders. The young girl was growing up so quickly. Leah couldn't help thinking what a good mother Amy would make someday.

Linda and Carrie stood very still, with their hands over their mouths, as though holding back a squeal as the chipmunks ate the nuts. Amy turned and smiled at Leah. No words were needed as they shared their unspoken happiness.

Lord, thank You for Adam, Leah prayed, *and for allowing me the privilege of helping him raise his nieces. Thank You for helping Amy overcome her initial fears about me having a baby.* She placed her hand against her stomach, patting it gently. *Help me to be a good mother to this little one I am carrying.*

Chicago

It had been a few days since David returned home, but he felt no better about things. In fact, he felt worse. This morning he'd received a letter from Priscilla, most of which he couldn't make out because it was smudged, making most of the words unreadable. The envelope looked like it had been dropped in a mud puddle, causing water to seep through the envelope. Well, it didn't matter. Nothing she said would change his mind. He was not going back to Arthur or joining the Amish church.

David rubbed his temples as he sat at the kitchen table staring at the rumpled letter he'd been unable to fully read. He wouldn't bother to reply to it. *It's better for everyone that I left Arthur. Priscilla's in love with Elam, and I was wrong for trying to horn in. I've been selfish and inconsiderate, only thinking of what I want. Just look where it got me. I should have stuck with my plans to become a veterinarian. At least my folks would have been happy, and I do like working with animals, so maybe in the end, I'd have been happy, too.*

"Are you all right, David? You look upset." Mom put her hands on David's shoulders.

"I am. Or as the Amish would say, 'I'm feeling umgerennt right now.'"

"Umgerennt? What does that mean?"

"It's the Pennsylvania Dutch word for 'upset.'"

Mom took a seat at the kitchen table beside David. "I've known since you returned to Chicago that something was troubling you, son. Would you like to talk about it?"

If it had been David's father asking the question, David would have declined, but Mom had always been more understanding. David took a deep breath and poured out his story. He ended by saying he felt guilty because Priscilla had gotten burned.

Mom sat several seconds, fingering the tablecloth. "I understand now why you came home, but you're being too hard on yourself, David."

David continued to rub his temples. "What do you mean?"

"You didn't purposely leave the stove on, right?"

"Course not. I thought I'd turned it off, but I've gone over it again and again, and now I'm not really sure."

"I understand how that can be. I've done many things without realizing I'd done them." Mom tapped his arm. "Blaming yourself for Priscilla's accident will do no good for you or her.

What's done is done. You need to put this all behind you and move on."

"How am I supposed to get that awful night out of my head, Mom?" A lump crept into David's throat, making it hard to swallow. He couldn't get rid of the image of Priscilla on the kitchen floor, trying to put out the flames on her dress.

"You could go back to college and finish the courses you need to prepare for veterinary school."

"I may consider going back in the fall." David pushed away from the table. "In the meantime, I'll talk to Dad about helping out at his veterinary clinic. Even if all I do is clean up the place after hours, it'll be better than sitting around here feeling sorry for myself." His forehead wrinkled. "I'm still not sure becoming a vet and working with Dad is what I want to do with the rest of my life. I really did like the slower pace of the Amish life."

"Do you have to become Amish in order to slow down and enjoy the simpler things?" Mom asked.

"No, I suppose not. I just. . . Oh, never mind. I'll be fine once I've been here awhile and figure out what I want to do."

Arthur

No matter how hard Elam tried, he couldn't seem to concentrate on his work. He'd gone to see Priscilla last night, but she'd barely said two words. Later, when he got ready to leave, Priscilla's mother had whispered to Elam that her daughter had been struggling with depression.

"After what happened to her, how could she not be depressed?" Elam mumbled.

"Did you say something, son?"

Elam jumped at the sound of his dad's deep voice. He thought he'd been working alone at the back of their bulk food store, where he'd been putting several new items on the shelves.

Elam whirled around. "Uh. . .guess ya caught me talkin' to myself."

"Don't be doin' too much of that, because a lot needs to be done yet today. The only good thing about talkin' to yourself is you usually get the answer you're looking for." Dad studied Elam a few seconds. "You okay? You look kind of sullen."

Elam blew out his breath. "I'm worried about Priscilla. Just can't get her out of my mind."

"It's understandable, since you two have been courting so long. She's going through a lot right now and needs all the support she can get."

"I asked Priscilla to marry me, but she said she couldn't give me an answer yet." Elam bit his bottom lip so hard, he tasted blood. "If David hadn't left Arthur, she may have chosen him instead of me. Guess I waited too long to ask her. If I hadn't been so worried about saving up enough money for us to have a home, Priscilla and I may have been married by now."

"I'm sure she still cares for you, Elam," Dad said. "It's going to be awhile before her burns have healed. She needs time to deal with things. It would be distressing for anyone to go through what she's had to face." He gave Elam's shoulder a squeeze. "Try to be patient, and keep giving her your love and support. Every woman needs reassurance, whether she's going through a traumatic event or not."

Elam nodded. "Guess that's all I can do. Now that David is gone, at least I have a better chance with Priscilla." He lowered his gaze. *Now if I could only come to grips with what's happened to her.*

CHAPTER 43

Days turned into weeks, and by the end of July, Priscilla felt better. The areas where she'd been burned were no longer painful or blistered. But as the skin peeled off and new skin appeared underneath, it remained red. As instructed, she'd have to stay out of the direct sun for a while. Hopefully, none of the red areas would leave a scar, but only time would tell. She'd also been getting plenty of rest and doing exercises to keep her skin supple. She didn't want it to draw up and leave her handicapped.

As Priscilla sat in the covered area on the back porch, breathing in the warm air, she thought about David. She still hadn't heard anything from him, and couldn't help feeling disappointed. Elaine had assured Priscilla that she'd sent the letter. Apparently, David had chosen not to respond. She'd even tried calling his cell number, but he'd never returned any of her messages. Was David deliberately trying to avoid her? How could he say he loved her and then take off like he did and not bother to respond to her letter or phone calls? Could David have only been pretending to care about her? If so, he'd sure had her fooled.

Sure wish I could talk to him, she thought. *If I saw David face-to-face, maybe I could make him understand I don't blame him for what happened to me. If he was serious about becoming Amish, he shouldn't have left.*

"Would you like some company?" Mom took a seat on the bench beside Priscilla, halting her thoughts.

Priscilla moved her head slowly up and down. "Of course I would."

"It started out to be a pleasantly warm day, but it's gotten hotter now—especially in the house." Mom sighed. "I'm glad I got all my baking done this morning, because I wouldn't want to do it now. The kitchen would soon feel like an oven."

The mention of the kitchen feeling like an oven caused Priscilla to shudder. She would never forget the stifling smoke and the horrific pain she'd endured from the corn popper catching fire. She felt thankful the whole kitchen hadn't been ablaze, which it could have been if the fire on the stove hadn't been put out. A few days after Priscilla's accident, Dad had repainted the kitchen, which removed any signs of the smoke.

"It won't be long and it'll be time to pick and can our corn," Mom said. "Your burns are healing so nicely you should be able to help with that."

Priscilla nodded. "I'm glad Elaine came over to assist you when the strawberries were ripe, since I wasn't able to do anything to help."

Mom smiled. "You're fortunate to have good friends like Elaine and Leah."

"I know." Priscilla drank from the glass of lemonade she'd brought outside after lunch. "Mind if I ask you something, Mom?"

"Of course not. What do you want to know?"

"Have I received any letters from David?"

"None that I know of." Mom leaned closer to Priscilla. "I hope you don't think I'd throw his letters away. I'd promised you before that I would never do it again."

Priscilla took another drink and set her glass on the table near her chair. "I wonder why he hasn't responded to my letter."

"I didn't even know you had written to David. How long ago was that?"

"Soon after you gave me the note he left in our mailbox. I asked Elaine to write it for me."

"Are you sure she mailed it?"

"She said she did." She sighed deeply. "I really expected he would have answered by now."

"Maybe he's been busy."

"I can't imagine him being too busy to write back, or at least call and leave a message for me." Priscilla rubbed a spot on her arm that had begun to itch, being careful not to scratch. "I thought we were good friends, but friends don't ignore each other like that." *I thought he had feelings for me that went beyond friendship, too.* Of course, Priscilla didn't voice her thoughts to her mother. Like Elam, Mom was probably glad David had gone back to Chicago and given up his plans to become Amish. It was a shame Mom hadn't gotten to know David better. She may have seen him in a different light.

Of course, Priscilla conceded, *I thought I knew him fairly well, but I guess I was wrong, for I never expected him to turn his back on me when I was going through a difficult time.*

Mom looked like she might say something more to Priscilla, but a horse and buggy had just pulled up to the area near their store. "Guess I'd better see who it is and what they need to buy from our store." Mom rose from her seat. "We'll talk more later, Priscilla."

After Mom left, Priscilla decided to go back inside. She was tired and thought a short nap might help, so she curled up on the couch. In no time at all she drifted off.

Elam yawned as he headed down the road in his open buggy toward the Hershbergers' place. Turning his head from side to side, he tried to get the spasms in his neck to relax. He hadn't slept well last night and had been plagued with the same reoccurring dream about Priscilla and David.

Maybe I should have stepped aside and let David have her. Since she still hasn't accepted my marriage proposal, it could be a clue that she cares more for him than me.

Frowning, he clutched the horse's reins tighter as the troubling thoughts whirled in his head. *I don't think I can do that. I love her too much.*

If Elam could clear the slate and start over with Priscilla, he surely would. If he'd proposed to her before David moved to Arthur, she'd have probably accepted, and none of this would be an issue right now. It was his fault, though, for worrying too much about having enough money to begin a life with Priscilla. He should have at least explained that he wanted to marry her but felt the need to wait until he was better prepared financially.

It didn't do any good to fret about that now. He just hoped Priscilla would give him an answer to his proposal today. He couldn't imagine living the rest of his life without her, but if she rejected him, he'd have to find a way to deal with it.

Elam snapped the reins to get his horse moving faster. For some reason, Gus was being a slowpoke this Saturday afternoon.

When Elam pulled his rig up to the hitching rack near the barn, he spotted Priscilla's mother coming out of the store where she sold jams and other home-canned items. She waved, and when he approached, she smiled and said, "*Wie geht's*, Elam?"

"Good day," he replied. Glancing past Iva, his gaze came to rest on a ruby-red cardinal that had landed in the tree nearby. "I'm doing okay. How 'bout you?"

"I'm fine, but I'd be better if it hadn't turned out so hot and muggy today." She lifted a corner of her apron and fanned her face with it. "It was much cooler this morning when Priscilla and I sat on the porch visiting."

Elam glanced toward the house. "Speaking of Priscilla, is she inside right now?"

Iva nodded. "But I just checked on her a few minutes ago, and she was sleeping."

"Oh, I see. Guess I'd better not disturb her then." Elam's gaze dropped to the ground. He couldn't hide his disappointment. He'd really wanted—no needed—to see her today.

"You can wait till she wakes up if you want to." Iva bent down and pulled a handful of weeds from the flower bed close to the house.

"I'd better not. She might be asleep for a while, and I need to get back to the store soon to help my daed with an afternoon delivery that's supposed to come."

"I'll tell Priscilla you were here. She'll be sorry she missed you."

"Will she be at church tomorrow?" Elam asked. Priscilla hadn't been there at all since her accident. At first it was because of her pain, but then later she'd mentioned that she didn't want people making a fuss over her, or worse yet, staring at her hands and arms with pity.

"I believe she will go." Iva reached for another clump of weeds. "If you don't get to visit with her after church, we'd love to have you come by here tomorrow evening for a meal."

Elam smiled. "That'd be nice. Mom's been wanting to have Priscilla to our place for a meal, too, but we can do that some other time." He turned to go, calling over his shoulder. "Tell Priscilla I'll see her tomorrow morning."

*

As Iva watched Elam's horse and buggy pull out, she couldn't help thinking something about him had changed. Ever since Priscilla's accident he'd acted a bit strange. Today she'd noticed he seemed to have trouble making eye contact with her. Elam had dark circles under his eyes, too. No doubt from lack of sleep.

I wonder if Elam fears Priscilla won't marry him if she ends up with scars from her burns. Surely she knows he's not concerned with how she looks. Maybe I should talk with her about it.

Iva arched her back, hoping to get the kinks out. She'd done enough weeding for one day and had some more things she needed to get done in the store. The weeding could wait for another day. If she kept at it now, she'd probably end up at the chiropractor's or seeing Leah for a foot treatment.

Iva had just started walking toward the store when Elaine rode in on her bike. She parked it near the house and joined Iva on the lawn.

"I just dropped by Adam's store to give Ben a fawn rock I'd made for him and decided to come by here to see how Priscilla is doing." Elaine smiled. "I've been wondering how long it'll be before she can help me host the dinners again."

"She's napping right now, but I can already tell you she won't be up to helping you for several more weeks." Iva brushed some dirt off her hands. She'd need to wash them when she went in the store.

"I was hoping it might be sooner. The two young women I hired to take her place have a wedding to attend next weekend, and I have a dinner scheduled for the same Friday evening." Elaine stared across the yard. "Guess I'll try to manage it myself, but things would go much easier if I had some help."

Iva tapped her chin, contemplating things. "Say, I wonder if Adam's oldest niece, Amy, would be of any help to you. She's almost twelve years old. Leah's told Priscilla that Amy's a big help around the house."

Elaine smiled. "You know, I've never even thought about asking Amy. Danki for the suggestion. Since Priscilla's sleeping, I don't want to bother her, so I think I'll head over to the Beachys' place right now and ask."

Elaine mounted her bike, and as she pedaled down the driveway,

Iva stepped into her store. It seemed like things were working out for many in their community these days. Now if only everything went well for Priscilla in the days ahead, Iva would be happy.

As Elaine headed down the road in the direction of Leah's, her thoughts turned to Jonah. Truth was, she seemed to be thinking about him a lot lately.

Oh, Jonah, why can't I get you out of my mind? In the year Jonah had been married to Sara, Elaine had managed to push her thoughts of him behind—almost like a distant dream. She'd moved on with her life, and he'd moved on with his. Why, now, did she think of him nearly every day? They were both unattached, and free to begin a romance, but she knew Jonah wasn't seeking that.

I wonder if he knows Ben and I broke up. If Jonah has heard, does he even care? Elaine wished she felt free to tell Jonah herself that she and Ben were no longer a couple, but that would be too bold. Jonah might think she was dropping a hint she was available and interested in him courting her again.

I'm sure Jonah will eventually find out about me and Ben, so I'll leave it in God's hands. In the meantime, I'll pray and seek God's will for both me and Jonah.

CHAPTER 44

Priscilla didn't know why, but she felt nervous this morning. It wasn't like she'd never gone to church before. She just hadn't gone with red blotches on her hands and arms. Her dress sleeves covered most of them, but her lower arms and hands showed, and she felt self-conscious about it.

"It's good to see you here today," Elaine whispered as she took a seat beside Priscilla on the women's side of the room, waiting for the service to begin. Today church was being held in the addition Elaine's grandfather had built many years ago for the large dinners her grandmother hosted. It looked much different now than when Elaine held the dinners. The tables she used to serve guests had been folded and put away. In their place were backless wooden benches, providing enough seating for those in attendance. A few folding chairs had also been set up for some of the older folks who couldn't sit for a long period of time without back support.

"I'm glad to be back," Priscilla responded. "And I'm sorry I missed seeing you yesterday. Mom said both you and Elam came by while I was napping. I wish she would have woken me up."

Elaine shook her head. "I'm glad she didn't. You needed your rest."

"Seems all I've done since my accident is rest." Priscilla huffed. "I'm anxious to get back to the task of living."

"Coming here today is the first step of many."

Priscilla glanced across at Elam and smiled when he gave her a nod. She noticed his leg twitching and then bouncing up and down, like he had a nervous tremor. *What does Elam have to be jumpy about? I'm the one full of anxiety today.*

It seemed strange not to see David. He'd sat on the same bench as Elam during the last church service Priscilla had attended. It really bothered her that he hadn't called or written.

Maybe I should write to him again or try calling his cell number. Maybe that's what I'll do. Don't know why I didn't think of it till now.

Priscilla's thoughts were redirected when everyone began singing. Their varied but blended voices bounced off the walls, lifting to the ceiling in worshipful praise to the Father. It was good to be back in church among her people. She needed to focus on that.

Elaine tried to concentrate on the song they were singing, but it was hard not to watch Jonah as he struggled to keep Mark from fidgeting. Sara had always kept him well occupied during church services. No doubt the boy still missed his mother.

I'm sure Jonah still misses Sara, too. I wonder if he loved her more than he did me. I'm sure Jonah's feelings for me died when he married Sara. Elaine's fingers dug into her palms. *I shouldn't be thinking such thoughts—especially not here in church.*

She glanced at Leah and noticed her fanning her face with a piece of paper, while squirming on the bench. She was clearly uncomfortable today. The warmth and humidity likely played a part in that, and she was no doubt having trouble finding a comfortable position. It wouldn't be long before Leah would be holding her baby in her arms. Elaine tried not to be envious, but having children of her own had always been a dream. It didn't seem likely to happen, since she wouldn't be marrying Ben, and Jonah had no interest in her. Perhaps someday she would meet someone else and fall in love, but that seemed doubtful.

Elaine drew in a quick breath, forcing her attention to the first sermon being preached.

Jonah felt relieved when his dad offered to take Mark. Due to the oppressive heat they'd been having lately, Jonah hadn't been sleeping well, and dealing with a restless boy who was also tired caused him to feel more stressed. He couldn't blame his son for fidgeting. Several other children in the service were fussy, too.

It was hard to concentrate on the bishop's sermon, and Jonah knew he shouldn't, but he glanced at the women's section. His gaze came to rest on Elaine. Unexpectedly, she made eye contact with him, and he quickly looked away. He hoped no one had noticed.

Glancing at the bench where Ben sat, Jonah wondered once again what had really happened between Ben and Elaine. Were they still friends? Was there a chance they might get back together?

Jonah fanned his face with his hand. *I need to stop thinking about this and focus on the bishop's message.*

Elam was pleased to see Priscilla here today. Since he hadn't seen her yesterday, he looked forward to visiting during the evening meal at her folks' house. If she felt up to it, maybe they could go for a buggy ride after they ate, which would help them cool off and give them time for visiting privately.

He pinned his arms against his stomach, troubled by the bishop's sermon topic on guilt. To make matters worse, the room they were in was so hot Elam could hardly breathe. Beneath his vest, Elam's shirt clung to him like flypaper on the wall, while rivulets of sweat rolled down his temples. He couldn't wait until the service was over so he could get outside, where he hoped the air would be less stifling.

The bishop's voice grew louder as he expounded on the need to confess one's sins, using Acts 3:19 as a reference. "'Repent ye. . .and be converted, that your sins may be blotted out.'" He also quoted John 8:32: "'Ye shall know the truth, and the truth shall make you free.'"

When the service was finally over, Elam made a dash for the door. Taking in several deep breaths he headed toward the barn, pausing to lean on the fence.

"Are you okay?" Adam asked, stepping up to Elam. "You look umgerennt."

Elam rubbed the back of his neck. "To tell ya the truth, I am upset."

"Do you want to talk about it, or should I mind my own business?"

Elam scrubbed his sweaty palms on the side of his trousers, struggling with the desire to flee. As much as he wanted to tell someone the way he felt, Elam wasn't sure he could spit the words out. Yet if he didn't get this off his chest, he feared it would eat him alive.

"Promise you won't say anything to Leah about what I'm going to tell you?"

Adam frowned. "What's this got to do with my fraa?"

"Nothing. It's just... Well, she's one of Priscilla's closest friends, and if Leah finds out what I did, she'll probably tell Priscilla."

"Tell me what?"

Elam whirled around. "Priscilla! I didn't know you were there. I thought you were helping the women get lunch on the tables."

"I was, and it's ready. I came to tell you that." She looked at Elam strangely, her eyes narrowing slightly. "What were you going to tell Adam you don't want me or Leah knowing about?"

Elam glanced at Adam then back at Priscilla. As hot as he'd felt inside, it was nothing compared to the way he felt now. If he didn't get this off his chest, he might never tell Priscilla the truth. He hoped when she found out, she would find it in her heart to forgive him.

CHAPTER 45

"Think I'd better go and leave you two alone." Adam gave Elam's shoulder a squeeze and headed back to the house, where lunch was being served. From Elam's somber expression, Adam had a hunch whatever he'd been about to tell him was something serious.

"Where have you been?" Ben asked when Adam entered the house and took a seat beside him at one of the tables. "Thought maybe I was gonna have to eat your share of the food."

Adam thumped his stomach. "It wouldn't be the end of the world. I could probably stand to lose a few pounds."

Ben rolled his eyes. "Are you kidding? You're about as fit and trim as any man I know. Must be all the hard work you do at your store."

They bowed their heads for silent prayer. When Adam opened his eyes, he glanced out the window and saw Elam and Priscilla near the barn. *Sure hope everything goes okay between them right now.*

"What is it you didn't want Adam telling Leah because you were afraid she'd tell me?" Priscilla moved closer to Elam.

As though needing support, he continued to lean on the fence post while clearing his throat. "It's. . .umm. . . about how you got burned."

Priscilla's eyebrows squeezed together. "What do you mean? I know how I got burned. The sleeve of my dress caught on fire when I tried to turn off the stove."

Elam shook his head. "I'm talking about how the pan caught fire."

"David forgot to turn off the burner before he went outside to check on his horse. Why are we talking about this again, Elam?" Shooing a pesky fly off her arm, Priscilla felt more confused than ever.

Elam shifted from one foot to the other. Priscilla couldn't figure out why he was acting so strange. Then she remembered during the service how fidgety and nervous he'd seemed. "What's wrong, Elam?

How come you seem so naerfich today?"

Elam blew out his breath. "The fire didn't happen the way you think, Priscilla."

She tipped her head. "How did it happen?"

"The truth is, I'm the one who left the stove on." Elam dropped his gaze to the ground.

Stunned, Priscilla backed up to the nearest tree. "Wh–what do you mean? I don't understand."

"When David went outside to check on his horse, he turned off the stove. Thinking it would be good to get the popcorn done, I turned the stove back on. Then I went to the bathroom, but before I was able to return to the kitchen, the pan must have gotten too hot, and it caught fire."

Priscilla's eyes narrowed. "This whole time you knew David had turned it off, but you let him take the blame? How could you, Elam?"

He lifted his face to look at her. "I was ashamed to admit I had done it, and I was angry at David, because—"

"So you let David and me think he was the one responsible?" Priscilla's finger shook as she pointed at Elam. "You're not the man I thought you were."

Elam reached his hand out to her, but she pulled back. "I know what I did was wrong, Priscilla, and I'm begging you to forgive me. My only excuse is I love you so much and was afraid if you knew I was the one who caused the fire, you would choose David instead of me."

Priscilla's voice trembled. "Oh, really? Is that how you show your love for me—by lying?" She turned away. "Well, Elam, know this. It's over between us."

"Oh, please, Priscilla, you can't mean it. We've been a couple for a long time, and I want to marry you."

"I'm sorry, Elam, but it's over." Trembling, Priscilla dashed back to Elaine's house, where the others were eating. Struggling to hold back tears, she sought her mother and said she needed to go home.

Mom looked at her with concern. "Are you *grank*?"

"I'm not sick. I just need to go home."

"Maybe today has been too much for you." Mom slipped her arm around Priscilla's waist. "We'll go as soon as your daed finishes eating. Why don't you come over and try to eat something, too? You might feel better once you have some food in your stomach."

Priscilla shook her head. "If you and Dad want to finish your meals, that's fine, but I'm not hungry. I'll wait for you in the buggy."

Mom looked hesitant but finally nodded. "Okay, I'll get your daed."

Choking on sobs rising in her throat, Priscilla sprinted for the buggy. She needed to be alone to think things through. She was still in shock over Elam's confession. Did he expect her to accept this news and go on as though nothing had happened?

"How are things with you, Ben?" Adam asked as he enjoyed vanilla ice cream and the brownies Leah had made for dessert.

"Guess you heard Elaine and I broke up." Ben took the last bite of his apple pie.

Adam's brows furrowed. "I didn't know. Sorry to hear that, Ben." Adam wondered if Leah knew this and just hadn't said anything. "Since we're done eating, would you like to take a walk?"

"Sure. It'll give us a chance to talk in private."

Adam and Ben got more coffee then ventured outdoors. No one else was around the corner of the yard they'd chosen.

"When did this happen with you and Elaine?" Adam blew on his coffee, waiting for Ben to respond.

"Around the end of May. It was the same night Priscilla got burned," Ben answered. "With everything else going on, maybe Elaine forgot to say anything to Leah."

"Could be." Adam paused, searching for the right words. "Are you okay with all of this?"

"I'm good now, since I've had time to think about everything." Ben took a deep breath. "I realize I was just fooling myself, thinking Elaine would marry me. When we talked that Saturday night, she said I could never be more than her friend. I pretended it didn't matter, but truthfully, while we were courting, I'd hoped her feelings for me would turn into love. Guess it wasn't supposed to be."

"I'm sorry it didn't work out." Adam placed his hand on Ben's shoulder. "Are you and Elaine still on good terms?"

"Jah. Since Elaine was the first person I developed a friendship with after my family and I moved to Arthur, it would be hard to turn off our friendship, just like that." Ben snapped his fingers. "I really have to wonder, though, if Elaine might still be in love with Jonah."

Adam shrugged. From what Leah had told him, before Elaine's grandmother became ill, she and Jonah almost got married. He wondered if Elaine had ever stopped loving Jonah.

"It's good you can remain friends with Elaine." Adam took a seat in one of the chairs on the lawn. Ben did the same. "It would be difficult any other way. Like today, for instance, seeing her here at church."

"I'll admit it was kind of hard seeing her this morning, knowing we're no longer courting. Guess I'll get used to the idea, though."

Adam felt bad for his friend. He hoped someday Ben would find someone special who'd love him the way he deserved.

Ben extended his hand to shake Adam's. "I'm glad we talked, but now I think I'd better head home."

"I need to go, too, so I'll round up my girls. See you at work tomorrow." As Ben headed for his horse, Adam walked to the back of the house, where several people mingled. He spotted Carrie, Linda, and Amy playing with a group of children, and waved them over.

"Are you about ready to head home?" Leah asked, joining Adam and the girls.

"I am if you are." Adam smiled. "How about you girls? Are you ready to go home?"

Amy bobbed her head. "We've gotta fill the hummingbird feeders. They were almost empty when we left this morning."

"I wanna check on Chippy." Linda hopped up and down, and Carrie joined in, squealing, "Chippy! Chippy! Chippy!"

Leah laughed as the girls raced to the buggy. "I helped Elaine clear the tables, and a few other women said they would stay to help her finish."

Adam looked toward the girls to make sure they were out of earshot. "Did Elaine say anything to you about Ben?"

"She said he won't be courting her anymore, but they'll remain friends."

Adam nodded. "That's what Ben told me. It's too bad, but hopefully things will work out for both of them."

"I hope so." Leah's eyes glistened. "Oh, Adam, feel this." She took his hand and placed it against her stomach. "The boppli's been kicking up a storm since I ate. Maybe he likes those brownies I made."

Adam chuckled. "You seem so sure it's a boy."

She smiled. "I have a feeling it might be, but either way is fine with me."

"Same here." Grinning, Adam's heart overflowed with joy.

As they walked hand in hand, he reflected on the reasons he and Leah had gotten married and how their relationship had blossomed. Helping his wife climb into the buggy, where Amy, Linda, and Carrie were waiting, Adam couldn't imagine life without Leah and those precious girls. God had surely blessed him.

Elam's legs trembled so bad, he could barely remain standing. He'd struggled with the need to tell Priscilla what he'd done ever since she'd gotten burned, but he hadn't been able to work up the nerve until today. Even then, he'd felt he had no other choice. This morning when the bishop preached on guilt and the need to confess one's sins, Elam had fallen under conviction and had to tell someone. He'd chosen Adam, hoping for advice, but ended up confessing to Priscilla instead. If he'd been able to discuss it with Adam and there'd been more time before she'd shown up, things may have gone better. Since Iva had invited Elam over this evening, it would have given him an opportunity to be alone with Priscilla so they could talk privately. Now he wouldn't be going to dinner at the Hershbergers'. Elam reminded himself that he'd had plenty of time since Priscilla's accident to confess, but unfortunately, he'd blown it.

Elam started walking, kicking up gravel as he headed for his horse. *I should have told Priscilla right away. If I'd explained as soon as it happened, maybe she would have forgiven me, like she did when she thought it was David.*

Tears blurred Elam's vision so he could hardly see to hitch his horse to the buggy. If he could only go back and do things over again, he would never have turned the stove burner back on after David went outside. He'd have used the bathroom and waited for Priscilla to come back downstairs. He'd hoped to have the popcorn made so she'd be impressed that he'd done it for her. It may have given him an edge over David, who seemed to always be trying to win Priscilla's favor.

If the accident hadn't occurred, and Priscilla was given the chance to choose between me and David, I wonder who she would pick. Would she choose David or agree to become my wife? Elam drew in a sharp breath as a new realization hit him: *Priscilla will never marry me now that she knows what I did. There's nothing I can do to repair the damage.*

As Elam climbed in his buggy and backed the horse from the hitching rack, he made a decision. Priscilla deserved to be happy, and he would make sure it happened.

CHAPTER 46

Shelly Howe will be coming by to pick me up soon," Priscilla announced during breakfast Monday morning. "I arranged it with her last night."

"Oh? Where are you going?" Mom asked.

"To Chicago, to see David."

"Priscilla, you can't go running off to Chicago by yourself to see a man who doesn't want to be here anymore."

Priscilla thrust out her chin. "David didn't want to go, Mom. He left because he believed he was responsible for my burns. He needs to know the truth."

"What truth?" Mom glanced at Dad, as if looking to him for an answer, but he merely shrugged in response.

"What truth?" Mom repeated, this time looking at Priscilla.

"Elam left the stove on, not David."

Mom's fingers touched her parted lips as she let out a gasp.

Dad looked at Priscilla with a dazed expression. "Come again?"

"After church yesterday, Elam confessed that he'd left the stove on." Priscilla paused to collect her thoughts and take a drink of water. "I'm not upset because he went to the bathroom and left the stove unattended. I'm disappointed that he didn't admit it right away. Instead, he allowed David to take the blame."

"I—I don't know what to say," Mom stammered. "I never would have expected Elam to do something like that."

"Nor I," Dad spoke up. "What in the world was he thinking?"

Priscilla stared at her plate of untouched pancakes. "He's jealous of David and wanted to drive him away."

Mom let out a little gasp. "Oh my!"

"Now do you see why I need to speak with David?" Priscilla lifted her hand. "I can't let him go on thinking he did this to me."

"You're right. He does need to know," Dad interjected. "You

have my blessing to go."

Mom pursed her lips. "What Elam did was wrong, but I still believe he loves you, Priscilla. If you choose David instead of Elam, I know he will be crushed."

Priscilla shook her head. "This isn't about choosing anyone, Mom. I'm just going to tell David the truth. If he does come back to Arthur, it'll be his decision. Whatever happens after that will be in God's hands."

Dad gave a decisive nod. "That's absolutely right."

Priscilla glanced at the kitchen clock. "Shelly will be here for me soon, so I need to finish breakfast and be ready when she arrives. I have his parents' address, and hopefully we'll find him there."

Mom looked at Dad. "Can't you persuade her not to go?"

He shook his head. "Priscilla is not a little girl anymore, Iva. She's a grown woman and can make her own decisions. If Priscilla thinks it's important to visit David, then we should support her decision."

"I suppose you're right." Mom reached over and gently touched Priscilla's arm. "Are you sure you're up to the trip?"

Priscilla nodded. "And even if I'm not, I feel it's important for me to go."

A short time later, a horn honked outside. Priscilla rose from her chair. "That must be my driver, Mom. Should I run out and tell her to come in while I help you do the dishes?"

Mom shook her head. "No, that's okay. I'll do them myself this morning."

"Danki, Mom." Priscilla gave both parents a hug.

"Have a safe trip," Dad said as Priscilla grabbed her purse and moved toward the door. "We'll be praying everything goes well when you see David today."

As Iva washed the breakfast dishes, she couldn't stop thinking about the things Priscilla had told them. *What will happen when our daughter gets to Chicago and sees David?* Iva wondered. *Will she convince him to come back to Arthur and join the Amish church? Could David try to persuade Priscilla to leave her family and faith and become part of his English world?*

Iva continued to fret as she sloshed the soapy sponge over Daniel's favorite coffee mug. *I wish Elam would have been up-front with Priscilla and told her right away that he was the one who'd left the stove on. Even though what Elam did was wrong, I hope he and Priscilla will get back together.* She'd known for some time that they cared for each other. It would be a shame if their relationship ended now. Iva felt sure Elam loved Priscilla and probably felt guilty for what he'd done. Surely, Priscilla knew that, too.

Iva wished she could discuss this more with Daniel, but he'd gone outside to work in his shop shortly after Priscilla left. He'd mentioned a gazebo their bishop wanted to give his wife as an anniversary surprise and hurried out the door before Iva could voice more of her concerns.

She sighed. "Oh well. Daniel probably wouldn't have listened to what I had to say about Priscilla anyhow. He always seems to side with her."

It wasn't that Iva was trying to control her daughter's life. She only wanted the best for her. And to her way of thinking, David Morgan was not a good choice.

"I appreciate you letting me take the day off," Elam told his dad as they sat at the kitchen table, eating breakfast. "I hope things don't get too busy at the bulk food store while I'm gone."

Dad thumped Elam's arm. "We'll be fine. Just go do what ya need to do."

Relieved and appreciative of his dad's understanding, Elam nodded. "I messed things up with Priscilla, but maybe it's not too late to make things right with David."

Yesterday, after they'd returned home from church, Elam had admitted to his folks that he was the one responsible for Priscilla's burns. Telling them that had been hard enough, but explaining his reasons for letting David take the blame made it seem even worse. Mom had been shocked, and Dad said he was ashamed of Elam for being so deceitful. Then they'd both encouraged him to make things right—first with God and then those he had hurt. That was exactly what he planned to do, and the sooner the better.

A horn honked, and Elam pushed away from the table. "My driver's here. I'd better go." He leaned down and gave Mom a peck on the cheek. "Would you keep me in your prayers today?"

She smiled up at him. "Of course. I pray for my kinner every day."

"I'll be praying, too," Dad said as Elam slipped on his hat and started for the door. "And remember, son, God is in control. You just need to pray and ask for His will to be done."

"I know, but danki for the reminder." As Elam headed out the door, he lifted a silent prayer. *Lord, please give me the right words to say to David, and help me accept whatever happens today.*

Elaine parked her bike near Leah's house then stepped onto the porch and knocked on the door. She'd slept fitfully last night due to the unrelenting heat and had woken up with a headache. Since she didn't have an appointment, she hoped she would find Leah at home and able to fit in a reflexology treatment for her.

Coal got up to greet her from the corner of the porch. "How ya doing, boy?" Elaine bent down to scratch behind the Lab's ears. Coal gave out a whiny yawn then plodded back to his spot to lie down. "I know how you feel," Elaine murmured. "This heat is getting to me, too."

Despite her pounding headache, Elaine couldn't help smiling at the hummingbirds as they chattered noisily, flitting from one tree to the other.

Leah opened the door and smiled. "Guder mariye, Elaine."

"Good morning."

"You look like you're under the weather. Are you grank?"

"I woke up with a koppweh and was wondering if you'd have time to give me a foot treatment." Elaine touched her forehead.

"Of course. Come in." Leah stepped aside and Elaine entered the house. "The girls are in the barn looking at the newborn kittens. I'm sure they'll be awhile so we won't be disturbed. Let's go in the living room and you can sit in the recliner."

"Danki. I feel bad asking you to do this without making an appointment."

Leah shook her head. "It's not a problem."

Elaine removed her shoes and socks then leaned back into the chair, while Leah went to get her massage lotion. When she returned, she took a seat on the footstool in front of Elaine.

"Before you came to the door I was watching your hummingbirds. You have a feisty one that likes to chase the other males away."

"I know. A few out of the bunch act as if they own the feeders. You can learn so much by watching those little birds' antics." Leah poured massage lotion into the palm of her hand and rubbed some on Elaine's right foot. "I'll work on this foot first and see if you get any relief. Then I'll move on to the left foot."

"You know best."

"Are you feeling stressed over your breakup with Ben?" Leah asked as she began to pressure-point the heel of Elaine's foot. "Is that what brought the headache on?"

"No, Ben and I realized we can never be more than friends." Elaine drew in a deep breath and released it slowly. "I doubt my headache is from stress over that. What brought this on is lack of sleep, which was caused from the heat. Even with all the windows open, not a hint of cool air came into my bedroom last night."

"It was the same way here. Amy, Linda, and Carrie slept in the living room because their rooms upstairs were too hot. Guess we'd better get used to it, though. If it's this warm in July, can you imagine how it will be in August?"

Elaine winced when Leah touched a sore spot, but she didn't say anything about it. From previous treatments, finding a tender area was a good thing, because it meant Leah was getting to the root of her problem.

In an effort to relax, Elaine closed her eyes. An unbidden image of Jonah came to mind. *Sure wish I could stop thinking about him. It only causes me more stress. What I need to think about is hiring someone to paint the dining room so it'll look better when I host the next dinner.*

By the time Leah finished the treatment, Elaine felt more relaxed, and her headache had eased. "That was just what I needed. I'm feeling much better now." She reached for her purse to get some money.

Leah shook her head. "You don't owe me anything today." She gave Elaine a hug. "I'm just glad you're feeling better."

"Danki." Elaine put her shoes and stockings on. "How are you feeling these days?"

"With the exception of the heat, I'm doing pretty well." Leah patted her protruding stomach. "I'll be even better once the boppli is born."

"I'll bet." Elaine moved toward the door. "I'd best be on my way now. I'd like to stop and see Priscilla before I go home."

"It was nice to see her at church yesterday, wasn't it?"

"Jah, but she didn't stay long. In fact, I don't think she stayed for the meal. Since it was her first Sunday back, I'm wondering if it was too much for her."

Leah's brows creased. "I probably shouldn't say anything, but Elam was about to tell Adam something and then Priscilla showed up, so Adam left the two of them alone so they could talk. It wasn't long after that when I saw Priscilla heading over to her folks' buggy. From her grim expression, I'd have to say she was upset about something."

Elaine smoothed the wrinkles in her dress. "I hope nothing is wrong between Priscilla and Elam. He's gone over to her place a lot since her accident, and I think it's only a matter of time before he proposes."

Leah smiled. "I hope so. If ever two people should be together, it's them."

Priscilla and her driver had been on the road a little over an hour, and they had a ways to go before reaching Chicago. So far, the trip had been uneventful. In fact, other than Priscilla's anxiousness to get there, she enjoyed the ride and diversion from the normal routine.

Although, Priscilla thought regretfully, *my routine has been anything from normal these last several weeks.*

Priscilla was thankful Shelly had air-conditioning in her vehicle, which made traveling on a hot day like this more comfortable. Since Priscilla's burns were healing nicely, she felt better physically. However, after Elam's confession, emotionally, she was a mess. Maybe after speaking to David, she would feel better.

Priscilla had called David's cell number, but he didn't answer. When she tried to leave him a message to let him know she was coming, a computerized voice said his voice mailbox was full. She hoped David would be home, or the trip would be for nothing, but she'd felt compelled to make the trip anyway. This was one of those times when she probably shouldn't be spontaneous, but impulsive decisions seemed to be in her nature.

"I don't know about you, but I could use a break about now." Shelly cut into Priscilla's thoughts. "I need some coffee and something to eat."

"Okay, whatever you think is best." Even though Priscilla's breakfast had worn off, she wasn't hungry. All she really wanted was to get to David's house and speak to him.

Shelly mentioned seeing a sign for food up ahead, about the same time as Priscilla noticed the passenger in a car passing them. He looked like Elam. But that was ridiculous. Why would he be traveling on the interstate on a weekday? He usually helped in his parents' store for part of each day. Priscilla wished she could have gotten a closer look, but the car had already passed and was way up ahead.

My imagination must be playing tricks on me, she mused. *I just thought he looked like Elam because he and David are all I've been thinking about lately.*

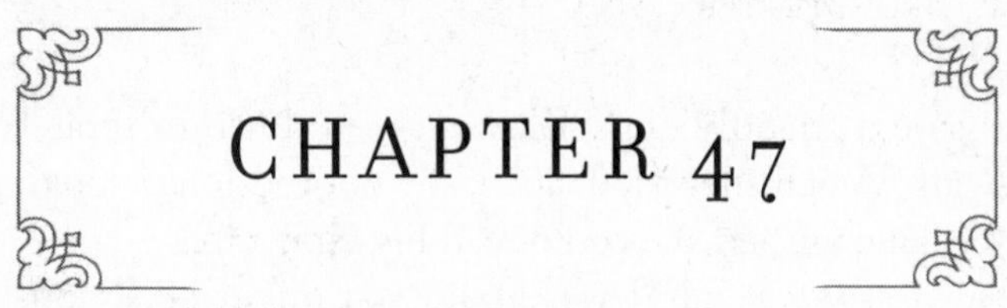

CHAPTER 47

As Elaine approached Jonah's buggy shop on her way home from Leah's, a lump formed in her throat. She wished she felt free to stop by and say hello, but with no legitimate reason, she quickly dismissed the idea. Elaine longed for the days when things were open and easy between her and Jonah. They used to be close, and she'd been comfortable discussing anything with him. But that was before Grandma took ill and Elaine felt she had to break things off with Jonah. Everything between them had changed after that. They couldn't remain good friends because Elaine needed to sever all ties. This was to allow Jonah the freedom to find what he needed with someone else, who ended up being Sara.

Nearing the entrance to Jonah's place, Elaine noticed Jonah heading down the driveway in the direction of the mailbox. Suddenly, a border collie ran past Jonah and darted in front of her bike. She put on her brakes in time to keep from hitting the dog but spun out in some gravel near the side of the road. The next thing Elaine knew, she was on the ground, with the dog licking her face.

Jonah rushed forward. "Are you hurt?" He dropped to his knees beside her.

"I don't think so." She gladly accepted his extended hand and clambered to her feet. "When Herbie darted in front of me, it took me by surprise, and I lost control of my bike." She brushed the dirt from the skirt of her dress, feeling suddenly shaky. She didn't know whether it was from the scare of the fall or from seeing the look of concern in Jonah's eyes. Elaine cocked her head and looked at the dog again. "It is Herbie, isn't it?"

"He does look a lot like my parents' dog, but this is Champ. I got him from a friend this morning. He reminded me so much of Herbie, I couldn't resist. Thought it would be good for my kinner to have a pet—especially Mark. He's the one who named the pooch Champ."

"He's sure a friendly dog." Elaine leaned down to scratch behind Champ's ears. When she stood again, she noticed Jonah looking at her strangely. Elaine wished she could read his expression.

"When I saw you fall, I was afraid you might be seriously hurt." Jonah continued to hold her hand. "You must feel kind of shaky right now. Maybe you should come up to the house and rest before you continue on. I'll see what my mamm has cold for us to drink, and we can sit on the porch and visit awhile. Your bike fender is bent, too, so I'll fix it for you."

"It's nice of you to offer, but I don't want to trouble you. I'm sure you have plenty of work to do in your shop."

"My daed and Timothy are there. They can manage without me for a bit." Jonah let go of Elaine's hand and picked up her bicycle. "I'll take this up to the yard and make sure everything's working okay. Wouldn't want you to try and ride it if something else is amiss."

"Danki for offering." She smiled. "I'm not quite ready to get back on it yet anyway."

They headed up the driveway, with Jonah's new dog barking and frolicking all the way. When they got to the house Jonah parked the bike and told Elaine to make herself comfortable on the porch. After he went inside, she took a seat on the wooden glider, with Champ lying near her feet.

Several minutes passed, until Jonah returned with two glasses of lemonade. He handed one to Elaine and took a seat beside her.

"Is. . .is your mamm going to j–join us?" With Jonah sitting so close, Elaine struggled to breathe and could barely speak without stuttering.

"No, she just put Mark down for a nap and needs to diaper and feed Martha Jean." Jonah sighed. "Don't know what I'd have done after Sara died without my parents' help."

"How are the children?"

"Doing well." Jonah took a drink, and Elaine did the same. They sat quietly until Jonah spoke again. "I heard you and Ben broke up."

Elaine nodded.

"Mind if I ask why?"

Her heart began to pound. Should she make light of this or tell Jonah the truth? "Well," she began, "Ben asked me to marry him, but I couldn't say yes, because I'm not in love with him."

"It seems like I've heard that before—only it was my marriage proposal you turned down." Jonah's brows furrowed as he stared into the yard. "Some folks might get the idea that you enjoy breaking men's hearts."

Elaine's spine stiffened. "Is that what you think, Jonah? Do you believe I intentionally wanted to hurt you when I said no to your proposal?"

"I guess not, but it hurt nonetheless." He turned to face her again. "As much as I thought I loved Meredith, it didn't compare to the way I felt about you."

Elaine's breath caught in her throat. "But you loved Sara—enough to marry her."

Jonah nodded. "Sara needed me, and I needed her. We did love each other, but I don't think Sara ever loved me as much as she did her first husband. And I. . ." Jonah's voice trailed off, and he quickly drank more lemonade.

"Did you love her as much as you used to love me?" Elaine dared to ask. She couldn't believe her boldness. It wasn't like her at all. But this was something she simply had to know.

He shook his head. "I loved her, but in a different way."

"I could tell. When I saw the two of you together your love and devotion to Sara and Mark was obvious." Elaine paused. *Should I say more? Should I tell Jonah the real reason I broke up with him?*

Throwing caution to the wind, Elaine looked at Jonah and said, "Remember that day when I said I didn't love you?"

"Course I remember. A man who loves a woman as much as I loved you isn't likely to forget something as painful as that."

She winced, reliving the agony of telling him good-bye and knowing how much it had hurt him, too. "I didn't mean it, Jonah. I only said I didn't love you because I had the responsibility of taking care of Grandma and didn't want to burden you with it." Elaine swallowed hard, hoping she wouldn't break down. Her tears were right on the surface.

"It wouldn't have been a burden, Elaine. I told you back then I would help with the care of Edna."

"I know, but Grandma was my responsibility, not yours. Being her caregiver was a full-time job. If we had gotten married I couldn't have been the wife you deserved."

"So you did love me then?"

She nodded, unable to keep the tears from falling.

"How do you feel about me now?"

"I love you with my whole heart, Jonah, but I realize you still love Sara, so I don't have any expectations of. . ."

He put his finger gently against her lips. "Sara will always have a place in my heart, but she's gone, and I believe she would want me to move on with my life."

Elaine sat quietly, unable to speak around the lump in her throat. Was Jonah saying what she thought he was saying? Could she even hope he was?

Jonah wiped Elaine's tears, and lifted her chin so she was looking directly at him. "I love you, Elaine, and if you don't think it's too late for us, I'd be honored if you would become my fraa. I don't want any more time to slip away between us."

"My answer is yes, Jonah." Elaine's voice trembled. "I'd very much like to be your wife."

He leaned forward and tenderly kissed her lips. "How long would it take you to plan a wedding? I'd like to get married as soon as possible."

Now tears of joy coursed down her cheeks. "Can you wait four months?"

He shook his head vigorously. "No, but if you need that long to prepare for the wedding, I'll try to be patient."

She smiled. "I might be able to make all the arrangements in three months. How about the first week of November? Would that be soon enough?"

Jonah pulled her gently into his arms. "It's not soon enough, but I'll wait until then. In the meantime, we have a lot of courting to do."

Chicago

Elam's heart pounded as he knocked on the Morgans' front door. He'd taken a chance coming here without phoning ahead, but he'd lost David's cell number. Fortunately, he'd found the Morgans' address on an old Christmas card David had sent him a few years ago.

Several minutes passed before the door opened. Elam recognized the woman standing at the entrance—she was David's mother.

"You're Elam, one of David's Amish friends, aren't you?" She tipped her head and looked at him curiously.

Elam nodded.

"If you've come to try and talk him into going back to Arthur and joining the Amish faith, you can turn around now and go home." She put both hands against her hips. "Because it's not going to happen. David's here to stay, and he'll be going back to college in the fall."

"I'm not here for that, but I do need to speak to David. Is he here? It's really important." Elam hoped David's mother wouldn't slam the door in his face. He'd come too far to be turned away now. Besides, he needed to say what was on his mind.

She hesitated but finally nodded. "David started working part-time for his father, but he won't go into the clinic until later this afternoon. Right now, he's in the living room, watching TV."

Elam followed her down the hall. When he entered the living room, he saw David lying on the couch. At first Elam thought he was sleeping, but as soon as he approached, David's eyes snapped open and he sat up. "Elam, what are you doing here?"

"I need to talk to you." Elam glanced at David's mother and was relieved when she left the room.

"How's Priscilla?" David gestured for Elam to take a seat in one of the chairs.

"She's doing better. Her burns are healing well, and I don't think she'll have any lasting scars." Elam lowered himself into the rocking chair, figuring if he got the chair moving it might help him relax.

"I'm glad to hear it. I've been praying for her."

"Same here."

"So, how are things with you? You look like you have something serious on your mind."

"Actually, I'm not doing so well," Elam said truthfully.

"Oh? What's wrong?"

"Priscilla and I broke up."

David's eyes widened. "Really? How come?"

"You need to know something important."

"What's that?"

Elam's voice lowered. He hoped David's mother couldn't overhear their conversation. "You're not the one responsible for Priscilla getting burned."

David leaned forward. "What was that?"

"You're not responsible for Priscilla's burns." Elam spoke a little louder.

David grabbed the throw pillow, hugging it to his chest. "What do you mean? I left the stove on. If I hadn't. . ."

Elam shook his head determinedly. "I'm the one responsible." Before David had a chance to say more, Elam blurted out everything that had happened that night.

David sat for several seconds, shaking his head, as though in disbelief. "Why did you let me believe I was the one responsible, Elam?"

"I was jealous of the attention you showed Priscilla. You hung around her a lot, and it seemed like you were trying to take her from me." Elam swallowed hard. He wanted to run and hide, but he'd come here to set things right with David, and he wouldn't take the coward's way out. "I thought if you believed you were the guilty one, you'd leave Arthur for good."

David rocked slowly back and forth, as though trying to take things in. "Well, you got your wish, so why'd you come here now and confess?"

"I had to, David. I've been struggling with guilt ever since Priscilla's accident. I couldn't live with the lie any longer." Elam paused to take a breath. "I've asked God's forgiveness. Now I'm asking yours. Can you find it in your heart to forgive me?"

"Yes, I can." David lifted his chin with an air of confidence. "I appreciate you coming all this way to tell me the truth. It's been really hard dealing with the thought that I was the cause of Priscilla getting hurt. You've taken a burden of guilt off my shoulders."

"Priscilla was upset when you left."

"I'm sorry for that, but it was better that way."

Elam drew in another quick breath. He'd have to say quickly what was on his mind, before he lost his nerve. "I believe Priscilla's in love with you, and I realize now you're the best person for her, not me. I destroyed any chance of Priscilla and me being together when I let you take the blame for what I had done. I'd understand if neither of you ever spoke to me again."

David opened his mouth like he was going to say more when his mother stepped into the room. "You have another visitor, David."

"Can it wait, Mom? Elam and I are having a discussion here."

His mother pursed her lips. "I suppose, but she says it's important."

"Okay." David turned to Elam. "Sit tight. I'll be right back."

Priscilla shifted nervously as she waited in the hall for David's mother to return. The woman hadn't greeted Priscilla any too cordially, but at least she hadn't slammed the door in her face. When Priscilla asked if David was there, his mother had said he was and that Priscilla should wait in the hall. *Lord, please give me the right words when I speak to David.*

A short time later David stepped into the hallway. "Oh, Priscilla, it's you? Did you come with Elam?"

She tipped her head. "Huh?"

"Elam's here, too. I figured you must have come together."

Priscilla's knees nearly buckled, and she grasped the door frame for support. So that must have been Elam she'd seen on the interstate. But what was he doing here?

"Elam and I did not come here together. I left a message last night, telling you I was coming," she said firmly. "We broke up yesterday when I found out he was the one who hadn't turned the burner off on the stove."

David nodded. "Elam told me about that. He came here to apologize for letting me take the blame."

"What did you say?"

"I'll admit, I was upset at first, but what's done is done. There's no reason for me to hold a grudge, so I've accepted his apology. I could barely live with myself, being the cause of what happened to you. Now Elam has lifted the burden from me, too."

"Did you get my letter or phone messages, David?"

He nodded. "But most of the words in the letter were smudged. Maybe it got wet. Oh, and I didn't get your phone message, either. My cell phone battery died soon after I returned home, and I haven't bothered to replace it." David thrust his hands into his jean pockets. "Guess I kinda got used to doing without it when I was trying to prepare for joining the Amish church. Course, I'll admit, I did use the cell phone a few times when it was necessary—like the night you got burned."

"The reason I wrote and tried to call is I wanted you to know I didn't blame you for my accident," Priscilla said. "Also, I had hoped to persuade you to come back to Arthur."

David shook his head. "I'll come back to visit Gram and Gramps from time to time, but I've decided not to join the Amish faith after all."

"How come?"

"It's just not for me. I realize now that Chicago is where I belong." David crossed his arms. "I'm going back to school in the fall and will eventually become my dad's partner at his veterinary clinic."

Priscilla studied David's face, unable to read his expression. Did he really think the Amish life wasn't for him, or was there some other reason he'd decided to stay here and pursue a career he'd previously said he wasn't interested in?

"Elam loves you," David said. "He knows he messed up, and you oughta give him another chance."

Priscilla bit down on her quivering lip. Knowing Elam had come here to apologize to David made her realize he truly was sorry for what he'd done and hadn't just said so in order to win her back. Truthfully, Priscilla had to admit, she did still love him and had for a long time. It was suddenly clear to her that what she'd felt for David had only been infatuation, not love. Apparently, since he wasn't returning to Arthur to join the Amish faith, he didn't love her, either.

"Why don't you go into the living room?" David suggested. "Elam is there, and I'll leave you two alone so you can talk."

"Okay." Despite what David had said, Priscilla hoped it wasn't too late for her and Elam. Since she'd rejected him yesterday, maybe he wouldn't want anything to do with her now.

Priscilla stepped into the other room and saw Elam sitting in a chair, holding his straw hat with a downcast expression.

When she approached, he leaped to his feet. "Ach, Priscilla! I didn't know you were here."

"Came to tell David he wasn't the one who left the stove on."

"Jah, I told him that, too."

"I know. David told me. He also said you apologized."

Elam nodded. "I've never been sorrier for anything in my life, because my deceitfulness caused me to lose you."

She stepped in front of him, placing her hands on his shoulders. "You haven't lost me, Elam. I forgive you, and if you still want me, I'd be honored to be your wife."

Tears pooled in Elam's eyes. "You mean it, Priscilla—after all I've done?"

Priscilla choked back a sob. "Matthew 6:14 says, 'If ye forgive men their trespasses, your heavenly Father will also forgive you.' I've done things in my life I'm ashamed of, too, and others have forgiven me." She leaned her head against Elam's chest. "I love you, Elam."

"I love you, too." Elam lifted Priscilla's chin and sealed their love with a kiss sweeter than any he'd ever given her before. How thankful she was for the chance to begin again, and for the restoration of their relationship, because of God's amazing grace.

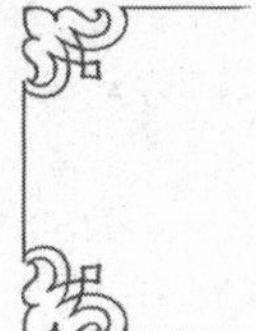

EPILOGUE

Six months later

"I can't believe how much all of our lives have changed," Priscilla commented to Elaine and Leah as they sat at her kitchen table, drinking tea and admiring the cookbook they had worked on together. It was nice to see it finally done and ready to sell to those who attended Elaine's dinners.

Elaine smiled. "I'm still amazed at how God has worked things out for each one of us."

Leah patted her baby Michael's back. "I remember when we were girls and talked about our future—how we hoped God would reveal His will for our lives and help us to choose the right husbands."

Priscilla nodded. "He's done that, all right. Elam and I are married. Elaine and Jonah are married. And you, Leah, have a husband and four kinner to raise. The Lord has truly blessed us all with good mates."

Leah reached over and touched Priscilla's arm. "You were blessed when your burns healed so well, too. It's good to see that you have no scars at all."

"Jah, and I'm grateful." Priscilla glanced at the letter she had received the other day. "By the way, Elam and I heard from David recently."

"Oh, what'd he have to say?" Elaine asked.

"He met a young woman while attending college and thinks she may be the right one for him."

"That's good news. I'm pleased to say that Ben is now seeing someone new as well."

Priscilla clasped her friends' hands. "I thank the Lord daily for the friendship we share. I can't imagine going through life without good friends. Your love and support has brought me through many difficult things I've had to face, and I hope we can all be friends for the rest of our lives."

Elaine and Leah nodded in agreement.

"And now," Priscilla announced, pushing away from the table, "it's time to eat lunch. Today, I am serving my friendship salad."

PRISCILLA'S FRIENDSHIP SALAD

INGREDIENTS:
1 head lettuce
3 slices swiss cheese
1 (10 ounce) box frozen peas
1 large onion, chopped
1 tablespoon sugar
5 tablespoons mayonnaise
½ pound bacon, fried and crumbled
2 eggs, hard boiled and sliced or chopped

Tear lettuce into small pieces and layer in large serving bowl. Tear swiss cheese into pieces and layer over lettuce. Layer peas and onion. Sprinkle sugar over all then spread with mayonnaise. Cover and let stand in refrigerator two to three hours. Before serving, top with crumbled bacon and chopped egg. Toss and serve.

DISCUSSION QUESTIONS

1. Priscilla was in a predicament falling for two men at the same time. To make matters worse, both Elam and David were vying for her attention. Have you or someone you know ever had two suitors at the same time? If so, how did you handle the situation?

2. Elam was worried about not having enough money to buy a home for him and Priscilla. Was he wrong in letting money hold him back from marrying her? Could they have lived with one of their parents until they had enough money saved to build a house? Should Elam have told Priscilla the reason he hadn't proposed?

3. David cared for Priscilla, but was it right for him to pursue her, knowing Elam loved her, too? Should David have walked away from his feelings? Did he really want to be Amish, or was it simply so he could get close to Priscilla?

4. What challenges did David face after living the English life for twenty-four years and then deciding to become Amish? Would you be able to give up all the material things the English are used to having?

5. After twenty-five years, Cora finally found her son Adam. Should she have tried harder to explain how sorry she was for messing up his life, or should she have held back, for fear of pushing him further away? After years of separation, if you were to find your adult child, would you be able to hold back like Cora did, knowing Adam was in the same community? Did Cora give up too easily trying to locate her first husband and children? Would you have kept trying no matter how long it took?

6. If you were Adam and grew up knowing your mother or father abandoned you but crossed paths with that parent as an adult, would you be able to forgive your parent after hearing the reasons he or she left? Would your forgiveness have taken as long as Adam's

did, or could you forgive right away in order to build a relationship? Would you try to inflict emotional pain on your parent because it had been done to you?

7. There comes a time when parents have to show their children that they can be trusted, but they need to discern when to allow them to do certain things, such as letting them go places with friends. Should Cora have kept a tighter rein on her son Jared instead of giving him so much freedom in things he wanted to do? When should a parent step in and say no if their child wants to do something?

8. Was it right for Cora not to tell her second husband, who was English, about her earlier life in the Amish community? Was it the wrong time for her to blurt out that information when they were waiting for news about their son, Jared?

9. Should Elaine have let Jonah know sooner that she still loved him, even though he was still grieving for Sara? If not, how long should she have waited? If you were Jonah, having had three relationships that failed in different ways, would you give up on love and marriage or keep trying, hoping to find the right mate?

10. Was it right for Elaine to keep Ben waiting for an answer to his proposal, when deep down she'd never given up her feelings and hopes of getting back with Jonah? If you were Ben, would you have been able to immediately come face-to-face with your suspicions, knowing Elaine wasn't sure about her feelings for you? Was he too patient about waiting, too complacent?

11. If someone hit you, would you be able to "turn the other cheek" like the Amish do? Would you be able not to strike back or retaliate in any way?

12. Several Bible verses were quoted at different times throughout this story. Were there any special verses in this book that spoke to your heart? If so, what were they, and how did they bolster your faith in God?

ABOUT THE AUTHOR

New York Times bestselling and award-winning author Wanda E. Brunstetter is one of the founders of the Amish fiction genre. She has written close to 90 books translated in four languages. With over 10 million copies sold, Wanda's stories consistently earn spots on the nation's most prestigious bestseller lists and have received numerous awards.

Wanda's ancestors were part of the Anabaptist faith, and her novels are based on personal research intended to accurately portray the Amish way of life. Her books are well read and trusted by many Amish, who credit her for giving readers a deeper understanding of the people and their customs.

When Wanda visits her Amish friends, she finds herself drawn to their peaceful lifestyle, sincerity, and close family ties. Wanda enjoys photography, ventriloquism, gardening, bird-watching, beachcombing, and spending time with her family. She and her husband, Richard, have been blessed with two grown children, six grandchildren, and two great-grandchildren.

To learn more about Wanda, visit her website at www.wandabrunstetter.com.

Other Books by Wanda E. Brunstetter:

Kentucky Brothers Series

The Journey
The Healing
The Struggle

Indiana Cousins Series

A Cousin's Promise
A Cousin's Prayer
A Cousin's Challenge

Brides of Lehigh Canal Series

Kelly's Chance
Betsy's Return
Sarah's Choice

The Discovery–A Lancaster County Saga

Goodbye to Yesterday
The Silence of Winter
The Hope of Spring
The Pieces of Summer
A Revelation in Autumn
A Vow for Always

Daughters of Lancaster County Series

The Storekeeper's Daughter
The Quilter's Daughter
The Bishop's Daughter

Brides of Lancaster County Series

A Merry Heart
Looking for a Miracle
Plain and Fancy
The Hope Chest

Sisters of Holmes County Series

A Sister's Secret
A Sister's Test
A Sister's Hope

Brides of Webster County Series

Going Home
On Her Own
Dear to Me
Allison's Journey

Amish Cooking Class Series

The Seekers
The Blessing
The Celebration
Amish Cooking Class Cookbook

The Half-Stitched Amish Quilting Club Series

The Half-Stitched Amish Quilting Club
The Tattered Quilt
The Healing Quilt

The Prayer Jars Series

The Hope Jar
The Forgiving Jar (February 2019)

Nonfiction

The Simple Life
A Celebration of the Simple Life
Wanda E. Brunstetter's Amish Friends Cookbook
Wanda E. Brunstetter's Amish Friends Cookbook, Vol. 2
Amish Friends Harvest Cookbook
Amish Friends Christmas Cookbook

Children's Books

Rachel Yoder—Always Trouble
Somewhere series (8 books)
The Wisdom of Solomon
Mattie and Mark Miller. . .Double Trouble series (5 books)

Other Novels

The Beloved Christmas Quilt
Lydia's Charm
Amish White Christmas Pie
Woman of Courage
The Hawaiian Quilt
The Hawaiian Discovery
The Amish Millionaire
The Christmas Secret
The Lopsided Christmas Cake
The Farmers' Market Mishap

IF YOU LIKED THIS BOOK, YOU'LL ALSO LIKE...

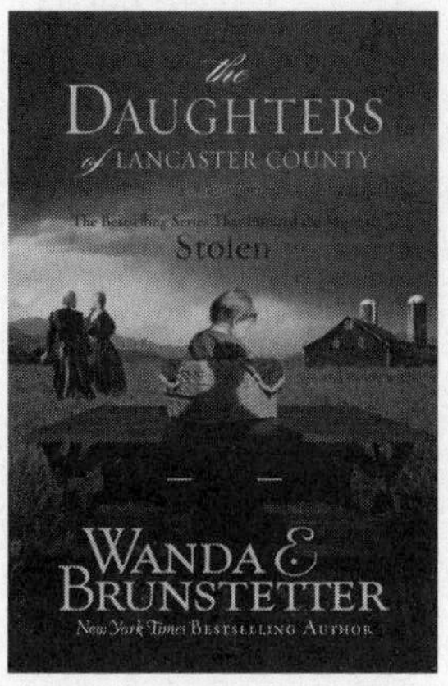

The Daughters of Lancaster County

Time stands still in Pennsylvania Amish Country where the Fisher family struggles to overcome devastating heartache.

Follow three young women who are pivotal to bringing faith, hope, love, and—most importantly—forgiveness back into this Amish family's lives.

Includes:
The Storekeeper's Daughter
The Quilter's Daughter
The Bishop's Daughter

Enjoy a heartfelt look into the lives of an endearing Amish family through the novels that inspired the made-for-stage musical, *Stolen*.

Paperback / 978-1-68322-649-9 / $15.99

Find This and More from Barbour Publishing
at Your Favorite Bookstore
www.barbourbooks.com

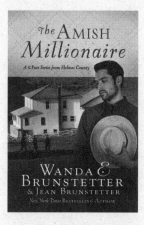